ONI PRESS
PRESENTS

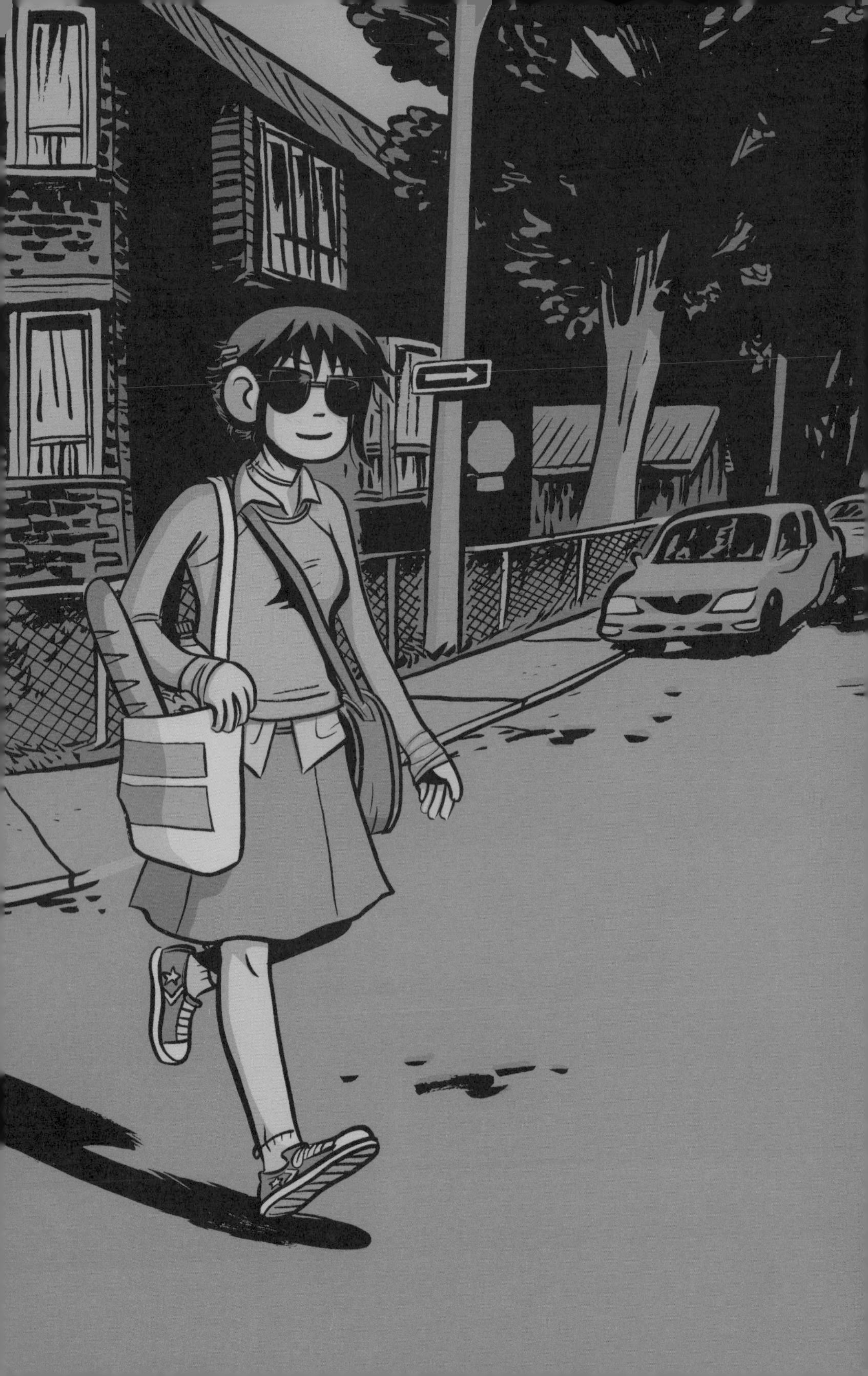

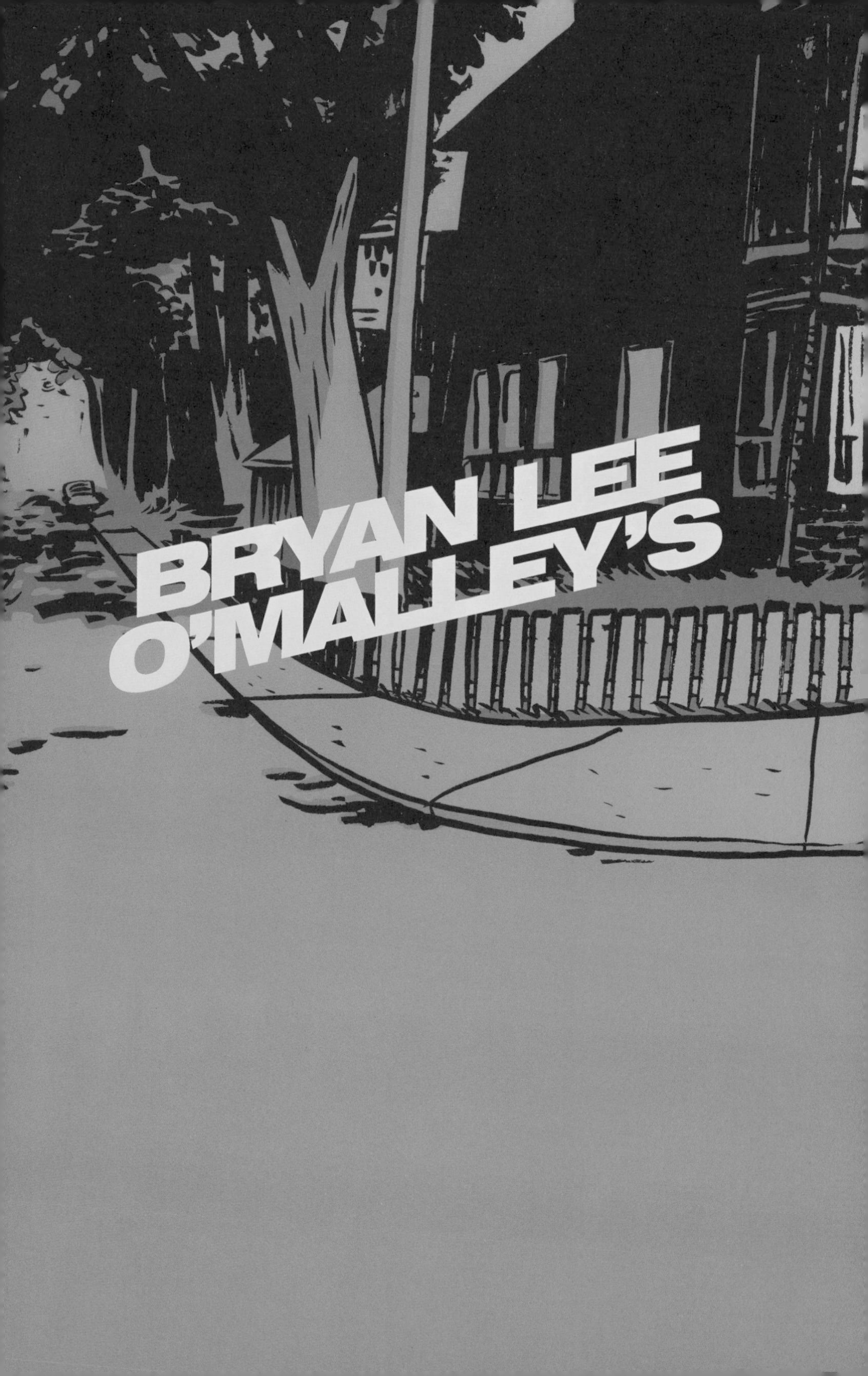
BRYAN LEE
O'MALLEY'S

Disco-Pig

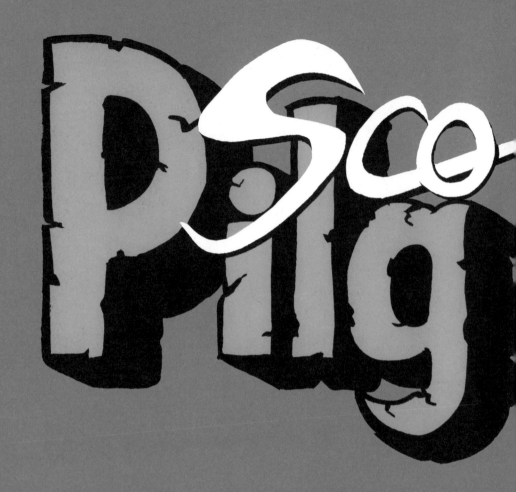

& THE

INFINITE

SADNESS

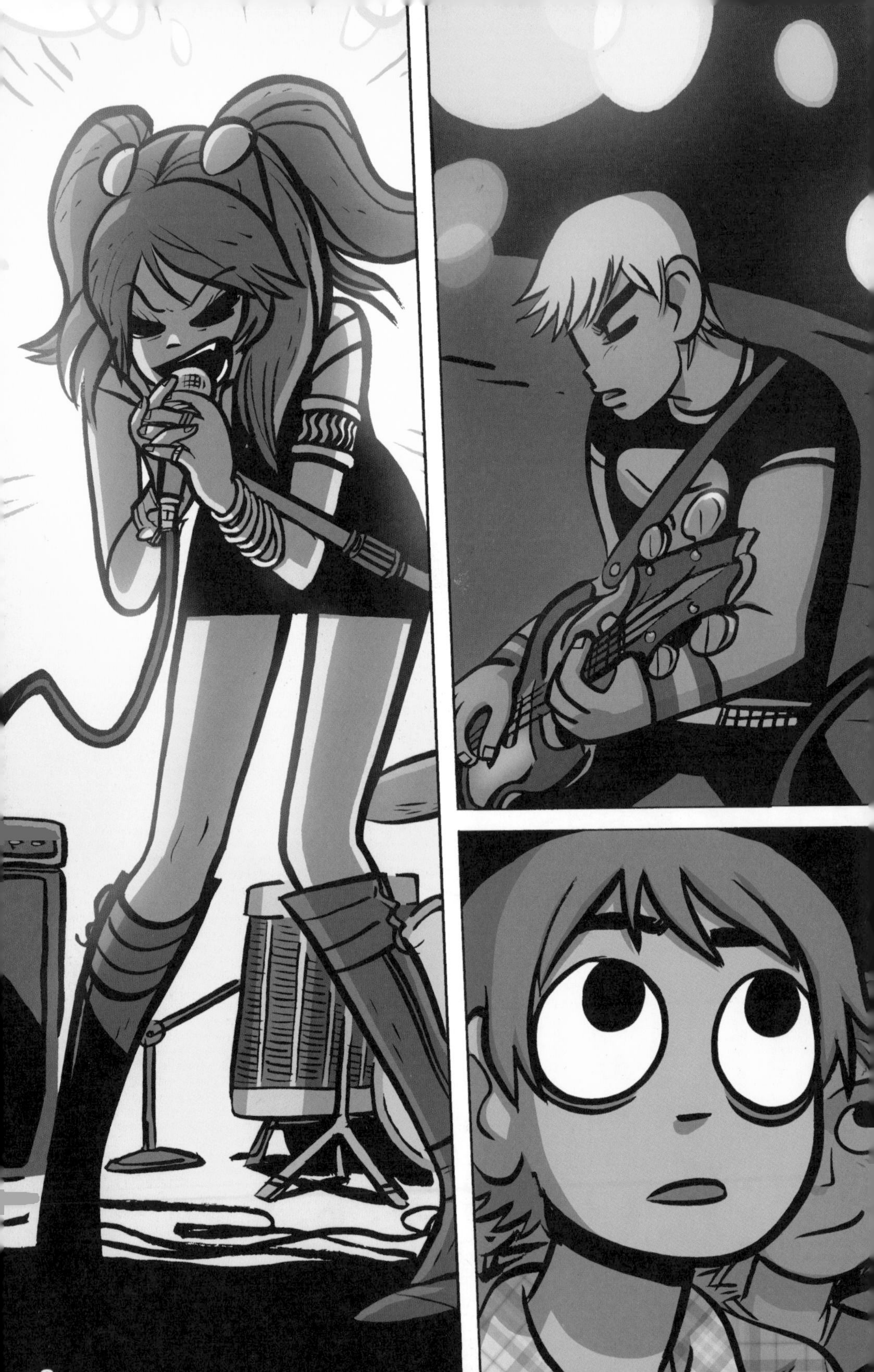

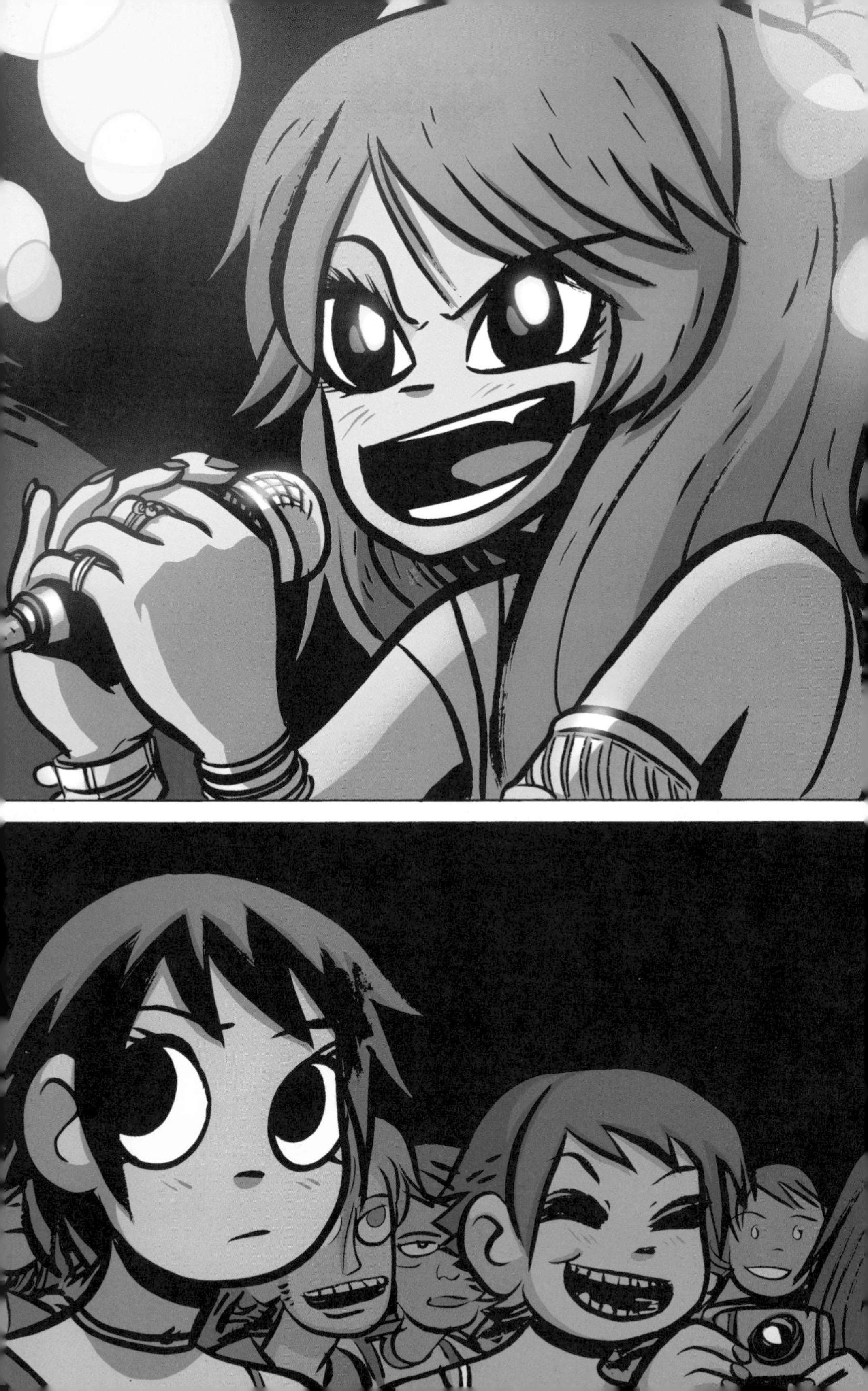

colored by Nathan Fairbairn • designed by Keith Wood with Bryan Lee O'Malley

cleanup & lettering remastered by **Troy Look** • edited by **James Lucas Jones**

Published by **Oni Press, Inc.**
Joe Nozemack publisher • **James Lucas Jones** editor in chief • **Keith Wood** art director
George Rohac operations director • **Tom Shimmin** marketing coordinator • **Jill Beaton** editor • **Charlie Chu** editor
Troy Look digital prepress lead • **Jason Storey** designer • **Robin Herrera** administrative assistant

ONI PRESS, INC.
1305 SE Martin Luther King Jr. Blvd.
Suite A
Portland, OR 97214

www.onipress.com
facebook.com/onipress • twitter.com/onipress • onipress.tumblr.com

www.scottpilgrim.com • www.radiomaru.com • twitter.com/radiomaru

First edition: May 2013

ISBN: 978-1-62010-002-8 • eISBN: 978-1-62010-045-5

Library of Congress Control Number: 2013933320

10 9 8 7 6 5 4 3 2 1

PRINTED IN THE U.S.A.
by Lake Book Manufacturing, Inc.

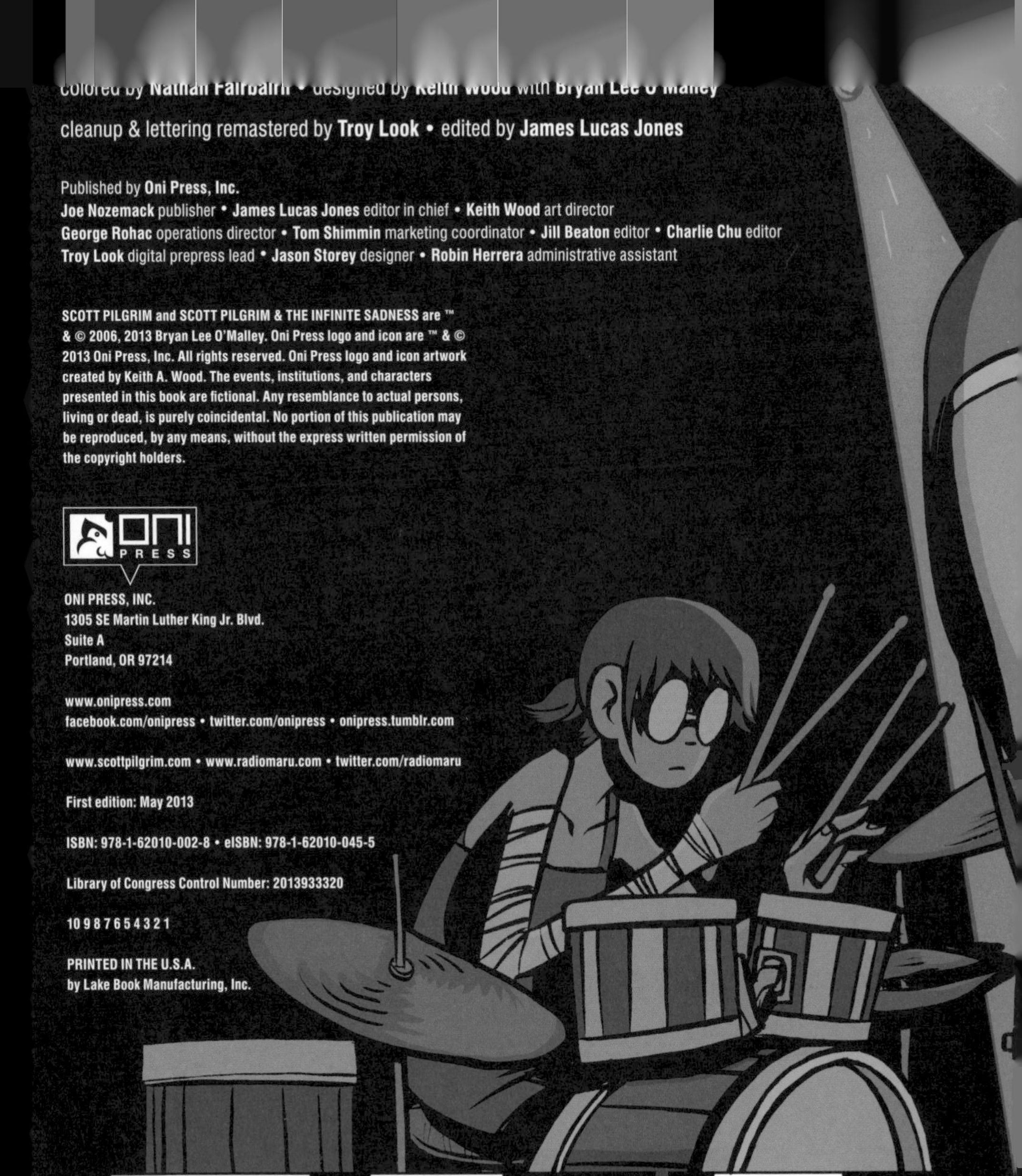

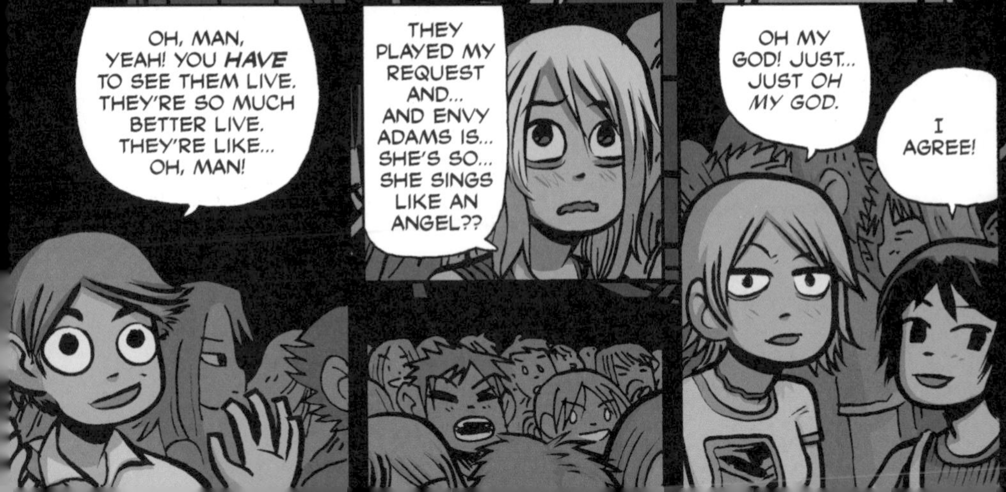
OH, MAN, YEAH! YOU *HAVE* TO SEE THEM LIVE. THEY'RE SO MUCH BETTER LIVE. THEY'RE LIKE... OH, MAN!
THEY PLAYED MY REQUEST AND... AND ENVY ADAMS IS... SHE'S SO... SHE SINGS LIKE AN ANGEL??
OH MY GOD! JUST... JUST *OH MY GOD.*
I AGREE!

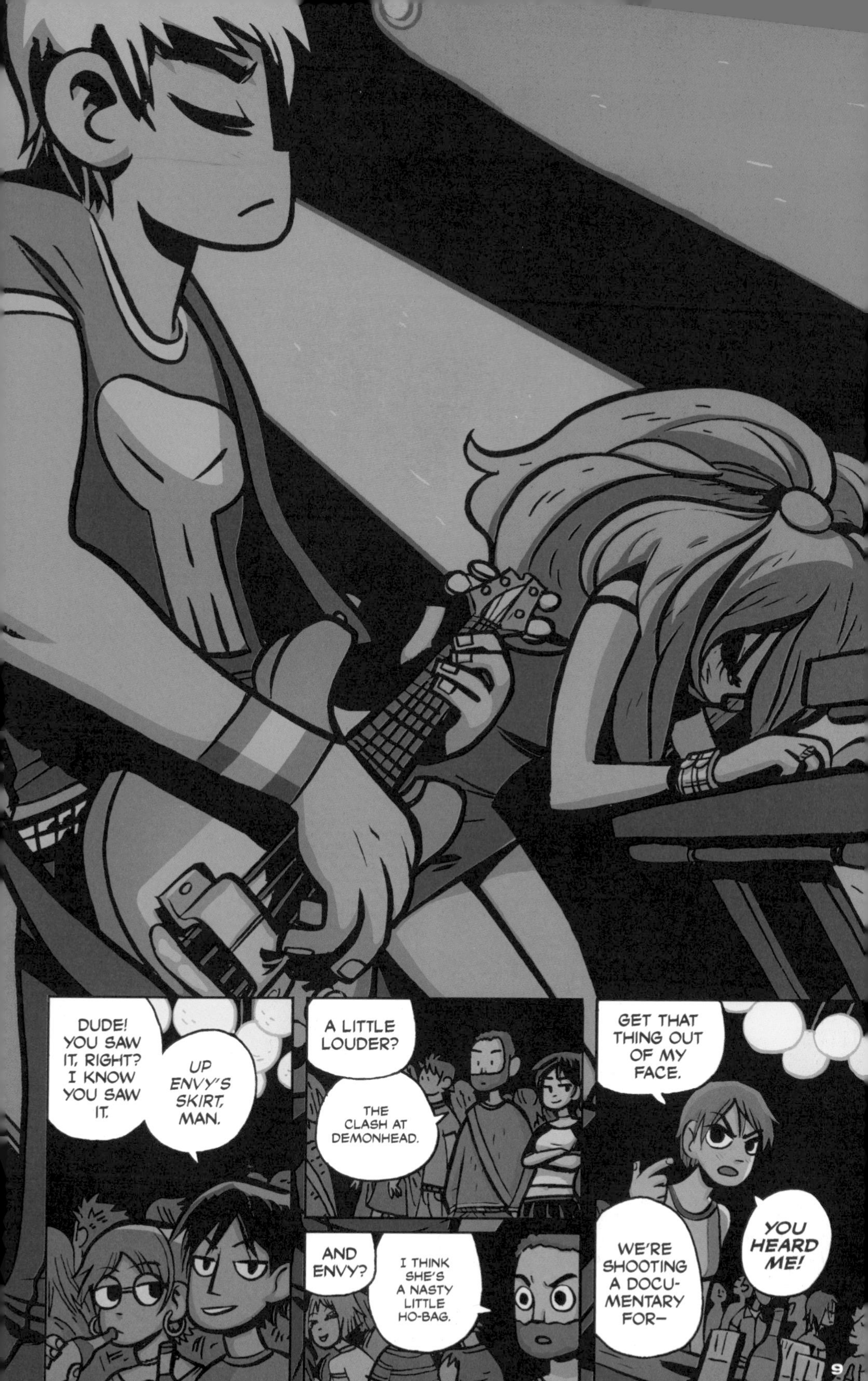
DUDE! YOU SAW IT, RIGHT? I KNOW YOU SAW IT.
UP ENVY'S SKIRT, MAN.
A LITTLE LOUDER?
THE CLASH AT DEMONHEAD.
AND ENVY?
I THINK SHE'S A NASTY LITTLE HO-BAG.
GET THAT THING OUT OF MY FACE.
WE'RE SHOOTING A DOCU-MENTARY FOR–
YOU HEARD ME!

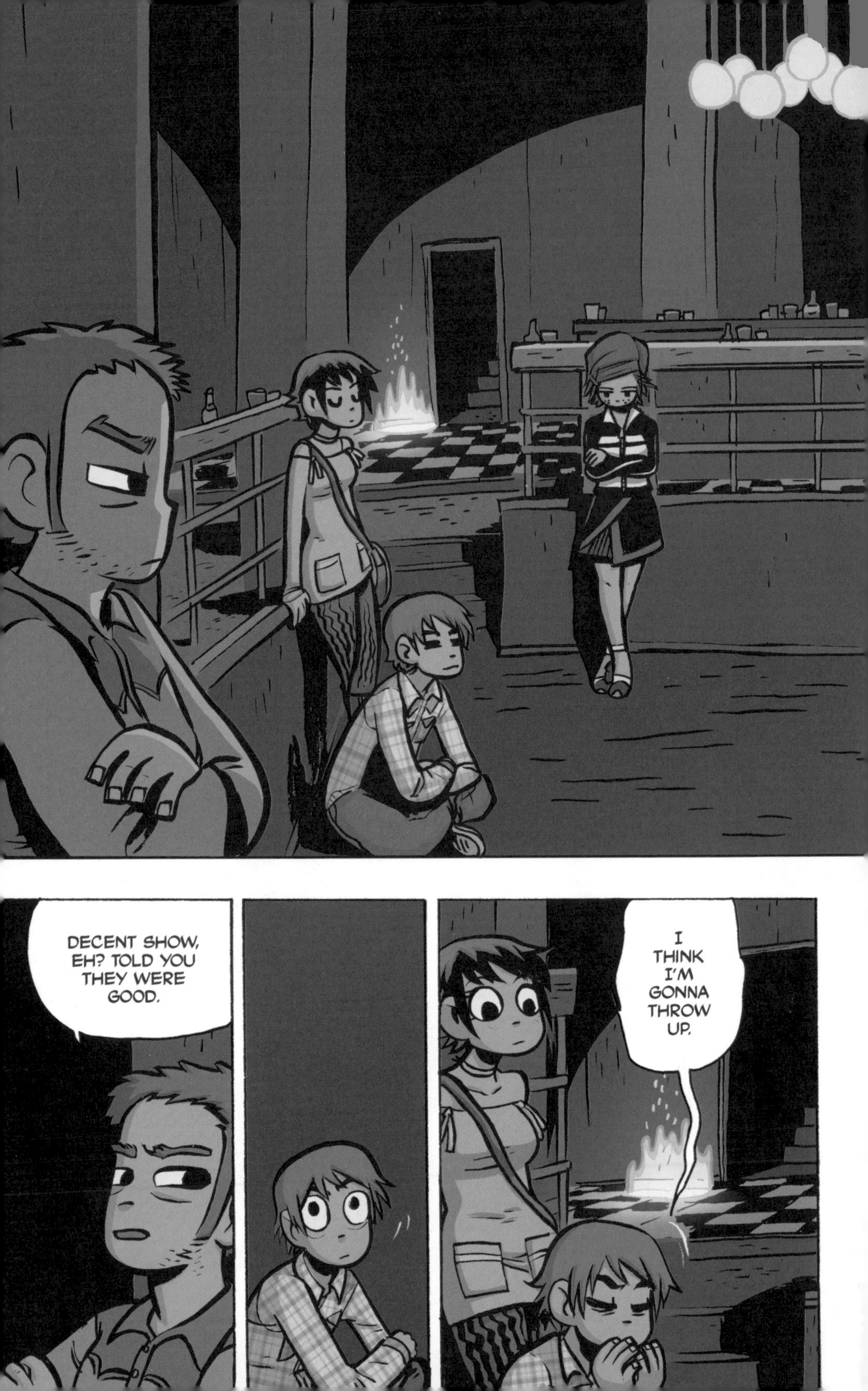
DECENT SHOW, EH? TOLD YOU THEY WERE GOOD.
I THINK I'M GONNA THROW UP.

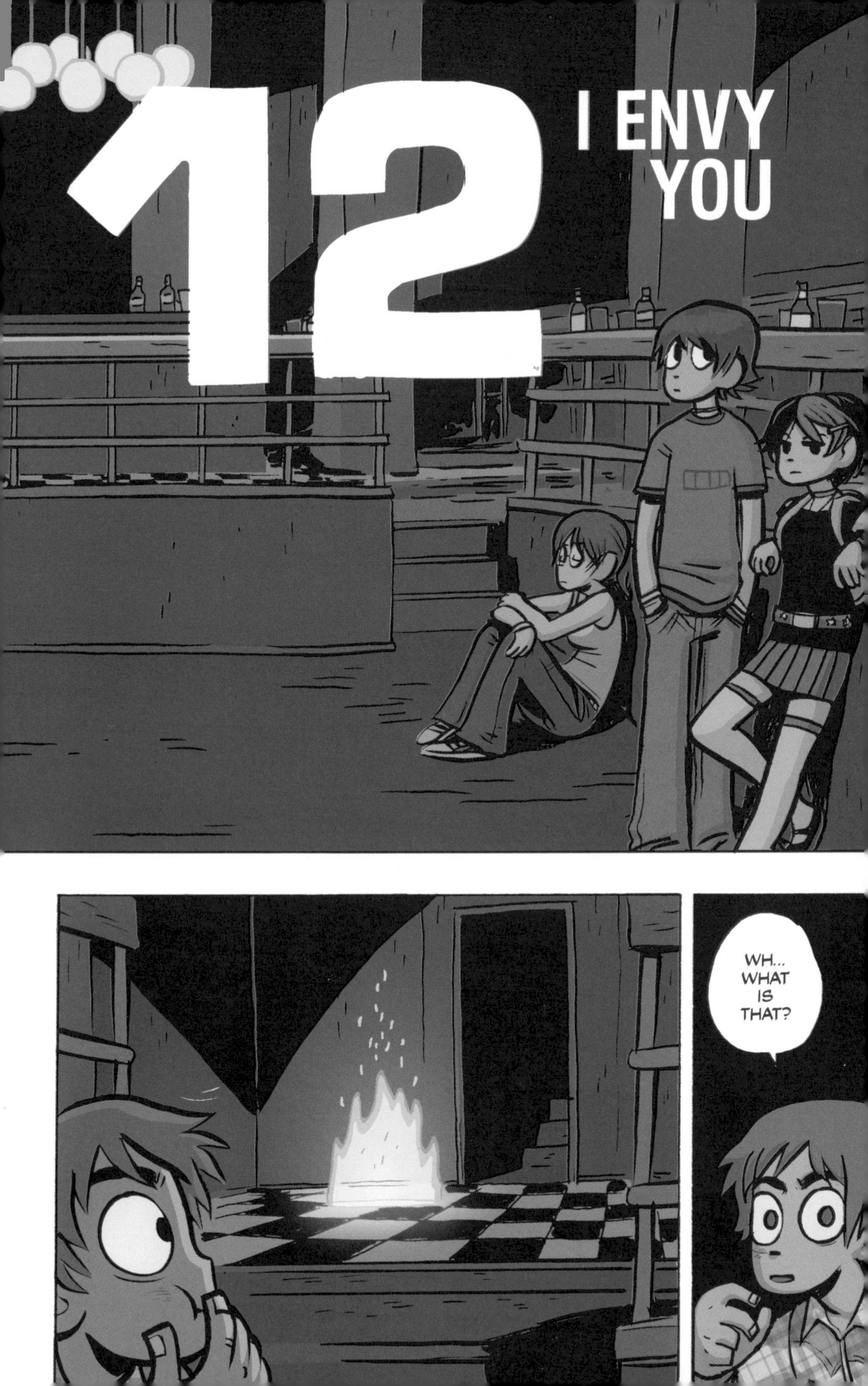
12
I ENVY YOU
WH... WHAT IS THAT?

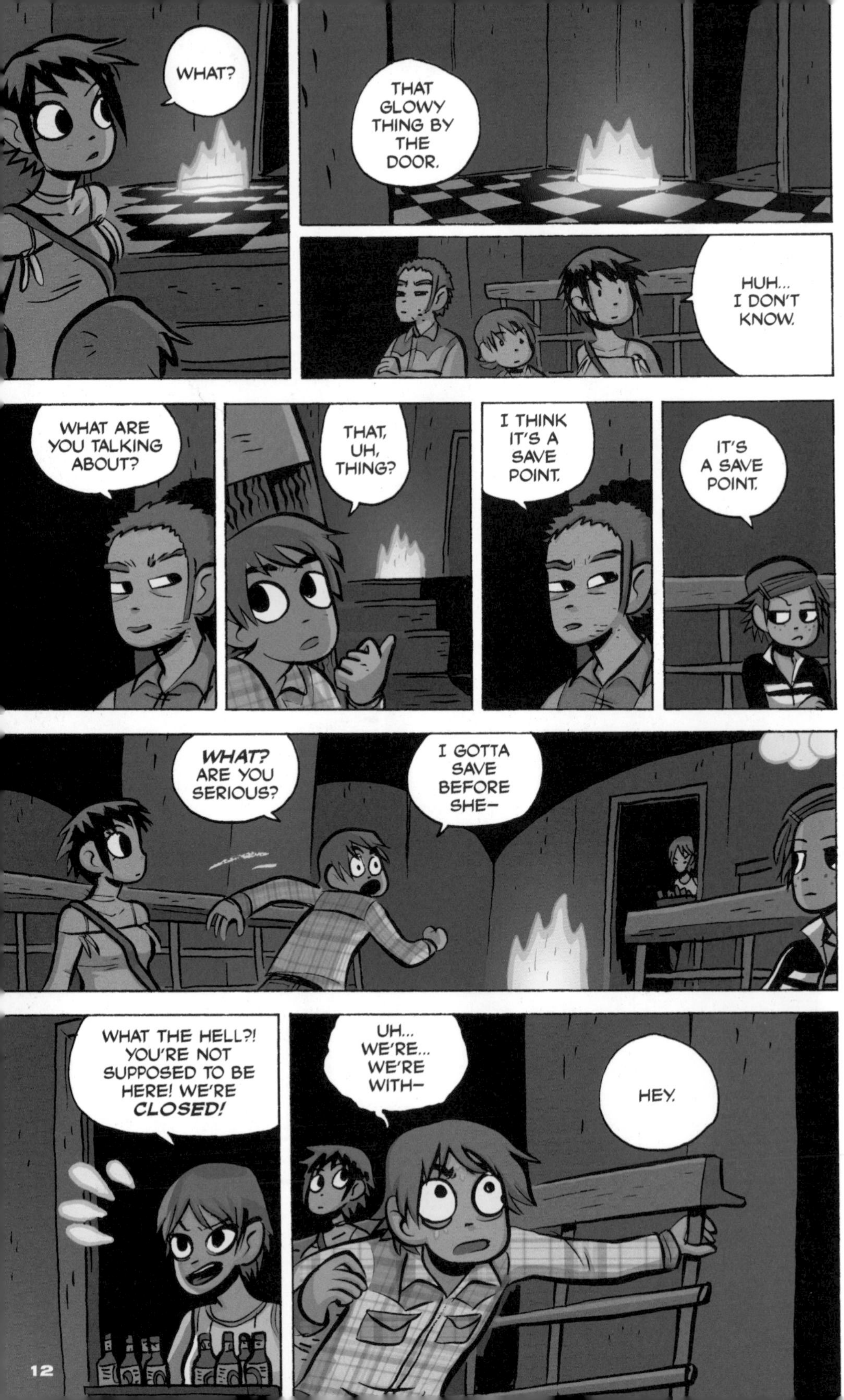
WHAT?
THAT GLOWY THING BY THE DOOR.
HUH... I DON'T KNOW.
WHAT ARE YOU TALKING ABOUT?
THAT, UH, THING?
I THINK IT'S A SAVE POINT.
IT'S A SAVE POINT.
WHAT? ARE YOU SERIOUS?
I GOTTA SAVE BEFORE SHE–
WHAT THE HELL?! YOU'RE NOT SUPPOSED TO BE HERE! WE'RE CLOSED!
UH... WE'RE... WE'RE WITH–
HEY.

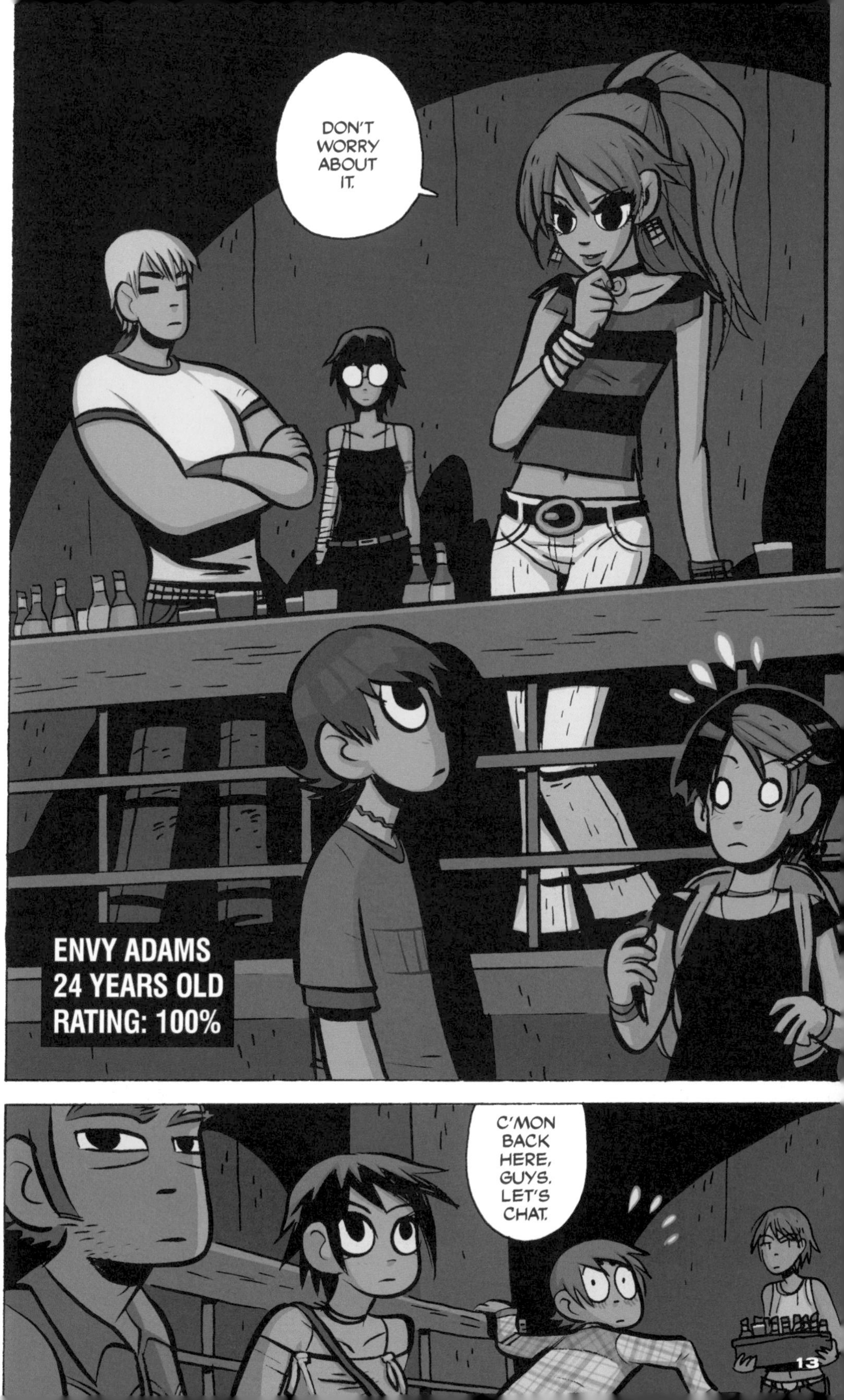
DON'T WORRY ABOUT IT.
ENVY ADAMS
24 YEARS OLD
RATING: 100%
C'MON BACK HERE, GUYS. LET'S CHAT.

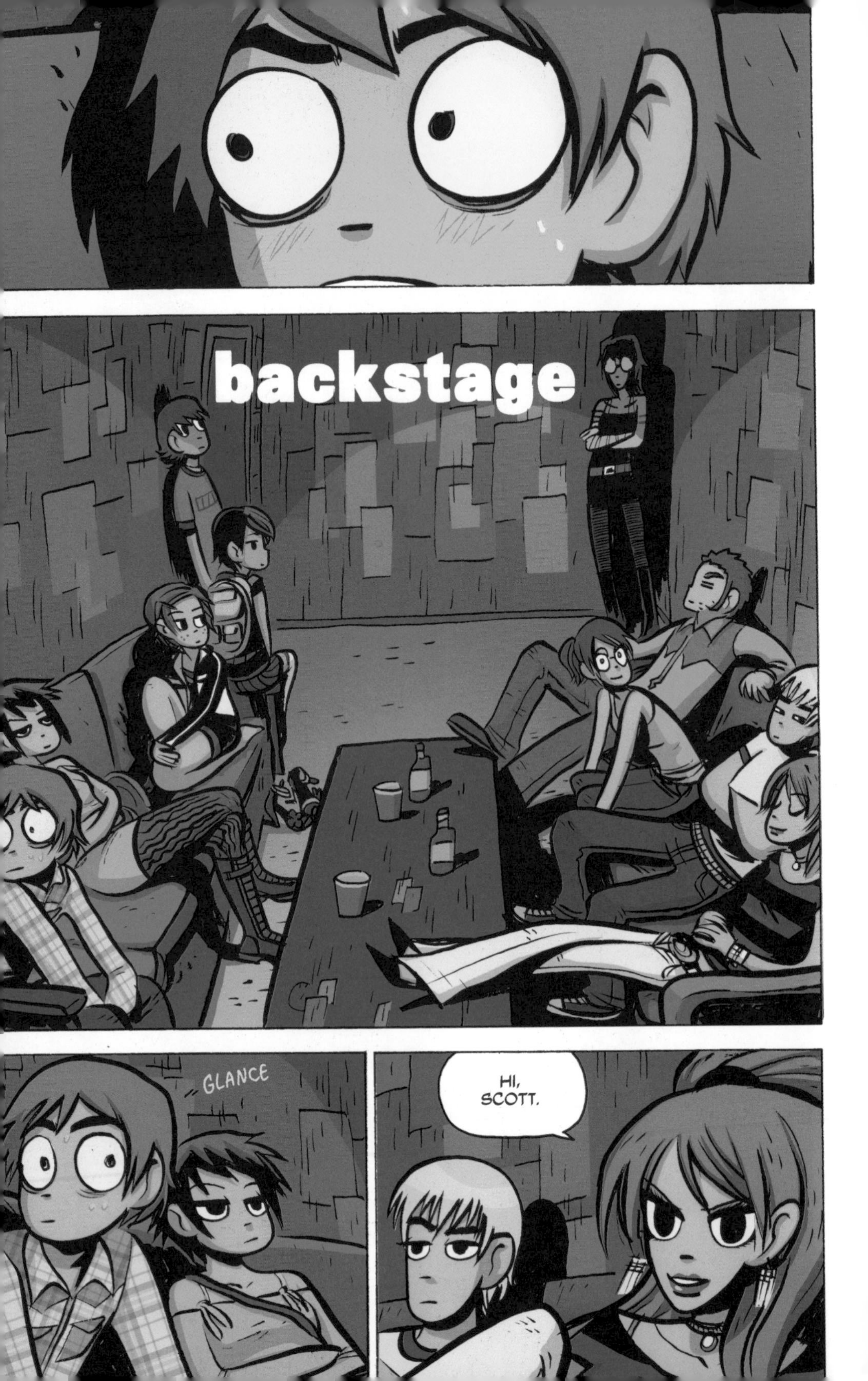
backstage
GLANCE
HI, SCOTT.

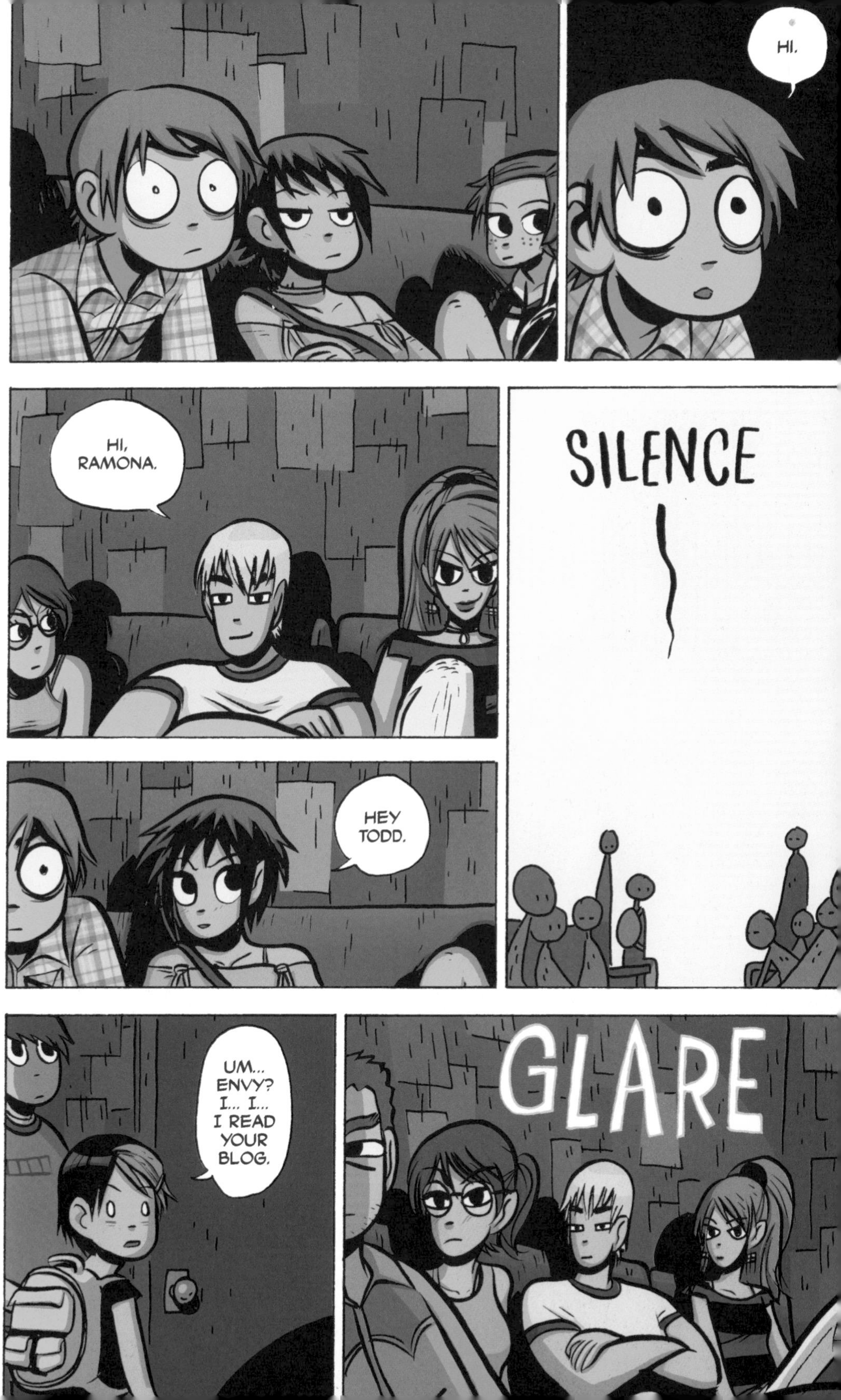
HI.
HI, RAMONA.
SILENCE
HEY TODD.
UM... ENVY? I... I... I READ YOUR BLOG.
GLARE

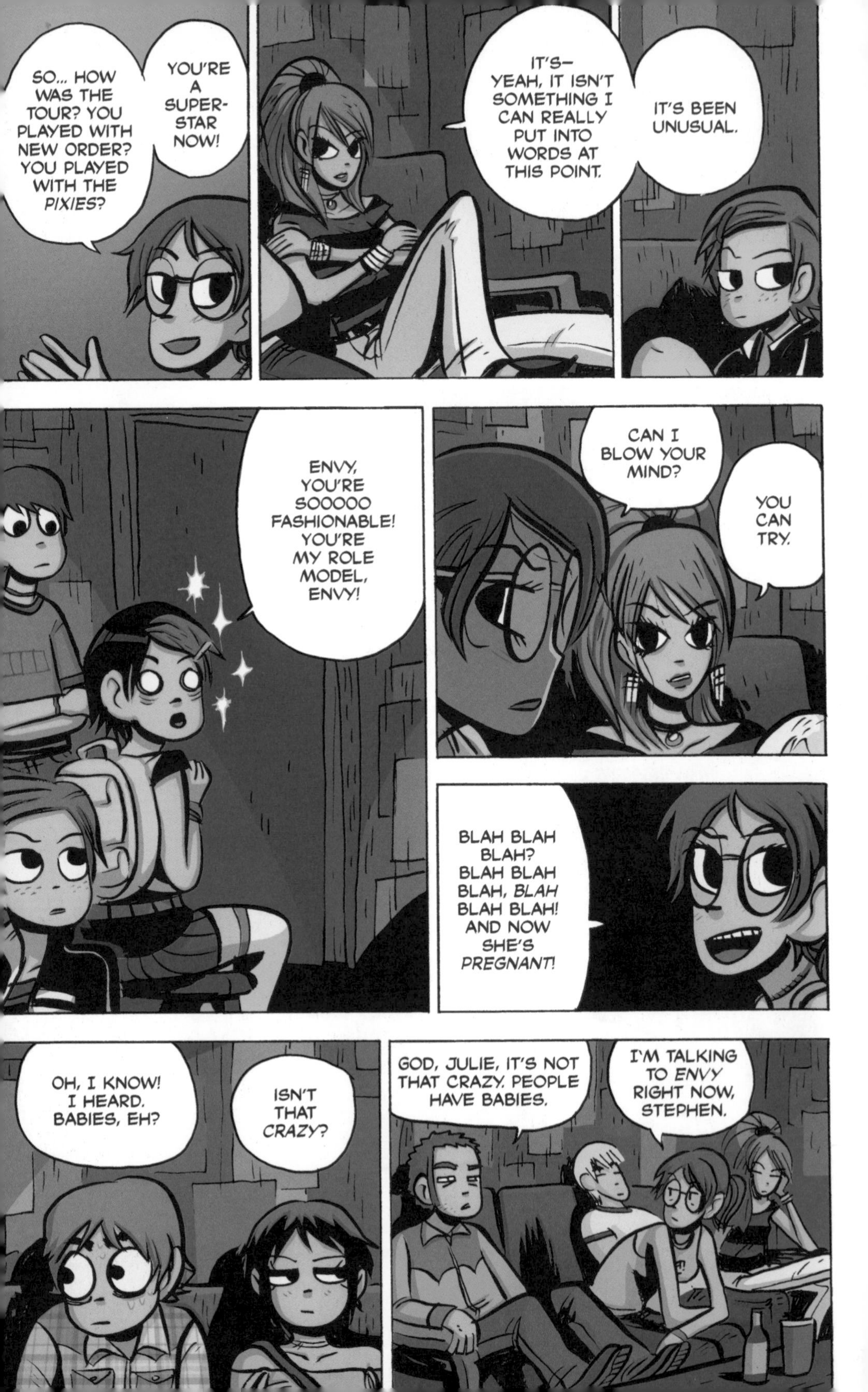
SO... HOW WAS THE TOUR? YOU PLAYED WITH NEW ORDER? YOU PLAYED WITH THE *PIXIES*?
YOU'RE A SUPER-STAR NOW!
IT'S— YEAH, IT ISN'T SOMETHING I CAN REALLY PUT INTO WORDS AT THIS POINT.
IT'S BEEN UNUSUAL.
ENVY, YOU'RE SOOOOO FASHIONABLE! YOU'RE MY ROLE MODEL, ENVY!
CAN I BLOW YOUR MIND?
YOU CAN TRY.
BLAH BLAH BLAH? BLAH BLAH BLAH, *BLAH* BLAH BLAH! AND NOW SHE'S *PREGNANT*!
OH, I KNOW! I HEARD. BABIES, EH?
ISN'T THAT *CRAZY*?
GOD, JULIE, IT'S NOT THAT CRAZY. PEOPLE HAVE BABIES.
I'M TALKING TO *ENVY* RIGHT NOW, STEPHEN.

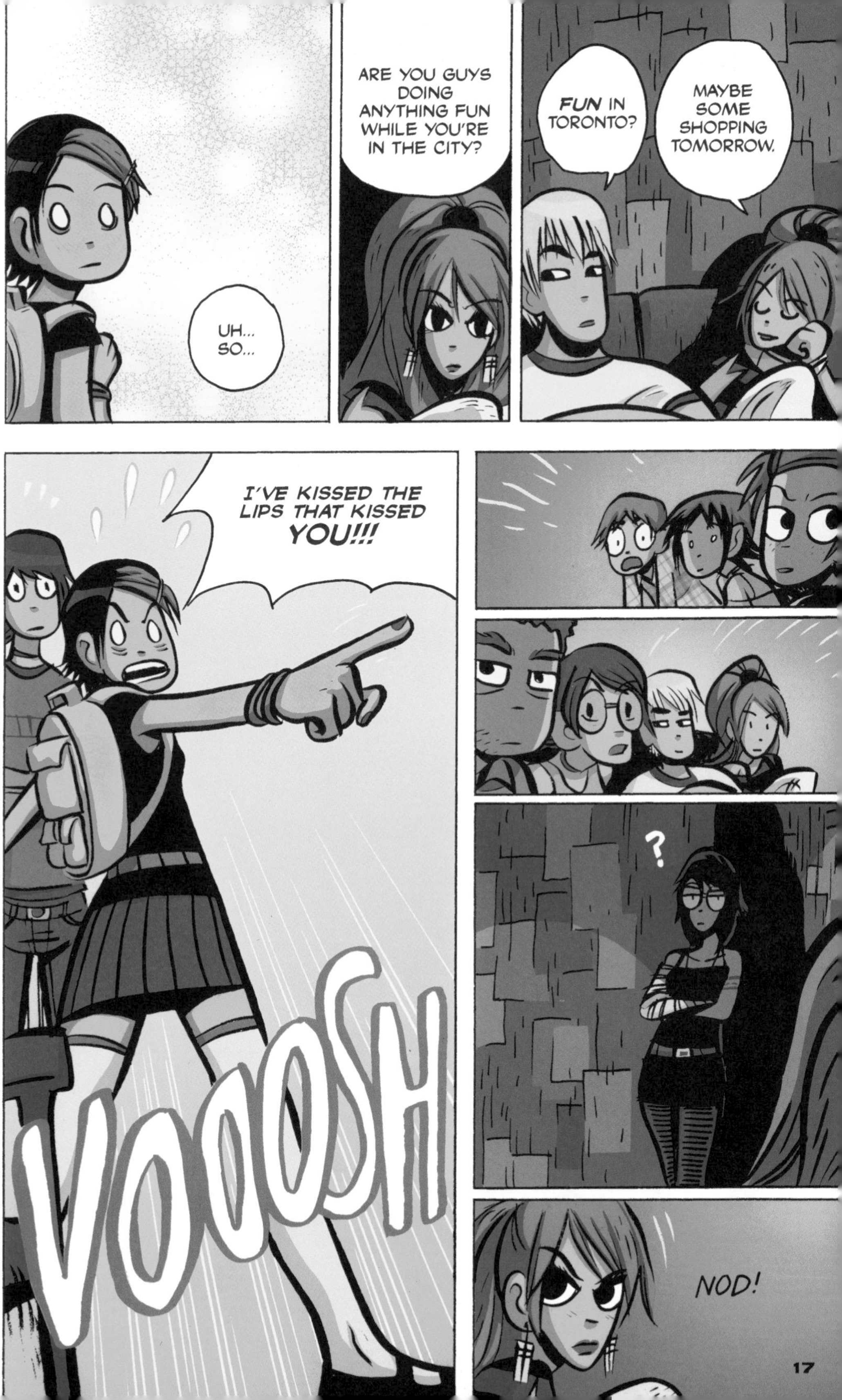

UH... SO...
ARE YOU GUYS DOING ANYTHING FUN WHILE YOU'RE IN THE CITY?
FUN IN TORONTO?
MAYBE SOME SHOPPING TOMORROW.
I'VE KISSED THE LIPS THAT KISSED YOU!!!
VOOOSH
?
NOD!

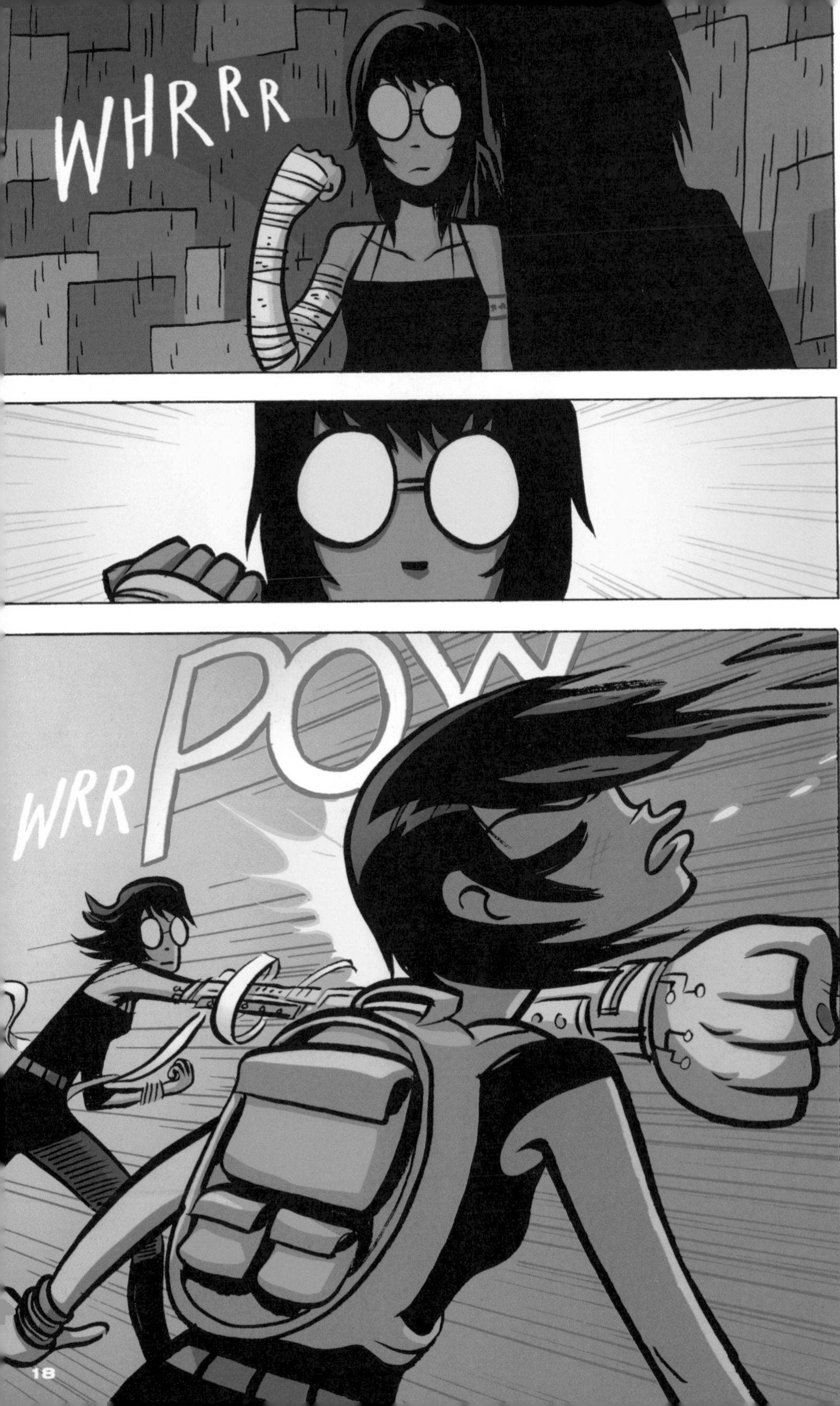
WHRRR
WRR
POW

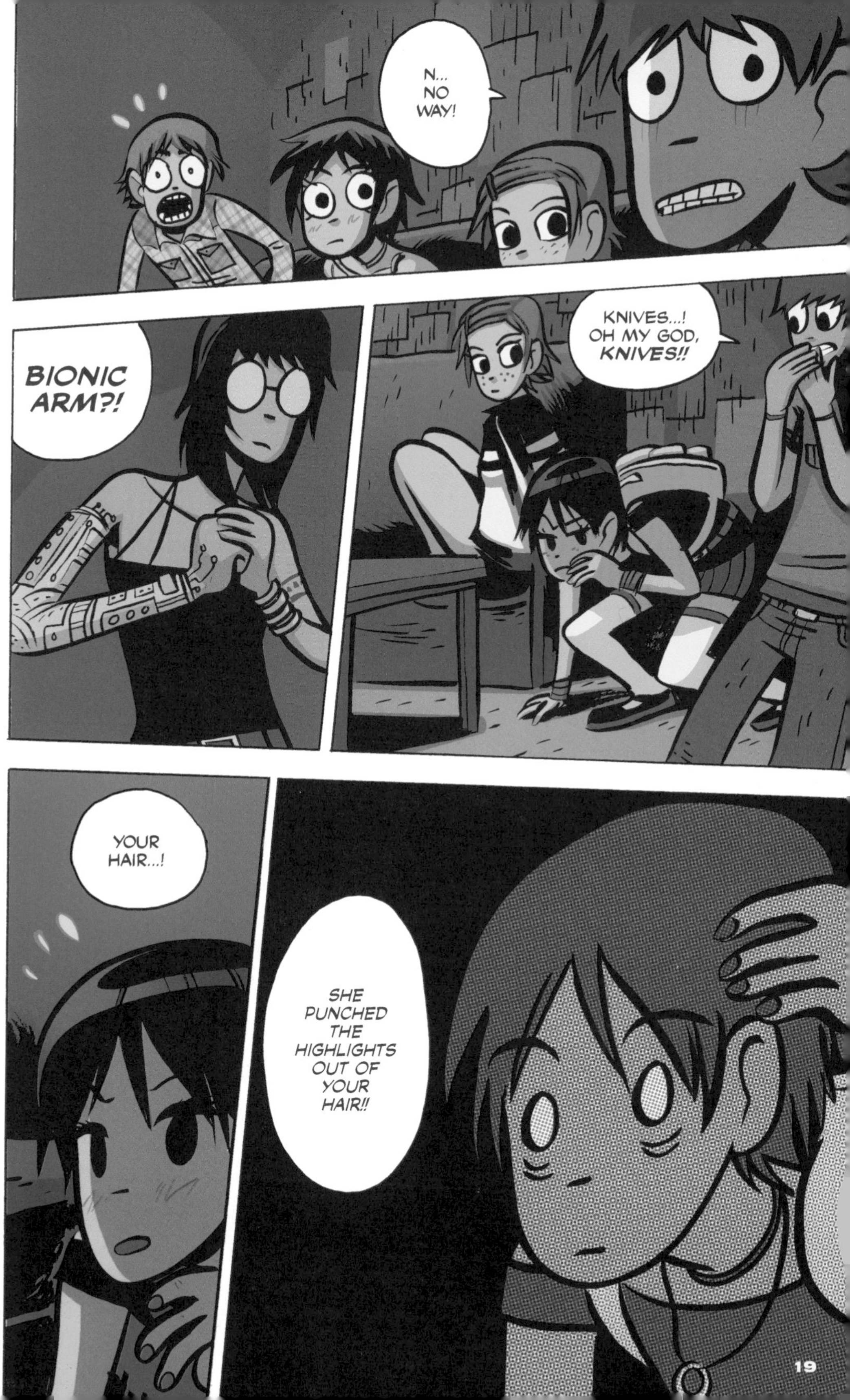
N...
NO
WAY!
BIONIC
ARM?!
KNIVES...!
OH MY GOD,
KNIVES!!
YOUR
HAIR...!
SHE
PUNCHED
THE
HIGHLIGHTS
OUT OF
YOUR
HAIR!!

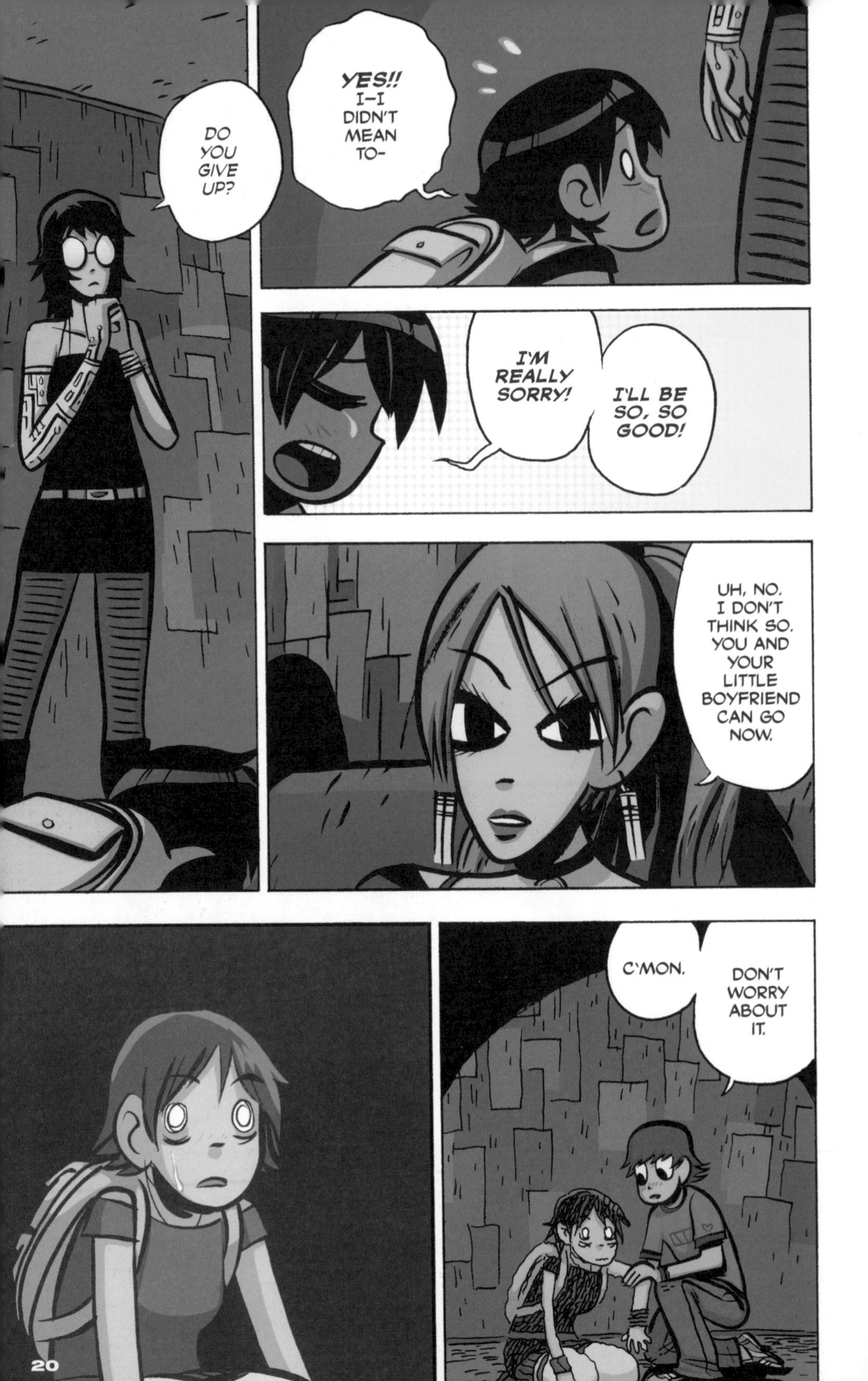
DO YOU GIVE UP?
YES!! I-I DIDN'T MEAN TO-
I'M REALLY SORRY!
I'LL BE SO, SO GOOD!
UH, NO. I DON'T THINK SO. YOU AND YOUR LITTLE BOYFRIEND CAN GO NOW.
C'MON.
DON'T WORRY ABOUT IT.

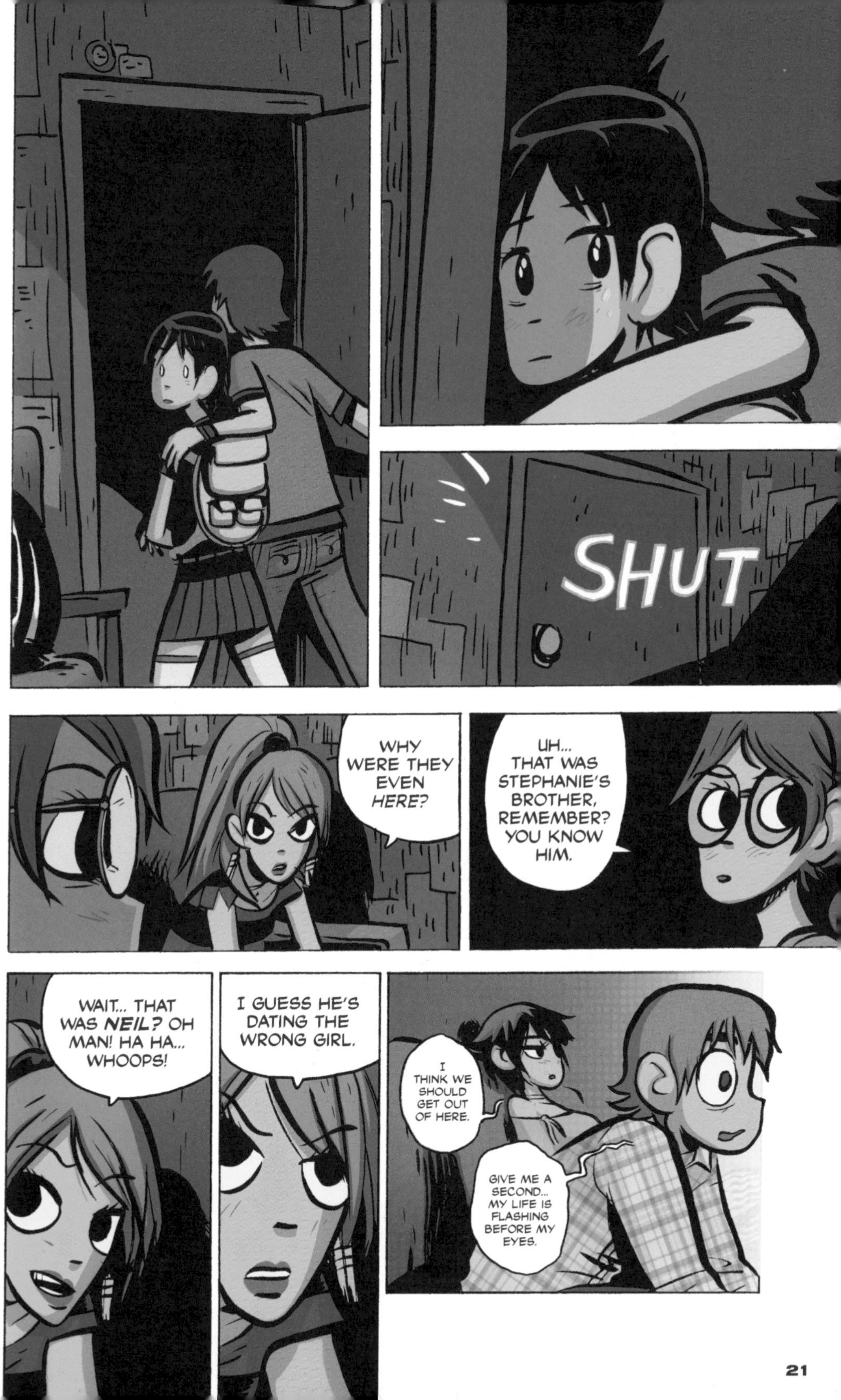
SHUT
WHY WERE THEY EVEN HERE?
UH... THAT WAS STEPHANIE'S BROTHER, REMEMBER? YOU KNOW HIM.
WAIT... THAT WAS NEIL? OH MAN! HA HA... WHOOPS!
I GUESS HE'S DATING THE WRONG GIRL.
I THINK WE SHOULD GET OUT OF HERE.
GIVE ME A SECOND... MY LIFE IS FLASHING BEFORE MY EYES.

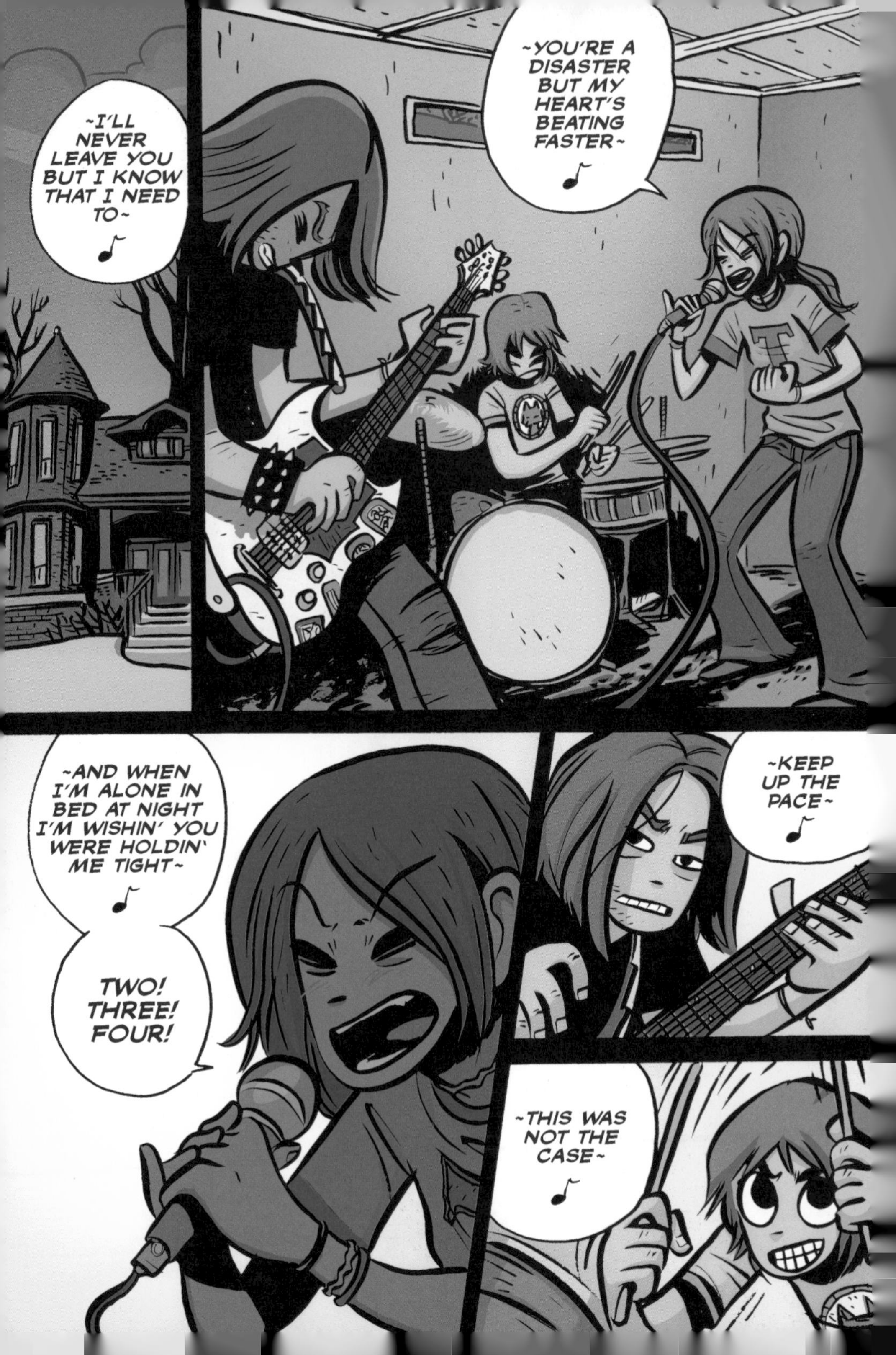
~I'LL NEVER LEAVE YOU BUT I KNOW THAT I NEED TO~
~YOU'RE A DISASTER BUT MY HEART'S BEATING FASTER~
~AND WHEN I'M ALONE IN BED AT NIGHT I'M WISHIN' YOU WERE HOLDIN' ME TIGHT~
TWO! THREE! FOUR!
~KEEP UP THE PACE~
~THIS WAS NOT THE CASE~

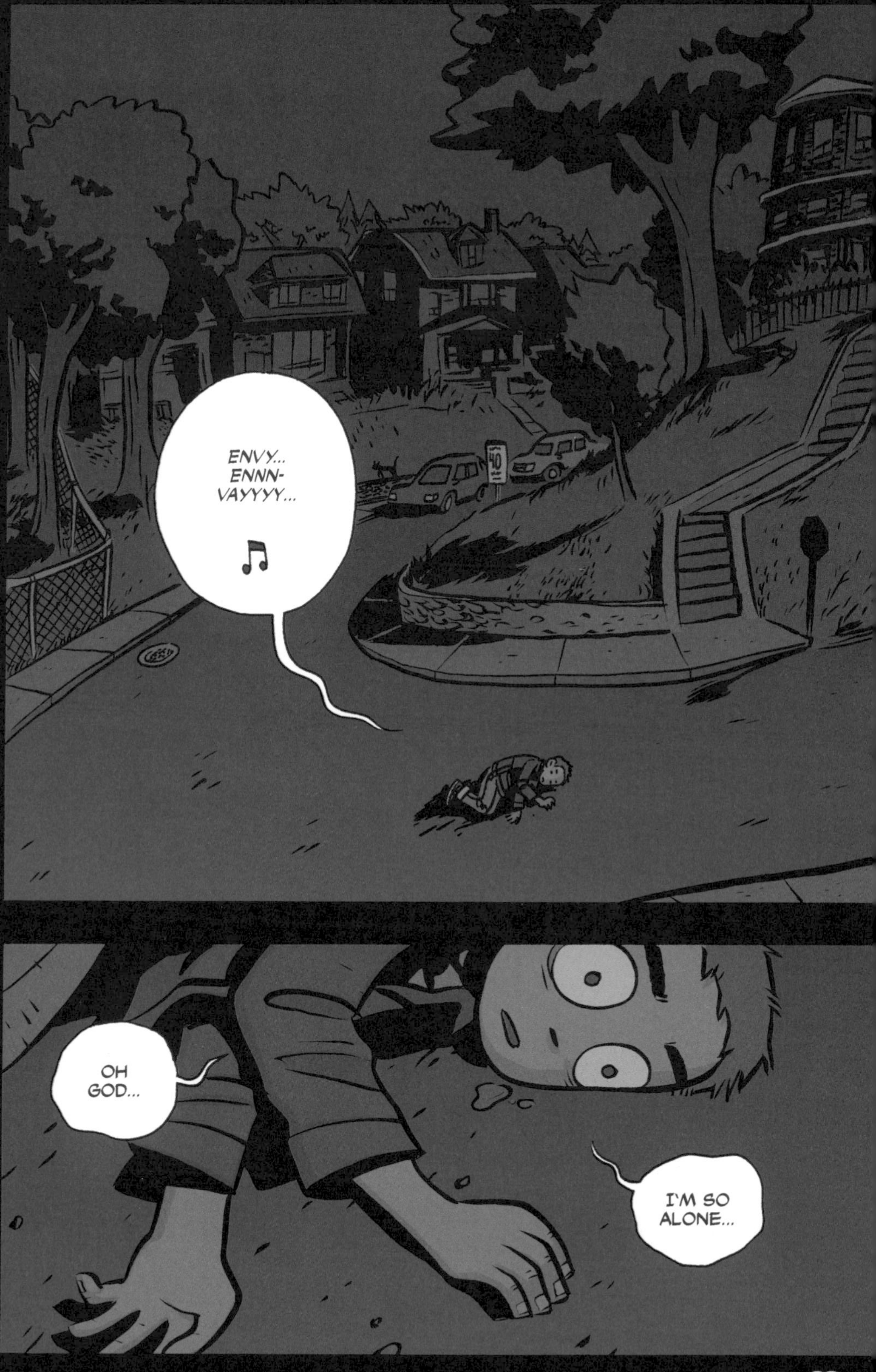
ENVY... ENNN- VAYYYY... ♫
40
OH GOD...
I'M SO ALONE...

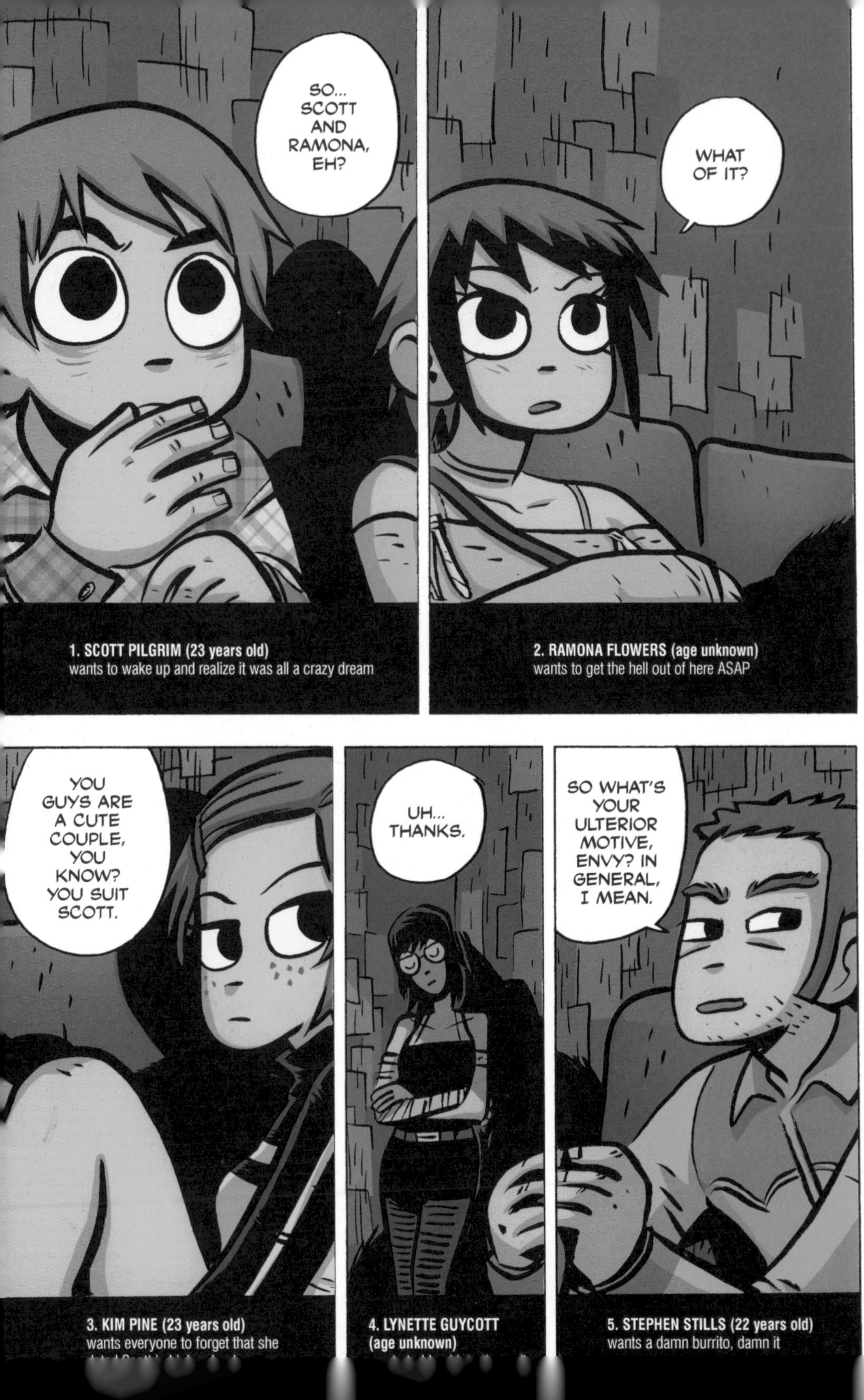

SO... SCOTT AND RAMONA, EH?
1. SCOTT PILGRIM (23 years old)
wants to wake up and realize it was all a crazy dream
WHAT OF IT?
2. RAMONA FLOWERS (age unknown)
wants to get the hell out of here ASAP
YOU GUYS ARE A CUTE COUPLE, YOU KNOW? YOU SUIT SCOTT.
3. KIM PINE (23 years old)
wants everyone to forget that she
UH... THANKS.
4. LYNETTE GUYCOTT
(age unknown)
SO WHAT'S YOUR ULTERIOR MOTIVE, ENVY? IN GENERAL, I MEAN.
5. STEPHEN STILLS (22 years old)
wants a damn burrito, damn it

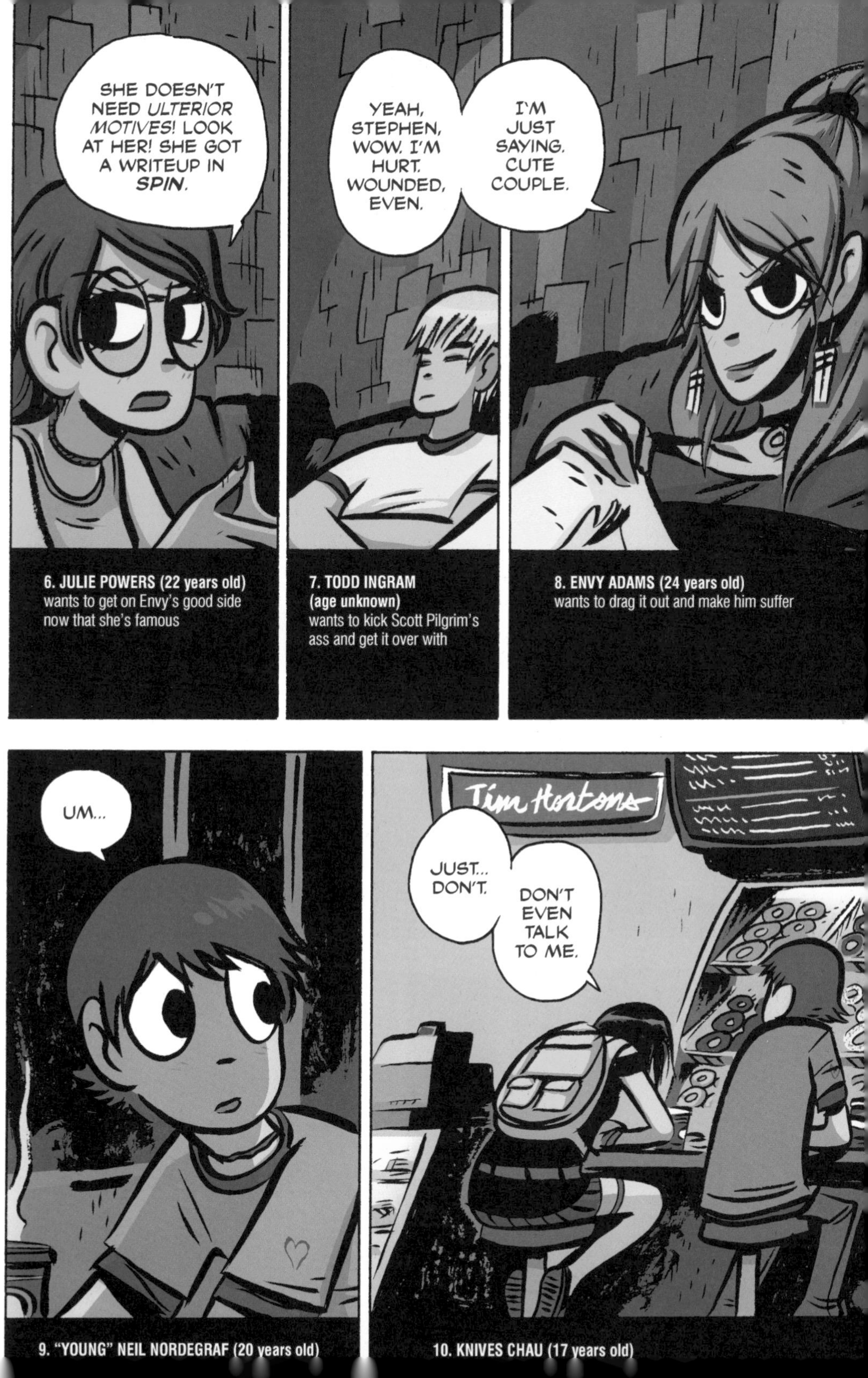
SHE DOESN'T NEED *ULTERIOR MOTIVES*! LOOK AT HER! SHE GOT A WRITEUP IN ***SPIN***.
6. JULIE POWERS (22 years old) wants to get on Envy's good side now that she's famous
YEAH, STEPHEN, WOW. I'M HURT. WOUNDED, EVEN.
I'M JUST SAYING. CUTE COUPLE.
7. TODD INGRAM (age unknown) wants to kick Scott Pilgrim's ass and get it over with
8. ENVY ADAMS (24 years old) wants to drag it out and make him suffer
UM...
9. "YOUNG" NEIL NORDEGRAF (20 years old)
Tim Hortons
JUST... DON'T.
DON'T EVEN TALK TO ME.
10. KNIVES CHAU (17 years old)

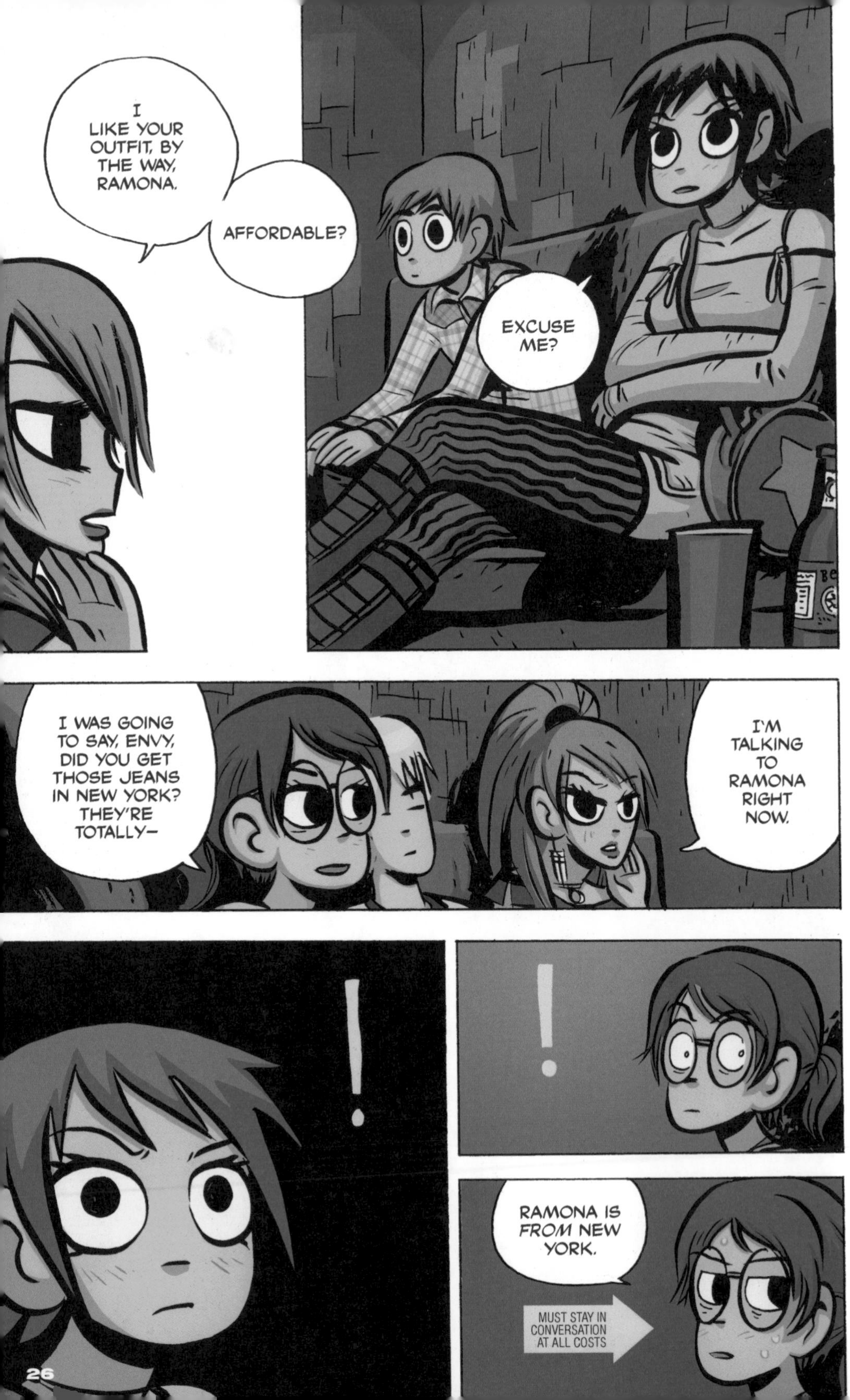
I LIKE YOUR OUTFIT, BY THE WAY, RAMONA.
AFFORDABLE?
EXCUSE ME?
I WAS GOING TO SAY, ENVY, DID YOU GET THOSE JEANS IN NEW YORK? THEY'RE TOTALLY—
I'M TALKING TO RAMONA RIGHT NOW.
!
!
RAMONA IS *FROM* NEW YORK.
MUST STAY IN CONVERSATION AT ALL COSTS

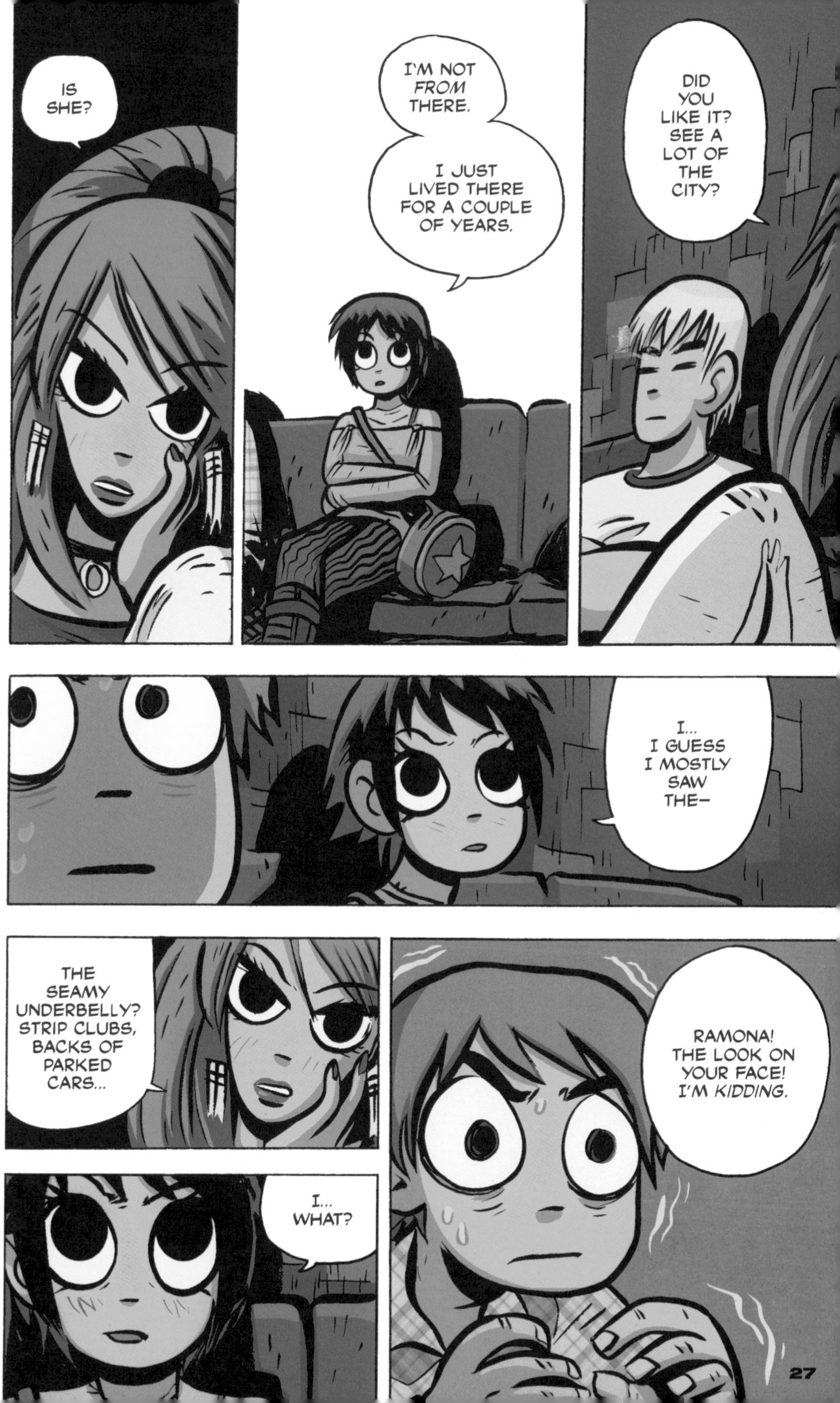
IS SHE?
I'M NOT *FROM* THERE.
I JUST LIVED THERE FOR A COUPLE OF YEARS.
DID YOU LIKE IT? SEE A LOT OF THE CITY?
I... I GUESS I MOSTLY SAW THE–
THE SEAMY UNDERBELLY? STRIP CLUBS, BACKS OF PARKED CARS...
RAMONA! THE LOOK ON YOUR FACE! I'M *KIDDING*.
I... WHAT?

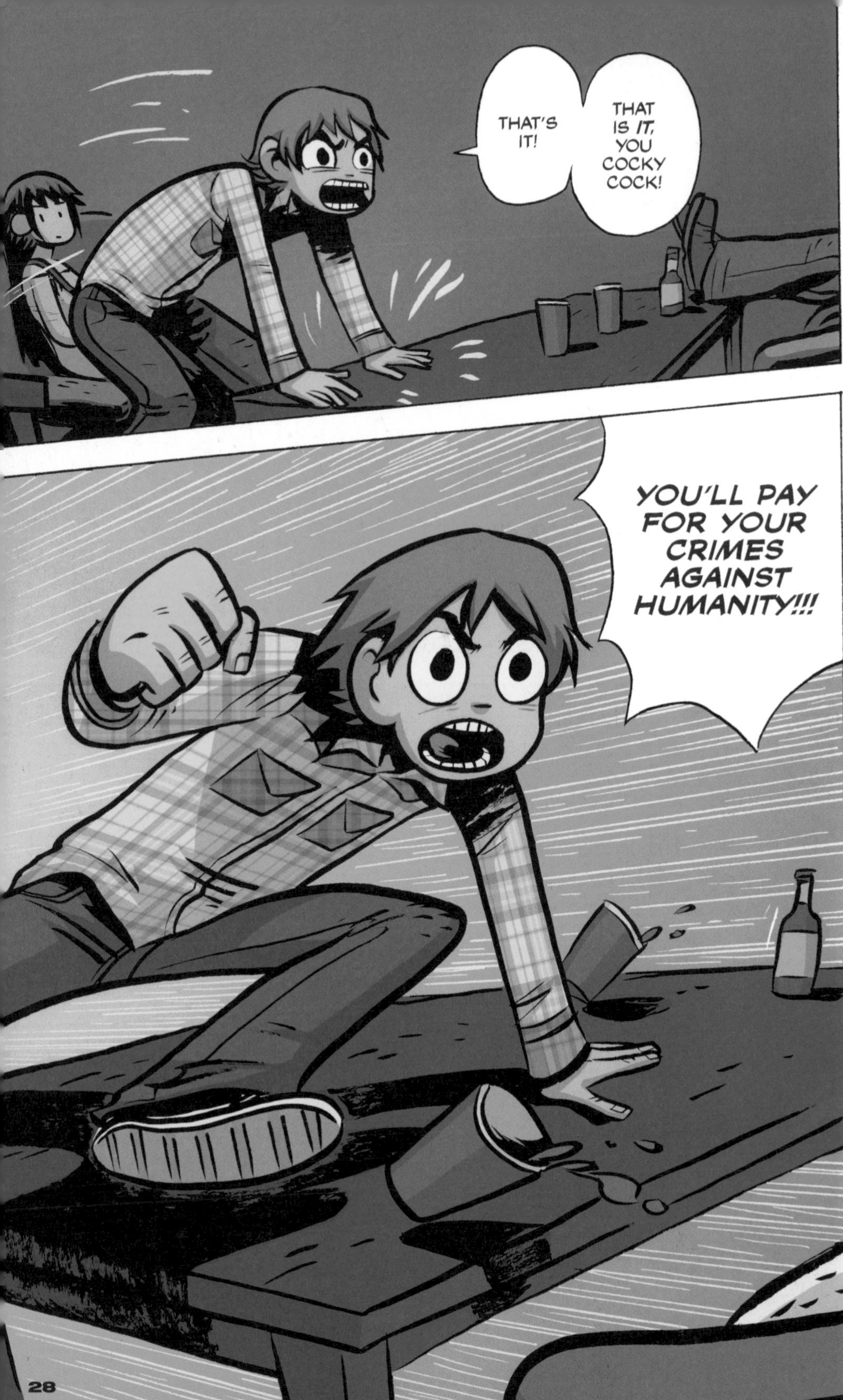
THAT'S IT!
THAT IS *IT*, YOU COCKY COCK!
YOU'LL PAY FOR YOUR CRIMES AGAINST HUMANITY!!!

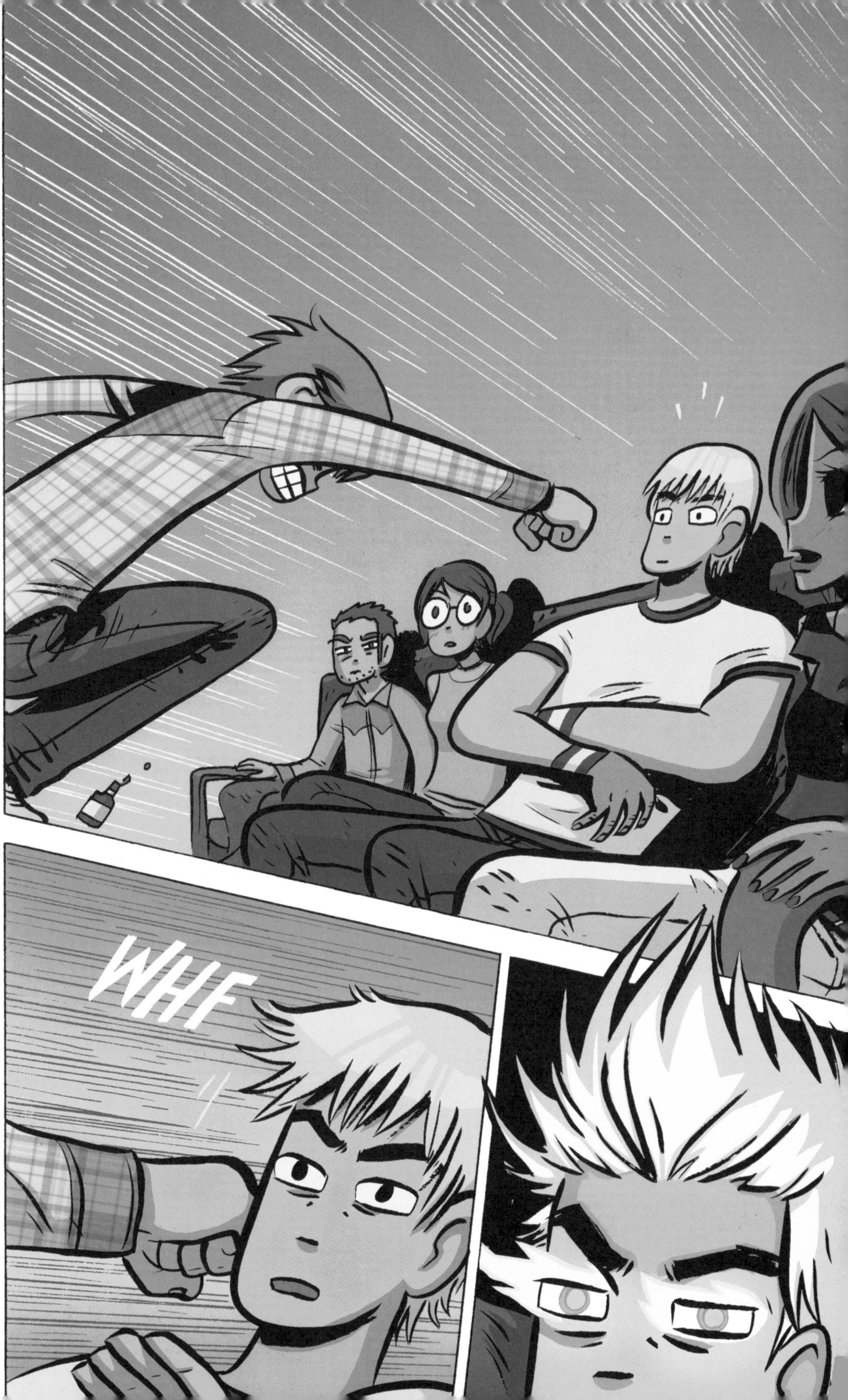
WHF

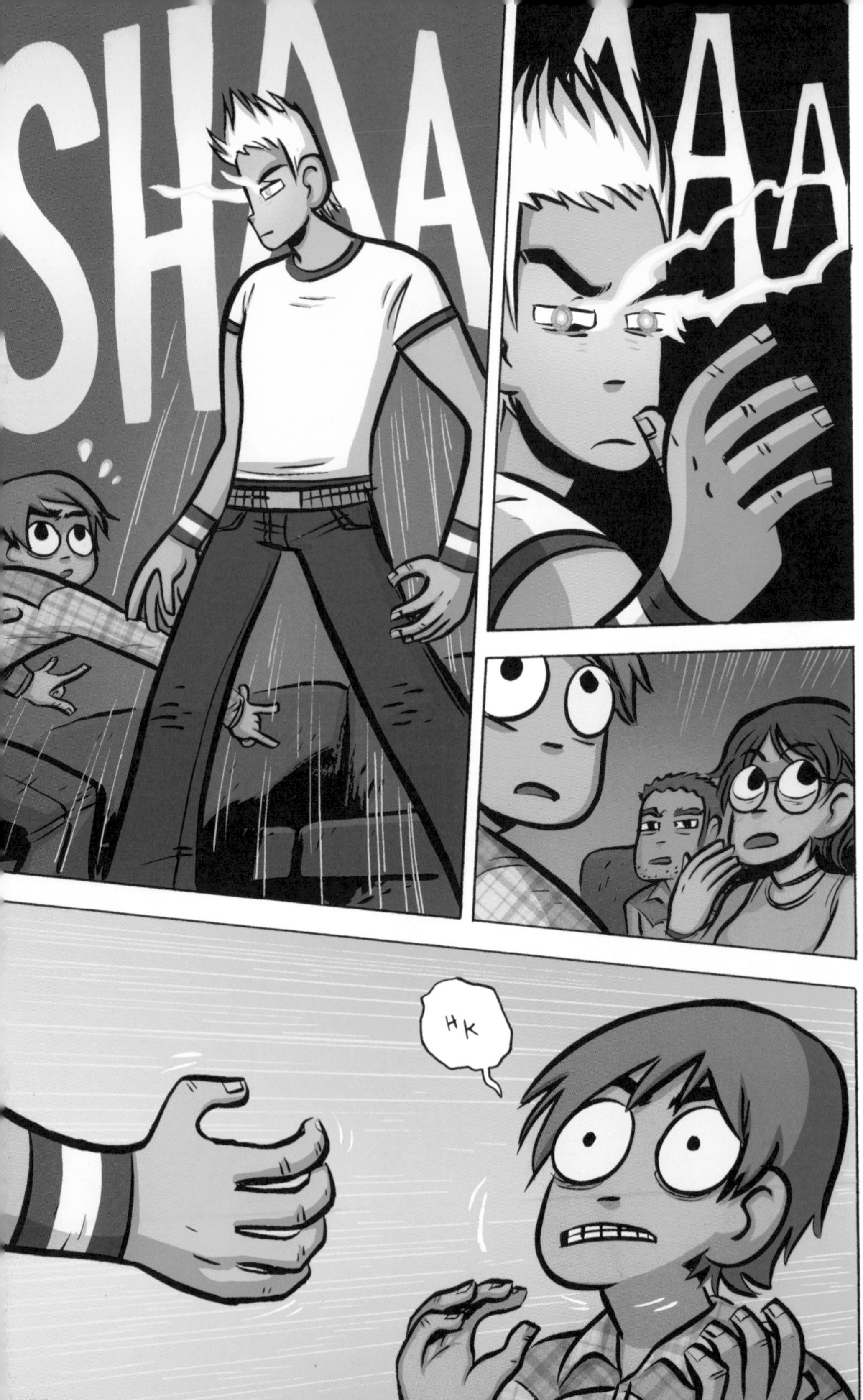
SHAAAAAA
HK

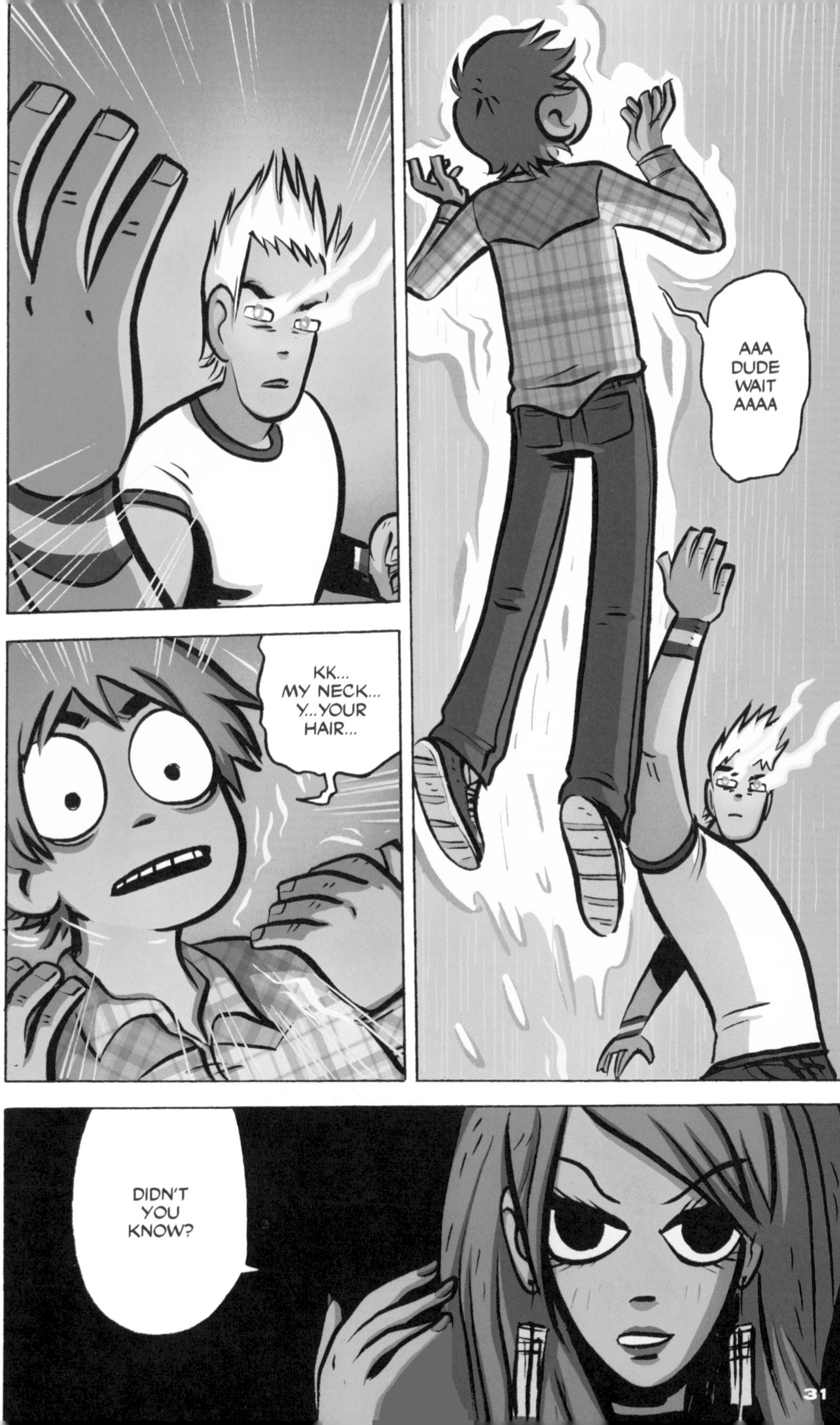
AAA DUDE WAIT AAAA
KK... MY NECK... Y...YOUR HAIR...
DIDN'T YOU KNOW?

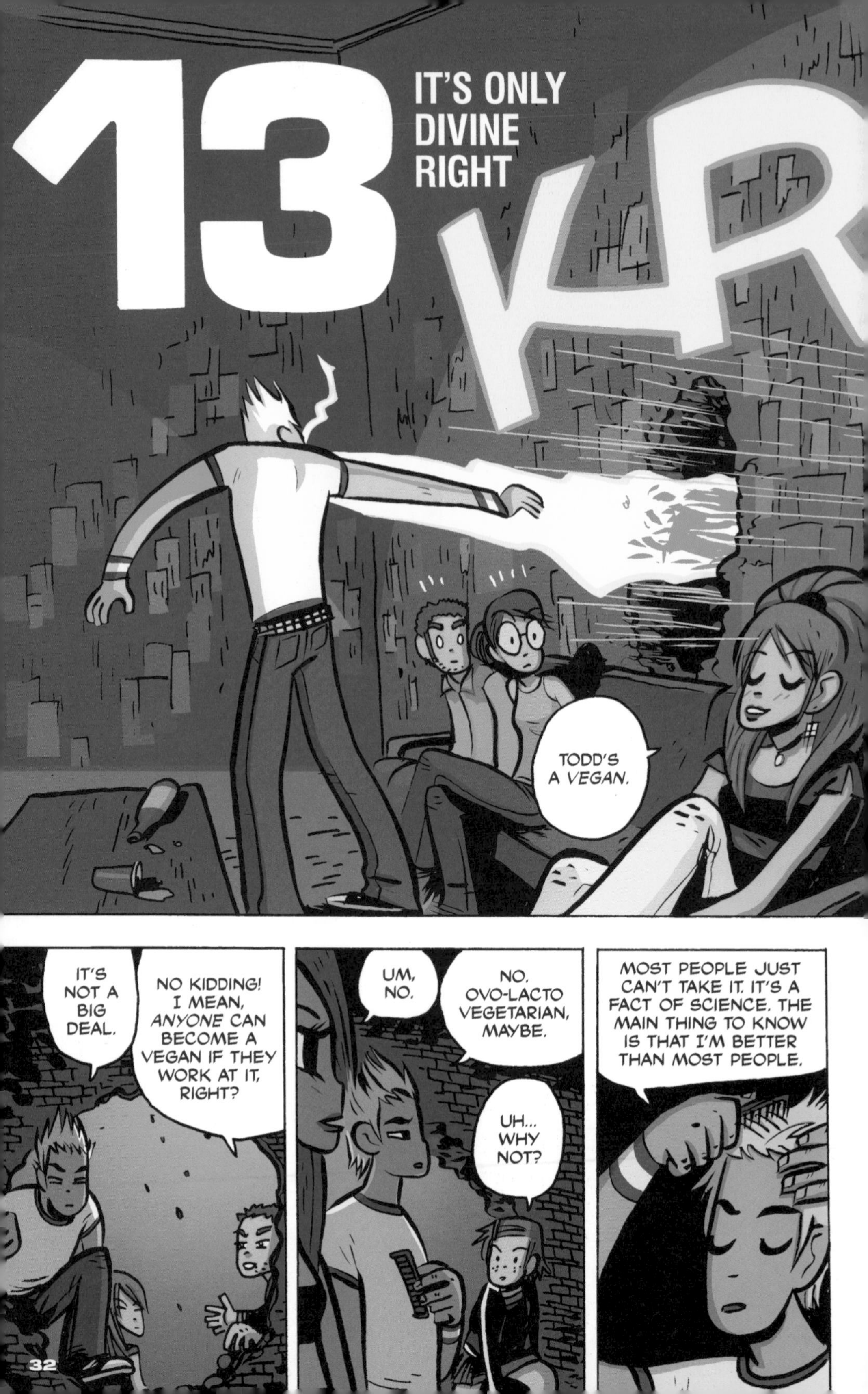
13
IT'S ONLY DIVINE RIGHT
KR
TODD'S A *VEGAN*.
IT'S NOT A BIG DEAL.
NO KIDDING! I MEAN, *ANYONE* CAN BECOME A VEGAN IF THEY WORK AT IT, RIGHT?
UM, NO.
NO. OVO-LACTO VEGETARIAN, MAYBE.
UH... WHY NOT?
MOST PEOPLE JUST CAN'T TAKE IT. IT'S A FACT OF SCIENCE. THE MAIN THING TO KNOW IS THAT I'M BETTER THAN MOST PEOPLE.

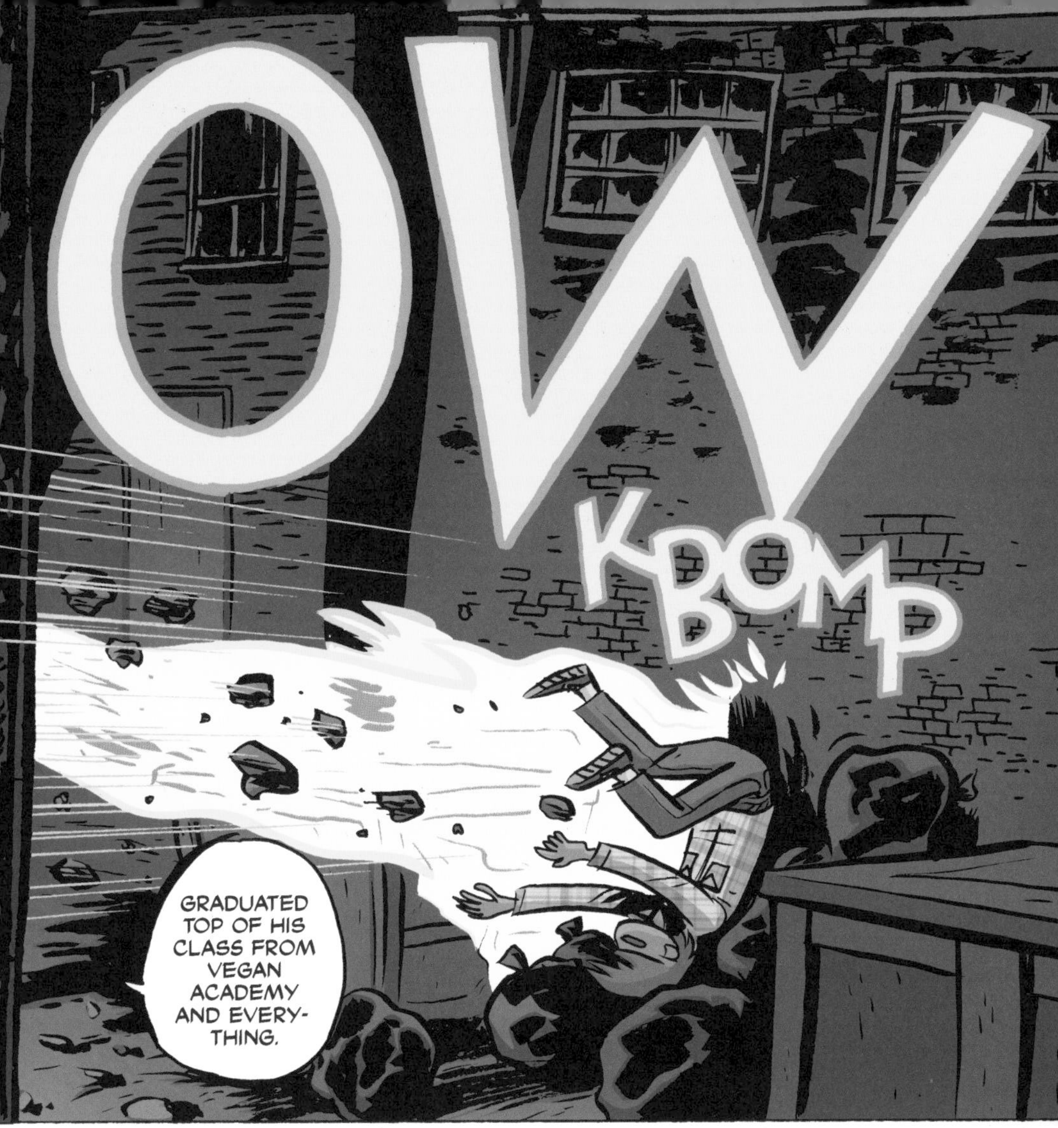
OW
KBOMP
GRADUATED TOP OF HIS CLASS FROM VEGAN ACADEMY AND EVERY-THING.

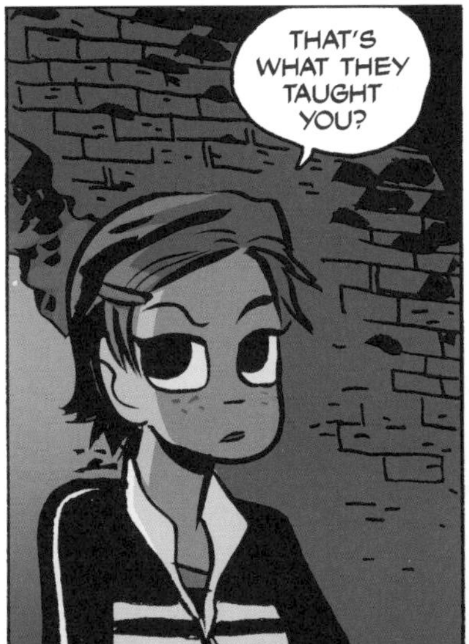
THAT'S WHAT THEY TAUGHT YOU?

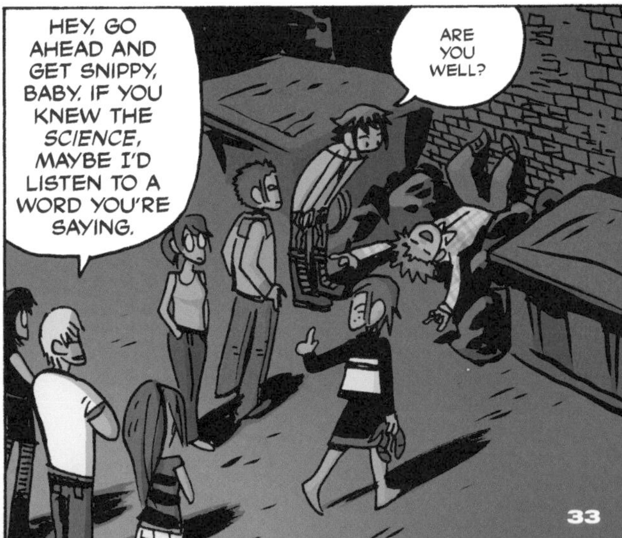
HEY, GO AHEAD AND GET SNIPPY, BABY. IF YOU KNEW THE *SCIENCE*, MAYBE I'D LISTEN TO A WORD YOU'RE SAYING.
ARE YOU WELL?

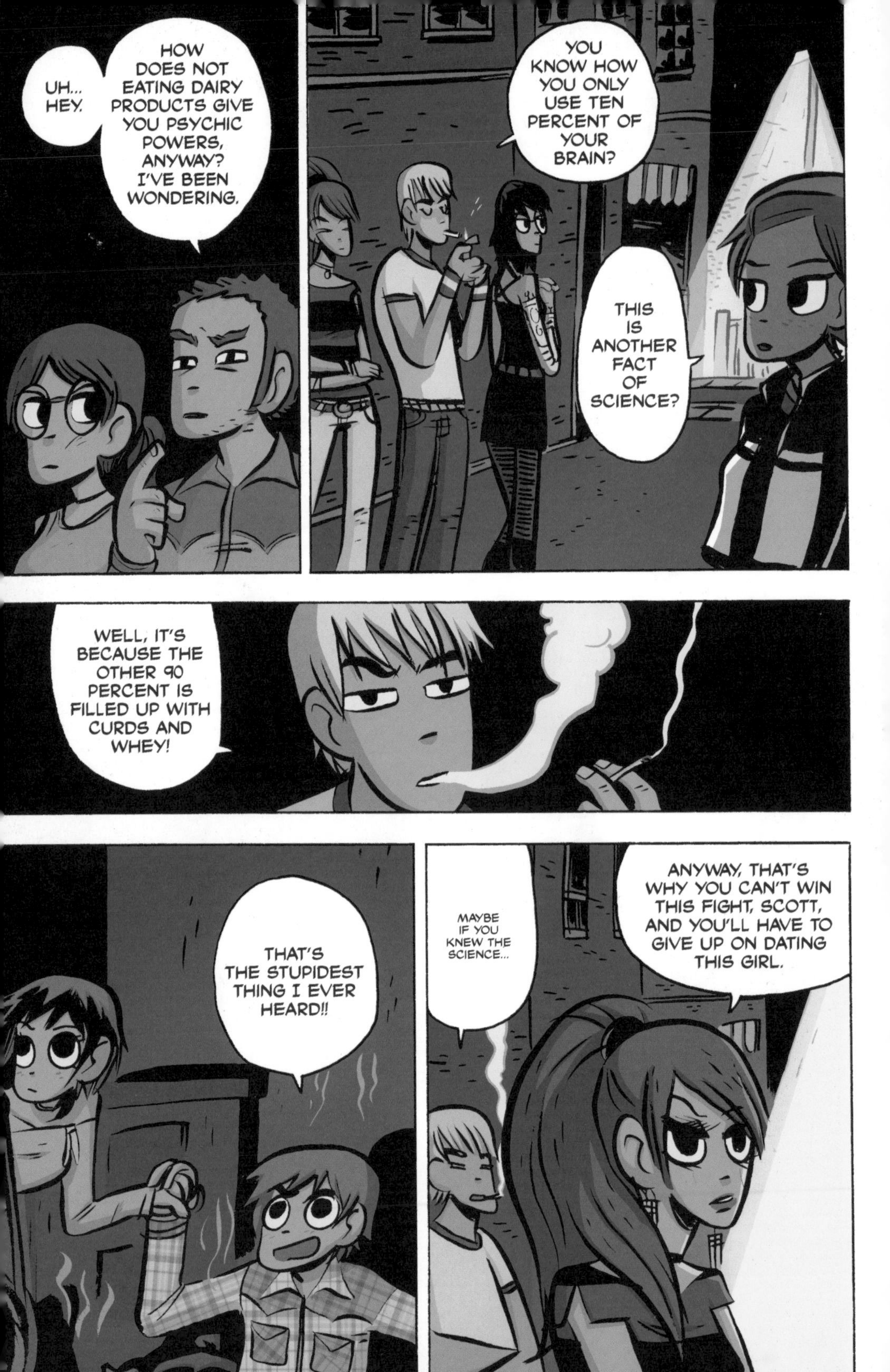
UH... HEY.
HOW DOES NOT EATING DAIRY PRODUCTS GIVE YOU PSYCHIC POWERS, ANYWAY? I'VE BEEN WONDERING.
YOU KNOW HOW YOU ONLY USE TEN PERCENT OF YOUR BRAIN?
THIS IS ANOTHER FACT OF SCIENCE?
WELL, IT'S BECAUSE THE OTHER 90 PERCENT IS FILLED UP WITH CURDS AND WHEY!
THAT'S THE STUPIDEST THING I EVER HEARD!!
ANYWAY, THAT'S WHY YOU CAN'T WIN THIS FIGHT, SCOTT, AND YOU'LL HAVE TO GIVE UP ON DATING THIS GIRL.
MAYBE IF YOU KNEW THE SCIENCE...

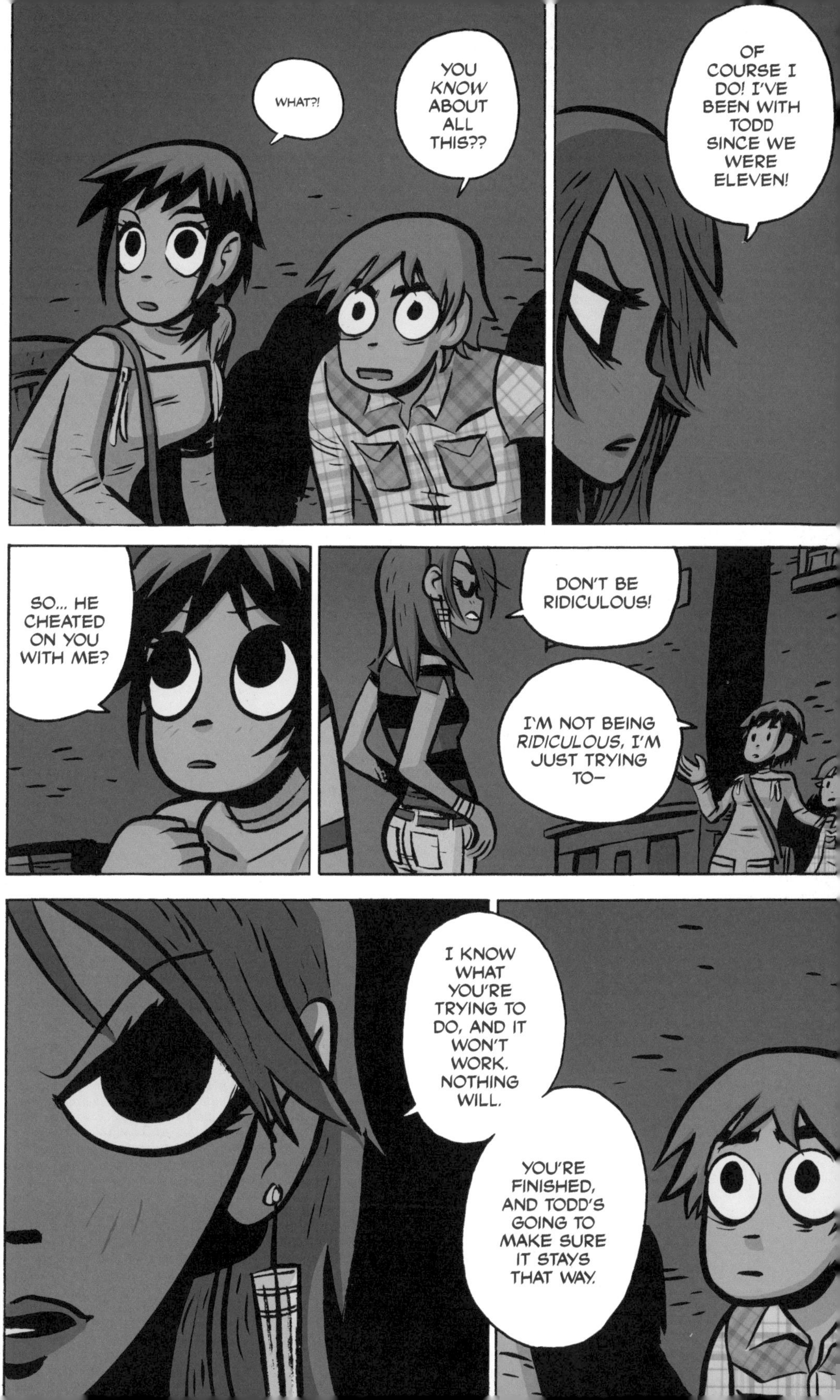
WHAT?!
YOU *KNOW* ABOUT ALL THIS??
OF COURSE I DO! I'VE BEEN WITH TODD SINCE WE WERE ELEVEN!
SO... HE CHEATED ON YOU WITH ME?
DON'T BE RIDICULOUS!
I'M NOT BEING *RIDICULOUS*, I'M JUST TRYING TO–
I KNOW WHAT YOU'RE TRYING TO DO, AND IT WON'T WORK. NOTHING WILL.
YOU'RE FINISHED, AND TODD'S GOING TO MAKE SURE IT STAYS THAT WAY.

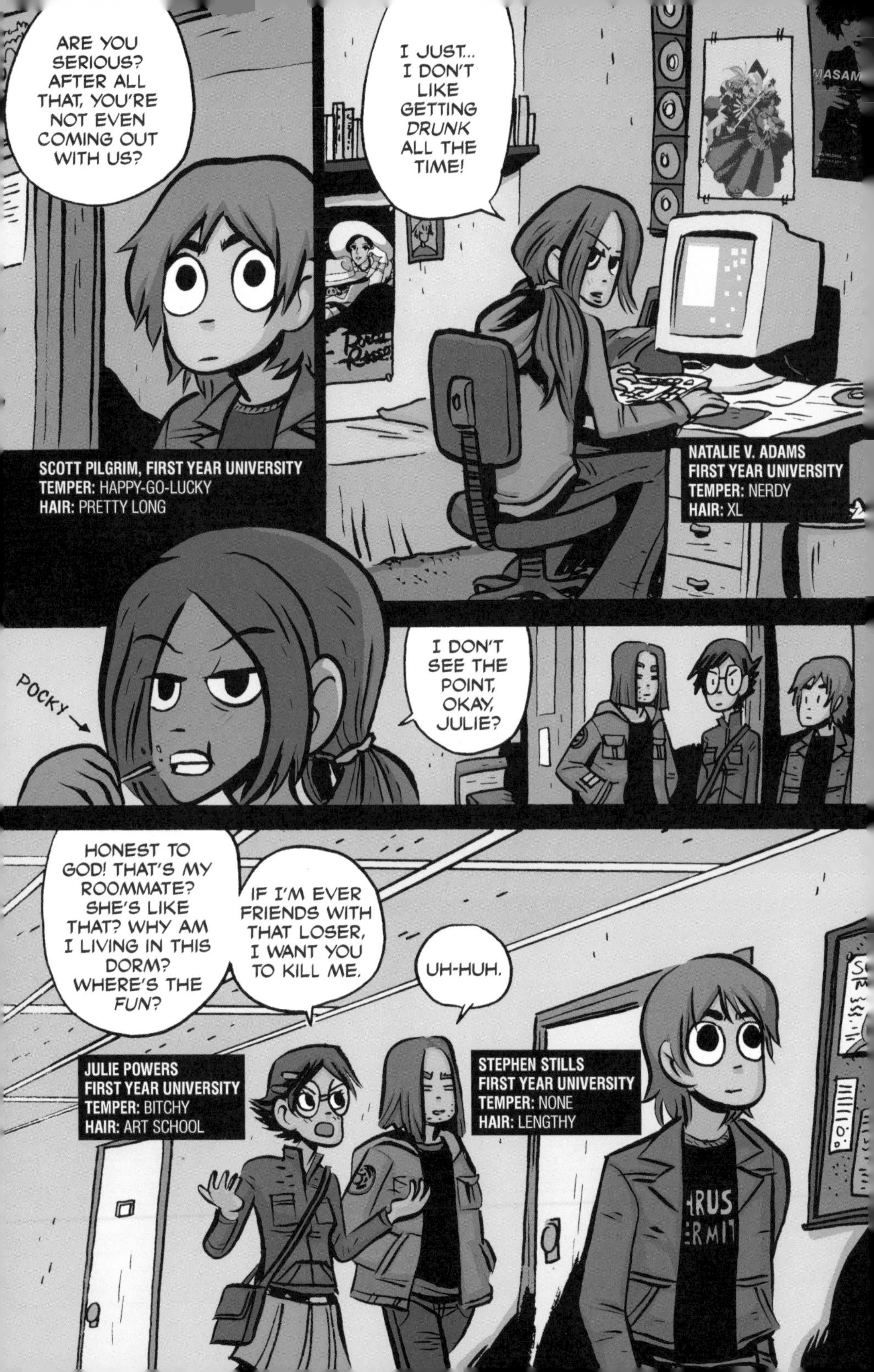
ARE YOU SERIOUS? AFTER ALL THAT, YOU'RE NOT EVEN COMING OUT WITH US?
I JUST... I DON'T LIKE GETTING DRUNK ALL THE TIME!
SCOTT PILGRIM, FIRST YEAR UNIVERSITY
TEMPER: HAPPY-GO-LUCKY
HAIR: PRETTY LONG
NATALIE V. ADAMS
FIRST YEAR UNIVERSITY
TEMPER: NERDY
HAIR: XL
POCKY
I DON'T SEE THE POINT, OKAY, JULIE?
HONEST TO GOD! THAT'S MY ROOMMATE? SHE'S LIKE THAT? WHY AM I LIVING IN THIS DORM? WHERE'S THE FUN?
IF I'M EVER FRIENDS WITH THAT LOSER, I WANT YOU TO KILL ME.
UH-HUH.
JULIE POWERS
FIRST YEAR UNIVERSITY
TEMPER: BITCHY
HAIR: ART SCHOOL
STEPHEN STILLS
FIRST YEAR UNIVERSITY
TEMPER: NONE
HAIR: LENGTHY

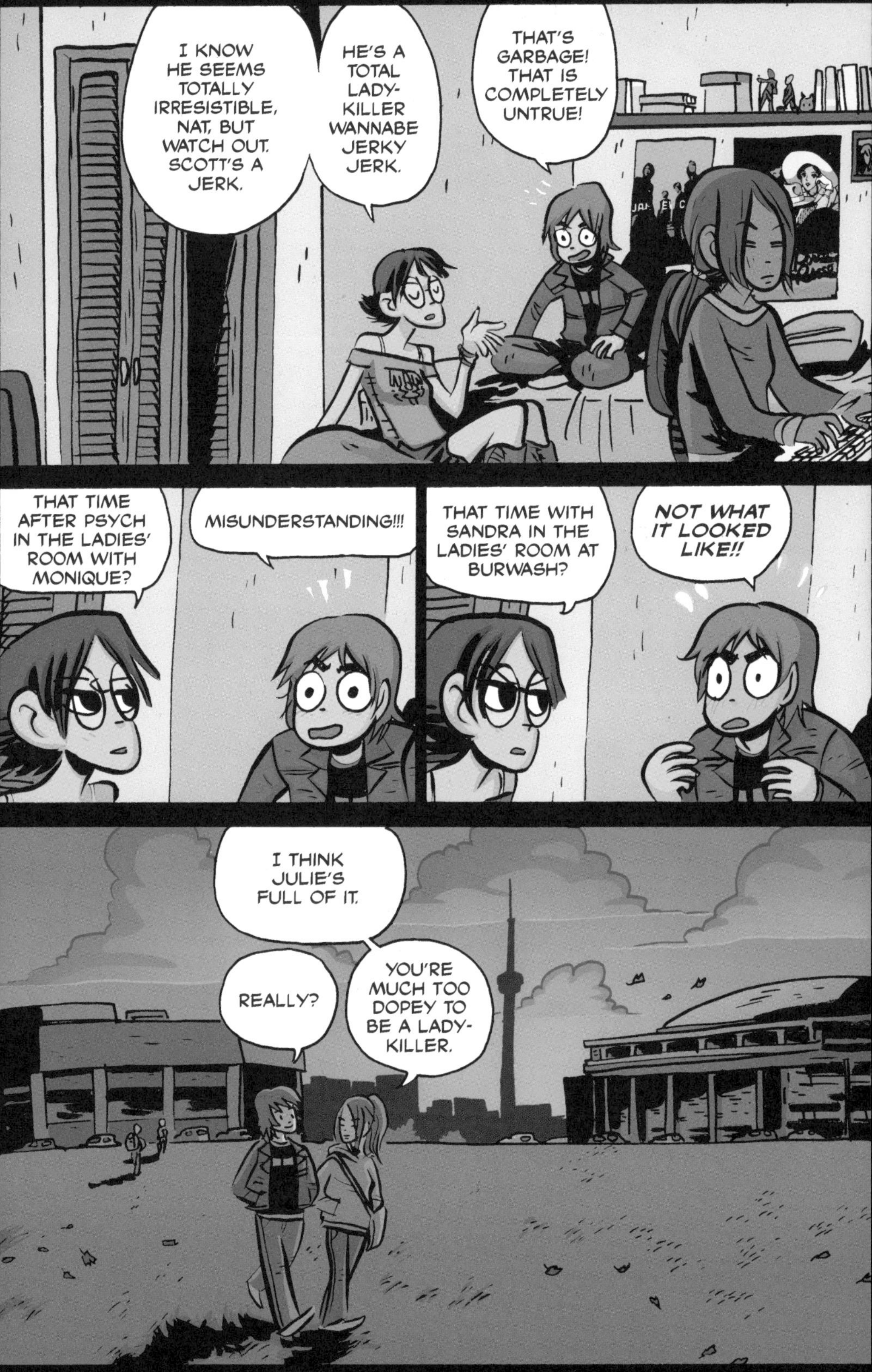
I KNOW HE SEEMS TOTALLY IRRESISTIBLE, NAT, BUT WATCH OUT. SCOTT'S A JERK.
HE'S A TOTAL LADY-KILLER WANNABE JERKY JERK.
THAT'S GARBAGE! THAT IS COMPLETELY UNTRUE!
THAT TIME AFTER PSYCH IN THE LADIES' ROOM WITH MONIQUE?
MISUNDERSTANDING!!!
THAT TIME WITH SANDRA IN THE LADIES' ROOM AT BURWASH?
NOT WHAT IT LOOKED LIKE!!
I THINK JULIE'S FULL OF IT.
REALLY?
YOU'RE MUCH TOO DOPEY TO BE A LADY-KILLER.

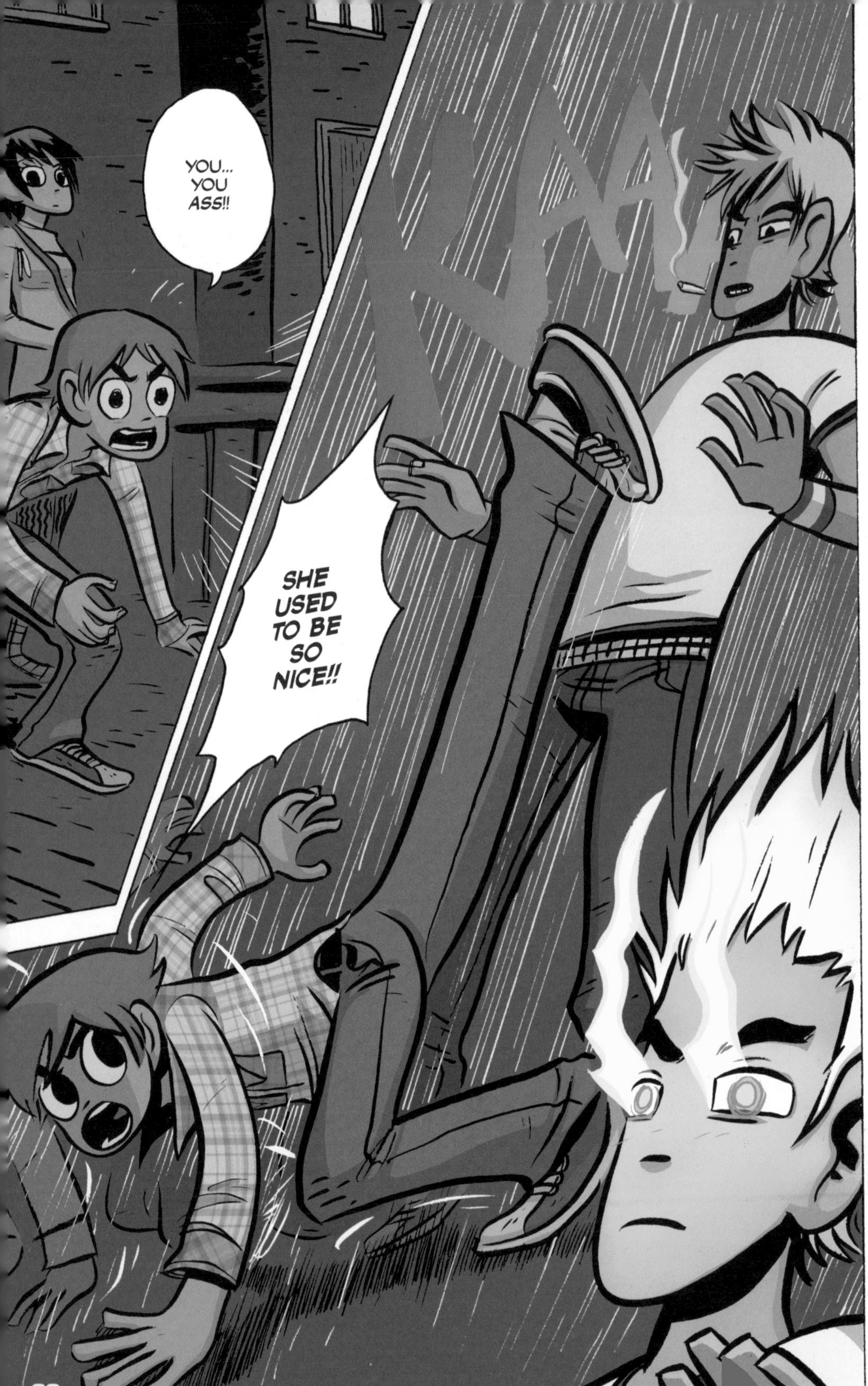
YOU... YOU ASS!!
SHE USED TO BE SO NICE!!

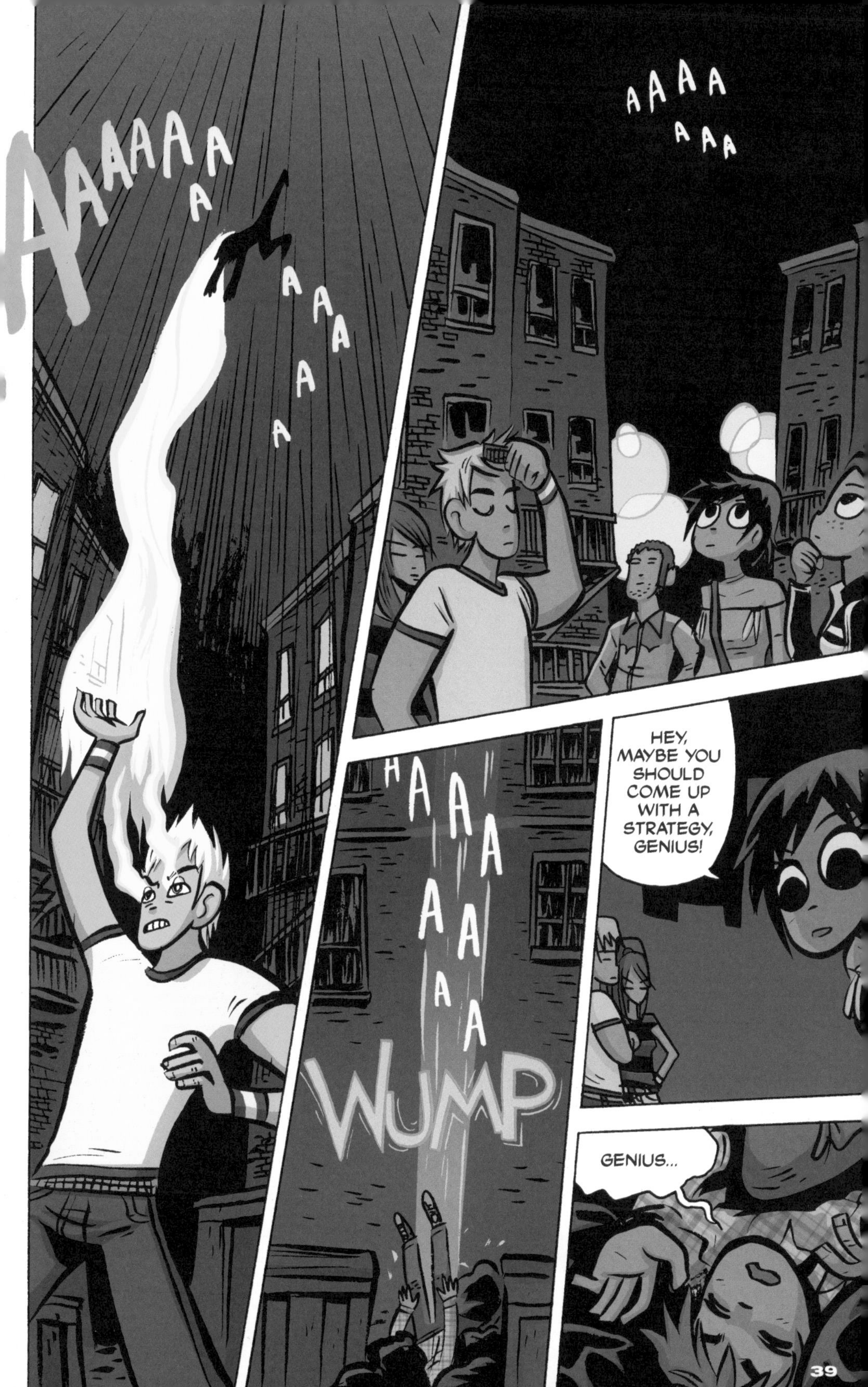
AAAAAAA
A
AAAA
A
A
AAAA
AAA
HAAAA
AAAA
A
A
WUMP
HEY, MAYBE YOU SHOULD COME UP WITH A STRATEGY, GENIUS!
GENIUS...

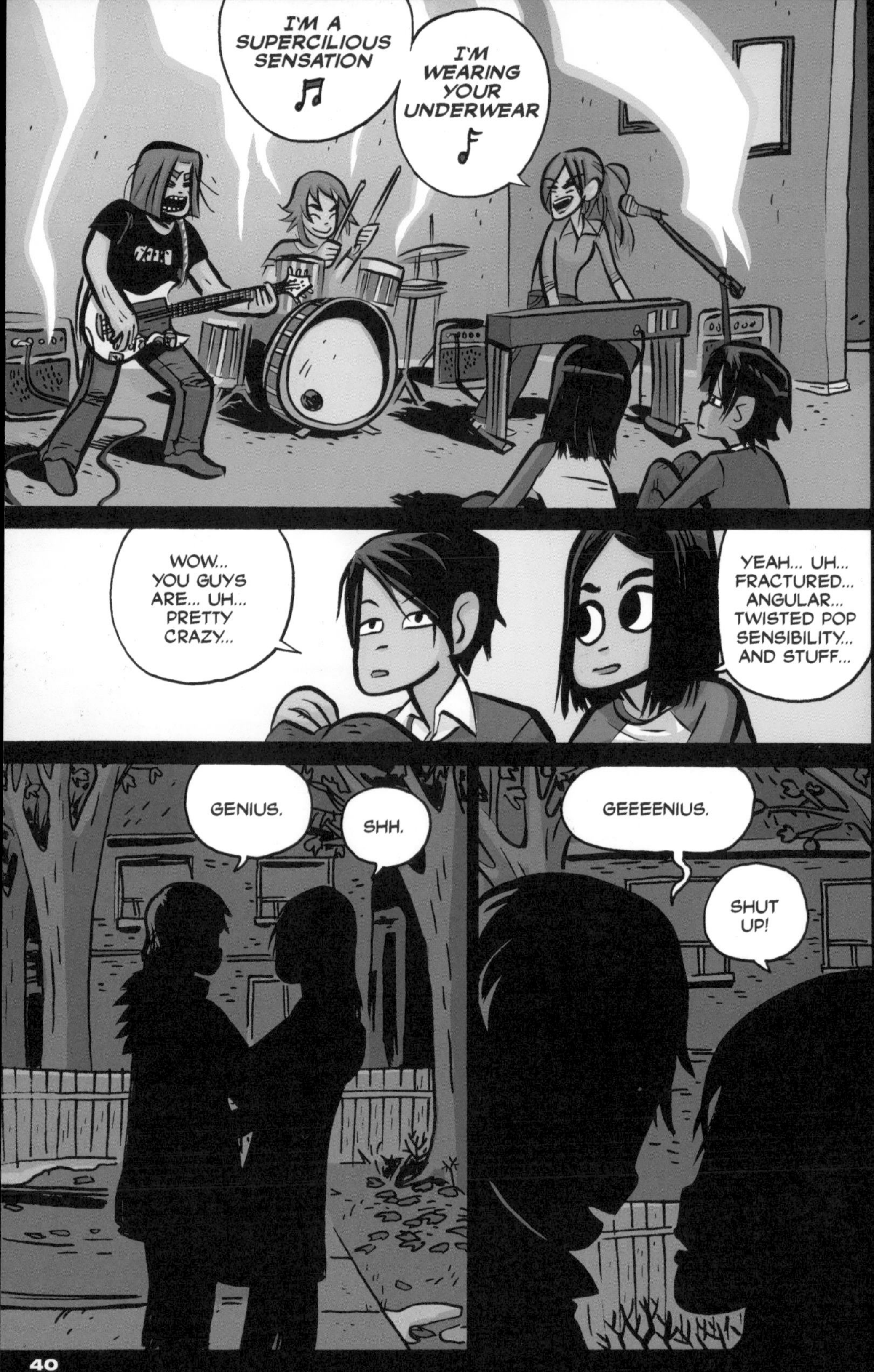
I'M A SUPERCILIOUS SENSATION
I'M WEARING YOUR UNDERWEAR
WOW... YOU GUYS ARE... UH... PRETTY CRAZY...
YEAH... UH... FRACTURED... ANGULAR... TWISTED POP SENSIBILITY... AND STUFF...
GENIUS.
SHH.
GEEEENIUS.
SHUT UP!

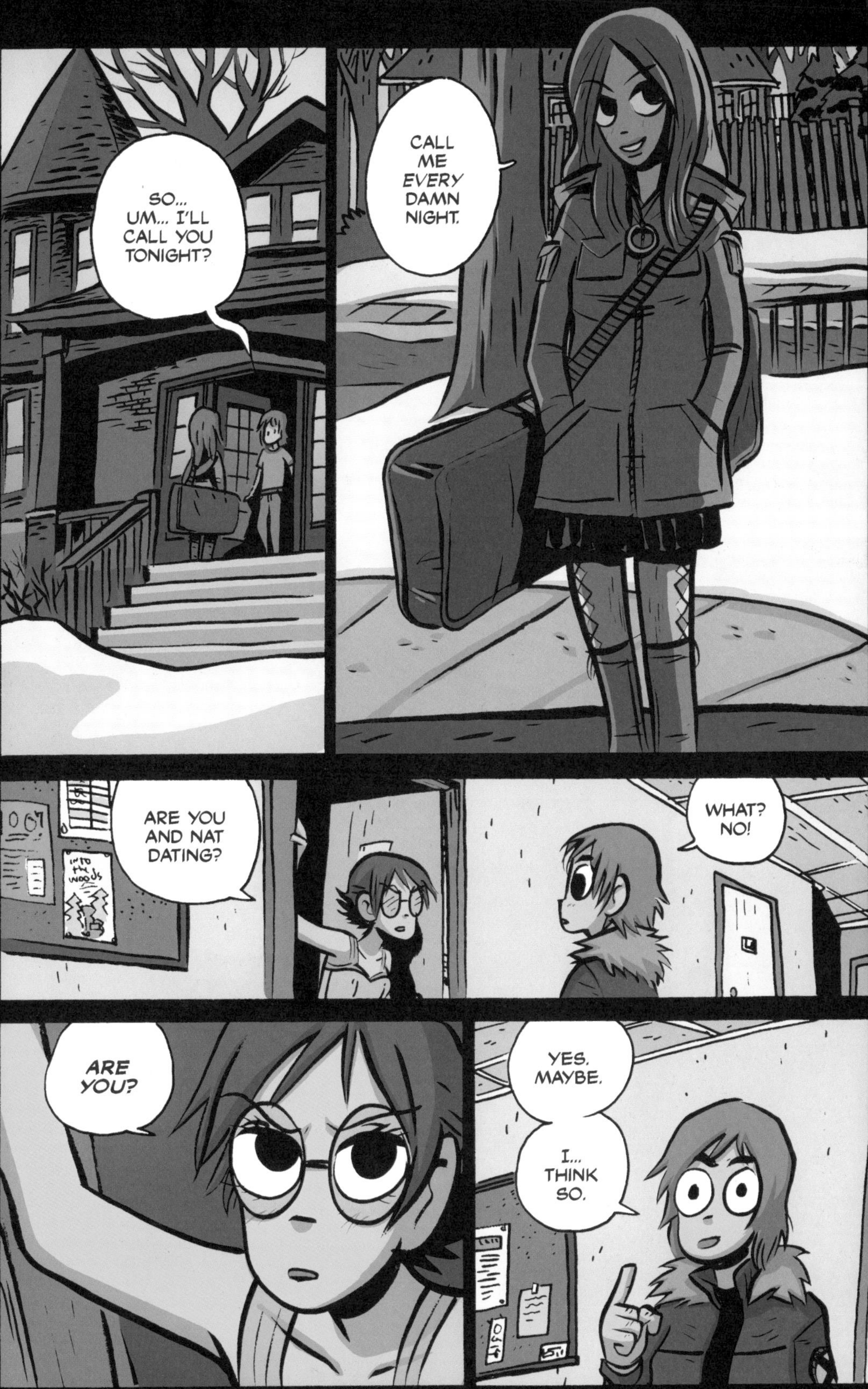
SO... UM... I'LL CALL YOU TONIGHT?
CALL ME *EVERY* DAMN NIGHT.
ARE YOU AND NAT DATING?
WHAT? NO!
ARE YOU?
YES. MAYBE.
I... THINK SO.

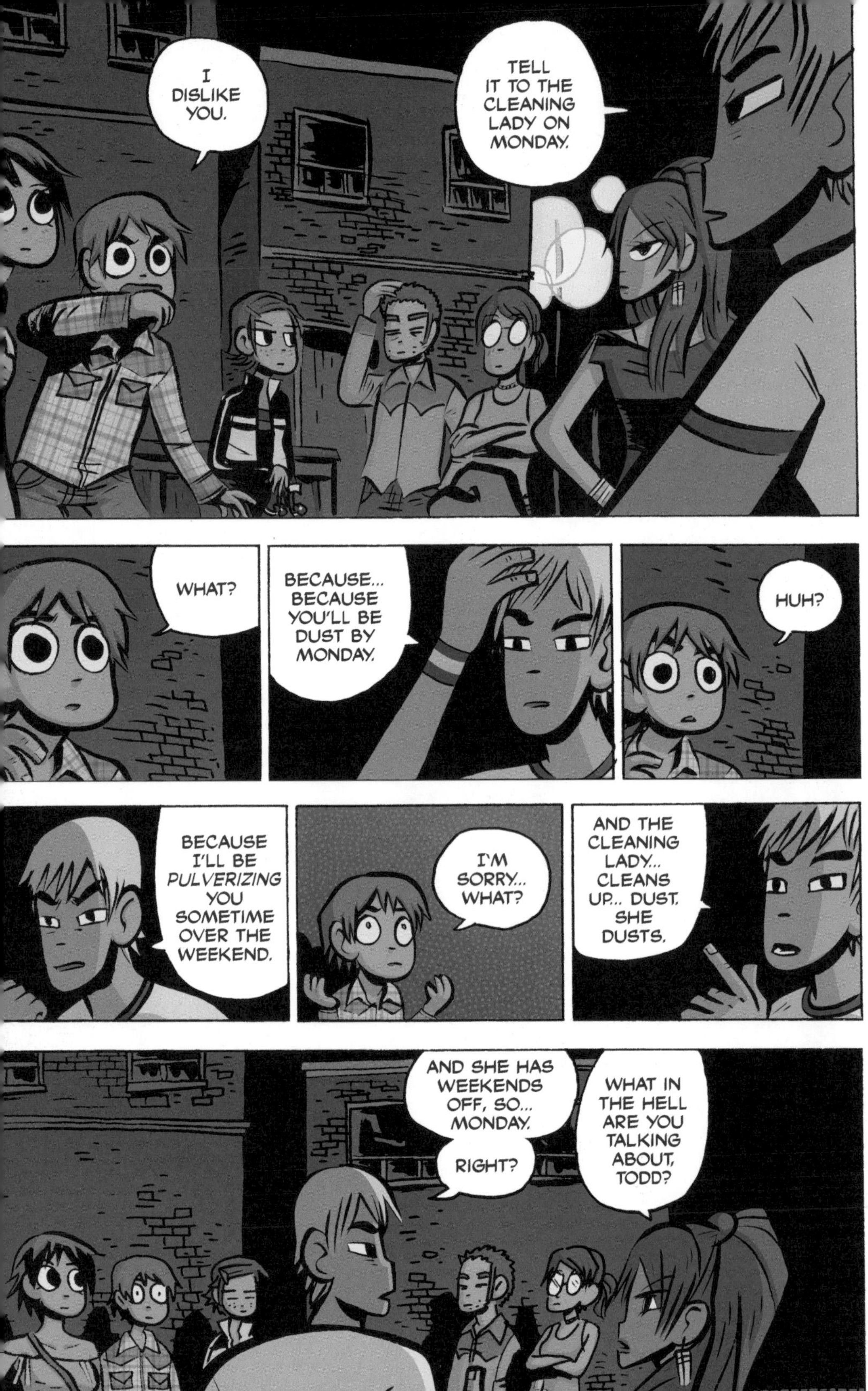
I DISLIKE YOU.
TELL IT TO THE CLEANING LADY ON MONDAY.
WHAT?
BECAUSE... BECAUSE YOU'LL BE DUST BY MONDAY.
HUH?
BECAUSE I'LL BE *PULVERIZING* YOU SOMETIME OVER THE WEEKEND.
I'M SORRY... WHAT?
AND THE CLEANING LADY... CLEANS UP... DUST. SHE DUSTS.
AND SHE HAS WEEKENDS OFF, SO... MONDAY.
RIGHT?
WHAT IN THE HELL ARE YOU TALKING ABOUT, TODD?

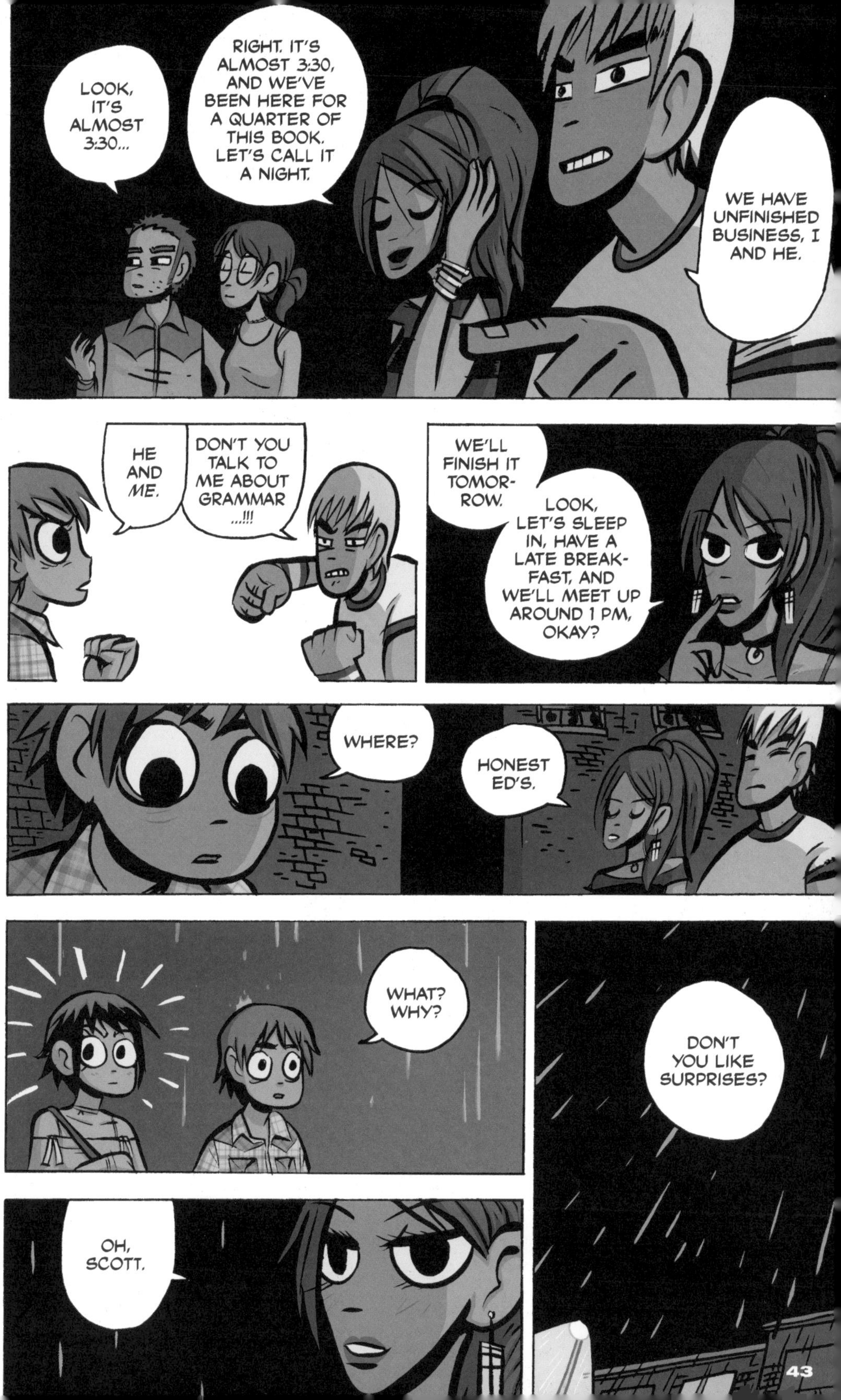
LOOK, IT'S ALMOST 3:30...
RIGHT. IT'S ALMOST 3:30, AND WE'VE BEEN HERE FOR A QUARTER OF THIS BOOK. LET'S CALL IT A NIGHT.
WE HAVE UNFINISHED BUSINESS, I AND HE.
HE AND *ME.*
DON'T YOU TALK TO ME ABOUT GRAMMAR ...!!!
WE'LL FINISH IT TOMORROW.
LOOK, LET'S SLEEP IN, HAVE A LATE BREAKFAST, AND WE'LL MEET UP AROUND 1 PM, OKAY?
WHERE?
HONEST ED'S.
WHAT? WHY?
DON'T YOU LIKE SURPRISES?
OH, SCOTT.

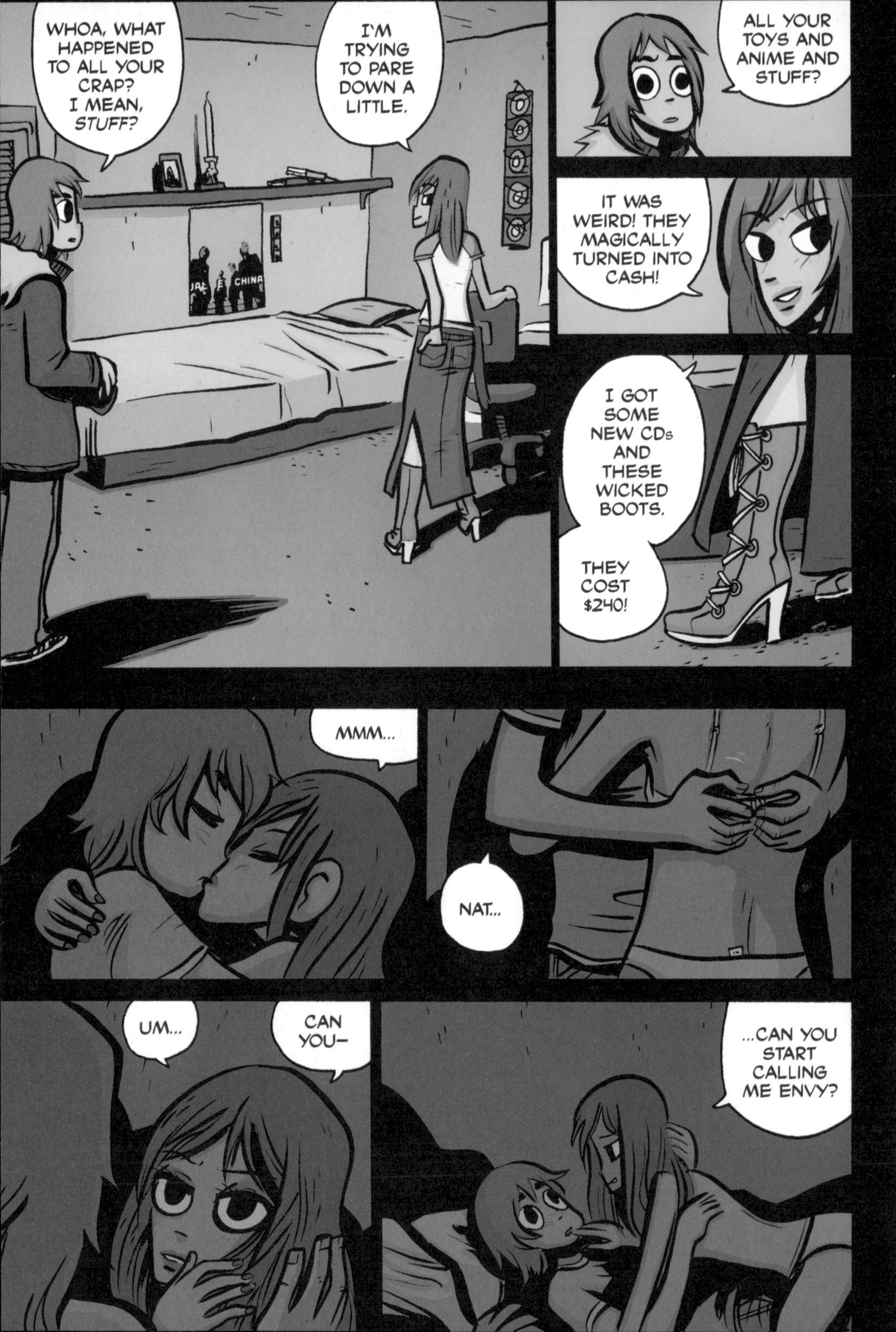

WHOA, WHAT HAPPENED TO ALL YOUR CRAP? I MEAN, STUFF?
I'M TRYING TO PARE DOWN A LITTLE.
JALE CHINA
ALL YOUR TOYS AND ANIME AND STUFF?
IT WAS WEIRD! THEY MAGICALLY TURNED INTO CASH!
I GOT SOME NEW CDs AND THESE WICKED BOOTS.
THEY COST $240!
MMM...
NAT...
UM...
CAN YOU–
...CAN YOU START CALLING ME ENVY?

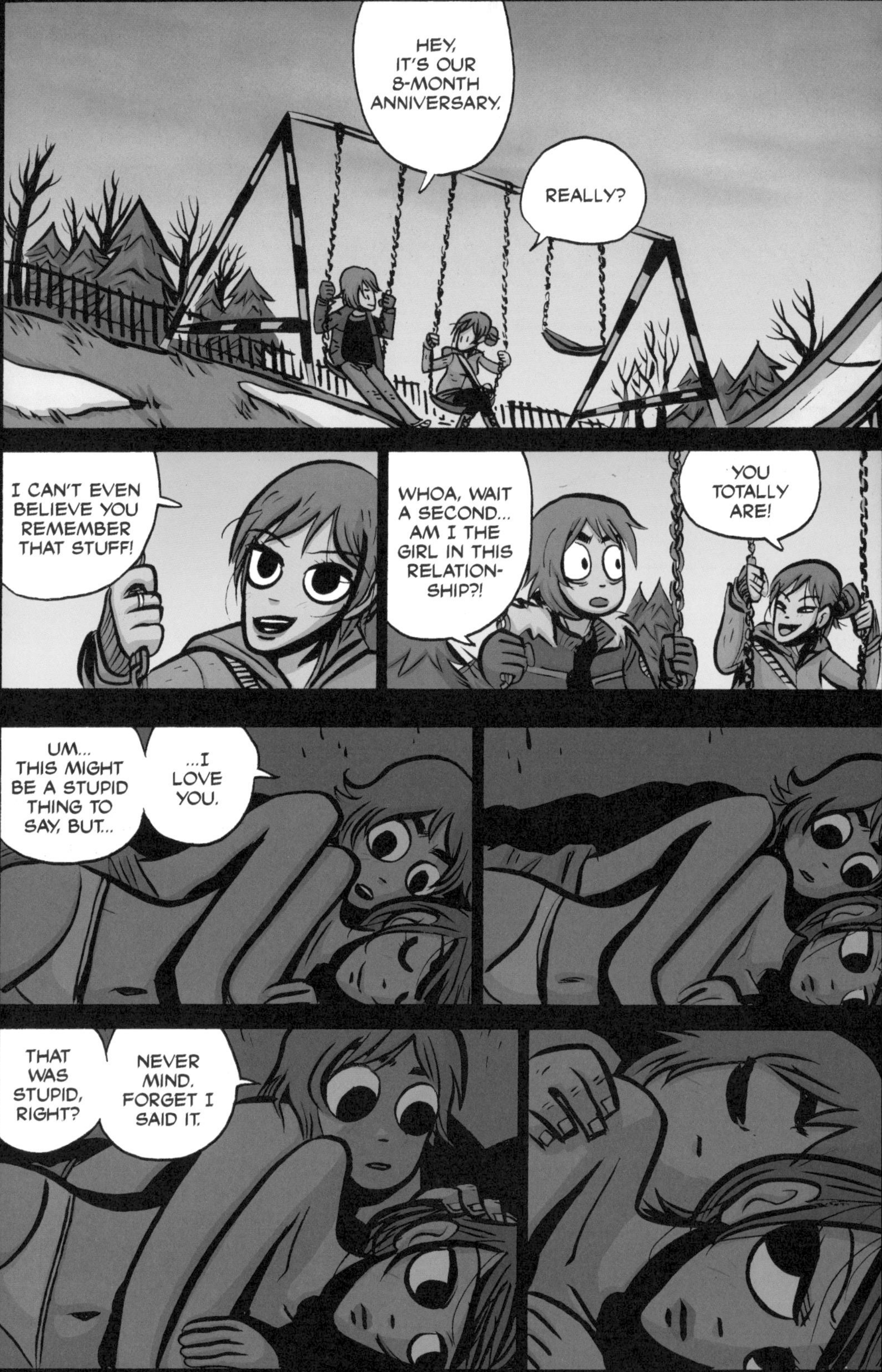
HEY, IT'S OUR 8-MONTH ANNIVERSARY.
REALLY?
I CAN'T EVEN BELIEVE YOU REMEMBER THAT STUFF!
WHOA, WAIT A SECOND... AM I THE GIRL IN THIS RELATION-SHIP?!
YOU TOTALLY ARE!
UM... THIS MIGHT BE A STUPID THING TO SAY, BUT...
...I LOVE YOU.
THAT WAS STUPID, RIGHT?
NEVER MIND. FORGET I SAID IT.

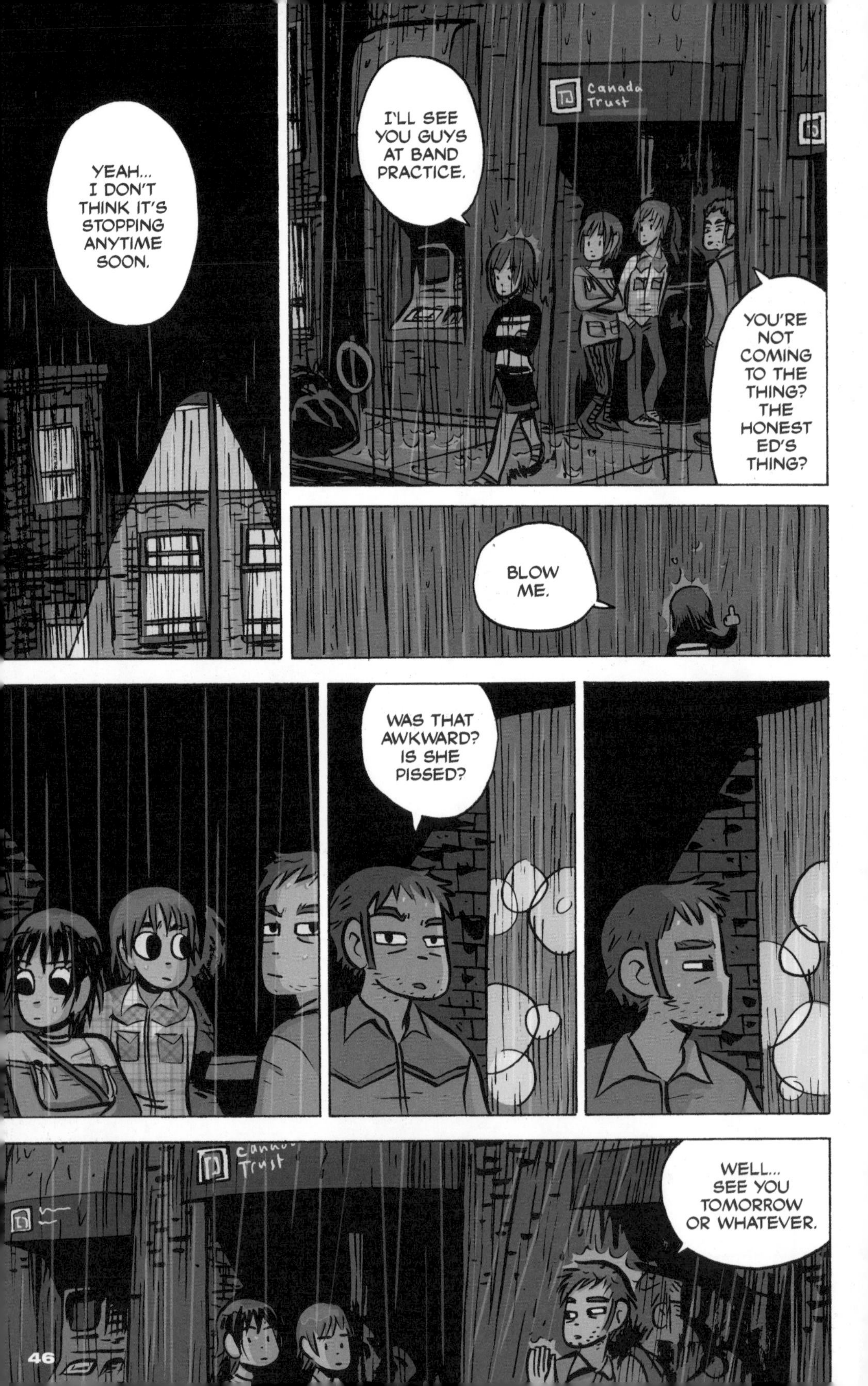
YEAH... I DON'T THINK IT'S STOPPING ANYTIME SOON.
I'LL SEE YOU GUYS AT BAND PRACTICE.
Canada Trust
YOU'RE NOT COMING TO THE THING? THE HONEST ED'S THING?
BLOW ME.
WAS THAT AWKWARD? IS SHE PISSED?
Trust
WELL... SEE YOU TOMORROW OR WHATEVER.

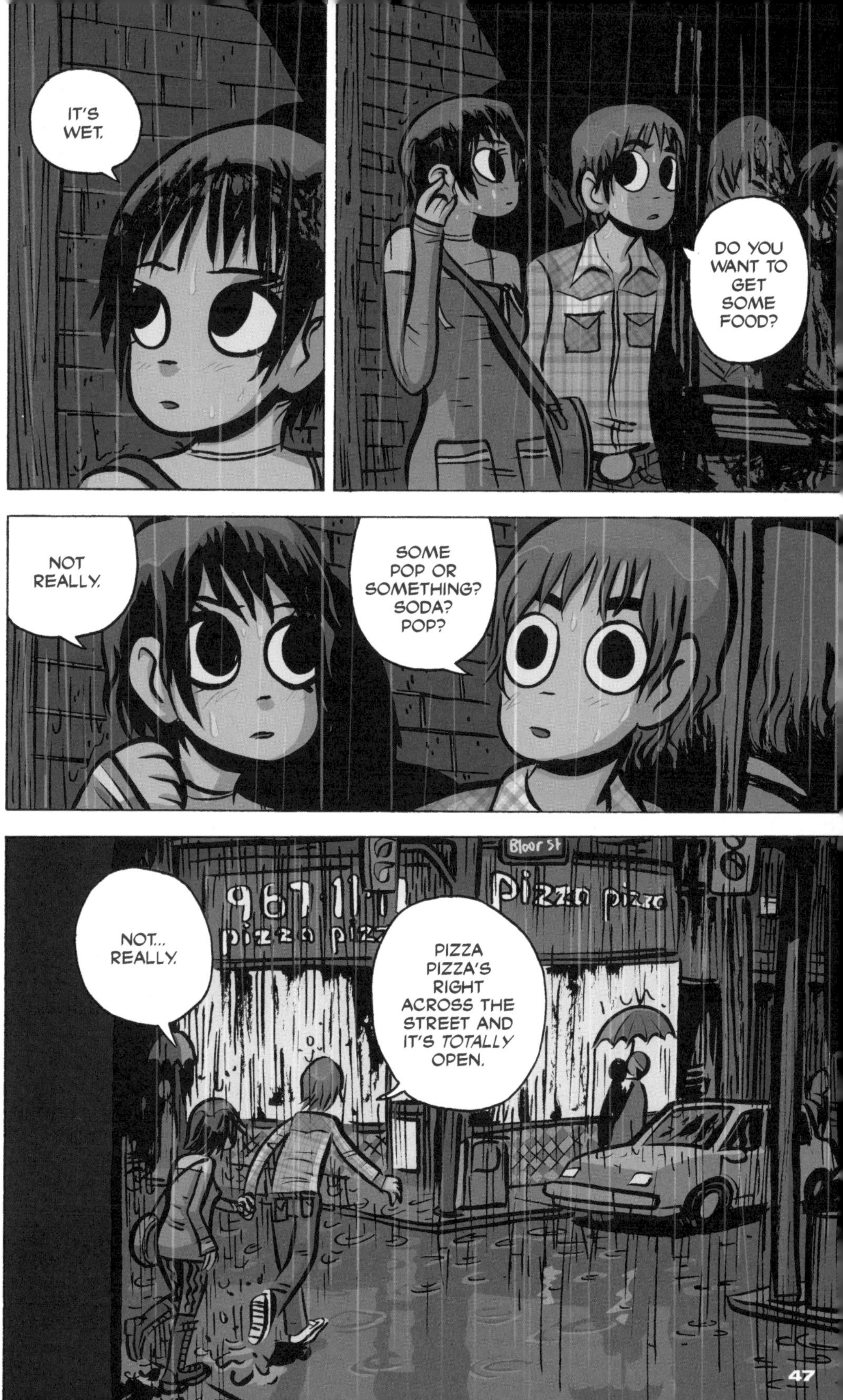
IT'S WET.
DO YOU WANT TO GET SOME FOOD?
NOT REALLY.
SOME POP OR SOMETHING? SODA? POP?
Bloor St
967-1111
pizza pizza
pizza pizza
NOT... REALLY.
PIZZA PIZZA'S RIGHT ACROSS THE STREET AND IT'S *TOTALLY* OPEN.

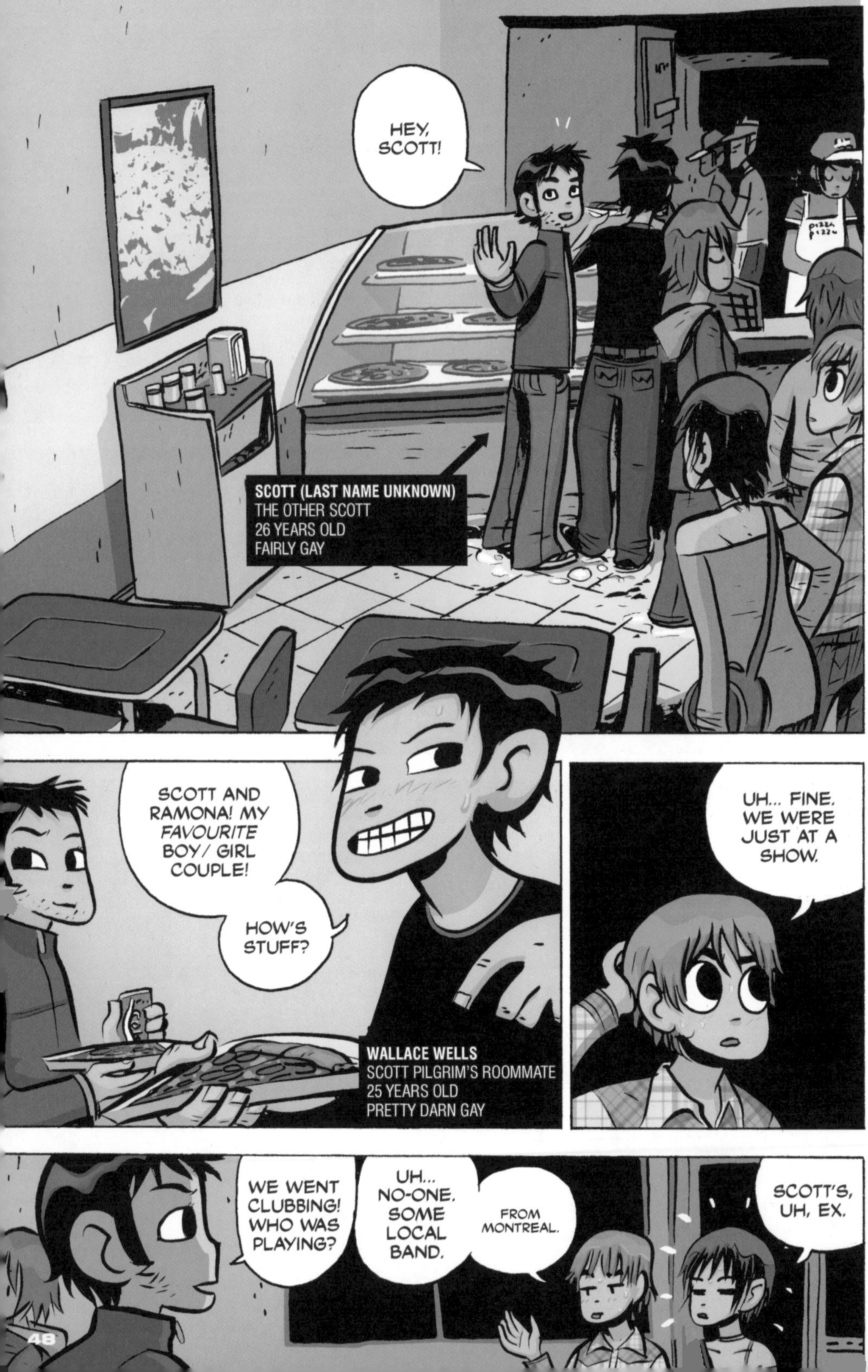
HEY, SCOTT!
SCOTT (LAST NAME UNKNOWN)
THE OTHER SCOTT
26 YEARS OLD
FAIRLY GAY
SCOTT AND RAMONA! MY *FAVOURITE* BOY/ GIRL COUPLE!
HOW'S STUFF?
WALLACE WELLS
SCOTT PILGRIM'S ROOMMATE
25 YEARS OLD
PRETTY DARN GAY
UH... FINE. WE WERE JUST AT A SHOW.
WE WENT CLUBBING! WHO WAS PLAYING?
UH... NO-ONE. SOME LOCAL BAND.
FROM MONTREAL.
SCOTT'S, UH, EX.

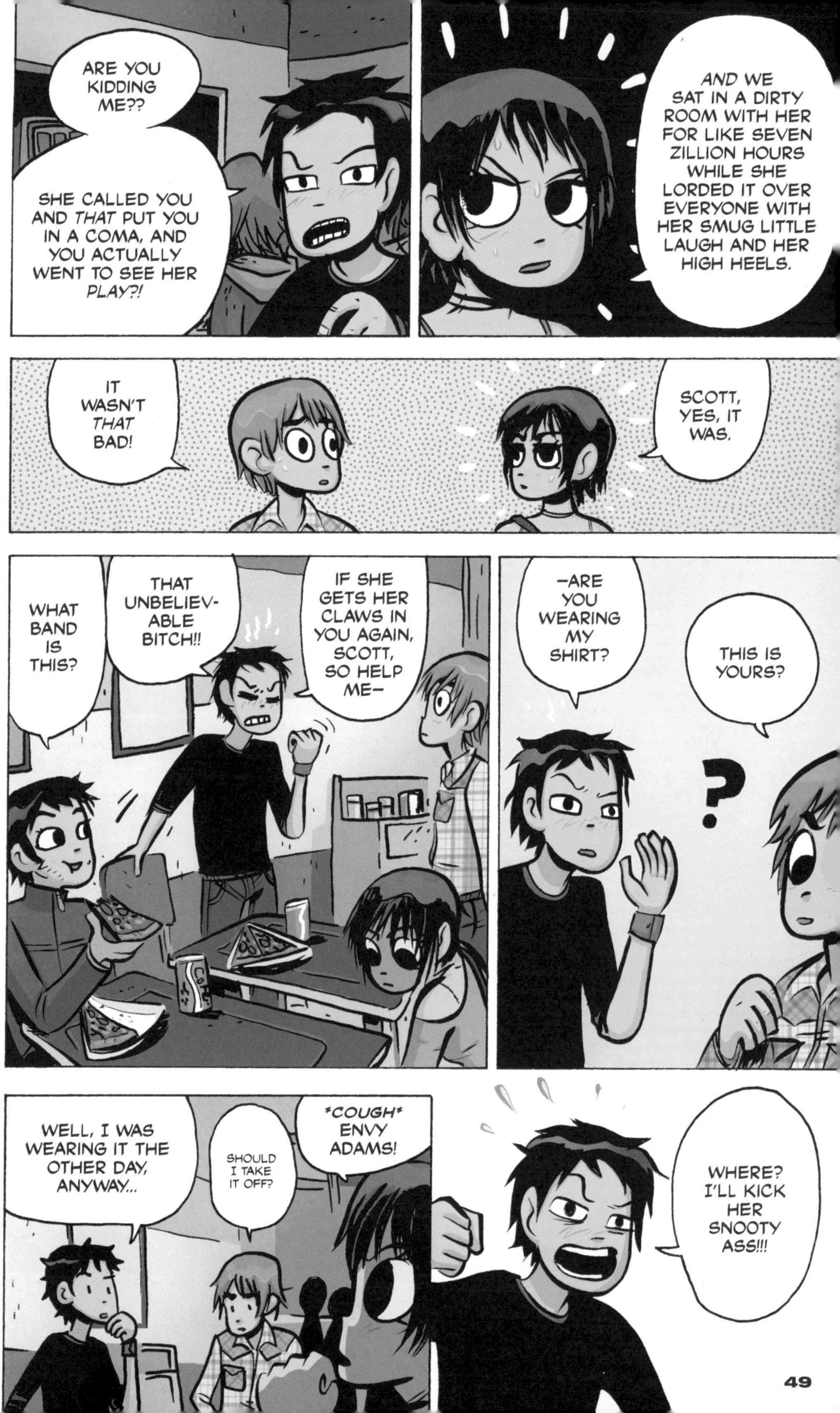
ARE YOU KIDDING ME??
SHE CALLED YOU AND *THAT* PUT YOU IN A COMA, AND YOU ACTUALLY WENT TO SEE HER *PLAY?!*
AND WE SAT IN A DIRTY ROOM WITH HER FOR LIKE SEVEN ZILLION HOURS WHILE SHE LORDED IT OVER EVERYONE WITH HER SMUG LITTLE LAUGH AND HER HIGH HEELS.
IT WASN'T *THAT* BAD!
SCOTT, YES, IT WAS.
WHAT BAND IS THIS?
THAT UNBELIEV-ABLE BITCH!!
IF SHE GETS HER CLAWS IN YOU AGAIN, SCOTT, SO HELP ME—
—ARE YOU WEARING MY SHIRT?
THIS IS YOURS?
WELL, I WAS WEARING IT THE OTHER DAY, ANYWAY...
SHOULD I TAKE IT OFF?
COUGH ENVY ADAMS!
WHERE? I'LL KICK HER SNOOTY ASS!!!

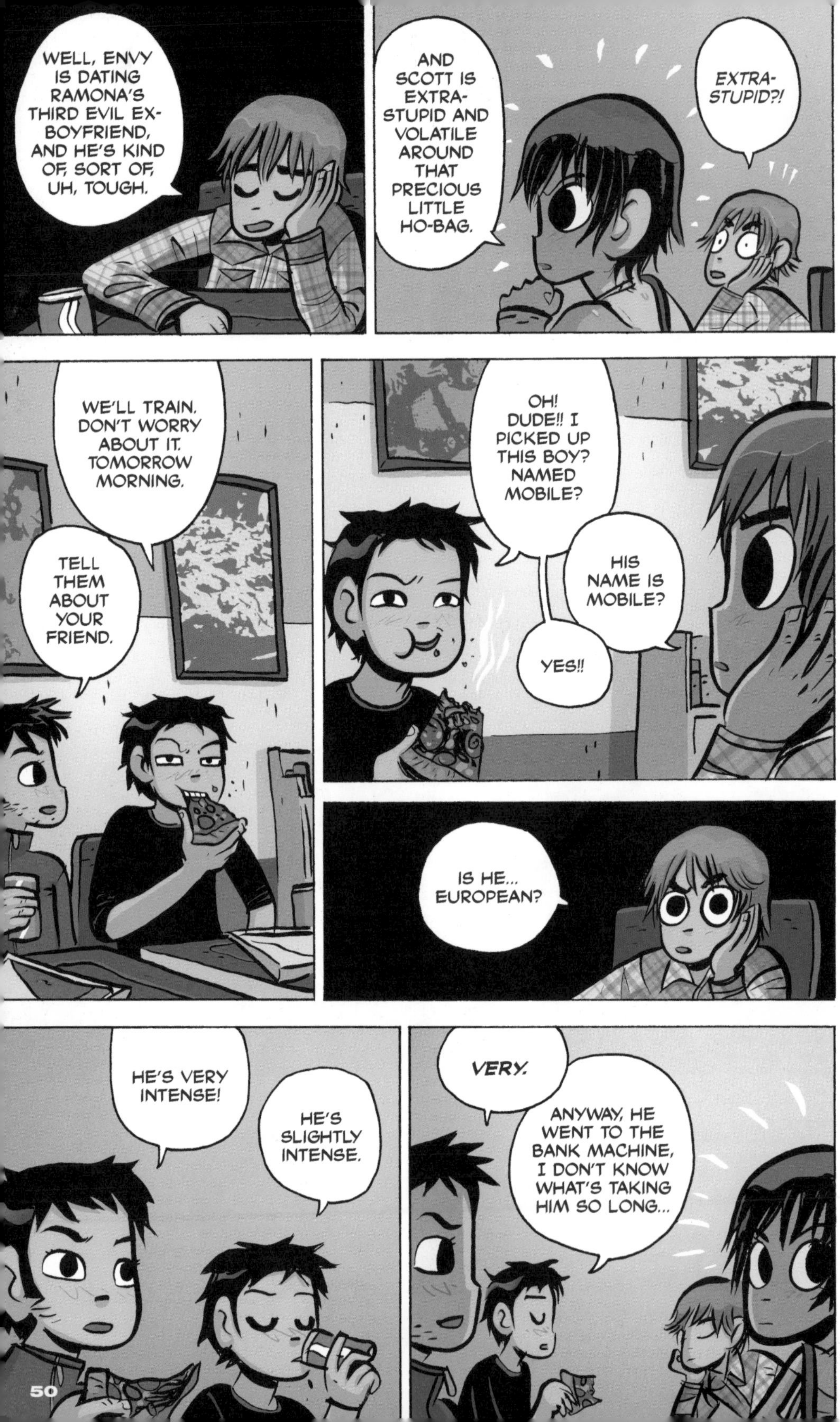
WELL, ENVY IS DATING RAMONA'S THIRD EVIL EX-BOYFRIEND, AND HE'S KIND OF, SORT OF, UH, TOUGH.
AND SCOTT IS EXTRA-STUPID AND VOLATILE AROUND THAT PRECIOUS LITTLE HO-BAG.
EXTRA-STUPID?!
WE'LL TRAIN. DON'T WORRY ABOUT IT. TOMORROW MORNING.
TELL THEM ABOUT YOUR FRIEND.
OH! DUDE!! I PICKED UP THIS BOY? NAMED MOBILE?
HIS NAME IS MOBILE?
YES!!
IS HE... EUROPEAN?
HE'S VERY INTENSE!
HE'S SLIGHTLY INTENSE.
VERY.
ANYWAY, HE WENT TO THE BANK MACHINE, I DON'T KNOW WHAT'S TAKING HIM SO LONG...

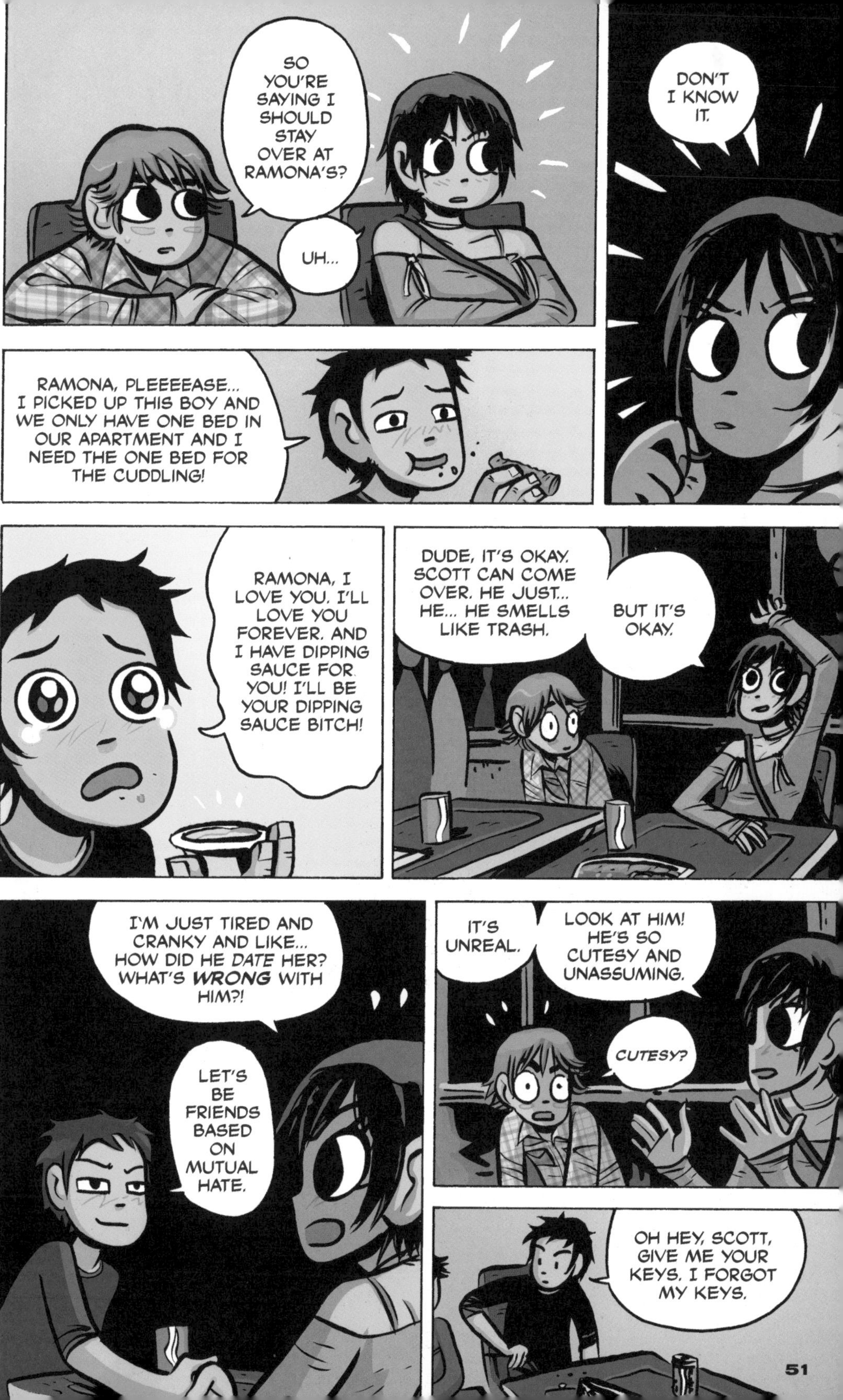
SO YOU'RE SAYING I SHOULD STAY OVER AT RAMONA'S?
UH...
DON'T I KNOW IT.
RAMONA, PLEEEEASE... I PICKED UP THIS BOY AND WE ONLY HAVE ONE BED IN OUR APARTMENT AND I NEED THE ONE BED FOR THE CUDDLING!
RAMONA, I LOVE YOU. I'LL LOVE YOU FOREVER. AND I HAVE DIPPING SAUCE FOR YOU! I'LL BE YOUR DIPPING SAUCE BITCH!
DUDE, IT'S OKAY. SCOTT CAN COME OVER. HE JUST... HE... HE SMELLS LIKE TRASH.
BUT IT'S OKAY.
I'M JUST TIRED AND CRANKY AND LIKE... HOW DID HE *DATE* HER? WHAT'S ***WRONG*** WITH HIM?!
LET'S BE FRIENDS BASED ON MUTUAL HATE.
IT'S UNREAL.
LOOK AT HIM! HE'S SO CUTESY AND UNASSUMING.
CUTESY?
OH HEY, SCOTT, GIVE ME YOUR KEYS. I FORGOT MY KEYS.

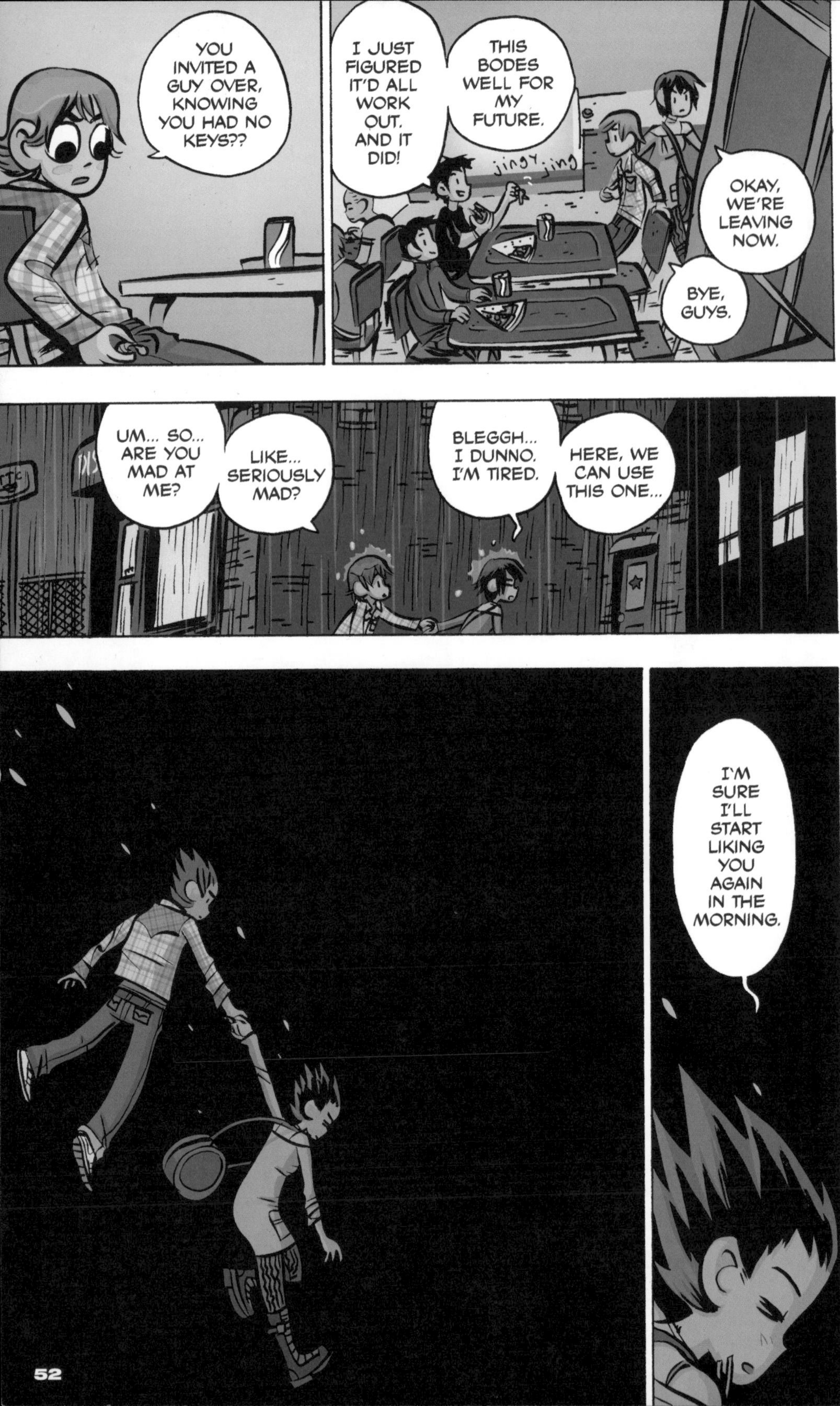
YOU INVITED A GUY OVER, KNOWING YOU HAD NO KEYS??
I JUST FIGURED IT'D ALL WORK OUT. AND IT DID!
THIS BODES WELL FOR MY FUTURE.
jingy jing
OKAY, WE'RE LEAVING NOW.
BYE, GUYS.
UM... SO... ARE YOU MAD AT ME?
LIKE... SERIOUSLY MAD?
BLEGGH... I DUNNO. I'M TIRED.
HERE, WE CAN USE THIS ONE...
I'M SURE I'LL START LIKING YOU AGAIN IN THE MORNING.

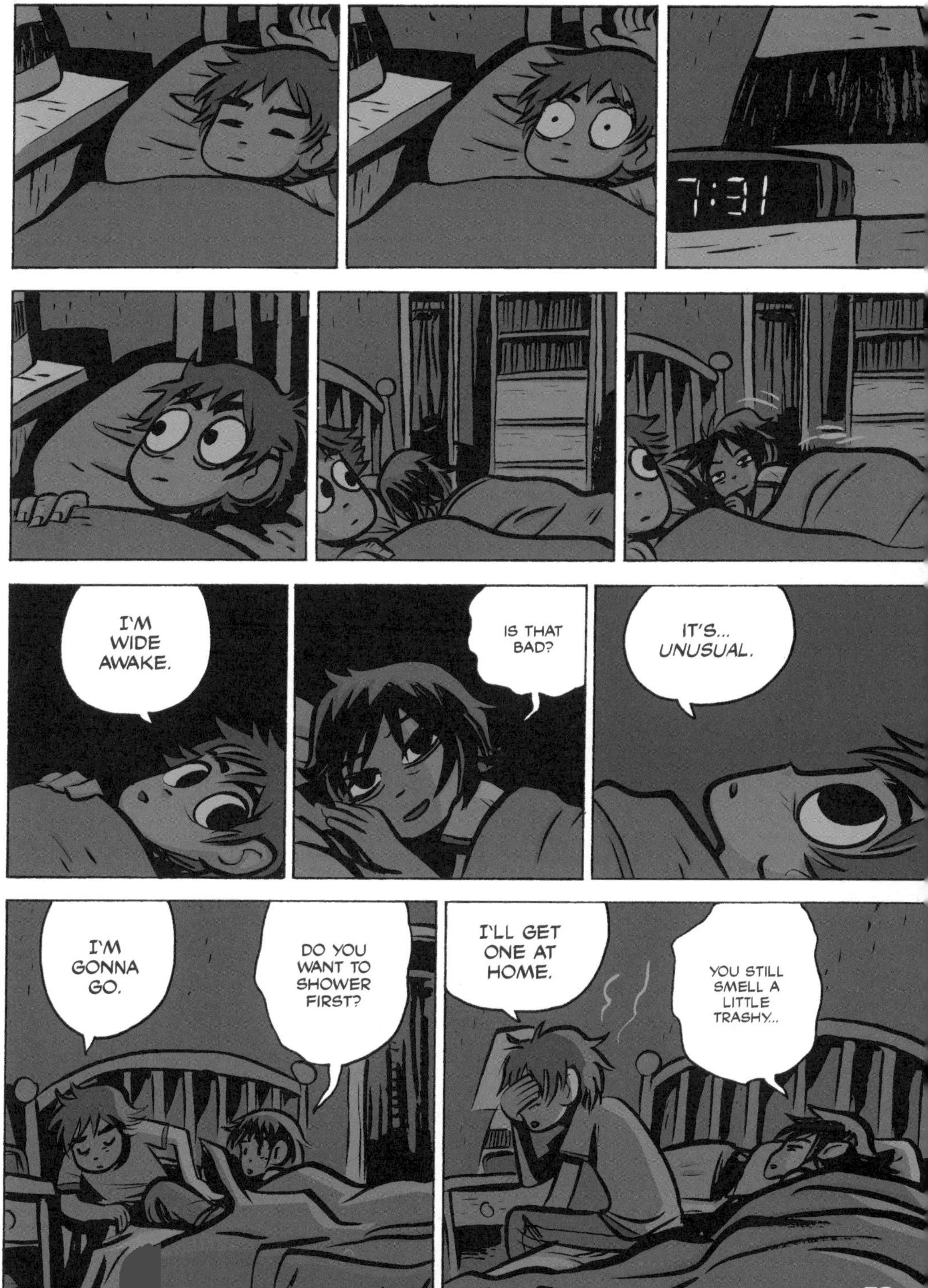
7:31
I'M WIDE AWAKE.
IS THAT BAD?
IT'S... UNUSUAL.
I'M GONNA GO.
DO YOU WANT TO SHOWER FIRST?
I'LL GET ONE AT HOME.
YOU STILL SMELL A LITTLE TRASHY...

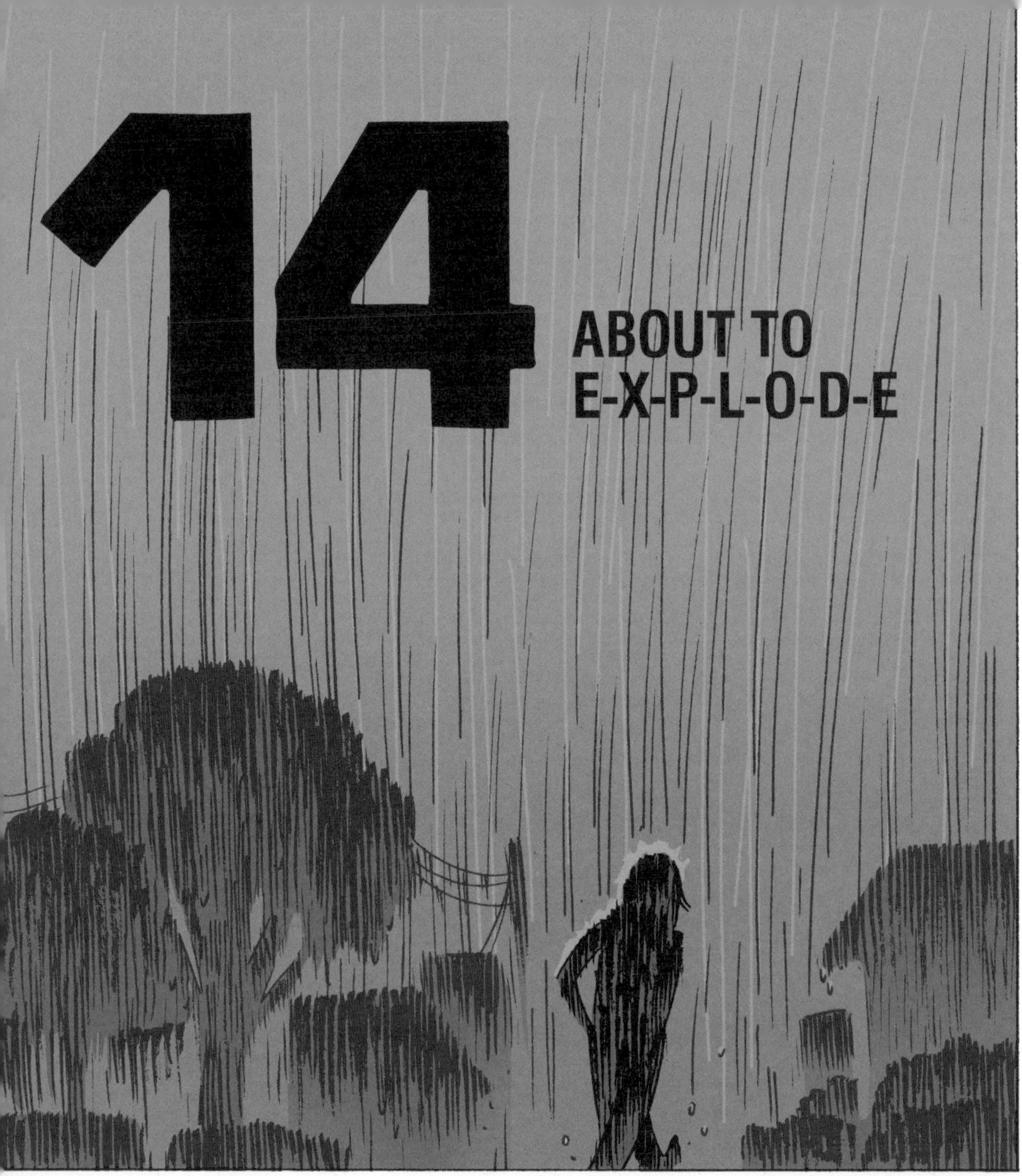
14
ABOUT TO
E-X-P-L-O-D-E

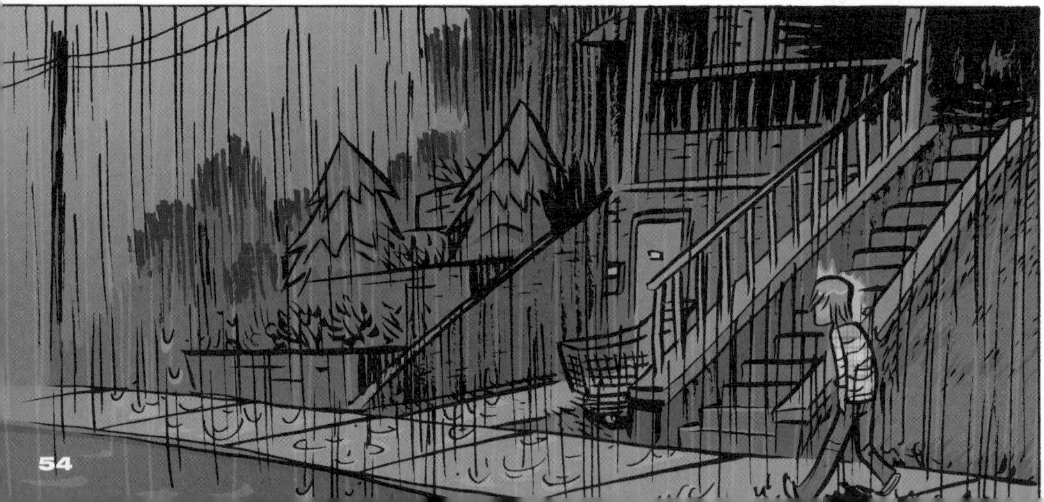

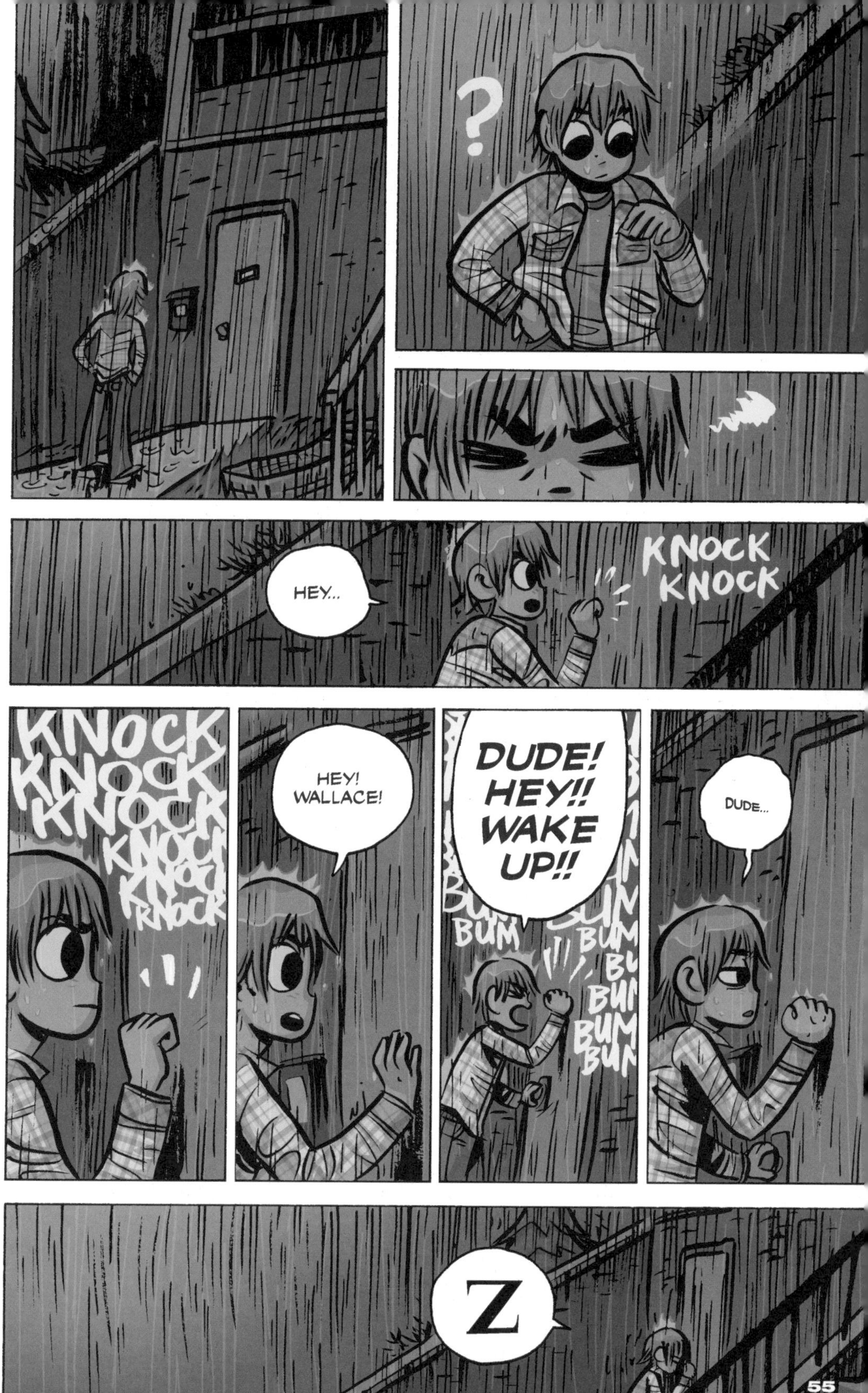
?
HEY...
KNOCK KNOCK
KNOCK KNOCK KNOCK KNOCK KNOCK KNOCK
HEY! WALLACE!
DUDE! HEY!! WAKE UP!!
BUM BUM BUM BUM BUM BUM BUM
DUDE...
Z

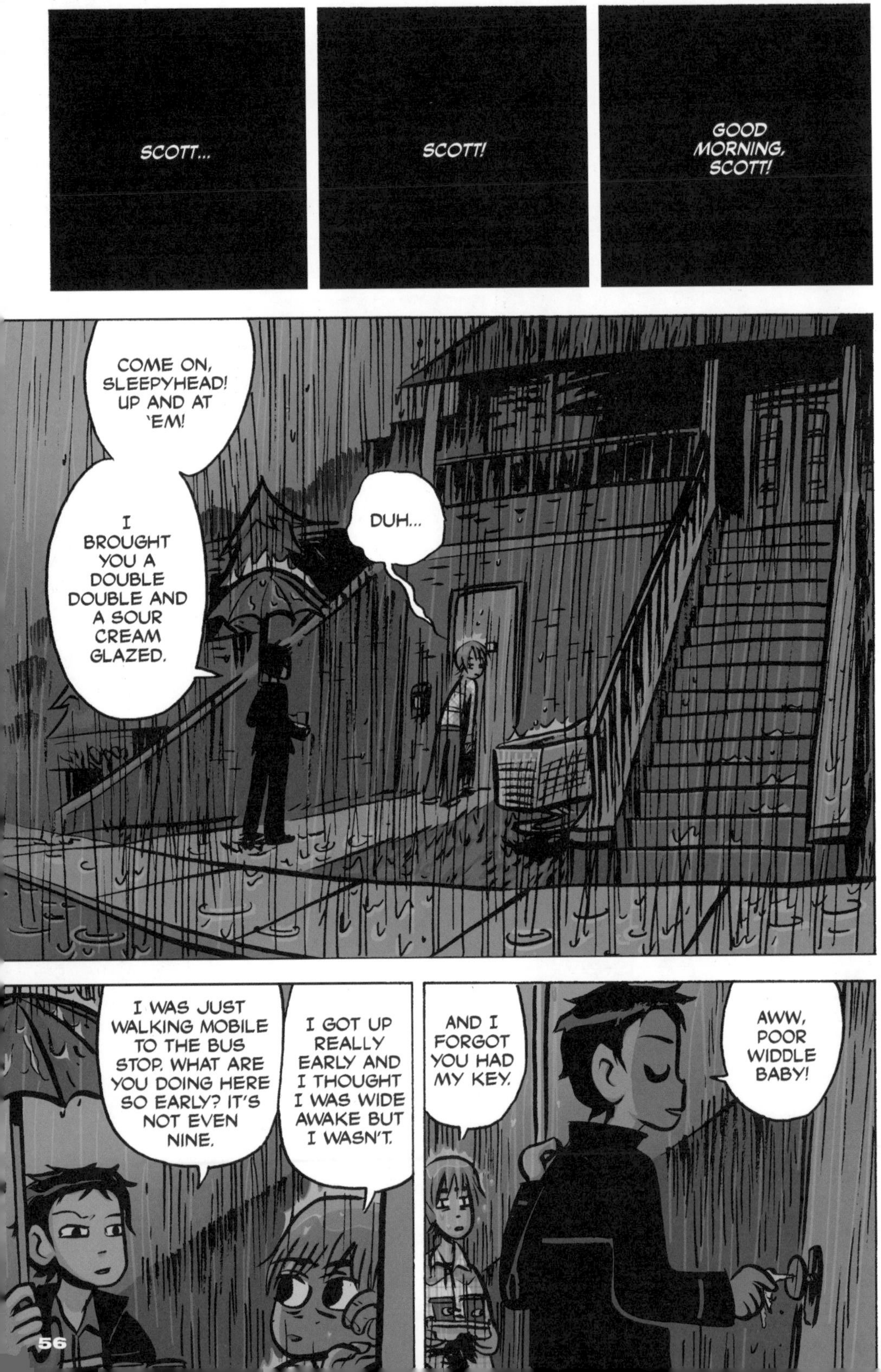
SCOTT...
SCOTT!
GOOD MORNING, SCOTT!
COME ON, SLEEPYHEAD! UP AND AT 'EM!
I BROUGHT YOU A DOUBLE DOUBLE AND A SOUR CREAM GLAZED.
DUH...
I WAS JUST WALKING MOBILE TO THE BUS STOP. WHAT ARE YOU DOING HERE SO EARLY? IT'S NOT EVEN NINE.
I GOT UP REALLY EARLY AND I THOUGHT I WAS WIDE AWAKE BUT I WASN'T.
AND I FORGOT YOU HAD MY KEY.
AWW, POOR WIDDLE BABY!

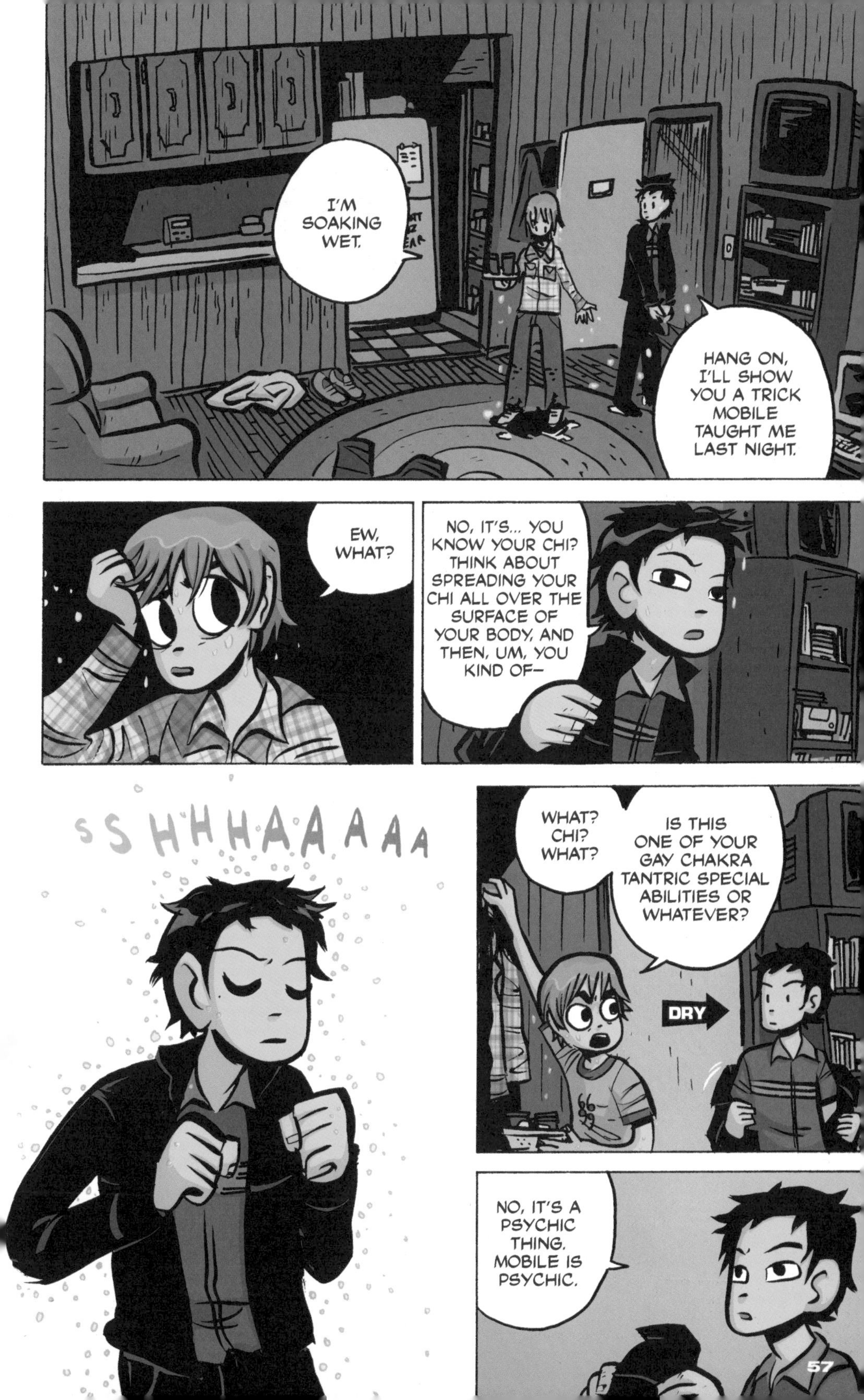
I'M SOAKING WET.
HANG ON, I'LL SHOW YOU A TRICK MOBILE TAUGHT ME LAST NIGHT.
EW, WHAT?
NO, IT'S... YOU KNOW YOUR CHI? THINK ABOUT SPREADING YOUR CHI ALL OVER THE SURFACE OF YOUR BODY, AND THEN, UM, YOU KIND OF—
SSHHHAAAAAA
WHAT? CHI? WHAT?
IS THIS ONE OF YOUR GAY CHAKRA TANTRIC SPECIAL ABILITIES OR WHATEVER?
DRY
NO, IT'S A PSYCHIC THING. MOBILE IS PSYCHIC.

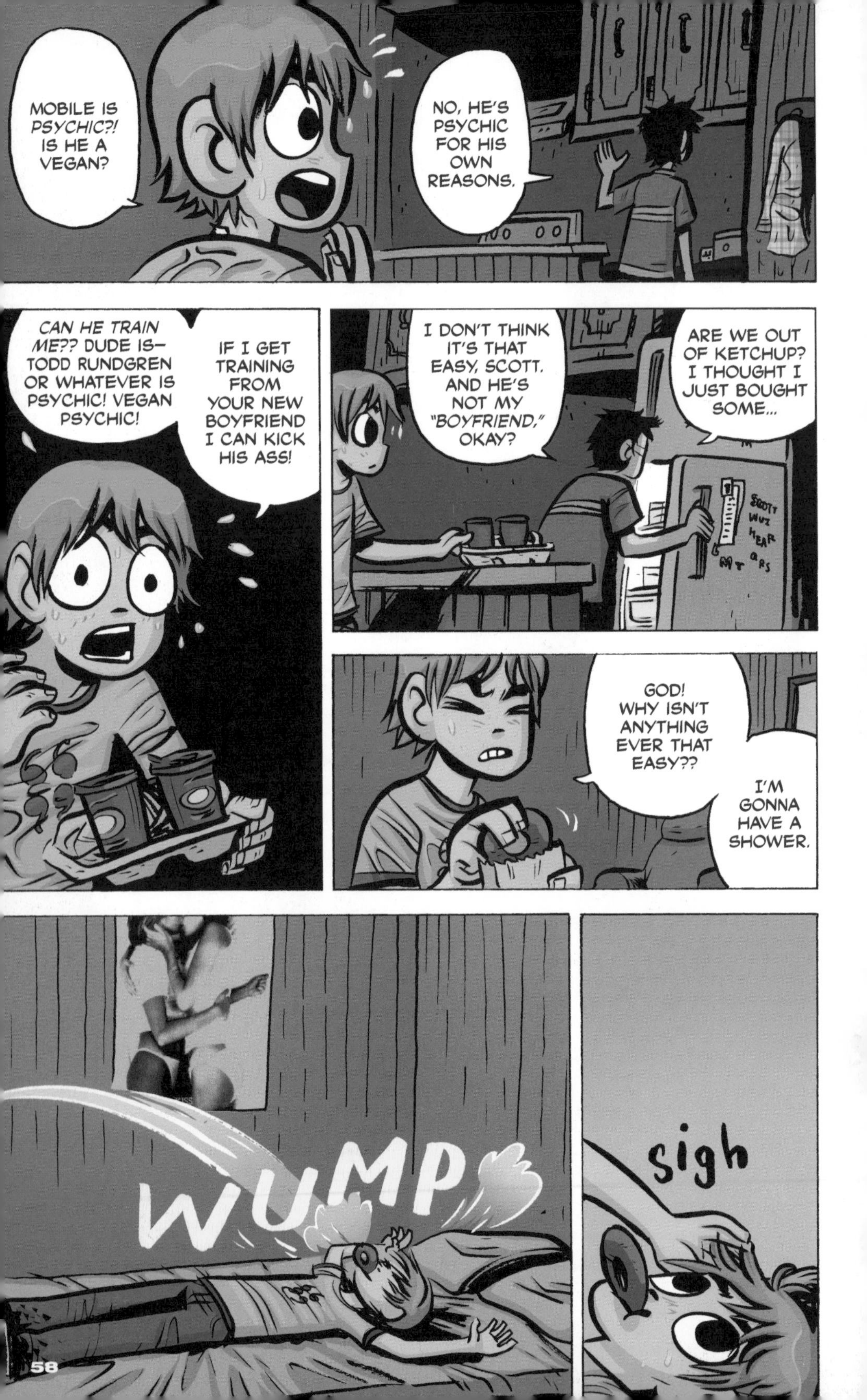
MOBILE IS *PSYCHIC?!* IS HE A VEGAN?
NO, HE'S PSYCHIC FOR HIS OWN REASONS.
CAN HE TRAIN ME?? DUDE IS— TODD RUNDGREN OR WHATEVER IS PSYCHIC! VEGAN PSYCHIC!
IF I GET TRAINING FROM YOUR NEW BOYFRIEND I CAN KICK HIS ASS!
I DON'T THINK IT'S THAT EASY, SCOTT. AND HE'S NOT MY *"BOYFRIEND,"* OKAY?
ARE WE OUT OF KETCHUP? I THOUGHT I JUST BOUGHT SOME...
GOD! WHY ISN'T ANYTHING EVER THAT EASY??
I'M GONNA HAVE A SHOWER.
WUMP
sigh

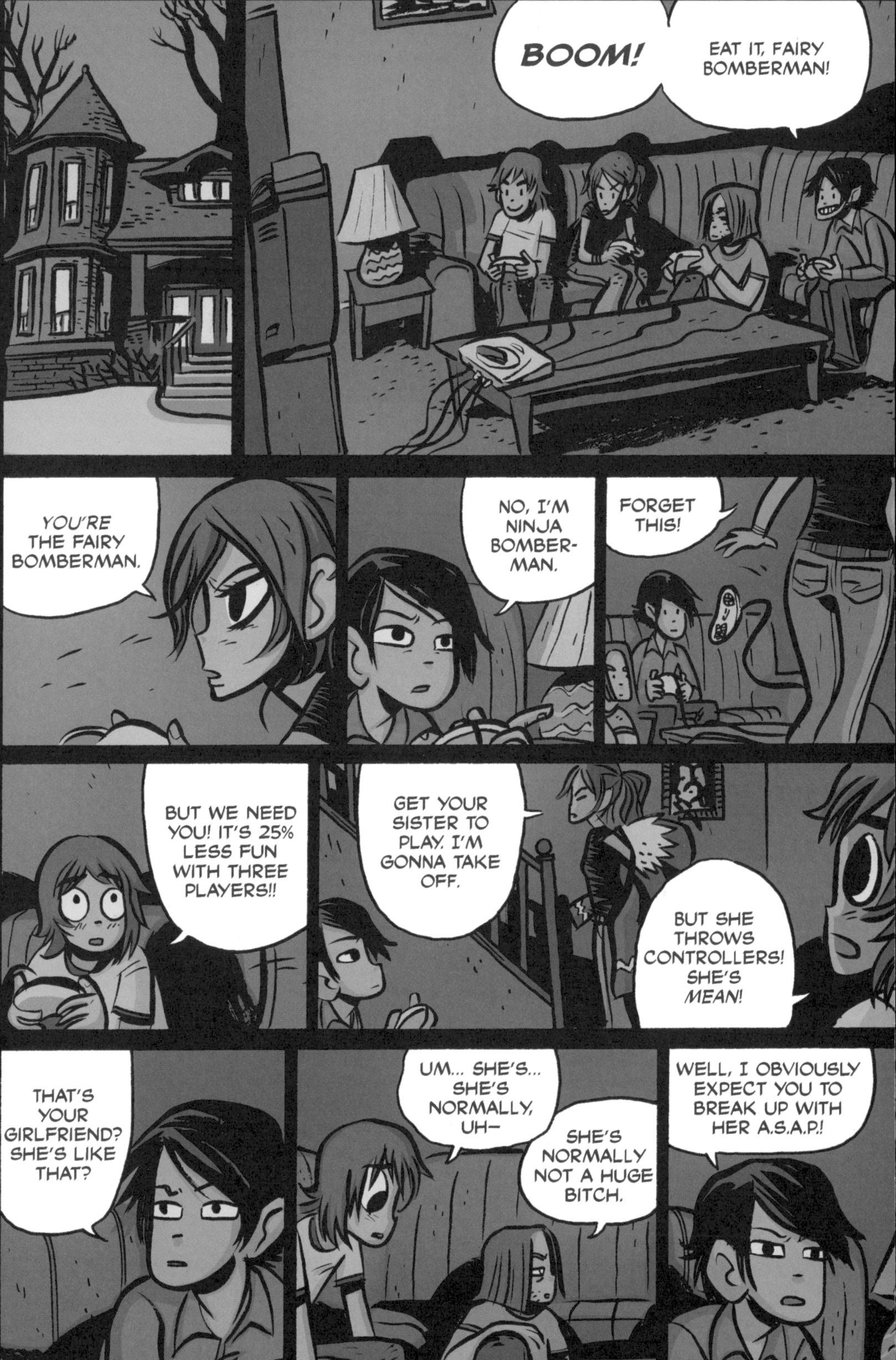
BOOM!
EAT IT, FAIRY BOMBERMAN!
YOU'RE THE FAIRY BOMBERMAN.
NO, I'M NINJA BOMBER-MAN.
FORGET THIS!
BUT WE NEED YOU! IT'S 25% LESS FUN WITH THREE PLAYERS!!
GET YOUR SISTER TO PLAY. I'M GONNA TAKE OFF.
BUT SHE THROWS CONTROLLERS! SHE'S MEAN!
THAT'S YOUR GIRLFRIEND? SHE'S LIKE THAT?
UM... SHE'S... SHE'S NORMALLY, UH—
SHE'S NORMALLY NOT A HUGE BITCH.
WELL, I OBVIOUSLY EXPECT YOU TO BREAK UP WITH HER A.S.A.P.!

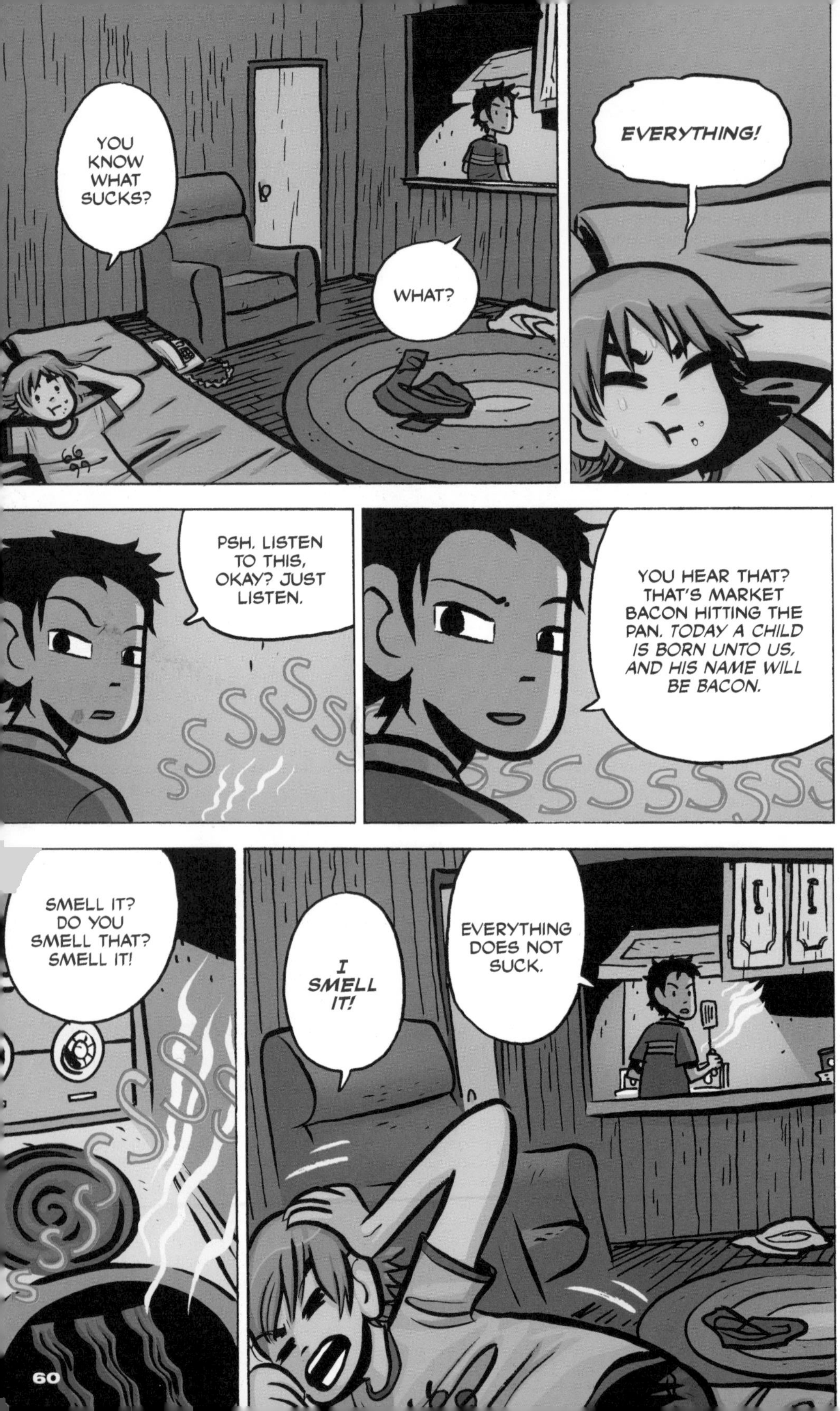
YOU KNOW WHAT SUCKS?
WHAT?
EVERYTHING!
PSH. LISTEN TO THIS, OKAY? JUST LISTEN.
YOU HEAR THAT? THAT'S MARKET BACON HITTING THE PAN. TODAY A CHILD IS BORN UNTO US, AND HIS NAME WILL BE BACON.
SMELL IT? DO YOU SMELL THAT? SMELL IT!
EVERYTHING DOES NOT SUCK.
I SMELL IT!

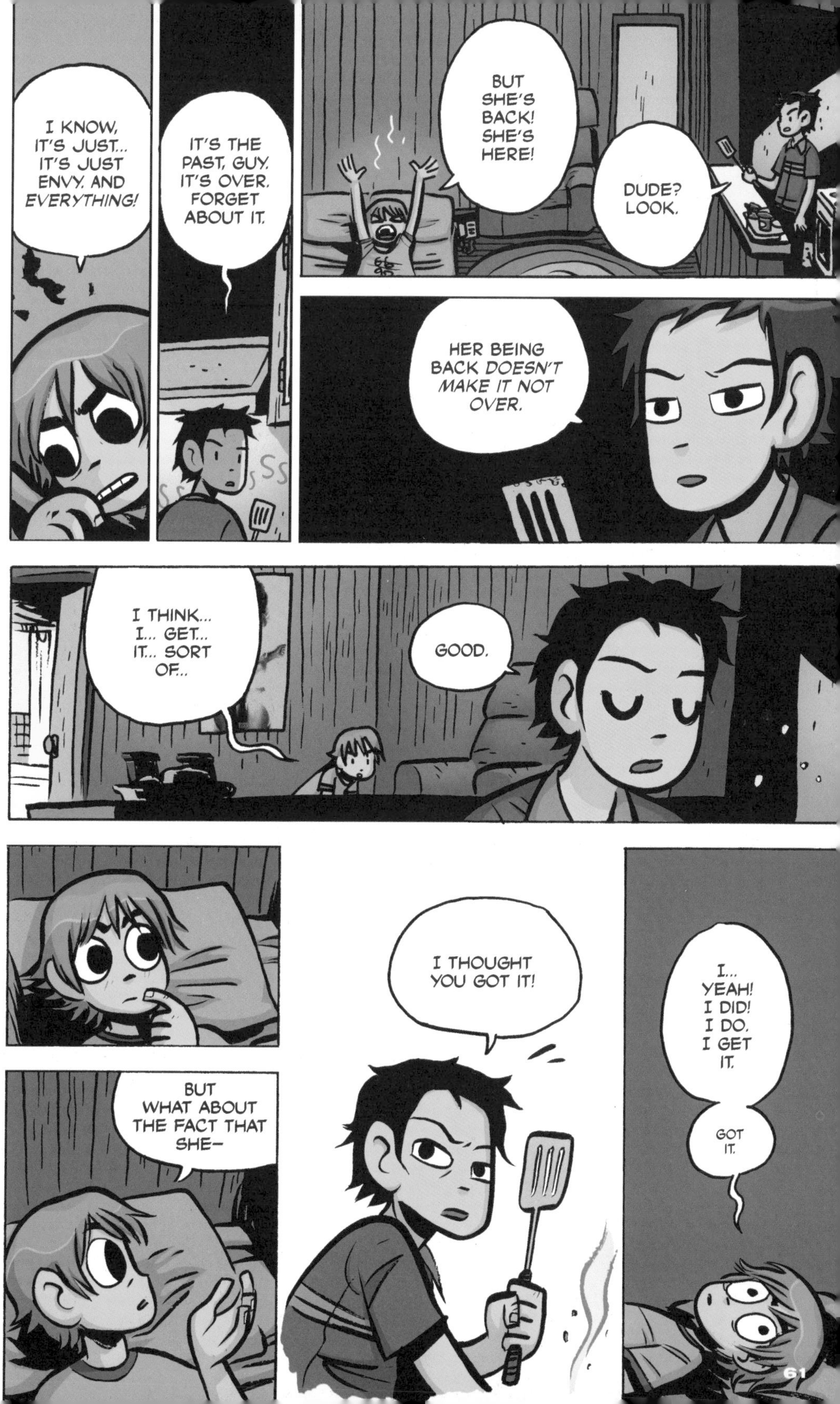
I KNOW, IT'S JUST... IT'S JUST ENVY. AND *EVERYTHING!*
IT'S THE PAST, GUY. IT'S OVER. FORGET ABOUT IT.
BUT SHE'S BACK! SHE'S HERE!
DUDE? LOOK.
HER BEING BACK *DOESN'T MAKE IT NOT OVER.*
I THINK... I... GET... IT... SORT OF...
GOOD.
BUT WHAT ABOUT THE FACT THAT SHE–
I THOUGHT YOU GOT IT!
I... YEAH! I DID! I DO. I GET IT.
GOT IT.

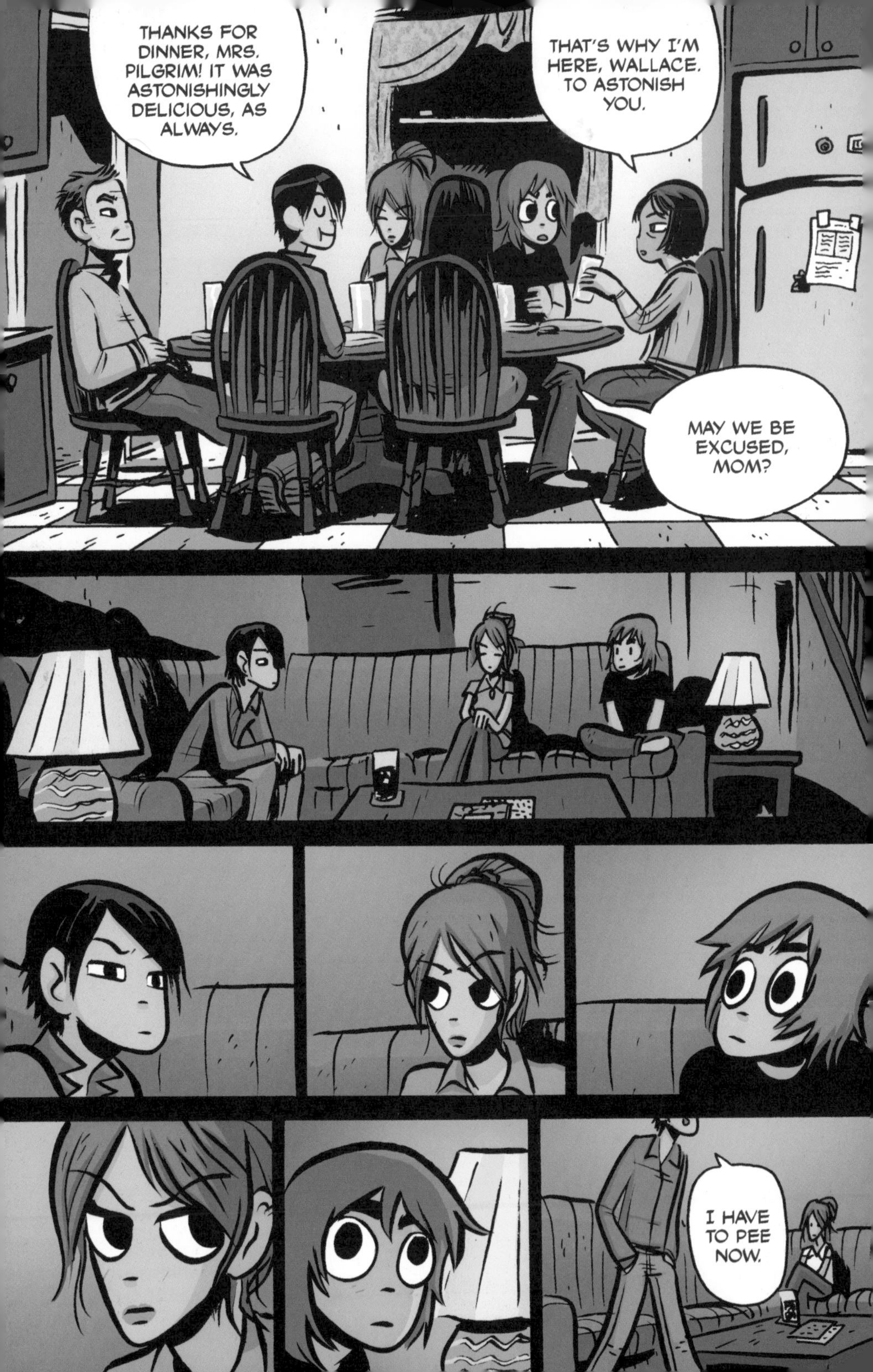
THANKS FOR DINNER, MRS. PILGRIM! IT WAS ASTONISHINGLY DELICIOUS, AS ALWAYS.
THAT'S WHY I'M HERE, WALLACE. TO ASTONISH YOU.
MAY WE BE EXCUSED, MOM?
I HAVE TO PEE NOW.

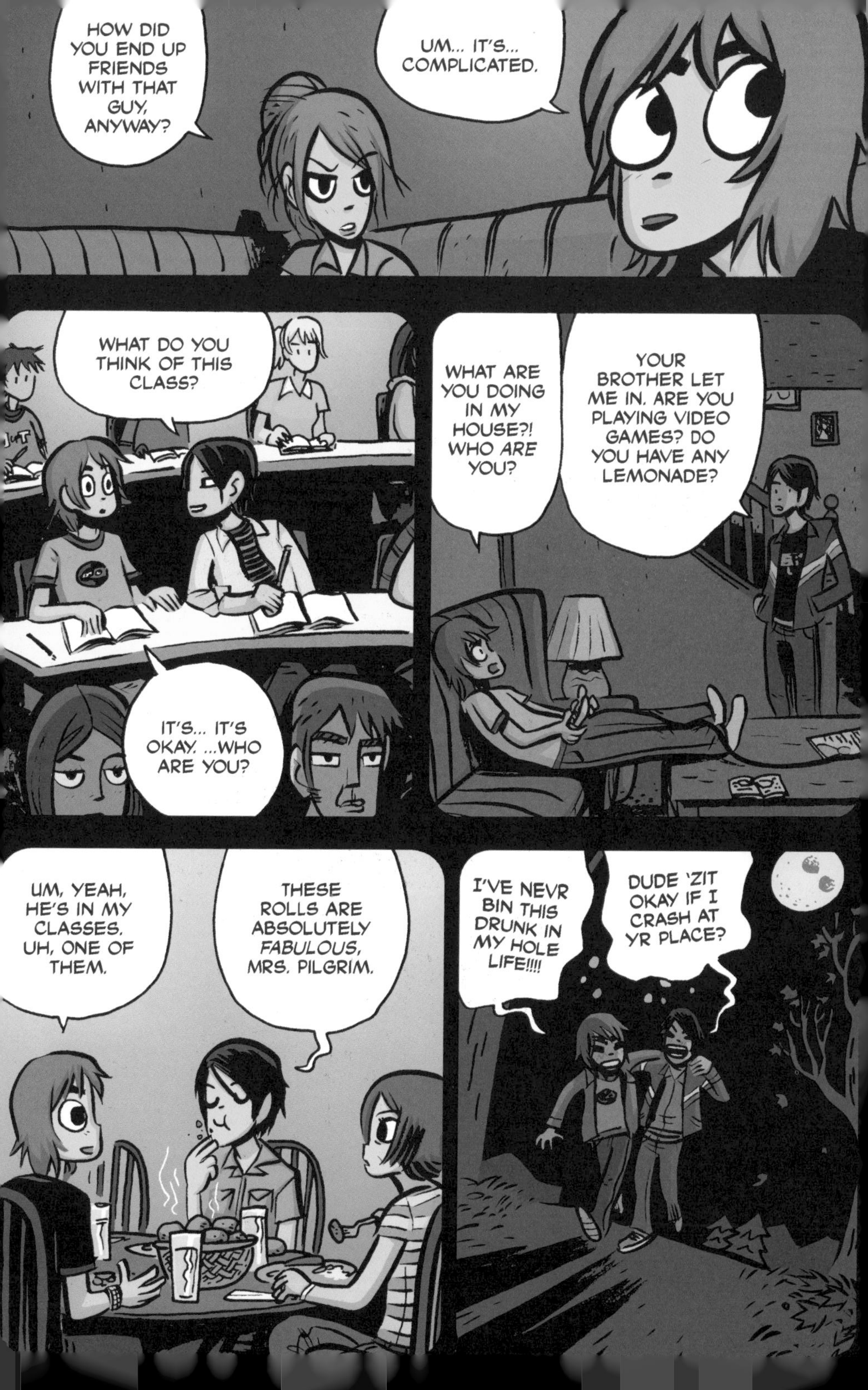
HOW DID YOU END UP FRIENDS WITH THAT GUY, ANYWAY?
UM... IT'S... COMPLICATED.
WHAT DO YOU THINK OF THIS CLASS?
IT'S... IT'S OKAY. ...WHO ARE YOU?
WHAT ARE YOU DOING IN MY HOUSE?! WHO *ARE* YOU?
YOUR BROTHER LET ME IN. ARE YOU PLAYING VIDEO GAMES? DO YOU HAVE ANY LEMONADE?
UM, YEAH, HE'S IN MY CLASSES. UH, ONE OF THEM.
THESE ROLLS ARE ABSOLUTELY *FABULOUS*, MRS. PILGRIM.
I'VE NEVR BIN THIS DRUNK IN MY HOLE LIFE!!!!
DUDE 'ZIT OKAY IF I CRASH AT YR PLACE?

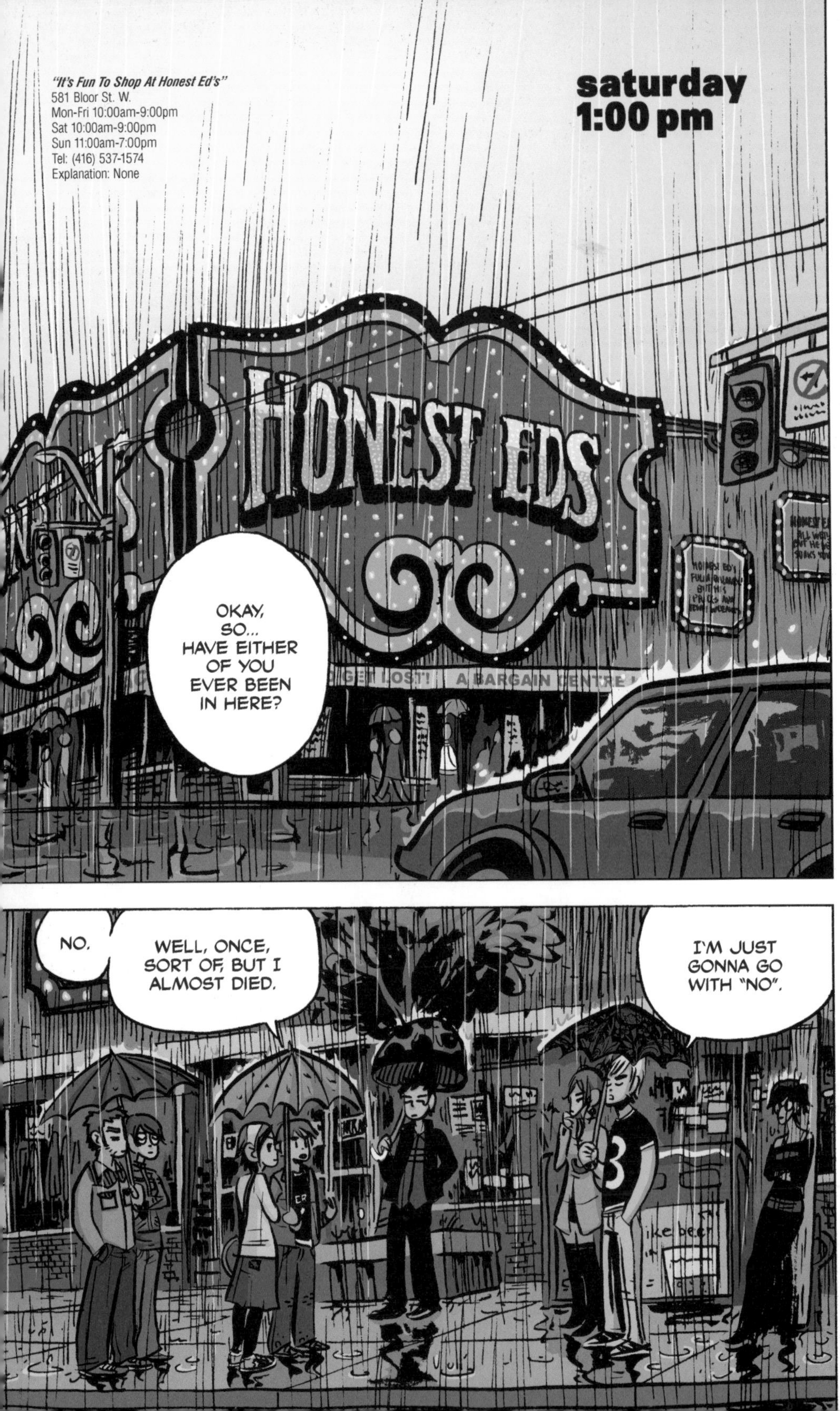
"It's Fun To Shop At Honest Ed's"
581 Bloor St. W.
Mon-Fri 10:00am-9:00pm
Sat 10:00am-9:00pm
Sun 11:00am-7:00pm
Tel: (416) 537-1574
Explanation: None
saturday 1:00 pm
HONEST EDS
OKAY, SO... HAVE EITHER OF YOU EVER BEEN IN HERE?
NO.
WELL, ONCE, SORT OF, BUT I ALMOST DIED.
I'M JUST GONNA GO WITH "NO".

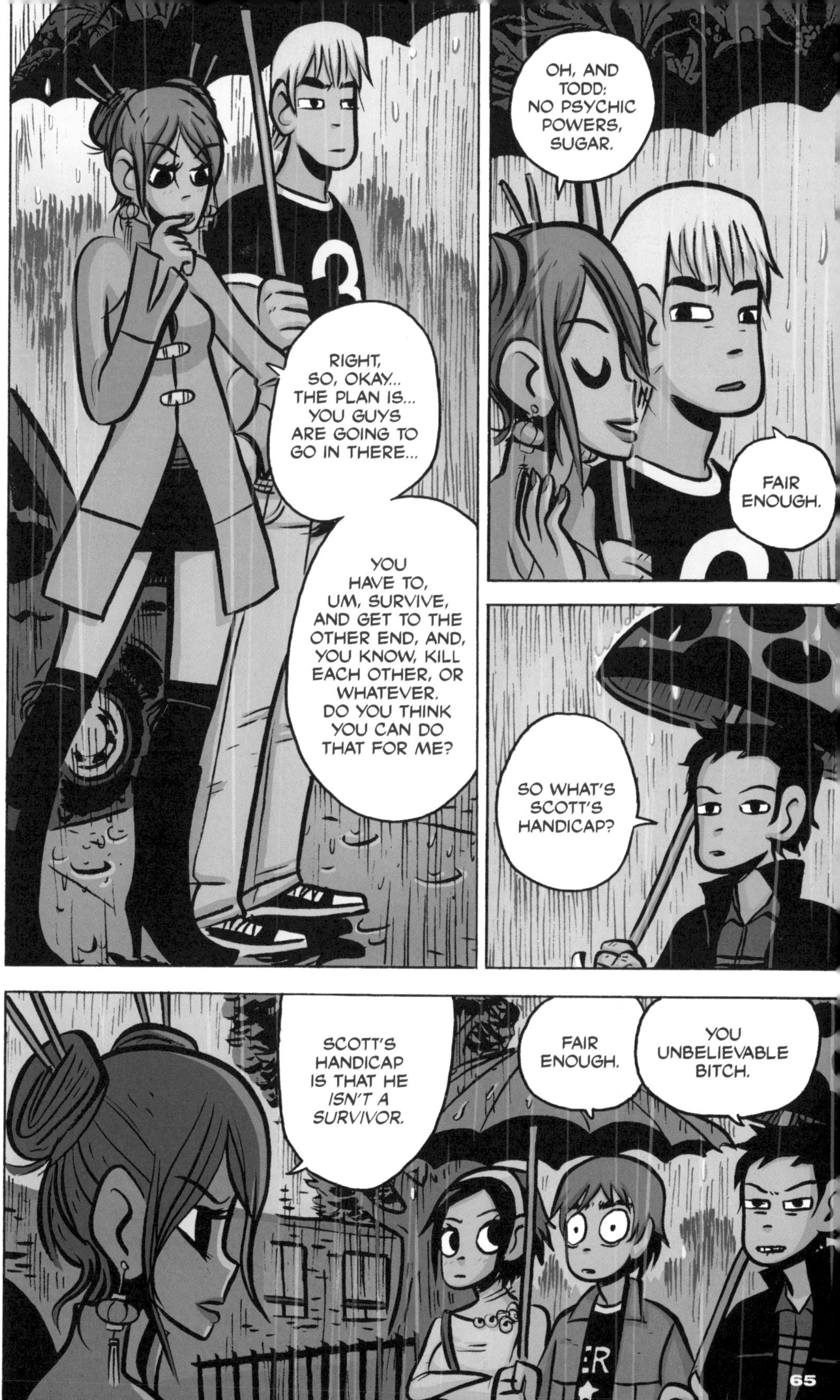
RIGHT, SO, OKAY... THE PLAN IS... YOU GUYS ARE GOING TO GO IN THERE...
YOU HAVE TO, UM, SURVIVE, AND GET TO THE OTHER END, AND, YOU KNOW, KILL EACH OTHER, OR WHATEVER. DO YOU THINK YOU CAN DO THAT FOR ME?
OH, AND TODD: NO PSYCHIC POWERS, SUGAR.
FAIR ENOUGH.
SO WHAT'S SCOTT'S HANDICAP?
SCOTT'S HANDICAP IS THAT HE *ISN'T A SURVIVOR.*
FAIR ENOUGH.
YOU UNBELIEVABLE BITCH.

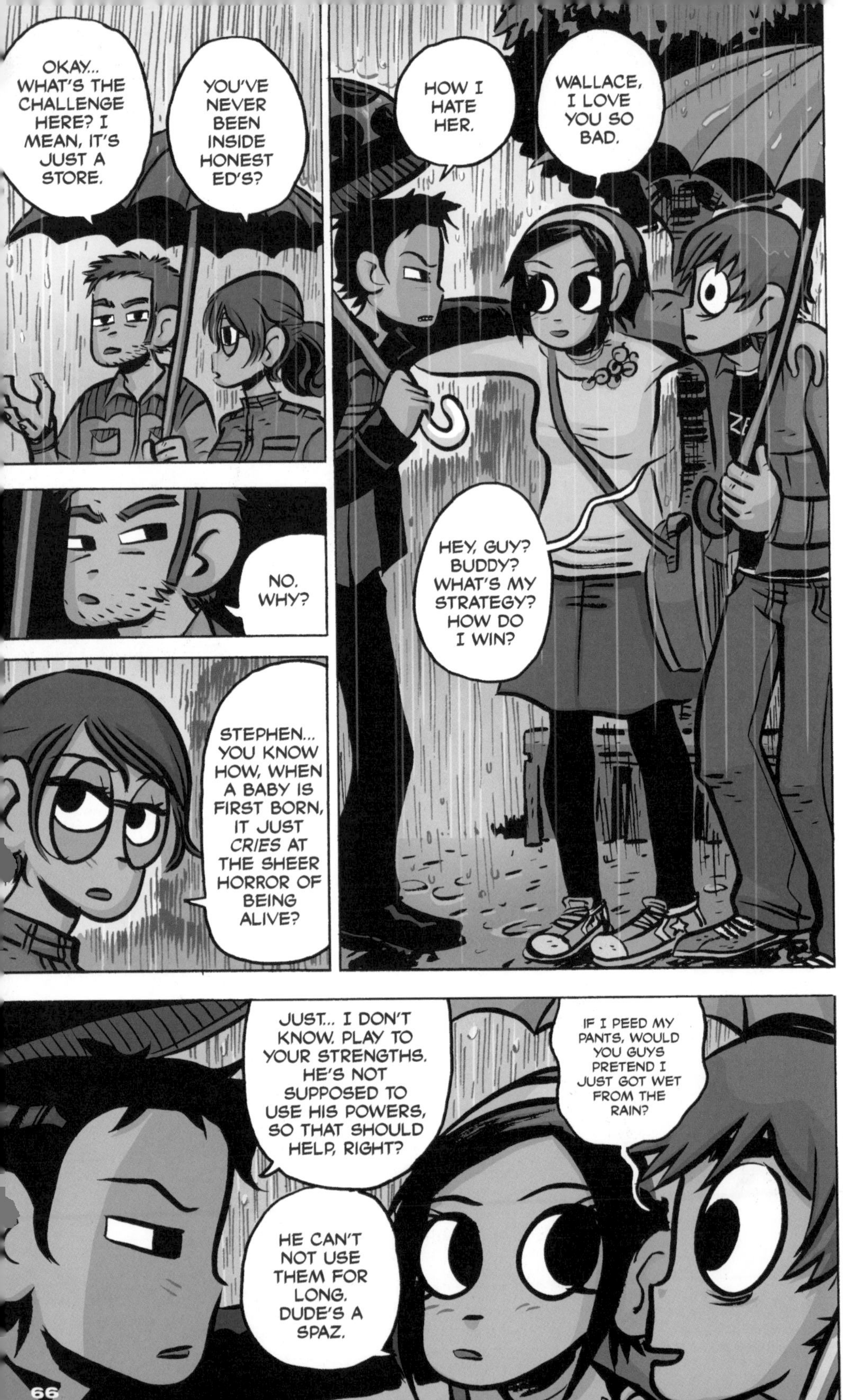
OKAY... WHAT'S THE CHALLENGE HERE? I MEAN, IT'S JUST A STORE.
YOU'VE NEVER BEEN INSIDE HONEST ED'S?
NO. WHY?
STEPHEN... YOU KNOW HOW, WHEN A BABY IS FIRST BORN, IT JUST *CRIES* AT THE SHEER HORROR OF BEING ALIVE?
HOW I HATE HER.
WALLACE, I LOVE YOU SO BAD.
HEY, GUY? BUDDY? WHAT'S MY STRATEGY? HOW DO I WIN?
JUST... I DON'T KNOW. PLAY TO YOUR STRENGTHS. HE'S NOT SUPPOSED TO USE HIS POWERS, SO THAT SHOULD HELP, RIGHT?
IF I PEED MY PANTS, WOULD YOU GUYS PRETEND I JUST GOT WET FROM THE RAIN?
HE CAN'T NOT USE THEM FOR LONG. DUDE'S A SPAZ.

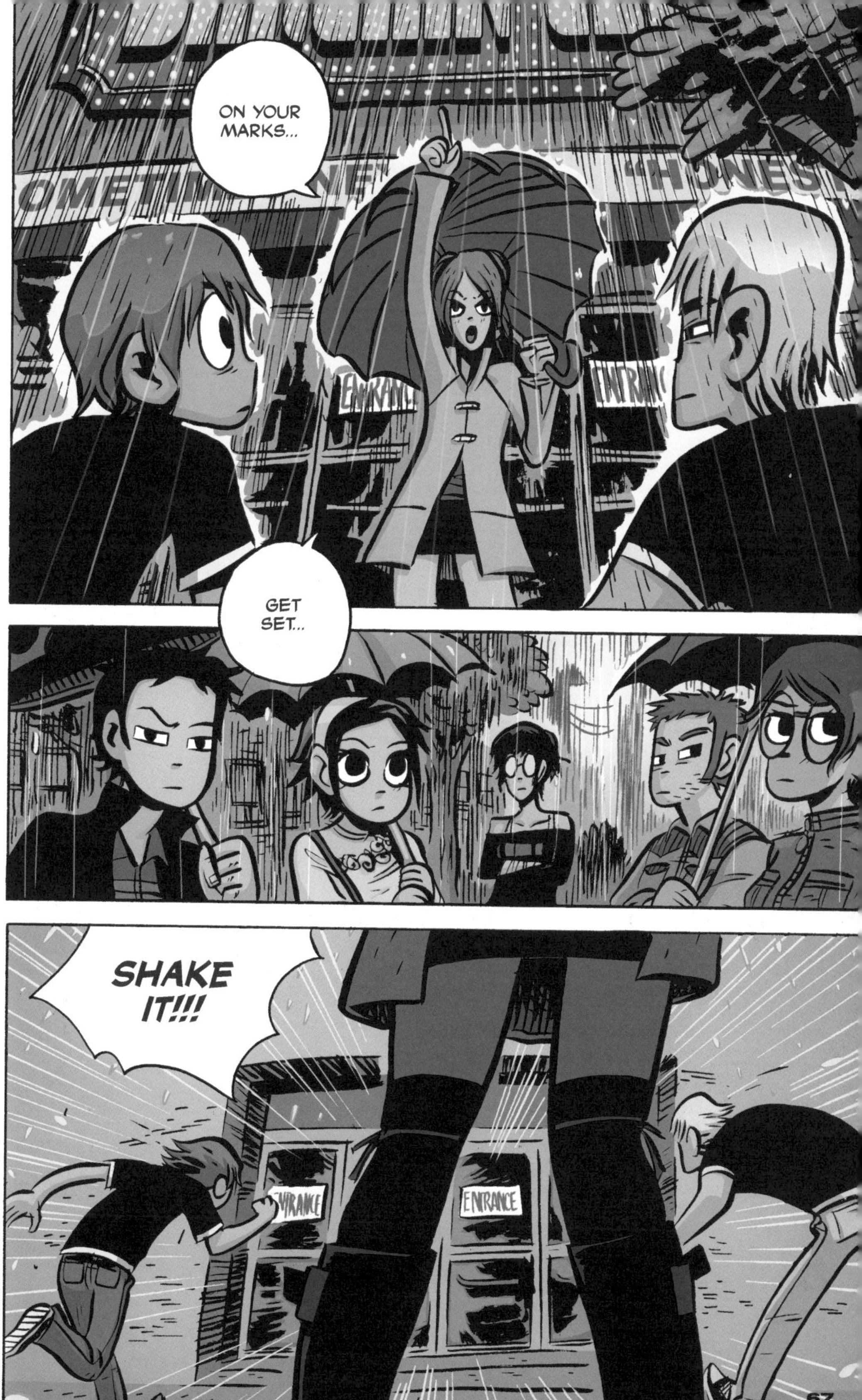
ON YOUR MARKS...
GET SET...
SHAKE IT!!!

THE STARK EXISTENTIAL HORROR OF HONEST ED'S

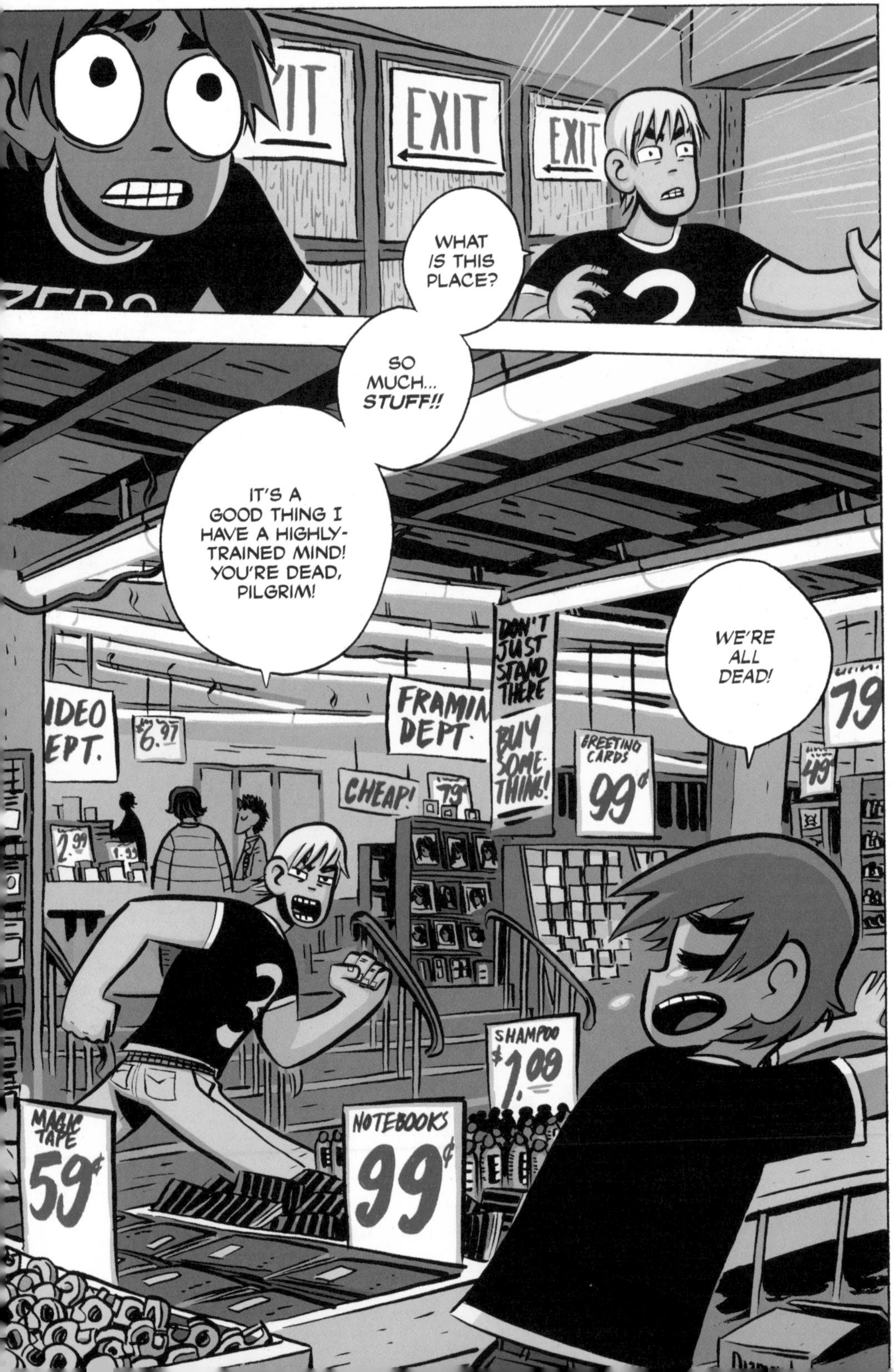
EXIT
EXIT
EXIT
WHAT IS THIS PLACE?
SO MUCH... STUFF!!
IT'S A GOOD THING I HAVE A HIGHLY-TRAINED MIND! YOU'RE DEAD, PILGRIM!
WE'RE ALL DEAD!
DON'T JUST STAND THERE BUY SOMETHING!
FRAMIN DEPT
CHEAP!
GREETING CARDS 99¢
SHAMPOO $1.00
MAGIC TAPE 59¢
NOTEBOOKS 99¢

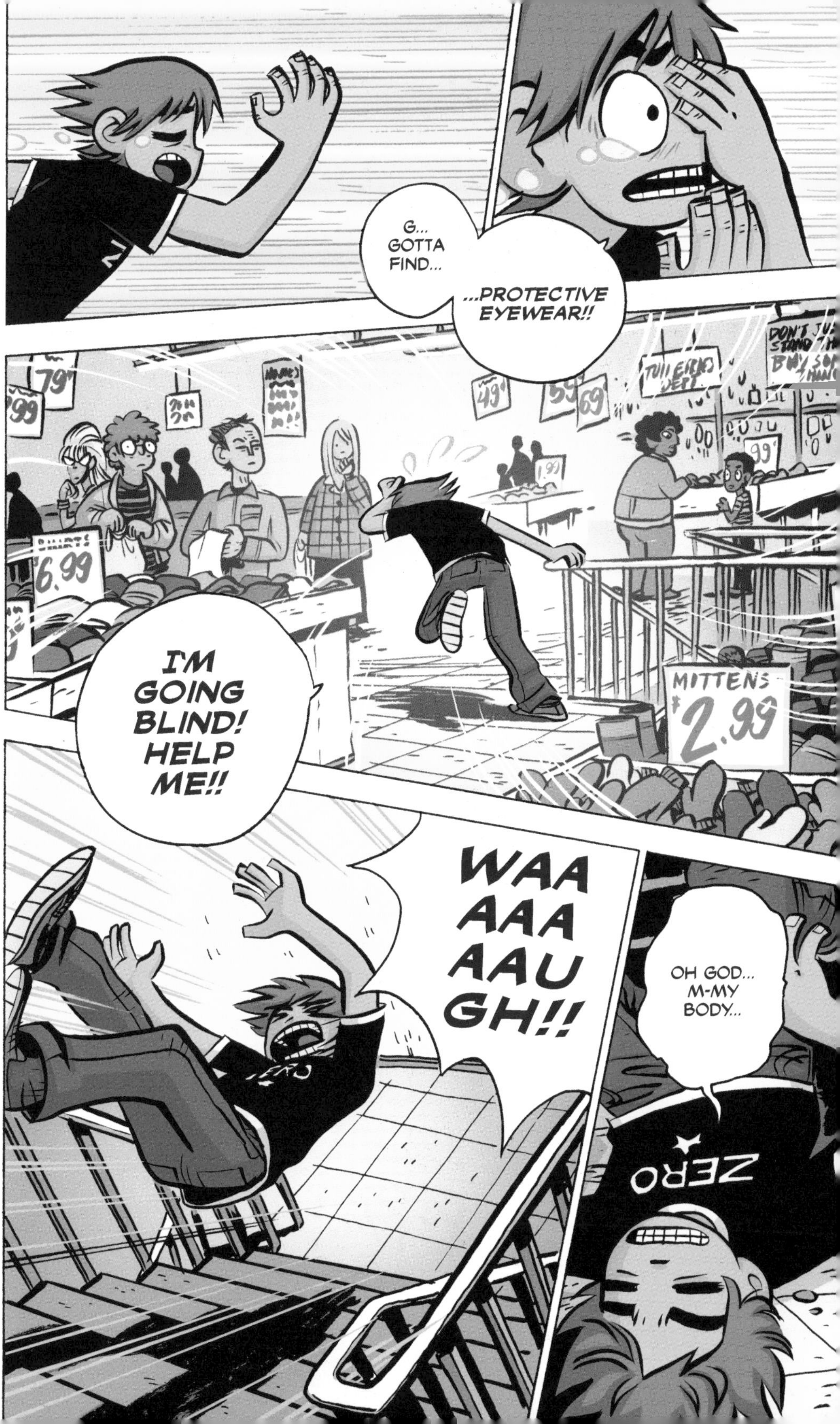
G... GOTTA FIND...
...PROTECTIVE EYEWEAR!!
MITTENS $2.99
I'M GOING BLIND! HELP ME!!
WAAAAAAAUGH!!
OH GOD... M-MY BODY...
ZERO

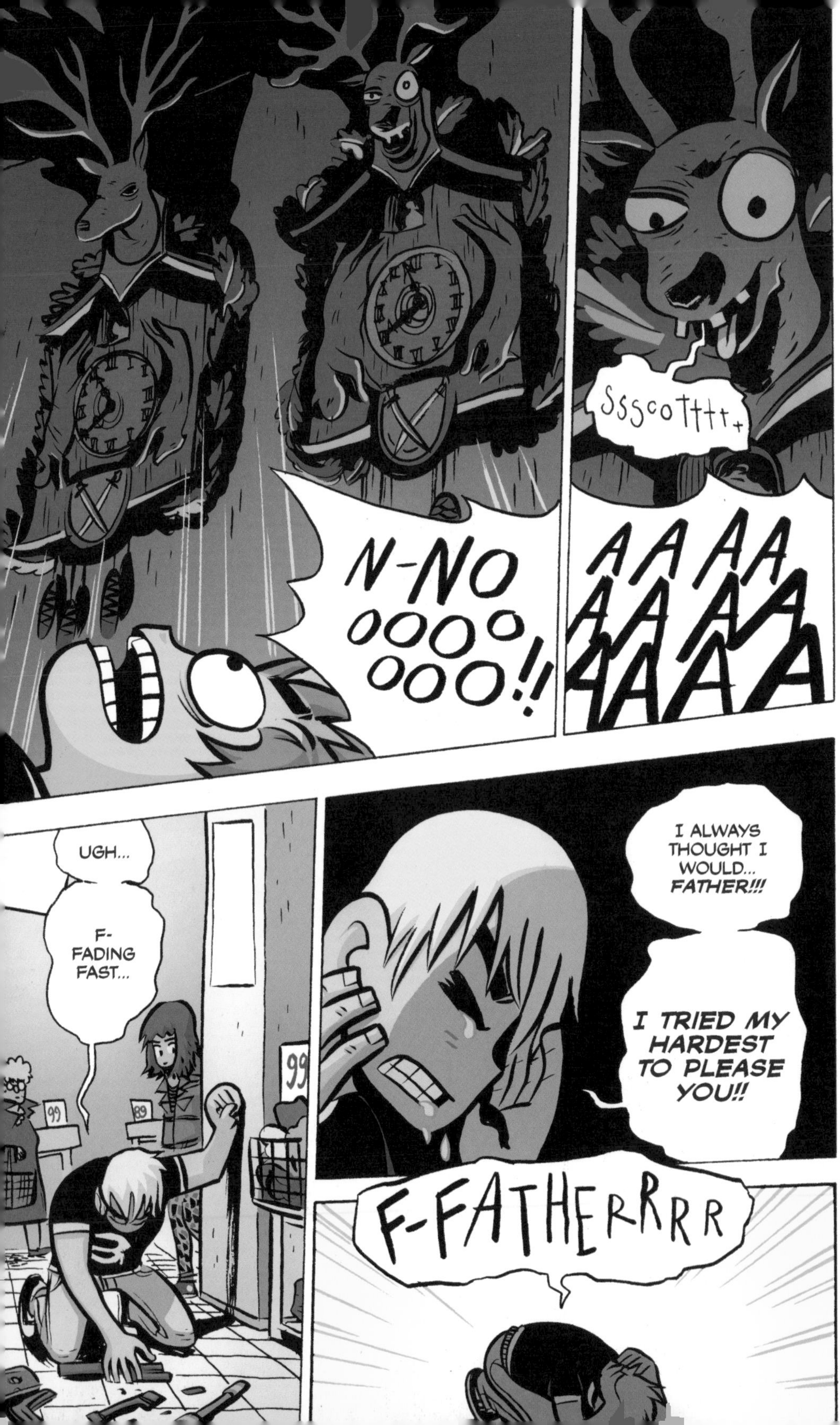
N-NOOOOOOOO!!
SSSCOTTTTT
AAAAAAAAAAAA
UGH...
F-FADING FAST...
99
89
99
I ALWAYS THOUGHT I WOULD... FATHER!!!
I TRIED MY HARDEST TO PLEASE YOU!!
F-FATHERRRRR

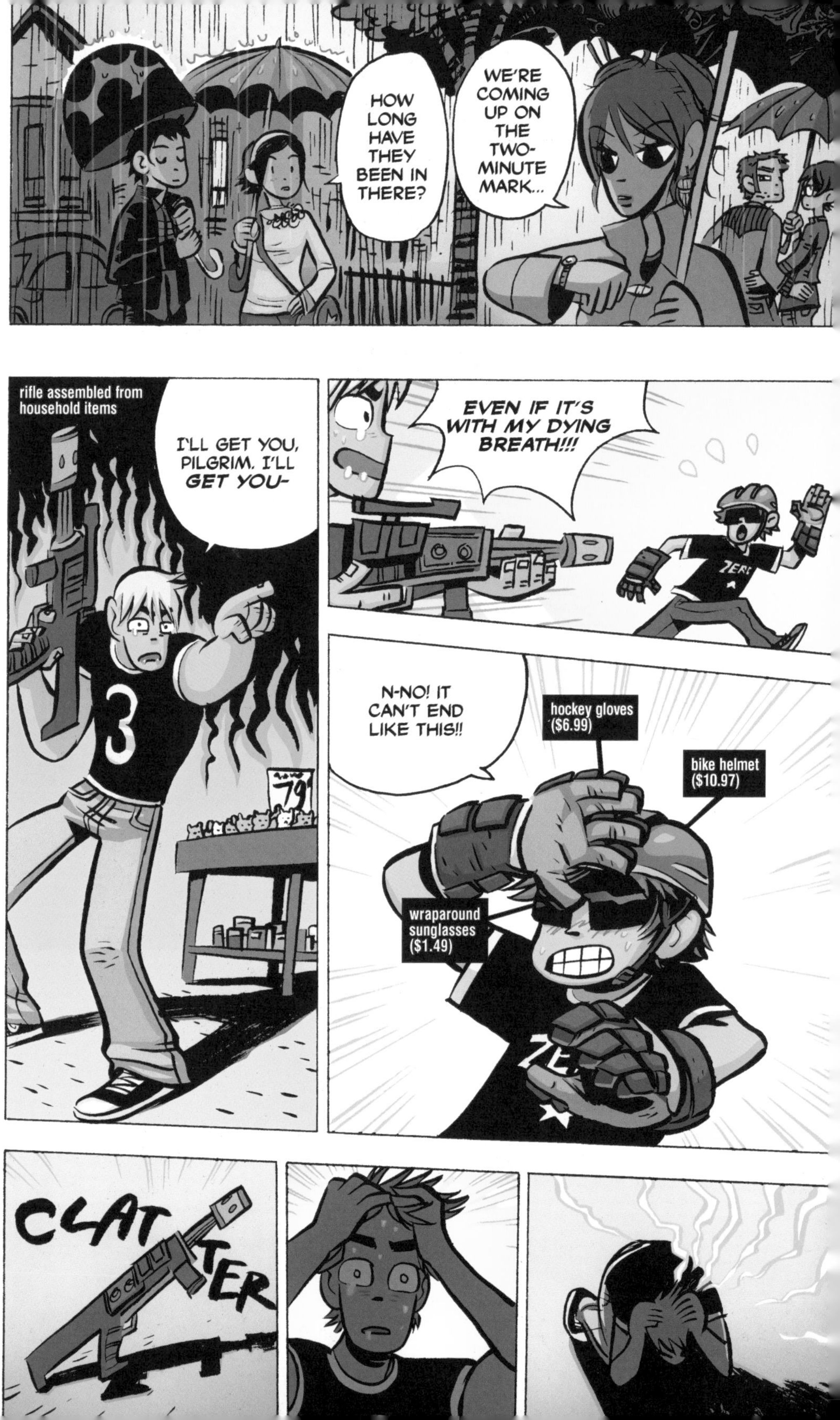

HOW LONG HAVE THEY BEEN IN THERE?
WE'RE COMING UP ON THE TWO-MINUTE MARK...
rifle assembled from household items
I'LL GET YOU, PILGRIM. I'LL GET YOU-
79
EVEN IF IT'S WITH MY DYING BREATH!!!
N-NO! IT CAN'T END LIKE THIS!!
hockey gloves ($6.99)
bike helmet ($10.97)
wraparound sunglasses ($1.49)
CLATTER

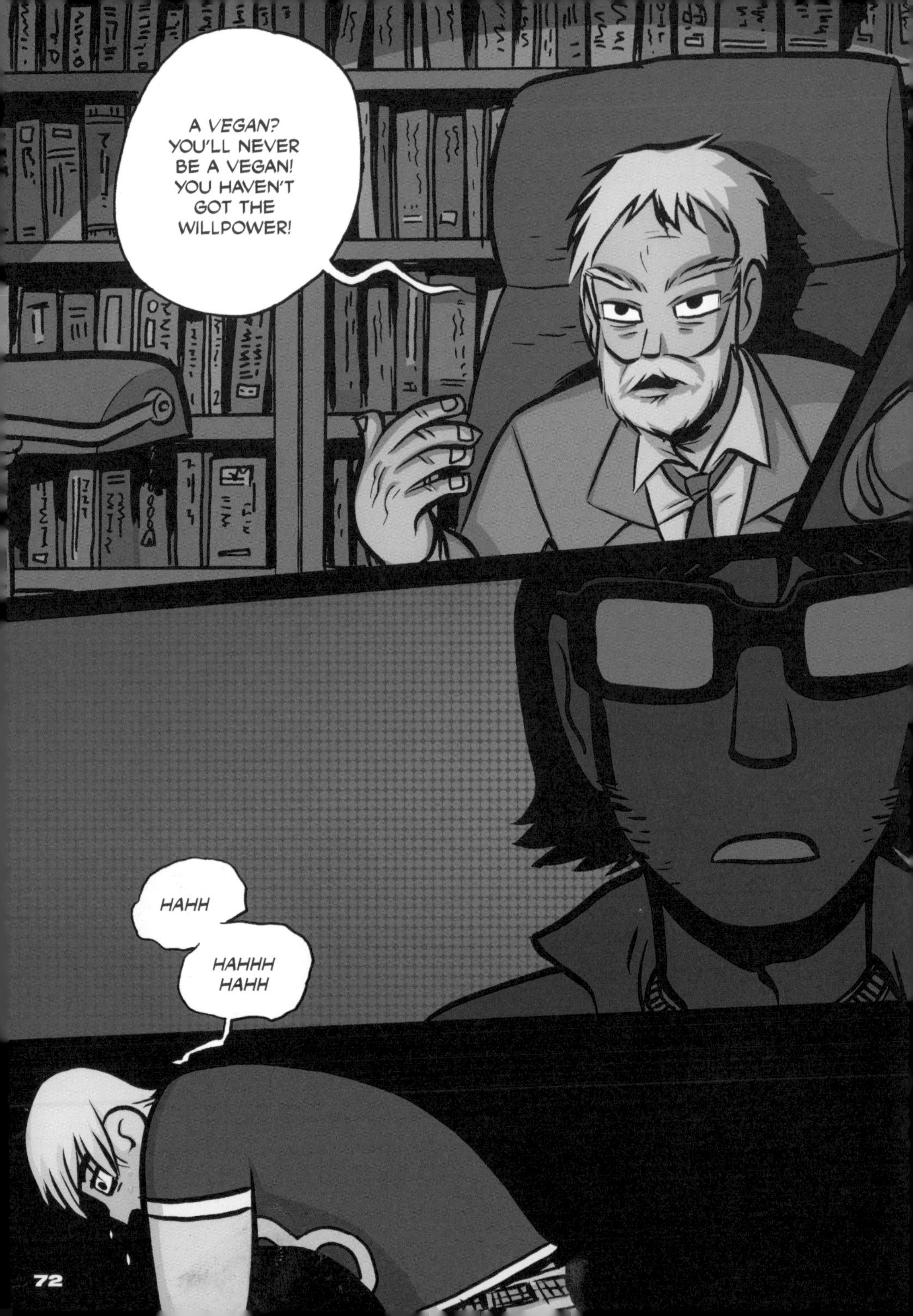
A *VEGAN*? YOU'LL NEVER BE A VEGAN! YOU HAVEN'T GOT THE WILLPOWER!
HAHH
HAHHH HAHH

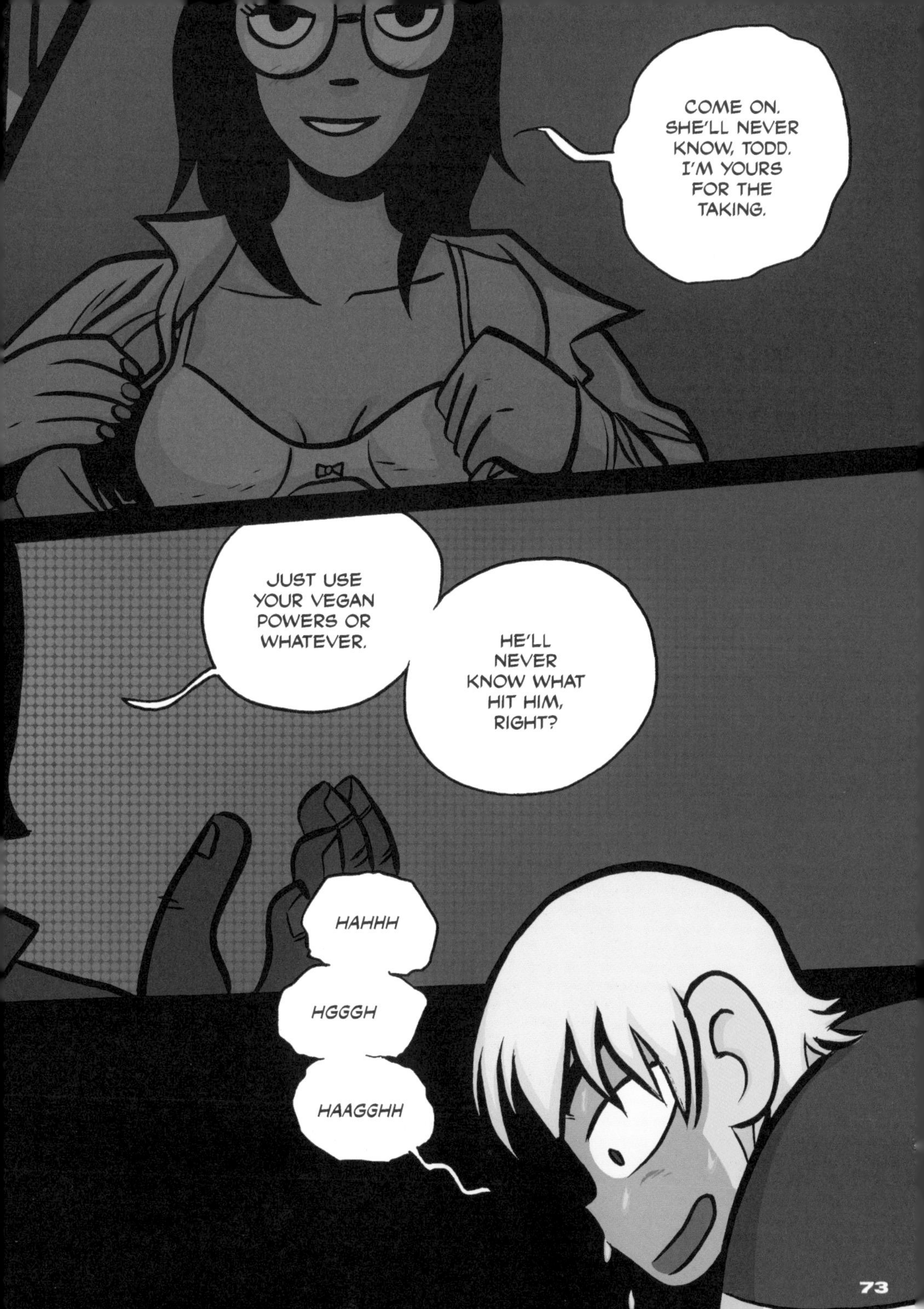
COME ON. SHE'LL NEVER KNOW, TODD. I'M YOURS FOR THE TAKING.
JUST USE YOUR VEGAN POWERS OR WHATEVER.
HE'LL NEVER KNOW WHAT HIT HIM, RIGHT?
HAHHH
HGGGH
HAAGGHH

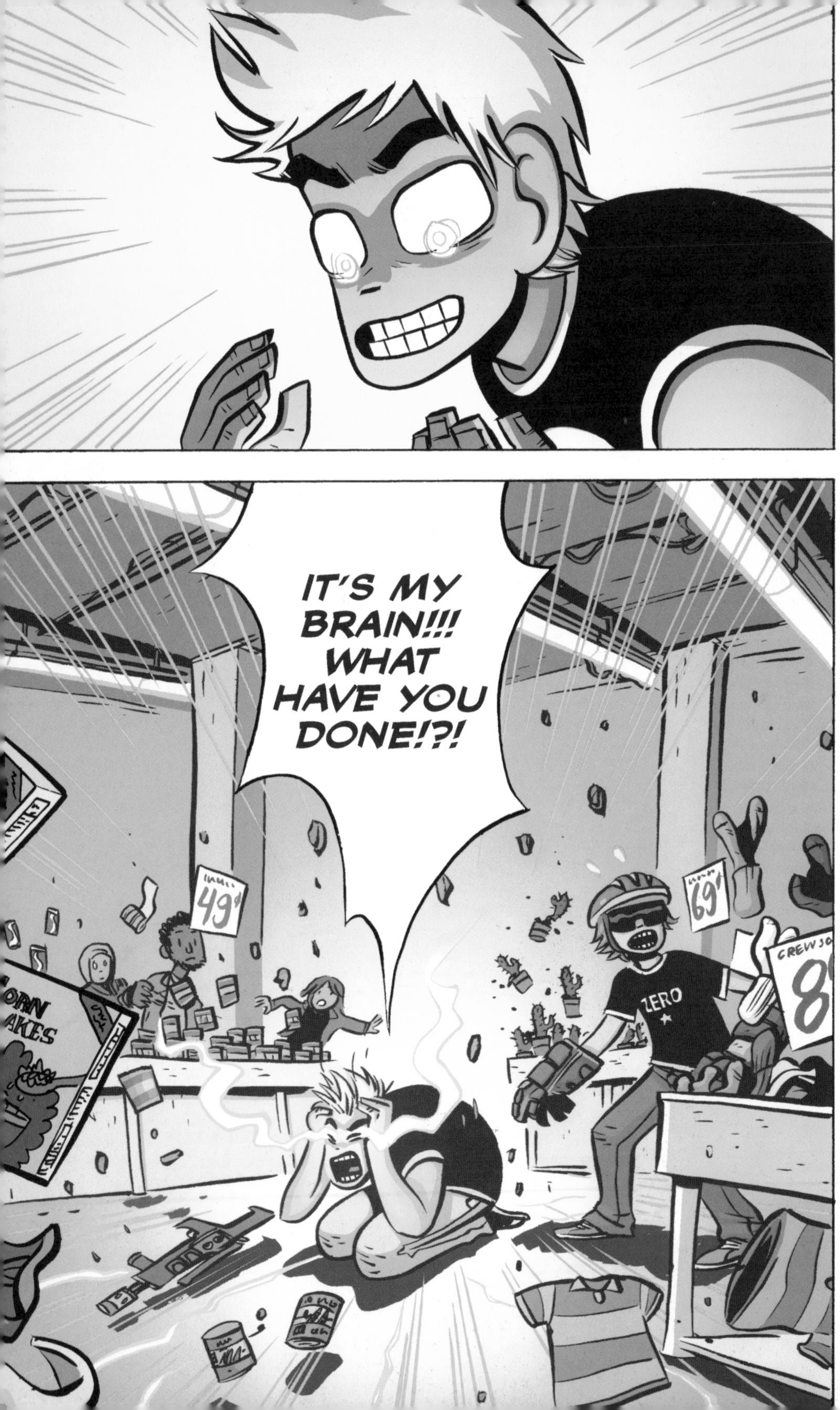
IT'S MY BRAIN!!! WHAT HAVE YOU DONE!?!
49¢
69¢
ZERO

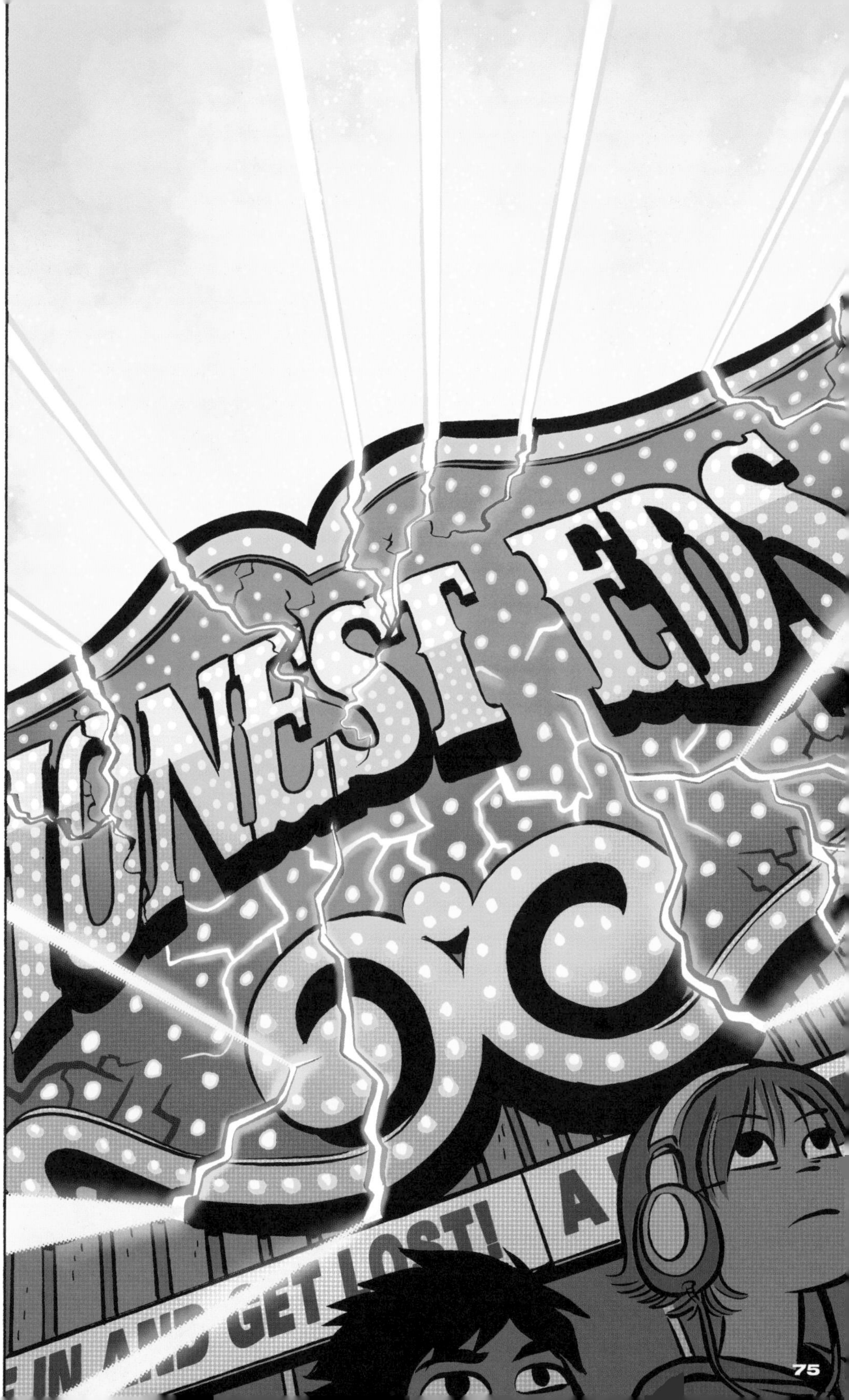
ONEST ED'S
IN AND GET LOST!

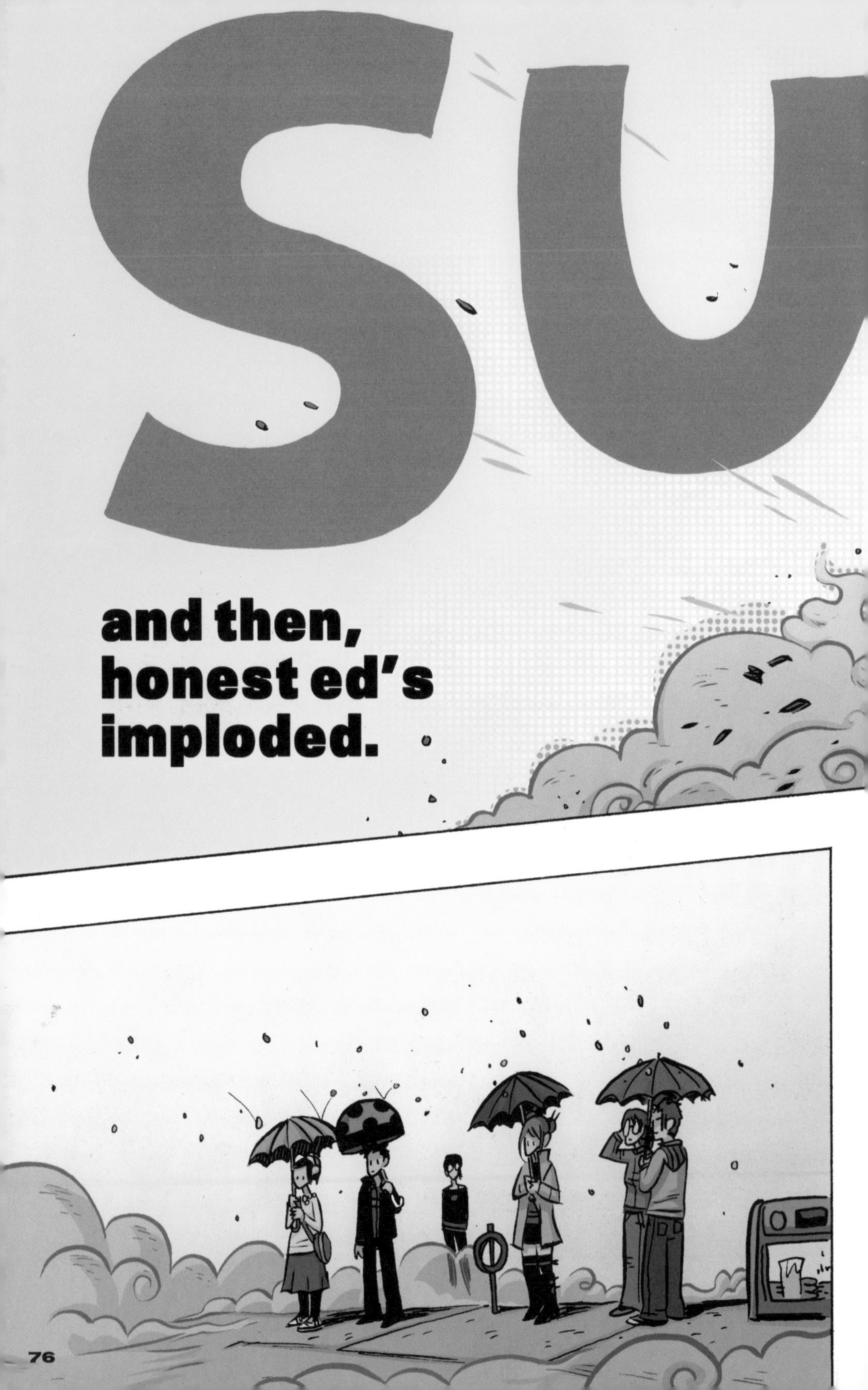
SU
and then, honest ed's imploded.

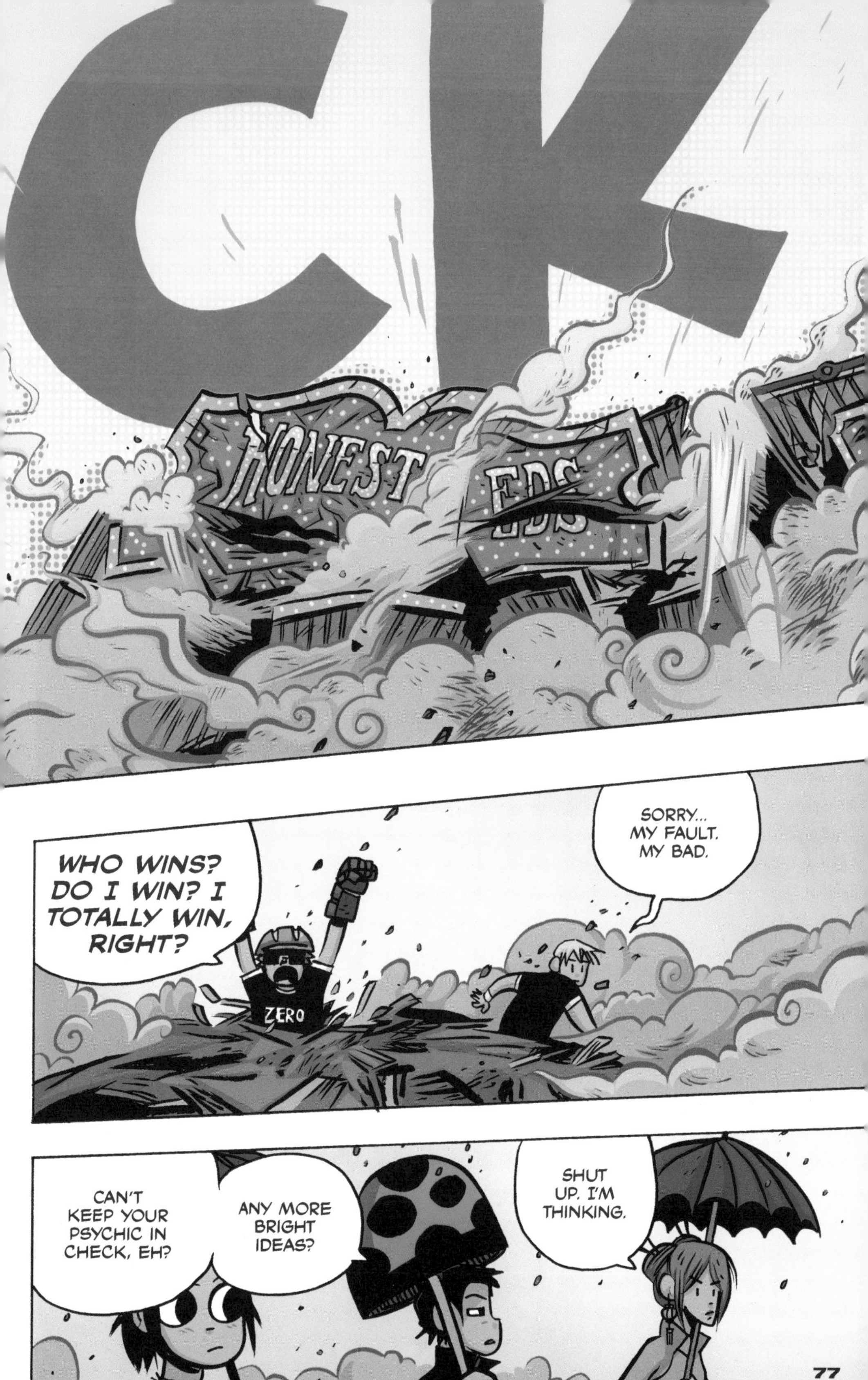
CK
HONEST EDS
WHO WINS? DO I WIN? I TOTALLY WIN, RIGHT?
SORRY... MY FAULT. MY BAD.
ZERO
CAN'T KEEP YOUR PSYCHIC IN CHECK, EH?
ANY MORE BRIGHT IDEAS?
SHUT UP. I'M THINKING.

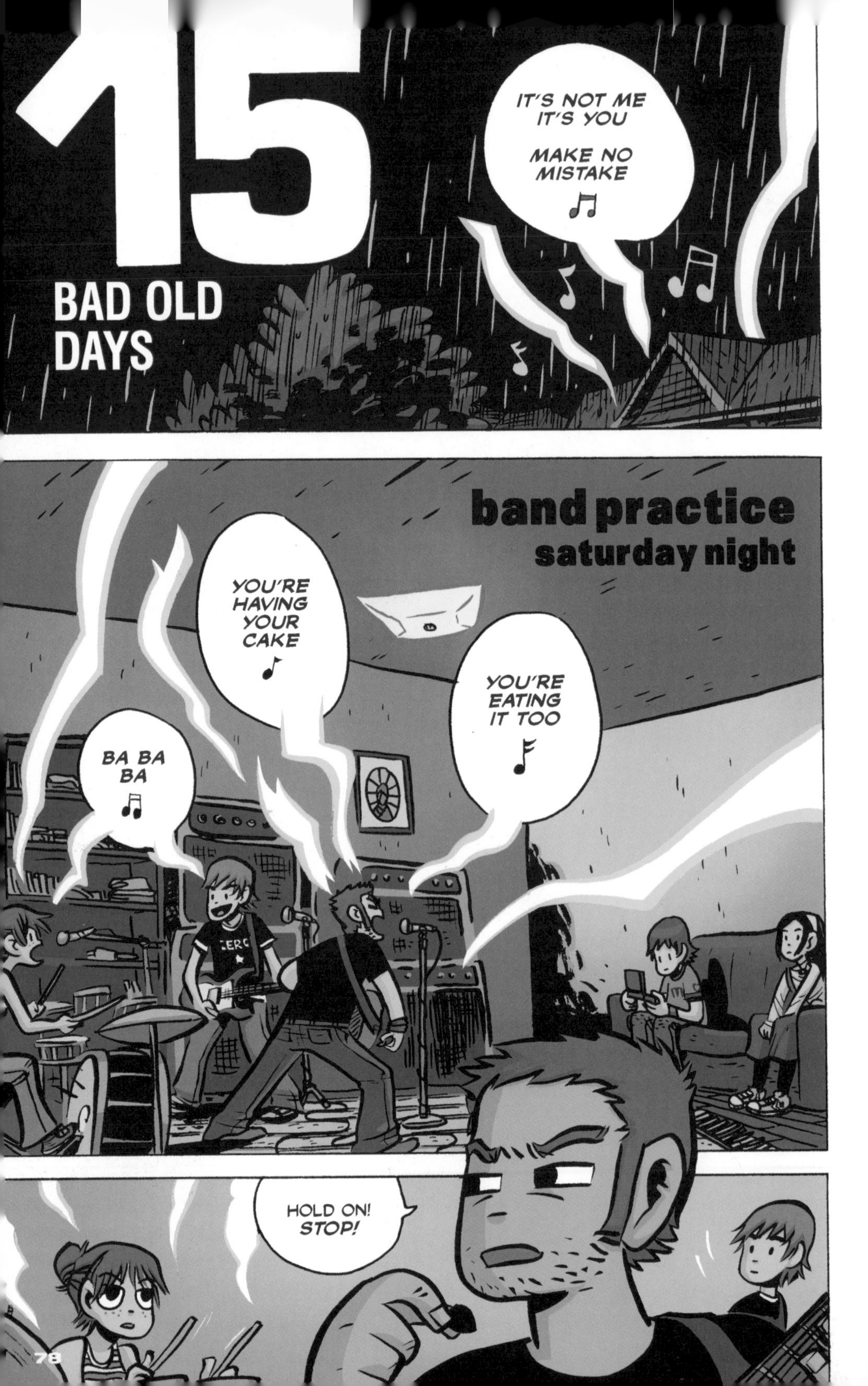

15
BAD OLD DAYS
IT'S NOT ME IT'S YOU
MAKE NO MISTAKE
band practice
saturday night
YOU'RE HAVING YOUR CAKE
YOU'RE EATING IT TOO
BA BA BA
HOLD ON! STOP!

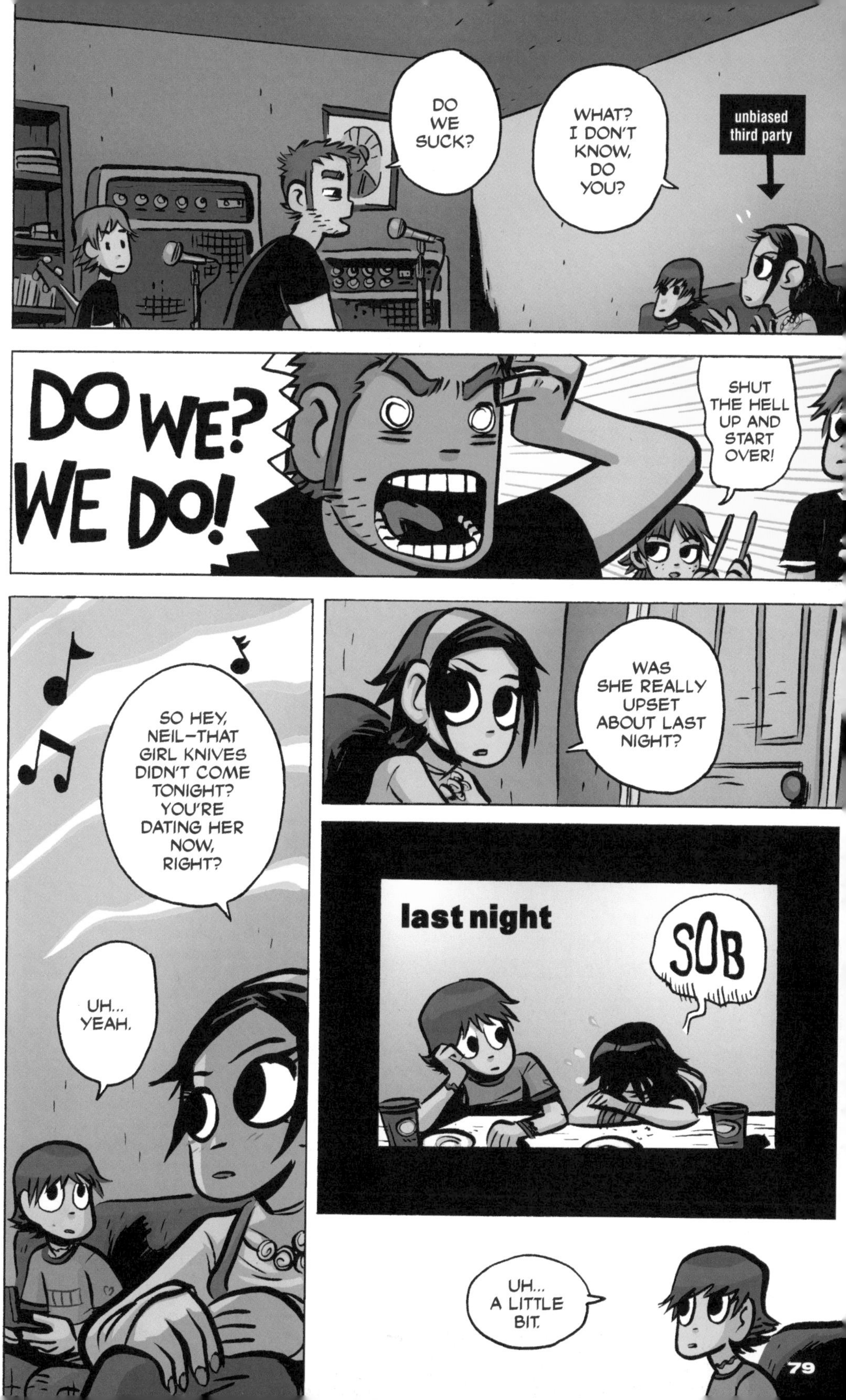
DO WE SUCK?
WHAT? I DON'T KNOW, DO YOU?
unbiased third party
DO WE? WE DO!
SHUT THE HELL UP AND START OVER!
SO HEY, NEIL—THAT GIRL KNIVES DIDN'T COME TONIGHT? YOU'RE DATING HER NOW, RIGHT?
UH... YEAH.
WAS SHE REALLY UPSET ABOUT LAST NIGHT?
last night
SOB
UH... A LITTLE BIT.

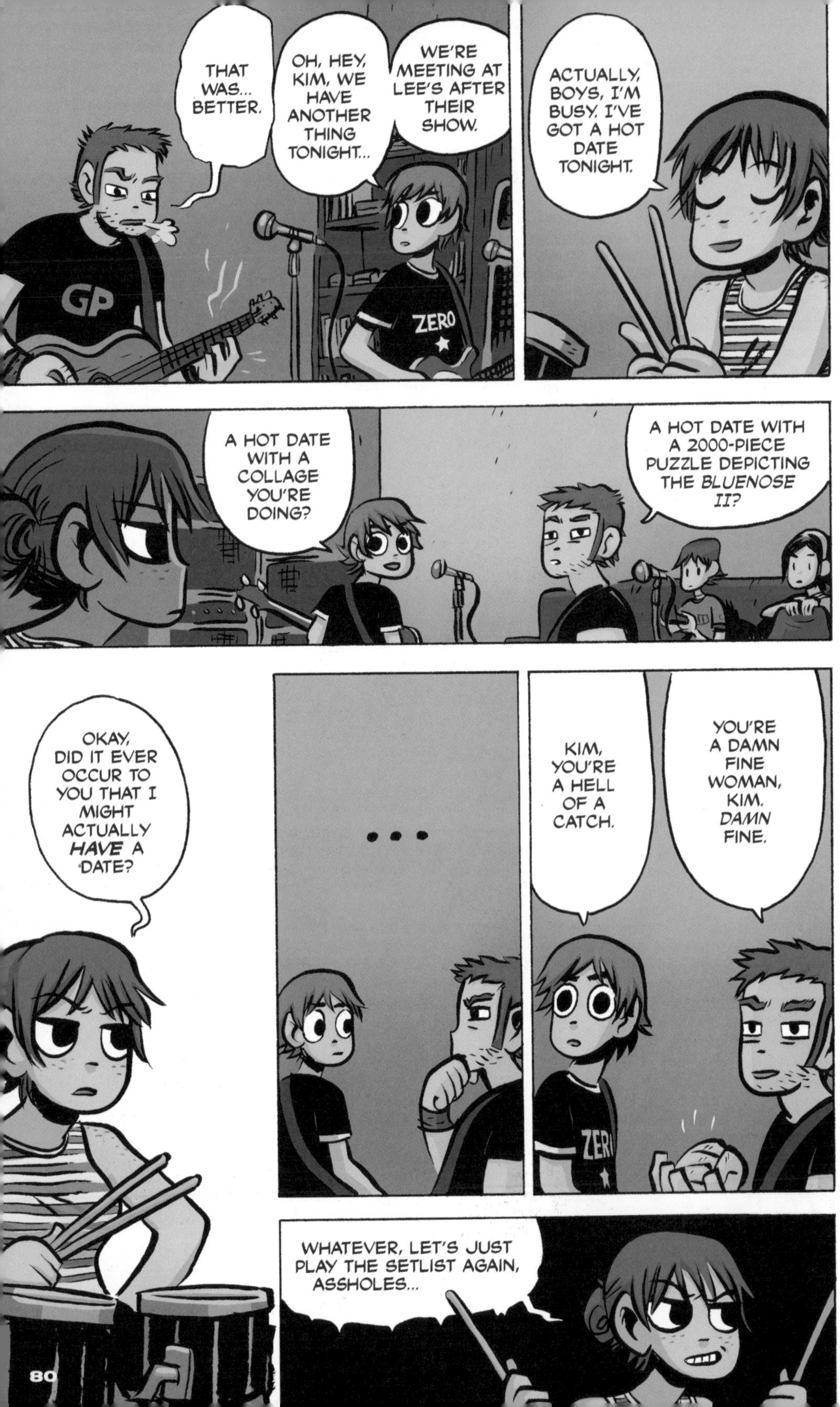
THAT WAS... BETTER.
OH, HEY, KIM, WE HAVE ANOTHER THING TONIGHT...
WE'RE MEETING AT LEE'S AFTER THEIR SHOW.
ACTUALLY, BOYS, I'M BUSY. I'VE GOT A HOT DATE TONIGHT.
A HOT DATE WITH A COLLAGE YOU'RE DOING?
A HOT DATE WITH A 2000-PIECE PUZZLE DEPICTING THE *BLUENOSE II*?
OKAY, DID IT EVER OCCUR TO YOU THAT I MIGHT ACTUALLY ***HAVE*** A DATE?
...
KIM, YOU'RE A HELL OF A CATCH.
YOU'RE A DAMN FINE WOMAN, KIM. *DAMN* FINE.
WHATEVER, LET'S JUST PLAY THE SETLIST AGAIN, ASSHOLES...

saturday night (later)

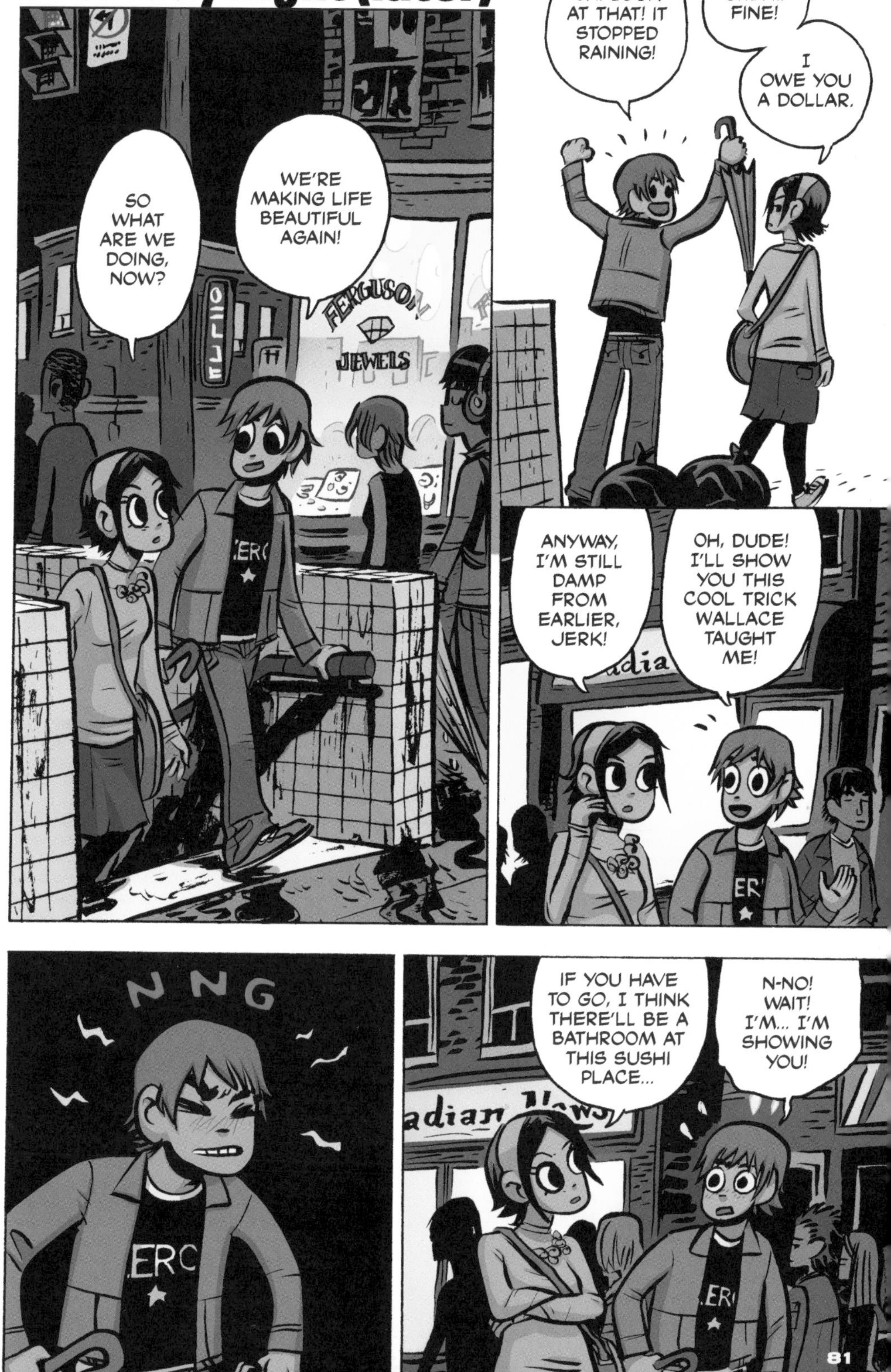

SO WHAT ARE WE DOING, NOW?
WE'RE MAKING LIFE BEAUTIFUL AGAIN!
FERGUSON
JEWELS
OH! LOOK AT THAT! IT STOPPED RAINING!
GREAT. FINE!
I OWE YOU A DOLLAR.
ANYWAY, I'M STILL DAMP FROM EARLIER, JERK!
OH, DUDE! I'LL SHOW YOU THIS COOL TRICK WALLACE TAUGHT ME!
NNG
IF YOU HAVE TO GO, I THINK THERE'LL BE A BATHROOM AT THIS SUSHI PLACE...
N-NO! WAIT! I'M... I'M SHOWING YOU!

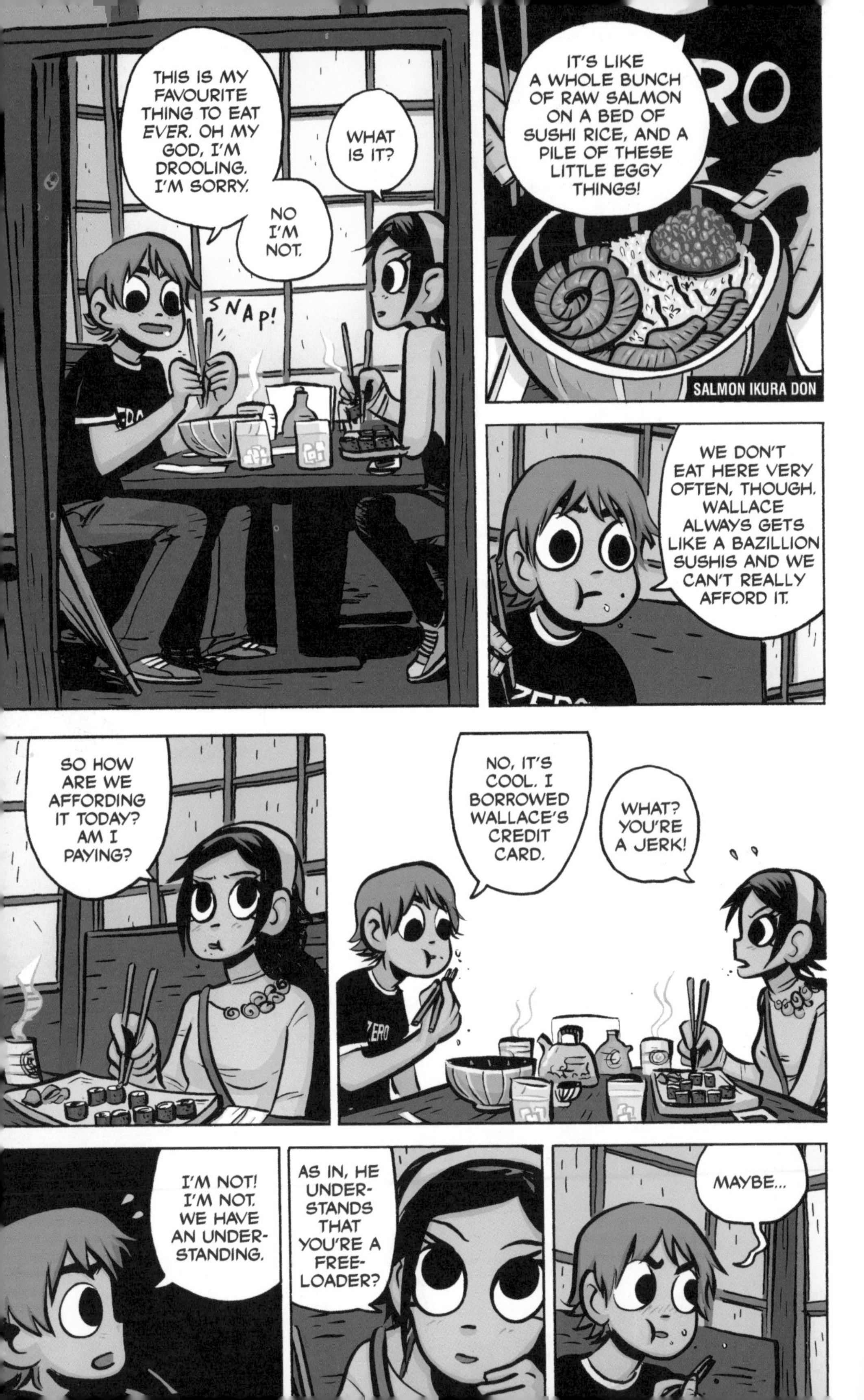
THIS IS MY FAVOURITE THING TO EAT EVER. OH MY GOD, I'M DROOLING. I'M SORRY.
WHAT IS IT?
NO I'M NOT.
SNAP!
IT'S LIKE A WHOLE BUNCH OF RAW SALMON ON A BED OF SUSHI RICE, AND A PILE OF THESE LITTLE EGGY THINGS!
SALMON IKURA DON
WE DON'T EAT HERE VERY OFTEN, THOUGH. WALLACE ALWAYS GETS LIKE A BAZILLION SUSHIS AND WE CAN'T REALLY AFFORD IT.
SO HOW ARE WE AFFORDING IT TODAY? AM I PAYING?
NO, IT'S COOL. I BORROWED WALLACE'S CREDIT CARD.
WHAT? YOU'RE A JERK!
I'M NOT! I'M NOT. WE HAVE AN UNDERSTANDING.
AS IN, HE UNDERSTANDS THAT YOU'RE A FREELOADER?
MAYBE...

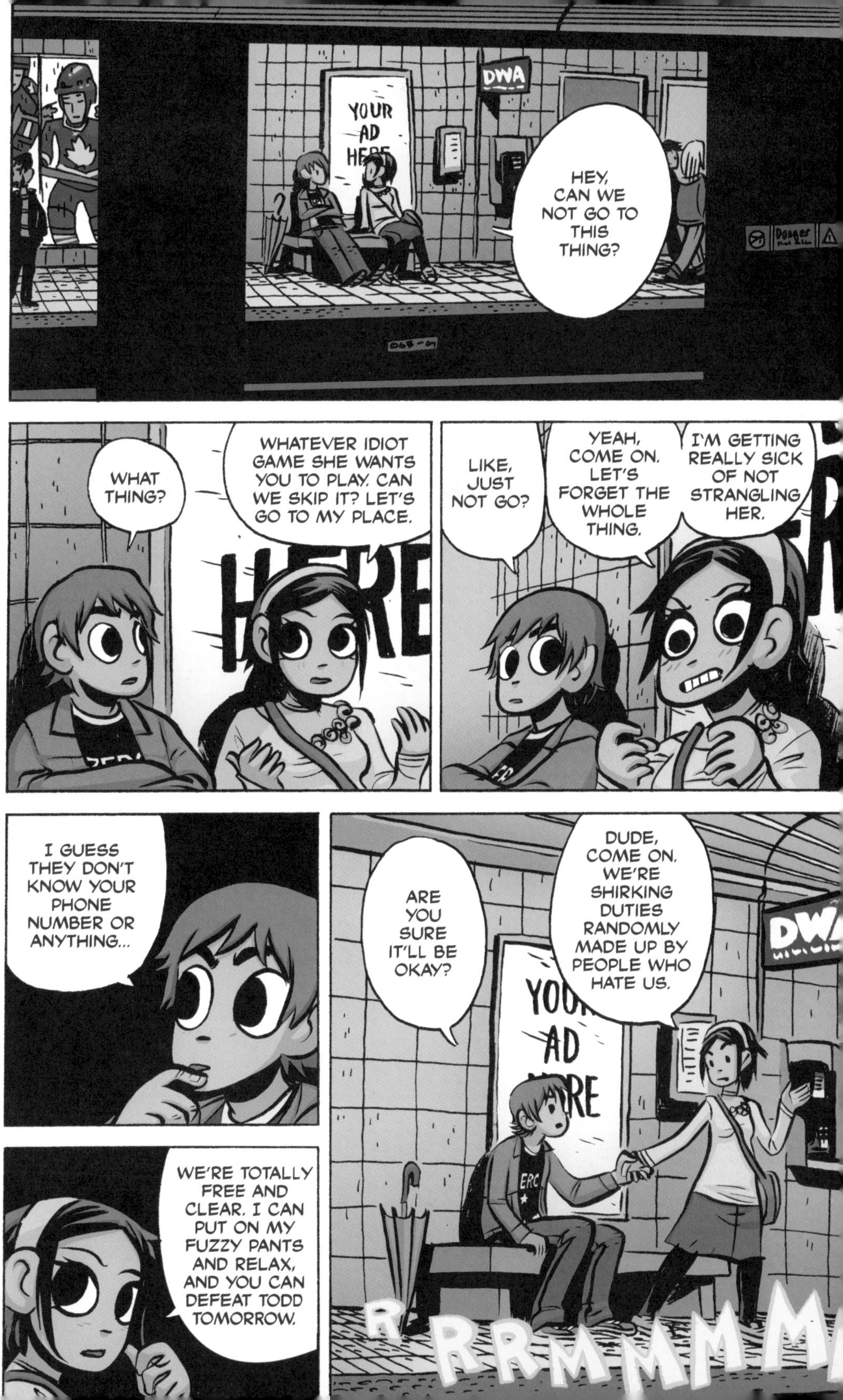

DWA
YOUR AD HERE
HEY, CAN WE NOT GO TO THIS THING?
WHAT THING?
WHATEVER IDIOT GAME SHE WANTS YOU TO PLAY. CAN WE SKIP IT? LET'S GO TO MY PLACE.
LIKE, JUST NOT GO?
YEAH, COME ON. LET'S FORGET THE WHOLE THING.
I'M GETTING REALLY SICK OF NOT STRANGLING HER.
I GUESS THEY DON'T KNOW YOUR PHONE NUMBER OR ANYTHING...
WE'RE TOTALLY FREE AND CLEAR. I CAN PUT ON MY FUZZY PANTS AND RELAX, AND YOU CAN DEFEAT TODD TOMORROW.
ARE YOU SURE IT'LL BE OKAY?
DUDE, COME ON. WE'RE SHIRKING DUTIES RANDOMLY MADE UP BY PEOPLE WHO HATE US.
RRRMMMMM

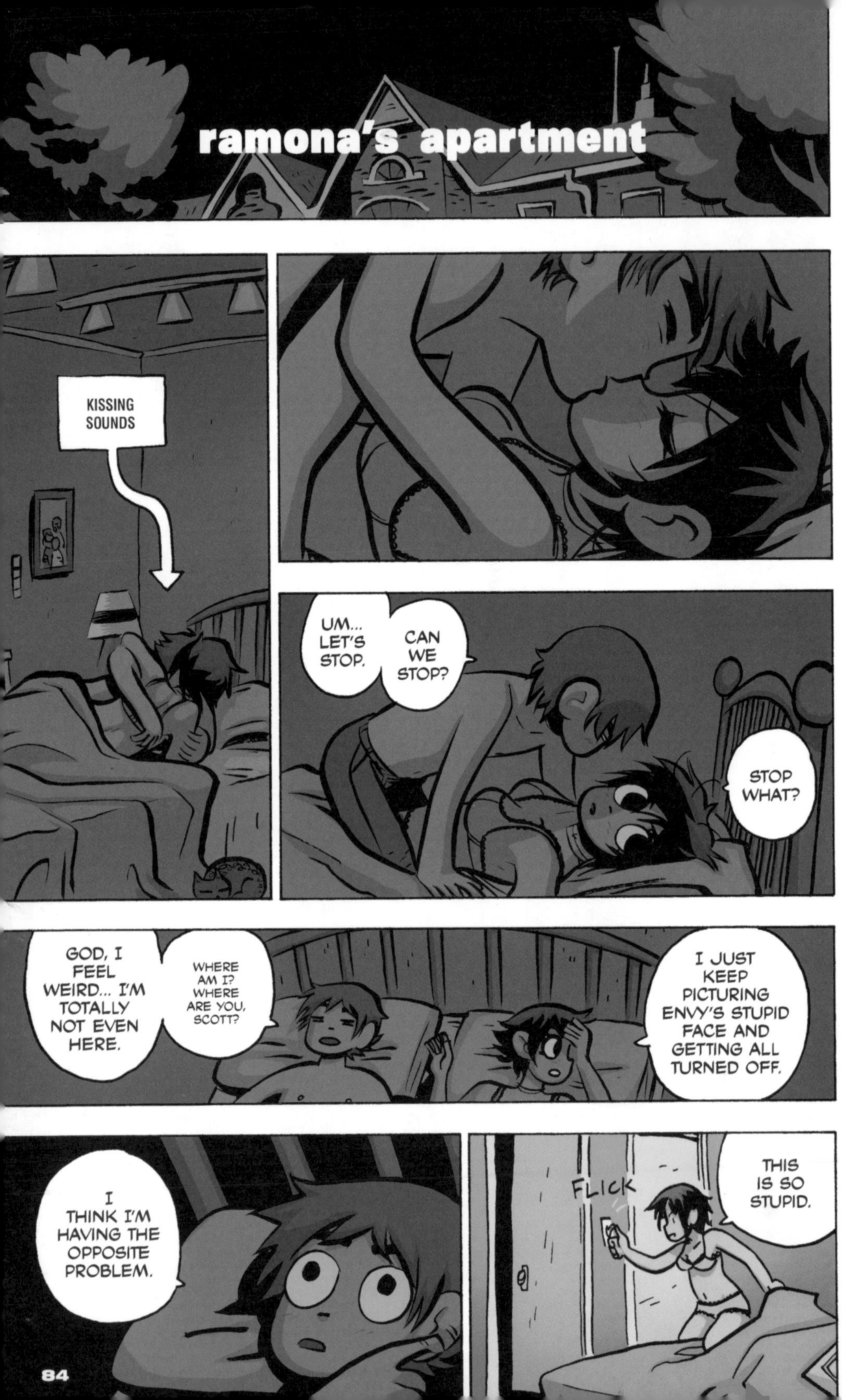
ramona's apartment
KISSING SOUNDS
UM... LET'S STOP.
CAN WE STOP?
STOP WHAT?
GOD, I FEEL WEIRD... I'M TOTALLY NOT EVEN HERE.
WHERE AM I? WHERE ARE YOU, SCOTT?
I JUST KEEP PICTURING ENVY'S STUPID FACE AND GETTING ALL TURNED OFF.
I THINK I'M HAVING THE OPPOSITE PROBLEM.
FLICK
THIS IS SO STUPID.

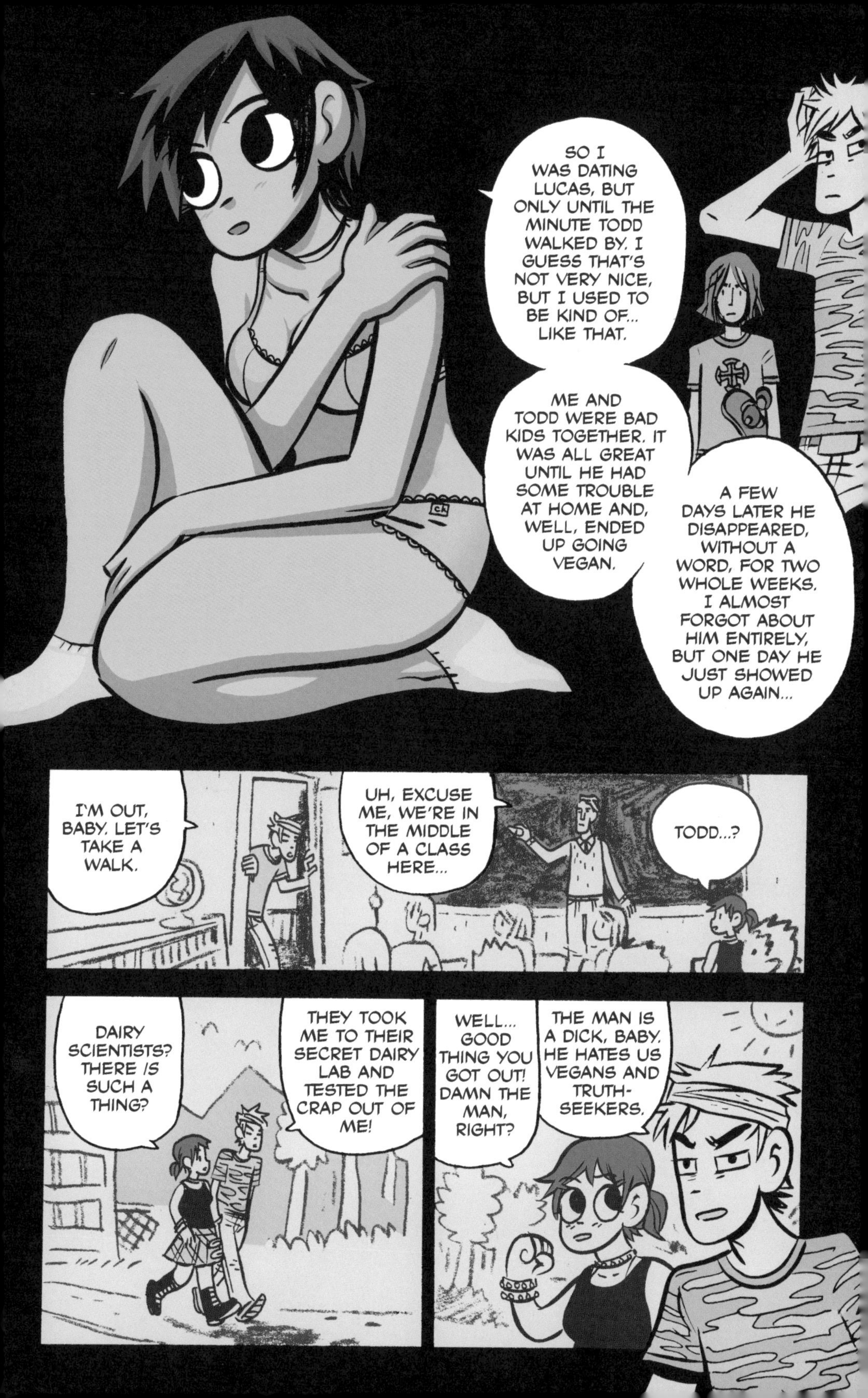
SO I WAS DATING LUCAS, BUT ONLY UNTIL THE MINUTE TODD WALKED BY. I GUESS THAT'S NOT VERY NICE, BUT I USED TO BE KIND OF... LIKE THAT.
ME AND TODD WERE BAD KIDS TOGETHER. IT WAS ALL GREAT UNTIL HE HAD SOME TROUBLE AT HOME AND, WELL, ENDED UP GOING VEGAN.
A FEW DAYS LATER HE DISAPPEARED, WITHOUT A WORD, FOR TWO WHOLE WEEKS. I ALMOST FORGOT ABOUT HIM ENTIRELY, BUT ONE DAY HE JUST SHOWED UP AGAIN...
I'M OUT, BABY. LET'S TAKE A WALK.
UH, EXCUSE ME, WE'RE IN THE MIDDLE OF A CLASS HERE...
TODD...?
DAIRY SCIENTISTS? THERE *IS* SUCH A THING?
THEY TOOK ME TO THEIR SECRET DAIRY LAB AND TESTED THE CRAP OUT OF ME!
WELL... GOOD THING YOU GOT OUT! DAMN THE MAN, RIGHT?
THE MAN IS A DICK, BABY. HE HATES US VEGANS AND TRUTH-SEEKERS.

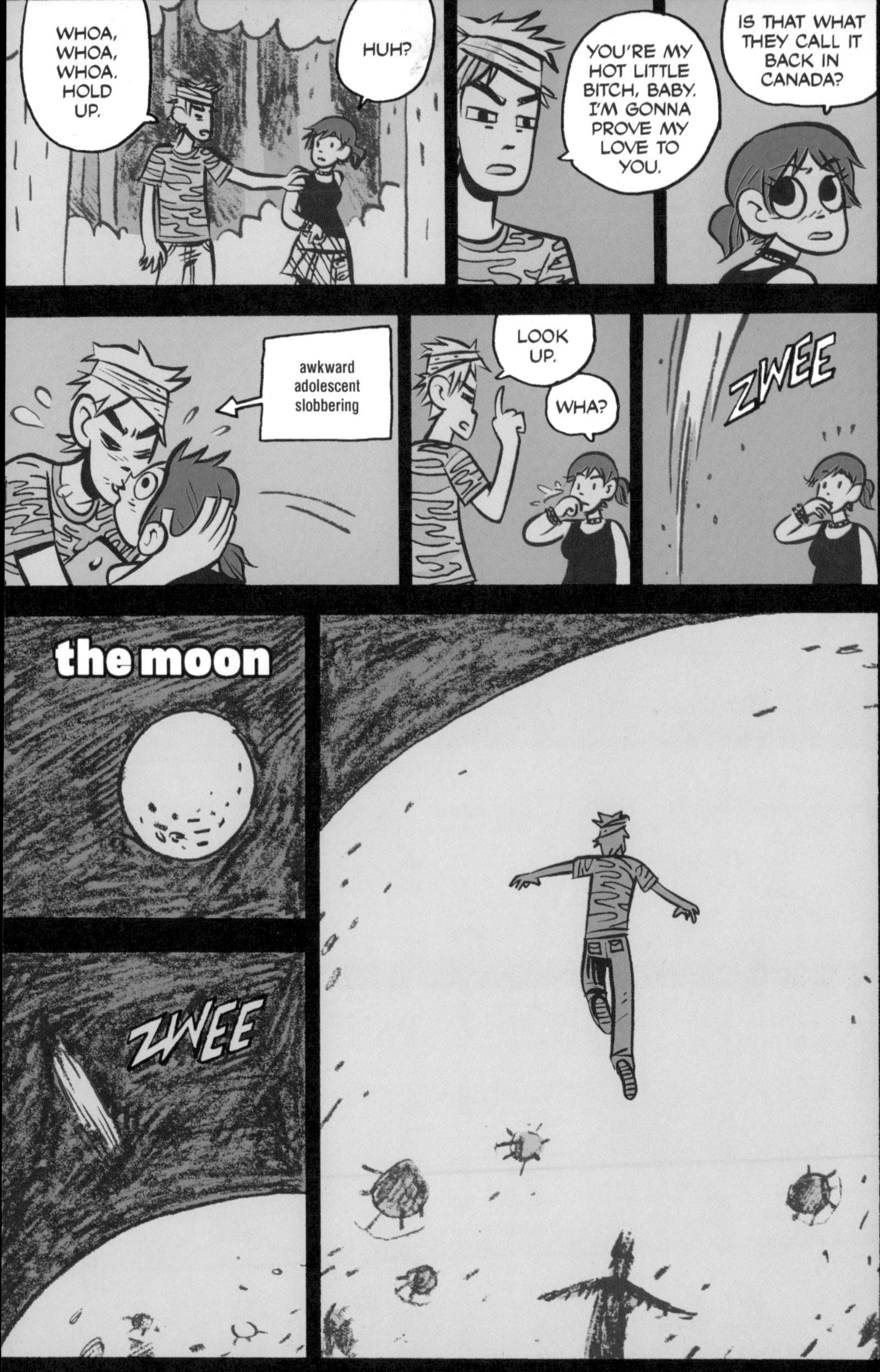
WHOA, WHOA, WHOA. HOLD UP.
HUH?
YOU'RE MY HOT LITTLE BITCH, BABY. I'M GONNA PROVE MY LOVE TO YOU.
IS THAT WHAT THEY CALL IT BACK IN CANADA?
awkward adolescent slobbering
LOOK UP.
WHA?
ZWEE
the moon
ZWEE

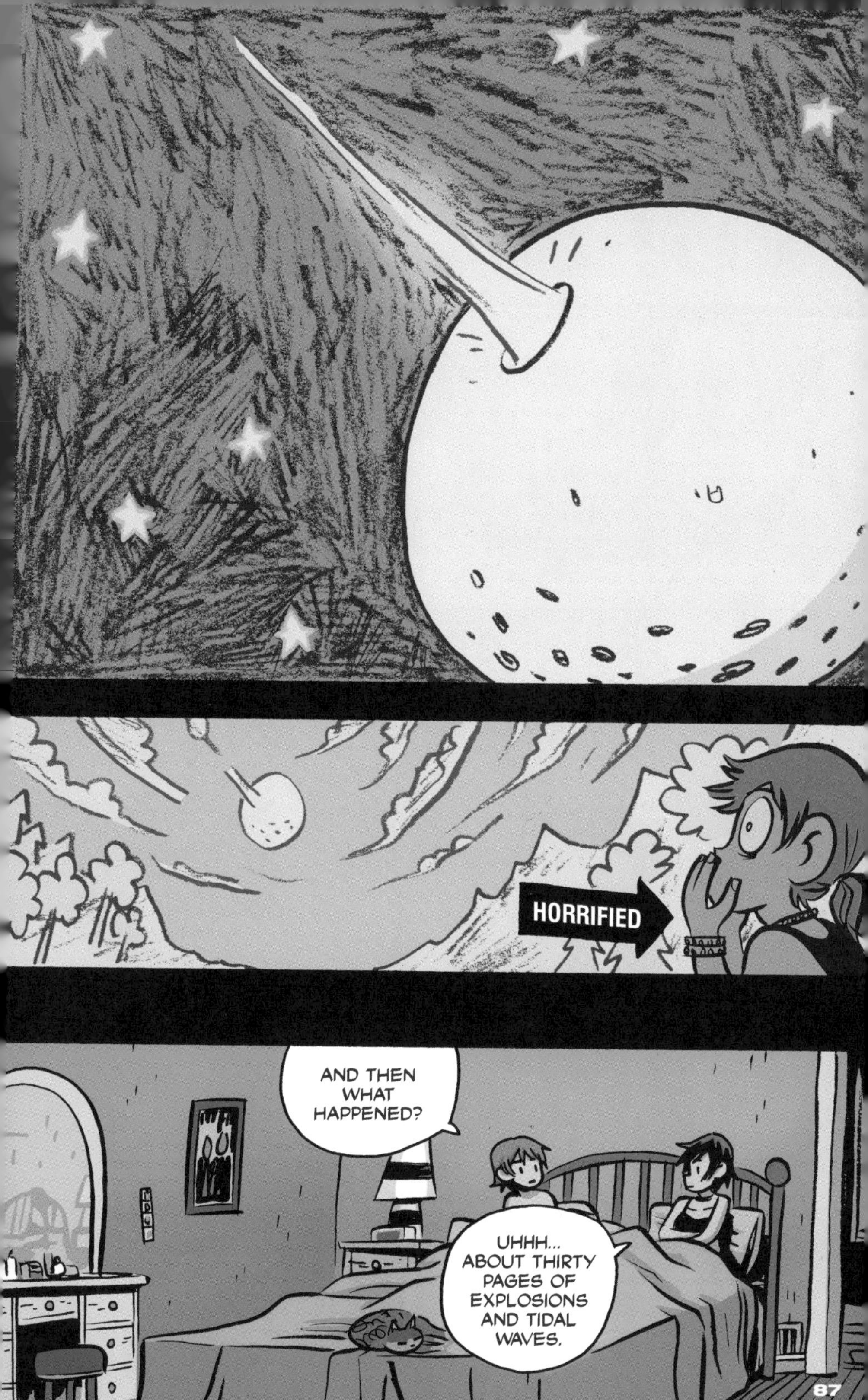

HORRIFIED
AND THEN WHAT HAPPENED?
UHHH... ABOUT THIRTY PAGES OF EXPLOSIONS AND TIDAL WAVES.

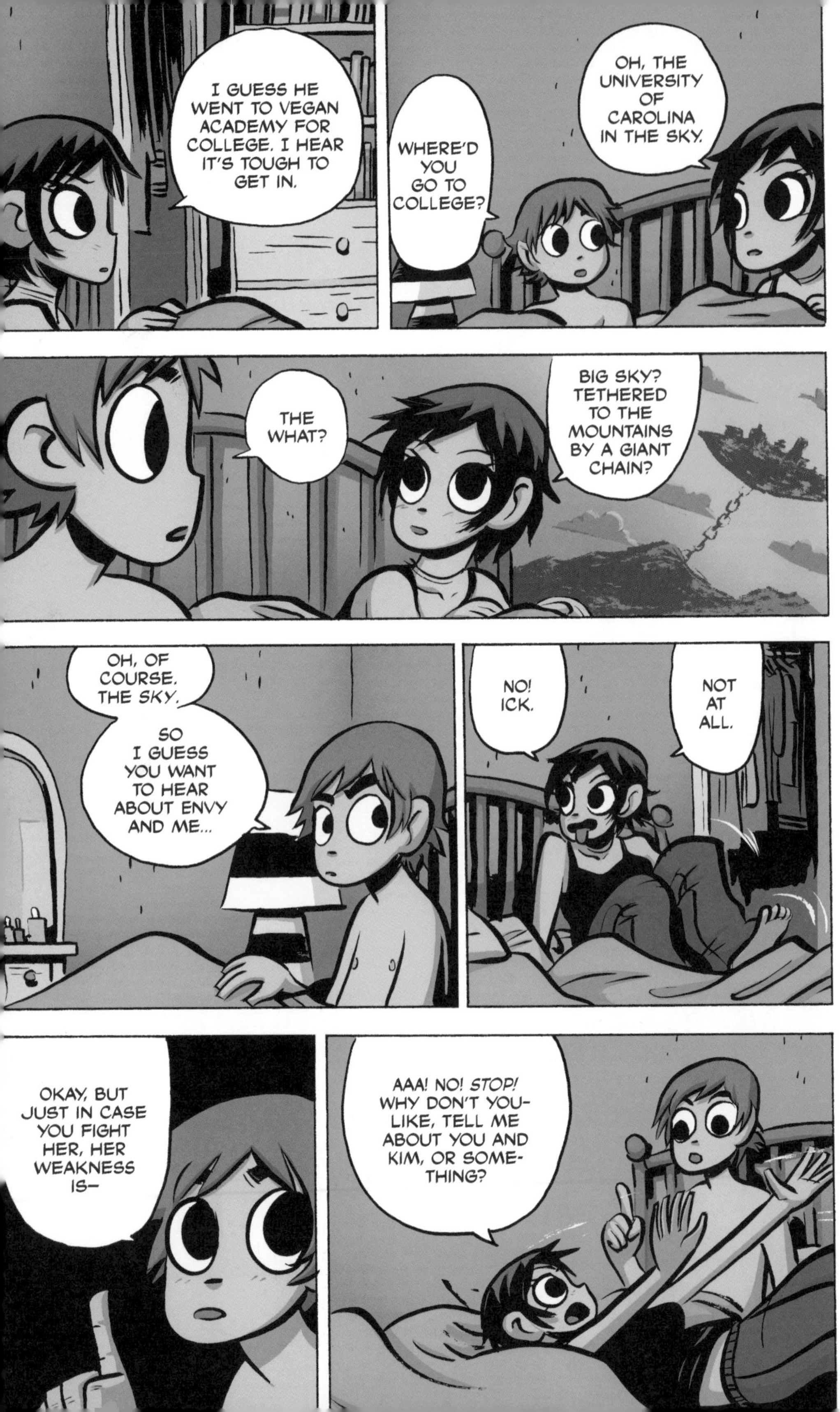
I GUESS HE WENT TO VEGAN ACADEMY FOR COLLEGE. I HEAR IT'S TOUGH TO GET IN.
WHERE'D YOU GO TO COLLEGE?
OH, THE UNIVERSITY OF CAROLINA IN THE SKY.
THE WHAT?
BIG SKY? TETHERED TO THE MOUNTAINS BY A GIANT CHAIN?
OH, OF COURSE. THE SKY.
SO I GUESS YOU WANT TO HEAR ABOUT ENVY AND ME...
NO! ICK.
NOT AT ALL.
OKAY, BUT JUST IN CASE YOU FIGHT HER, HER WEAKNESS IS—
AAA! NO! STOP! WHY DON'T YOU- LIKE, TELL ME ABOUT YOU AND KIM, OR SOME- THING?

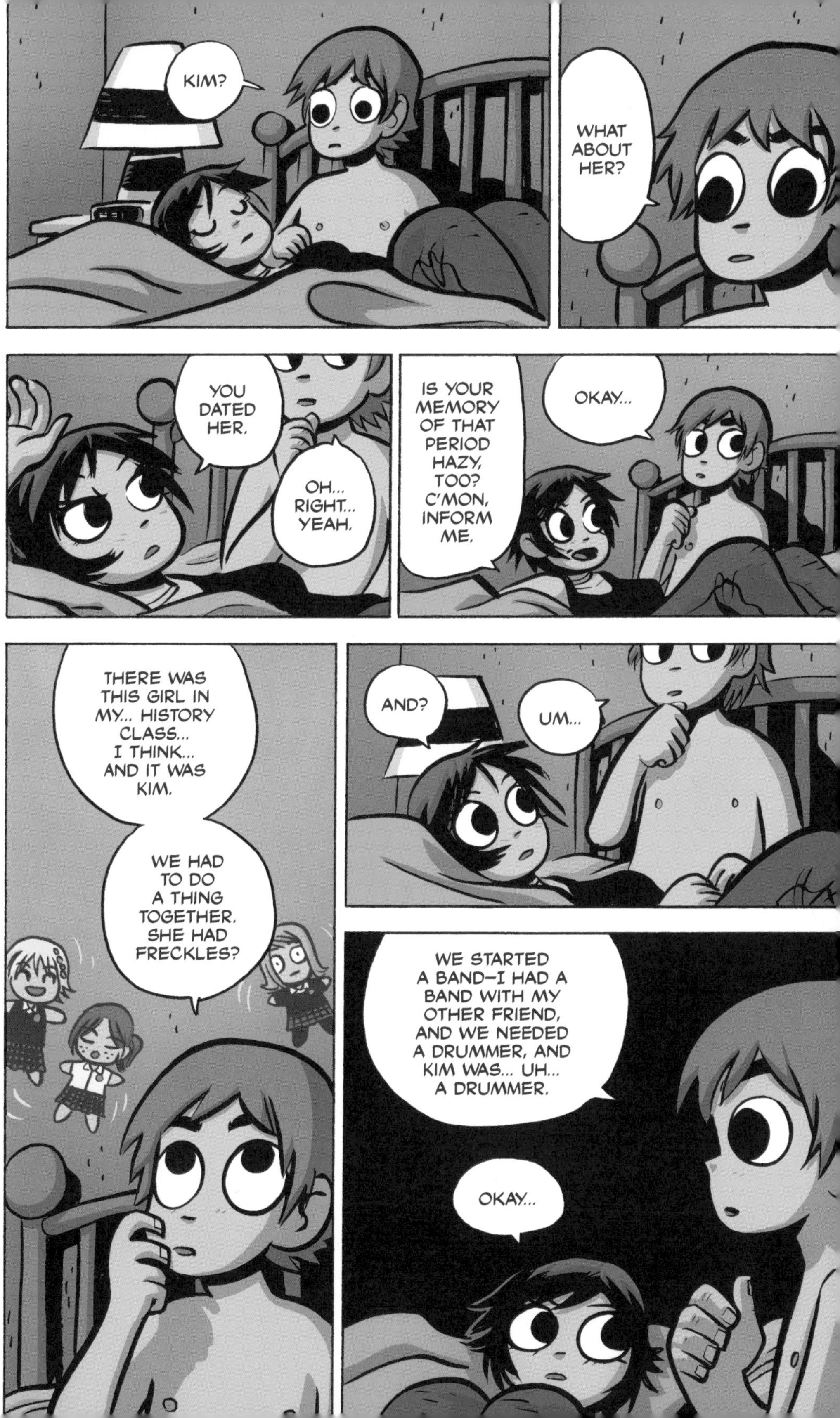
KIM?
WHAT ABOUT HER?
YOU DATED HER.
OH... RIGHT... YEAH.
OKAY...
IS YOUR MEMORY OF THAT PERIOD HAZY, TOO? C'MON, INFORM ME.
THERE WAS THIS GIRL IN MY... HISTORY CLASS... I THINK... AND IT WAS KIM.
WE HAD TO DO A THING TOGETHER. SHE HAD FRECKLES?
AND?
UM...
WE STARTED A BAND—I HAD A BAND WITH MY OTHER FRIEND, AND WE NEEDED A DRUMMER, AND KIM WAS... UH... A DRUMMER.
OKAY...

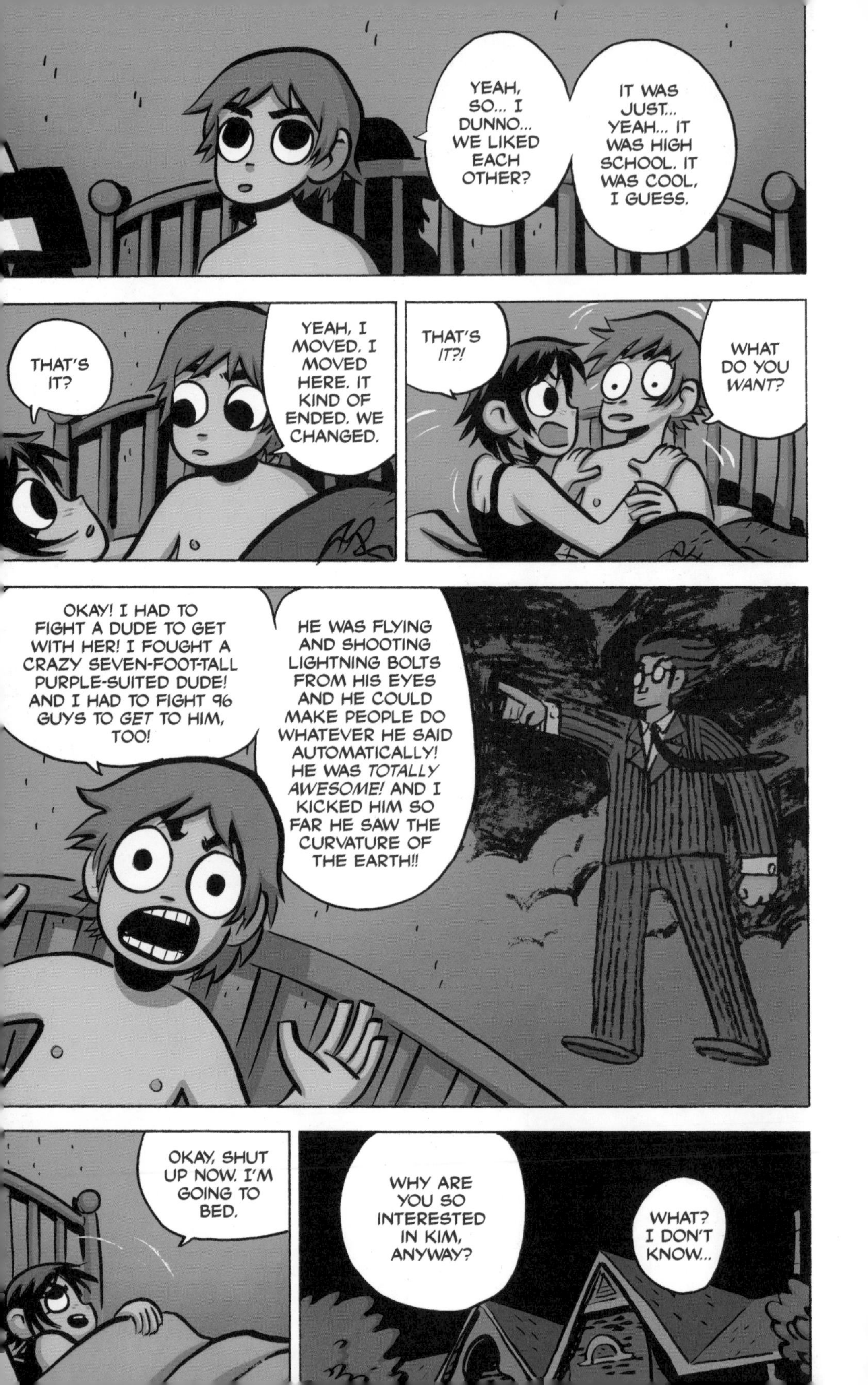
YEAH, SO... I DUNNO... WE LIKED EACH OTHER?
IT WAS JUST... YEAH... IT WAS HIGH SCHOOL. IT WAS COOL, I GUESS.
THAT'S IT?
YEAH, I MOVED. I MOVED HERE. IT KIND OF ENDED. WE CHANGED.
THAT'S *IT?!*
WHAT DO YOU *WANT?*
OKAY! I HAD TO FIGHT A DUDE TO GET WITH HER! I FOUGHT A CRAZY SEVEN-FOOT-TALL PURPLE-SUITED DUDE! AND I HAD TO FIGHT 96 GUYS TO *GET* TO HIM, TOO!
HE WAS FLYING AND SHOOTING LIGHTNING BOLTS FROM HIS EYES AND HE COULD MAKE PEOPLE DO WHATEVER HE SAID AUTOMATICALLY! HE WAS *TOTALLY AWESOME!* AND I KICKED HIM SO FAR HE SAW THE CURVATURE OF THE EARTH!!
OKAY, SHUT UP NOW. I'M GOING TO BED.
WHY ARE YOU SO INTERESTED IN KIM, ANYWAY?
WHAT? I DON'T KNOW...

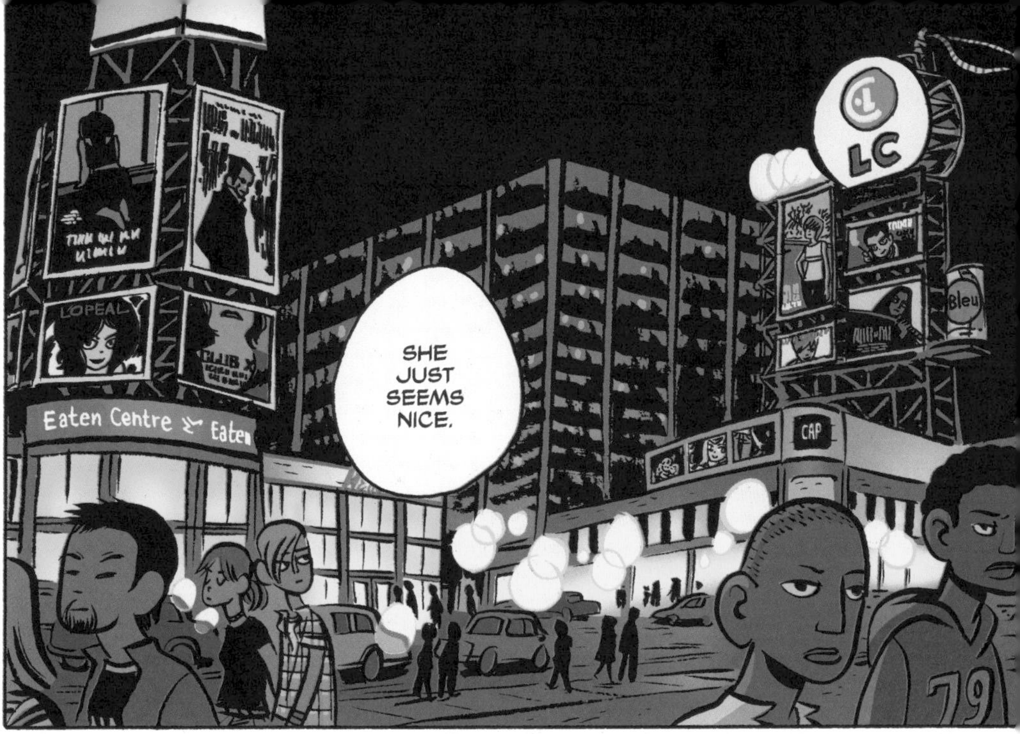
Eaten Centre
Eaten
LOPEAL
CLUB X
LC
CAP
Bleu
SHE JUST SEEMS NICE.
79

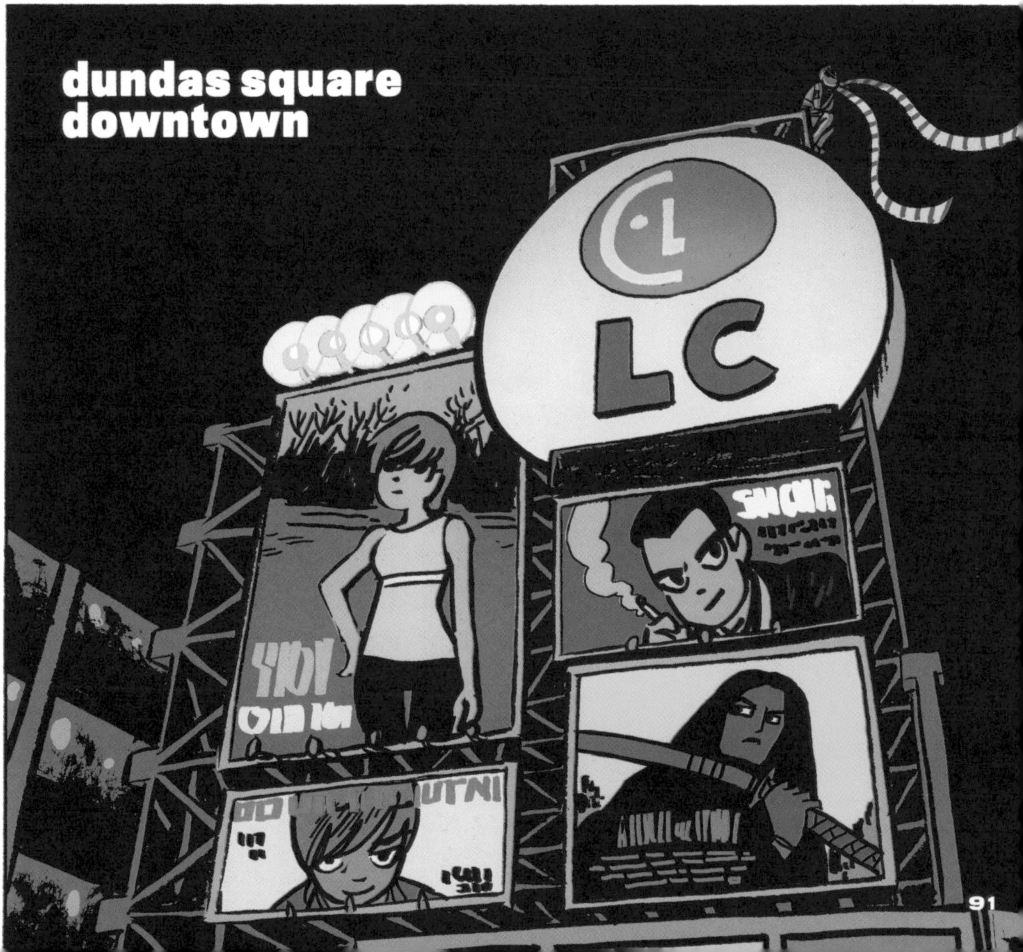
dundas square downtown
LC

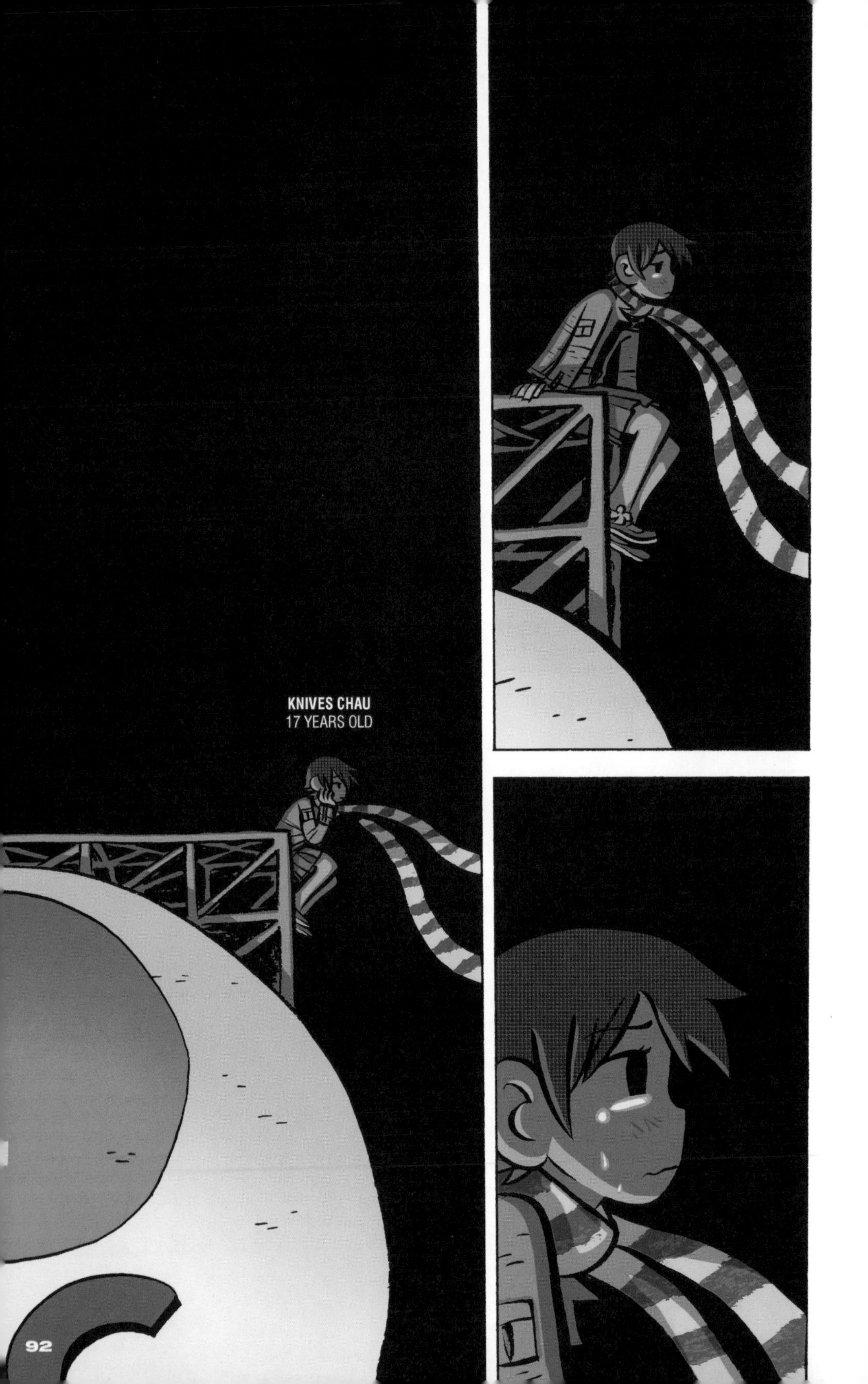
KNIVES CHAU
17 YEARS OLD

16
FRAIL & BEDAZZLED

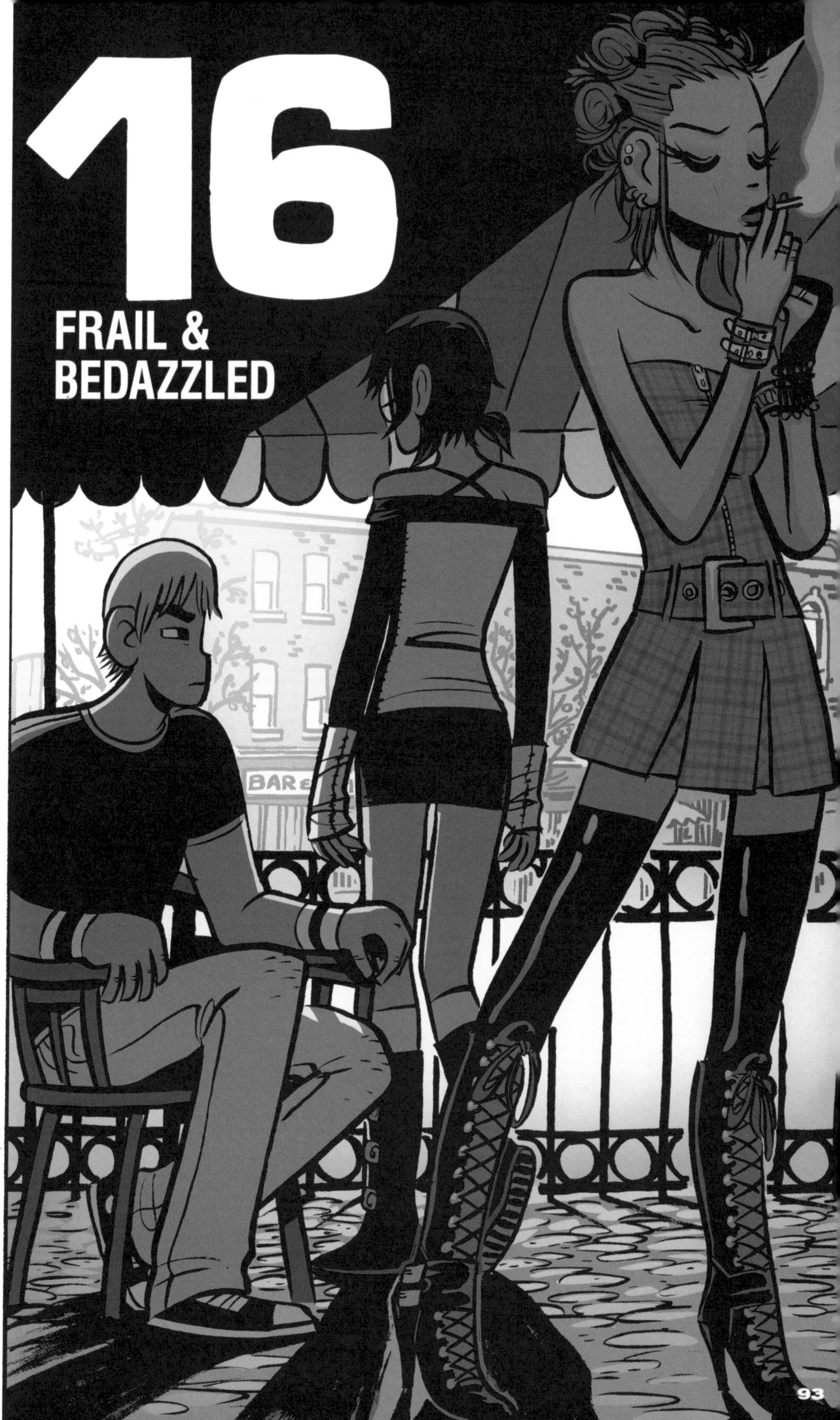
BAR

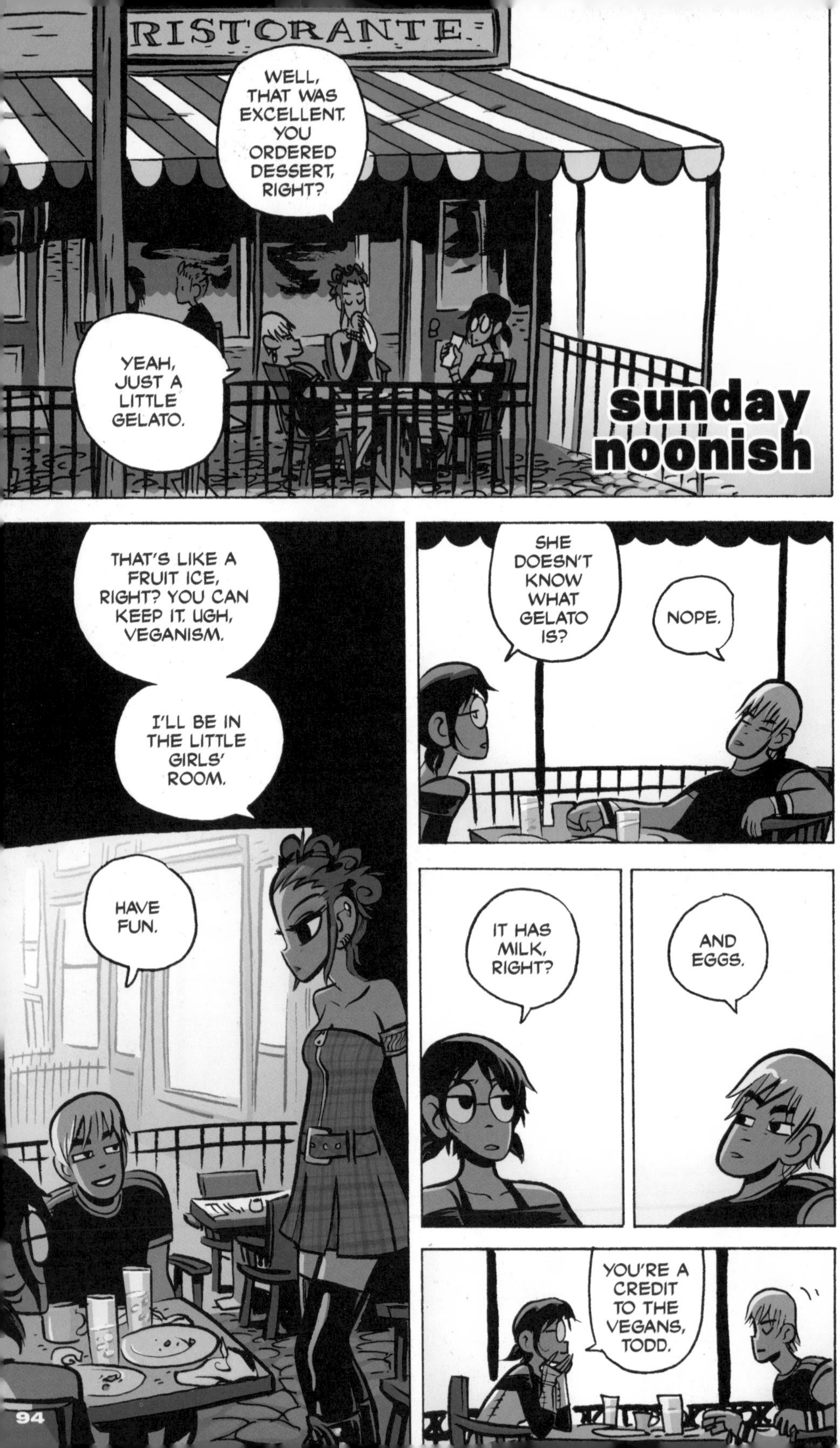
RISTORANTE
WELL, THAT WAS EXCELLENT. YOU ORDERED DESSERT, RIGHT?
YEAH, JUST A LITTLE GELATO.
sunday noonish
THAT'S LIKE A FRUIT ICE, RIGHT? YOU CAN KEEP IT. UGH, VEGANISM.
I'LL BE IN THE LITTLE GIRLS' ROOM.
HAVE FUN.
SHE DOESN'T KNOW WHAT GELATO IS?
NOPE.
IT HAS MILK, RIGHT?
AND EGGS.
YOU'RE A CREDIT TO THE VEGANS, TODD.

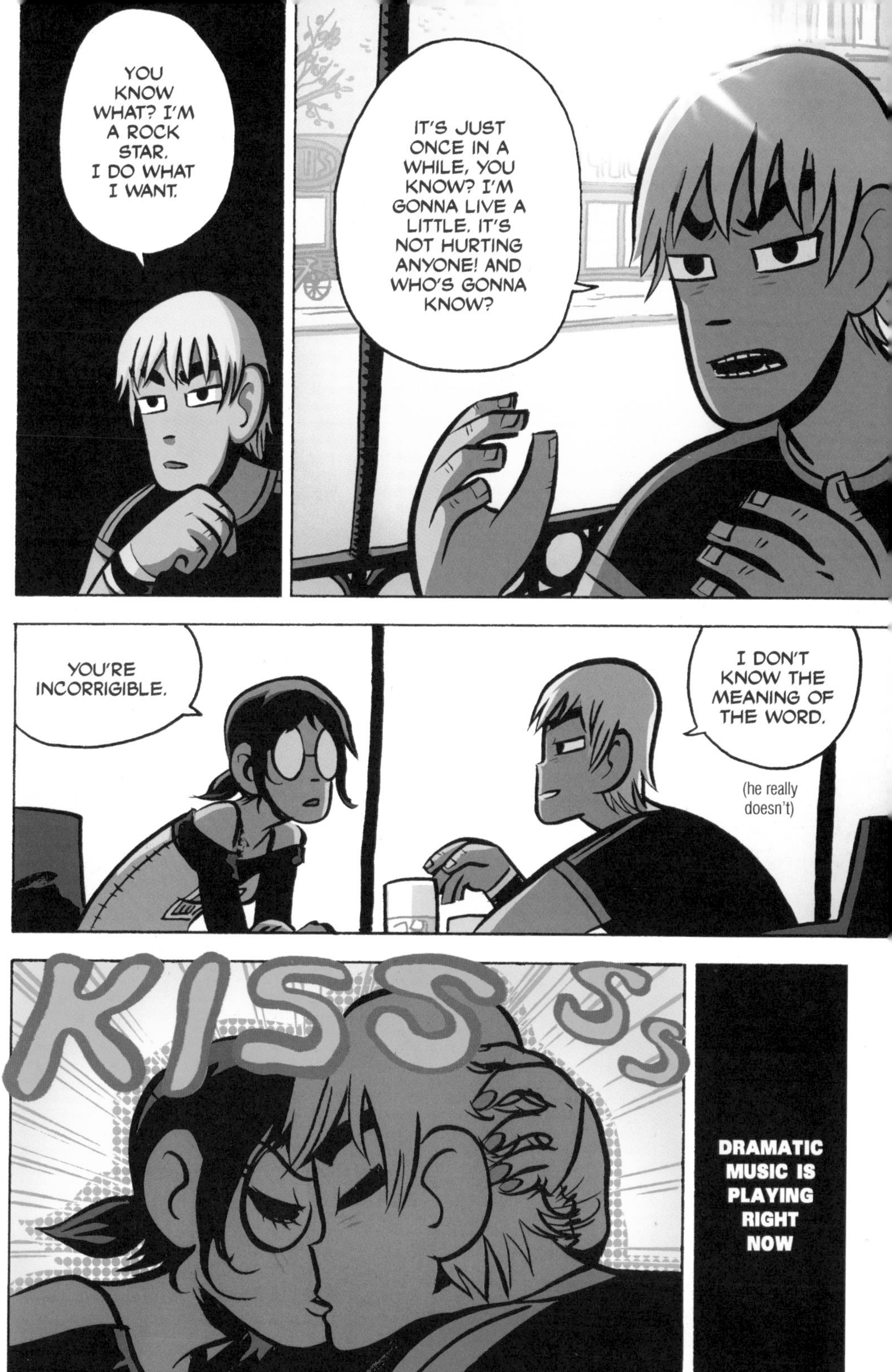

YOU KNOW WHAT? I'M A ROCK STAR. I DO WHAT I WANT.
IT'S JUST ONCE IN A WHILE, YOU KNOW? I'M GONNA LIVE A LITTLE. IT'S NOT HURTING ANYONE! AND WHO'S GONNA KNOW?
YOU'RE INCORRIGIBLE.
I DON'T KNOW THE MEANING OF THE WORD.
(he really doesn't)
KISSs
DRAMATIC MUSIC IS PLAYING RIGHT NOW

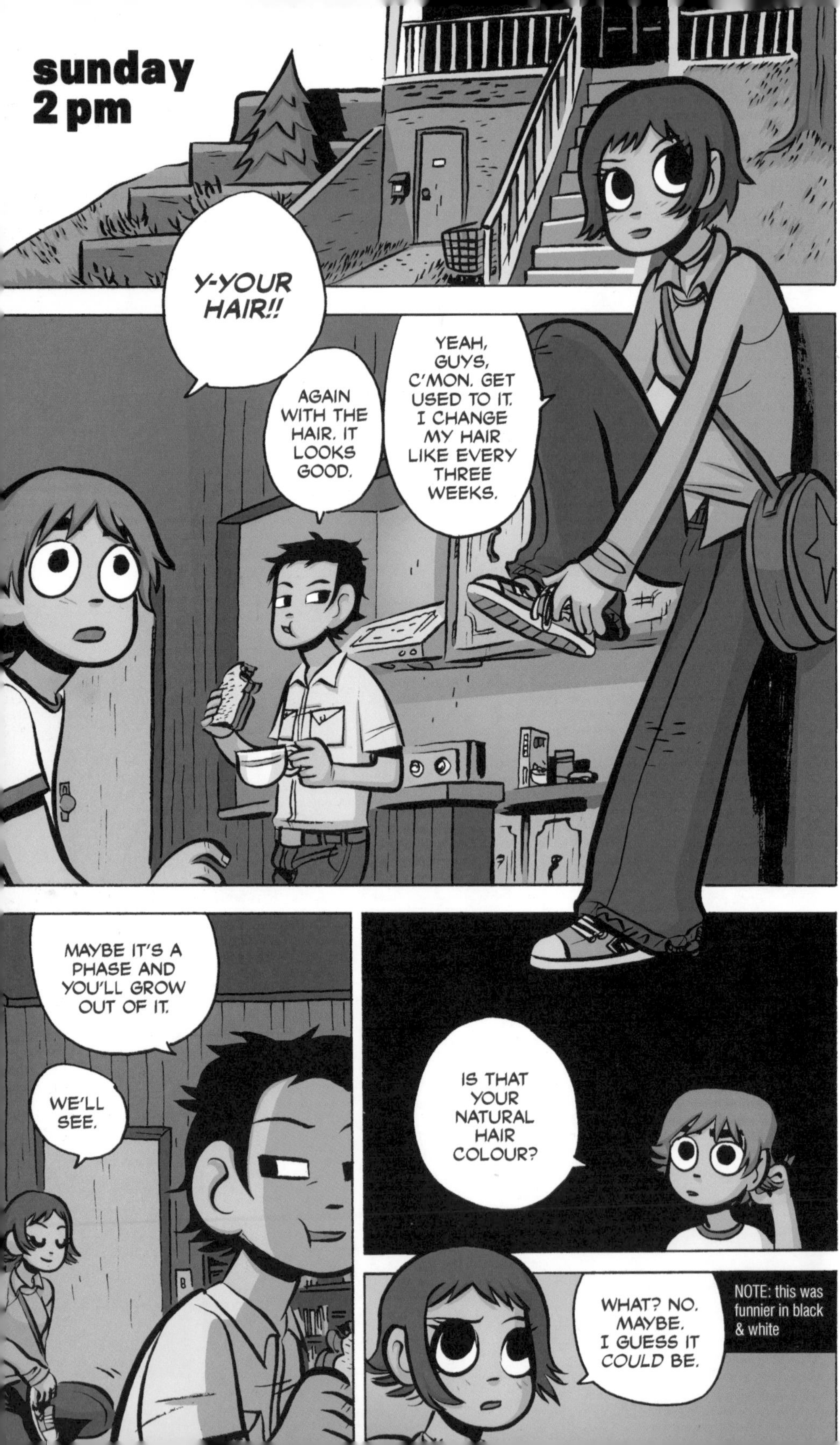
sunday
2 pm
Y-YOUR HAIR!!
AGAIN WITH THE HAIR. IT LOOKS GOOD.
YEAH, GUYS, C'MON. GET USED TO IT. I CHANGE MY HAIR LIKE EVERY THREE WEEKS.
MAYBE IT'S A PHASE AND YOU'LL GROW OUT OF IT.
WE'LL SEE.
IS THAT YOUR NATURAL HAIR COLOUR?
WHAT? NO. MAYBE. I GUESS IT COULD BE.
NOTE: this was funnier in black & white

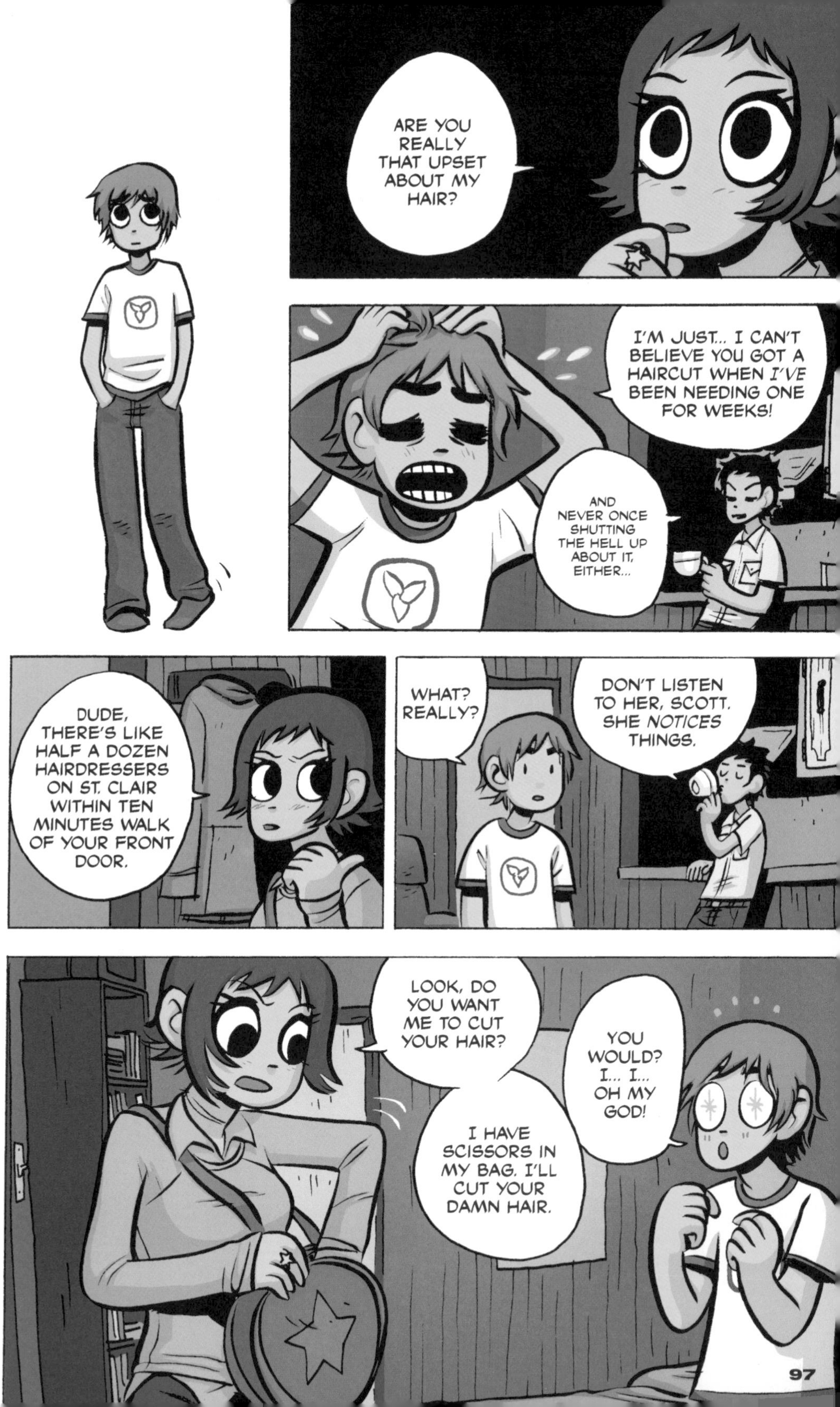
ARE YOU REALLY THAT UPSET ABOUT MY HAIR?
I'M JUST... I CAN'T BELIEVE YOU GOT A HAIRCUT WHEN *I'VE* BEEN NEEDING ONE FOR WEEKS!
AND NEVER ONCE SHUTTING THE HELL UP ABOUT IT, EITHER...
DUDE, THERE'S LIKE HALF A DOZEN HAIRDRESSERS ON ST. CLAIR WITHIN TEN MINUTES WALK OF YOUR FRONT DOOR.
WHAT? REALLY?
DON'T LISTEN TO HER, SCOTT. SHE *NOTICES* THINGS.
LOOK, DO YOU WANT ME TO CUT YOUR HAIR?
I HAVE SCISSORS IN MY BAG. I'LL CUT YOUR DAMN HAIR.
YOU WOULD? I... I... OH MY GOD!

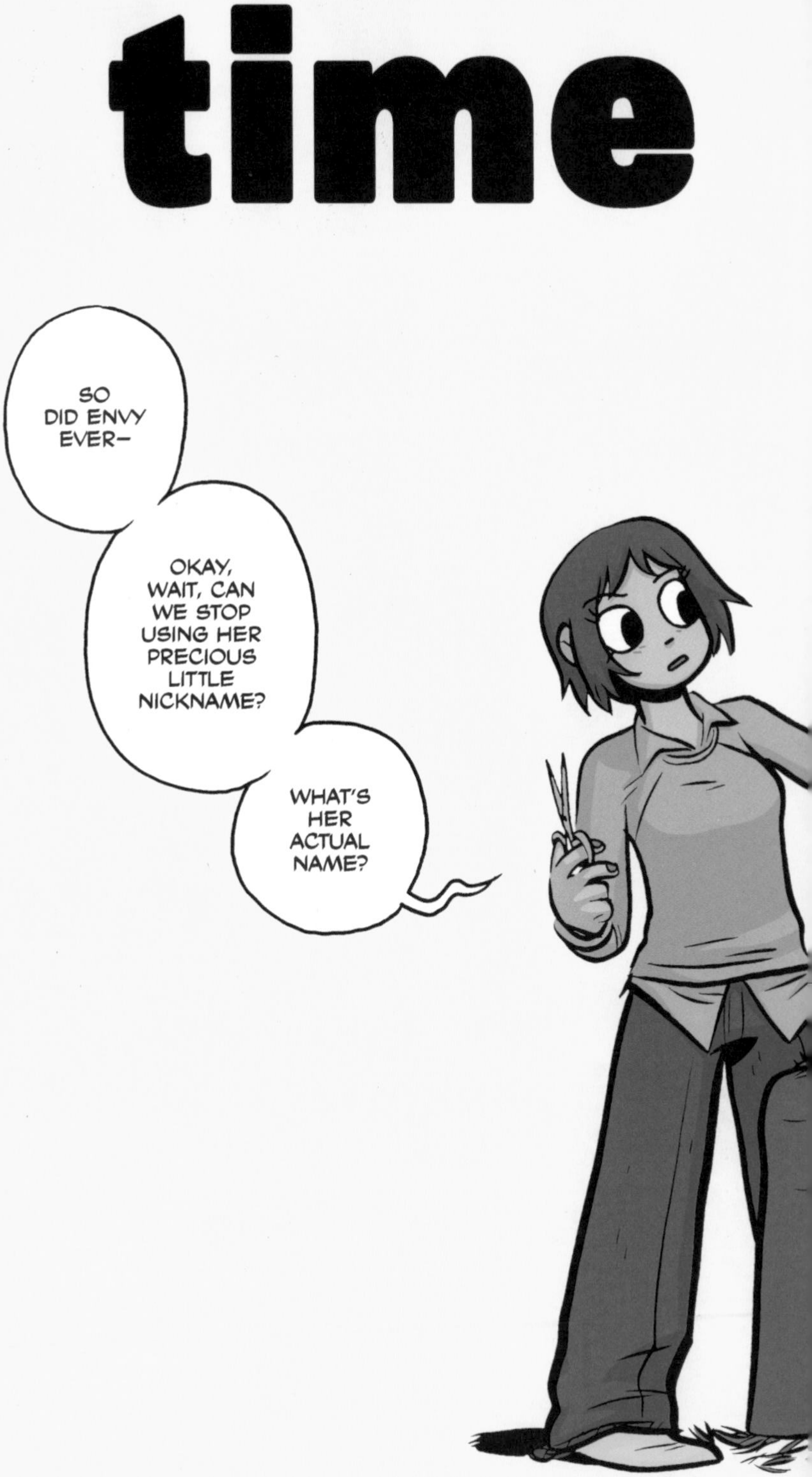
time
SO DID ENVY EVER–
OKAY, WAIT, CAN WE STOP USING HER PRECIOUS LITTLE NICKNAME?
WHAT'S HER ACTUAL NAME?

passed

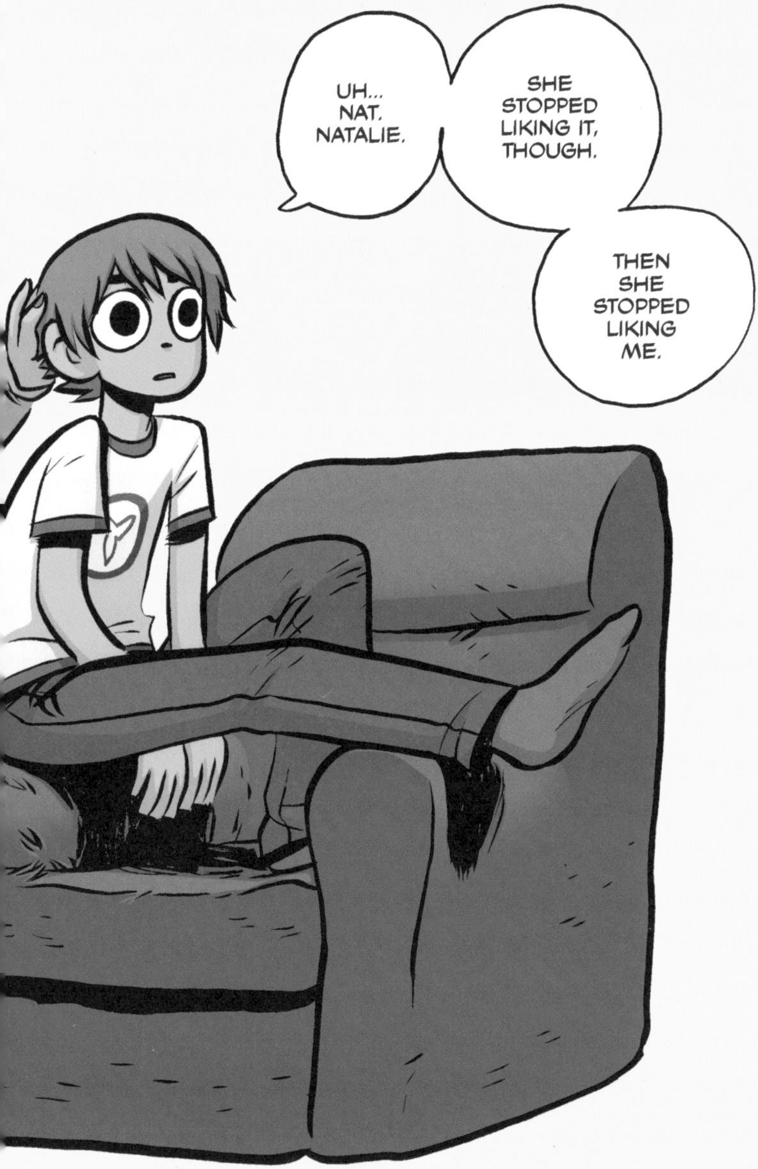
UH... NAT. NATALIE.
SHE STOPPED LIKING IT, THOUGH.
THEN SHE STOPPED LIKING ME.

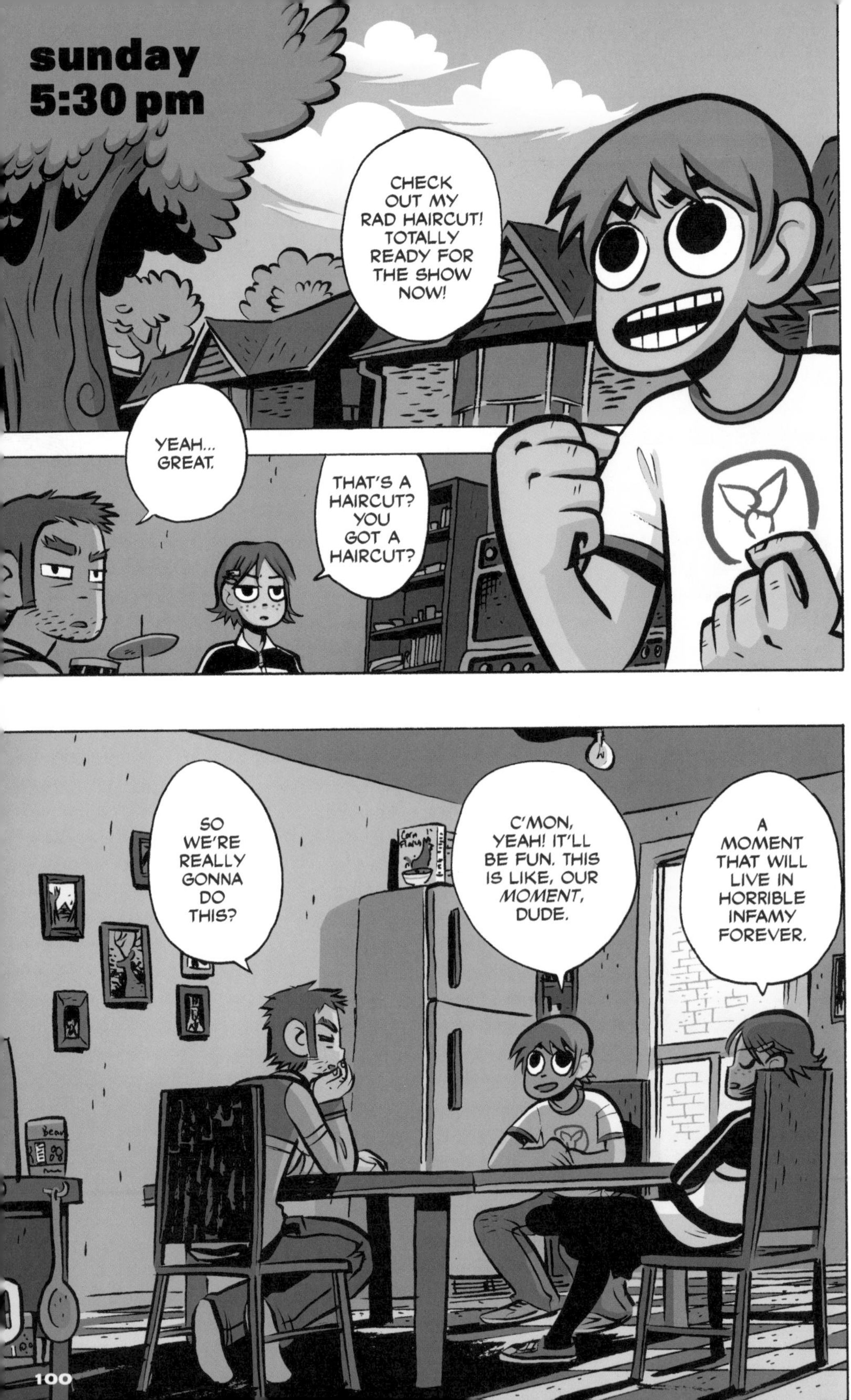
sunday 5:30 pm
CHECK OUT MY RAD HAIRCUT! TOTALLY READY FOR THE SHOW NOW!
YEAH... GREAT.
THAT'S A HAIRCUT? YOU GOT A HAIRCUT?
SO WE'RE REALLY GONNA DO THIS?
C'MON, YEAH! IT'LL BE FUN. THIS IS LIKE, OUR *MOMENT*, DUDE.
A MOMENT THAT WILL LIVE IN HORRIBLE INFAMY FOREVER.

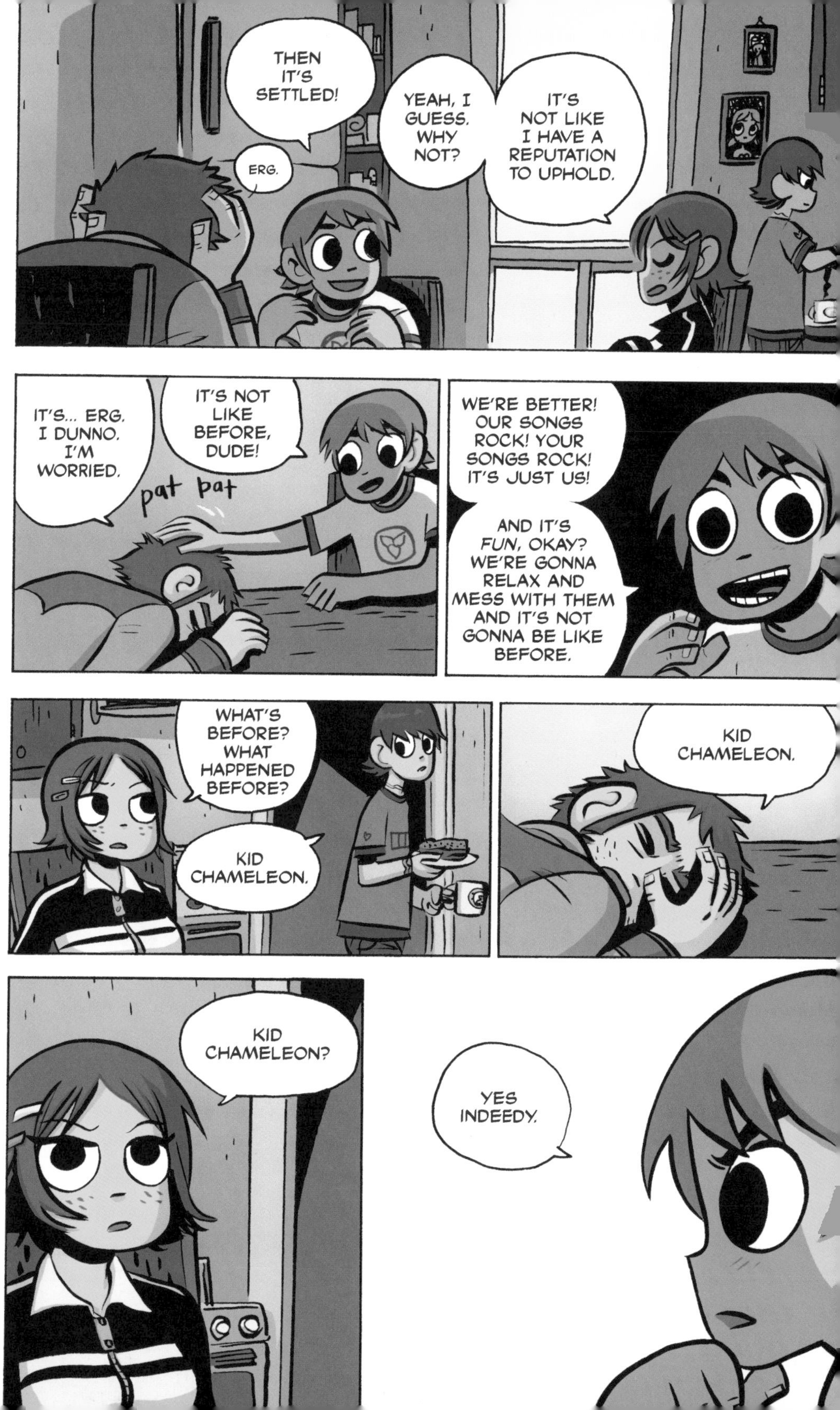

THEN IT'S SETTLED!
ERG.
YEAH, I GUESS. WHY NOT?
IT'S NOT LIKE I HAVE A REPUTATION TO UPHOLD.
IT'S... ERG. I DUNNO. I'M WORRIED.
IT'S NOT LIKE BEFORE, DUDE!
pat pat
WE'RE BETTER! OUR SONGS ROCK! YOUR SONGS ROCK! IT'S JUST US!
AND IT'S *FUN*, OKAY? WE'RE GONNA RELAX AND MESS WITH THEM AND IT'S NOT GONNA BE LIKE BEFORE.
WHAT'S BEFORE? WHAT HAPPENED BEFORE?
KID CHAMELEON.
KID CHAMELEON.
KID CHAMELEON?
YES INDEEDY.

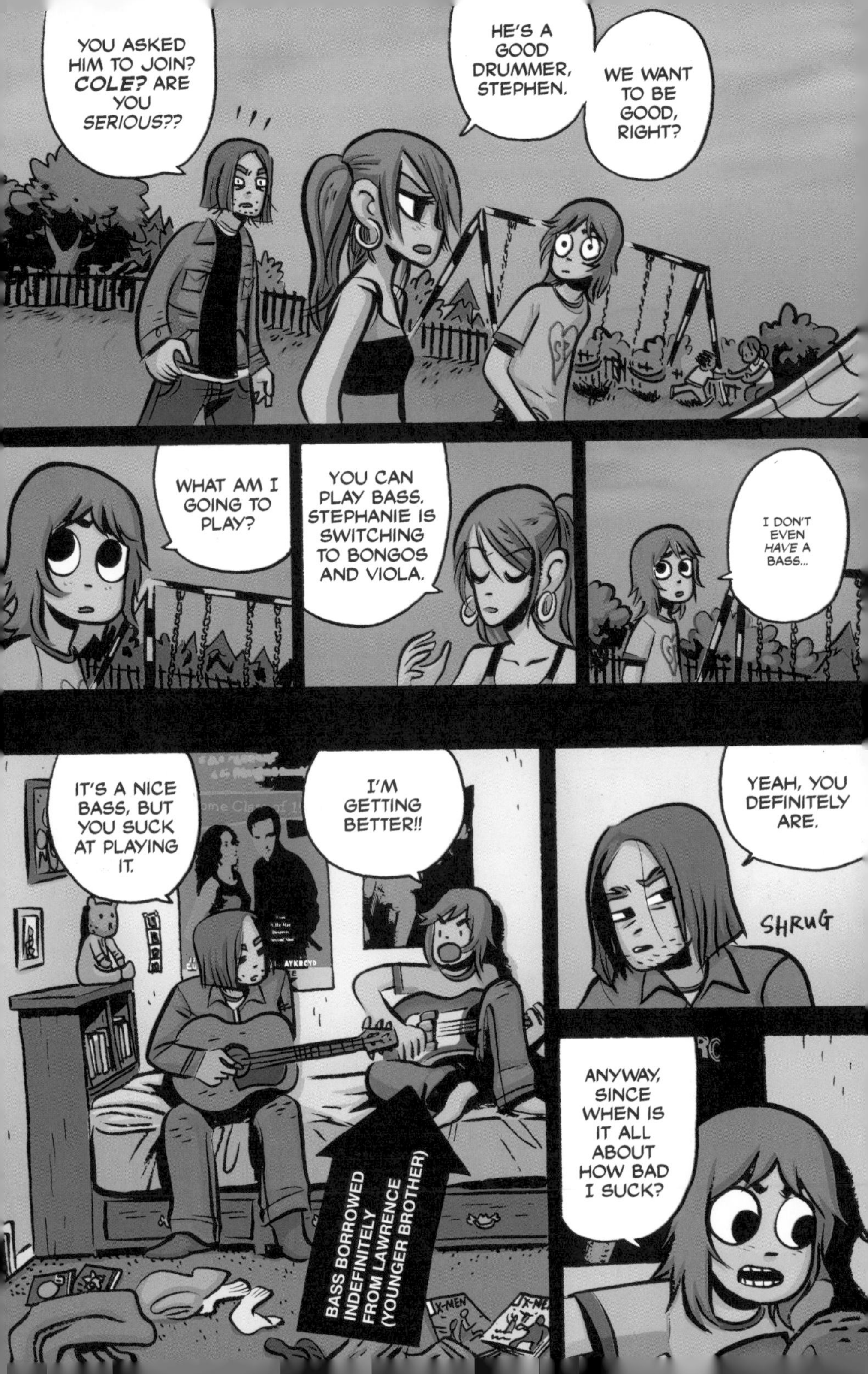
YOU ASKED HIM TO JOIN? COLE? ARE YOU SERIOUS??
HE'S A GOOD DRUMMER, STEPHEN.
WE WANT TO BE GOOD, RIGHT?
WHAT AM I GOING TO PLAY?
YOU CAN PLAY BASS. STEPHANIE IS SWITCHING TO BONGOS AND VIOLA.
I DON'T EVEN HAVE A BASS...
IT'S A NICE BASS, BUT YOU SUCK AT PLAYING IT.
I'M GETTING BETTER!!
BASS BORROWED INDEFINITELY FROM LAWRENCE (YOUNGER BROTHER)
YEAH, YOU DEFINITELY ARE.
SHRUG
ANYWAY, SINCE WHEN IS IT ALL ABOUT HOW BAD I SUCK?

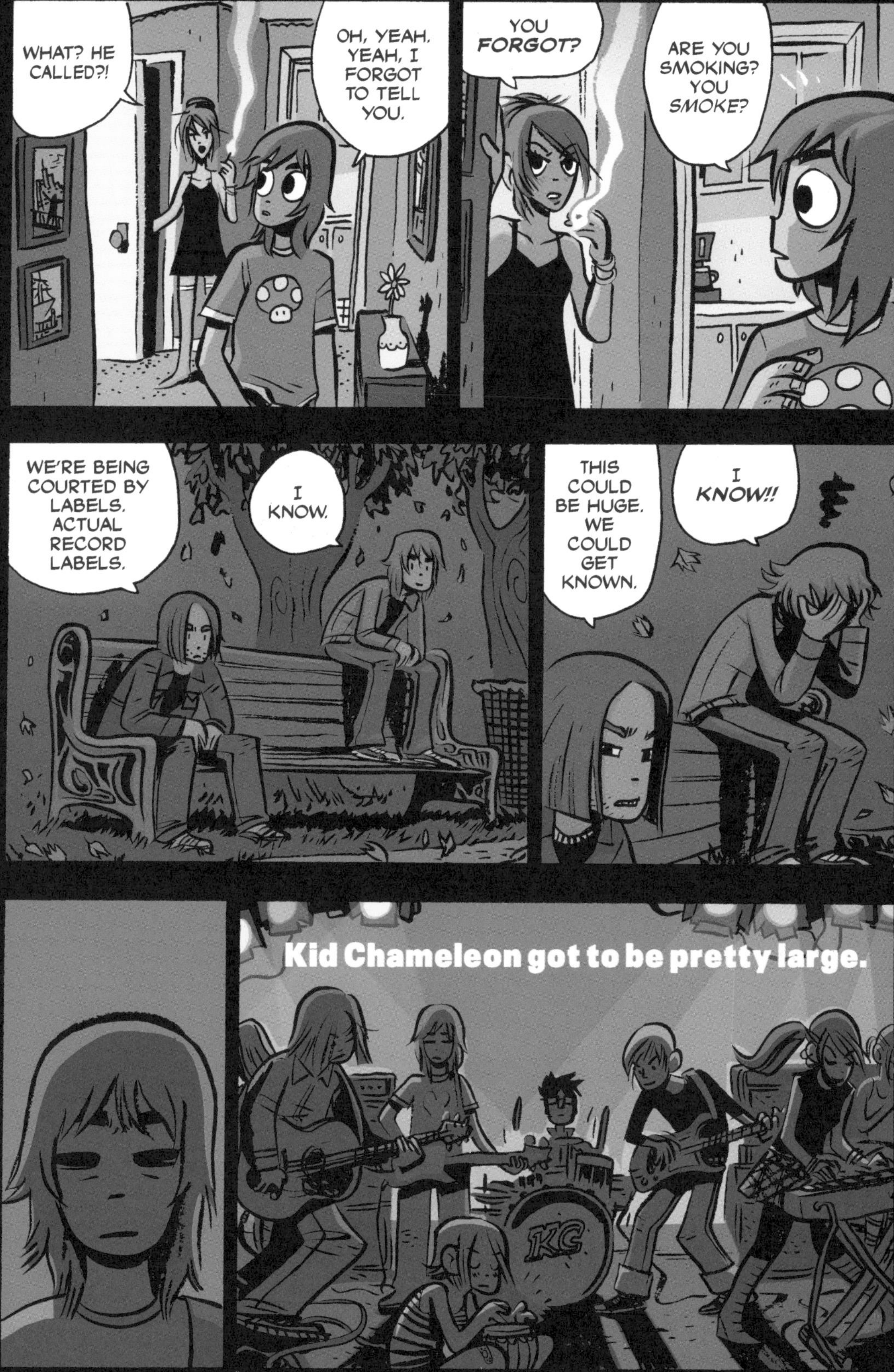
WHAT? HE CALLED?!
OH, YEAH. YEAH, I FORGOT TO TELL YOU.
YOU FORGOT?
ARE YOU SMOKING? YOU SMOKE?
WE'RE BEING COURTED BY LABELS. ACTUAL RECORD LABELS.
I KNOW.
THIS COULD BE HUGE. WE COULD GET KNOWN.
I KNOW!!
Kid Chameleon got to be pretty large.
KC

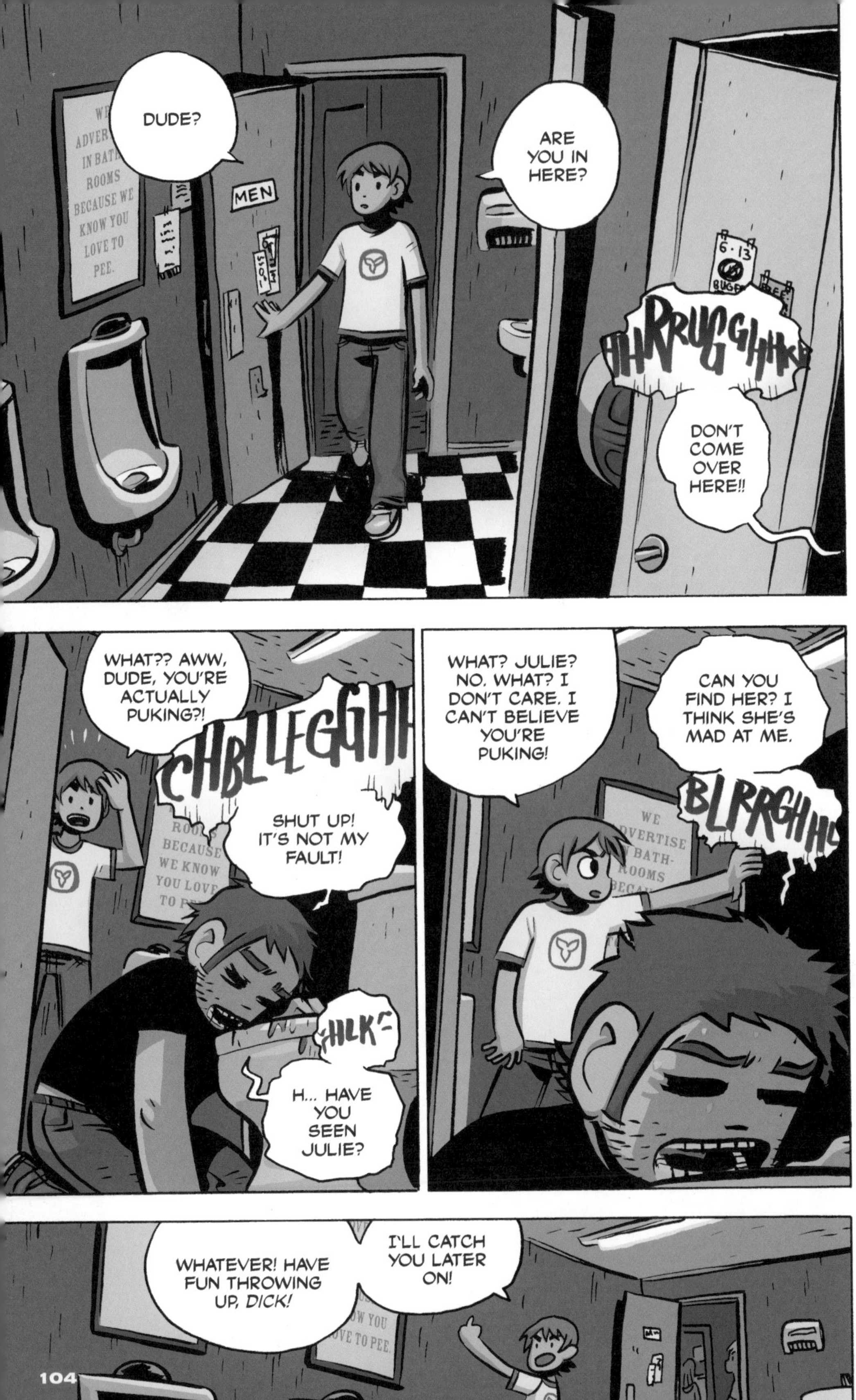
DUDE?
ARE YOU IN HERE?
MEN
HHRRUGGHHK
DON'T COME OVER HERE!!
WHAT?? AWW, DUDE, YOU'RE ACTUALLY PUKING?!
CHBLLEGGHH
SHUT UP! IT'S NOT MY FAULT!
HLK
H... HAVE YOU SEEN JULIE?
WHAT? JULIE? NO. WHAT? I DON'T CARE. I CAN'T BELIEVE YOU'RE PUKING!
CAN YOU FIND HER? I THINK SHE'S MAD AT ME.
BLRRGHHL
WE ADVERTISE IN BATH-ROOMS BECAUSE WE KNOW YOU LOVE TO PEE.
WHATEVER! HAVE FUN THROWING UP, *DICK!*
I'LL CATCH YOU LATER ON!

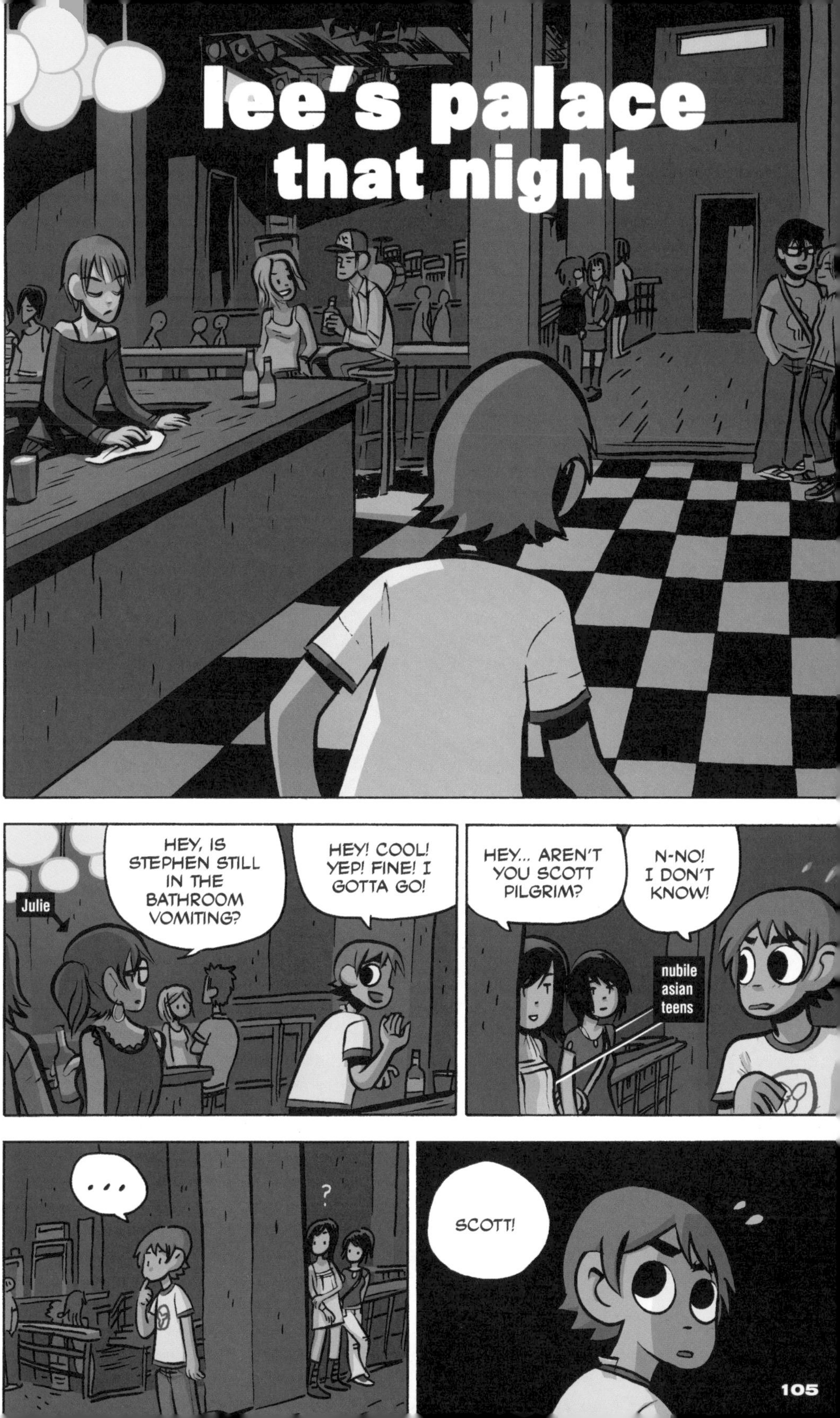

lee's palace that night
HEY, IS STEPHEN STILL IN THE BATHROOM VOMITING?
Julie
HEY! COOL! YEP! FINE! I GOTTA GO!
HEY... AREN'T YOU SCOTT PILGRIM?
N-NO! I DON'T KNOW!
nubile asian teens
...
?
SCOTT!

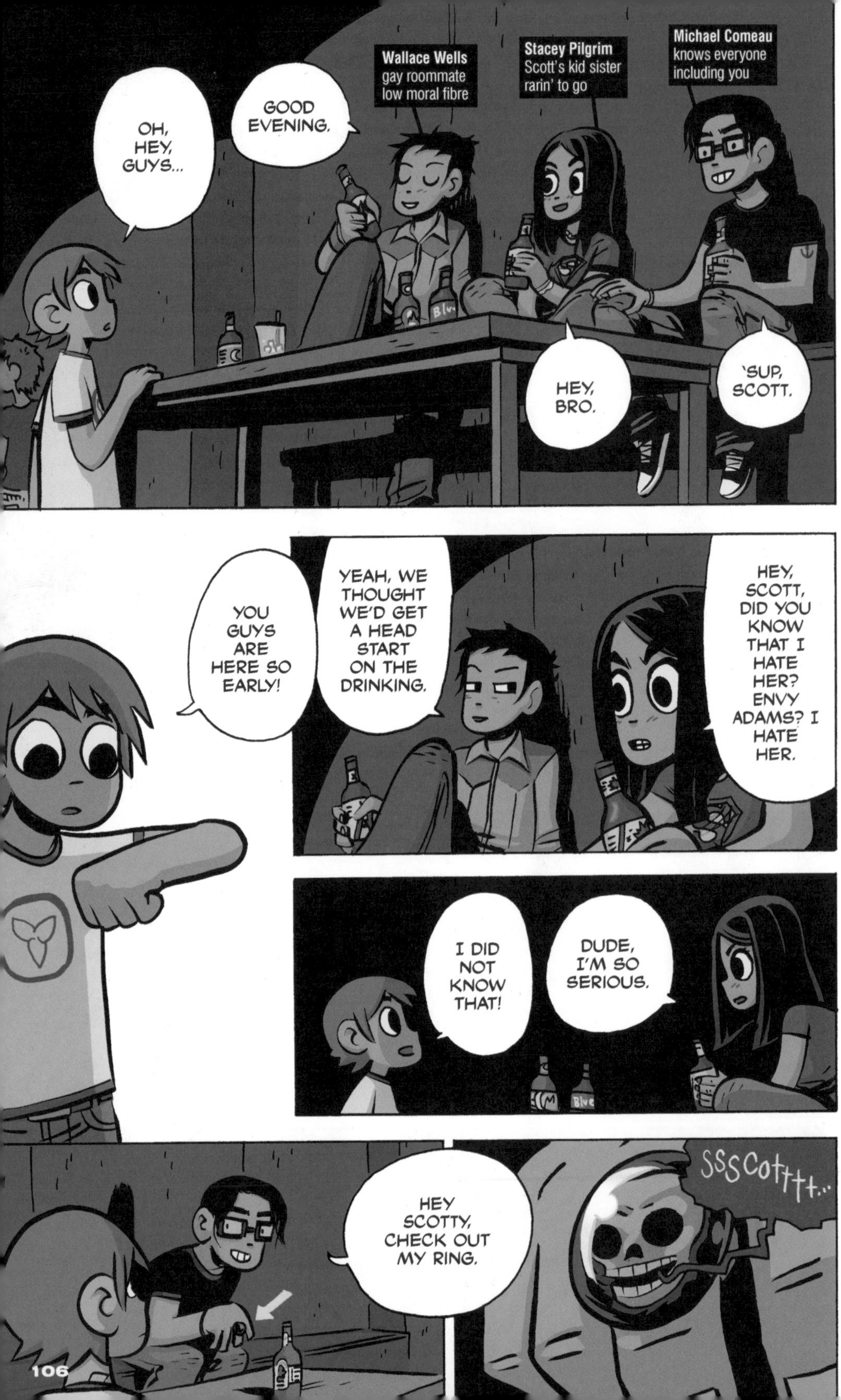
OH, HEY, GUYS...
GOOD EVENING.
Wallace Wells gay roommate low moral fibre
Stacey Pilgrim Scott's kid sister rarin' to go
Michael Comeau knows everyone including you
HEY, BRO.
'SUP, SCOTT.
YOU GUYS ARE HERE SO EARLY!
YEAH, WE THOUGHT WE'D GET A HEAD START ON THE DRINKING.
HEY, SCOTT, DID YOU KNOW THAT I HATE HER? ENVY ADAMS? I HATE HER.
I DID NOT KNOW THAT!
DUDE, I'M SO SERIOUS.
HEY SCOTTY, CHECK OUT MY RING.
SSSCotttt..

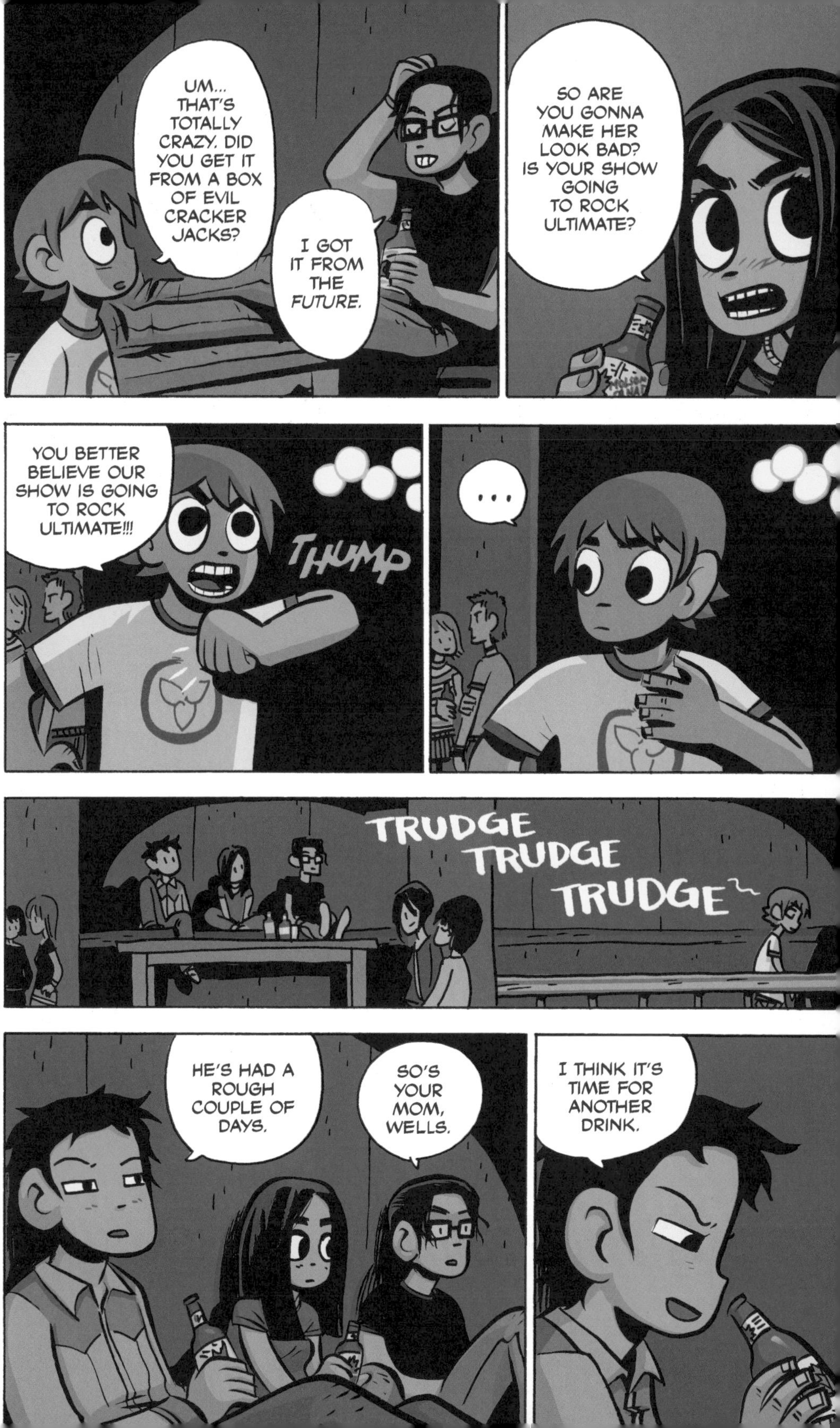
UM... THAT'S TOTALLY CRAZY. DID YOU GET IT FROM A BOX OF EVIL CRACKER JACKS?
I GOT IT FROM THE FUTURE.
SO ARE YOU GONNA MAKE HER LOOK BAD? IS YOUR SHOW GOING TO ROCK ULTIMATE?
YOU BETTER BELIEVE OUR SHOW IS GOING TO ROCK ULTIMATE!!!
THUMP
...
TRUDGE
TRUDGE
TRUDGE
HE'S HAD A ROUGH COUPLE OF DAYS.
SO'S YOUR MOM, WELLS.
I THINK IT'S TIME FOR ANOTHER DRINK.

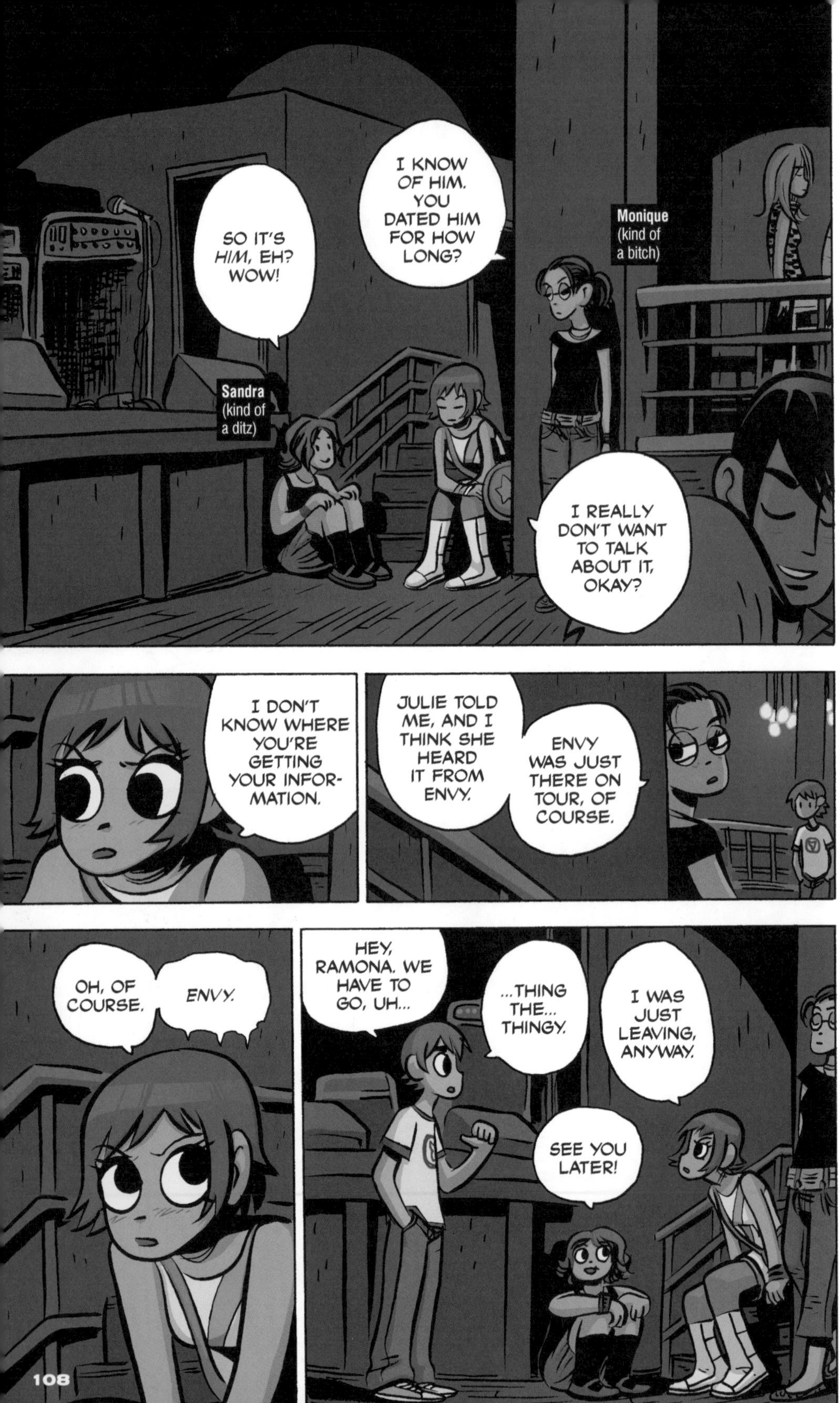
SO IT'S HIM, EH? WOW!
I KNOW OF HIM. YOU DATED HIM FOR HOW LONG?
Monique (kind of a bitch)
Sandra (kind of a ditz)
I REALLY DON'T WANT TO TALK ABOUT IT, OKAY?
I DON'T KNOW WHERE YOU'RE GETTING YOUR INFOR-MATION.
JULIE TOLD ME, AND I THINK SHE HEARD IT FROM ENVY.
ENVY WAS JUST THERE ON TOUR, OF COURSE.
OH, OF COURSE.
ENVY.
HEY, RAMONA, WE HAVE TO GO, UH...
...THING THE... THINGY.
I WAS JUST LEAVING, ANYWAY.
SEE YOU LATER!

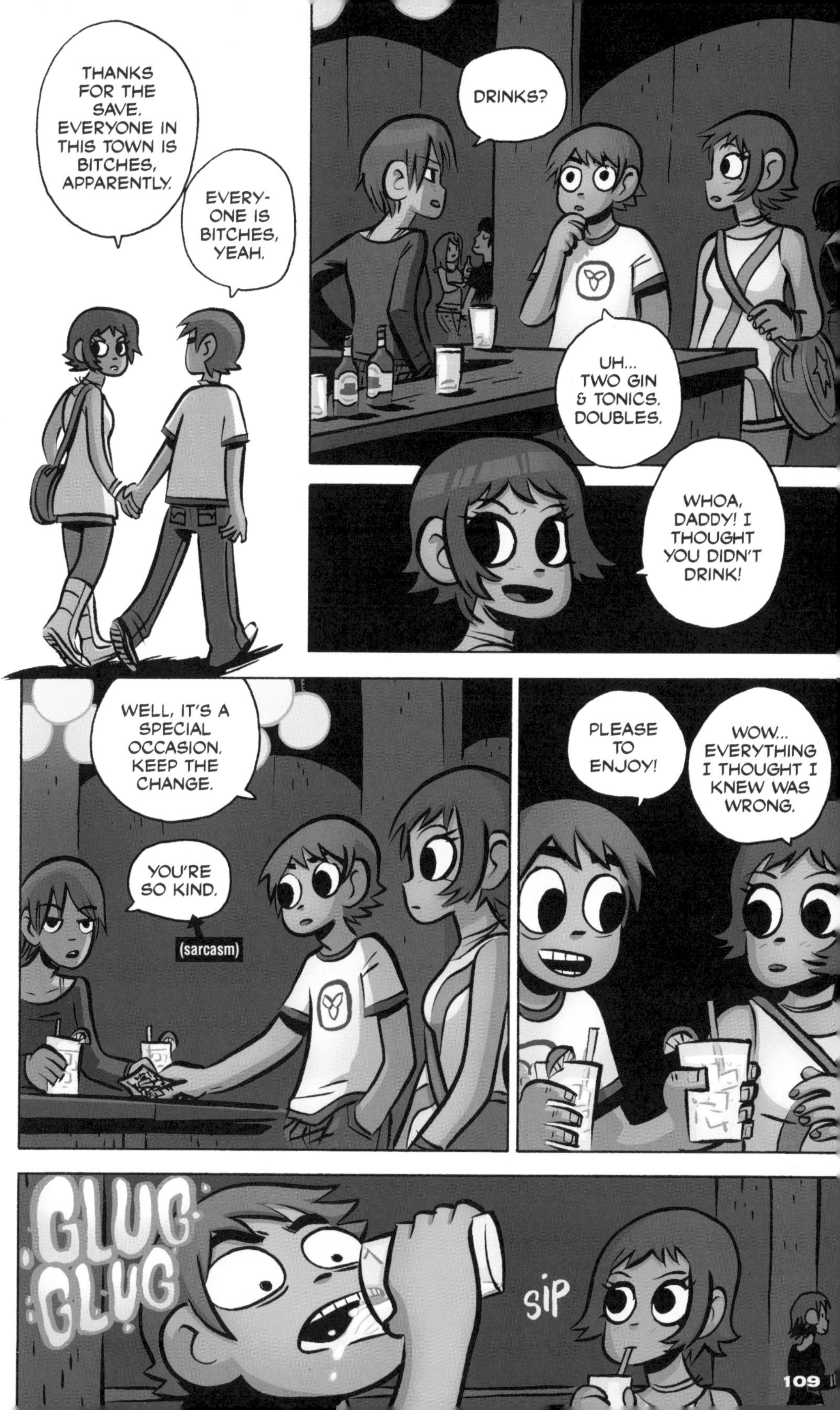
THANKS FOR THE SAVE. EVERYONE IN THIS TOWN IS BITCHES, APPARENTLY.
EVERY-ONE IS BITCHES, YEAH.
DRINKS?
UH... TWO GIN & TONICS. DOUBLES.
WHOA, DADDY! I THOUGHT YOU DIDN'T DRINK!
WELL, IT'S A SPECIAL OCCASION. KEEP THE CHANGE.
YOU'RE SO KIND.
(sarcasm)
PLEASE TO ENJOY!
WOW... EVERYTHING I THOUGHT I KNEW WAS WRONG.
GLUG GLUG
SIP

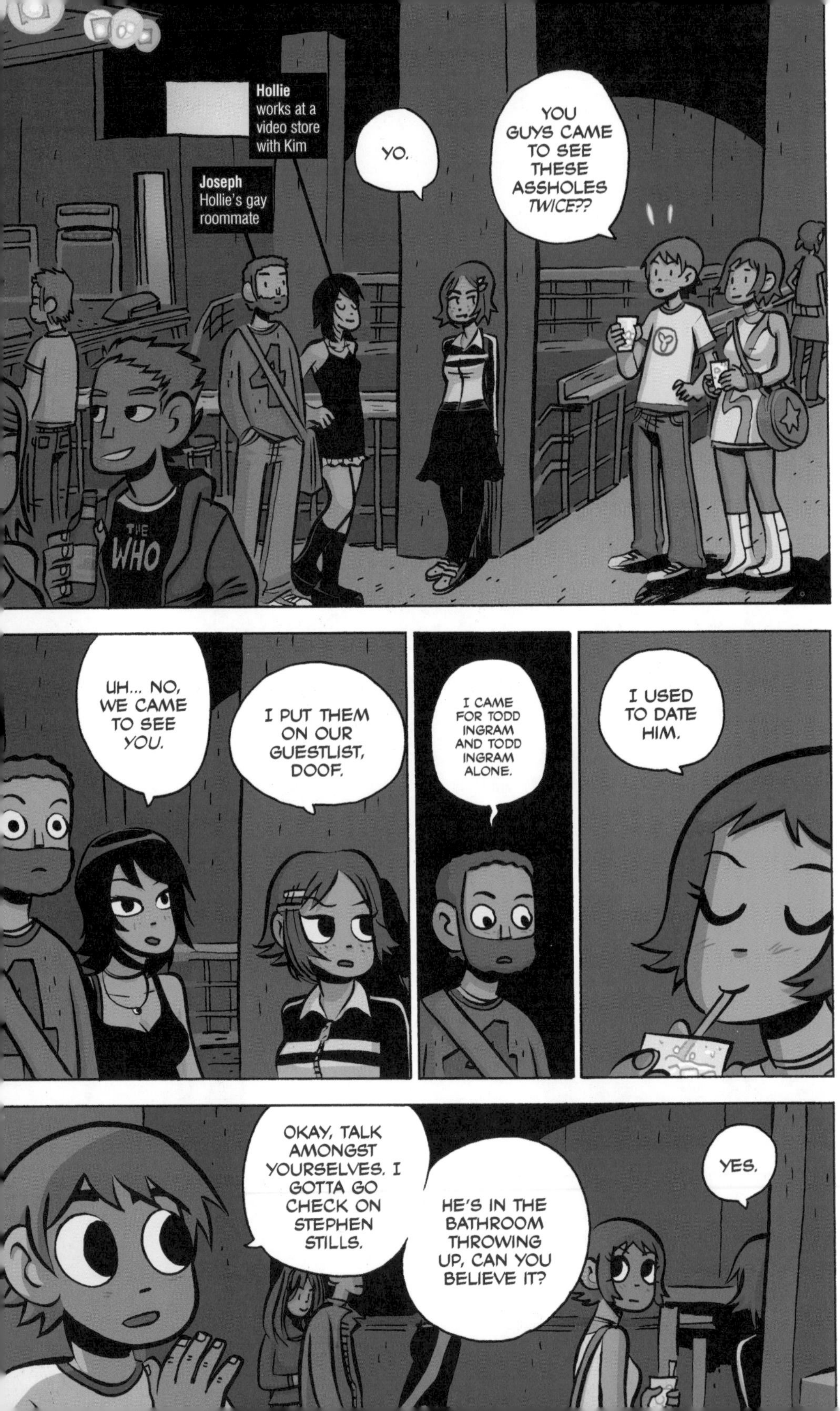
Hollie
works at a video store with Kim
Joseph
Hollie's gay roommate
YO.
YOU GUYS CAME TO SEE THESE ASSHOLES TWICE??
THE WHO
UH... NO, WE CAME TO SEE YOU.
I PUT THEM ON OUR GUESTLIST, DOOF.
I CAME FOR TODD INGRAM AND TODD INGRAM ALONE.
I USED TO DATE HIM.
OKAY, TALK AMONGST YOURSELVES. I GOTTA GO CHECK ON STEPHEN STILLS.
HE'S IN THE BATHROOM THROWING UP, CAN YOU BELIEVE IT?
YES.

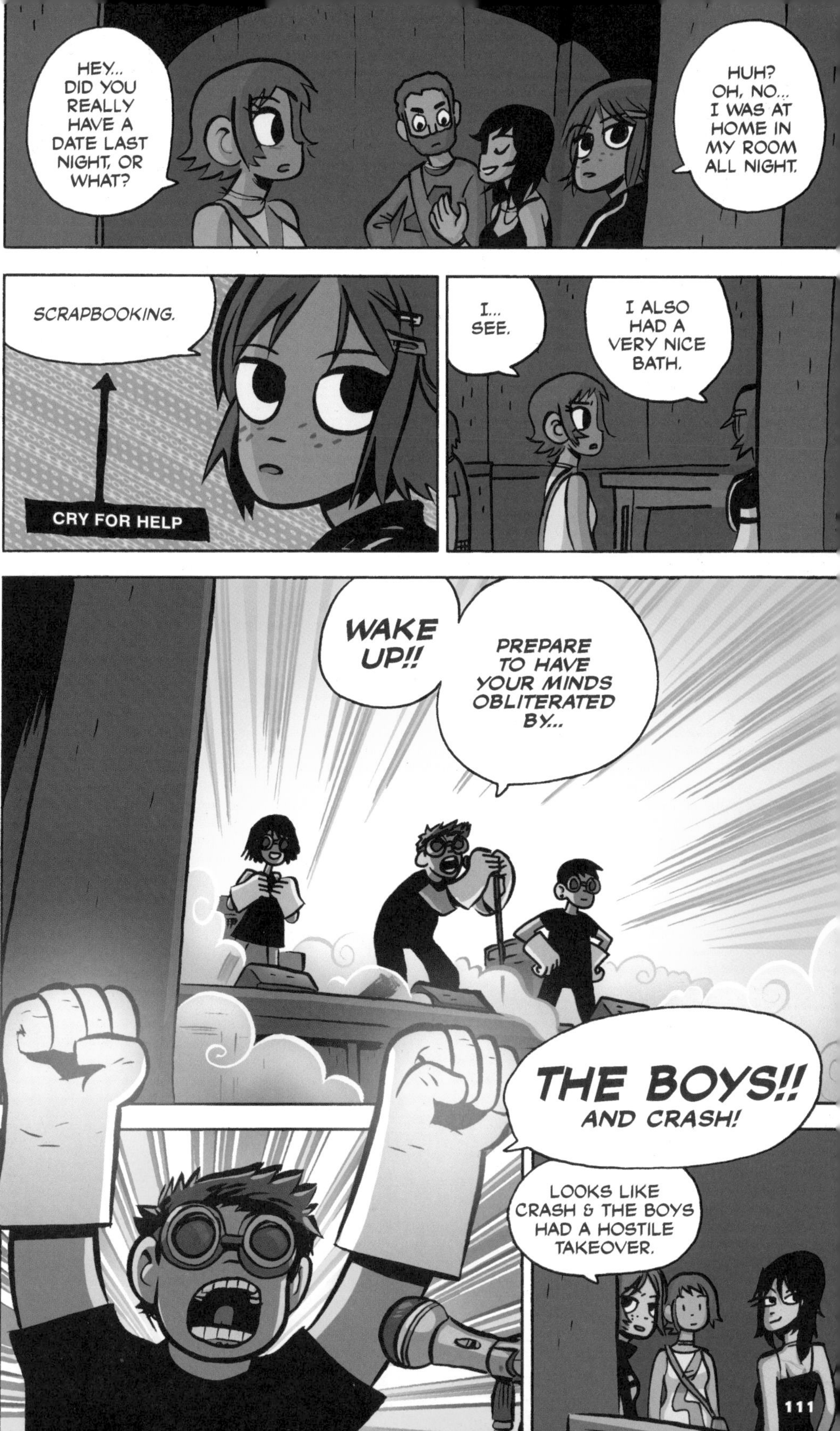
HEY... DID YOU REALLY HAVE A DATE LAST NIGHT, OR WHAT?
HUH? OH, NO... I WAS AT HOME IN MY ROOM ALL NIGHT.
SCRAPBOOKING.
CRY FOR HELP
I... SEE.
I ALSO HAD A VERY NICE BATH.
WAKE UP!!
PREPARE TO HAVE YOUR MINDS OBLITERATED BY...
THE BOYS!! AND CRASH!
LOOKS LIKE CRASH & THE BOYS HAD A HOSTILE TAKEOVER.

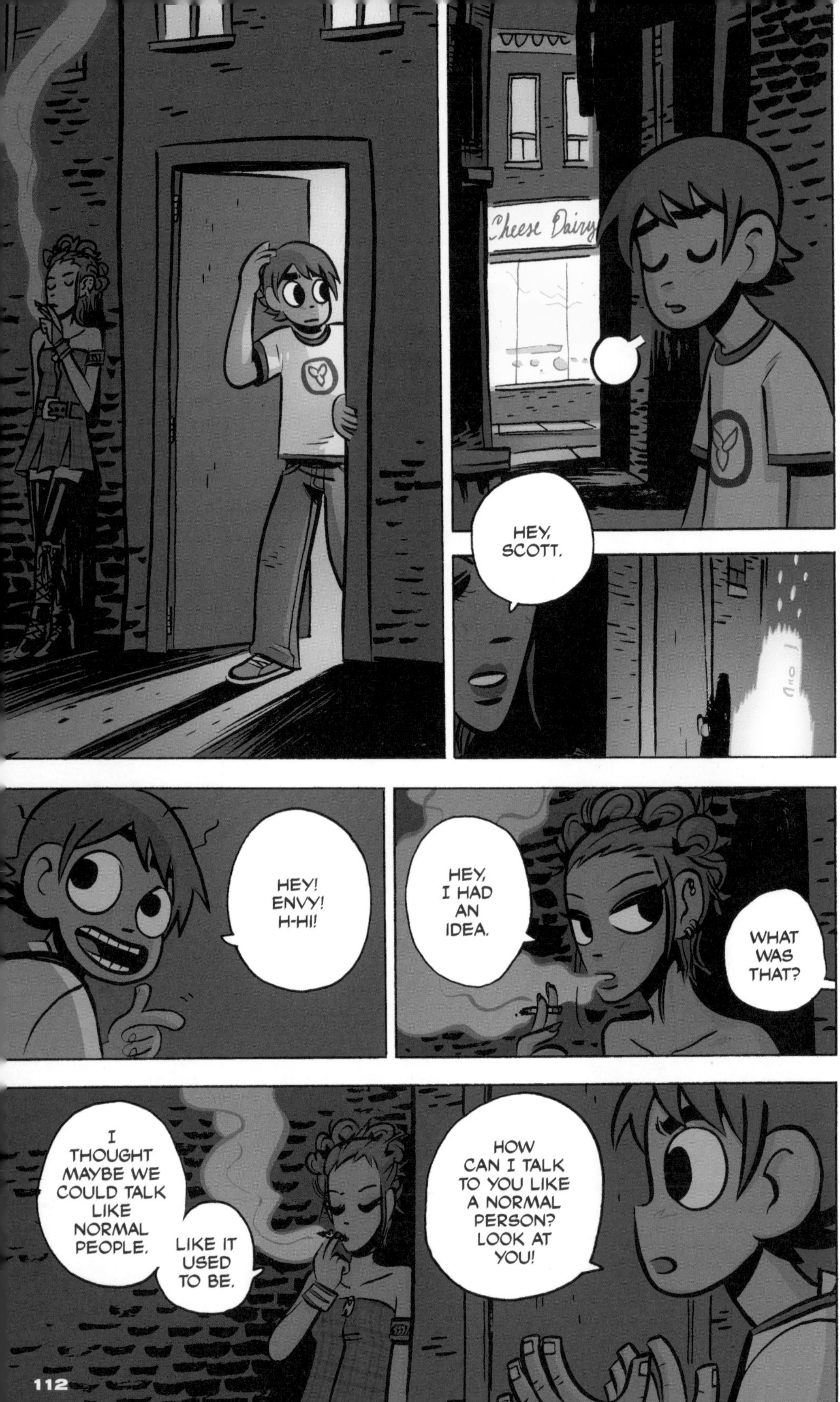
Cheese Dairy
HEY, SCOTT.
HEY! ENVY! H-HI!
HEY, I HAD AN IDEA.
WHAT WAS THAT?
I THOUGHT MAYBE WE COULD TALK LIKE NORMAL PEOPLE.
LIKE IT USED TO BE.
HOW CAN I TALK TO YOU LIKE A NORMAL PERSON? LOOK AT YOU!

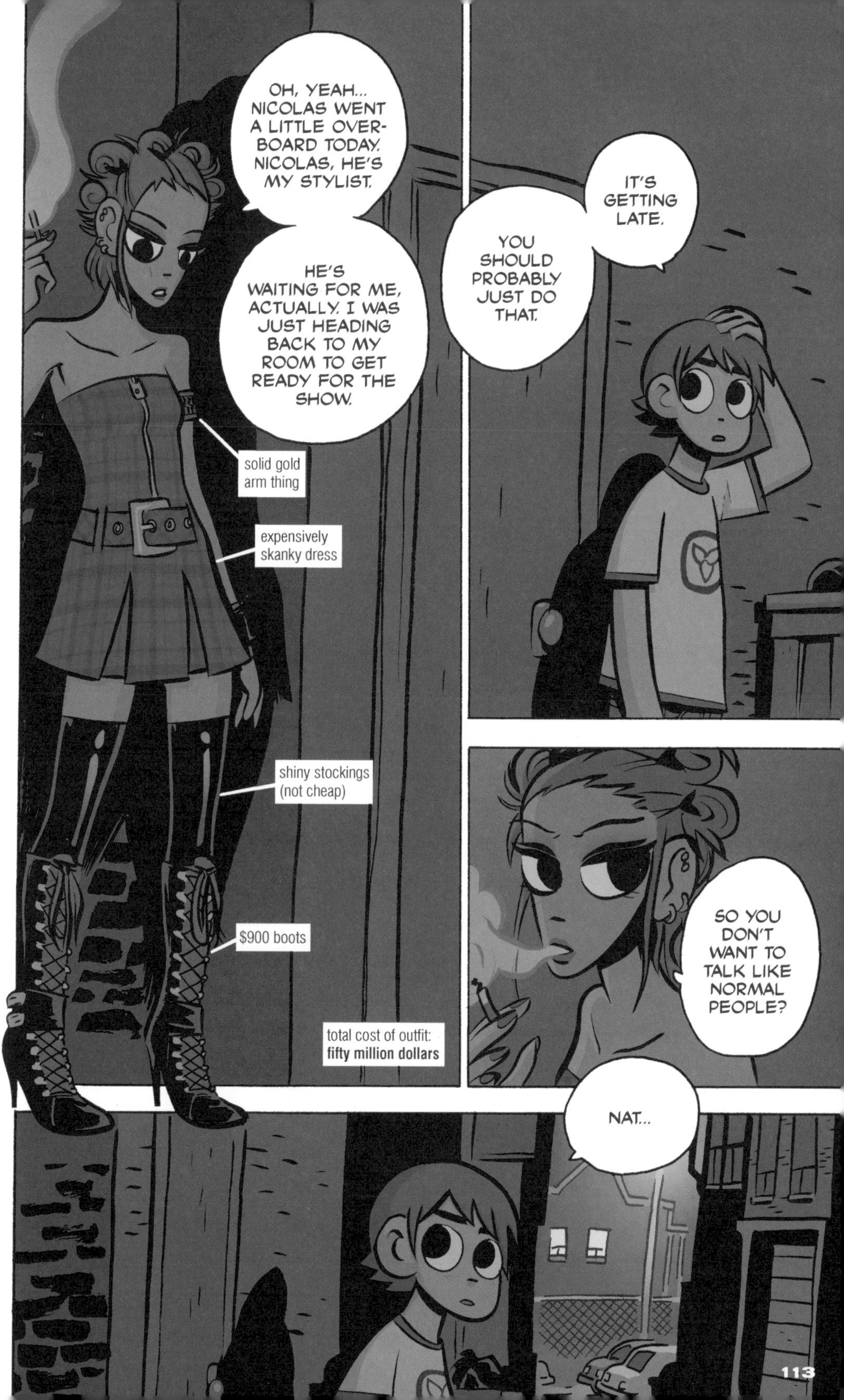
OH, YEAH... NICOLAS WENT A LITTLE OVER-BOARD TODAY. NICOLAS, HE'S MY STYLIST.
HE'S WAITING FOR ME, ACTUALLY. I WAS JUST HEADING BACK TO MY ROOM TO GET READY FOR THE SHOW.
solid gold arm thing
expensively skanky dress
shiny stockings (not cheap)
$900 boots
total cost of outfit: **fifty million dollars**
IT'S GETTING LATE.
YOU SHOULD PROBABLY JUST DO THAT.
SO YOU DON'T WANT TO TALK LIKE NORMAL PEOPLE?
NAT...

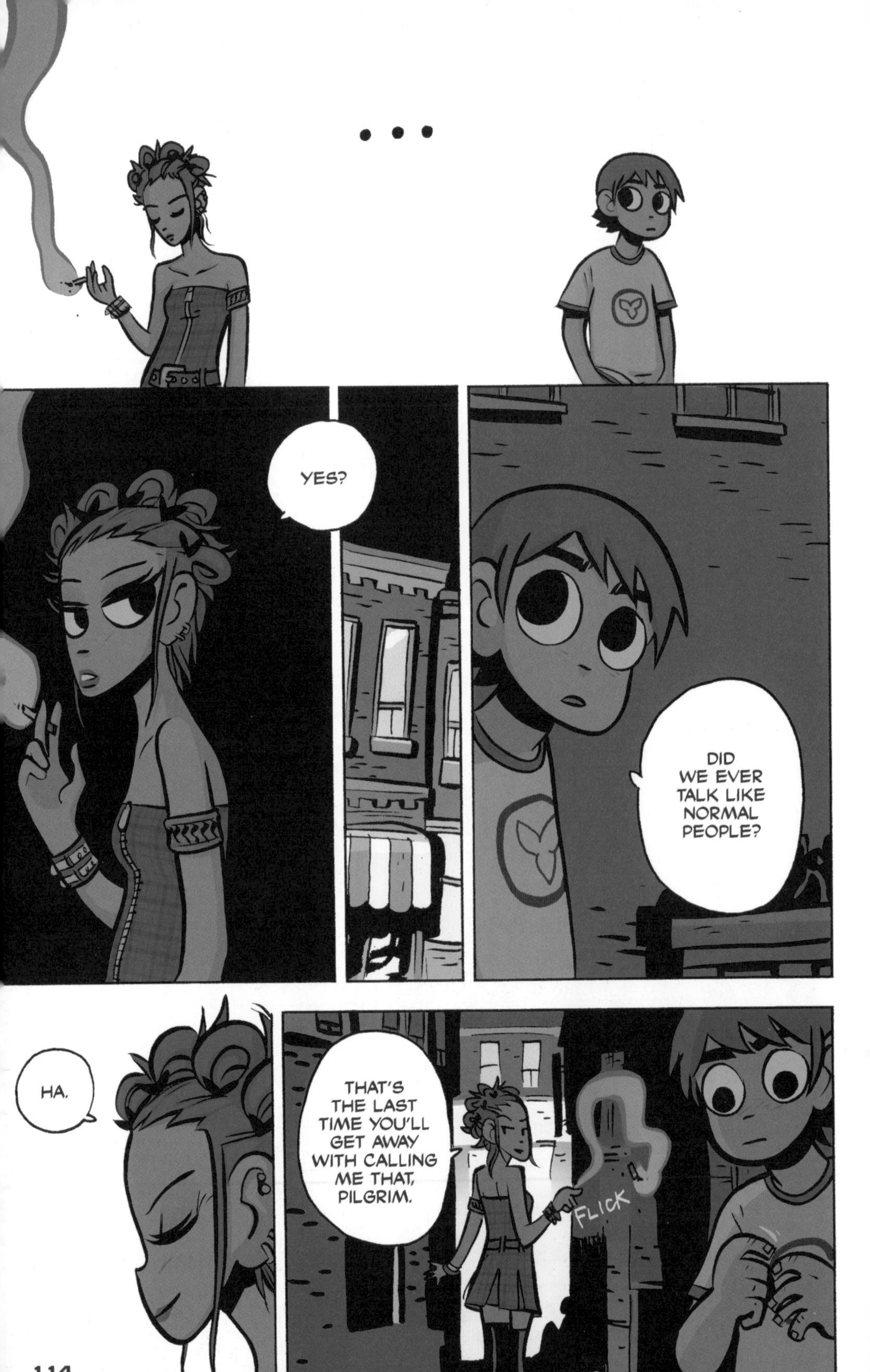
. . .
YES?
DID WE EVER TALK LIKE NORMAL PEOPLE?
HA.
THAT'S THE LAST TIME YOU'LL GET AWAY WITH CALLING ME THAT, PILGRIM.
FLICK

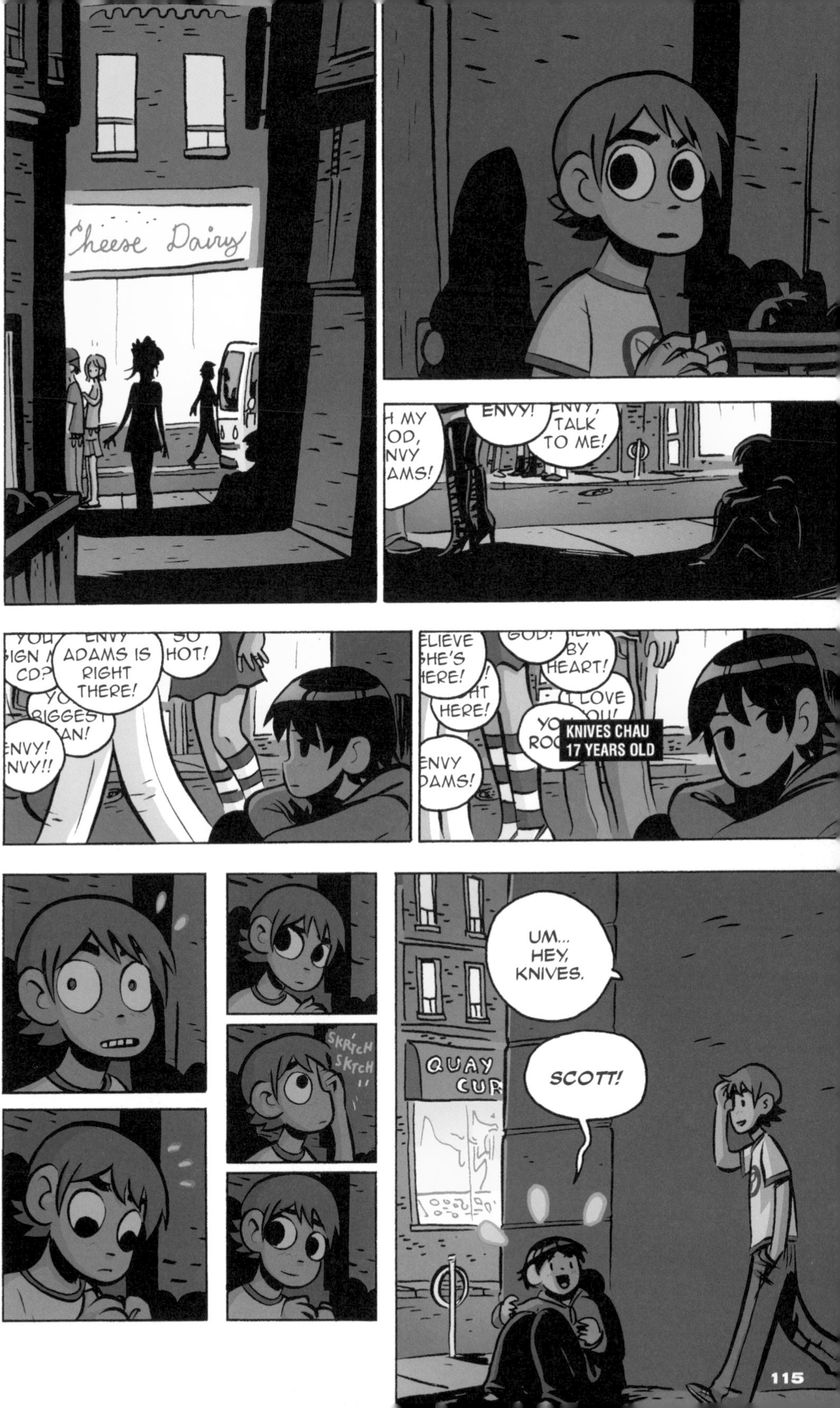
Cheese Dairy
ENVY!
TALK TO ME!
ADAMS IS RIGHT THERE!
HOT!
BY HEART!
HERE!
KNIVES CHAU
17 YEARS OLD
SKRTCH SKRTCH
UM... HEY, KNIVES.
SCOTT!

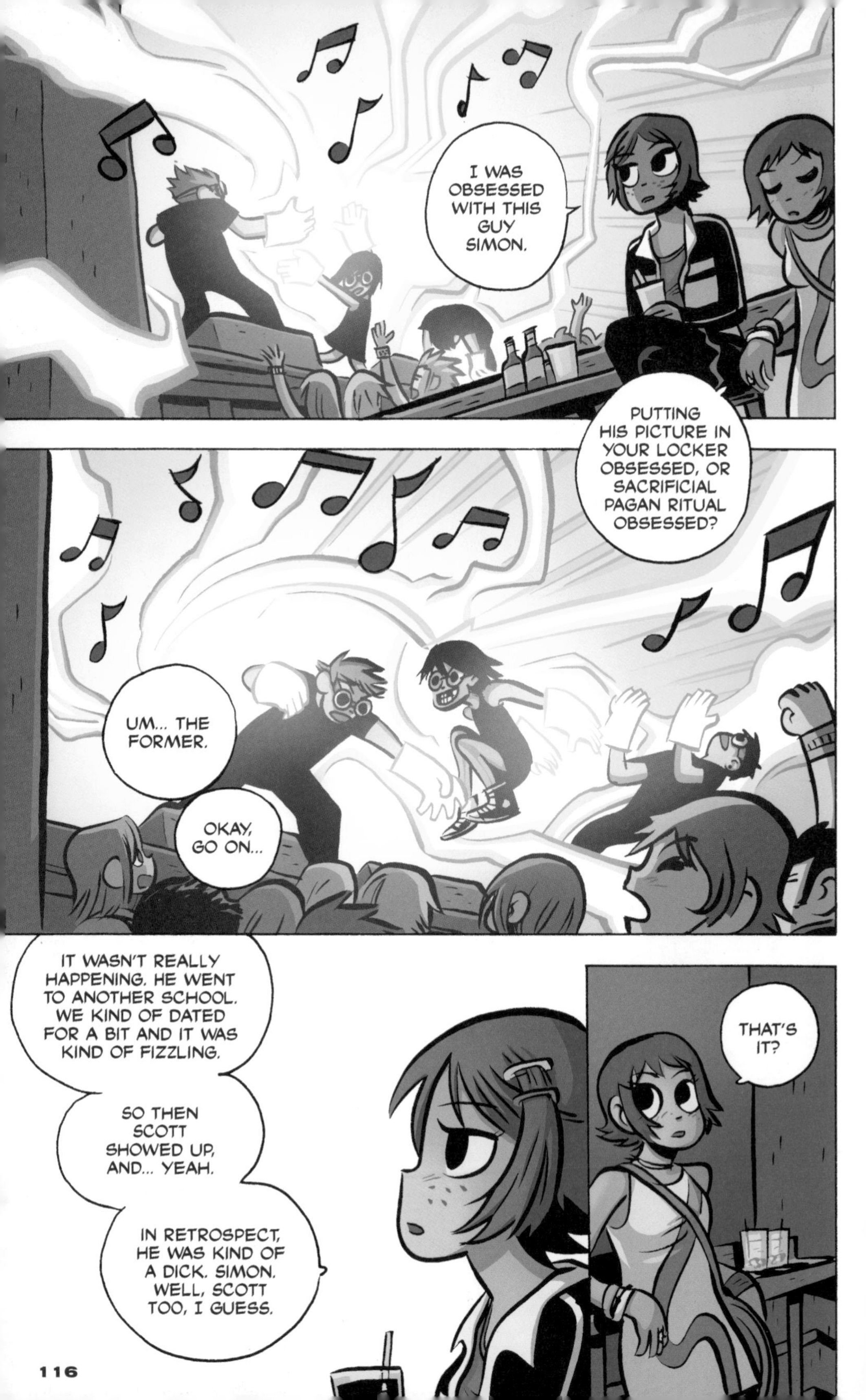
I WAS OBSESSED WITH THIS GUY SIMON.
PUTTING HIS PICTURE IN YOUR LOCKER OBSESSED, OR SACRIFICIAL PAGAN RITUAL OBSESSED?
UM... THE FORMER.
OKAY, GO ON...
IT WASN'T REALLY HAPPENING. HE WENT TO ANOTHER SCHOOL. WE KIND OF DATED FOR A BIT AND IT WAS KIND OF FIZZLING.
SO THEN SCOTT SHOWED UP, AND... YEAH.
IN RETROSPECT, HE WAS KIND OF A DICK. SIMON. WELL, SCOTT TOO, I GUESS.
THAT'S IT?

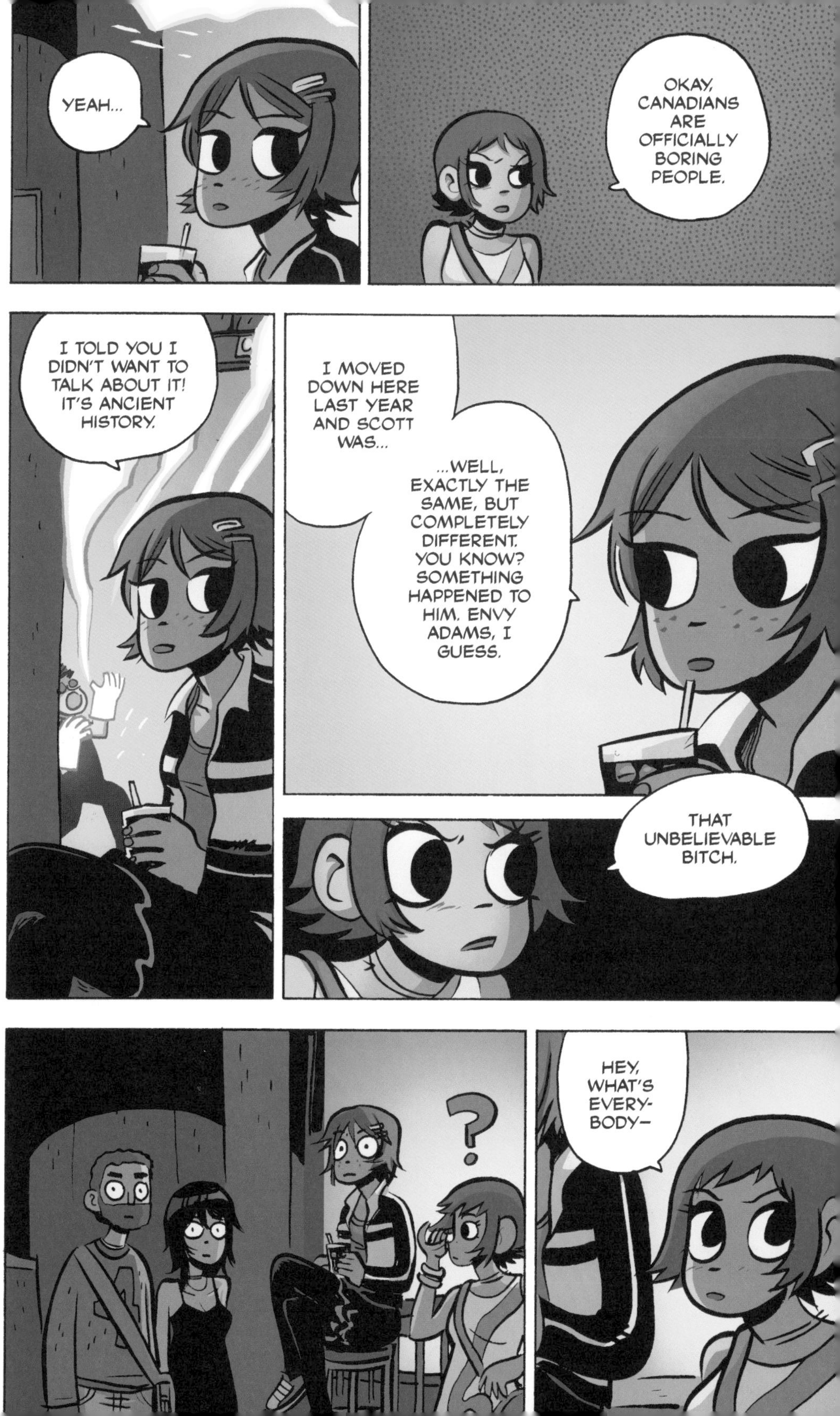
YEAH...
OKAY, CANADIANS ARE OFFICIALLY BORING PEOPLE.
I TOLD YOU I DIDN'T WANT TO TALK ABOUT IT! IT'S ANCIENT HISTORY.
I MOVED DOWN HERE LAST YEAR AND SCOTT WAS...
...WELL, EXACTLY THE SAME, BUT COMPLETELY DIFFERENT. YOU KNOW? SOMETHING HAPPENED TO HIM. ENVY ADAMS, I GUESS.
THAT UNBELIEVABLE BITCH.
?
HEY, WHAT'S EVERY-BODY—

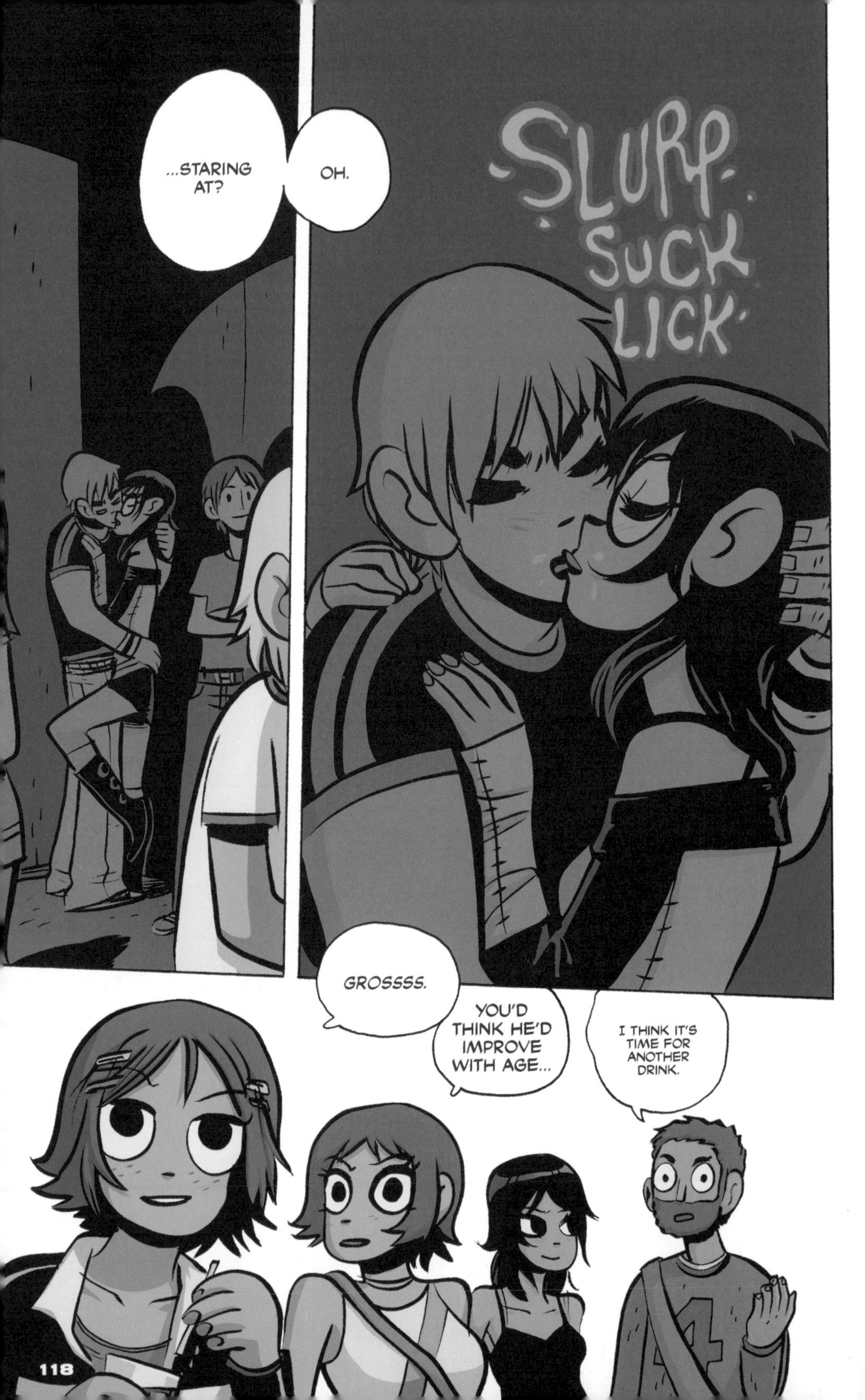

...STARING AT?
OH.
SLURP SUCK LICK
GROSSSS.
YOU'D THINK HE'D IMPROVE WITH AGE...
I THINK IT'S TIME FOR ANOTHER DRINK.

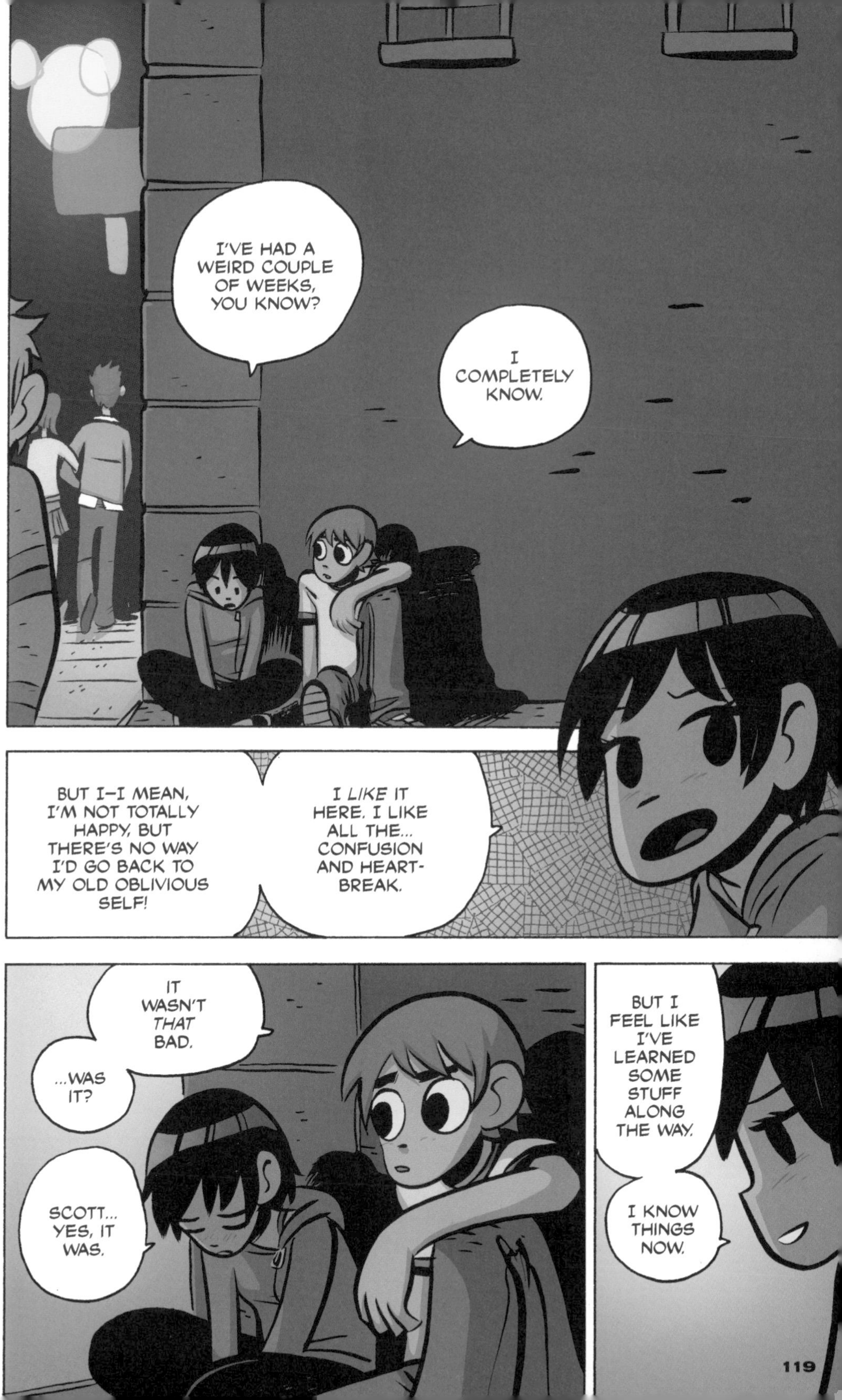

I'VE HAD A WEIRD COUPLE OF WEEKS, YOU KNOW?
I COMPLETELY KNOW.
BUT I—I MEAN, I'M NOT TOTALLY HAPPY, BUT THERE'S NO WAY I'D GO BACK TO MY OLD OBLIVIOUS SELF!
I *LIKE* IT HERE. I LIKE ALL THE... CONFUSION AND HEART-BREAK.
IT WASN'T *THAT* BAD.
...WAS IT?
SCOTT... YES, IT WAS.
BUT I FEEL LIKE I'VE LEARNED SOME STUFF ALONG THE WAY.
I KNOW THINGS NOW.

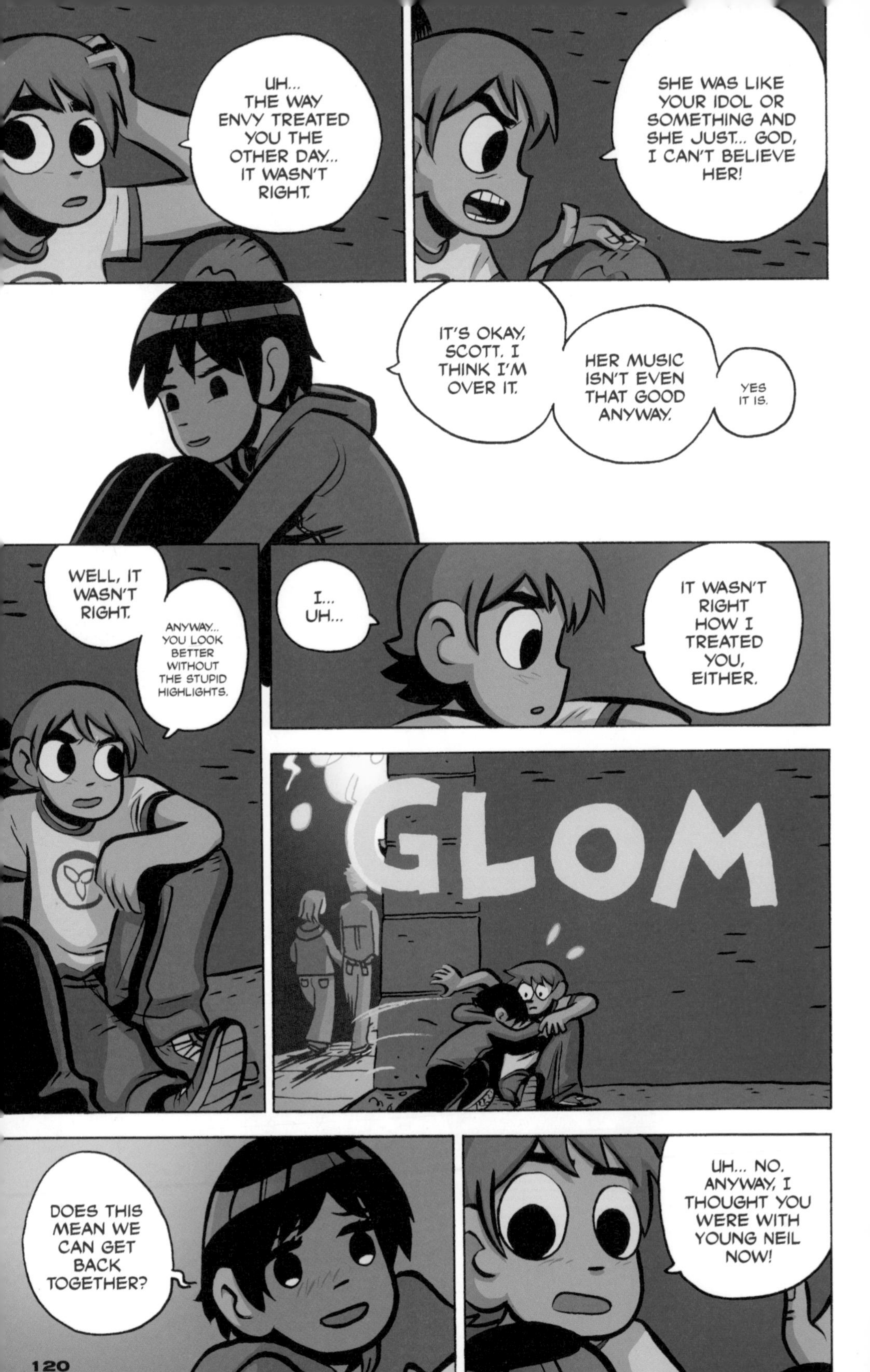
UH... THE WAY ENVY TREATED YOU THE OTHER DAY... IT WASN'T RIGHT.
SHE WAS LIKE YOUR IDOL OR SOMETHING AND SHE JUST... GOD, I CAN'T BELIEVE HER!
IT'S OKAY, SCOTT. I THINK I'M OVER IT.
HER MUSIC ISN'T EVEN THAT GOOD ANYWAY.
YES IT IS.
WELL, IT WASN'T RIGHT.
ANYWAY... YOU LOOK BETTER WITHOUT THE STUPID HIGHLIGHTS.
I... UH...
IT WASN'T RIGHT HOW I TREATED YOU, EITHER.
GLOM
DOES THIS MEAN WE CAN GET BACK TOGETHER?
UH... NO. ANYWAY, I THOUGHT YOU WERE WITH YOUNG NEIL NOW!

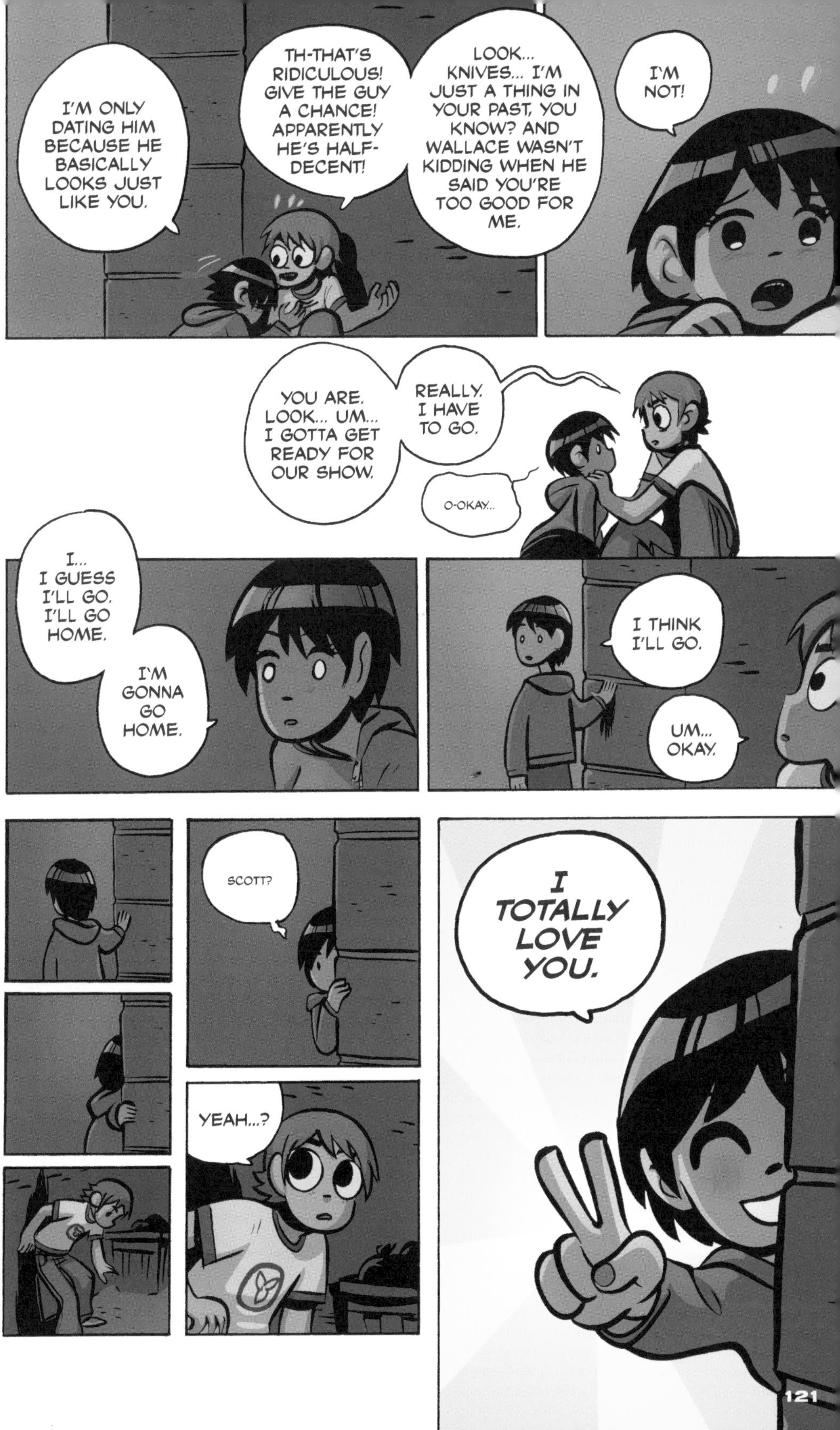

I'M ONLY DATING HIM BECAUSE HE BASICALLY LOOKS JUST LIKE YOU.
TH-THAT'S RIDICULOUS! GIVE THE GUY A CHANCE! APPARENTLY HE'S HALF-DECENT!
LOOK... KNIVES... I'M JUST A THING IN YOUR PAST, YOU KNOW? AND WALLACE WASN'T KIDDING WHEN HE SAID YOU'RE TOO GOOD FOR ME.
I'M NOT!
YOU ARE. LOOK... UM... I GOTTA GET READY FOR OUR SHOW.
REALLY. I HAVE TO GO.
O-OKAY...
I... I GUESS I'LL GO. I'LL GO HOME.
I'M GONNA GO HOME.
I THINK I'LL GO.
UM... OKAY.
SCOTT?
YEAH...?
I TOTALLY LOVE YOU.

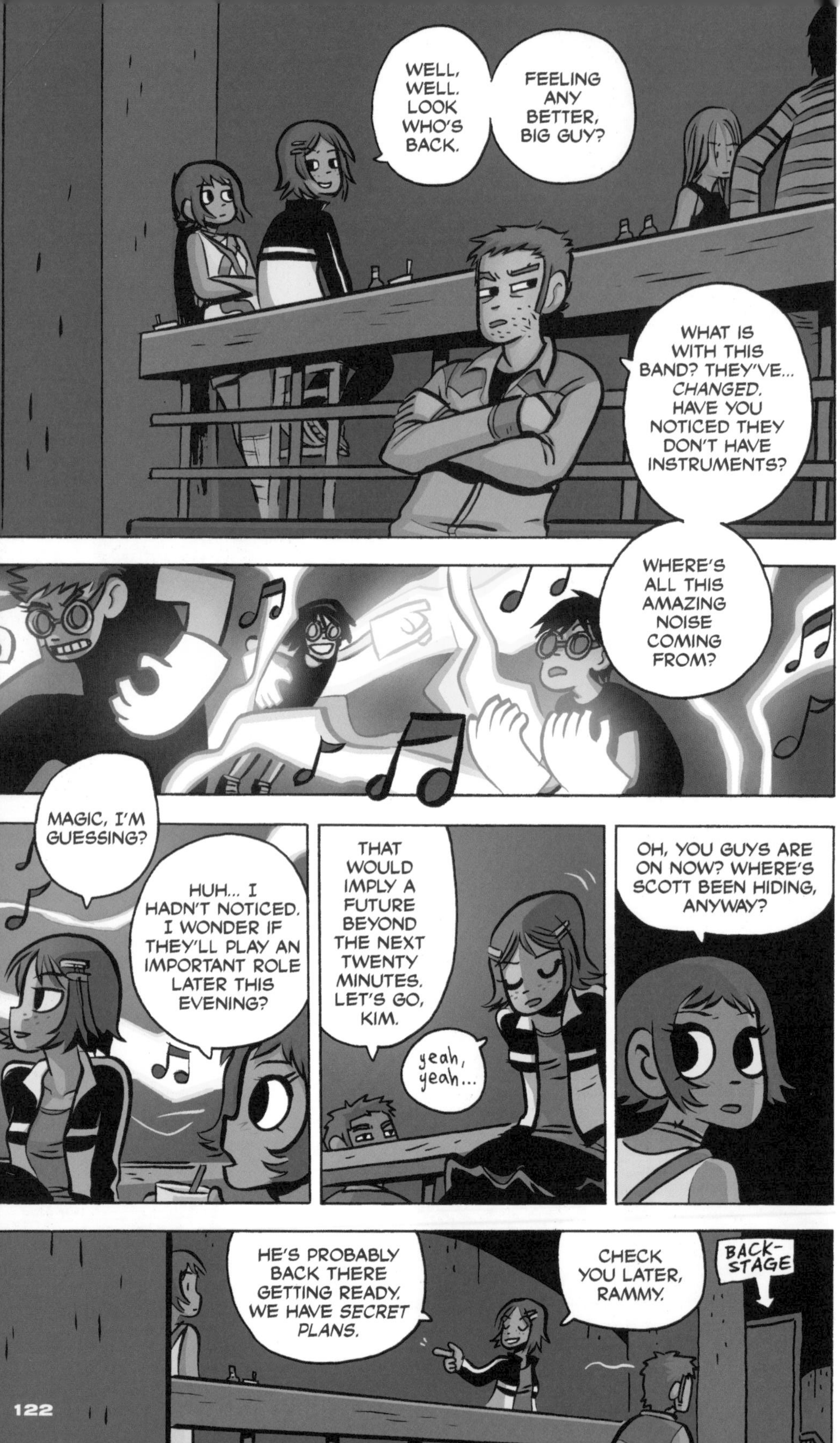
WELL, WELL. LOOK WHO'S BACK.
FEELING ANY BETTER, BIG GUY?
WHAT IS WITH THIS BAND? THEY'VE... CHANGED. HAVE YOU NOTICED THEY DON'T HAVE INSTRUMENTS?
WHERE'S ALL THIS AMAZING NOISE COMING FROM?
MAGIC, I'M GUESSING?
HUH... I HADN'T NOTICED. I WONDER IF THEY'LL PLAY AN IMPORTANT ROLE LATER THIS EVENING?
THAT WOULD IMPLY A FUTURE BEYOND THE NEXT TWENTY MINUTES. LET'S GO, KIM.
yeah, yeah...
OH, YOU GUYS ARE ON NOW? WHERE'S SCOTT BEEN HIDING, ANYWAY?
HE'S PROBABLY BACK THERE GETTING READY. WE HAVE SECRET PLANS.
CHECK YOU LATER, RAMMY.
BACK-STAGE

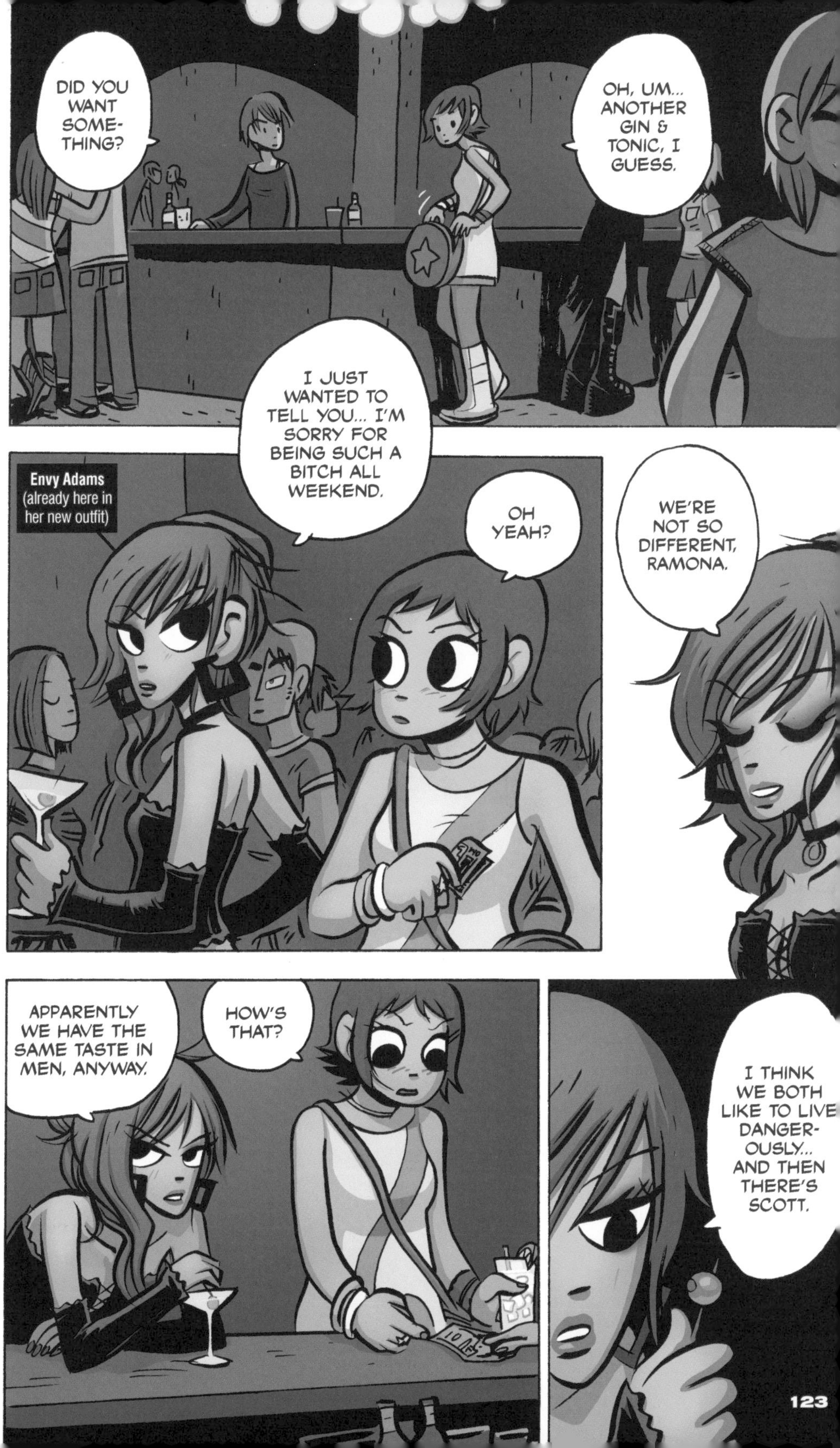
DID YOU WANT SOME-THING?
OH, UM... ANOTHER GIN & TONIC, I GUESS.
I JUST WANTED TO TELL YOU... I'M SORRY FOR BEING SUCH A BITCH ALL WEEKEND.
Envy Adams (already here in her new outfit)
OH YEAH?
WE'RE NOT SO DIFFERENT, RAMONA.
APPARENTLY WE HAVE THE SAME TASTE IN MEN, ANYWAY.
HOW'S THAT?
I THINK WE BOTH LIKE TO LIVE DANGER-OUSLY... AND THEN THERE'S SCOTT.

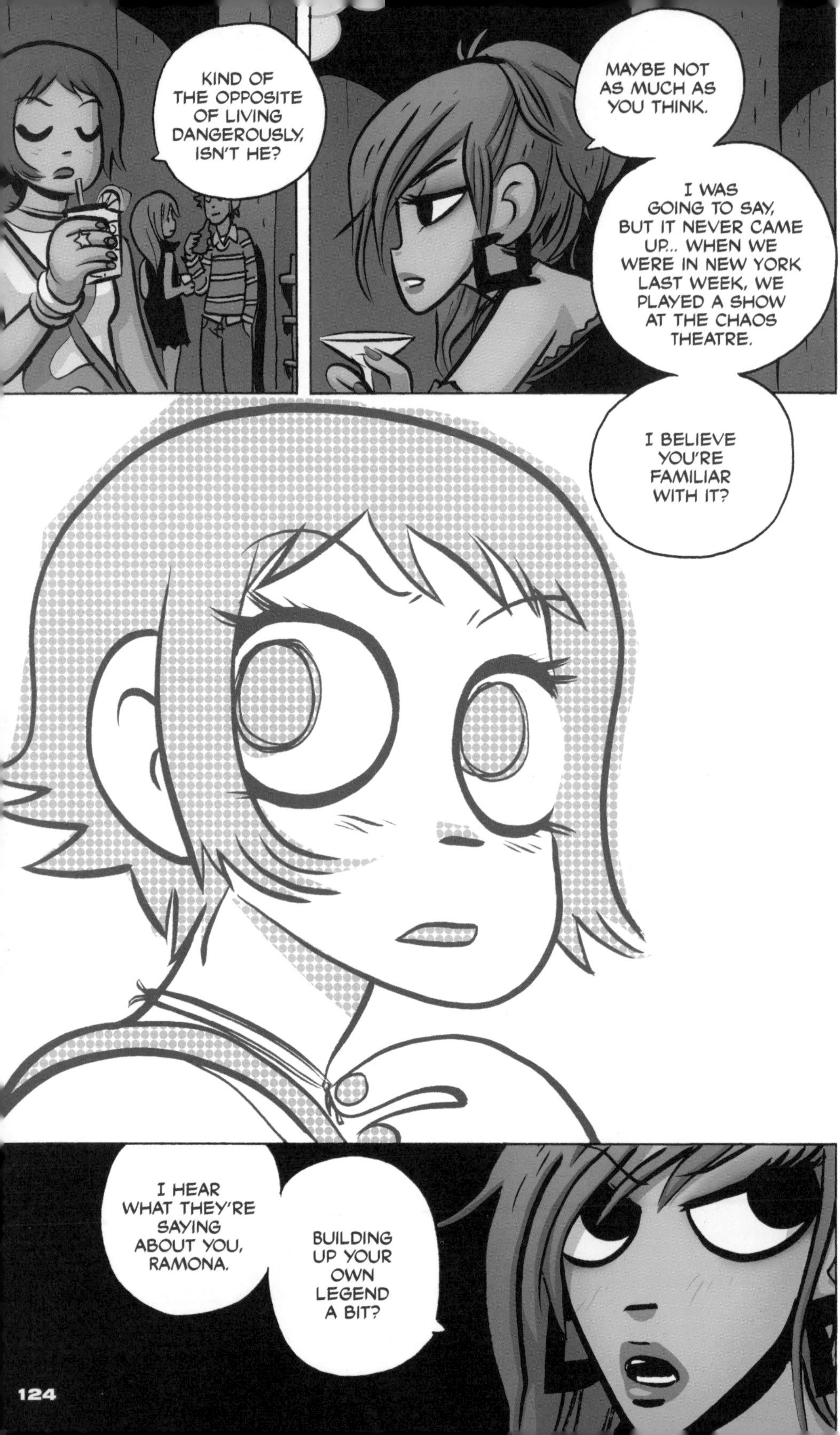
KIND OF THE OPPOSITE OF LIVING DANGEROUSLY, ISN'T HE?
MAYBE NOT AS MUCH AS YOU THINK.
I WAS GOING TO SAY, BUT IT NEVER CAME UP... WHEN WE WERE IN NEW YORK LAST WEEK, WE PLAYED A SHOW AT THE CHAOS THEATRE.
I BELIEVE YOU'RE FAMILIAR WITH IT?
I HEAR WHAT THEY'RE SAYING ABOUT YOU, RAMONA.
BUILDING UP YOUR OWN LEGEND A BIT?

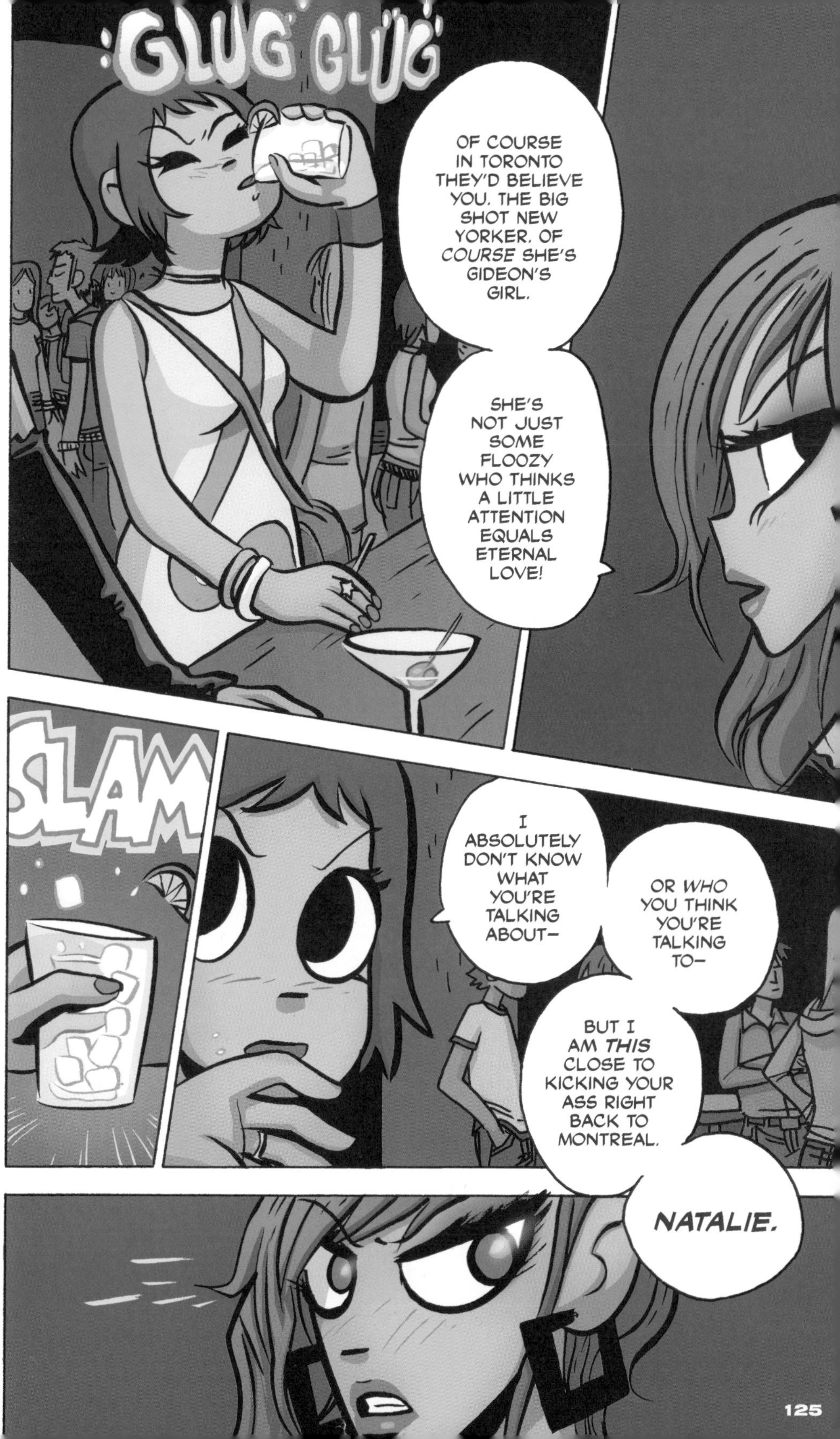
GLUG GLUG
OF COURSE IN TORONTO THEY'D BELIEVE YOU. THE BIG SHOT NEW YORKER. OF *COURSE* SHE'S GIDEON'S GIRL.
SHE'S NOT JUST SOME FLOOZY WHO THINKS A LITTLE ATTENTION EQUALS ETERNAL LOVE!
SLAM
I ABSOLUTELY DON'T KNOW WHAT YOU'RE TALKING ABOUT—
OR *WHO* YOU THINK YOU'RE TALKING TO—
BUT I AM *THIS* CLOSE TO KICKING YOUR ASS RIGHT BACK TO MONTREAL.
NATALIE.

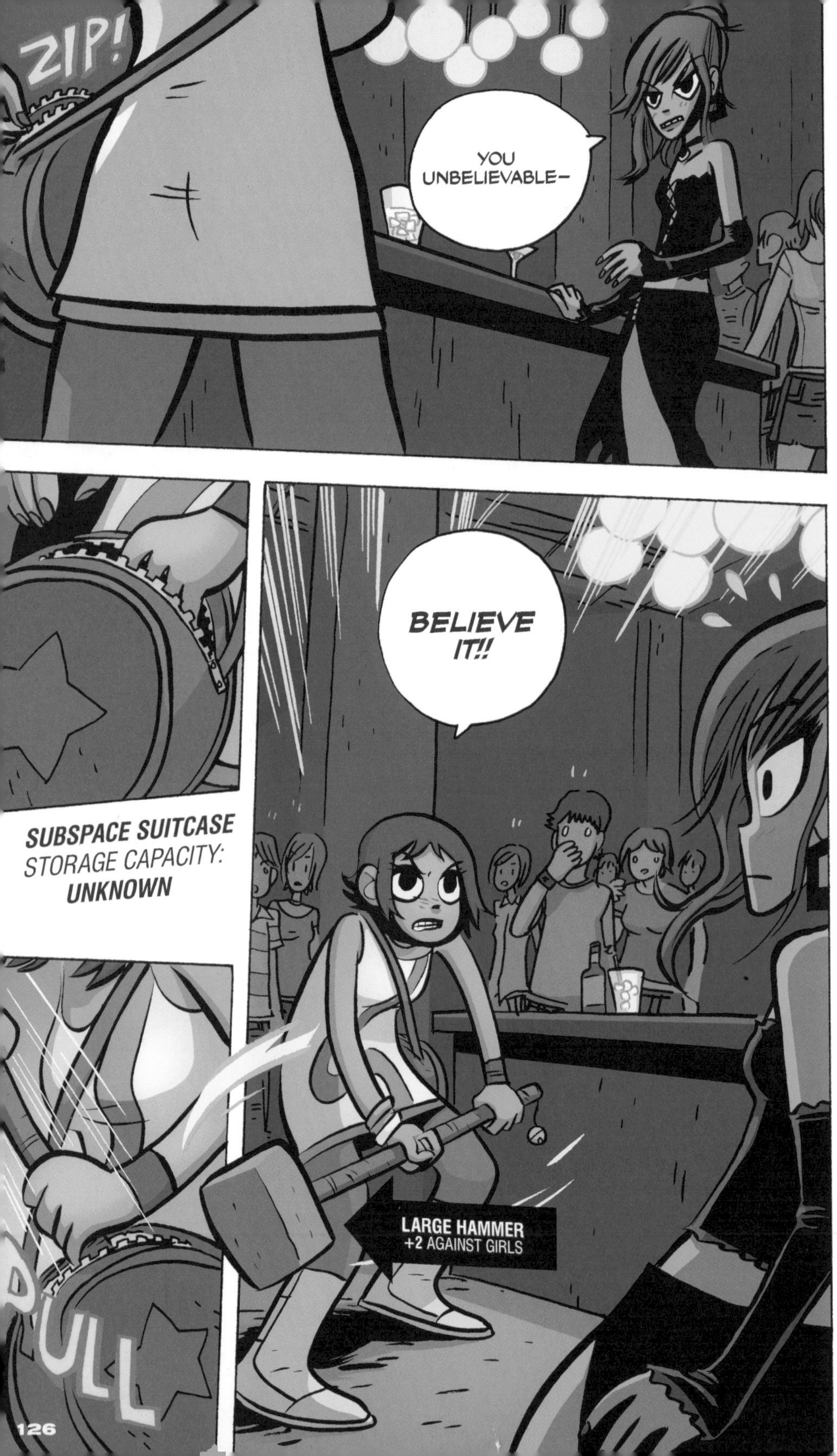
ZIP!
YOU UNBELIEVABLE–
SUBSPACE SUITCASE
STORAGE CAPACITY:
UNKNOWN
PULL
BELIEVE IT!!
LARGE HAMMER
+2 AGAINST GIRLS

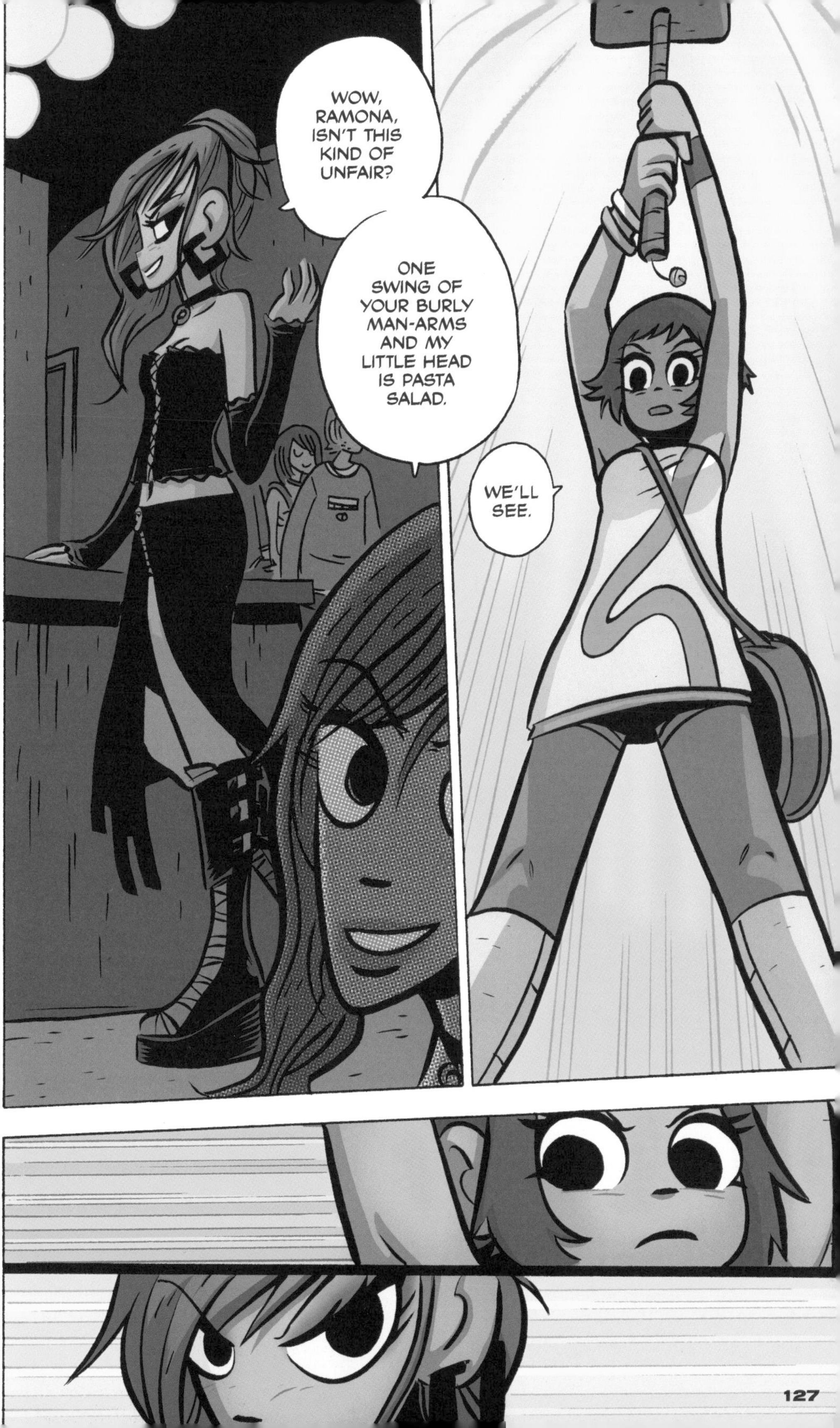
WOW, RAMONA, ISN'T THIS KIND OF UNFAIR?
ONE SWING OF YOUR BURLY MAN-ARMS AND MY LITTLE HEAD IS PASTA SALAD.
WE'LL SEE.

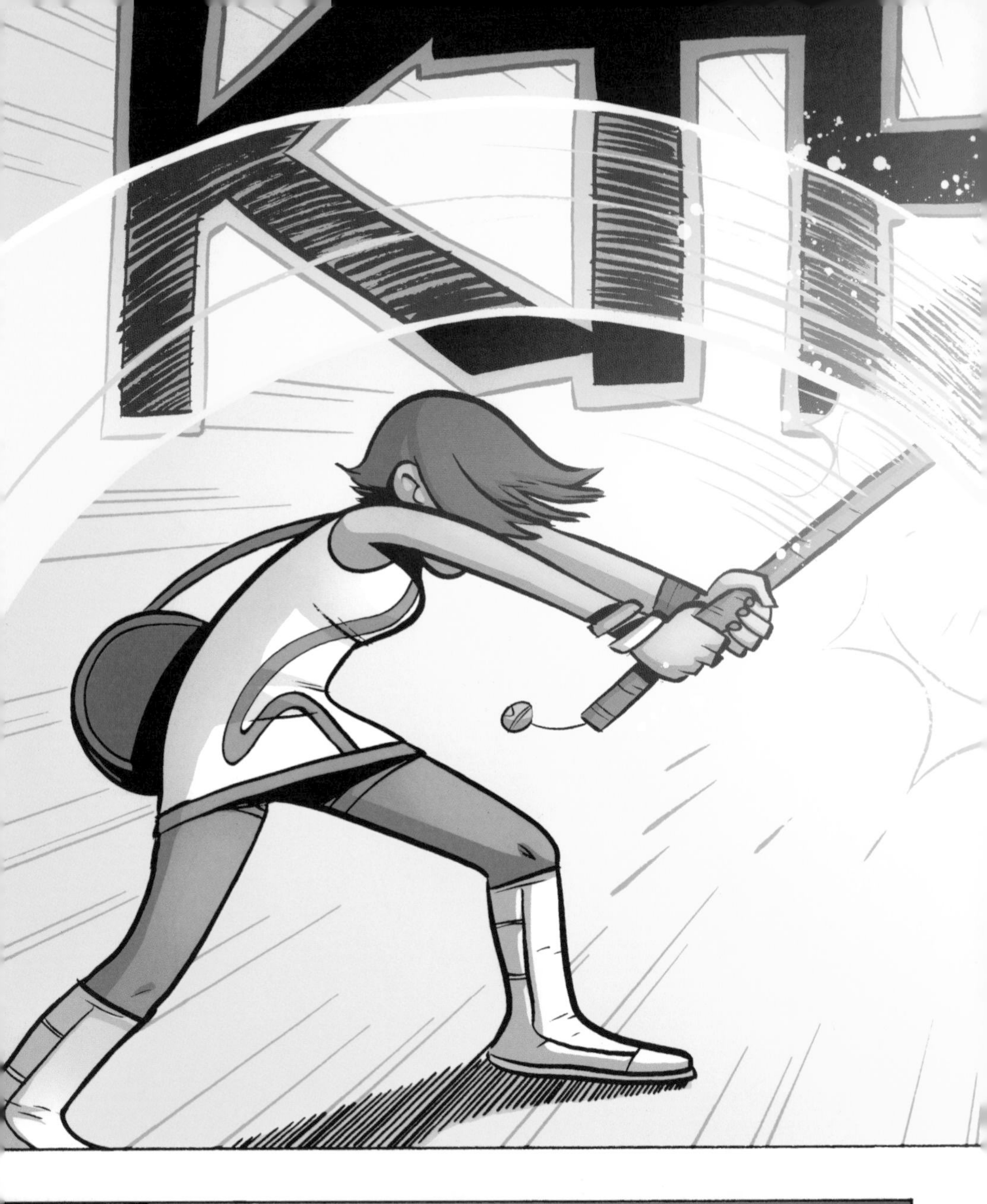

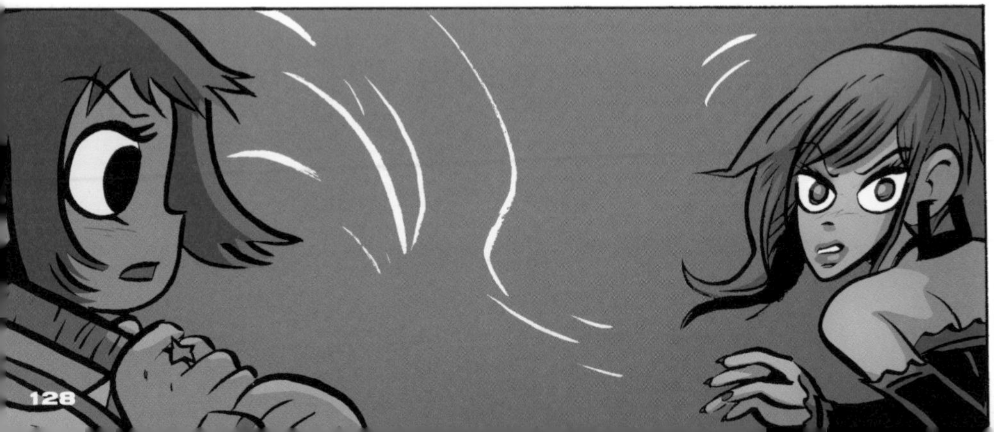

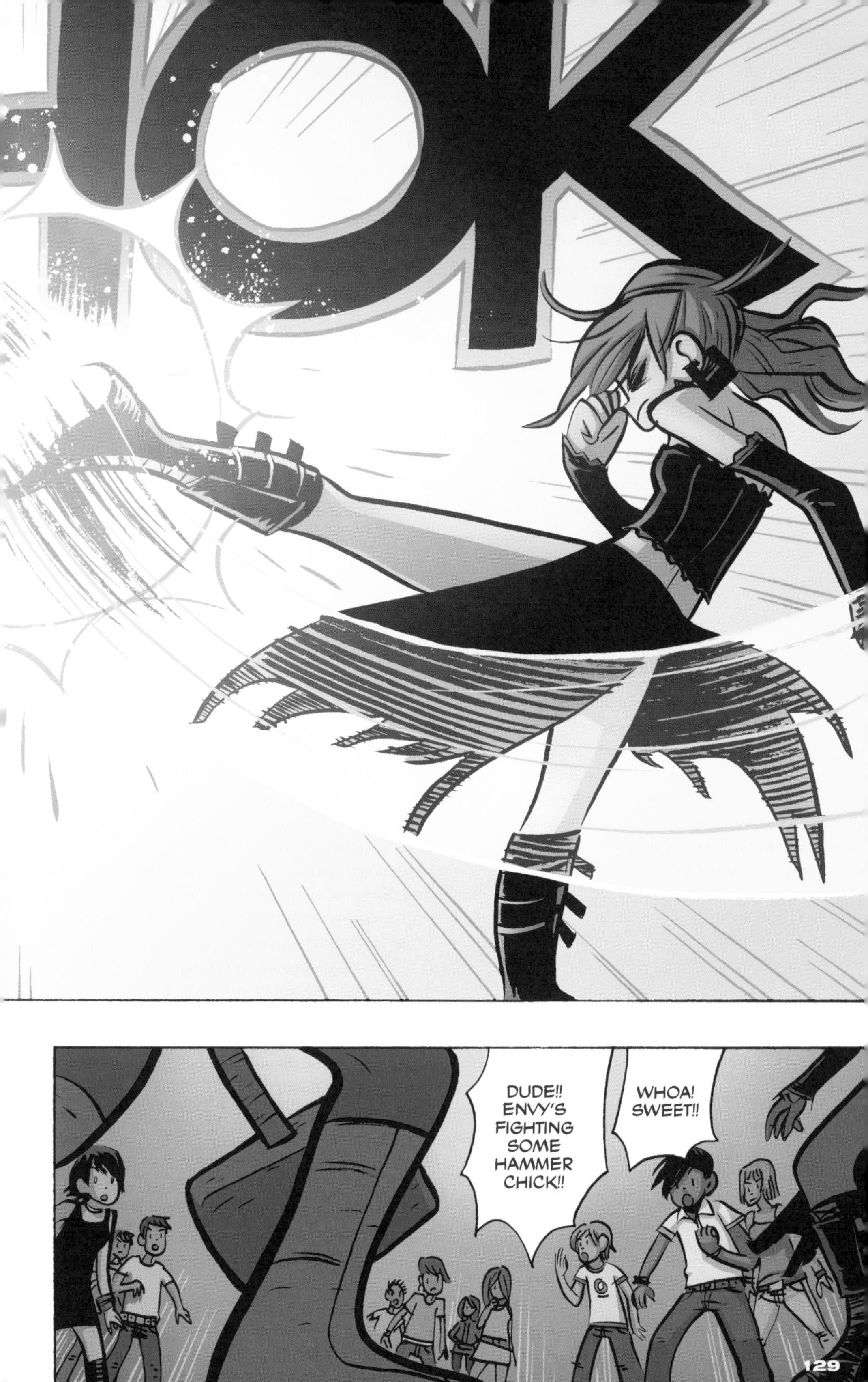
DUDE!! ENVY'S FIGHTING SOME HAMMER CHICK!!
WHOA! SWEET!!

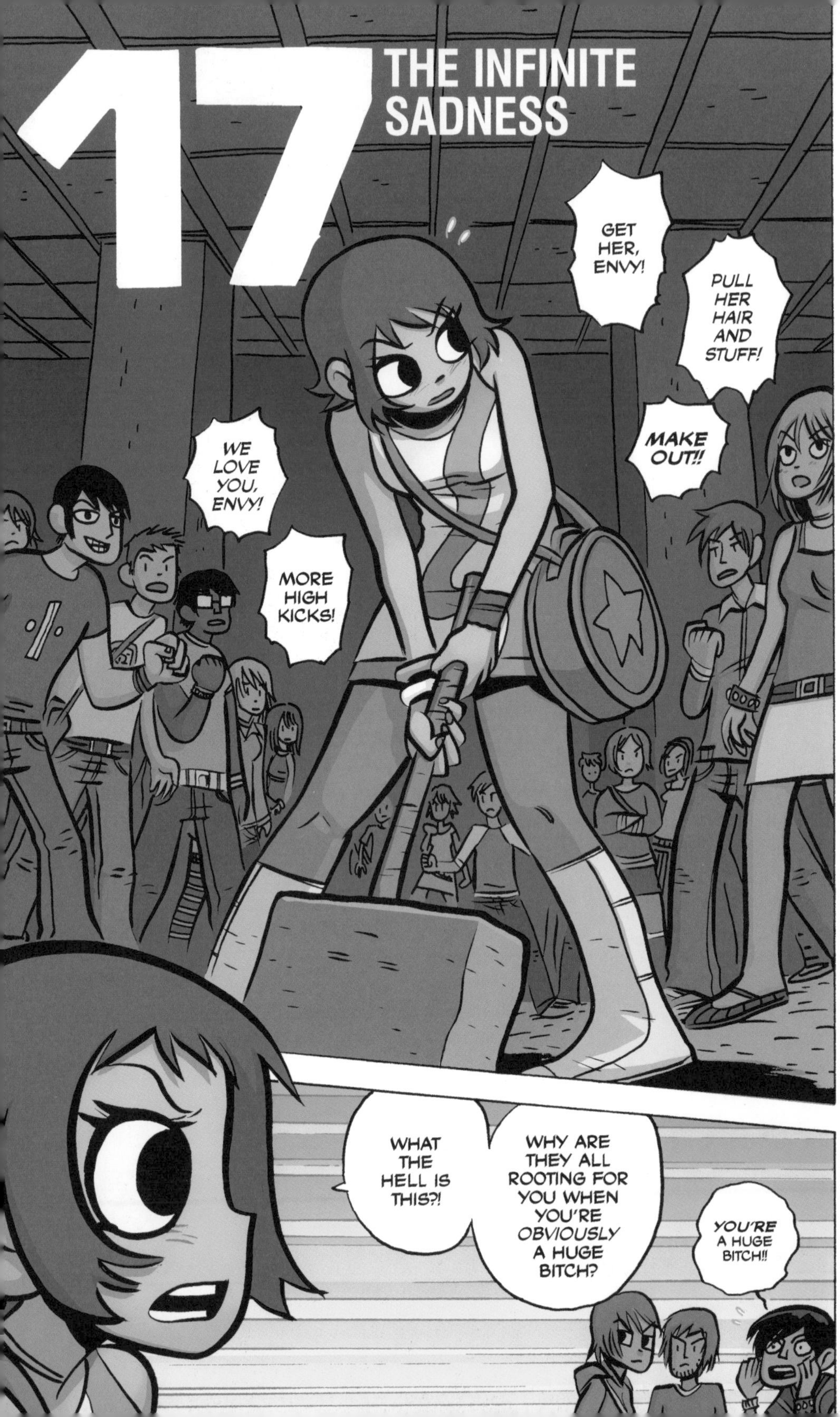17
THE INFINITE SADNESS
GET HER, ENVY!
PULL HER HAIR AND STUFF!
MAKE OUT!!
WE LOVE YOU, ENVY!
MORE HIGH KICKS!
WHAT THE HELL IS THIS?!
WHY ARE THEY ALL ROOTING FOR YOU WHEN YOU'RE OBVIOUSLY A HUGE BITCH?
YOU'RE A HUGE BITCH!!

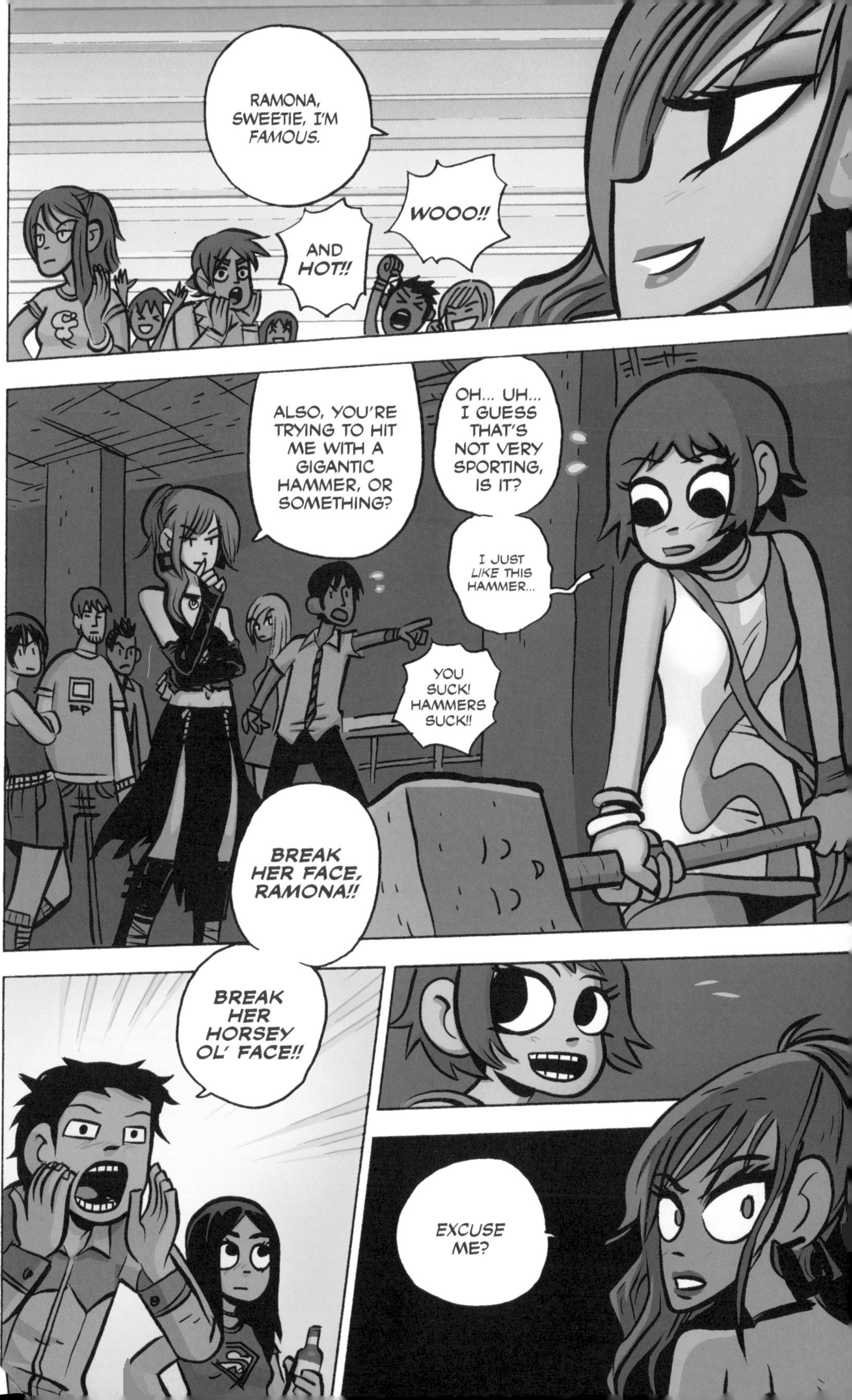
RAMONA, SWEETIE, I'M *FAMOUS.*
AND *HOT!!*
WOOO!!
ALSO, YOU'RE TRYING TO HIT ME WITH A GIGANTIC HAMMER, OR SOMETHING?
OH... UH... I GUESS THAT'S NOT VERY SPORTING, IS IT?
I JUST *LIKE* THIS HAMMER...
YOU SUCK! HAMMERS SUCK!!
BREAK HER FACE, RAMONA!!
BREAK HER HORSEY OL' FACE!!
EXCUSE ME?

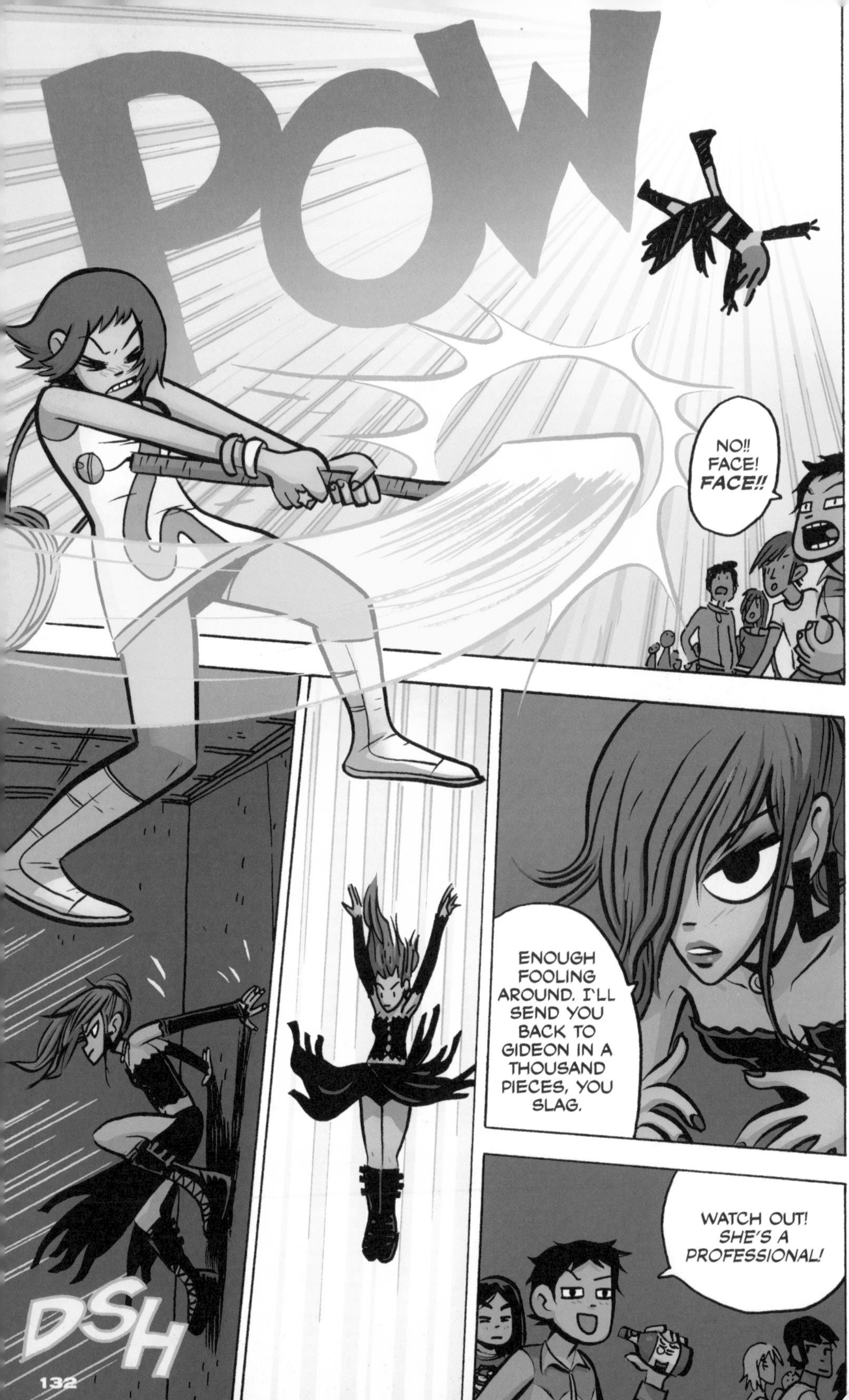
POW
NO!! FACE! FACE!!
ENOUGH FOOLING AROUND. I'LL SEND YOU BACK TO GIDEON IN A THOUSAND PIECES, YOU SLAG.
WATCH OUT! SHE'S A PROFESSIONAL!
DSH

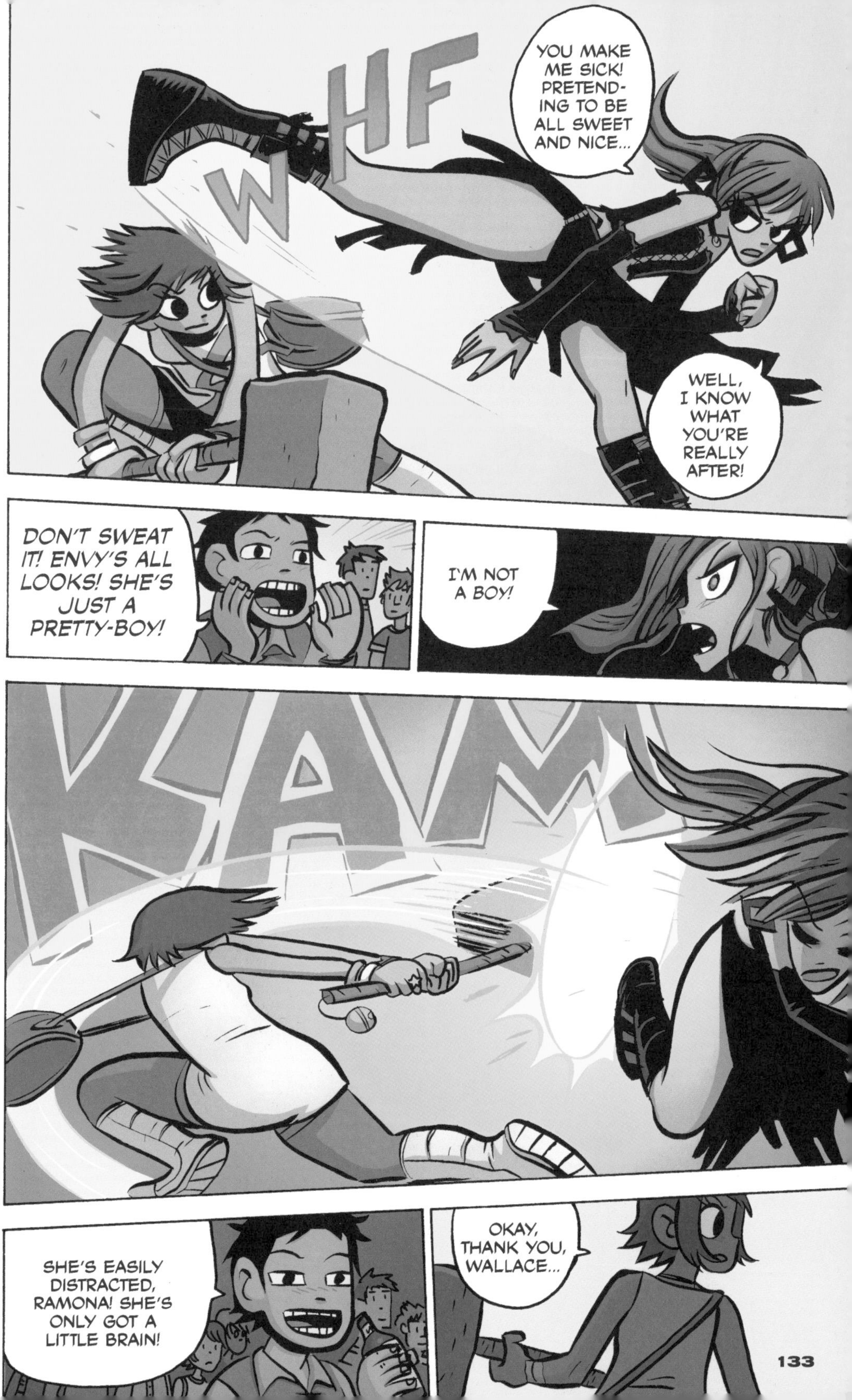
WHF
YOU MAKE ME SICK! PRETEND-ING TO BE ALL SWEET AND NICE...
WELL, I KNOW WHAT YOU'RE REALLY AFTER!
DON'T SWEAT IT! ENVY'S ALL LOOKS! SHE'S JUST A PRETTY-BOY!
I'M NOT A BOY!
KAM
SHE'S EASILY DISTRACTED, RAMONA! SHE'S ONLY GOT A LITTLE BRAIN!
OKAY, THANK YOU, WALLACE...

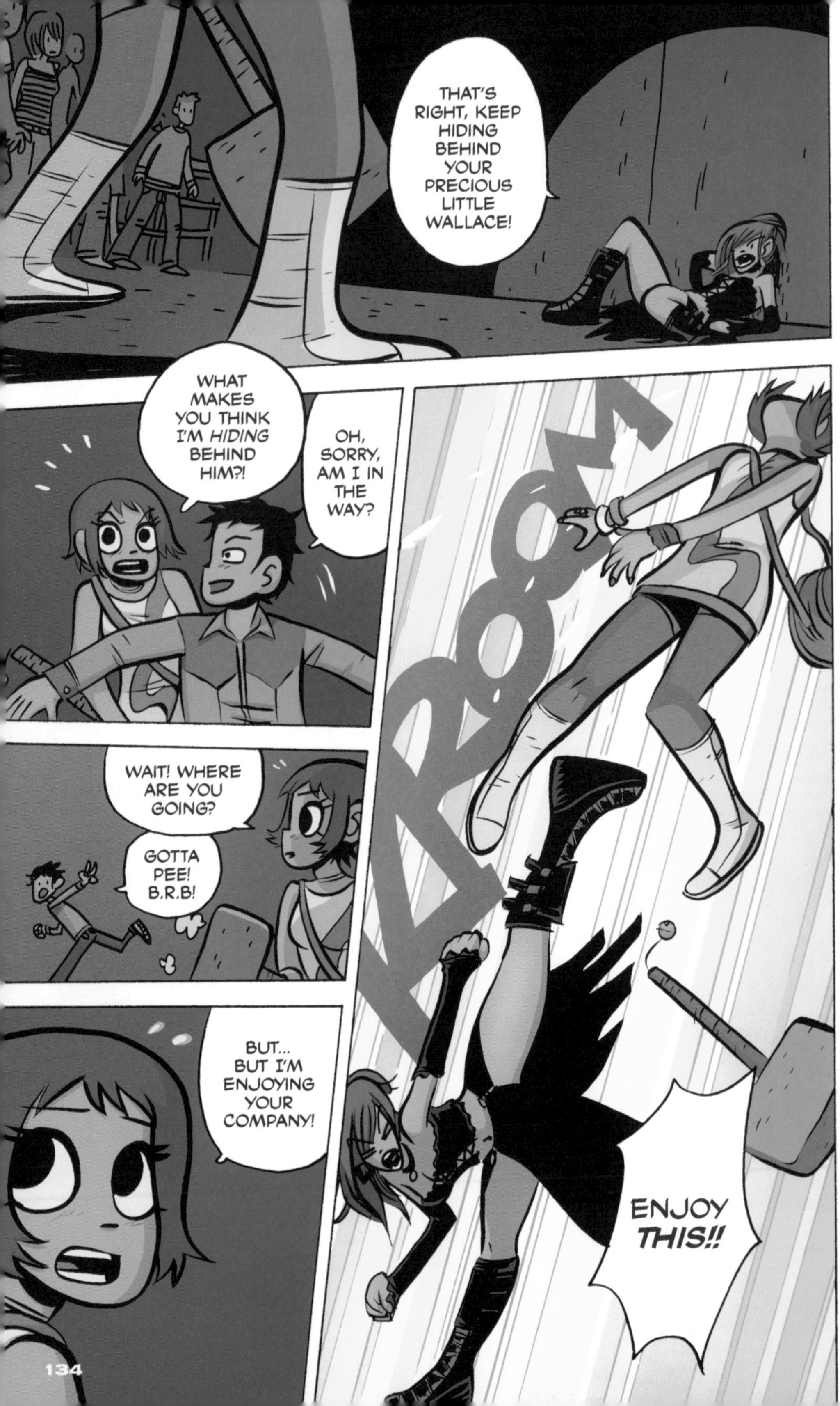
THAT'S RIGHT, KEEP HIDING BEHIND YOUR PRECIOUS LITTLE WALLACE!
WHAT MAKES YOU THINK I'M *HIDING* BEHIND HIM?!
OH, SORRY, AM I IN THE WAY?
WAIT! WHERE ARE YOU GOING?
GOTTA PEE! B.R.B!
BUT... BUT I'M ENJOYING YOUR COMPANY!
KRROOM
ENJOY *THIS!!*

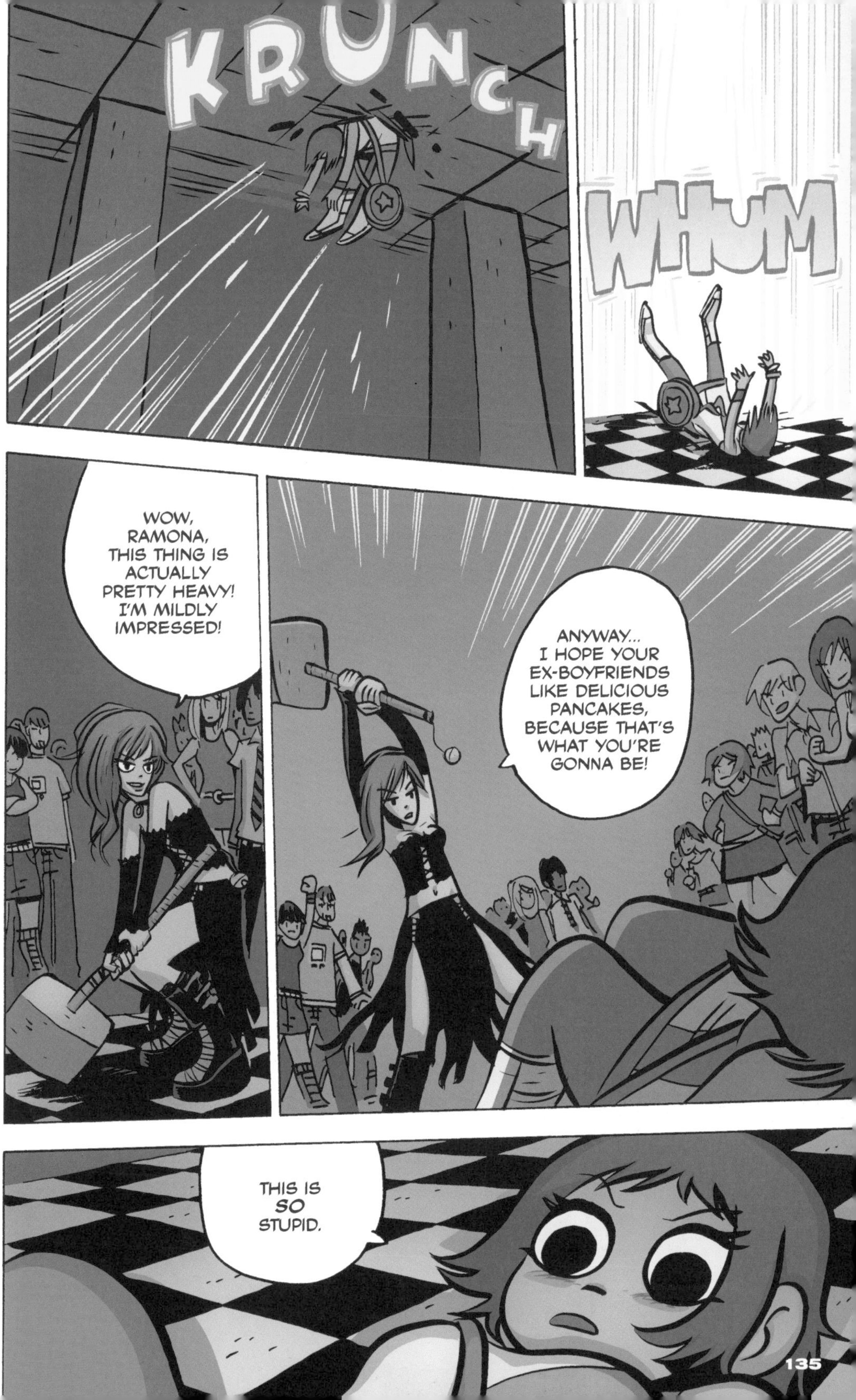
KRUNCH
WHUM
WOW, RAMONA, THIS THING IS ACTUALLY PRETTY HEAVY! I'M MILDLY IMPRESSED!
ANYWAY... I HOPE YOUR EX-BOYFRIENDS LIKE DELICIOUS PANCAKES, BECAUSE THAT'S WHAT YOU'RE GONNA BE!
THIS IS SO STUPID.

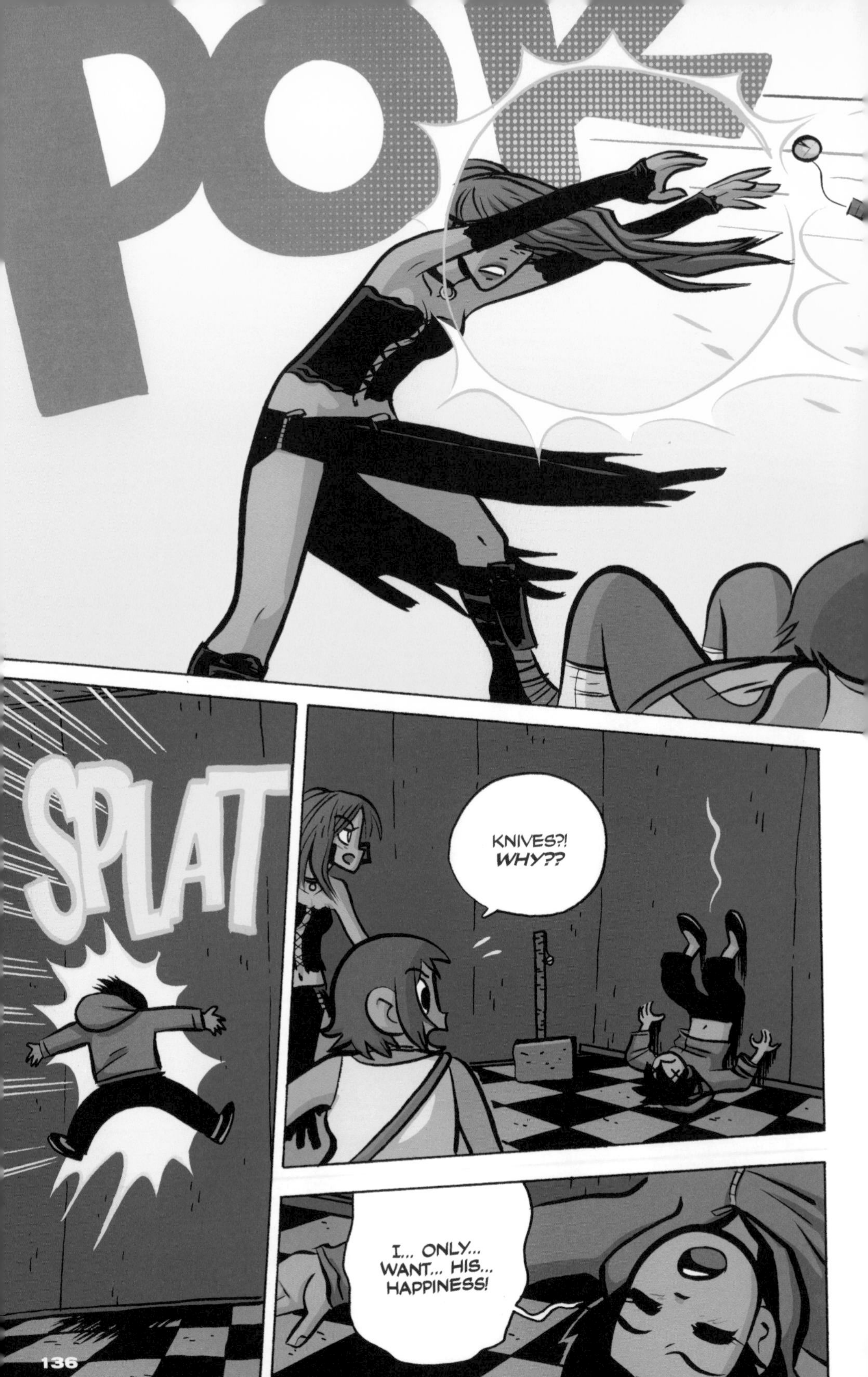
POK
SPLAT
KNIVES?! *WHY??*
I... ONLY... WANT... HIS... HAPPINESS!

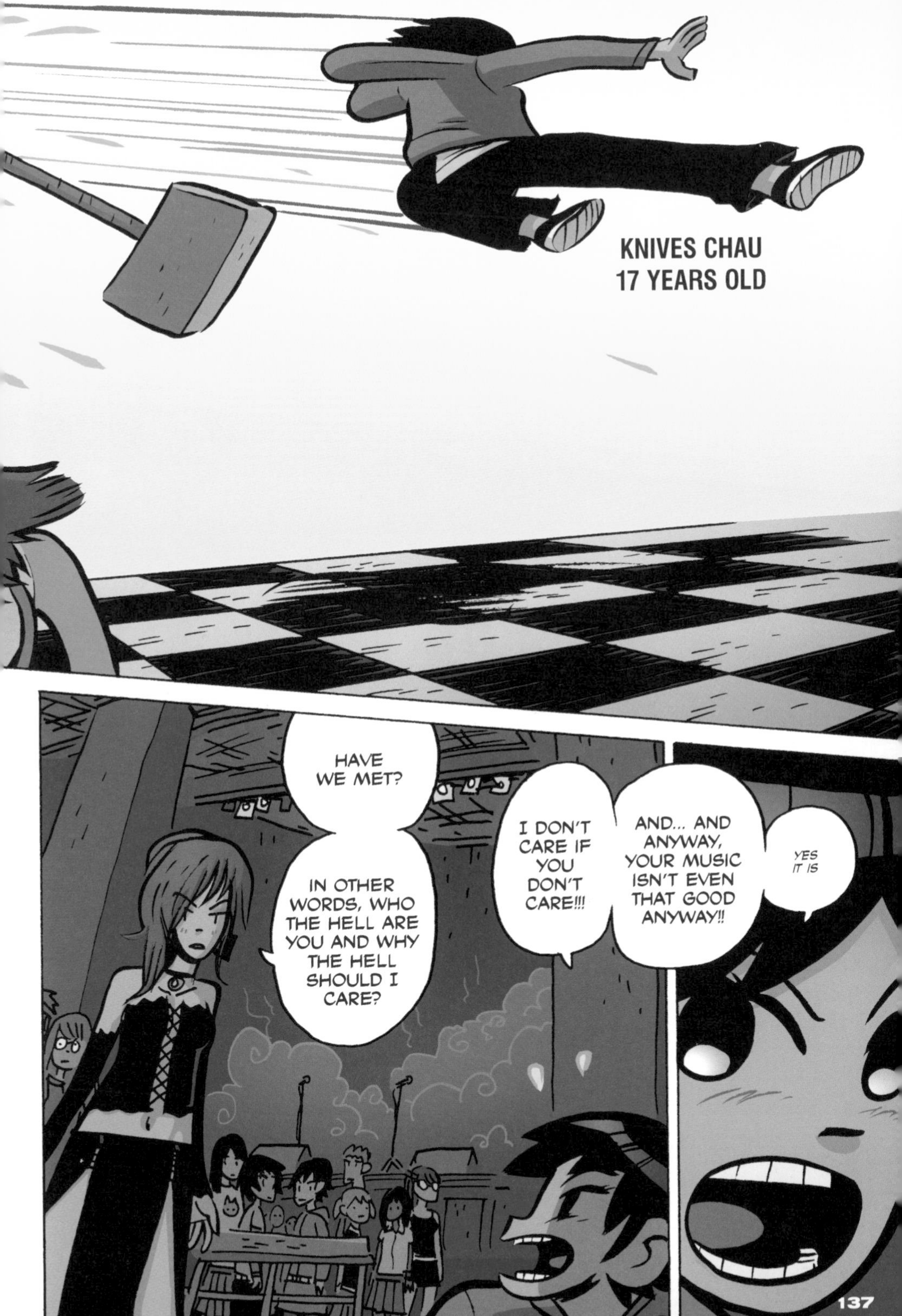
KNIVES CHAU
17 YEARS OLD
HAVE WE MET?
IN OTHER WORDS, WHO THE HELL ARE YOU AND WHY THE HELL SHOULD I CARE?
I DON'T CARE IF YOU DON'T CARE!!!
AND... AND ANYWAY, YOUR MUSIC ISN'T EVEN THAT GOOD ANYWAY!!
YES IT IS

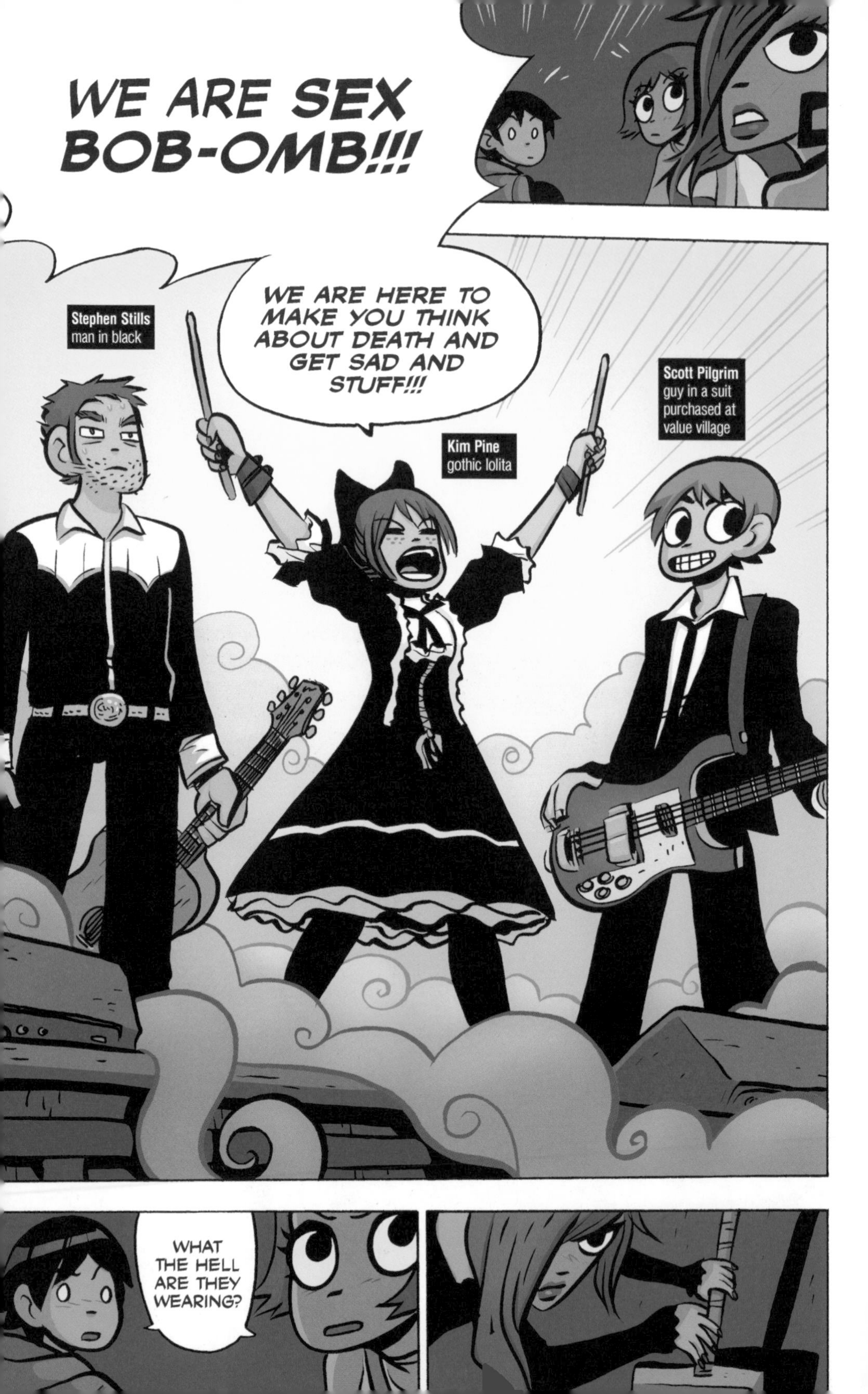
WE ARE SEX BOB-OMB!!!
WE ARE HERE TO MAKE YOU THINK ABOUT DEATH AND GET SAD AND STUFF!!!
Stephen Stills man in black
Kim Pine gothic lolita
Scott Pilgrim guy in a suit purchased at value village
WHAT THE HELL ARE THEY WEARING?

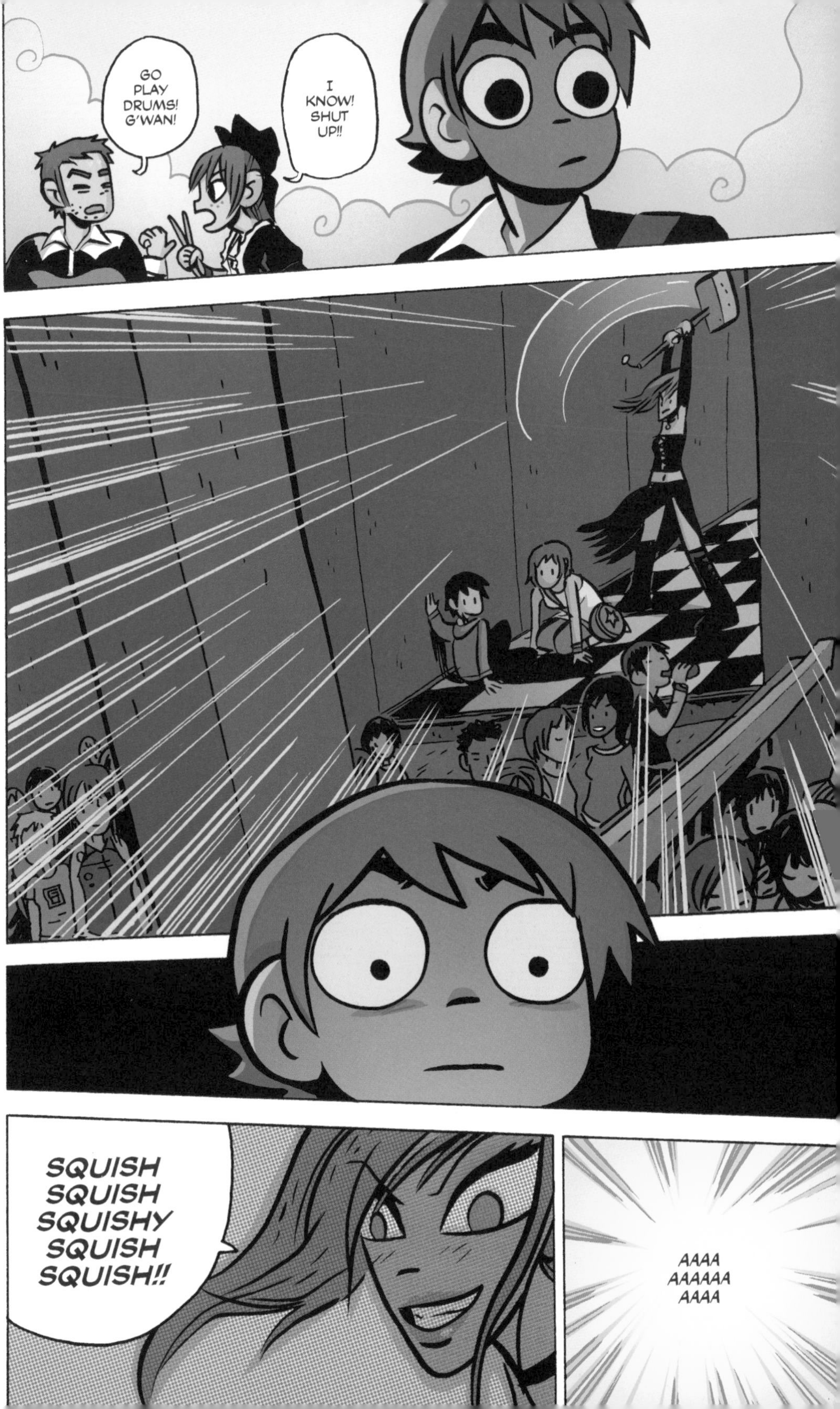
GO PLAY DRUMS! G'WAN!
I KNOW! SHUT UP!!
SQUISH SQUISH SQUISHY SQUISH SQUISH!!
AAAA AAAAAA AAAA

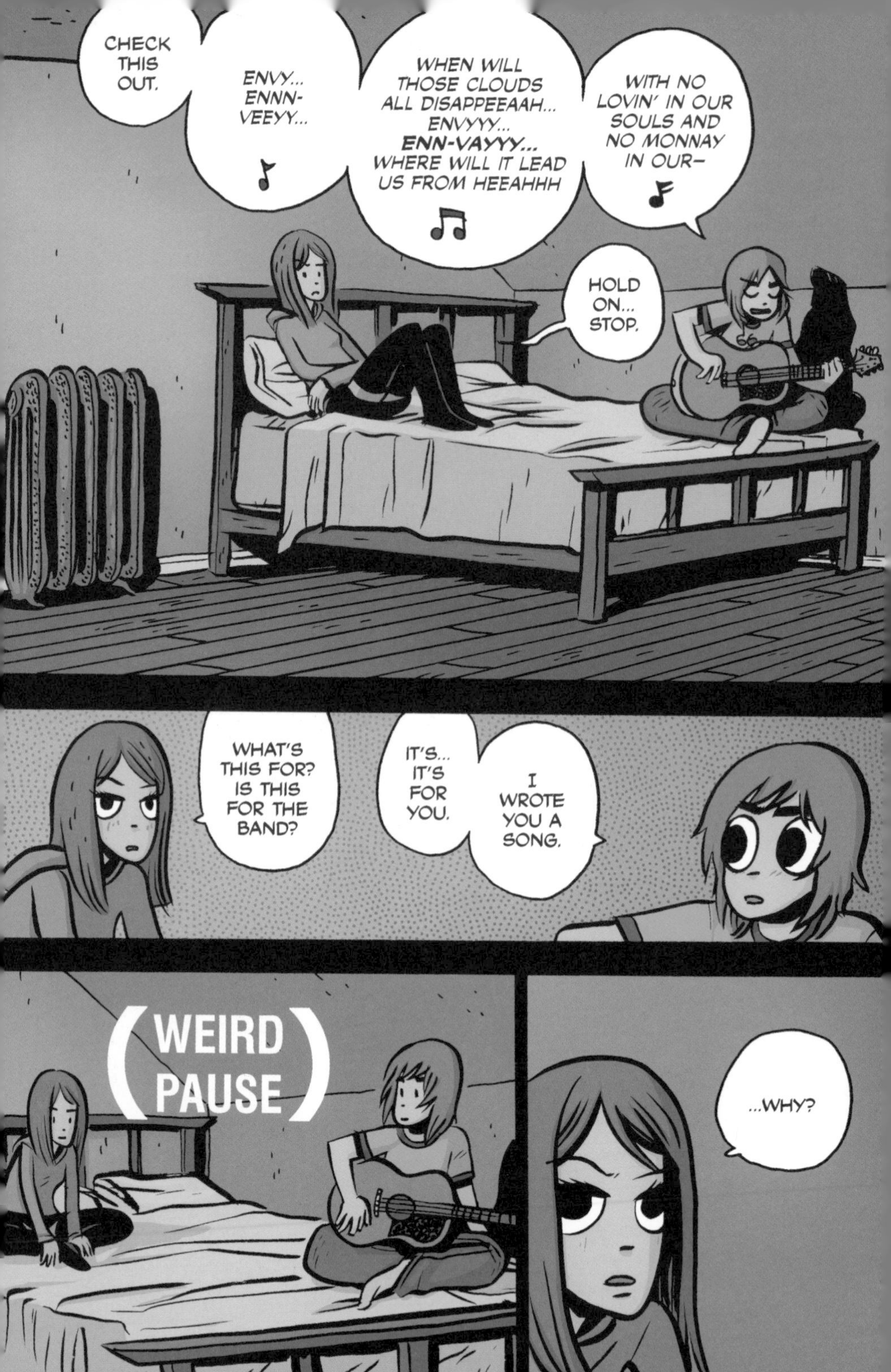
CHECK THIS OUT.
ENVY... ENNN-VEEYY...
WHEN WILL THOSE CLOUDS ALL DISAPPEEAAH... ENVYYY... **ENN-VAYYY...** WHERE WILL IT LEAD US FROM HEEAHHH
WITH NO LOVIN' IN OUR SOULS AND NO MONNAY IN OUR–
HOLD ON... STOP.
WHAT'S THIS FOR? IS THIS FOR THE BAND?
IT'S... IT'S FOR YOU.
I WROTE YOU A SONG.
(WEIRD PAUSE)
...WHY?

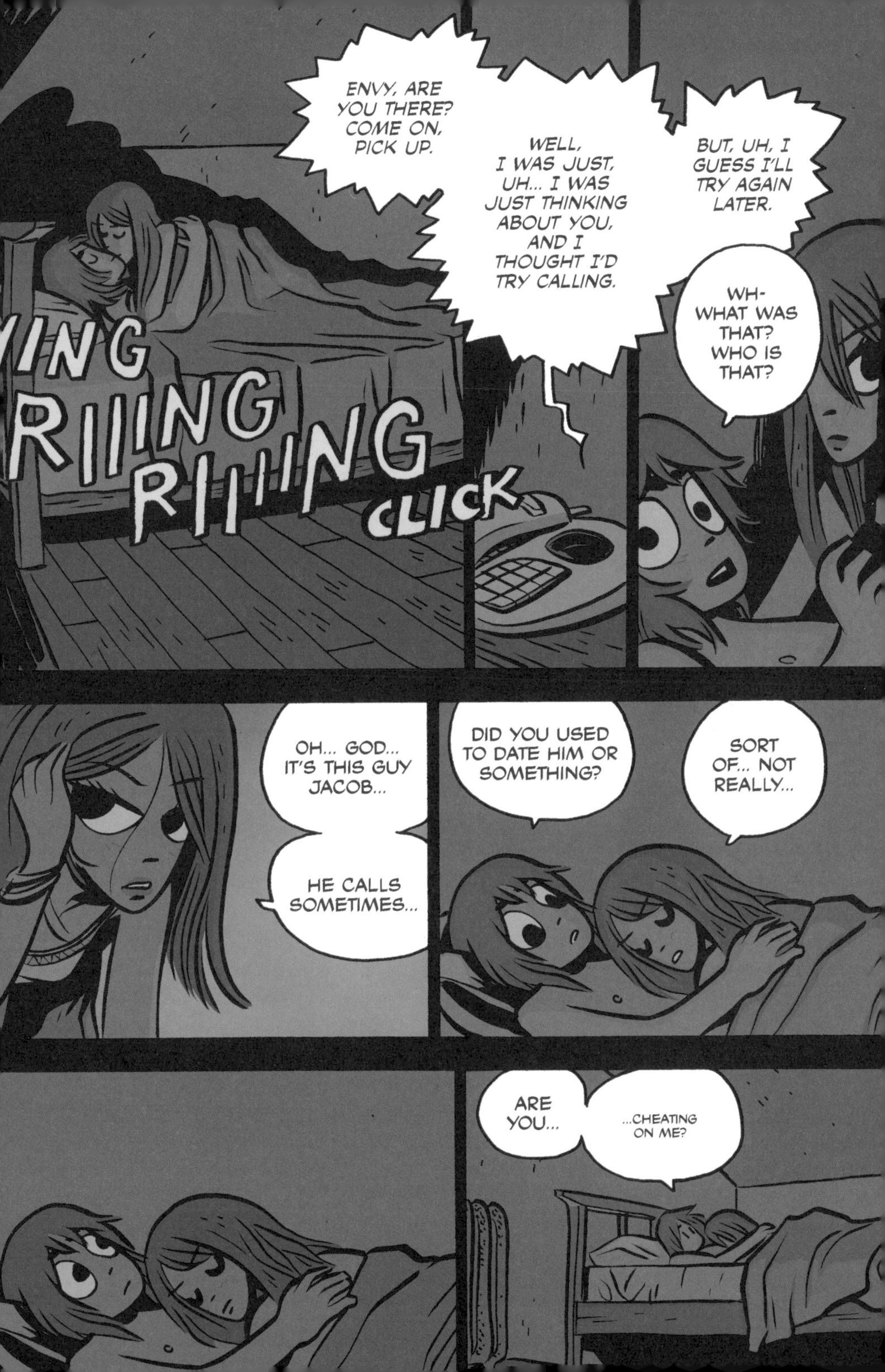
ENVY, ARE YOU THERE? COME ON, PICK UP.
WELL, I WAS JUST, UH... I WAS JUST THINKING ABOUT YOU, AND I THOUGHT I'D TRY CALLING.
BUT, UH, I GUESS I'LL TRY AGAIN LATER.
ING RIIING RIIIING
CLICK
WH- WHAT WAS THAT? WHO IS THAT?
OH... GOD... IT'S THIS GUY JACOB...
HE CALLS SOMETIMES...
DID YOU USED TO DATE HIM OR SOMETHING?
SORT OF... NOT REALLY...
ARE YOU...
...CHEATING ON ME?

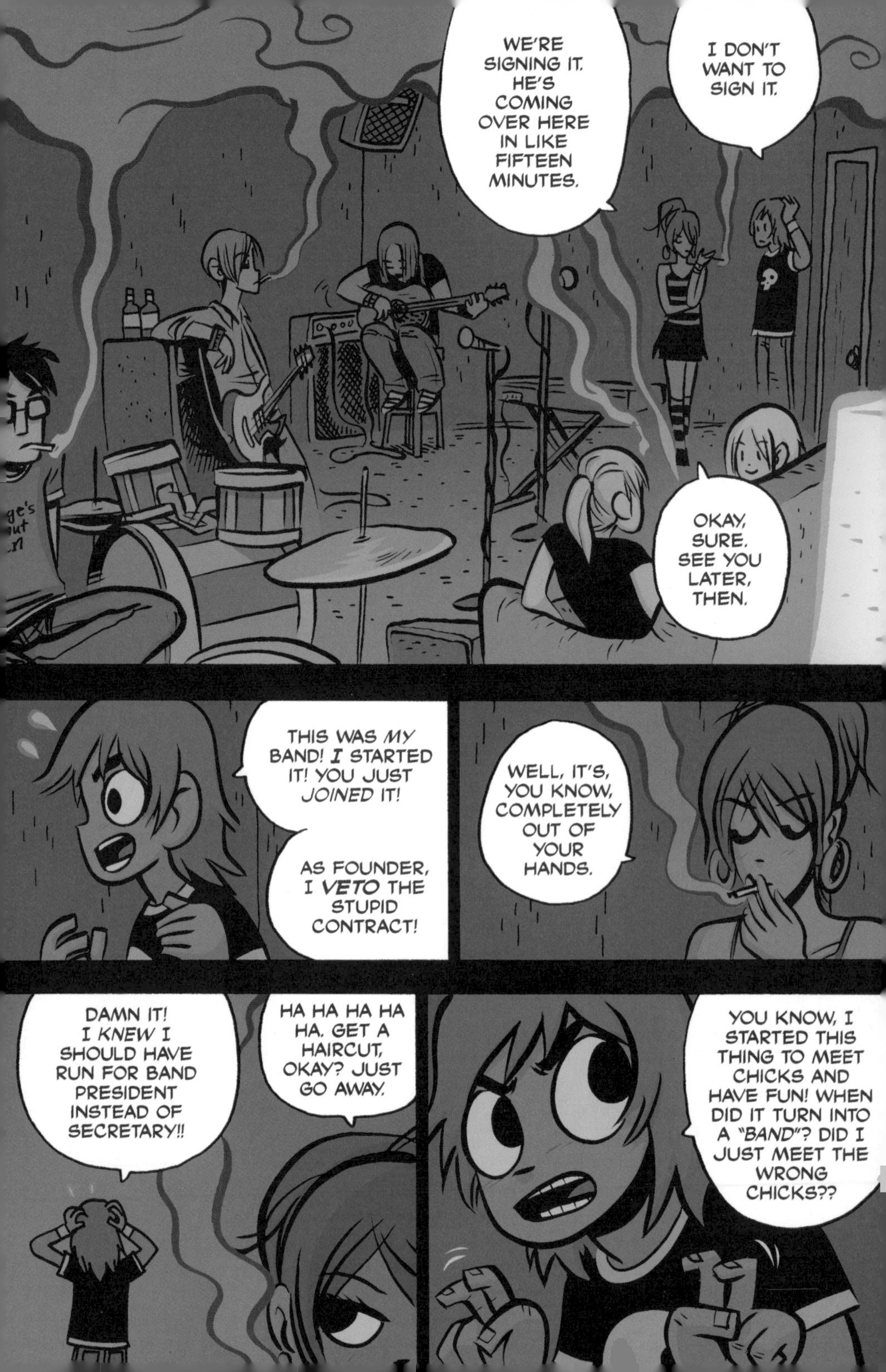

WE'RE SIGNING IT. HE'S COMING OVER HERE IN LIKE FIFTEEN MINUTES.
I DON'T WANT TO SIGN IT.
OKAY, SURE. SEE YOU LATER, THEN.
THIS WAS *MY* BAND! *I* STARTED IT! YOU JUST *JOINED* IT!
AS FOUNDER, I ***VETO*** THE STUPID CONTRACT!
WELL, IT'S, YOU KNOW, COMPLETELY OUT OF YOUR HANDS.
DAMN IT! I *KNEW* I SHOULD HAVE RUN FOR BAND PRESIDENT INSTEAD OF SECRETARY!!
HA HA HA HA HA. GET A HAIRCUT, OKAY? JUST GO AWAY.
YOU KNOW, I STARTED THIS THING TO MEET CHICKS AND HAVE FUN! WHEN DID IT TURN INTO A "*BAND*"? DID I JUST MEET THE WRONG CHICKS??

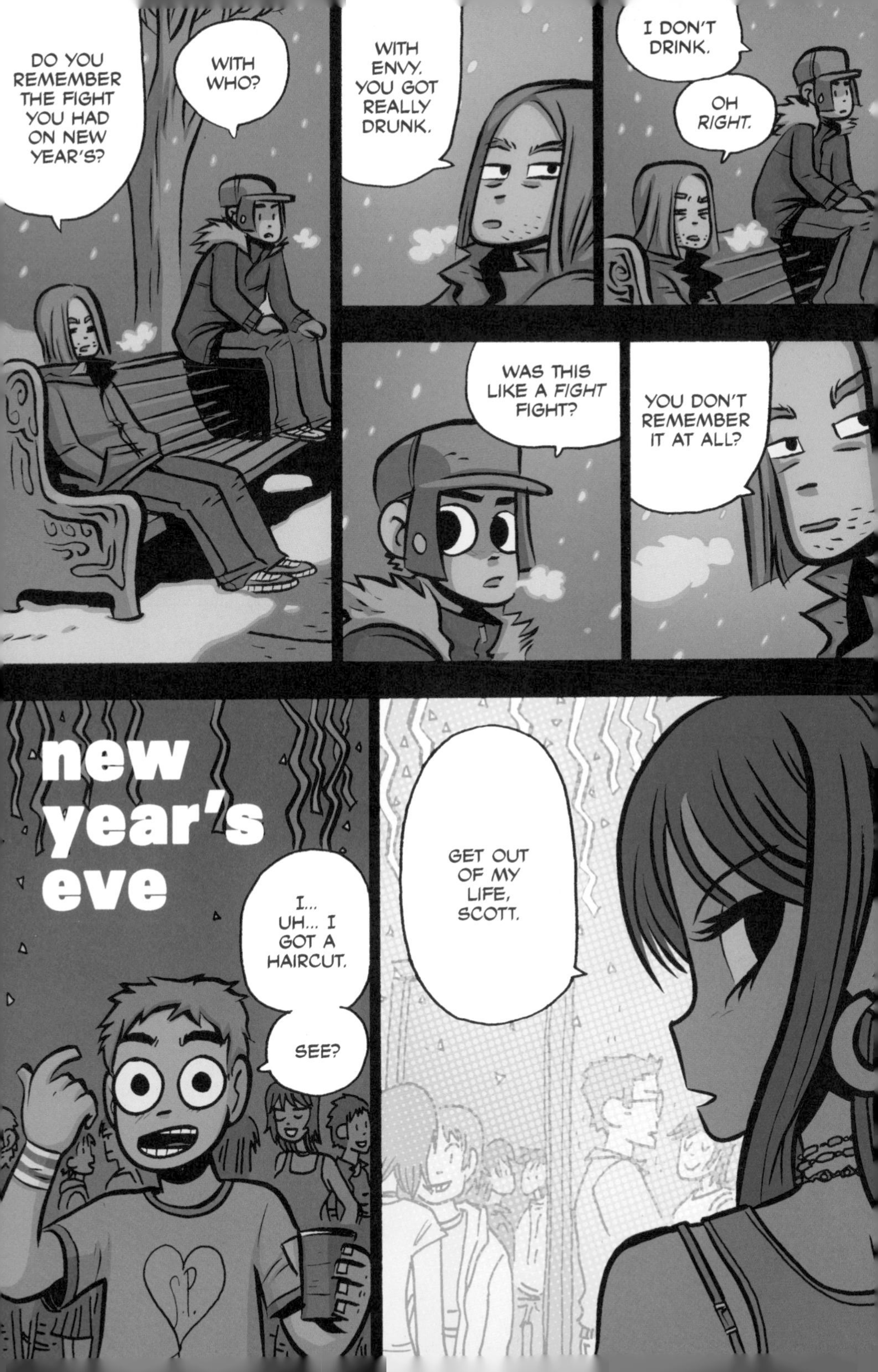
DO YOU REMEMBER THE FIGHT YOU HAD ON NEW YEAR'S?
WITH WHO?
WITH ENVY. YOU GOT REALLY DRUNK.
I DON'T DRINK.
OH RIGHT.
WAS THIS LIKE A FIGHT FIGHT?
YOU DON'T REMEMBER IT AT ALL?
new year's eve
I... UH... I GOT A HAIRCUT.
SEE?
GET OUT OF MY LIFE, SCOTT.

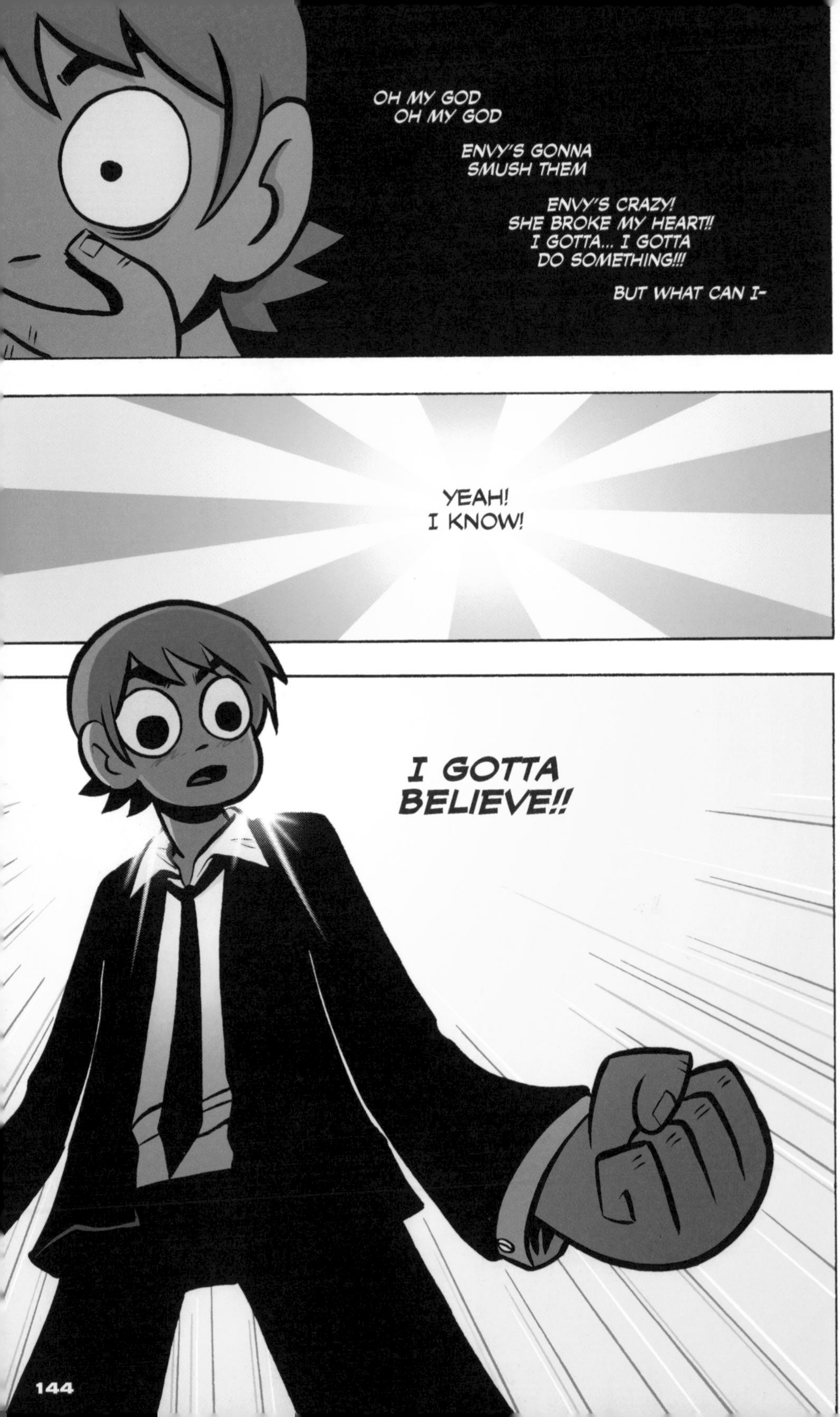
OH MY GOD
OH MY GOD
ENVY'S GONNA SMUSH THEM
ENVY'S CRAZY! SHE BROKE MY HEART!! I GOTTA... I GOTTA DO SOMETHING!!!
BUT WHAT CAN I-
YEAH! I KNOW!
I GOTTA BELIEVE!!

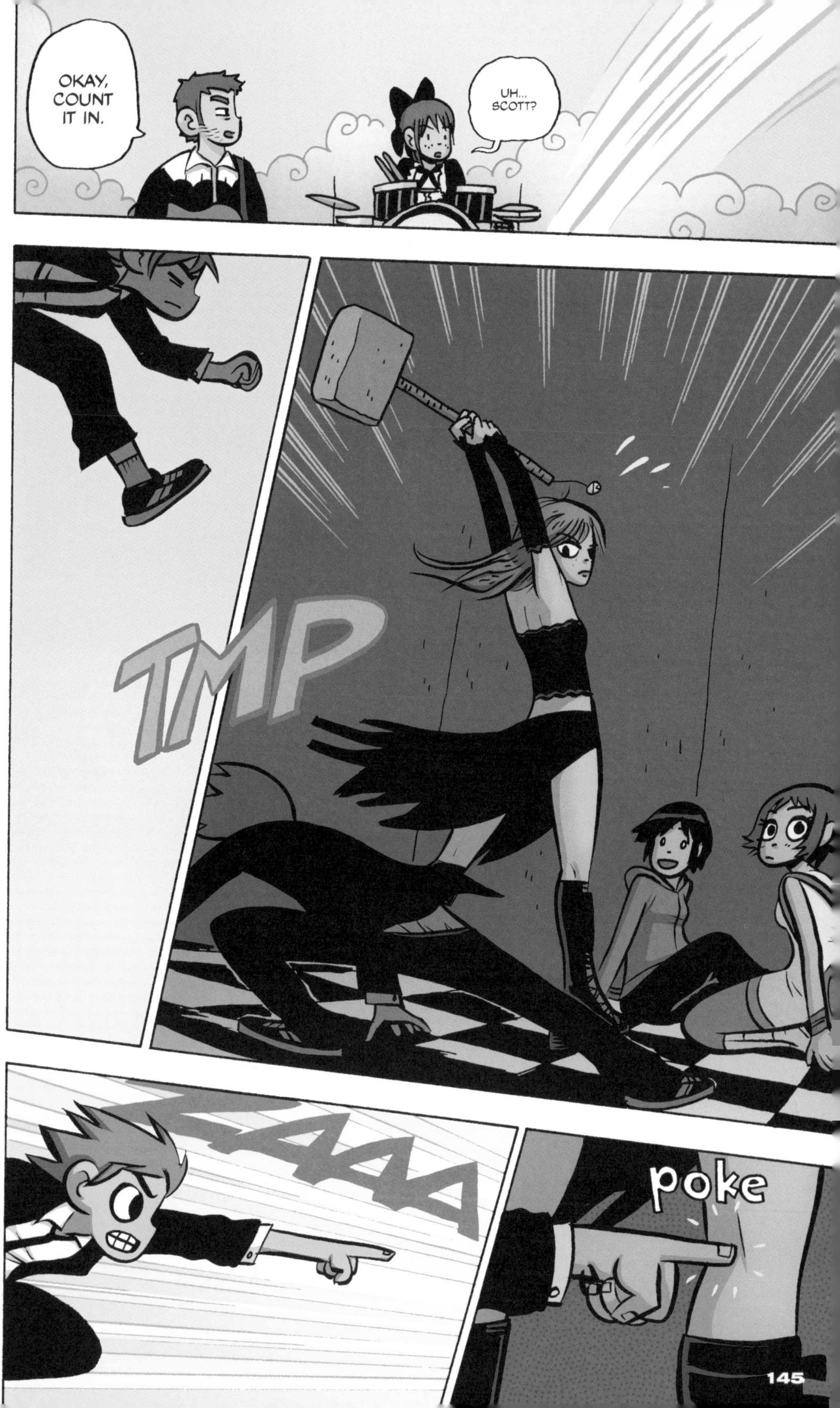
OKAY, COUNT IT IN.
UH... SCOTT?
TMP
ZAAAA
poke

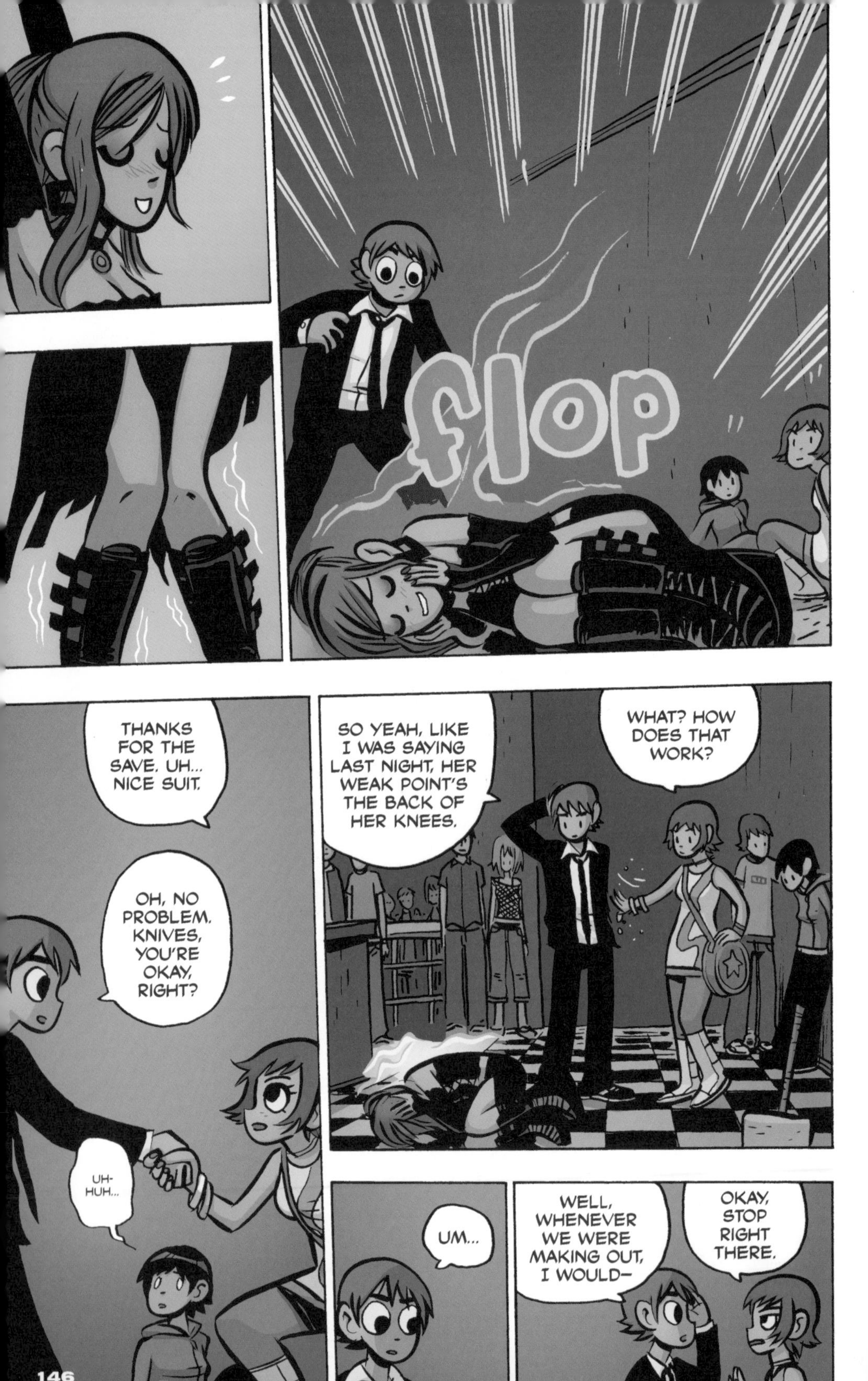
FLOP
THANKS FOR THE SAVE. UH... NICE SUIT.
OH, NO PROBLEM. KNIVES, YOU'RE OKAY, RIGHT?
UH-HUH...
SO YEAH, LIKE I WAS SAYING LAST NIGHT, HER WEAK POINT'S THE BACK OF HER KNEES.
WHAT? HOW DOES THAT WORK?
UM...
WELL, WHENEVER WE WERE MAKING OUT, I WOULD—
OKAY, STOP RIGHT THERE.

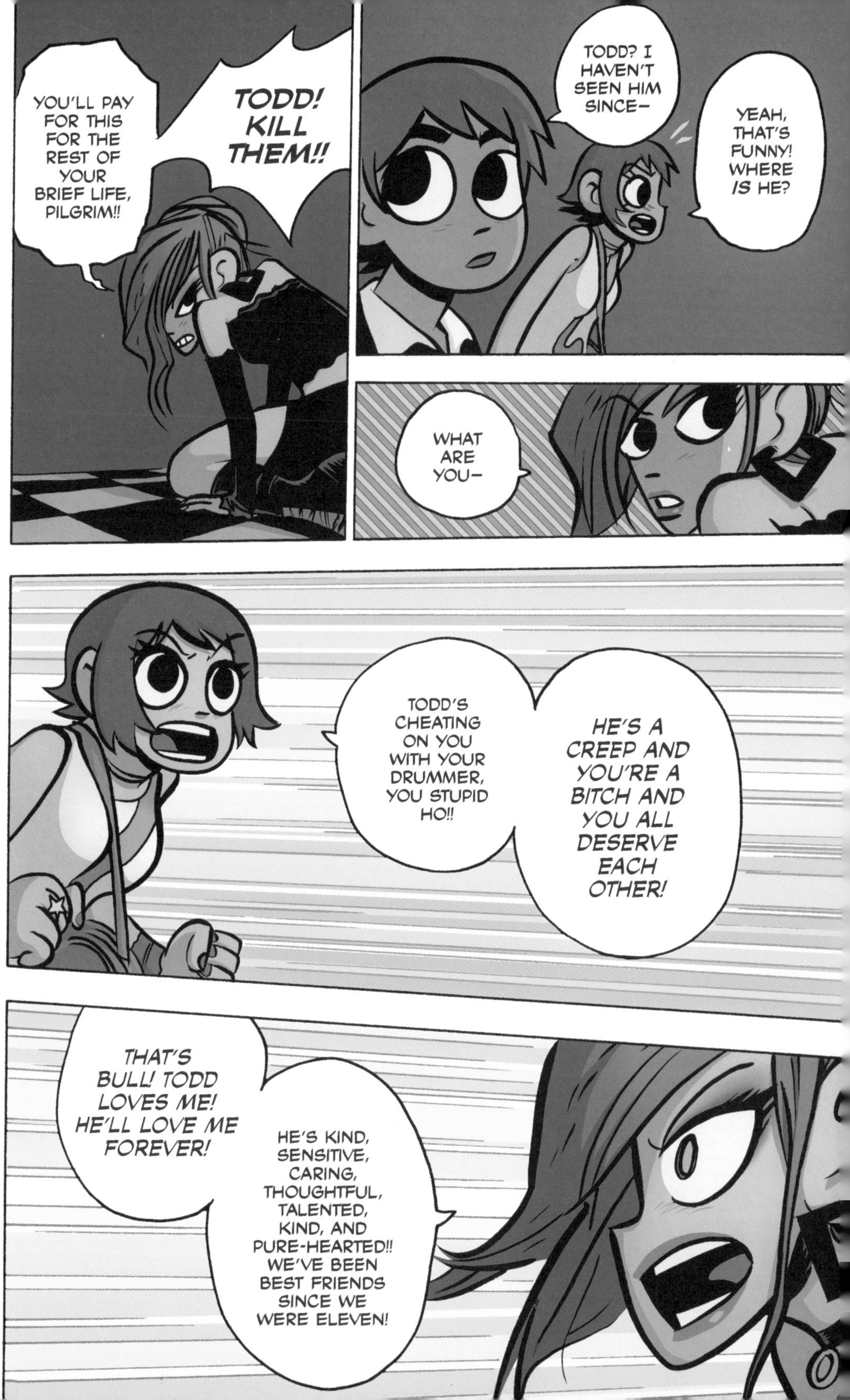
YOU'LL PAY FOR THIS FOR THE REST OF YOUR BRIEF LIFE, PILGRIM!!
TODD! KILL THEM!!
TODD? I HAVEN'T SEEN HIM SINCE–
YEAH, THAT'S FUNNY! WHERE IS HE?
WHAT ARE YOU–
TODD'S CHEATING ON YOU WITH YOUR DRUMMER, YOU STUPID HO!!
HE'S A CREEP AND YOU'RE A BITCH AND YOU ALL DESERVE EACH OTHER!
THAT'S BULL! TODD LOVES ME! HE'LL LOVE ME FOREVER!
HE'S KIND, SENSITIVE, CARING, THOUGHTFUL, TALENTED, KIND, AND PURE-HEARTED!! WE'VE BEEN BEST FRIENDS SINCE WE WERE ELEVEN!

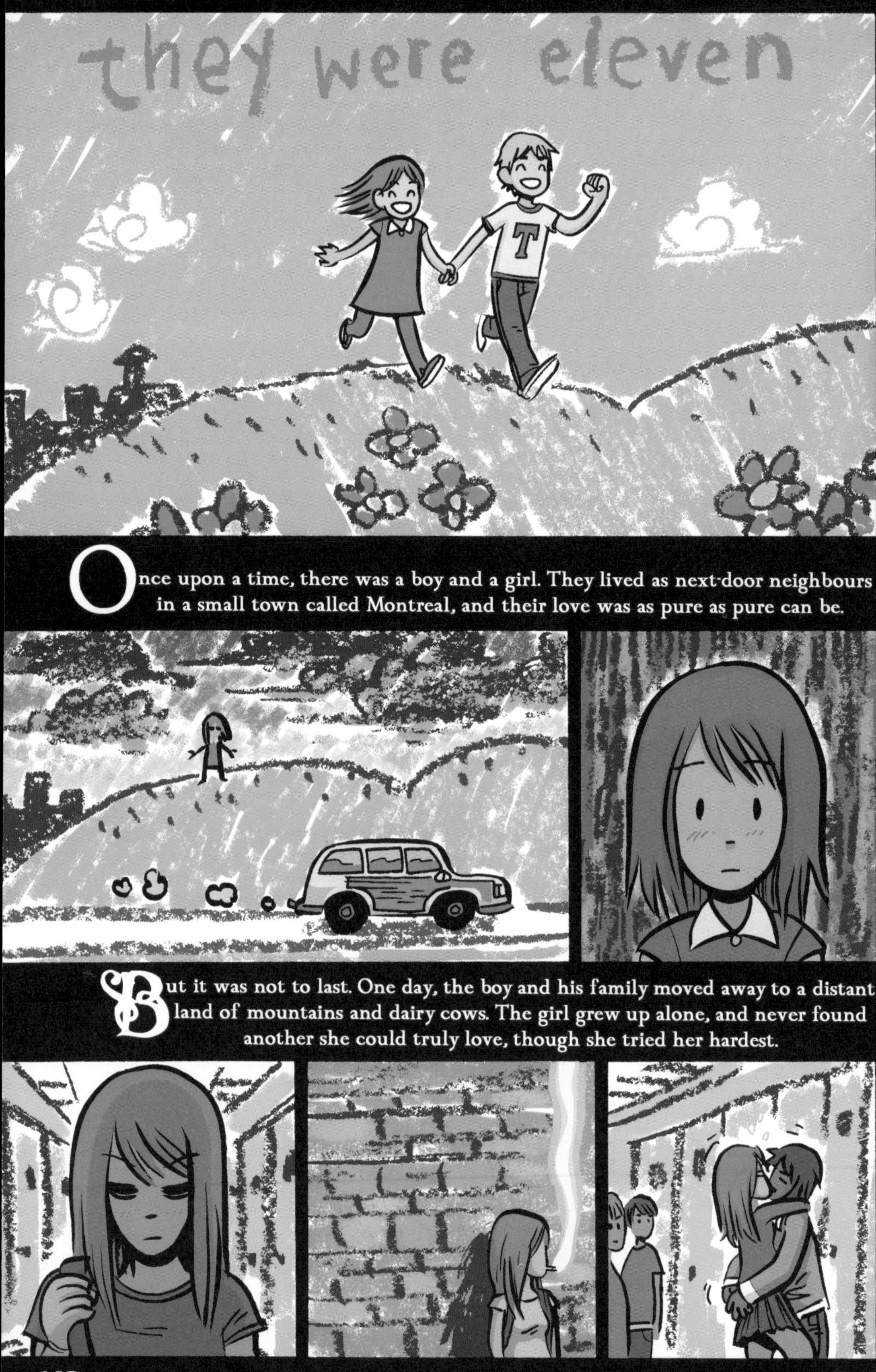
they were eleven
Once upon a time, there was a boy and a girl. They lived as next-door neighbours in a small town called Montreal, and their love was as pure as pure can be.
But it was not to last. One day, the boy and his family moved away to a distant land of mountains and dairy cows. The girl grew up alone, and never found another she could truly love, though she tried her hardest.

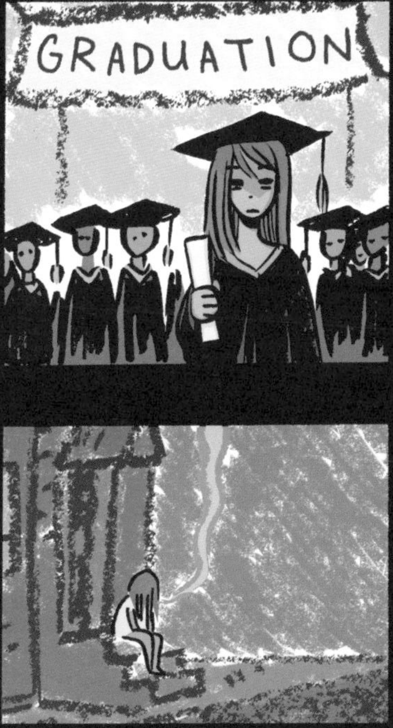
GRADUATION

And then, at last, when all seemed lost, the boy returned.

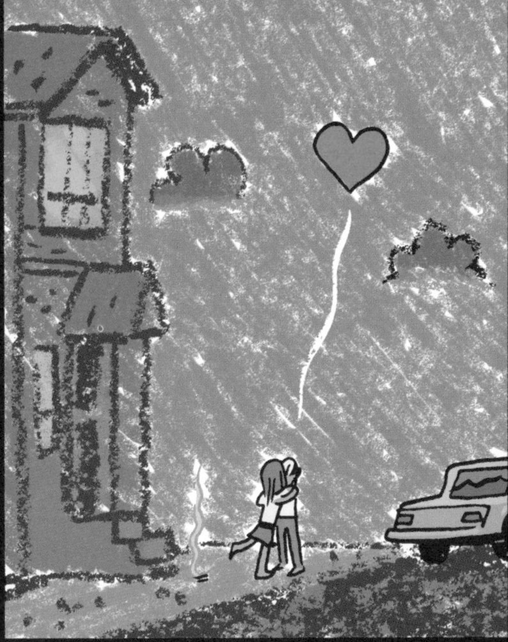

Promising they would never again part, the boy displayed his affection in a most remarkable and *unprecedented* fashion...

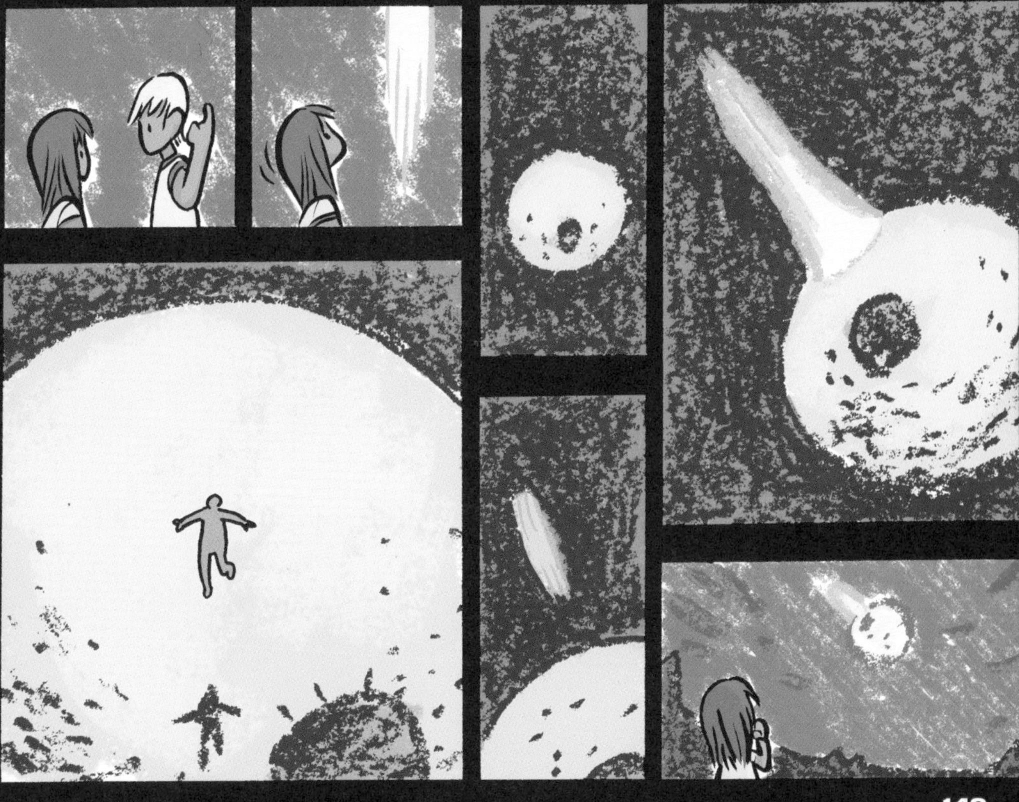

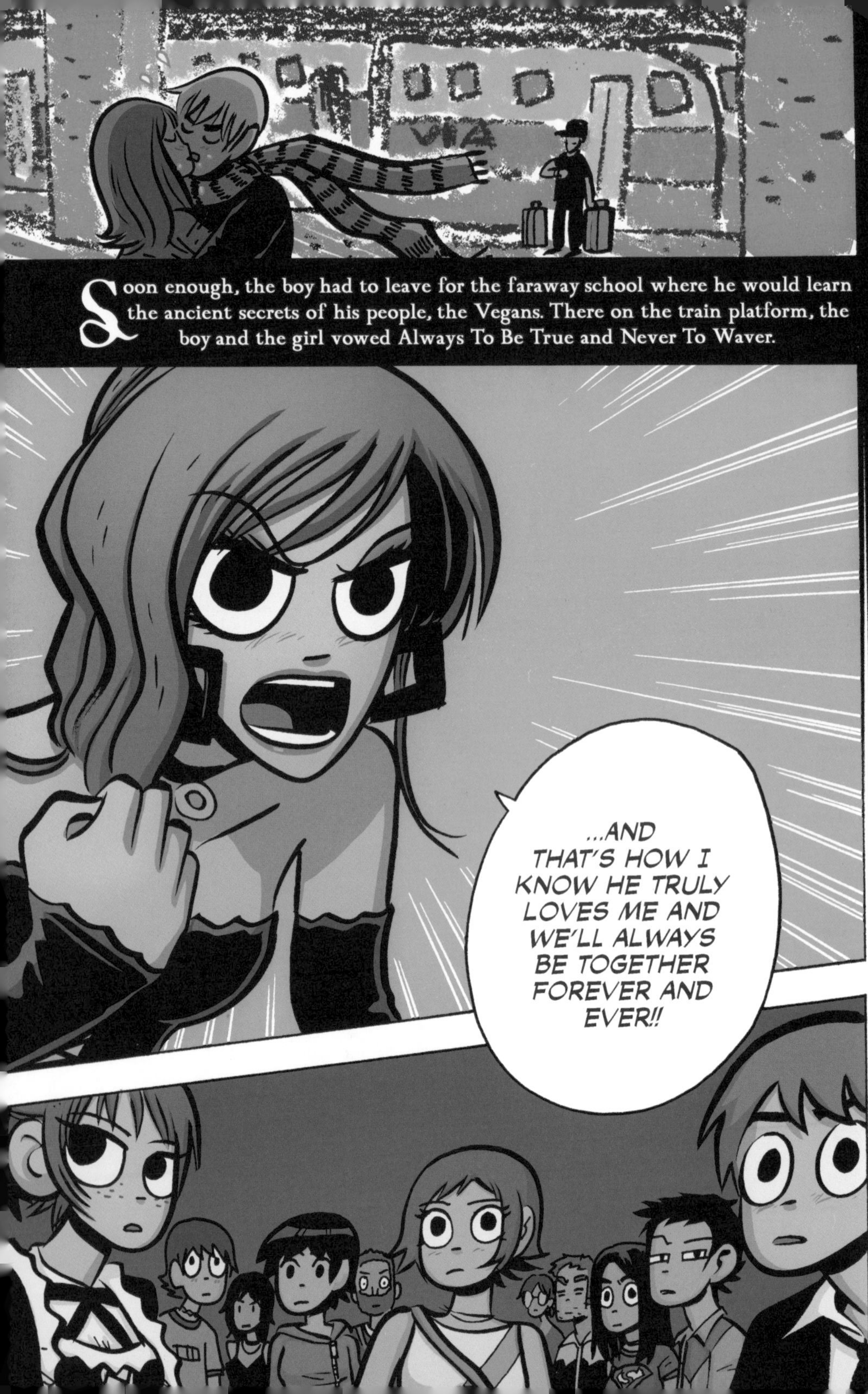
VIA
Soon enough, the boy had to leave for the faraway school where he would learn the ancient secrets of his people, the Vegans. There on the train platform, the boy and the girl vowed Always To Be True and Never To Waver.
...AND THAT'S HOW I KNOW HE TRULY LOVES ME AND WE'LL ALWAYS BE TOGETHER FOREVER AND EVER!!

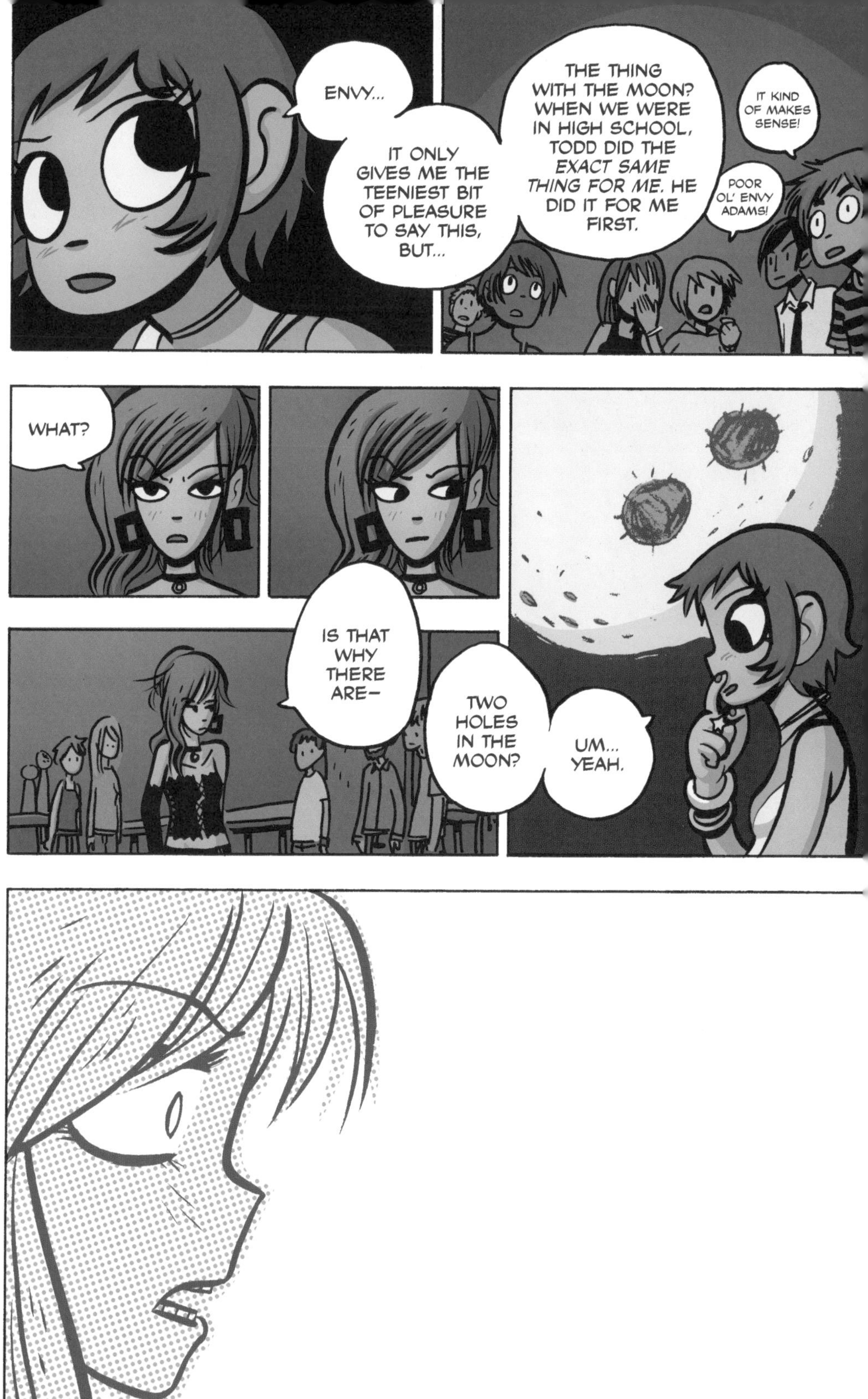
ENVY...
IT ONLY GIVES ME THE TEENIEST BIT OF PLEASURE TO SAY THIS, BUT...
THE THING WITH THE MOON? WHEN WE WERE IN HIGH SCHOOL, TODD DID THE *EXACT SAME THING FOR ME.* HE DID IT FOR ME FIRST.
IT KIND OF MAKES SENSE!
POOR OL' ENVY ADAMS!
WHAT?
IS THAT WHY THERE ARE–
TWO HOLES IN THE MOON?
UM... YEAH.

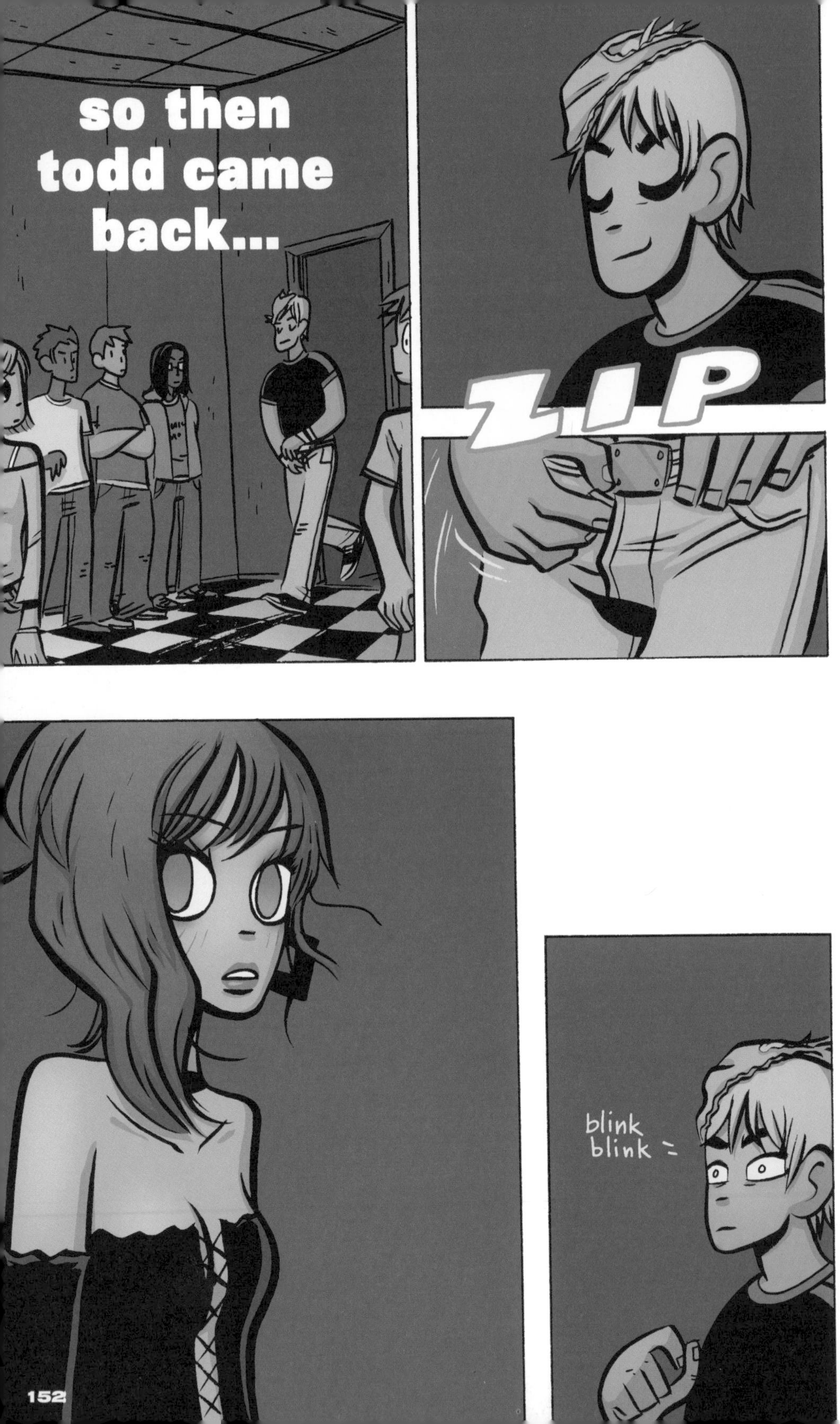
so then todd came back...
ZIP
blink
blink

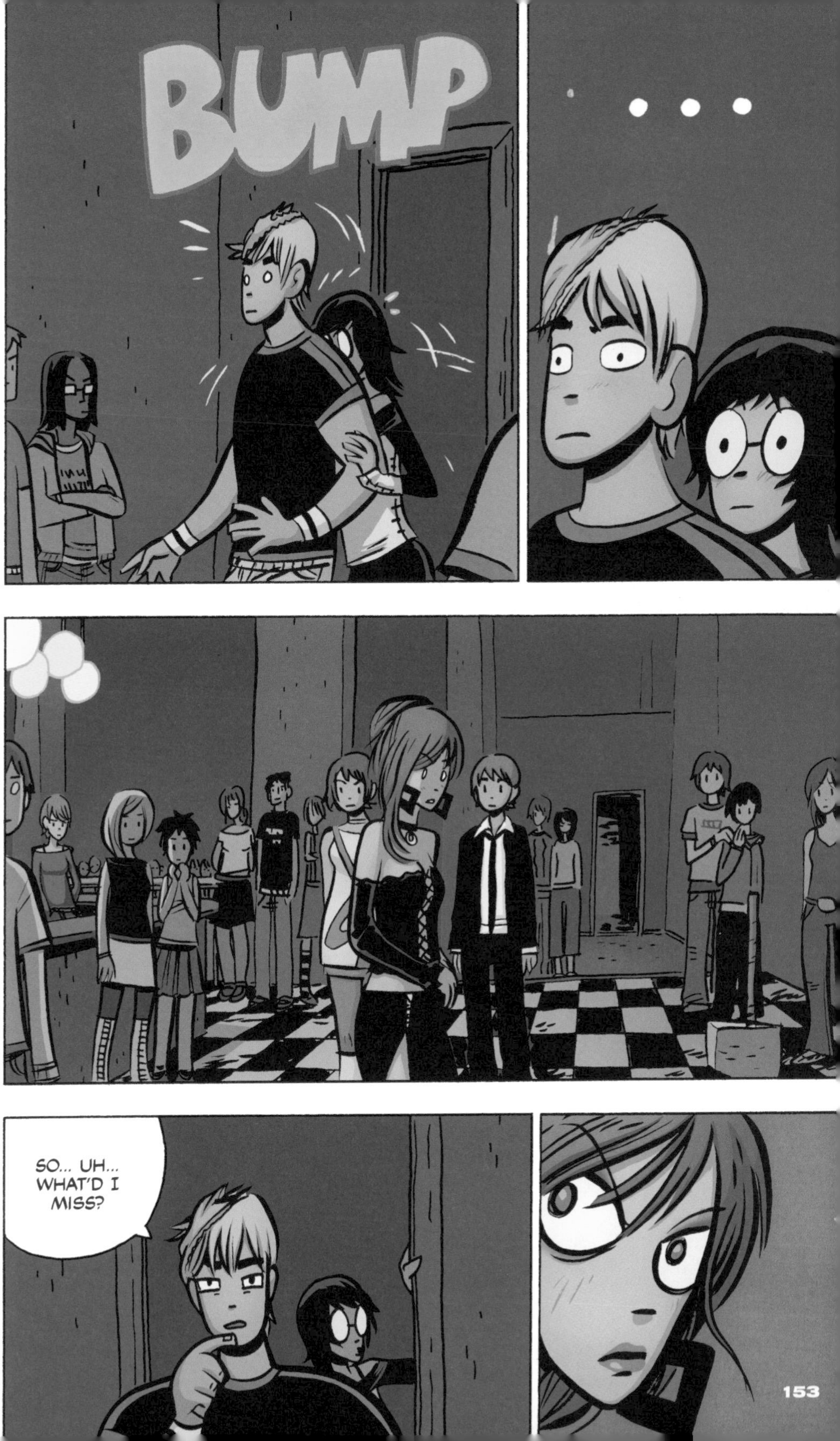
BUMP
...
SO... UH... WHAT'D I MISS?

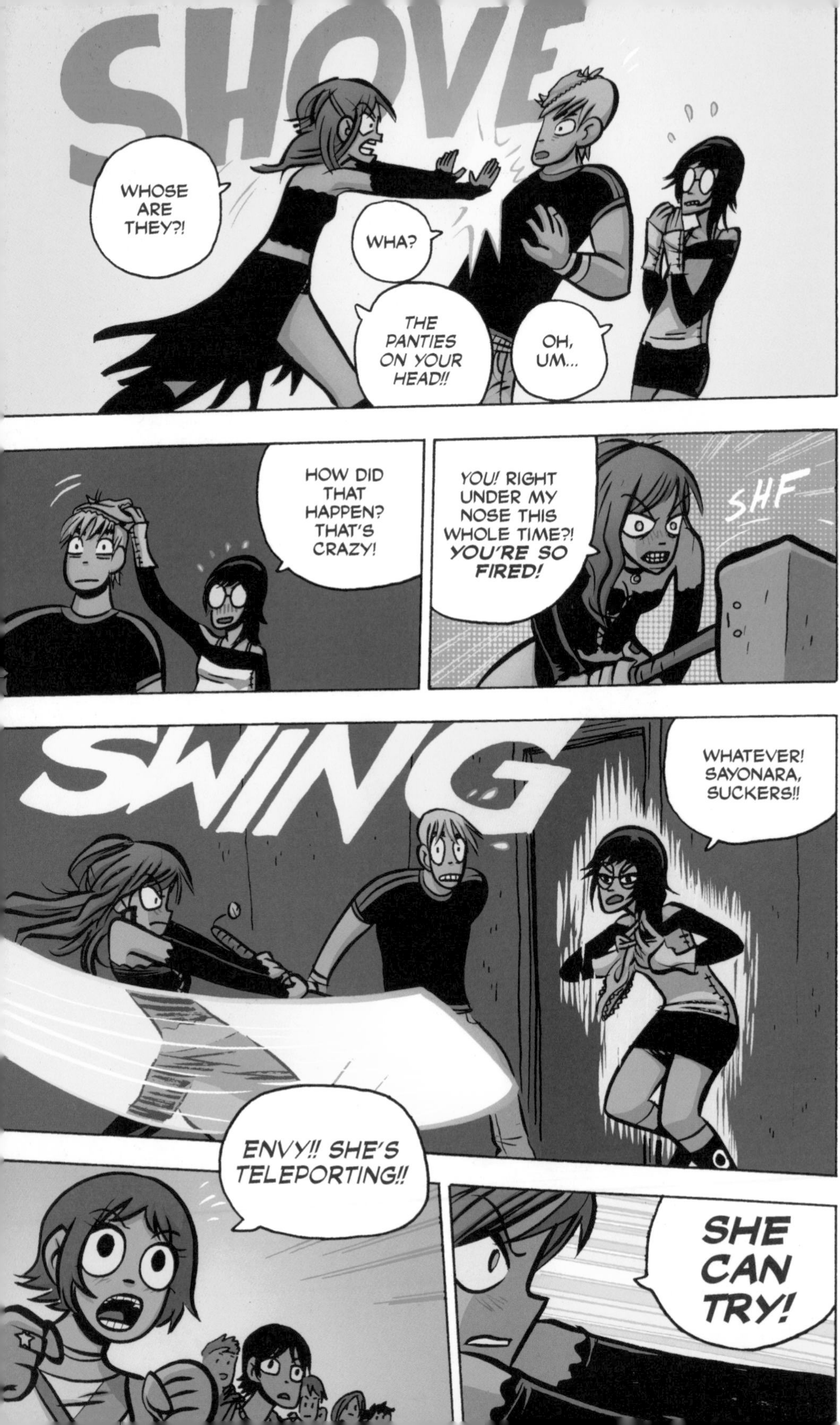
SHOVE
WHOSE ARE THEY?!
WHA?
THE PANTIES ON YOUR HEAD!!
OH, UM...
HOW DID THAT HAPPEN? THAT'S CRAZY!
YOU! RIGHT UNDER MY NOSE THIS WHOLE TIME?! YOU'RE SO FIRED!
SHF
SWING
WHATEVER! SAYONARA, SUCKERS!!
ENVY!! SHE'S TELEPORTING!!
SHE CAN TRY!

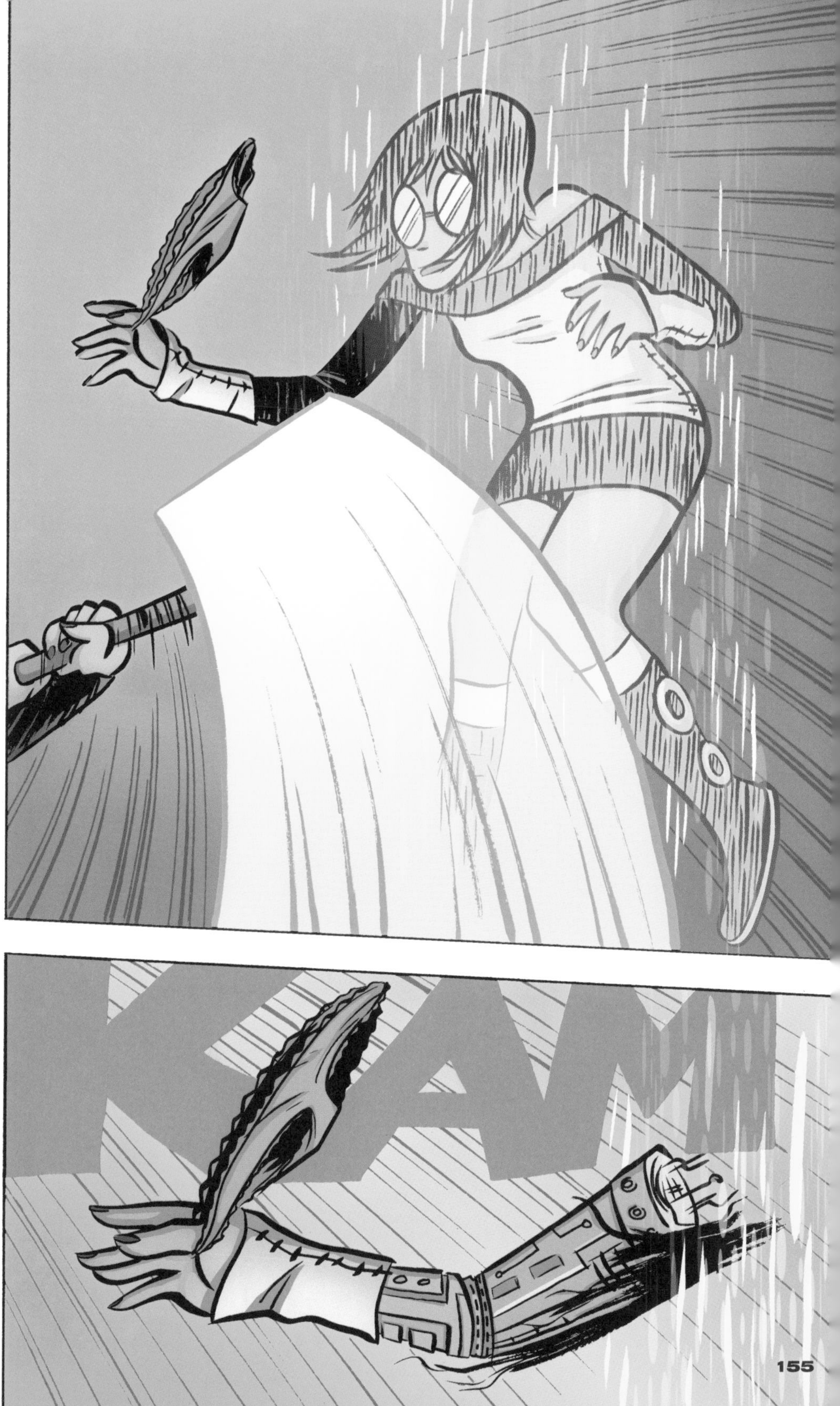
KAM

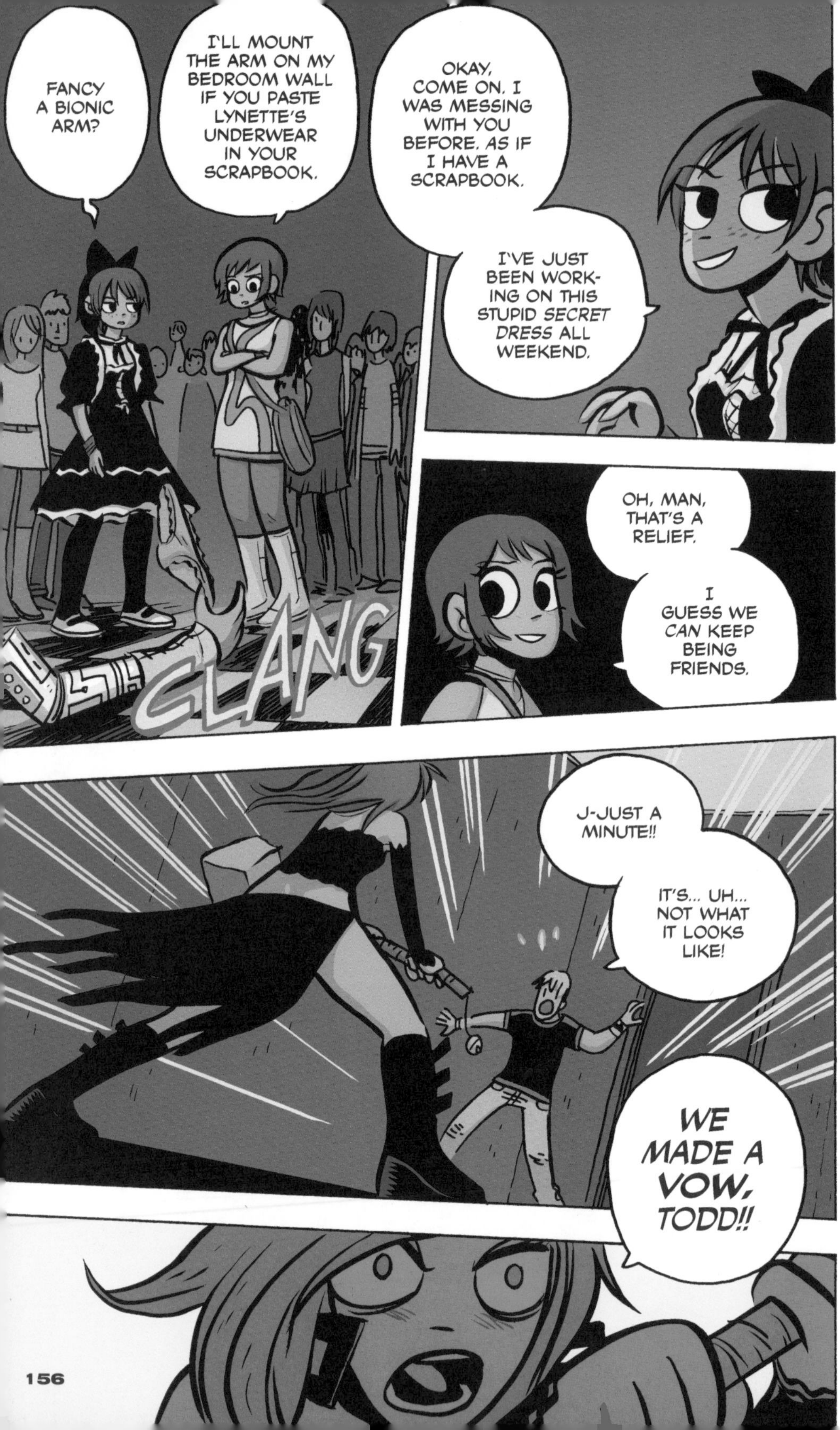
FANCY A BIONIC ARM?
I'LL MOUNT THE ARM ON MY BEDROOM WALL IF YOU PASTE LYNETTE'S UNDERWEAR IN YOUR SCRAPBOOK.
OKAY, COME ON. I WAS MESSING WITH YOU BEFORE. AS IF I HAVE A SCRAPBOOK.
I'VE JUST BEEN WORKING ON THIS STUPID *SECRET DRESS* ALL WEEKEND.
CLANG
OH, MAN, THAT'S A RELIEF.
I GUESS WE *CAN* KEEP BEING FRIENDS.
J-JUST A MINUTE!!
IT'S... UH... NOT WHAT IT LOOKS LIKE!
WE MADE A VOW, TODD!!

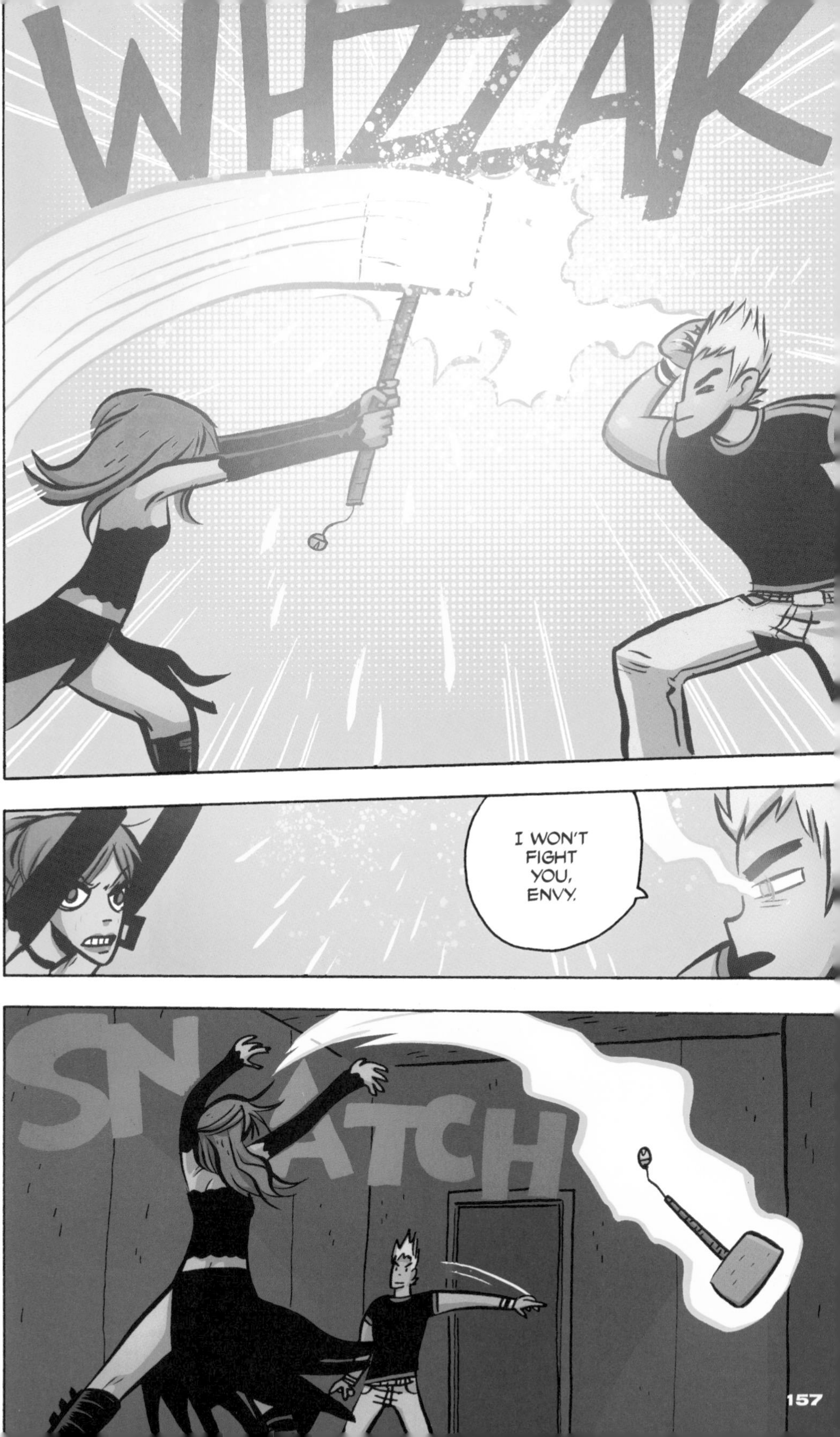
WHZZAK
I WON'T FIGHT YOU, ENVY.
SNATCH

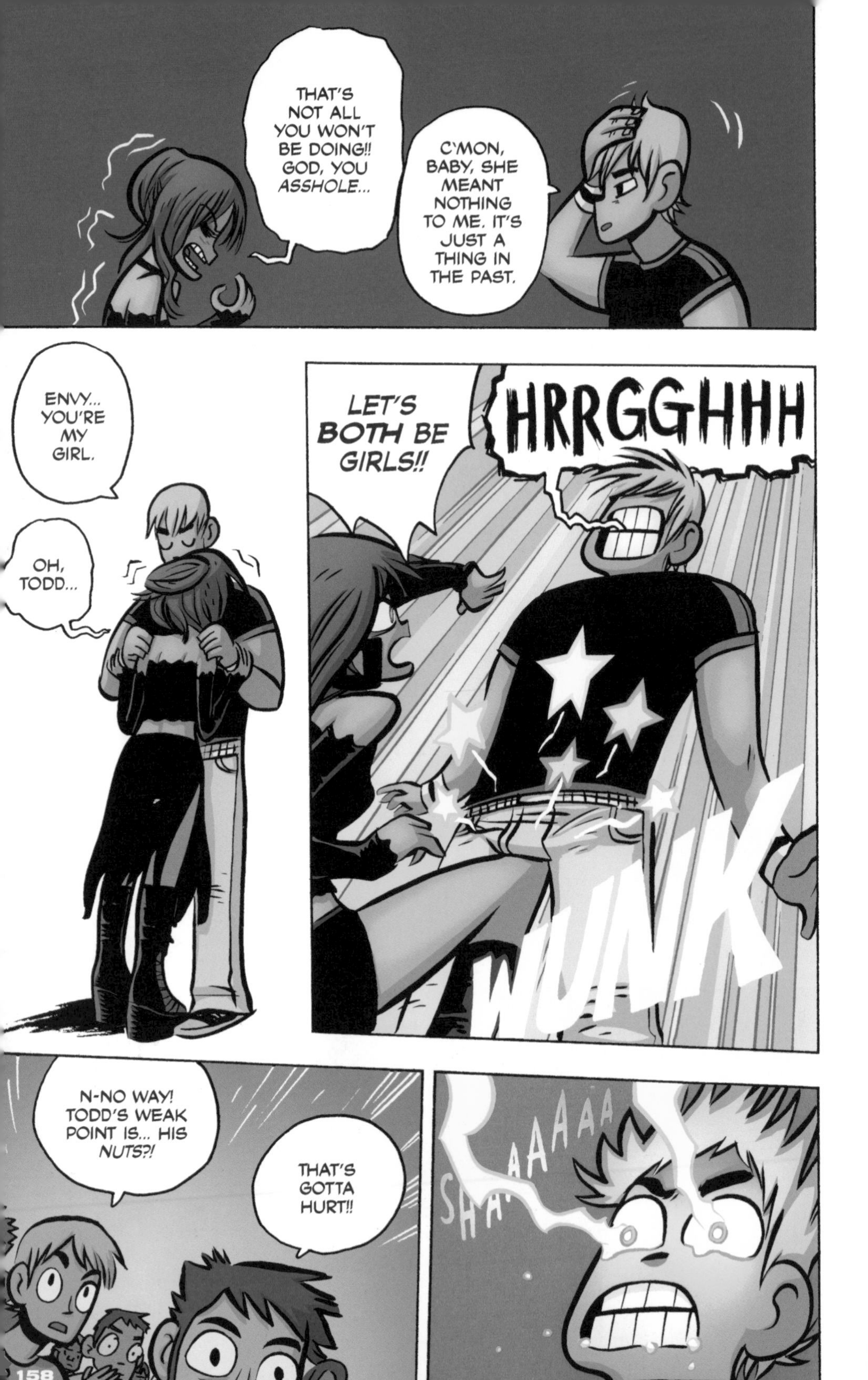
THAT'S NOT ALL YOU WON'T BE DOING!! GOD, YOU ASSHOLE...
C'MON, BABY, SHE MEANT NOTHING TO ME. IT'S JUST A THING IN THE PAST.
ENVY... YOU'RE MY GIRL.
OH, TODD...
LET'S BOTH BE GIRLS!!
HRRGGHHH
WUNK
N-NO WAY! TODD'S WEAK POINT IS... HIS NUTS?!
THAT'S GOTTA HURT!!
AAAAAA
SHA

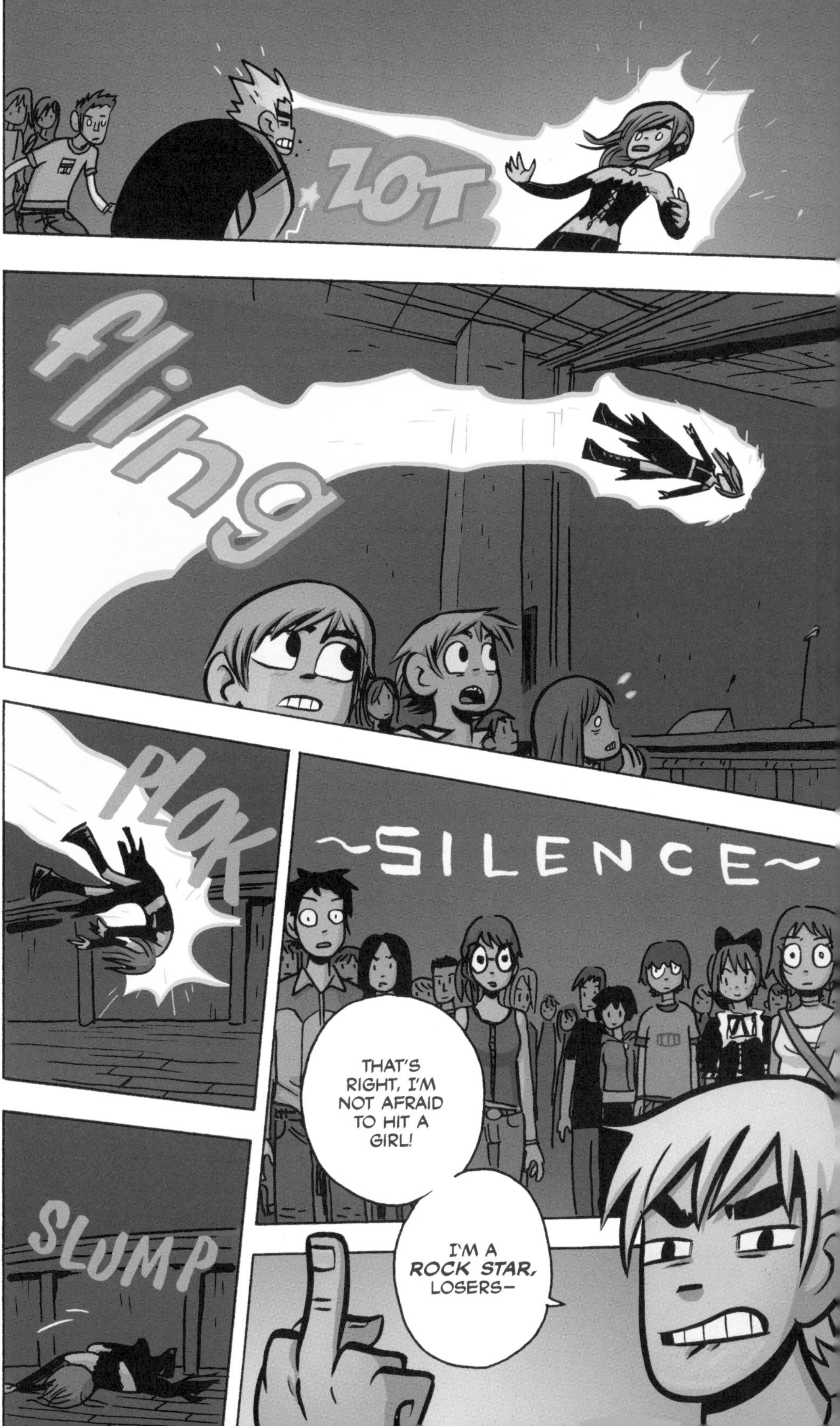
ZOT
fling
PLOK
~SILENCE~
SLUMP
THAT'S RIGHT, I'M NOT AFRAID TO HIT A GIRL!
I'M A ROCK STAR, LOSERS—

18 DESTROY ALL VEGANS

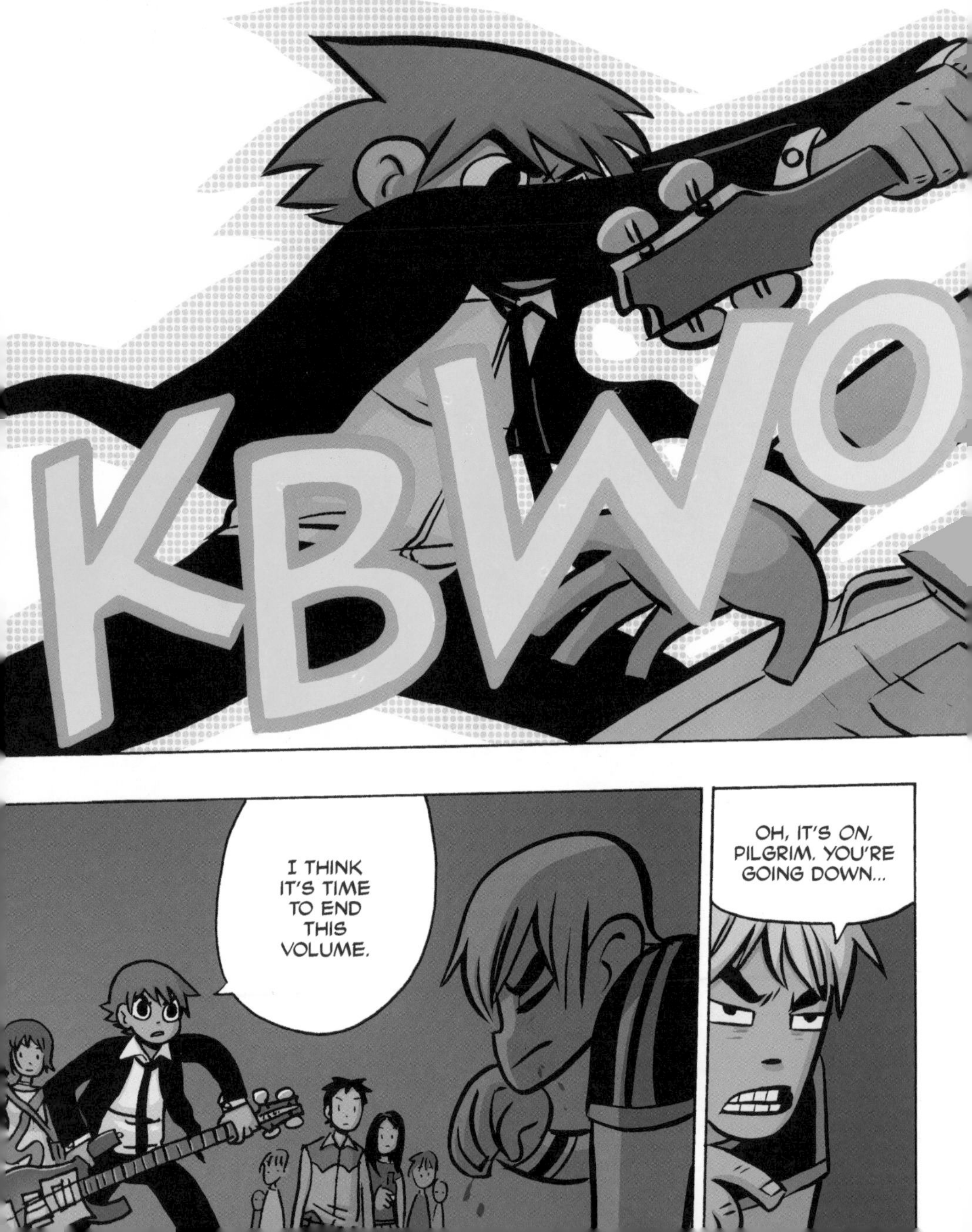
KBWO
I THINK IT'S TIME TO END THIS VOLUME.
OH, IT'S ON, PILGRIM. YOU'RE GOING DOWN...

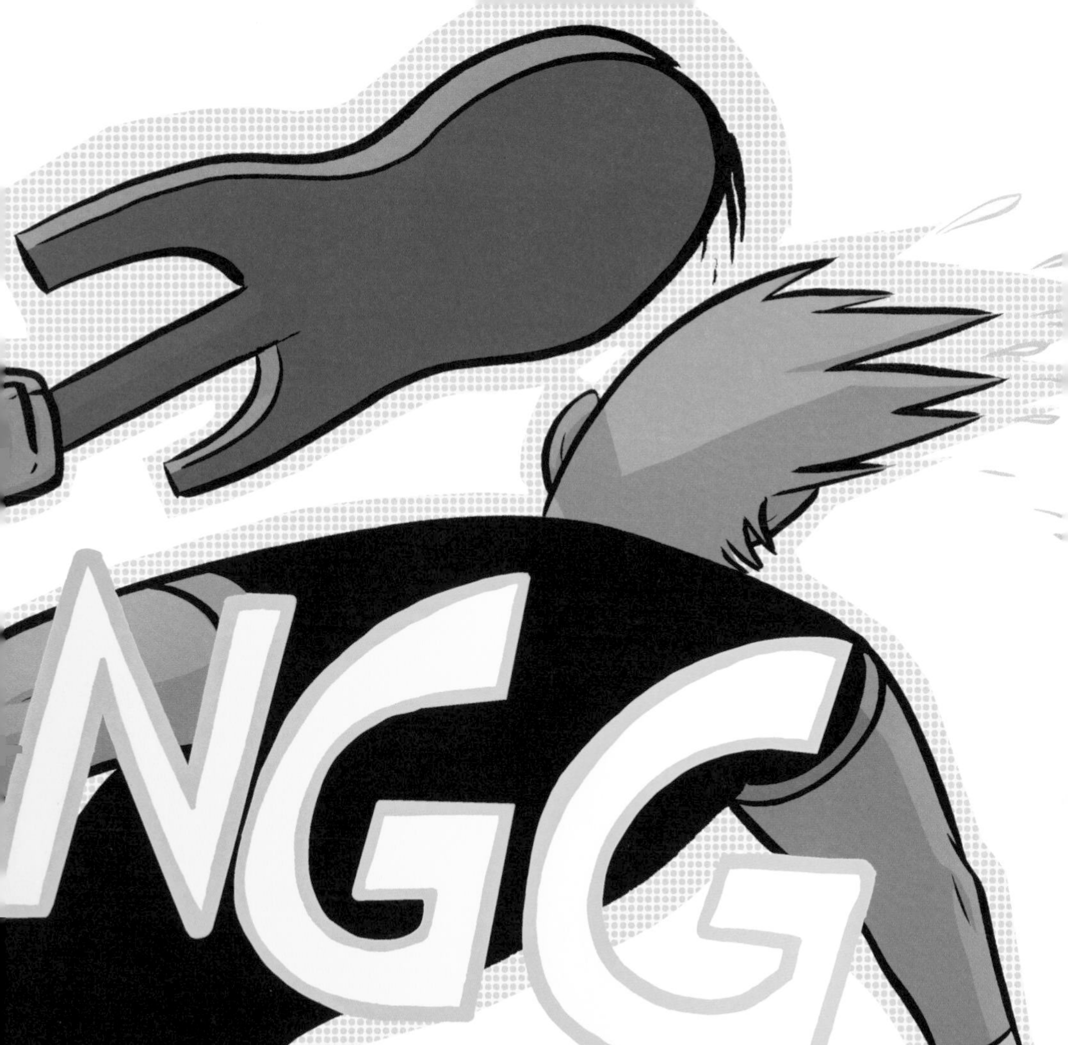
NGG
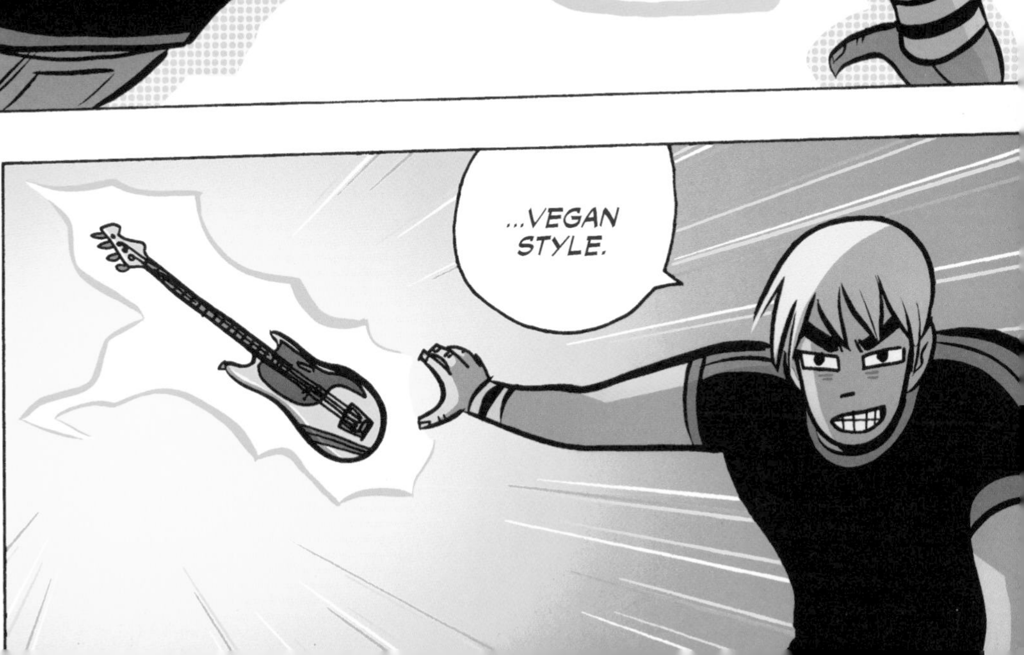
...VEGAN STYLE.

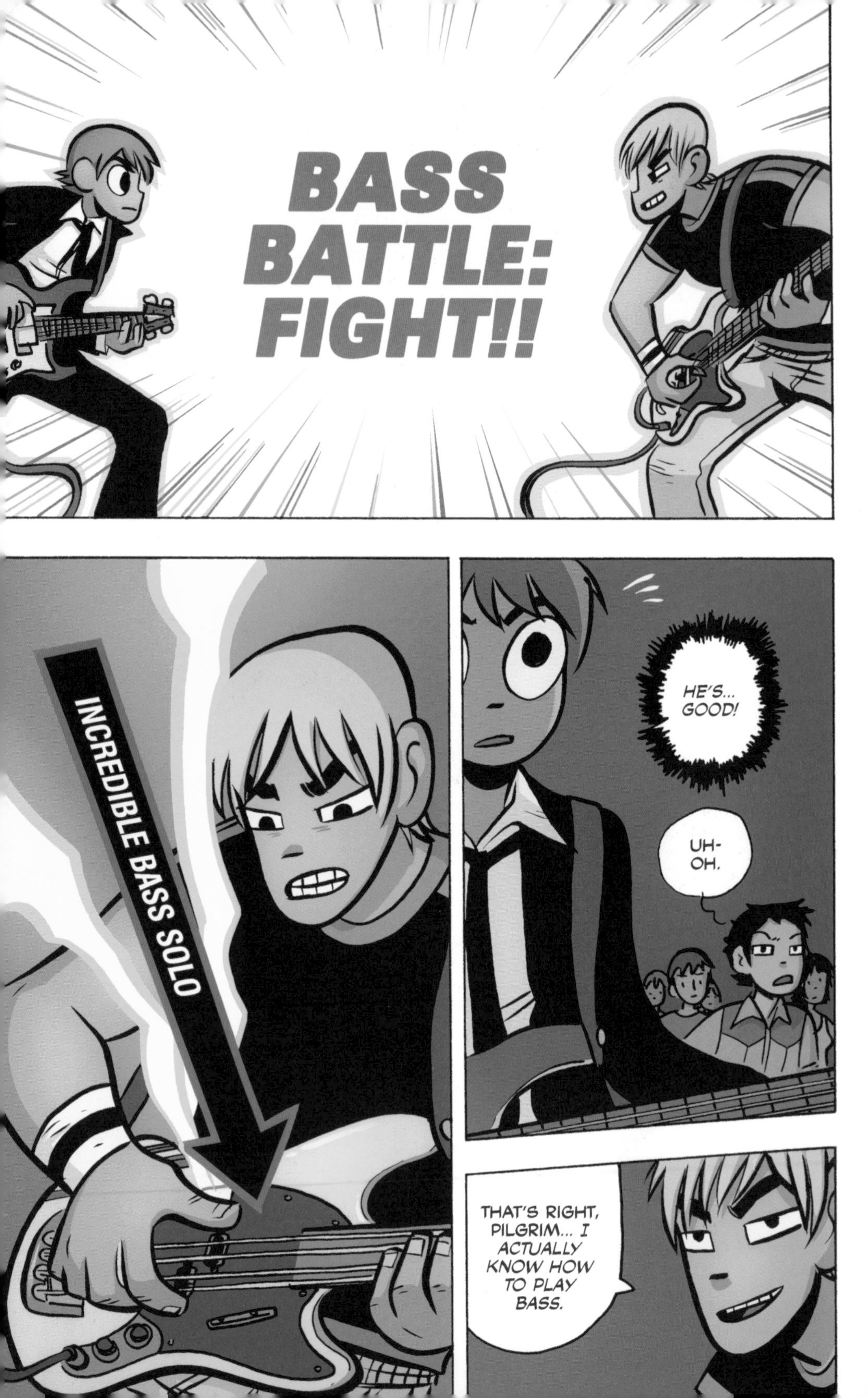
BASS BATTLE: FIGHT!!
INCREDIBLE BASS SOLO
HE'S... GOOD!
UH-OH.
THAT'S RIGHT, PILGRIM... I ACTUALLY KNOW HOW TO PLAY BASS.

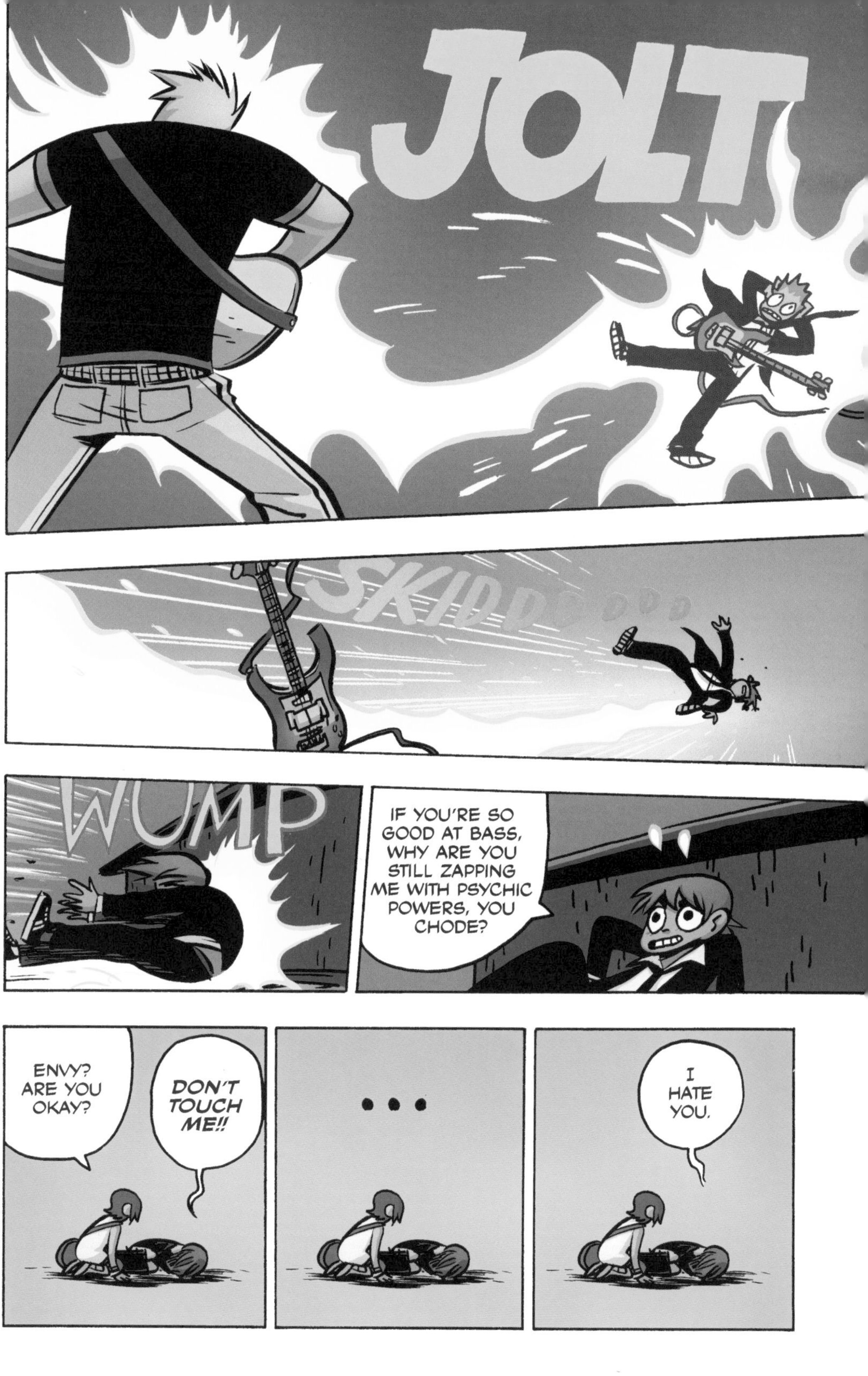
JOLT
SKIDDDDDD
WUMP
IF YOU'RE SO GOOD AT BASS, WHY ARE YOU STILL ZAPPING ME WITH PSYCHIC POWERS, YOU CHODE?
ENVY? ARE YOU OKAY?
DON'T TOUCH ME!!
...
I HATE YOU.

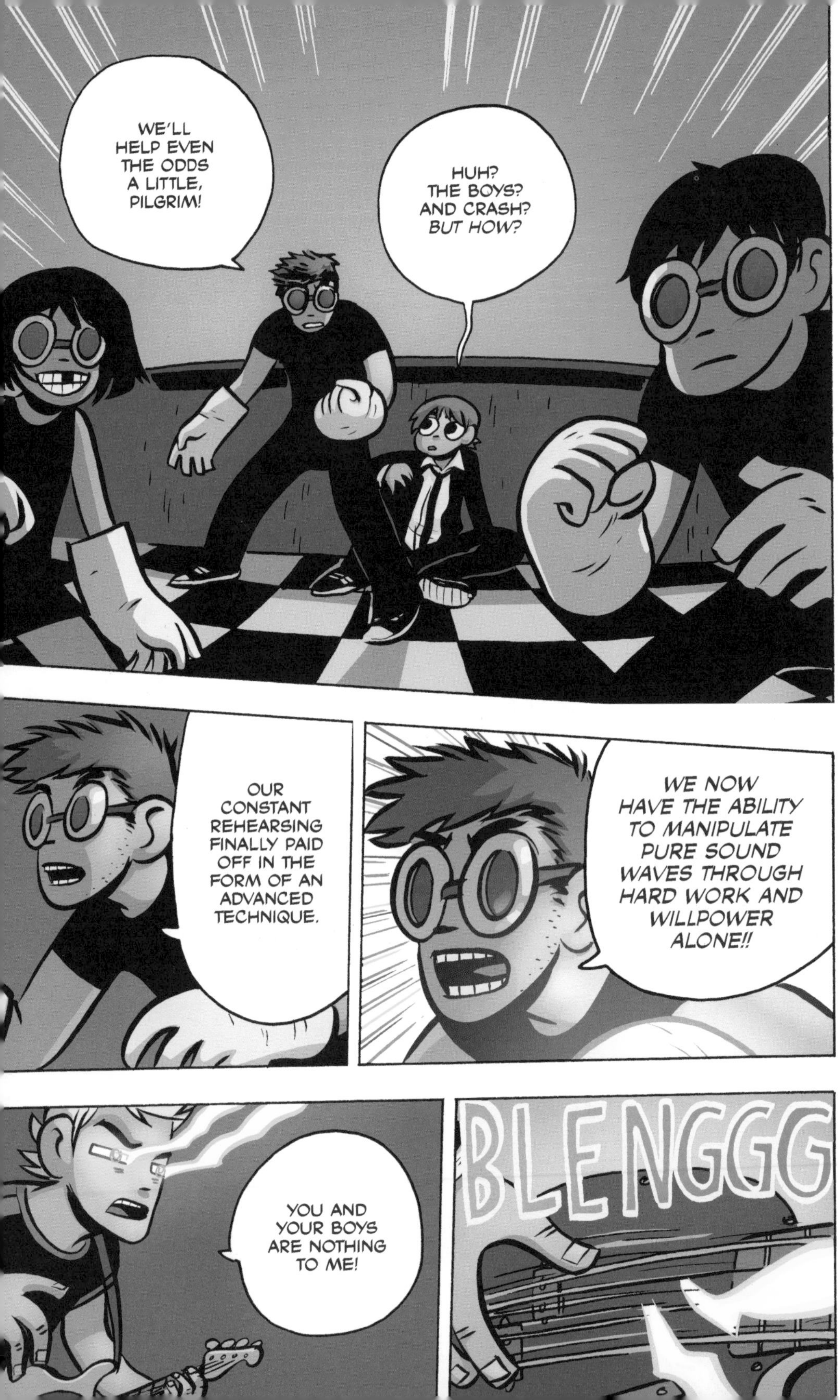
WE'LL HELP EVEN THE ODDS A LITTLE, PILGRIM!
HUH? THE BOYS? AND CRASH? *BUT HOW?*
OUR CONSTANT REHEARSING FINALLY PAID OFF IN THE FORM OF AN ADVANCED TECHNIQUE.
WE NOW HAVE THE ABILITY TO MANIPULATE PURE SOUND WAVES THROUGH HARD WORK AND WILLPOWER ALONE!!
YOU AND YOUR BOYS ARE NOTHING TO ME!
BLENGGG

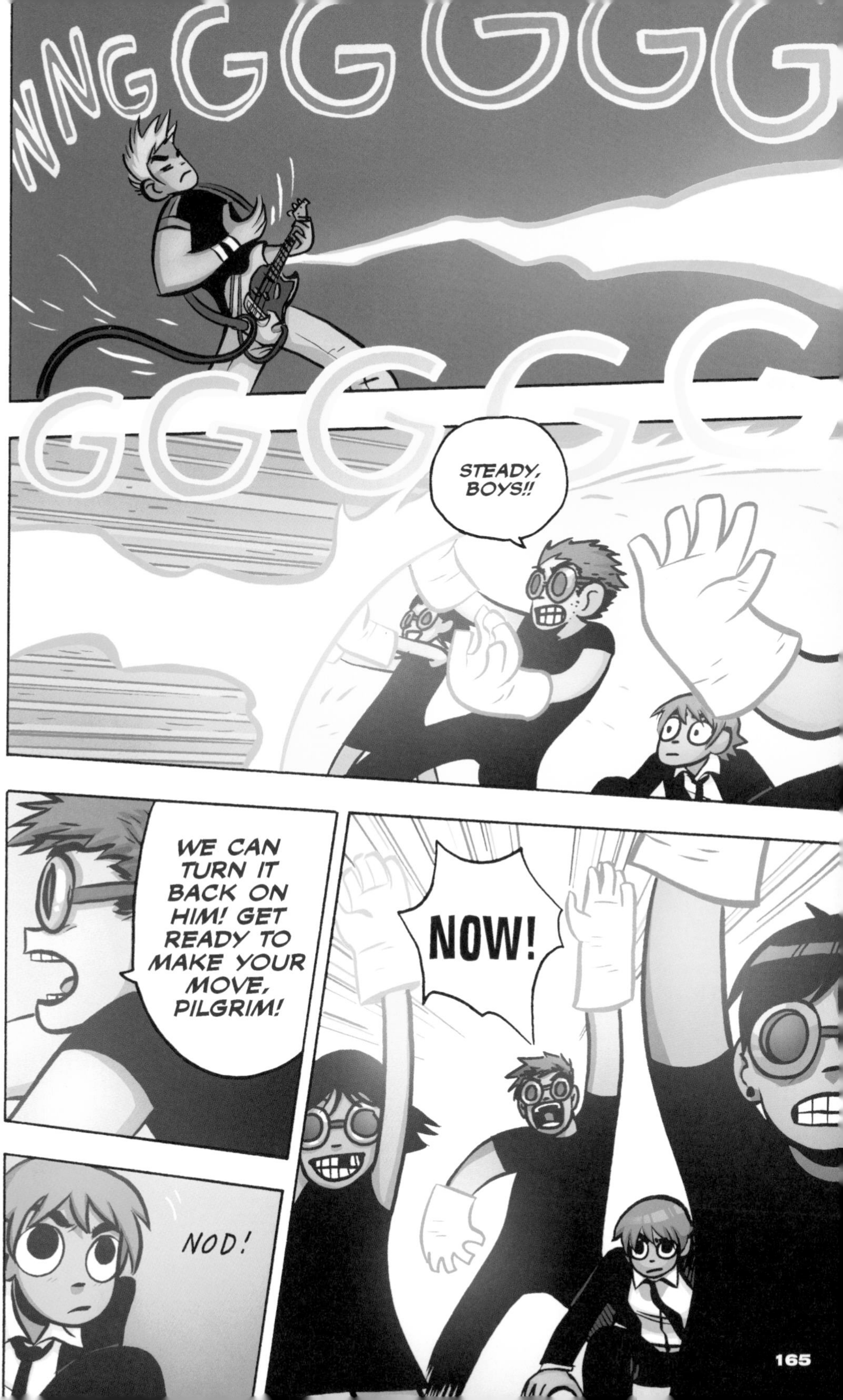
WNGGGGGG
GGGGGG
STEADY, BOYS!!
WE CAN TURN IT BACK ON HIM! GET READY TO MAKE YOUR MOVE, PILGRIM!
NOW!
NOD!

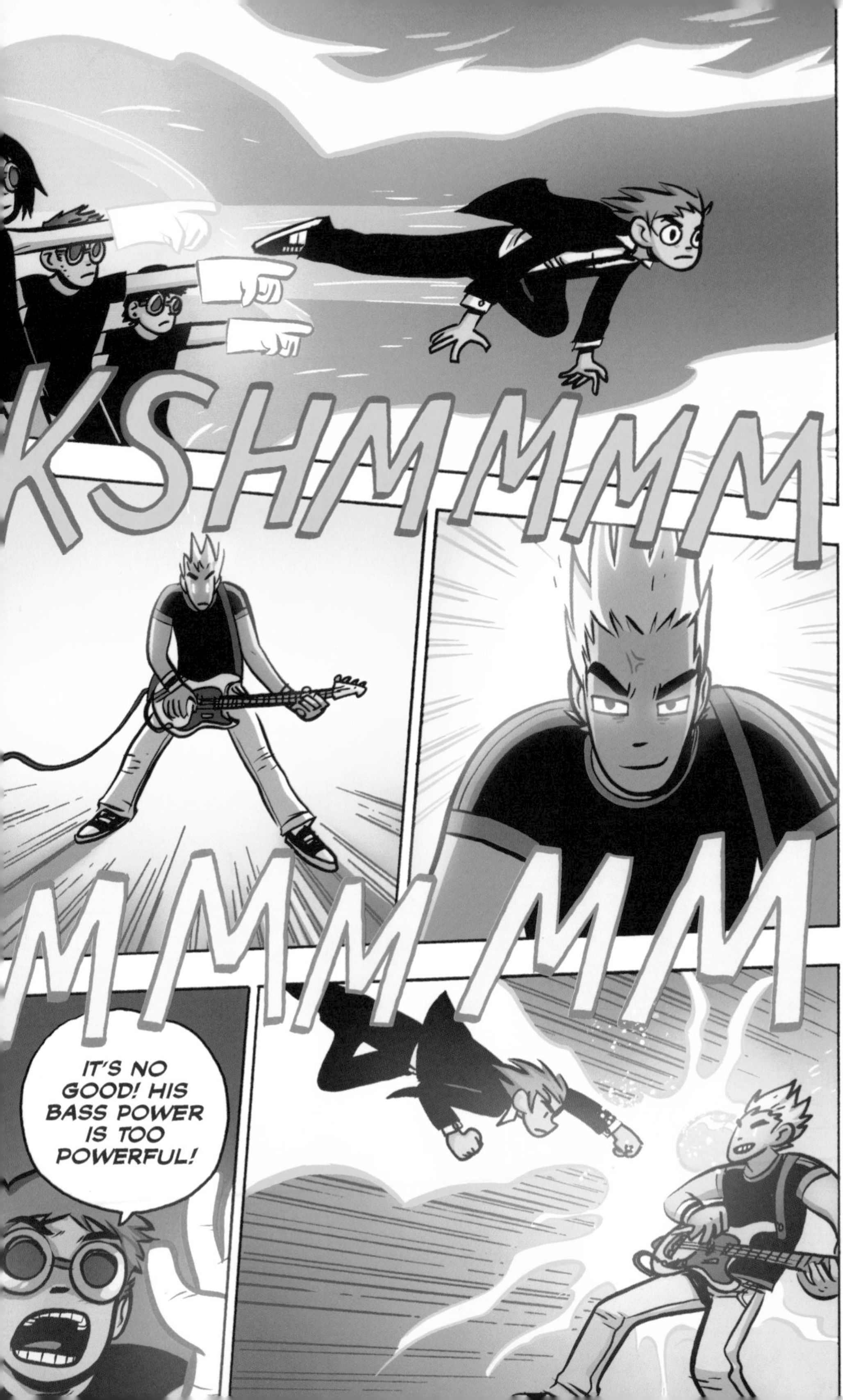
KSHMMMM
MMMMM
IT'S NO GOOD! HIS BASS POWER IS TOO POWERFUL!

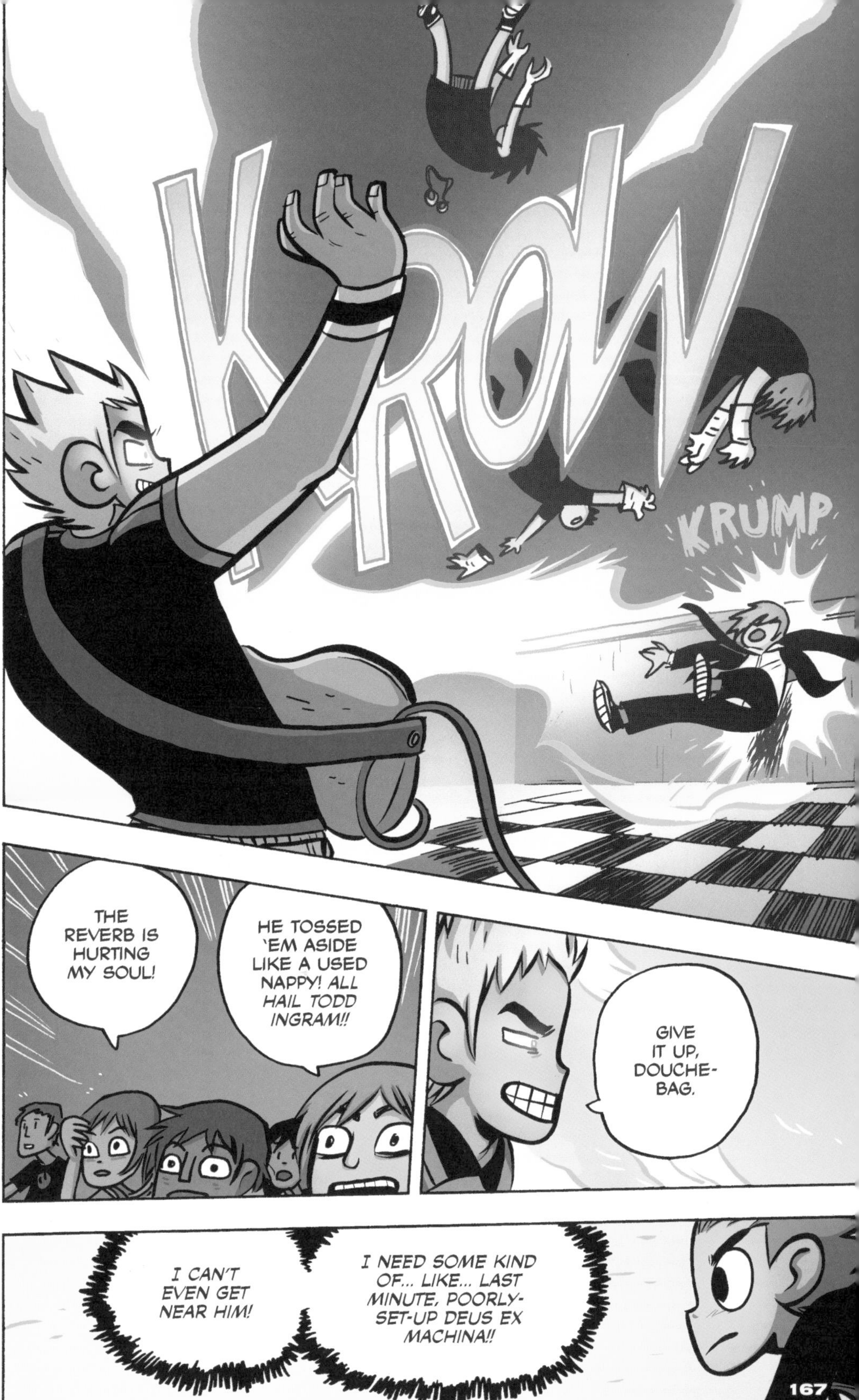
KROW
KRUMP
THE REVERB IS HURTING MY SOUL!
HE TOSSED 'EM ASIDE LIKE A USED NAPPY! ALL HAIL TODD INGRAM!!
GIVE IT UP, DOUCHE-BAG.
I CAN'T EVEN GET NEAR HIM!
I NEED SOME KIND OF... LIKE... LAST MINUTE, POORLY-SET-UP DEUS EX MACHINA!!

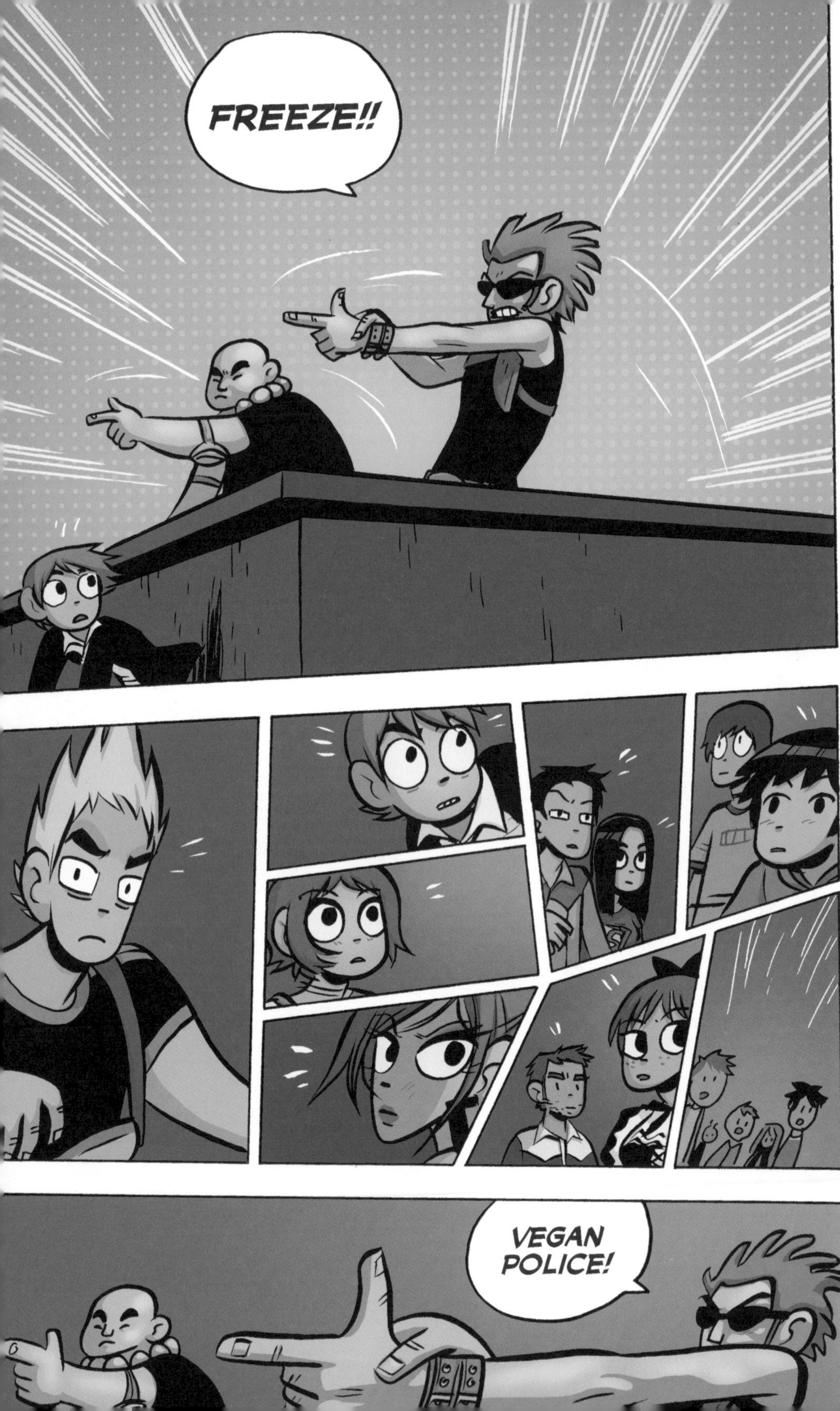
FREEZE!!
VEGAN POLICE!

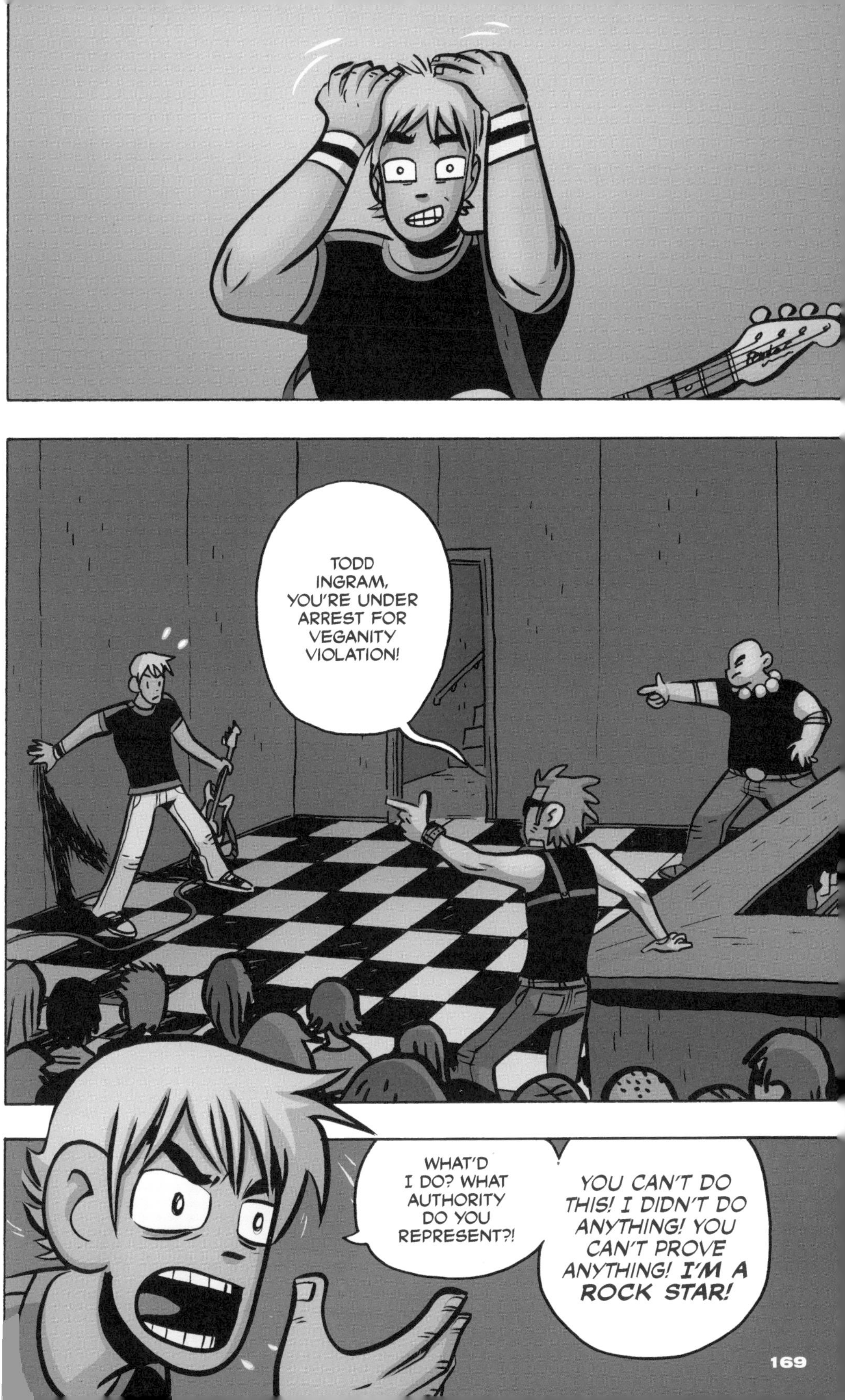
TODD INGRAM, YOU'RE UNDER ARREST FOR VEGANITY VIOLATION!
WHAT'D I DO? WHAT AUTHORITY DO YOU REPRESENT?!
YOU CAN'T DO THIS! I DIDN'T DO ANYTHING! YOU CAN'T PROVE ANYTHING! I'M A ROCK STAR!

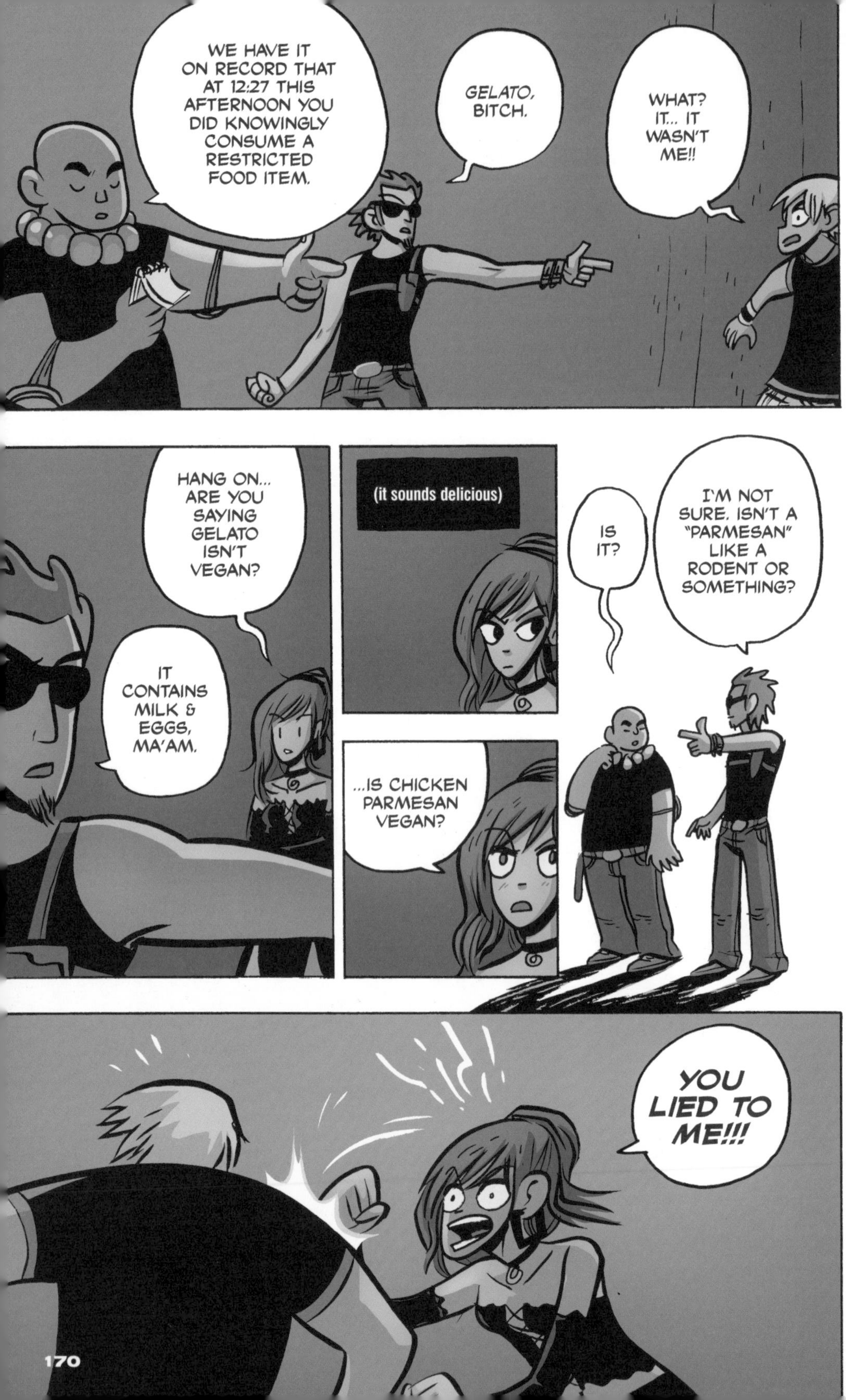
WE HAVE IT ON RECORD THAT AT 12:27 THIS AFTERNOON YOU DID KNOWINGLY CONSUME A RESTRICTED FOOD ITEM.
GELATO, BITCH.
WHAT? IT... IT WASN'T ME!!
HANG ON... ARE YOU SAYING GELATO ISN'T VEGAN?
IT CONTAINS MILK & EGGS, MA'AM.
(it sounds delicious)
...IS CHICKEN PARMESAN VEGAN?
IS IT?
I'M NOT SURE. ISN'T A "PARMESAN" LIKE A RODENT OR SOMETHING?
YOU LIED TO ME!!!

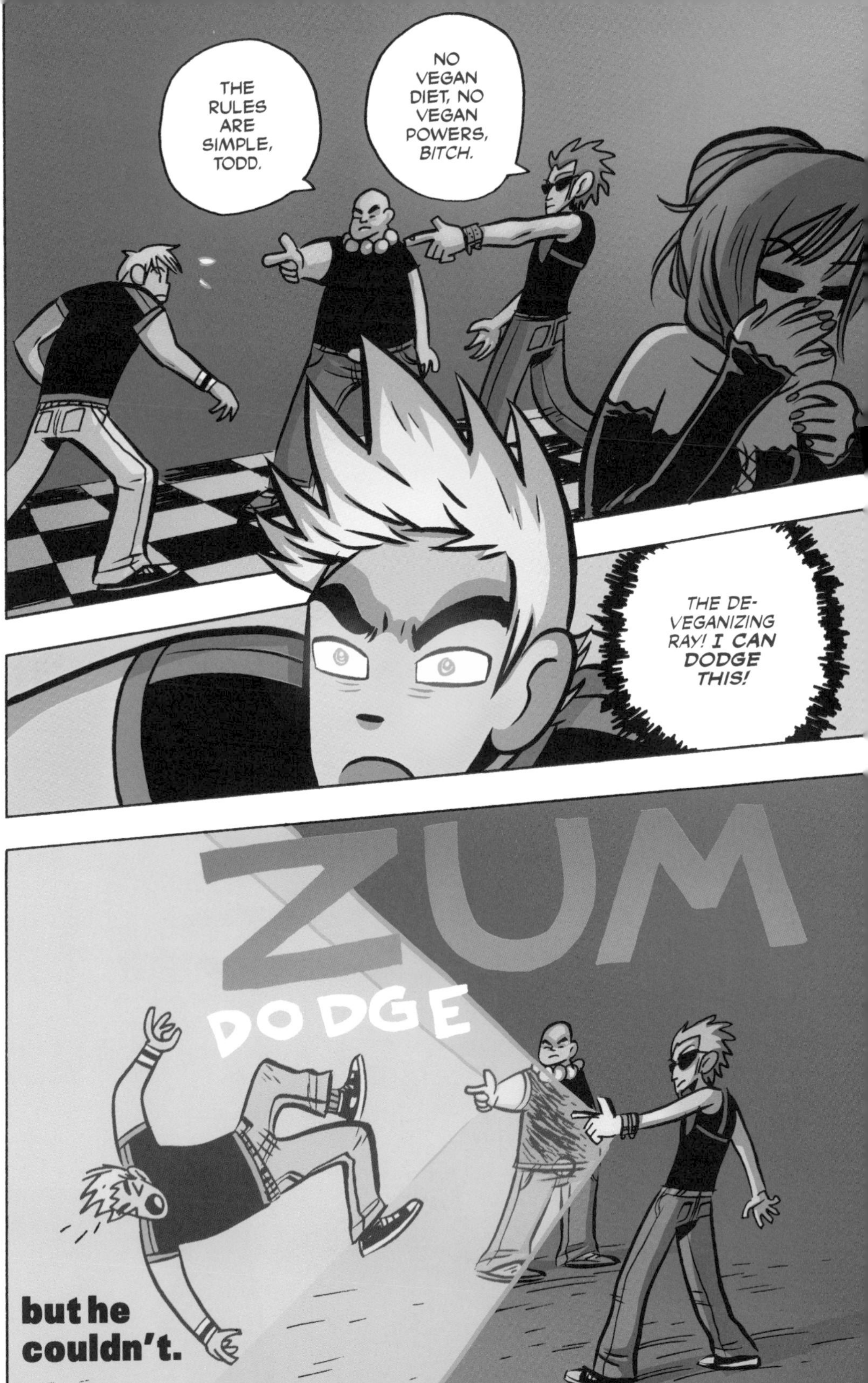
THE RULES ARE SIMPLE, TODD.
NO VEGAN DIET, NO VEGAN POWERS, BITCH.
THE DE-VEGANIZING RAY! I CAN DODGE THIS!
ZUM
DODGE
but he couldn't.

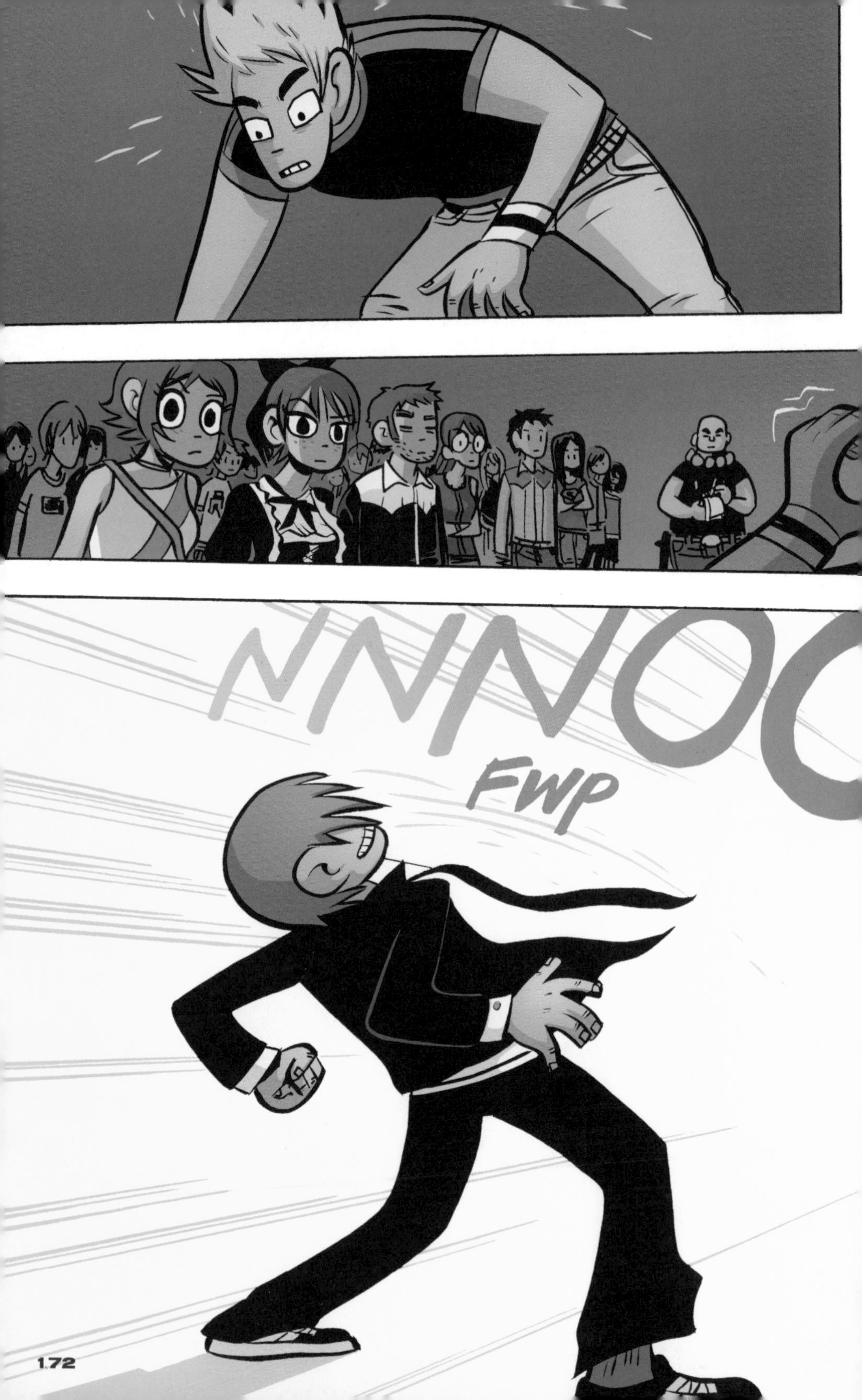
NNNOO
FWP

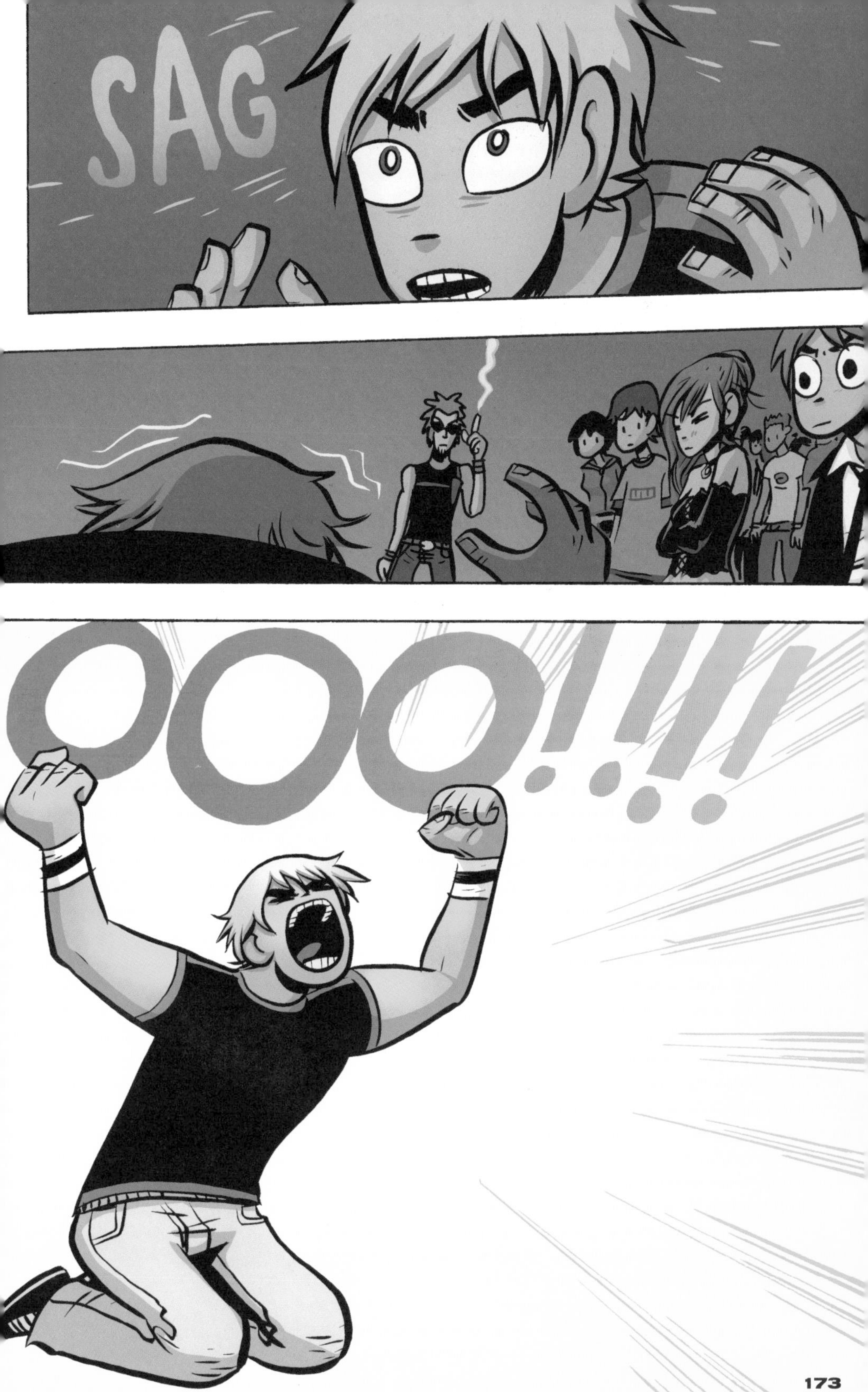
SAG
OOO!!!!

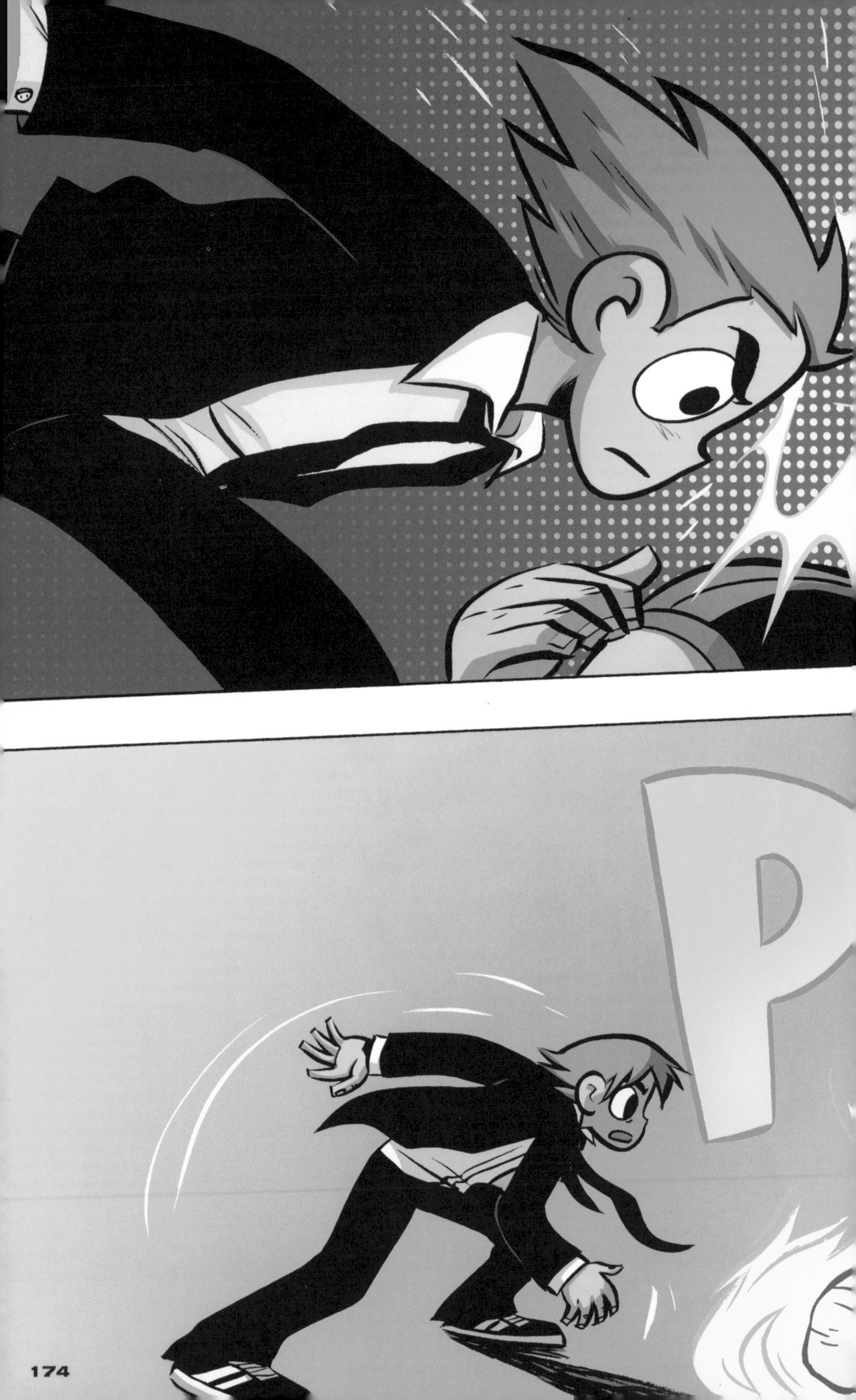
P

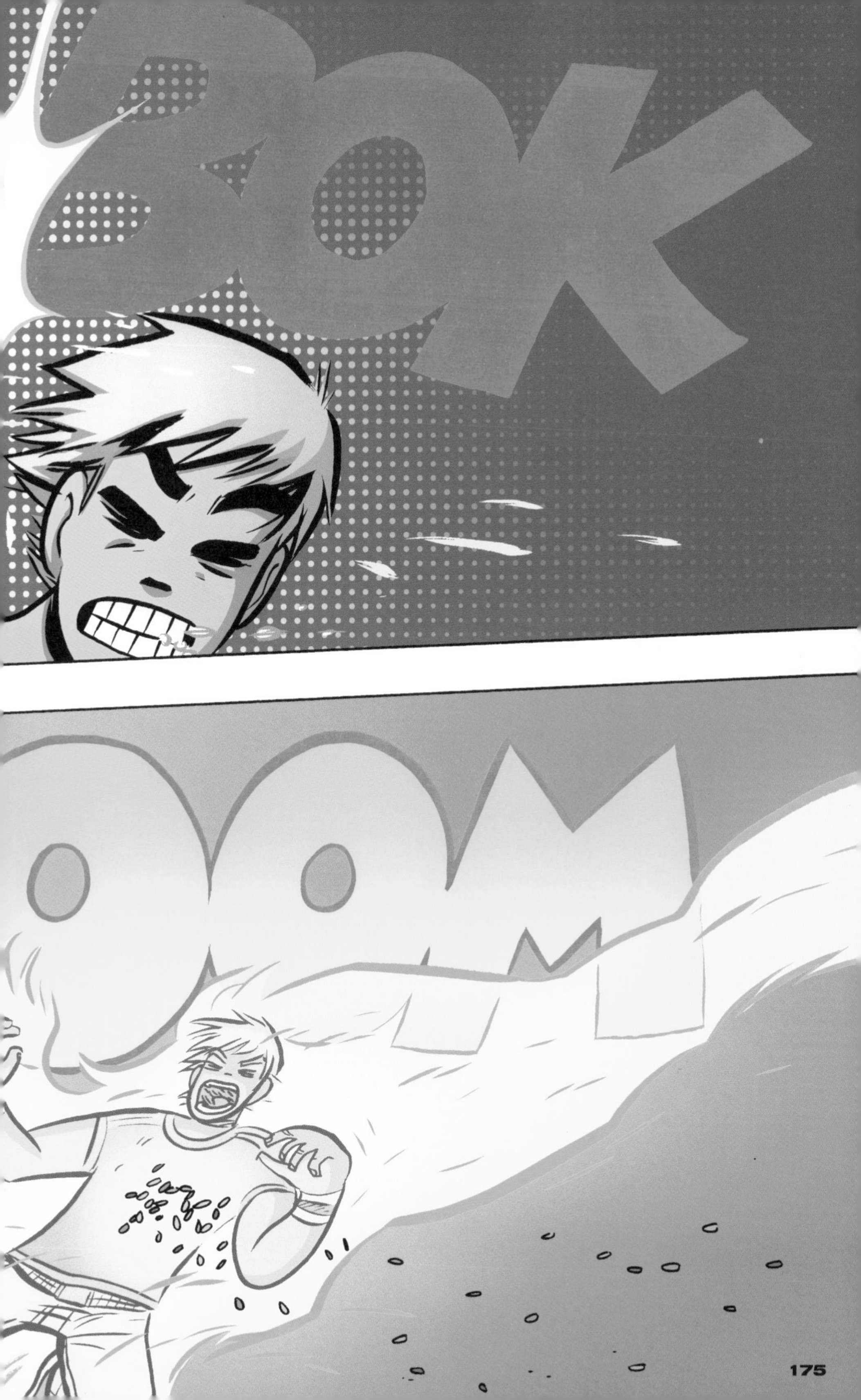
BOK
OOM

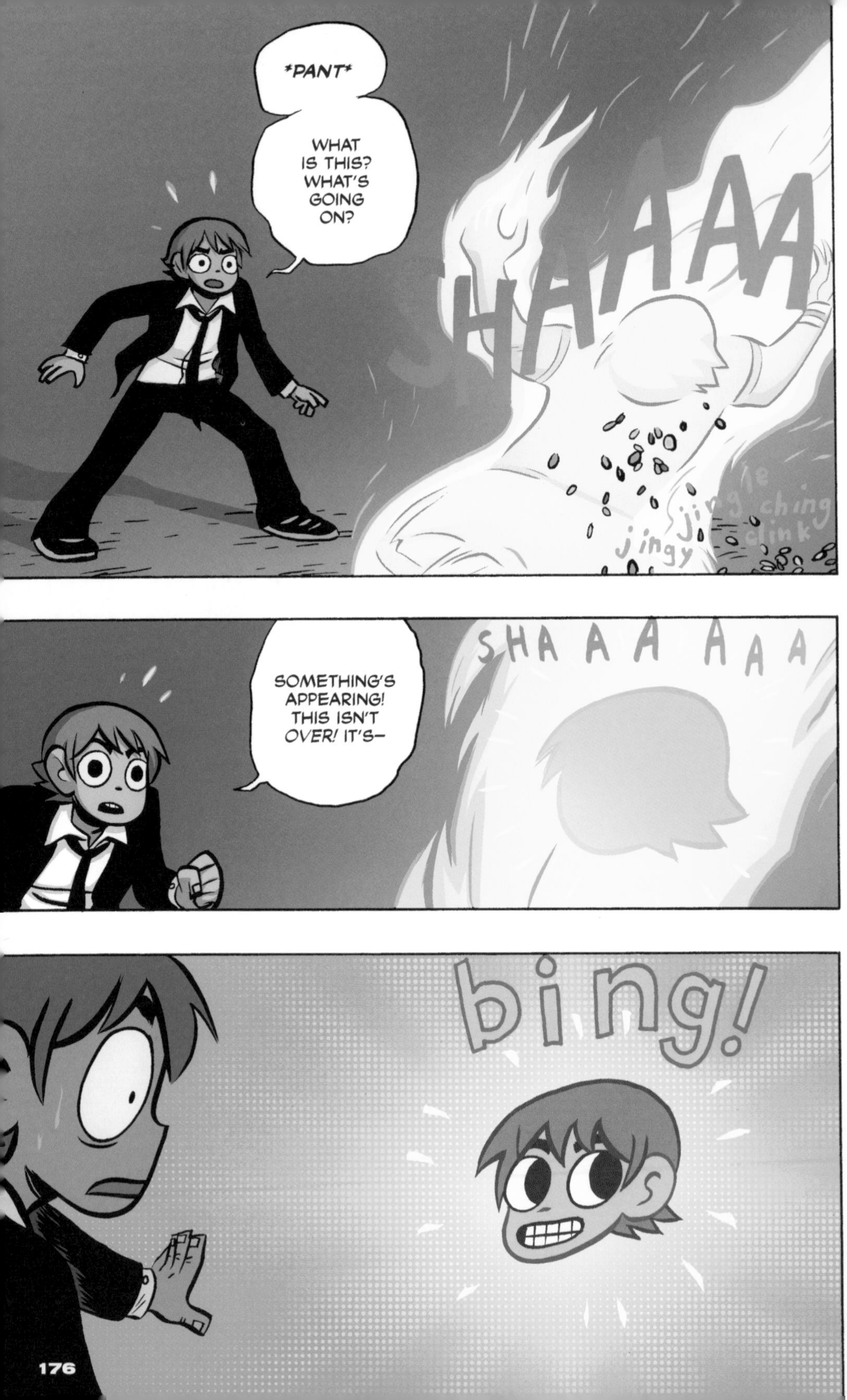
PANT
WHAT IS THIS? WHAT'S GOING ON?
SHAAAAA
jingy
jingle
ching
clink
SOMETHING'S APPEARING! THIS ISN'T OVER! IT'S—
SHAAAAAA
bing!

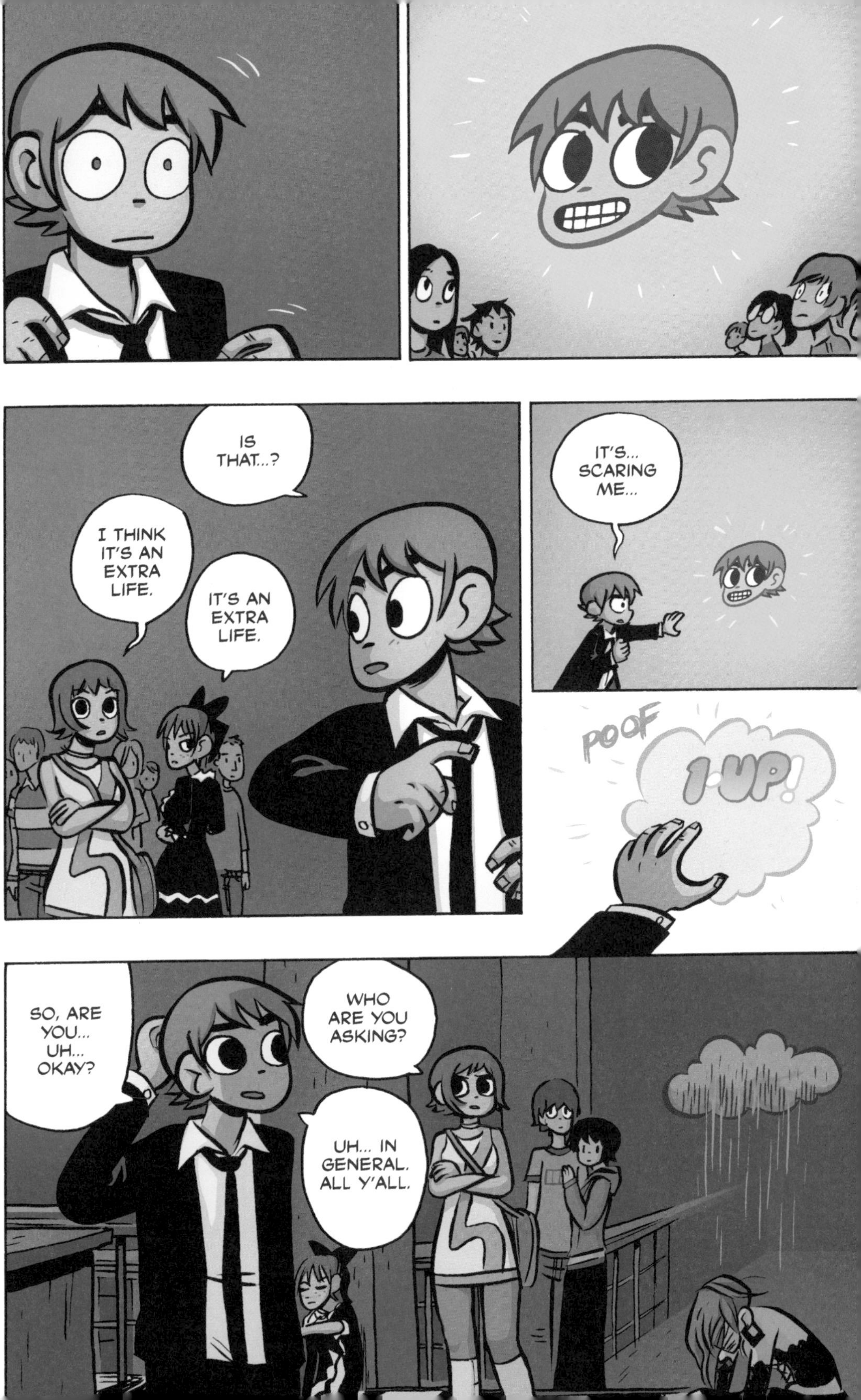
IS THAT...?
I THINK IT'S AN EXTRA LIFE.
IT'S AN EXTRA LIFE.
IT'S... SCARING ME...
POOF
1-UP!
SO, ARE YOU... UH... OKAY?
WHO ARE YOU ASKING?
UH... IN GENERAL. ALL Y'ALL.

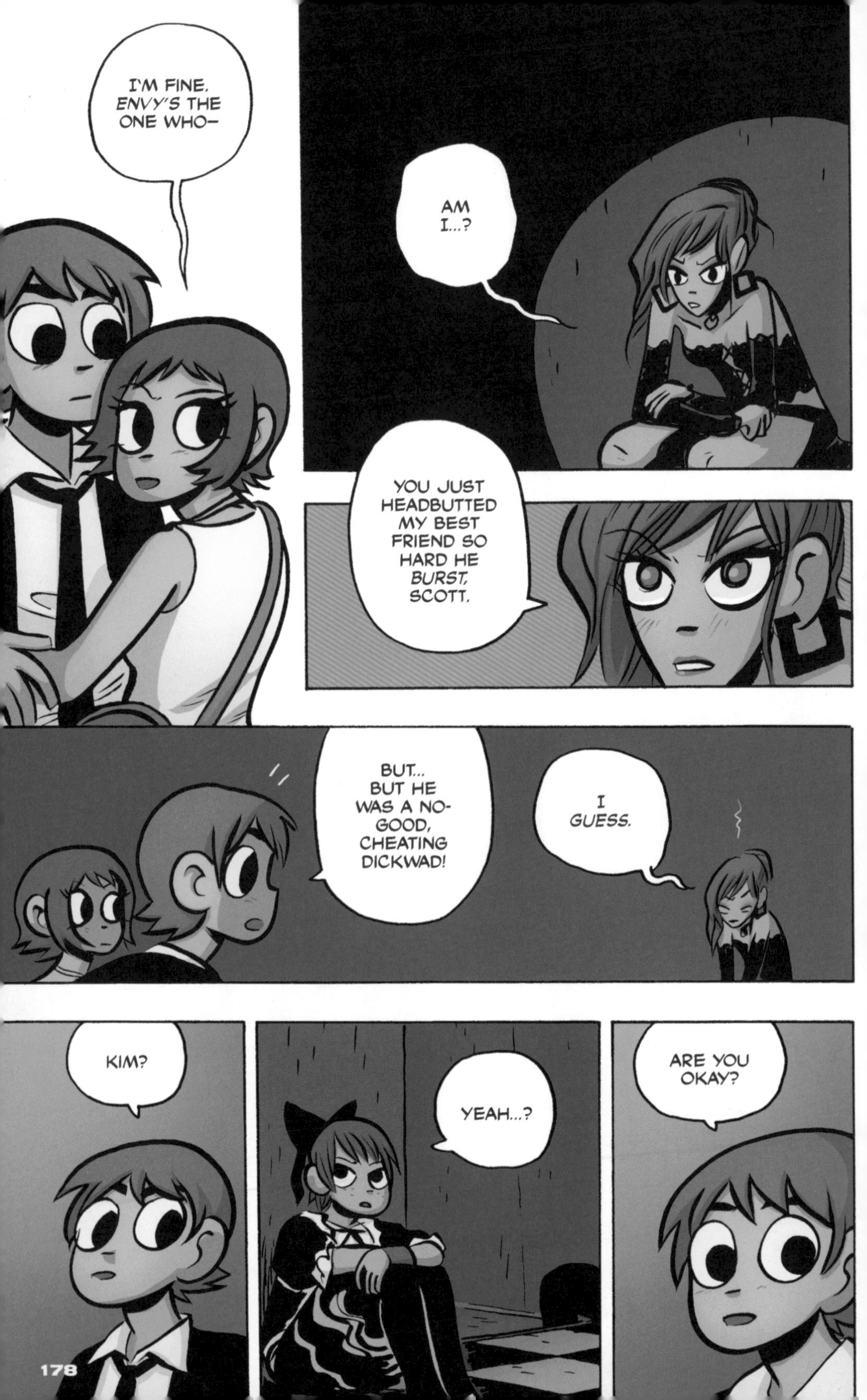

I'M FINE. *ENVY'S* THE ONE WHO–
AM I...?
YOU JUST HEADBUTTED MY BEST FRIEND SO HARD HE *BURST,* SCOTT.
BUT... BUT HE WAS A NO-GOOD, CHEATING DICKWAD!
I *GUESS.*
KIM?
YEAH...?
ARE YOU OKAY?

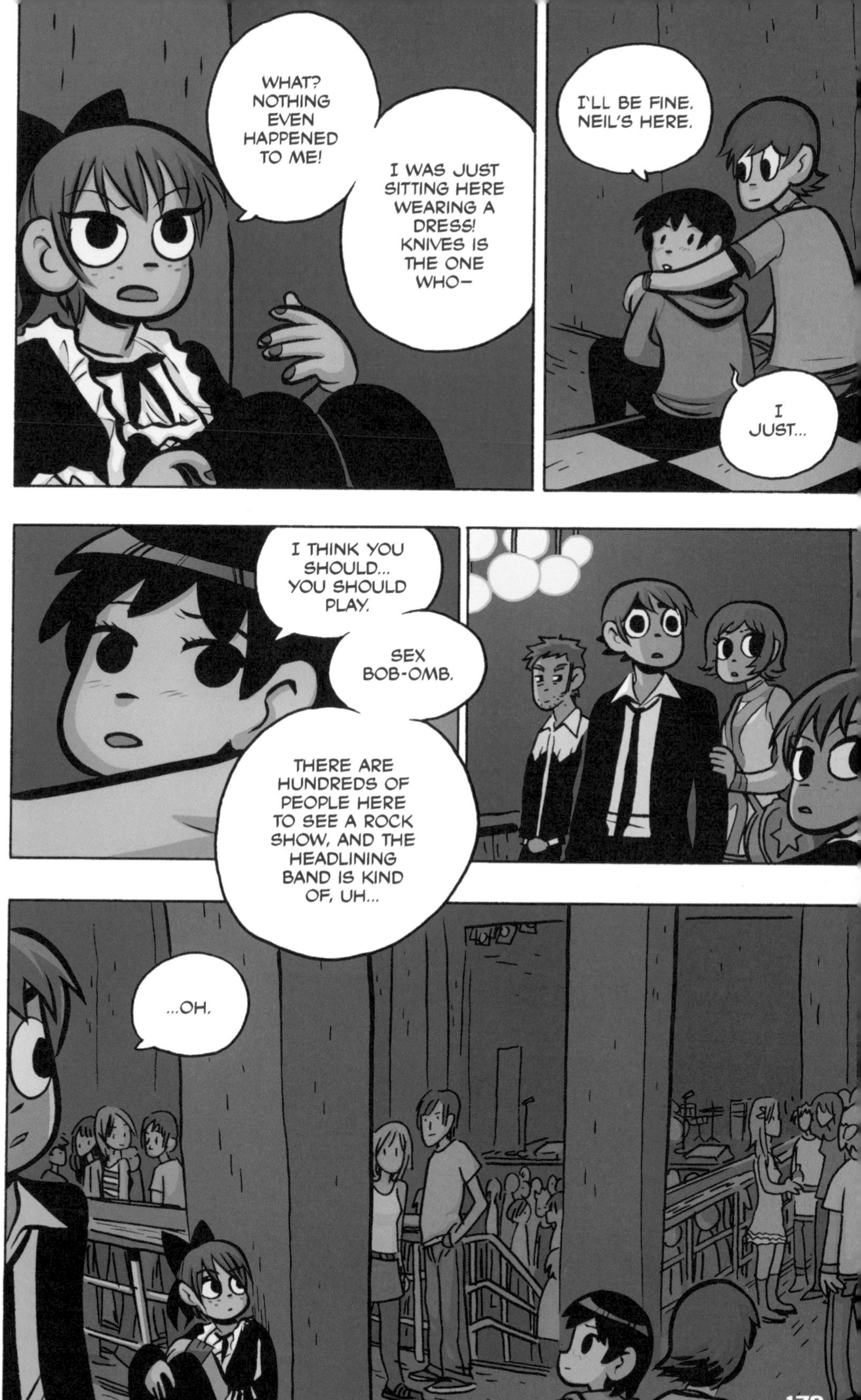
WHAT? NOTHING EVEN HAPPENED TO ME!
I WAS JUST SITTING HERE WEARING A DRESS! KNIVES IS THE ONE WHO—
I'LL BE FINE. NEIL'S HERE.
I JUST...
I THINK YOU SHOULD... YOU SHOULD PLAY.
SEX BOB-OMB.
THERE ARE HUNDREDS OF PEOPLE HERE TO SEE A ROCK SHOW, AND THE HEADLINING BAND IS KIND OF, UH...
...OH.

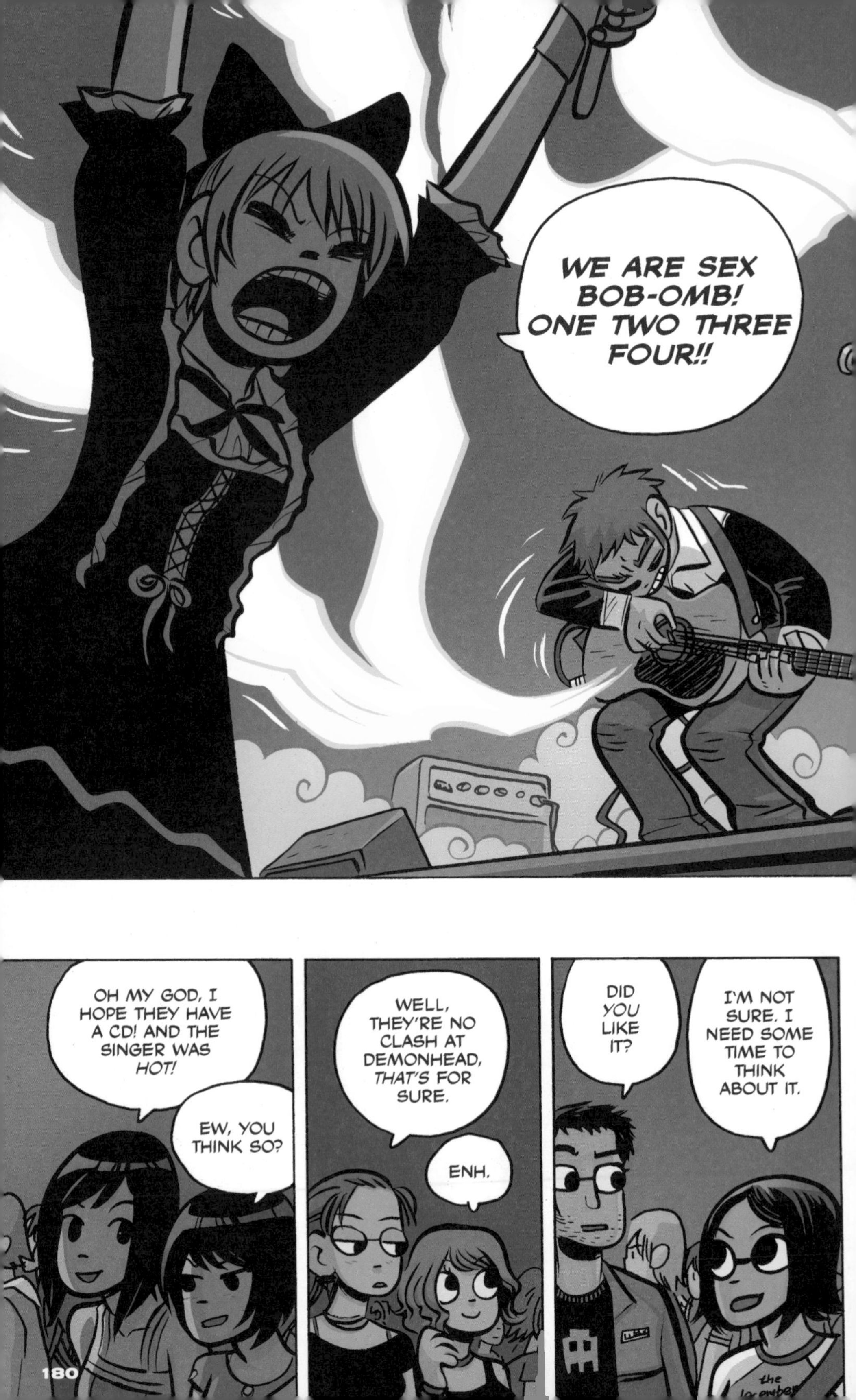
WE ARE SEX BOB-OMB! ONE TWO THREE FOUR!!
OH MY GOD, I HOPE THEY HAVE A CD! AND THE SINGER WAS *HOT!*
EW, YOU THINK SO?
WELL, THEY'RE NO CLASH AT DEMONHEAD, *THAT'S* FOR SURE.
ENH.
DID *YOU* LIKE IT?
I'M NOT SURE. I NEED SOME TIME TO THINK ABOUT IT.

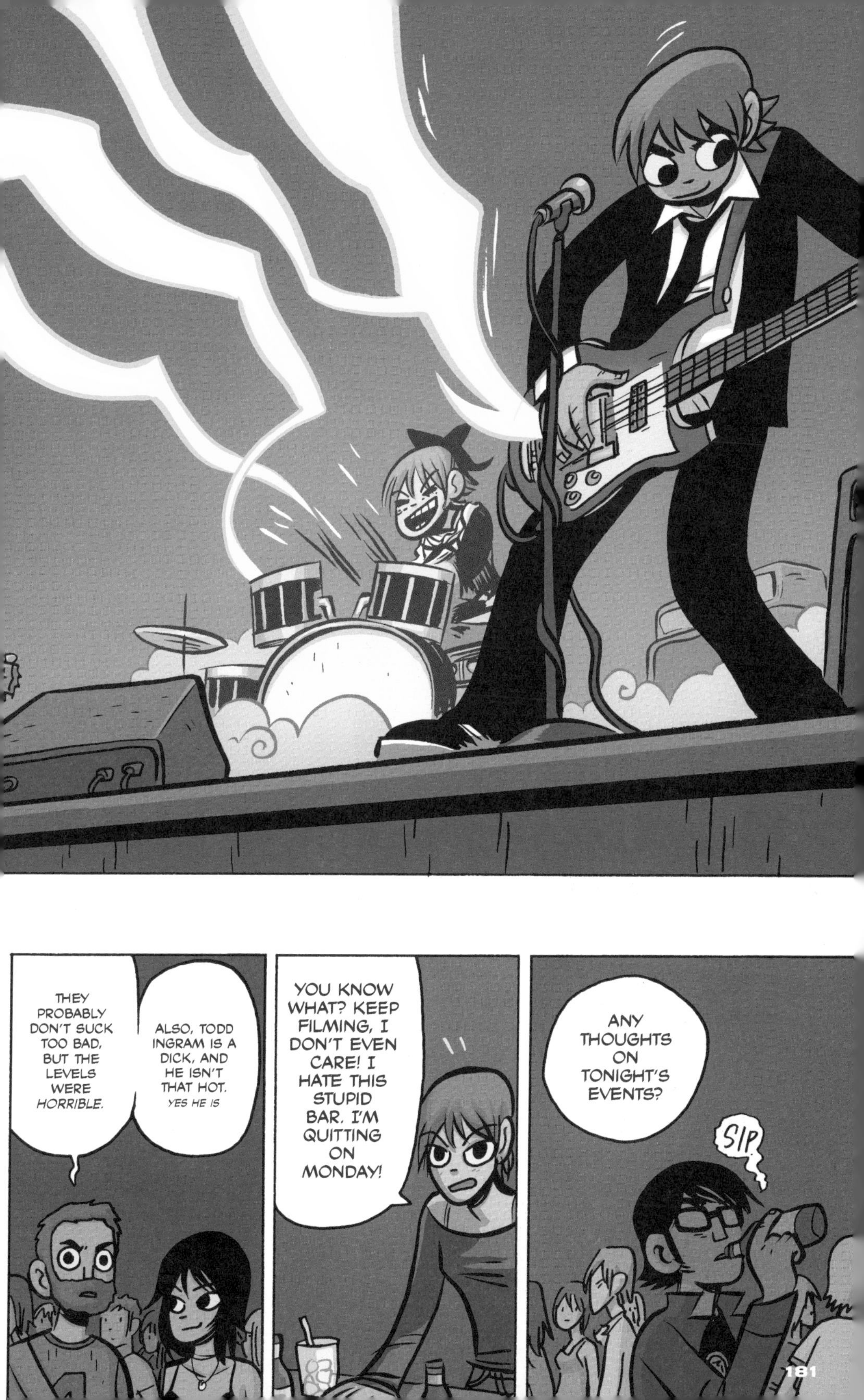
THEY PROBABLY DON'T SUCK TOO BAD, BUT THE LEVELS WERE *HORRIBLE.*
ALSO, TODD INGRAM IS A DICK, AND HE ISN'T THAT HOT.
YES HE IS
YOU KNOW WHAT? KEEP FILMING, I DON'T EVEN CARE! I HATE THIS STUPID BAR. I'M QUITTING ON MONDAY!
ANY THOUGHTS ON TONIGHT'S EVENTS?
SIP

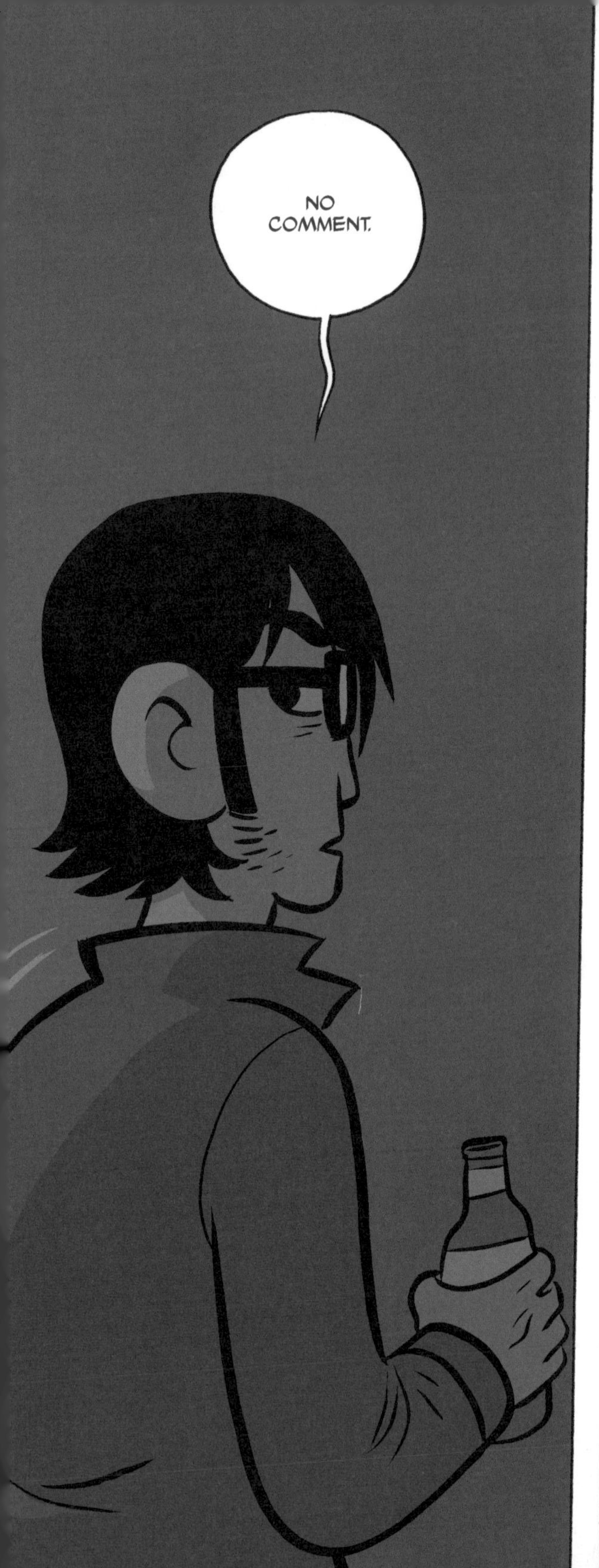
NO COMMENT.

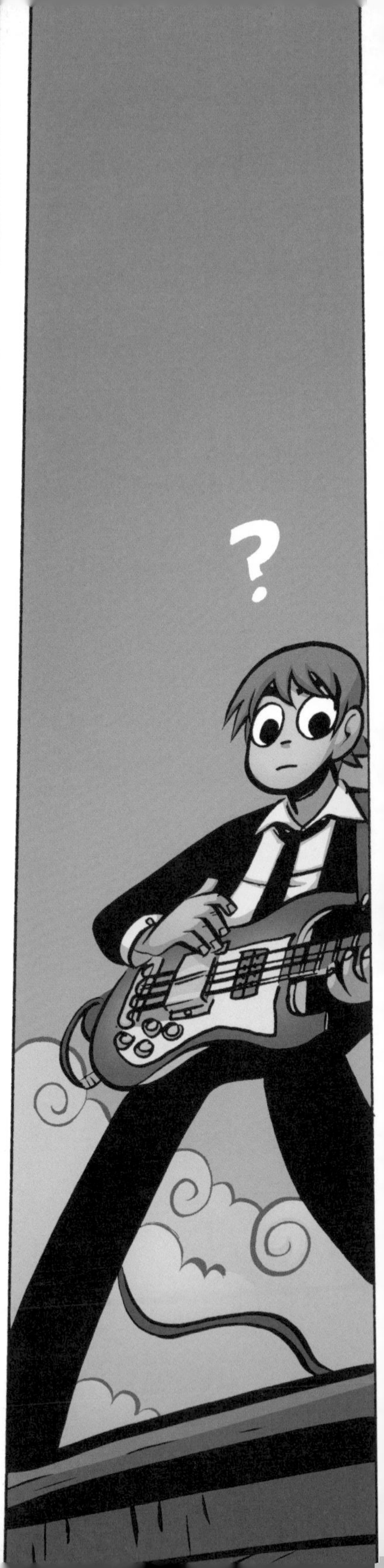
?

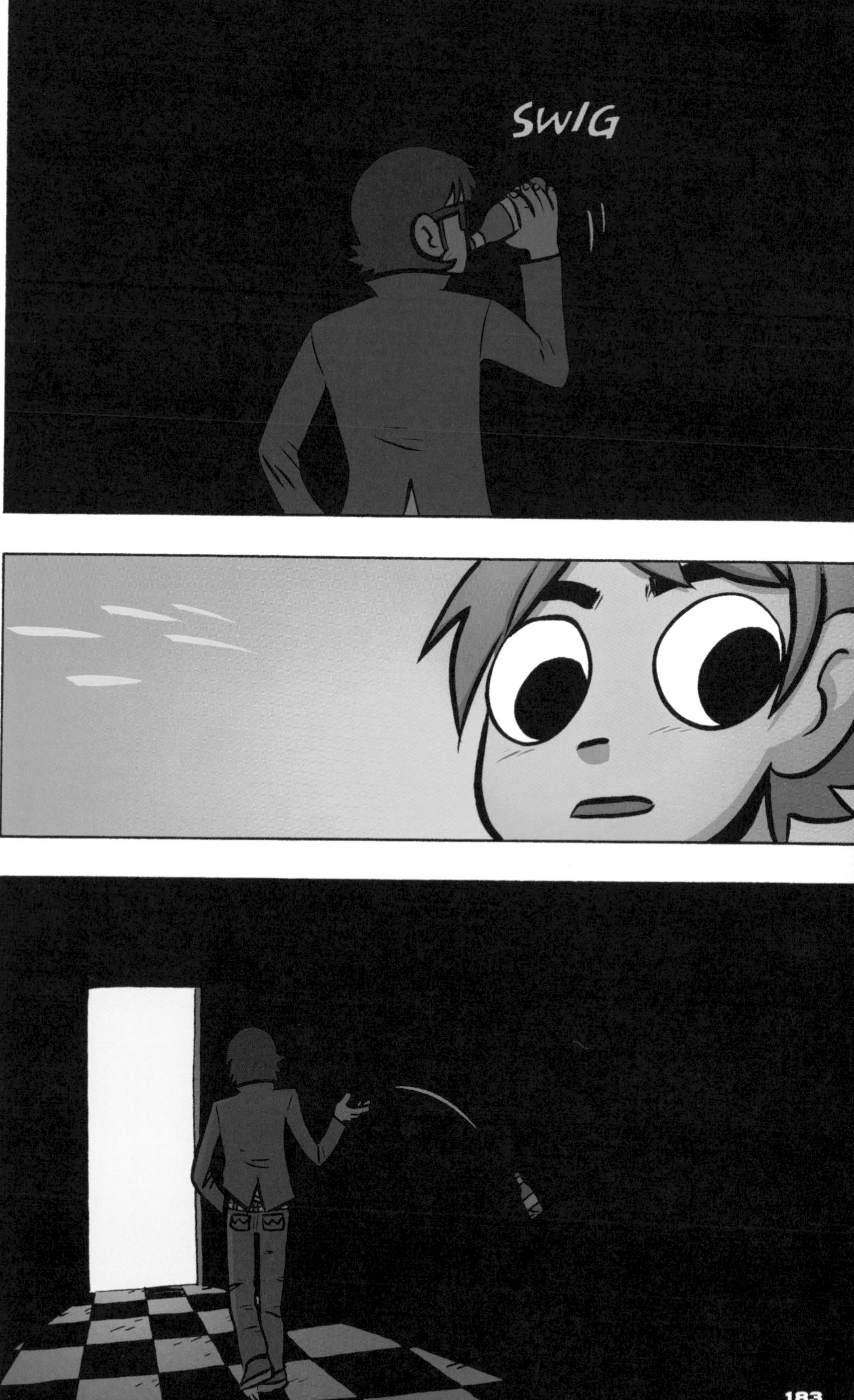
SWIG

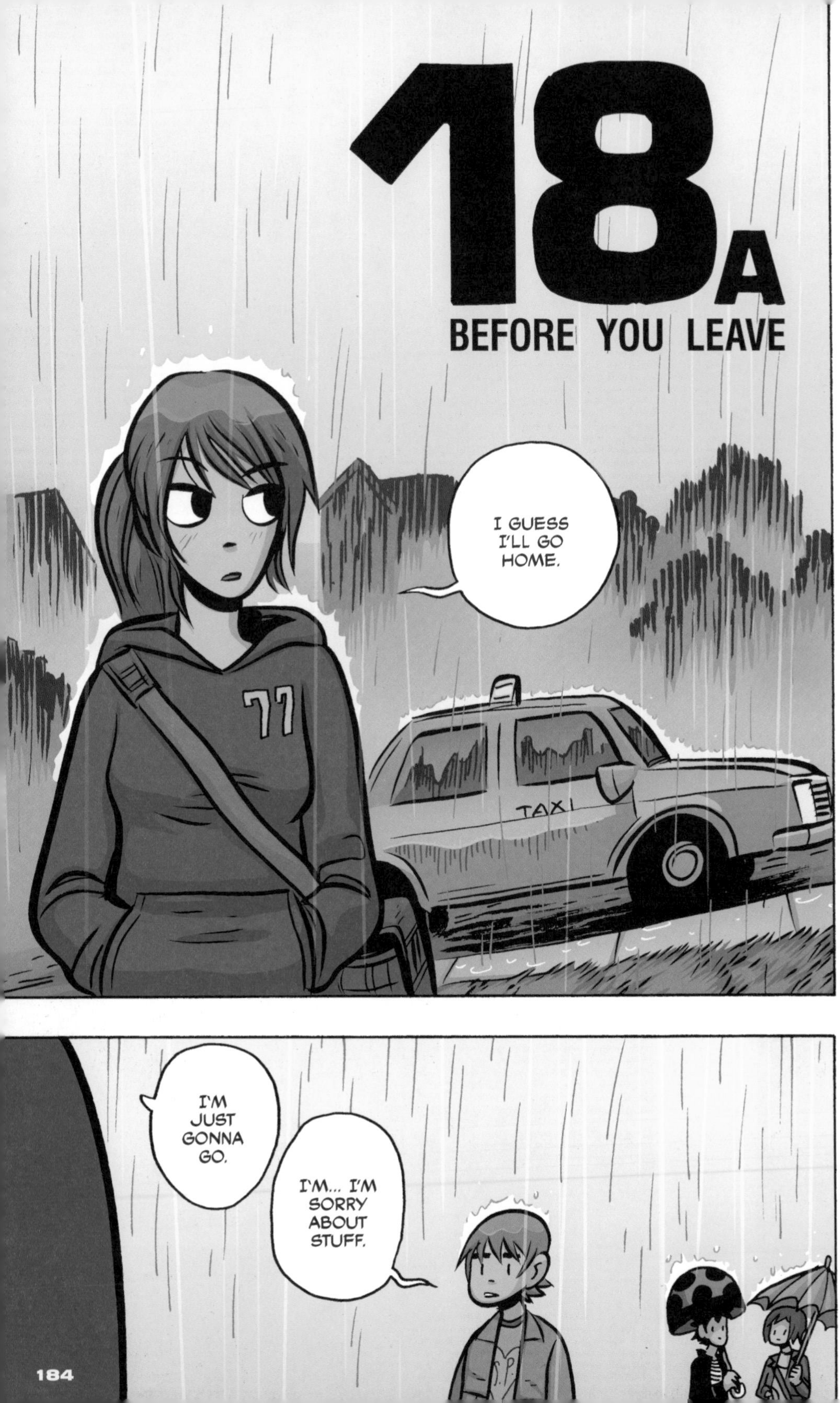
18A
BEFORE YOU LEAVE
I GUESS I'LL GO HOME.
77
TAXI
I'M JUST GONNA GO.
I'M... I'M SORRY ABOUT STUFF.

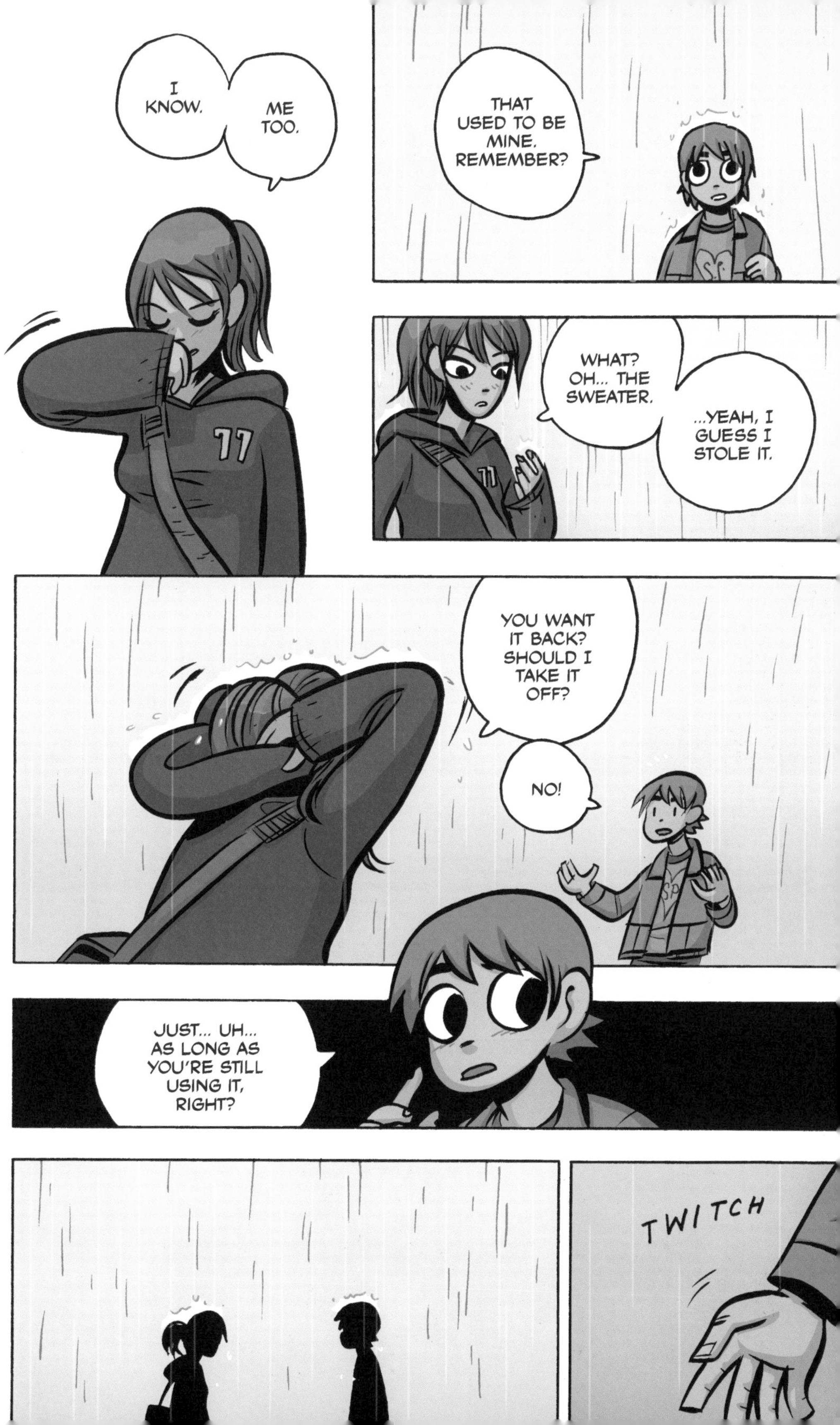
I KNOW.
ME TOO.
THAT USED TO BE MINE. REMEMBER?
WHAT? OH... THE SWEATER.
...YEAH, I GUESS I STOLE IT.
YOU WANT IT BACK? SHOULD I TAKE IT OFF?
NO!
JUST... UH... AS LONG AS YOU'RE STILL USING IT, RIGHT?
TWITCH

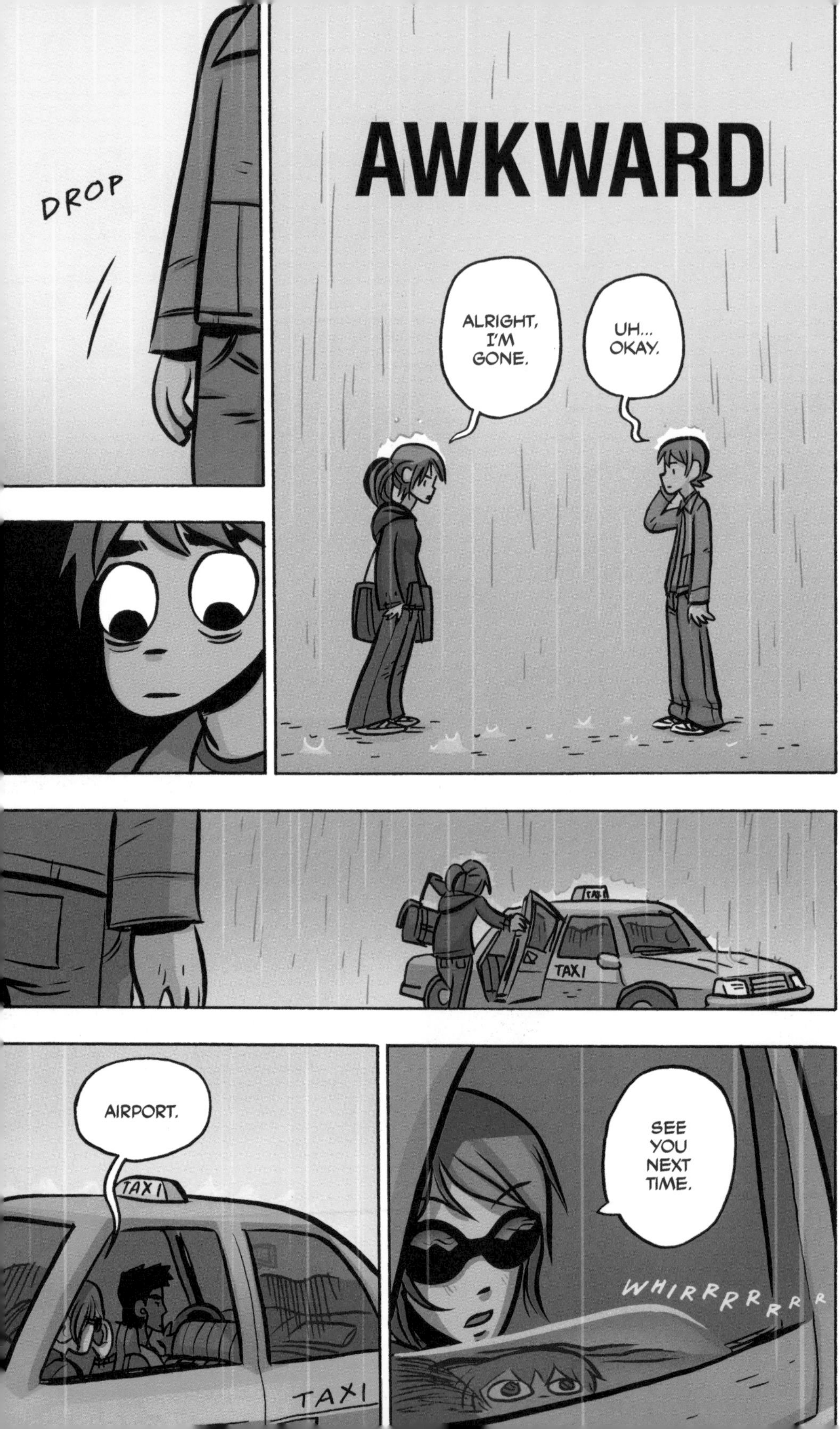
DROP
AWKWARD
ALRIGHT, I'M GONE.
UH... OKAY.
AIRPORT.
TAXI
TAXI
SEE YOU NEXT TIME.
WHIRRRRRRRR

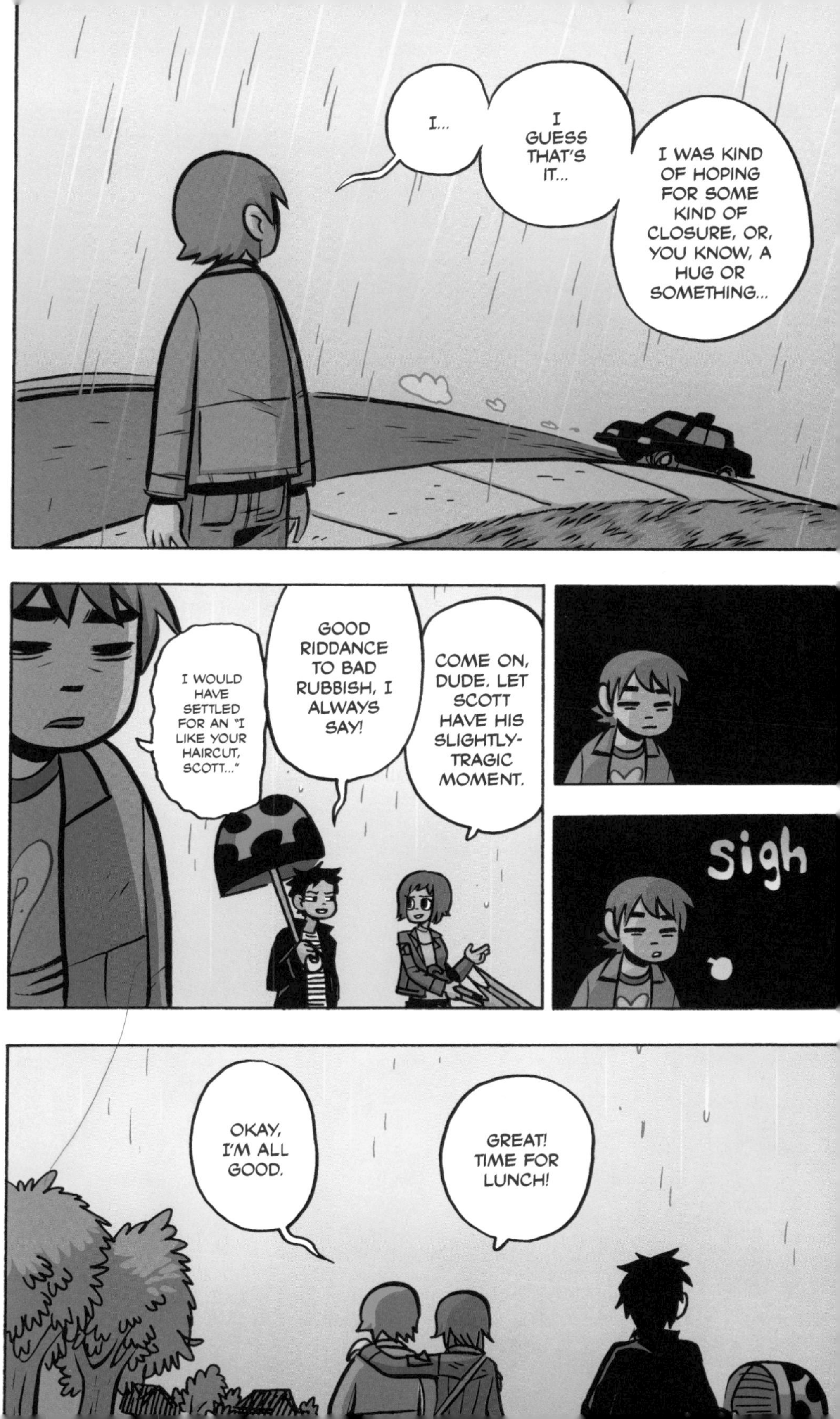
I...
I GUESS THAT'S IT...
I WAS KIND OF HOPING FOR SOME KIND OF CLOSURE, OR, YOU KNOW, A HUG OR SOMETHING...
I WOULD HAVE SETTLED FOR AN "I LIKE YOUR HAIRCUT, SCOTT..."
GOOD RIDDANCE TO BAD RUBBISH, I ALWAYS SAY!
COME ON, DUDE. LET SCOTT HAVE HIS SLIGHTLY-TRAGIC MOMENT.
sigh
OKAY, I'M ALL GOOD.
GREAT! TIME FOR LUNCH!

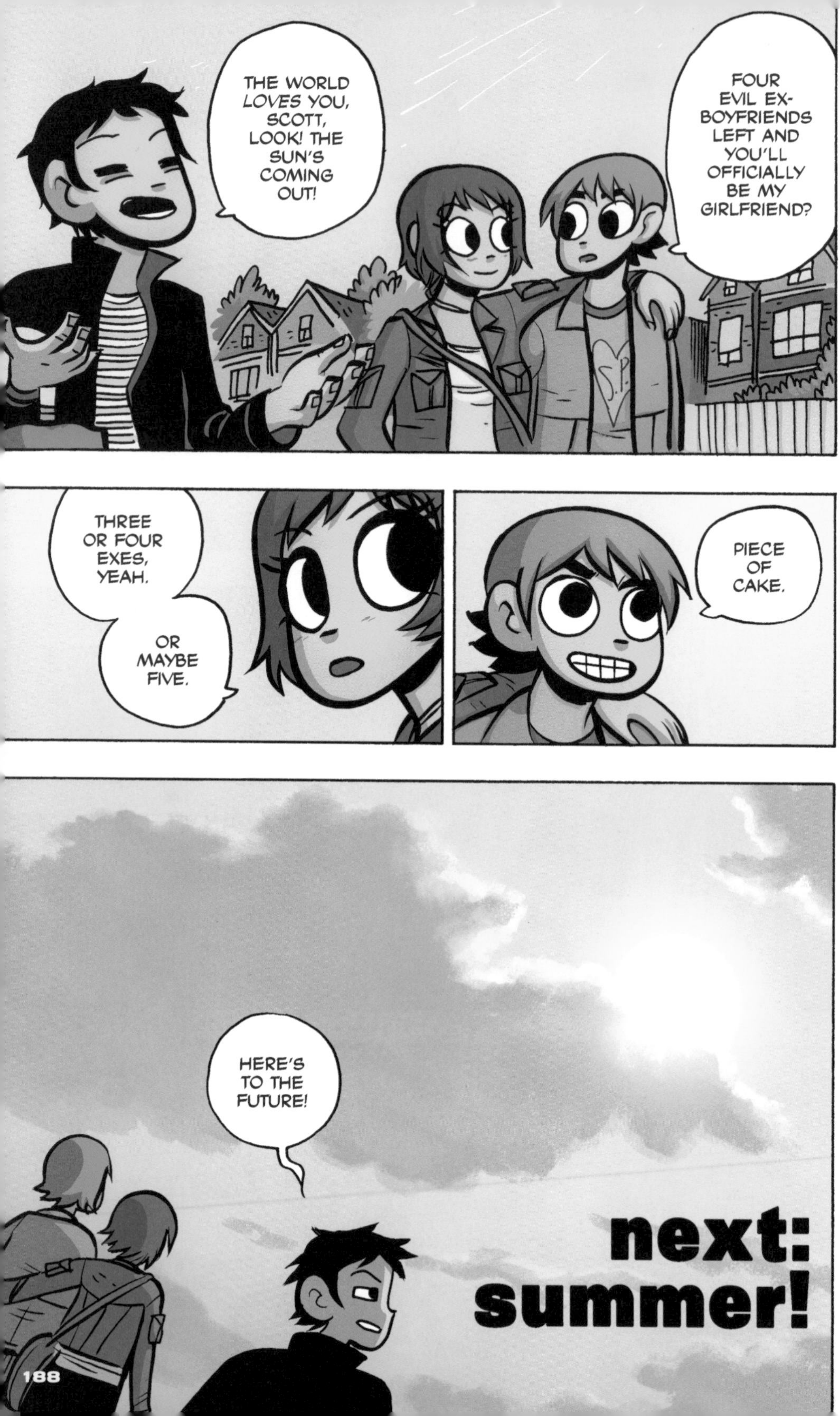
THE WORLD LOVES YOU, SCOTT, LOOK! THE SUN'S COMING OUT!
FOUR EVIL EX-BOYFRIENDS LEFT AND YOU'LL OFFICIALLY BE MY GIRLFRIEND?
THREE OR FOUR EXES, YEAH.
OR MAYBE FIVE.
PIECE OF CAKE.
HERE'S TO THE FUTURE!
next: summer!

EXTRAS

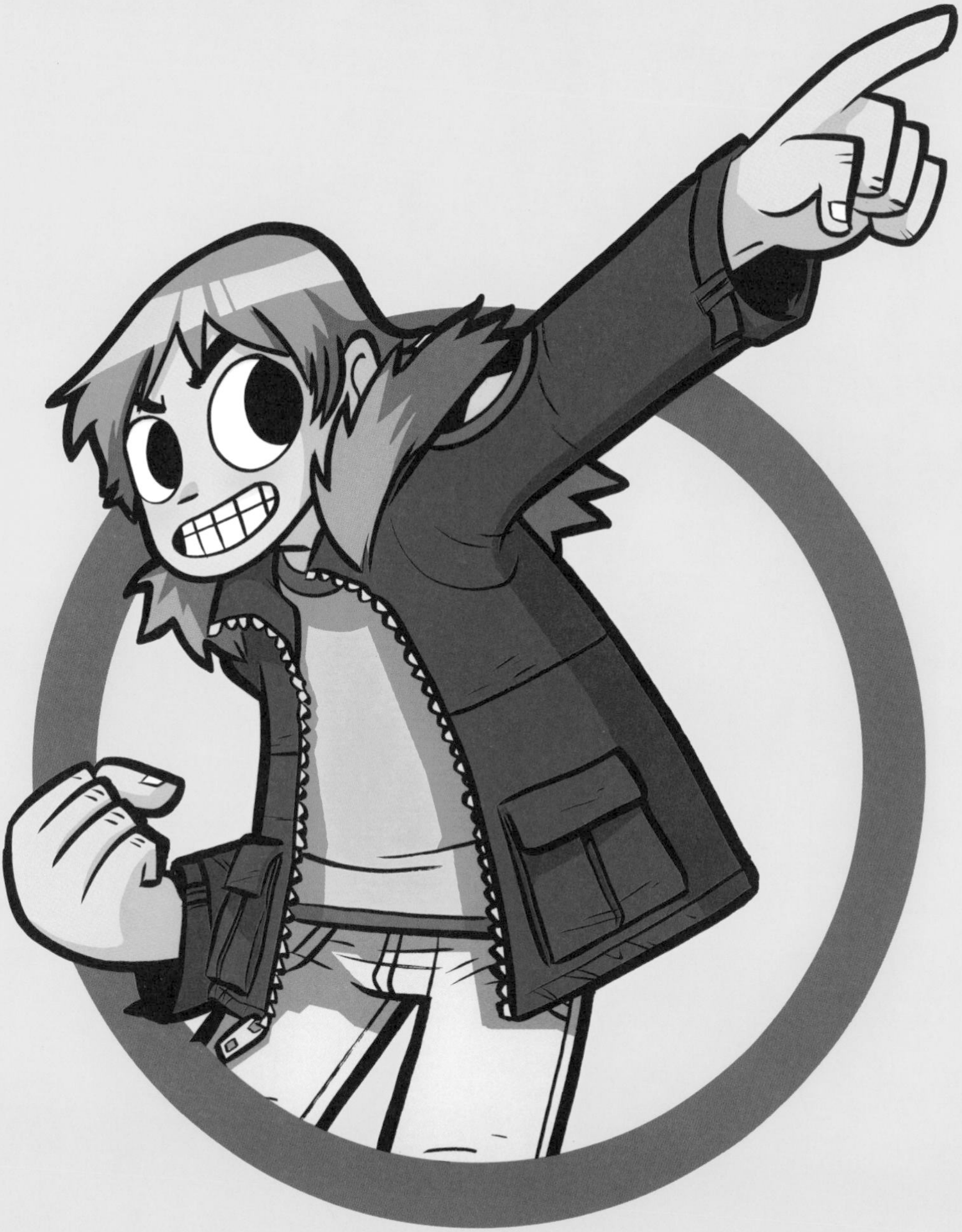

FREE SCOTT PILGRIM

This story, originally published in black-and-white for Free Comic Book Day 2006, takes place between volumes 3 and 4.

Colors by Nathan Fairbairn.

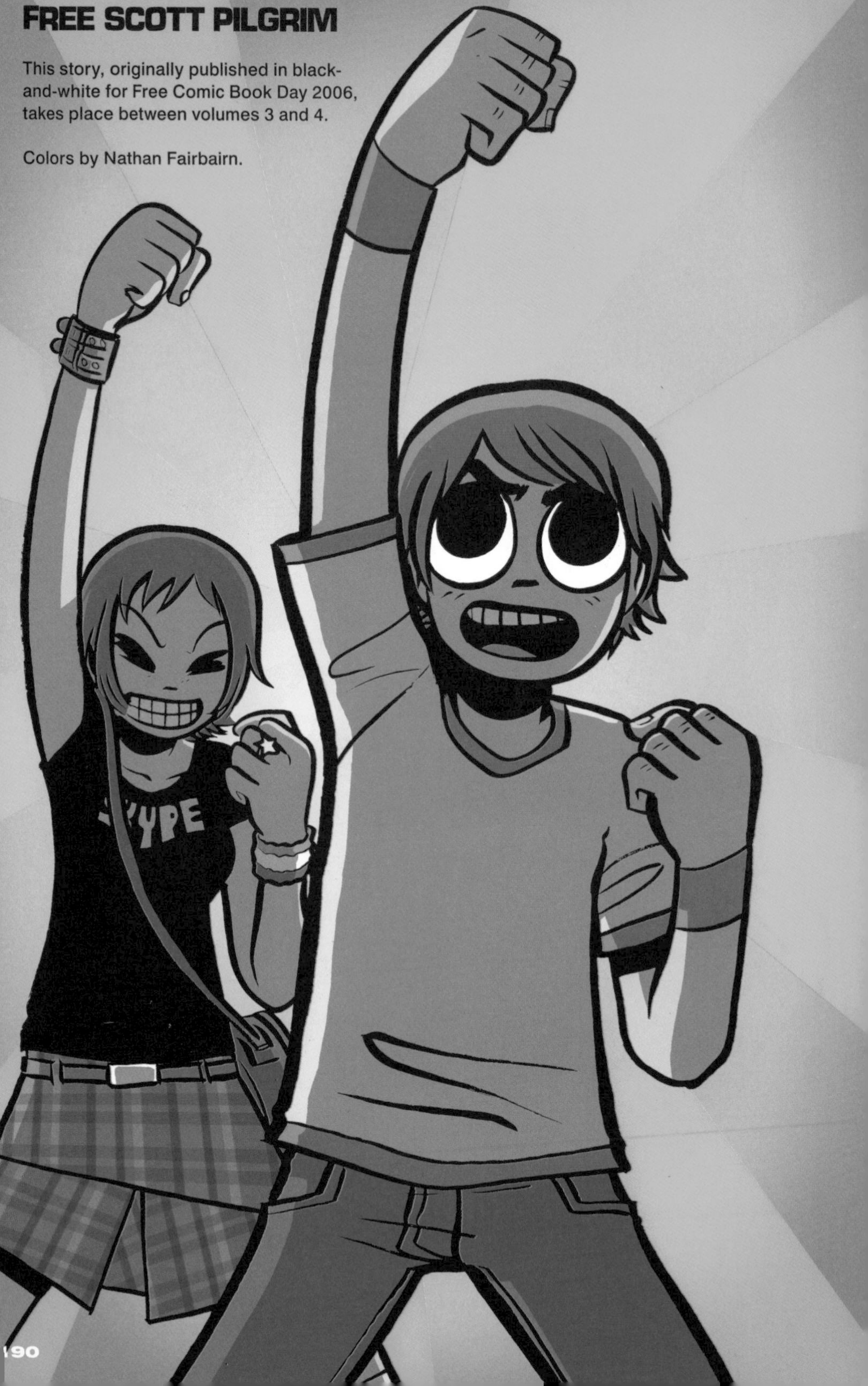

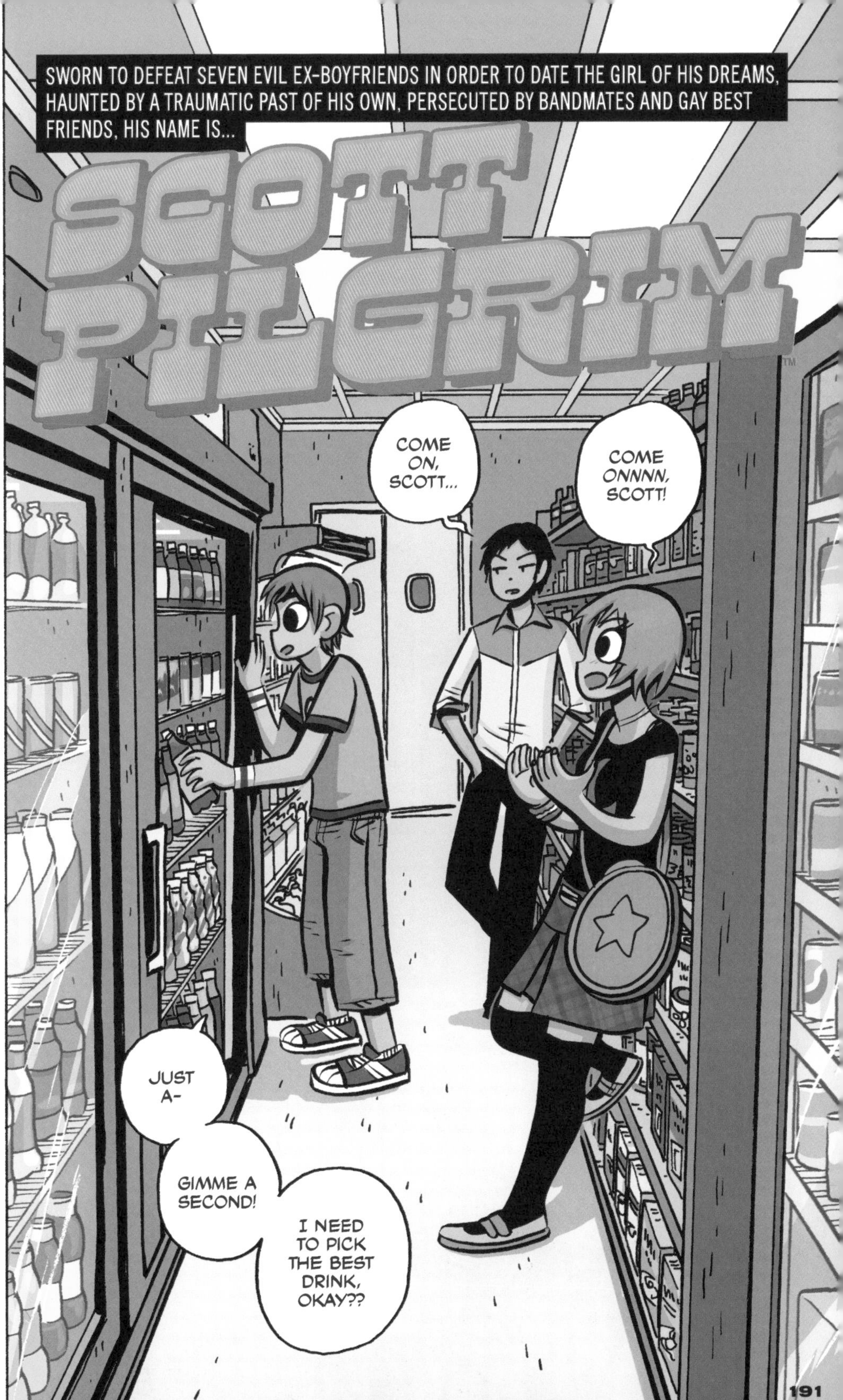
SWORN TO DEFEAT SEVEN EVIL EX-BOYFRIENDS IN ORDER TO DATE THE GIRL OF HIS DREAMS, HAUNTED BY A TRAUMATIC PAST OF HIS OWN, PERSECUTED BY BANDMATES AND GAY BEST FRIENDS, HIS NAME IS...
SCOTT PILGRIM™
COME ON, SCOTT...
COME ONNNN, SCOTT!
JUST A-
GIMME A SECOND!
I NEED TO PICK THE BEST DRINK, OKAY??

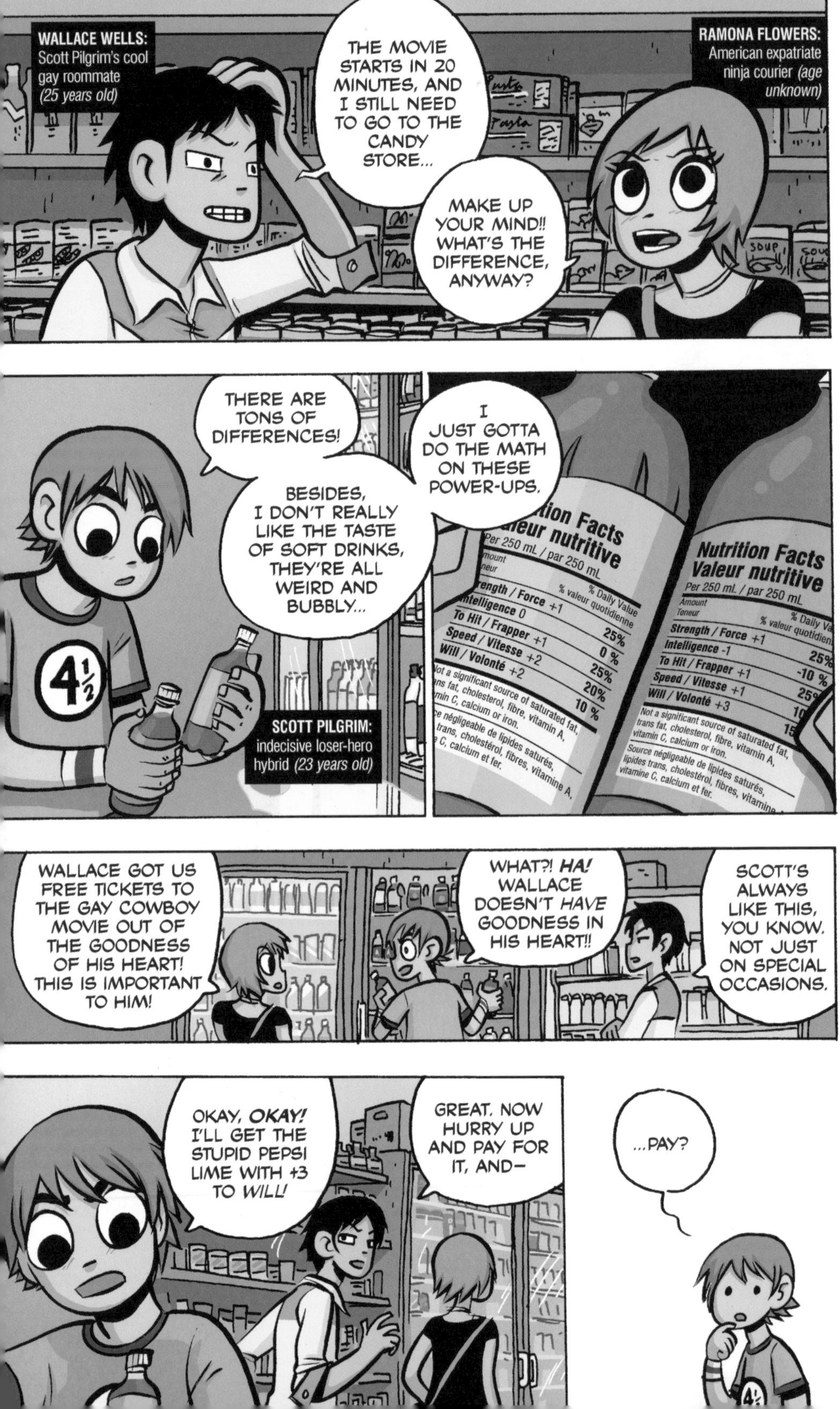

WALLACE WELLS: Scott Pilgrim's cool gay roommate (25 years old)
THE MOVIE STARTS IN 20 MINUTES, AND I STILL NEED TO GO TO THE CANDY STORE...
RAMONA FLOWERS: American expatriate ninja courier (age unknown)
MAKE UP YOUR MIND!! WHAT'S THE DIFFERENCE, ANYWAY?
THERE ARE TONS OF DIFFERENCES!
BESIDES, I DON'T REALLY LIKE THE TASTE OF SOFT DRINKS, THEY'RE ALL WEIRD AND BUBBLY...
SCOTT PILGRIM: indecisive loser-hero hybrid (23 years old)
I JUST GOTTA DO THE MATH ON THESE POWER-UPS.
Nutrition Facts Valeur nutritive
Per 250 mL / par 250 mL
Strength / Force +1
Intelligence 0
To Hit / Frapper +1
Speed / Vitesse +2
Will / Volonté +2
25%
0 %
25%
20%
10 %
Nutrition Facts Valeur nutritive
Per 250 mL / par 250 mL
Amount Teneur
Strength / Force +1
Intelligence -1
To Hit / Frapper +1
Speed / Vitesse +1
Will / Volonté +3
25%
-10 %
Not a significant source of saturated fat, trans fat, cholesterol, fibre, vitamin A, vitamin C, calcium or iron.
Source négligeable de lipides saturés, lipides trans, cholestérol, fibres, vitamine A, vitamine C, calcium et fer.
WALLACE GOT US FREE TICKETS TO THE GAY COWBOY MOVIE OUT OF THE GOODNESS OF HIS HEART! THIS IS IMPORTANT TO HIM!
WHAT?! HA! WALLACE DOESN'T HAVE GOODNESS IN HIS HEART!!
SCOTT'S ALWAYS LIKE THIS, YOU KNOW. NOT JUST ON SPECIAL OCCASIONS.
OKAY, OKAY! I'LL GET THE STUPID PEPSI LIME WITH +3 TO WILL!
GREAT. NOW HURRY UP AND PAY FOR IT, AND—
...PAY?

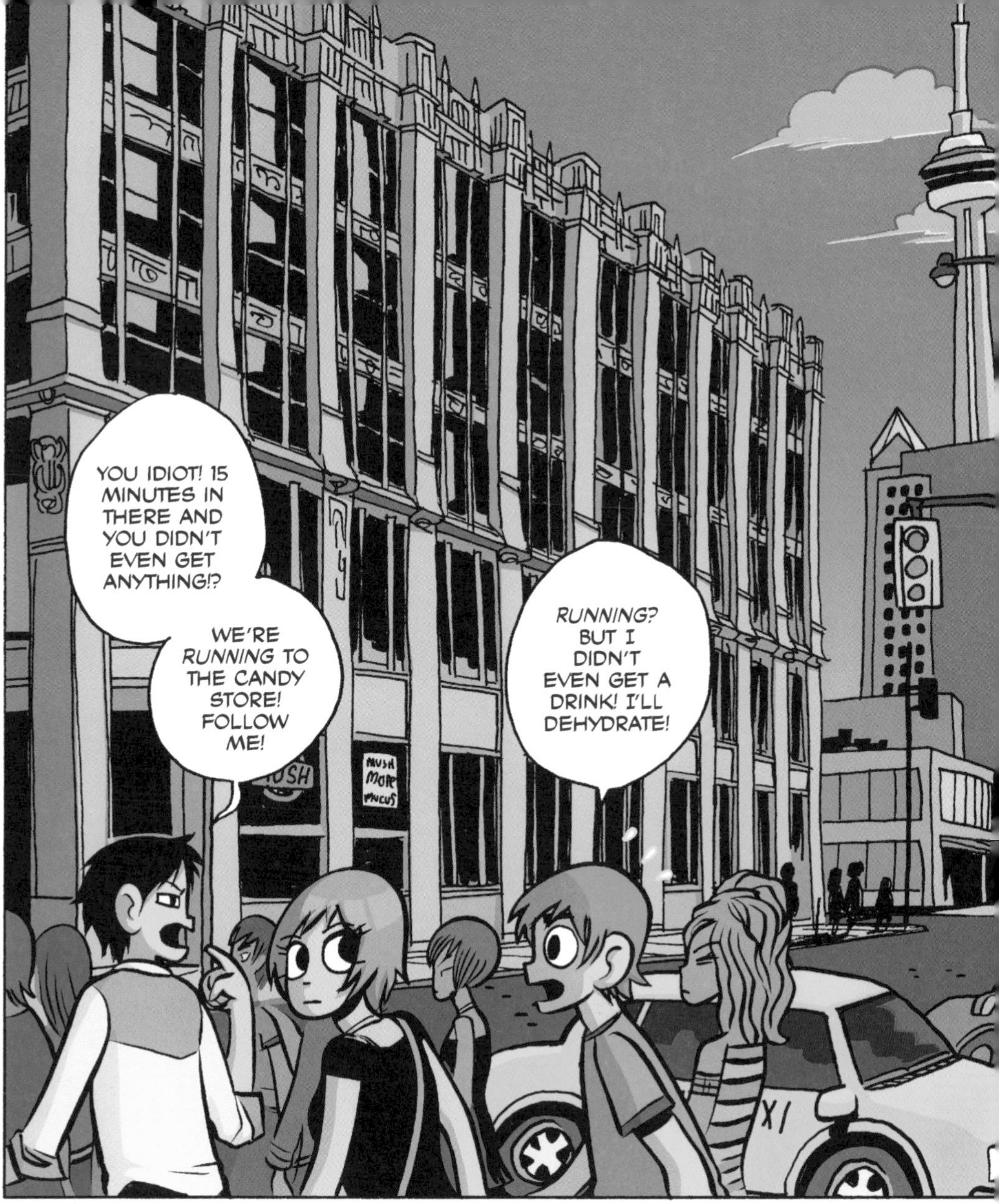
YOU IDIOT! 15 MINUTES IN THERE AND YOU DIDN'T EVEN GET ANYTHING!?
WE'RE *RUNNING* TO THE CANDY STORE! FOLLOW ME!
RUNNING? BUT I DIDN'T EVEN GET A DRINK! I'LL DEHYDRATE!
MUSH MORE MUCUS

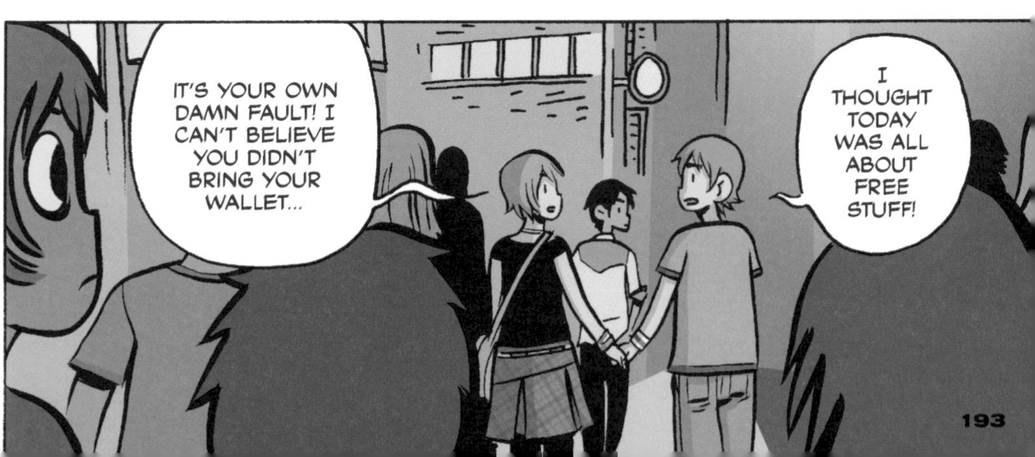
IT'S YOUR OWN DAMN FAULT! I CAN'T BELIEVE YOU DIDN'T BRING YOUR WALLET...
I THOUGHT TODAY WAS ALL ABOUT FREE STUFF!

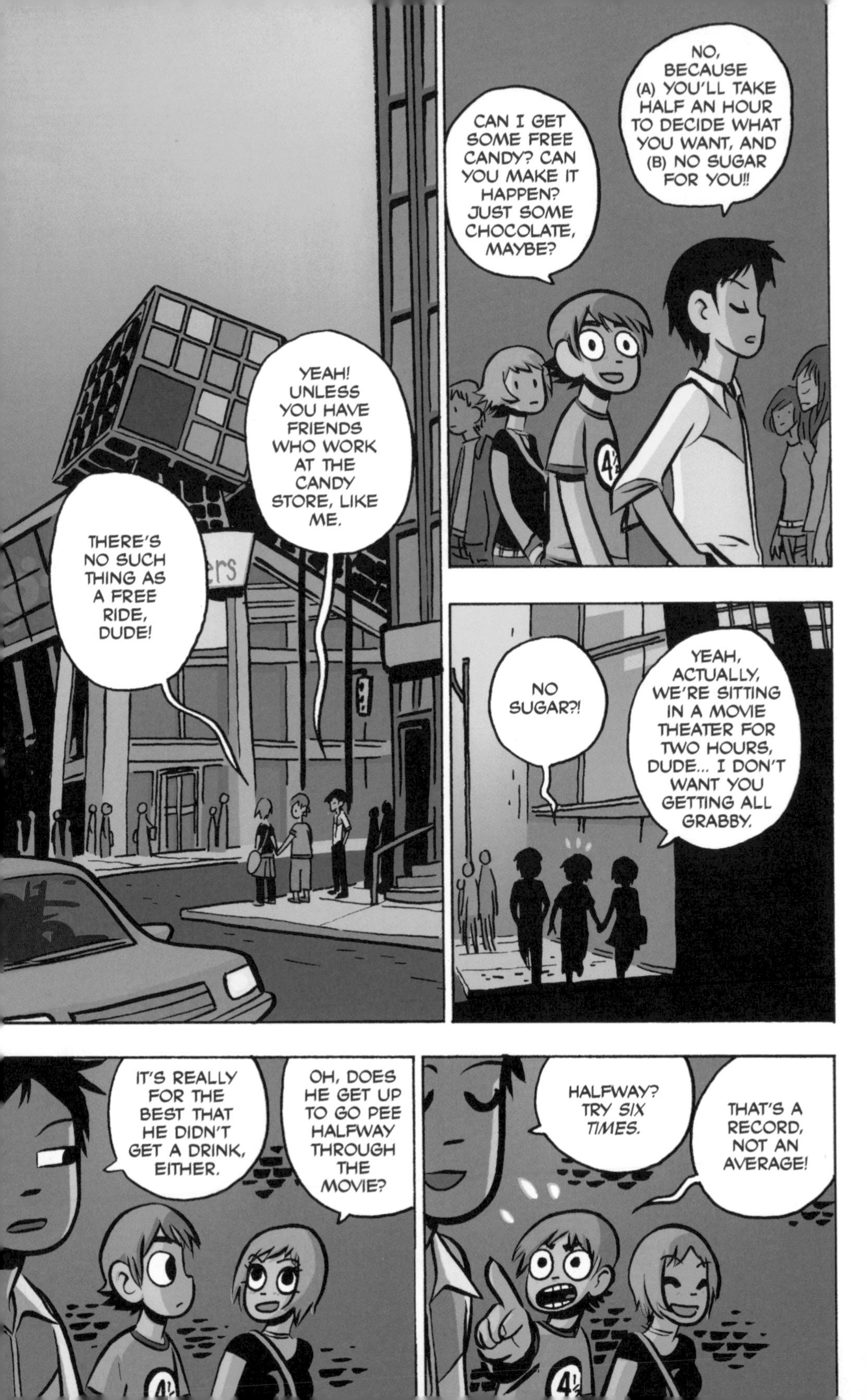
THERE'S NO SUCH THING AS A FREE RIDE, DUDE!
YEAH! UNLESS YOU HAVE FRIENDS WHO WORK AT THE CANDY STORE, LIKE ME.
CAN I GET SOME FREE CANDY? CAN YOU MAKE IT HAPPEN? JUST SOME CHOCOLATE, MAYBE?
NO, BECAUSE (A) YOU'LL TAKE HALF AN HOUR TO DECIDE WHAT YOU WANT, AND (B) NO SUGAR FOR YOU!!
NO SUGAR?!
YEAH, ACTUALLY, WE'RE SITTING IN A MOVIE THEATER FOR TWO HOURS, DUDE... I DON'T WANT YOU GETTING ALL GRABBY.
IT'S REALLY FOR THE BEST THAT HE DIDN'T GET A DRINK, EITHER.
OH, DOES HE GET UP TO GO PEE HALFWAY THROUGH THE MOVIE?
HALFWAY? TRY *SIX TIMES.*
THAT'S A RECORD, NOT AN AVERAGE!

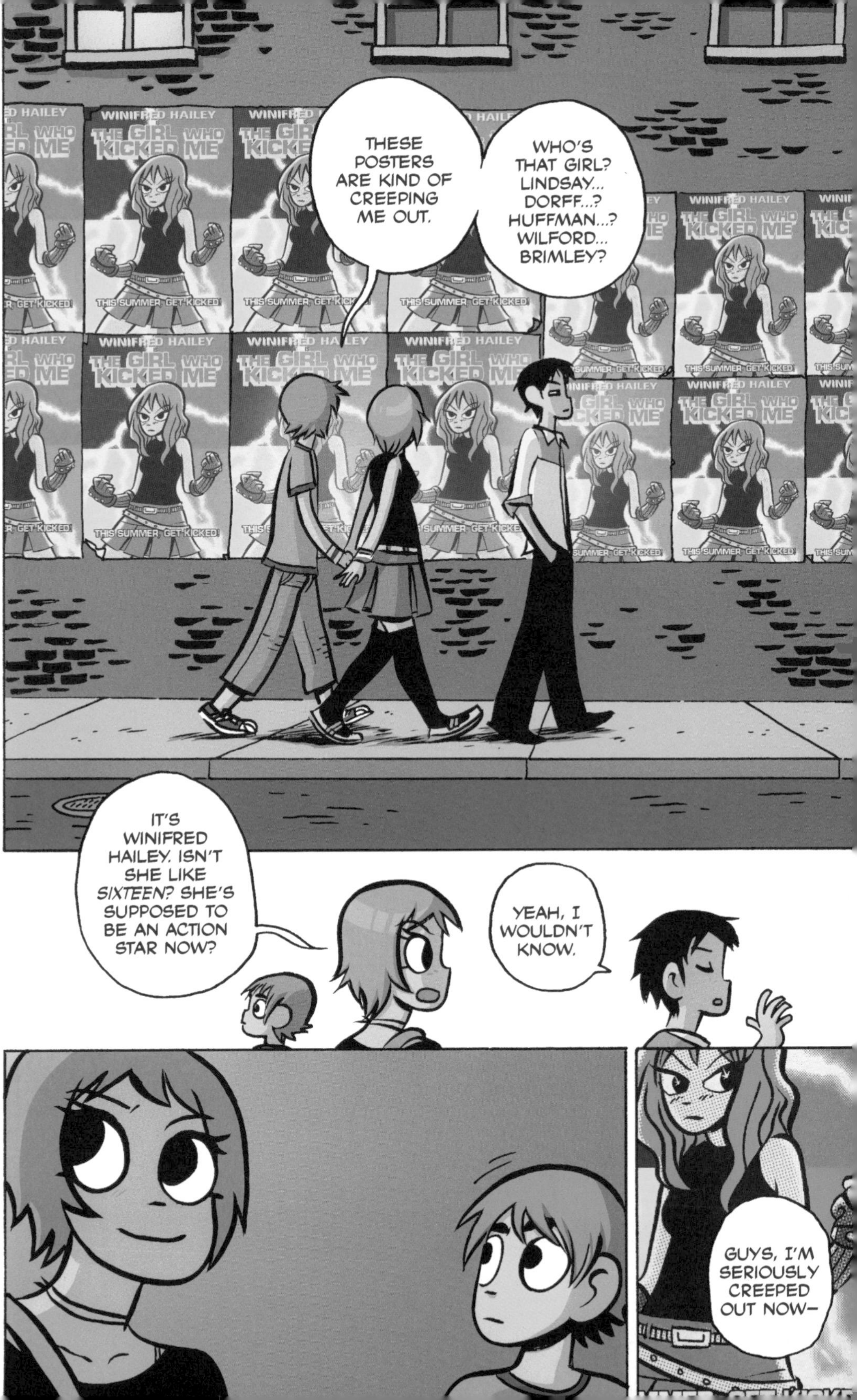
WINIFRED HAILEY
THE GIRL WHO KICKED ME
THIS SUMMER GET KICKED!
THESE POSTERS ARE KIND OF CREEPING ME OUT.
WHO'S THAT GIRL? LINDSAY... DORFF...? HUFFMAN...? WILFORD... BRIMLEY?
IT'S WINIFRED HAILEY. ISN'T SHE LIKE *SIXTEEN?* SHE'S SUPPOSED TO BE AN ACTION STAR NOW?
YEAH, I WOULDN'T KNOW.
GUYS, I'M SERIOUSLY CREEPED OUT NOW–

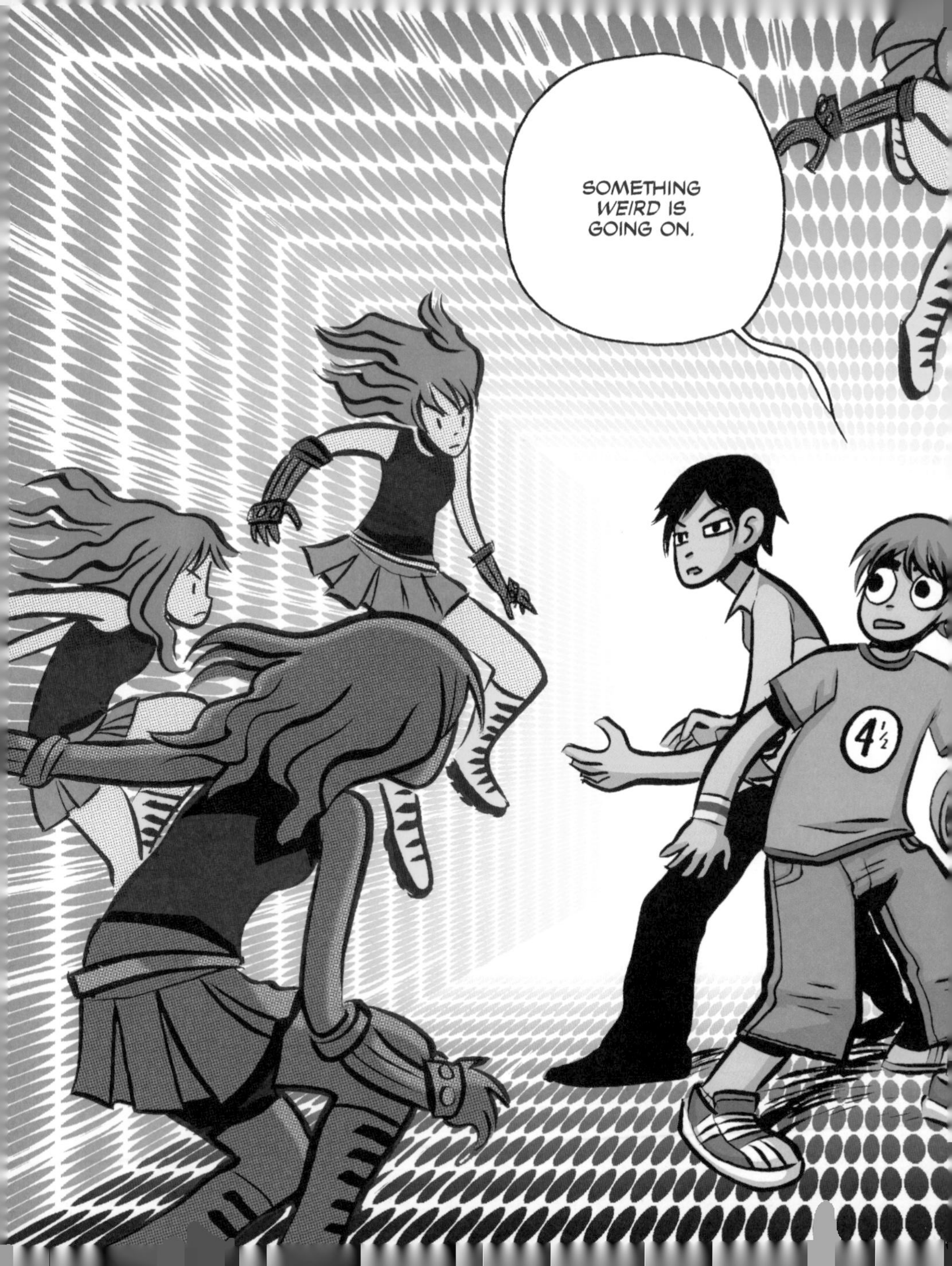
SOMETHING *WEIRD* IS GOING ON.
4½

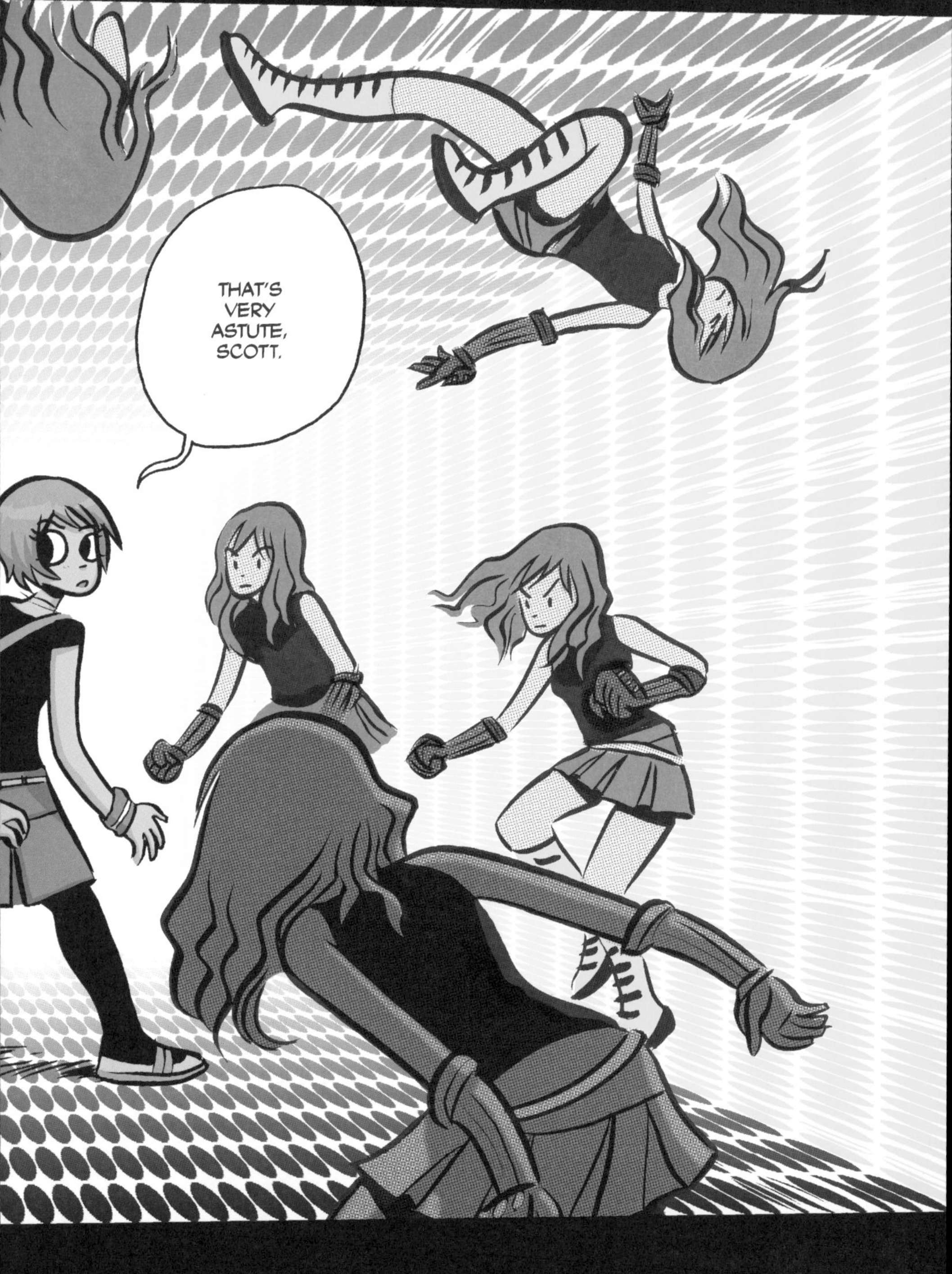
THAT'S VERY ASTUTE, SCOTT.

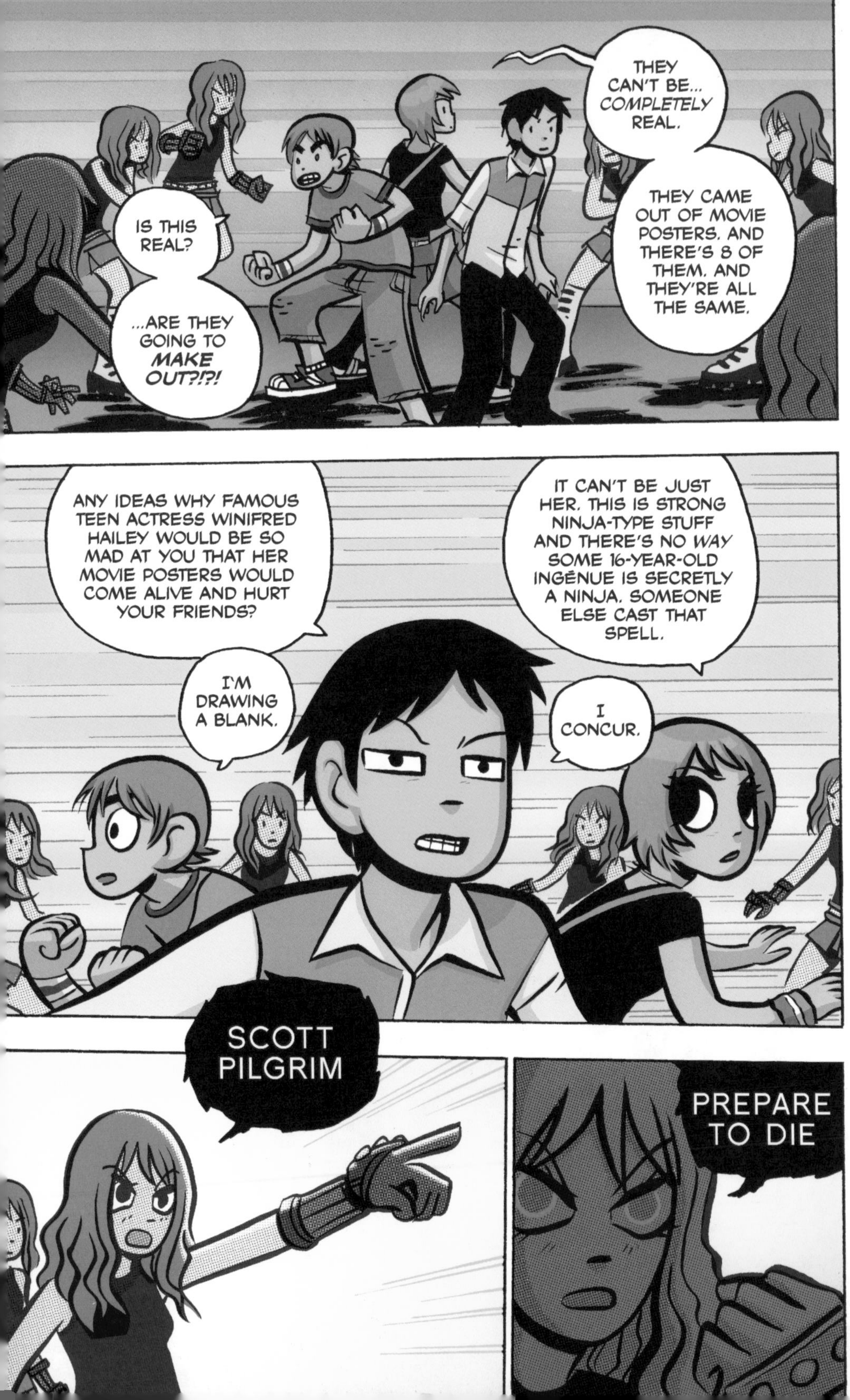
THEY CAN'T BE... COMPLETELY REAL.
THEY CAME OUT OF MOVIE POSTERS. AND THERE'S 8 OF THEM. AND THEY'RE ALL THE SAME.
IS THIS REAL?
...ARE THEY GOING TO MAKE OUT?!?!
ANY IDEAS WHY FAMOUS TEEN ACTRESS WINIFRED HAILEY WOULD BE SO MAD AT YOU THAT HER MOVIE POSTERS WOULD COME ALIVE AND HURT YOUR FRIENDS?
I'M DRAWING A BLANK.
IT CAN'T BE JUST HER. THIS IS STRONG NINJA-TYPE STUFF AND THERE'S NO WAY SOME 16-YEAR-OLD INGÉNUE IS SECRETLY A NINJA. SOMEONE ELSE CAST THAT SPELL.
I CONCUR.
SCOTT PILGRIM
PREPARE TO DIE

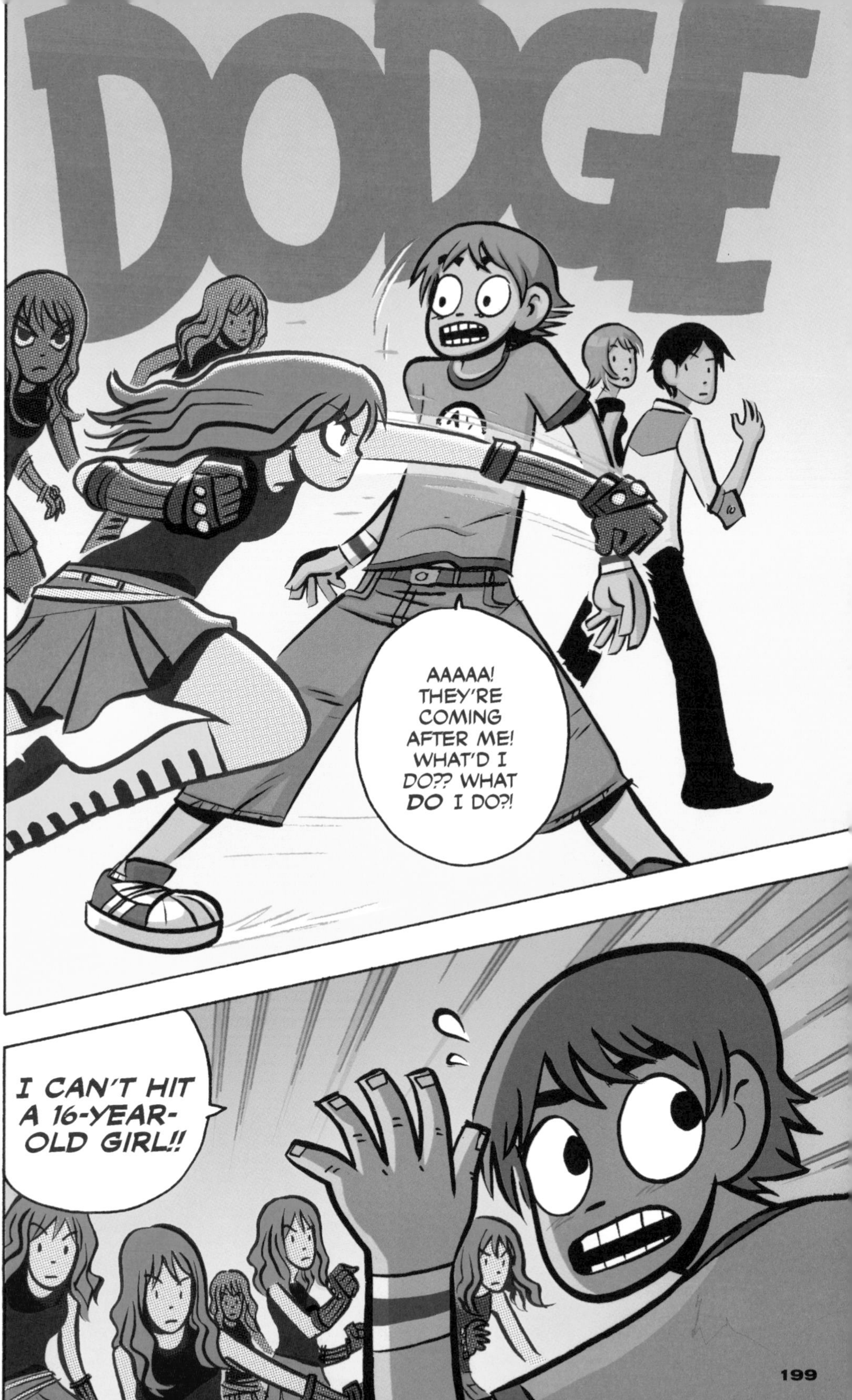
DODGE
AAAAA! THEY'RE COMING AFTER ME! WHAT'D I DO?? WHAT DO I DO?!
I CAN'T HIT A 16-YEAR-OLD GIRL!!

WHY ARE THE WINIFREDS IGNORING US?

THEY'RE JUST FOR SCOTT, IT LOOKS LIKE. CUTE AS A BUTTON, THOUGH, AREN'T THEY?

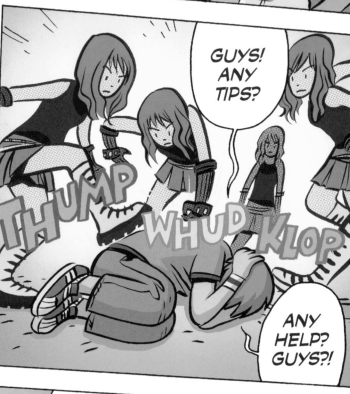

GUYS! ANY TIPS?

THUMP WHUD KLOP

ANY HELP? GUYS?!

BASH KROK SPOW

MAYBE SOME KIND OF NINJA MAGIC TRIGGERED WHEN HE WALKED BY THE POSTERS?

YOUR GUESS IS MORE OR LESS AS BAD AS MINE, DUDE.

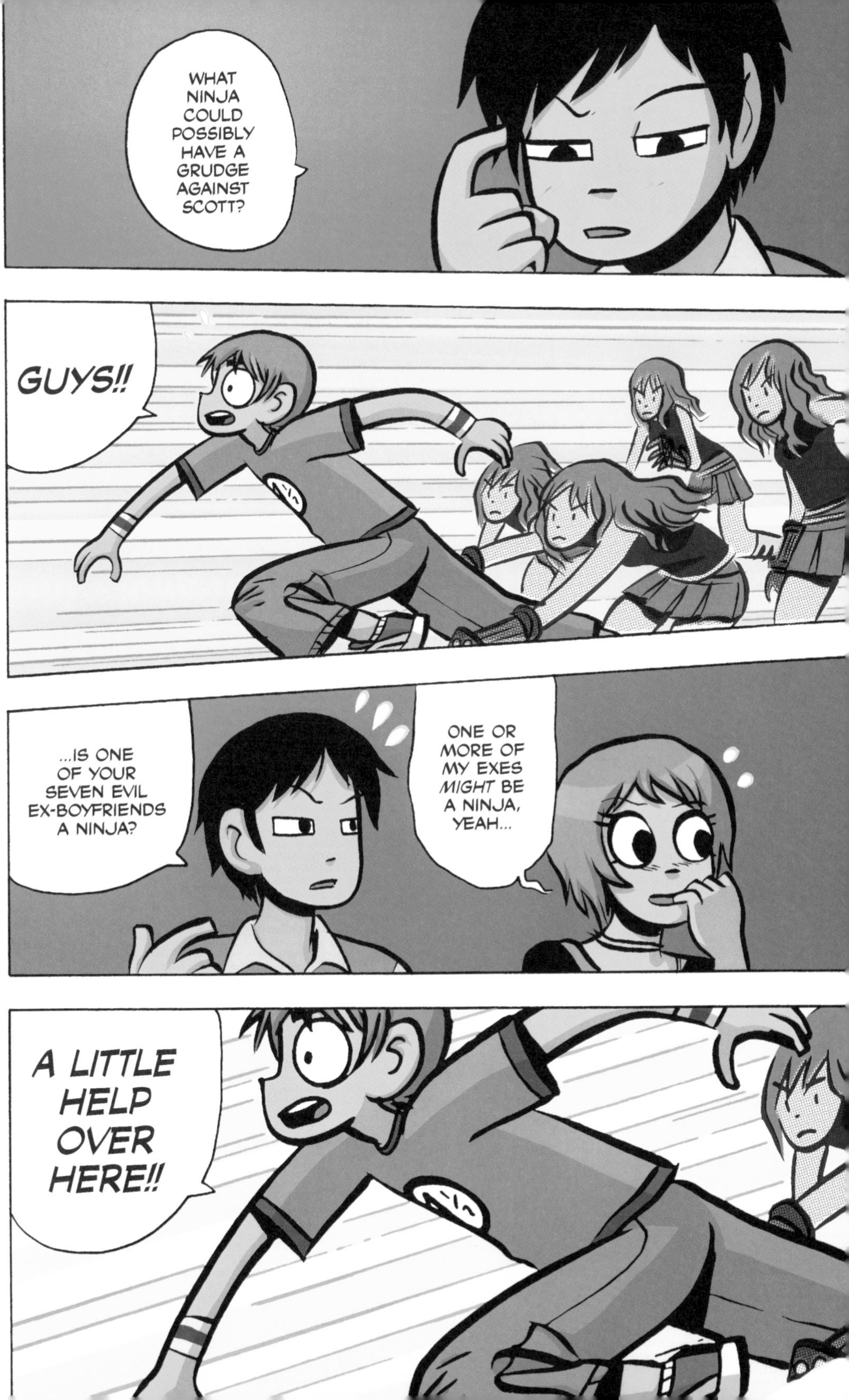
WHAT NINJA COULD POSSIBLY HAVE A GRUDGE AGAINST SCOTT?
GUYS!!
...IS ONE OF YOUR SEVEN EVIL EX-BOYFRIENDS A NINJA?
ONE OR MORE OF MY EXES *MIGHT* BE A NINJA, YEAH...
A LITTLE HELP OVER HERE!!

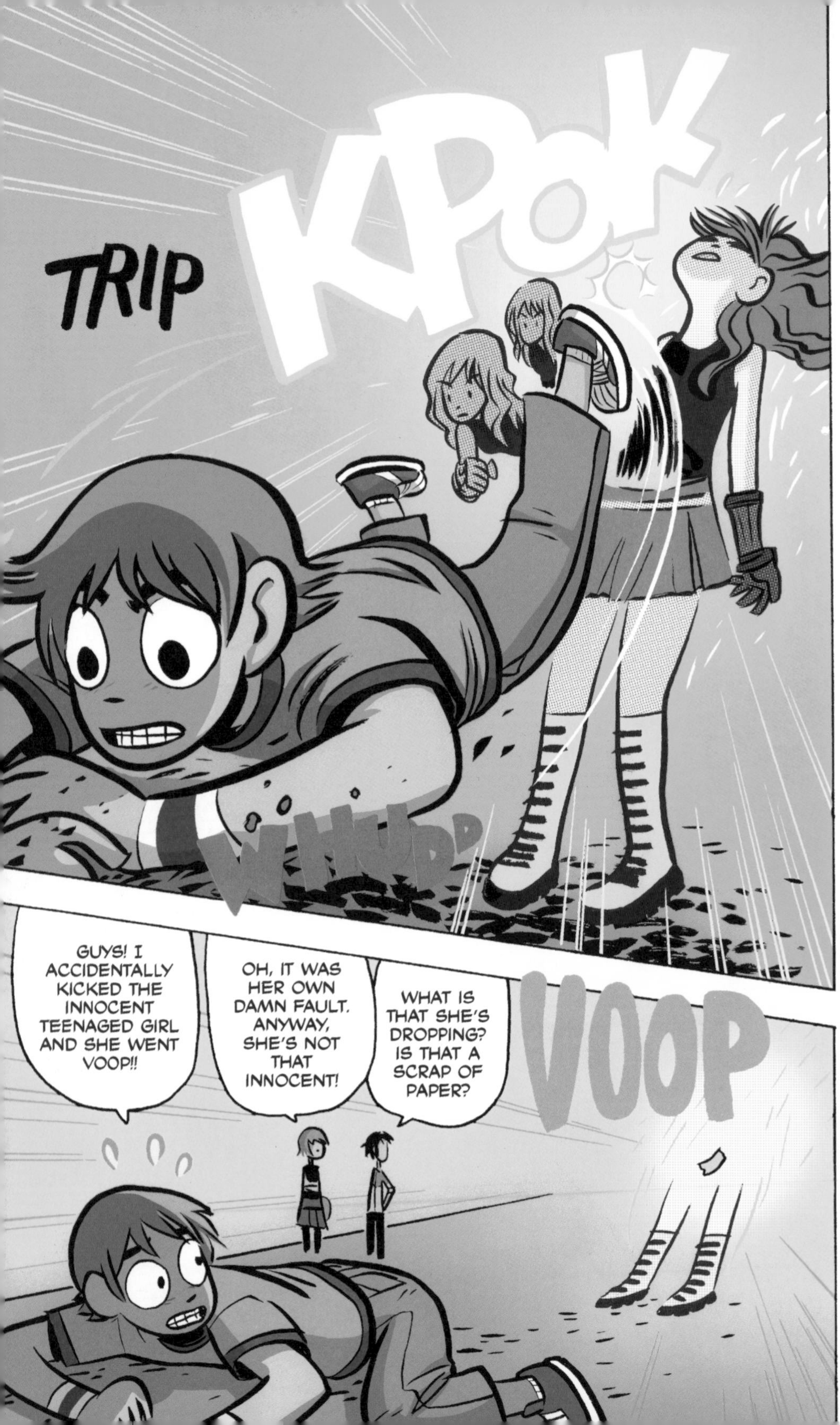
TRIP
KPOK
WHUDD
GUYS! I ACCIDENTALLY KICKED THE INNOCENT TEENAGED GIRL AND SHE WENT VOOP!!
OH, IT WAS HER OWN DAMN FAULT. ANYWAY, SHE'S NOT THAT INNOCENT!
WHAT IS THAT SHE'S DROPPING? IS THAT A SCRAP OF PAPER?
VOOP

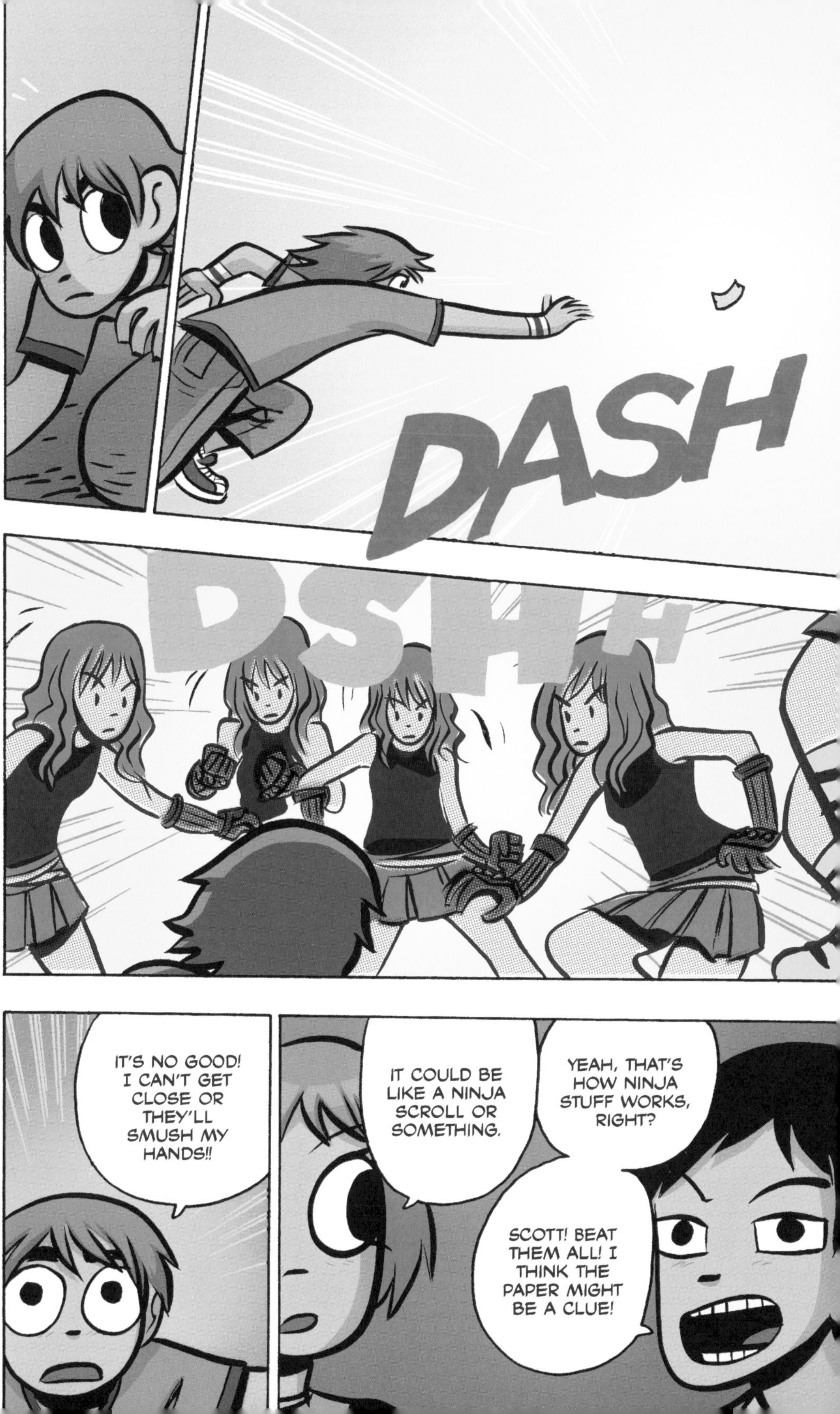
DASH
DSHH
IT'S NO GOOD! I CAN'T GET CLOSE OR THEY'LL SMUSH MY HANDS!!
IT COULD BE LIKE A NINJA SCROLL OR SOMETHING.
YEAH, THAT'S HOW NINJA STUFF WORKS, RIGHT?
SCOTT! BEAT THEM ALL! I THINK THE PAPER MIGHT BE A CLUE!

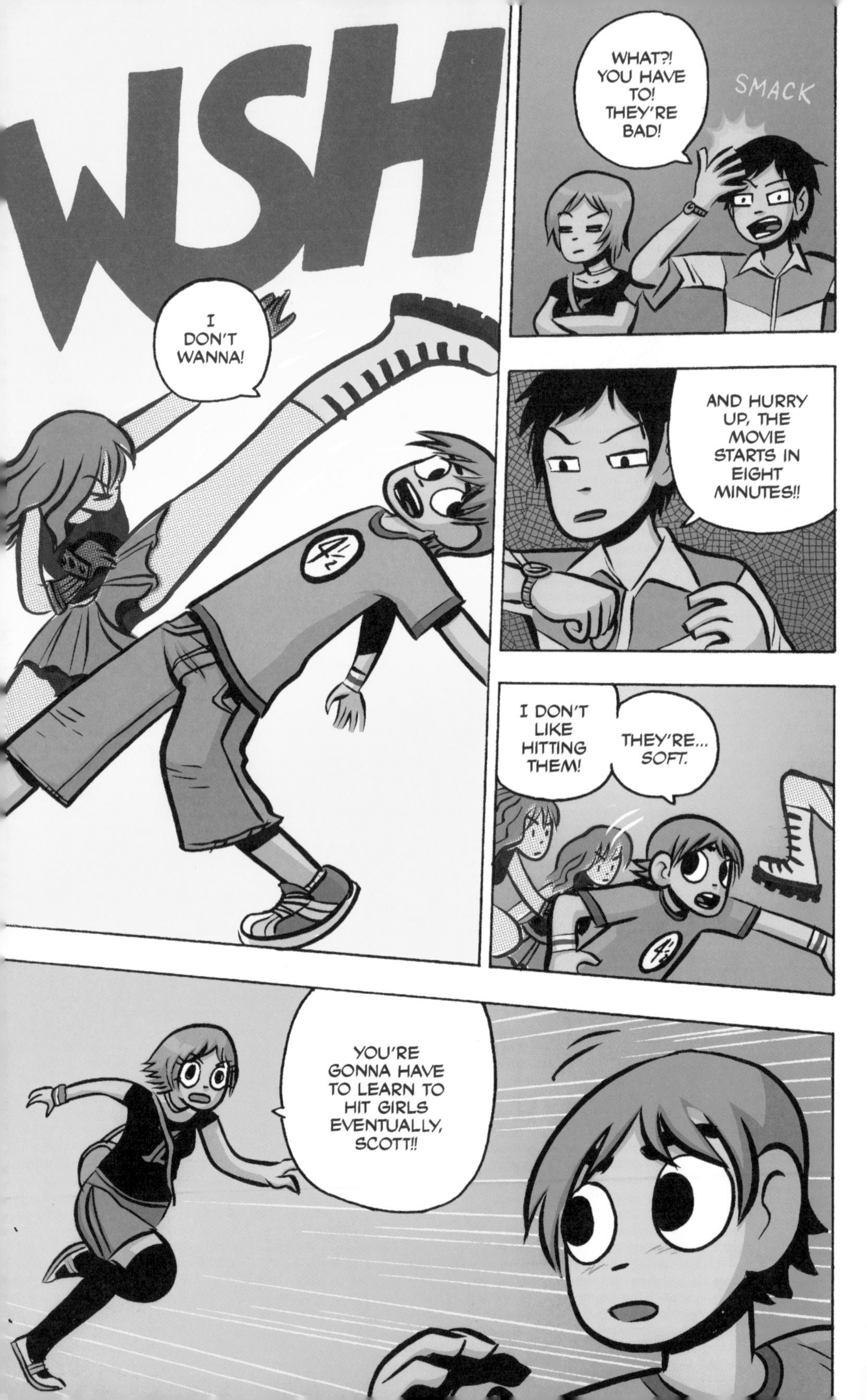
WSH
I DON'T WANNA!
WHAT?! YOU HAVE TO! THEY'RE BAD!
SMACK
AND HURRY UP, THE MOVIE STARTS IN EIGHT MINUTES!!
I DON'T LIKE HITTING THEM!
THEY'RE... SOFT.
YOU'RE GONNA HAVE TO LEARN TO HIT GIRLS EVENTUALLY, SCOTT!!

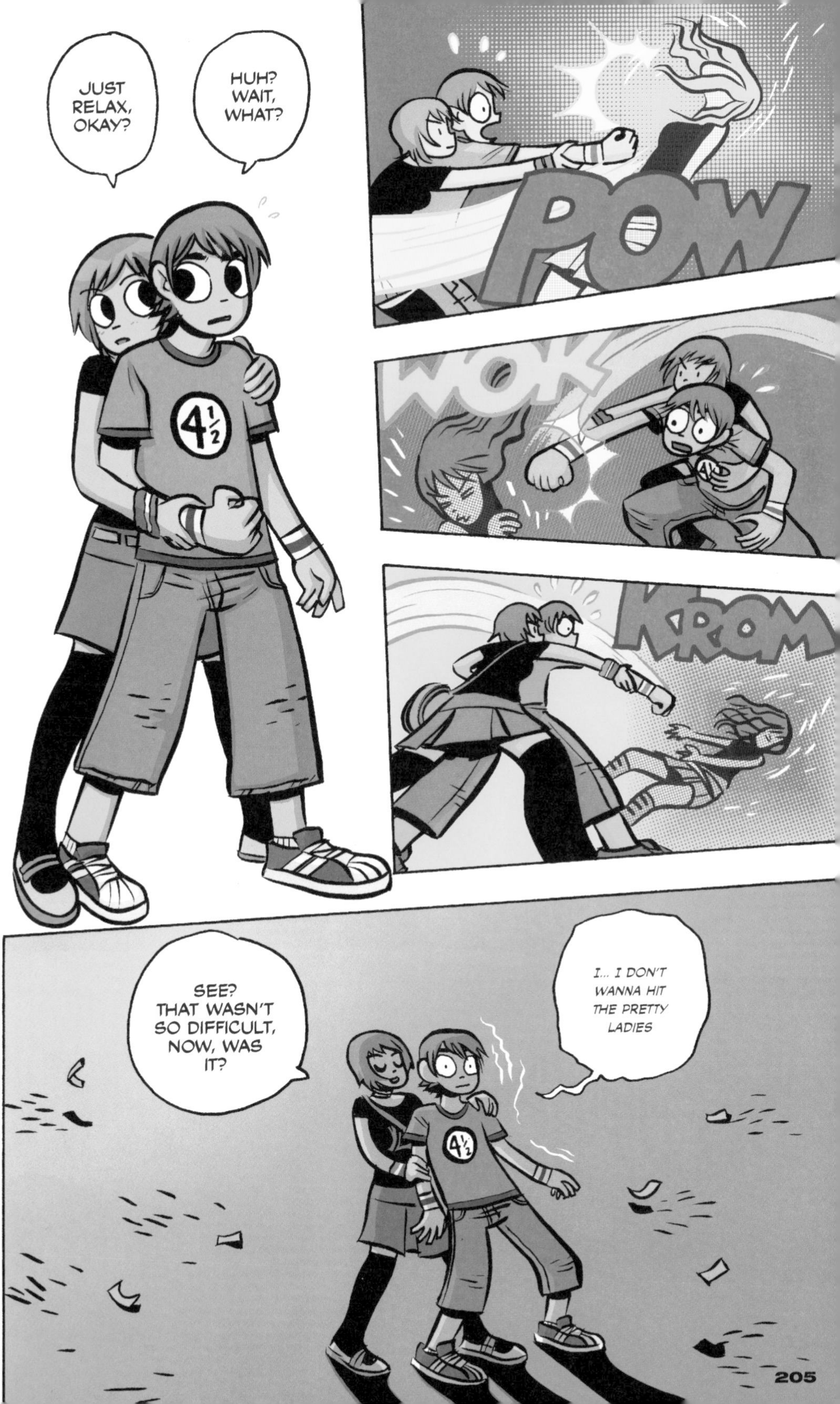
JUST RELAX, OKAY?
HUH? WAIT, WHAT?
POW
WOK
KROM
SEE? THAT WASN'T SO DIFFICULT, NOW, WAS IT?
I... I DON'T WANNA HIT THE PRETTY LADIES

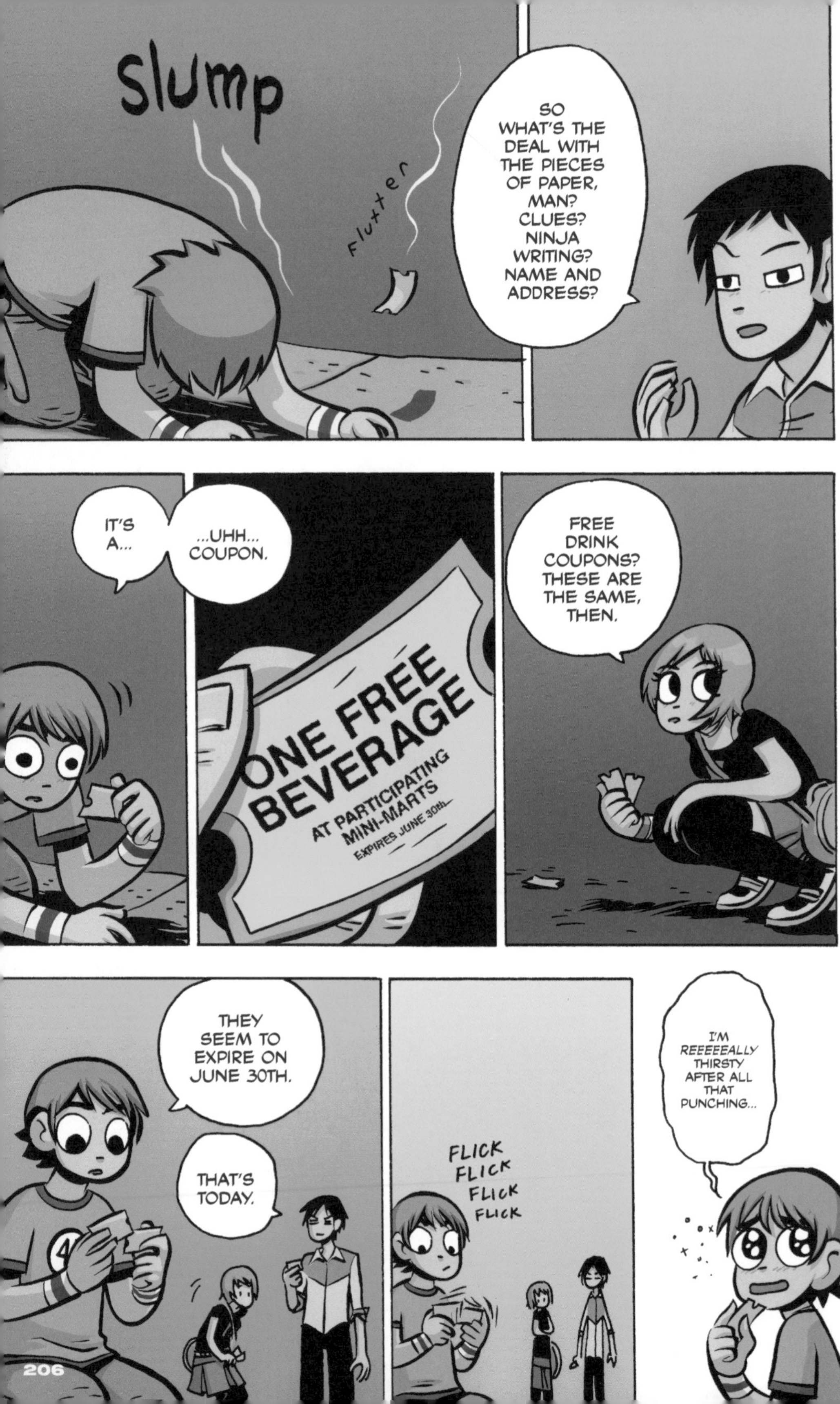
Slump
Flutter
SO WHAT'S THE DEAL WITH THE PIECES OF PAPER, MAN? CLUES? NINJA WRITING? NAME AND ADDRESS?
IT'S A...
...UHH... COUPON.
ONE FREE BEVERAGE
AT PARTICIPATING MINI-MARTS
EXPIRES JUNE 30th
FREE DRINK COUPONS? THESE ARE THE SAME, THEN.
THEY SEEM TO EXPIRE ON JUNE 30TH.
THAT'S TODAY.
FLICK FLICK FLICK FLICK
I'M REEEEEALLY THIRSTY AFTER ALL THAT PUNCHING...

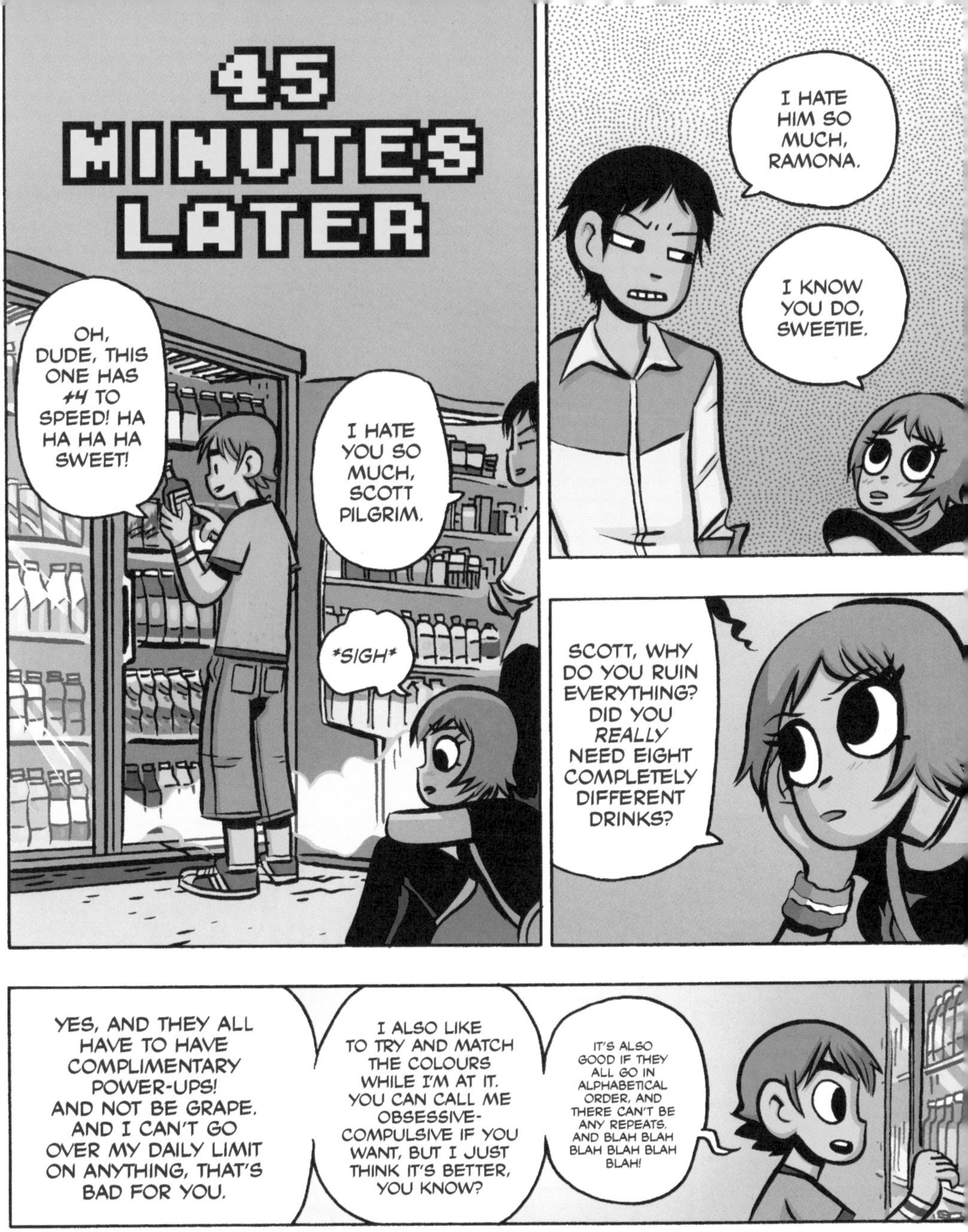
45 MINUTES LATER
OH, DUDE, THIS ONE HAS +4 TO SPEED! HA HA HA HA SWEET!
I HATE YOU SO MUCH, SCOTT PILGRIM.
SIGH
I HATE HIM SO MUCH, RAMONA.
I KNOW YOU DO, SWEETIE.
SCOTT, WHY DO YOU RUIN EVERYTHING? DID YOU *REALLY* NEED EIGHT COMPLETELY DIFFERENT DRINKS?
YES, AND THEY ALL HAVE TO HAVE COMPLIMENTARY POWER-UPS! AND NOT BE GRAPE. AND I CAN'T GO OVER MY DAILY LIMIT ON ANYTHING, THAT'S BAD FOR YOU.
I ALSO LIKE TO TRY AND MATCH THE COLOURS WHILE I'M AT IT. YOU CAN CALL ME OBSESSIVE-COMPULSIVE IF YOU WANT, BUT I JUST THINK IT'S BETTER, YOU KNOW?
IT'S ALSO GOOD IF THEY ALL GO IN ALPHABETICAL ORDER, AND THERE CAN'T BE ANY REPEATS, AND BLAH BLAH BLAH BLAH BLAH BLAH!

SCOTT PILGRIM SAYS...

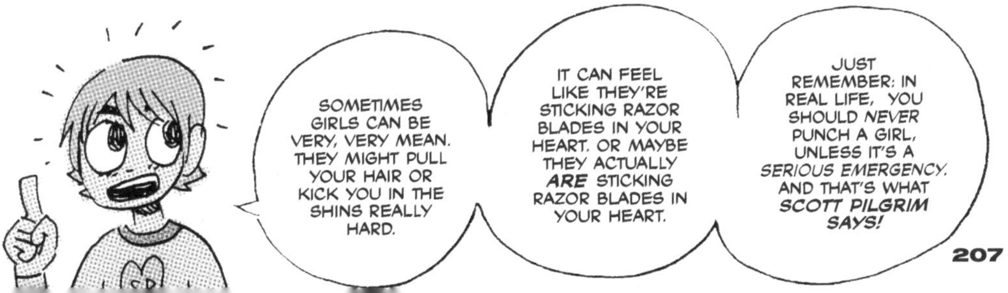
SOMETIMES GIRLS CAN BE VERY, VERY MEAN. THEY MIGHT PULL YOUR HAIR OR KICK YOU IN THE SHINS REALLY HARD.
IT CAN FEEL LIKE THEY'RE STICKING RAZOR BLADES IN YOUR HEART. OR MAYBE THEY ACTUALLY **ARE** STICKING RAZOR BLADES IN YOUR HEART.
JUST REMEMBER: IN REAL LIFE, YOU SHOULD *NEVER* PUNCH A GIRL, UNLESS IT'S A *SERIOUS EMERGENCY*. AND THAT'S WHAT ***SCOTT PILGRIM SAYS!***

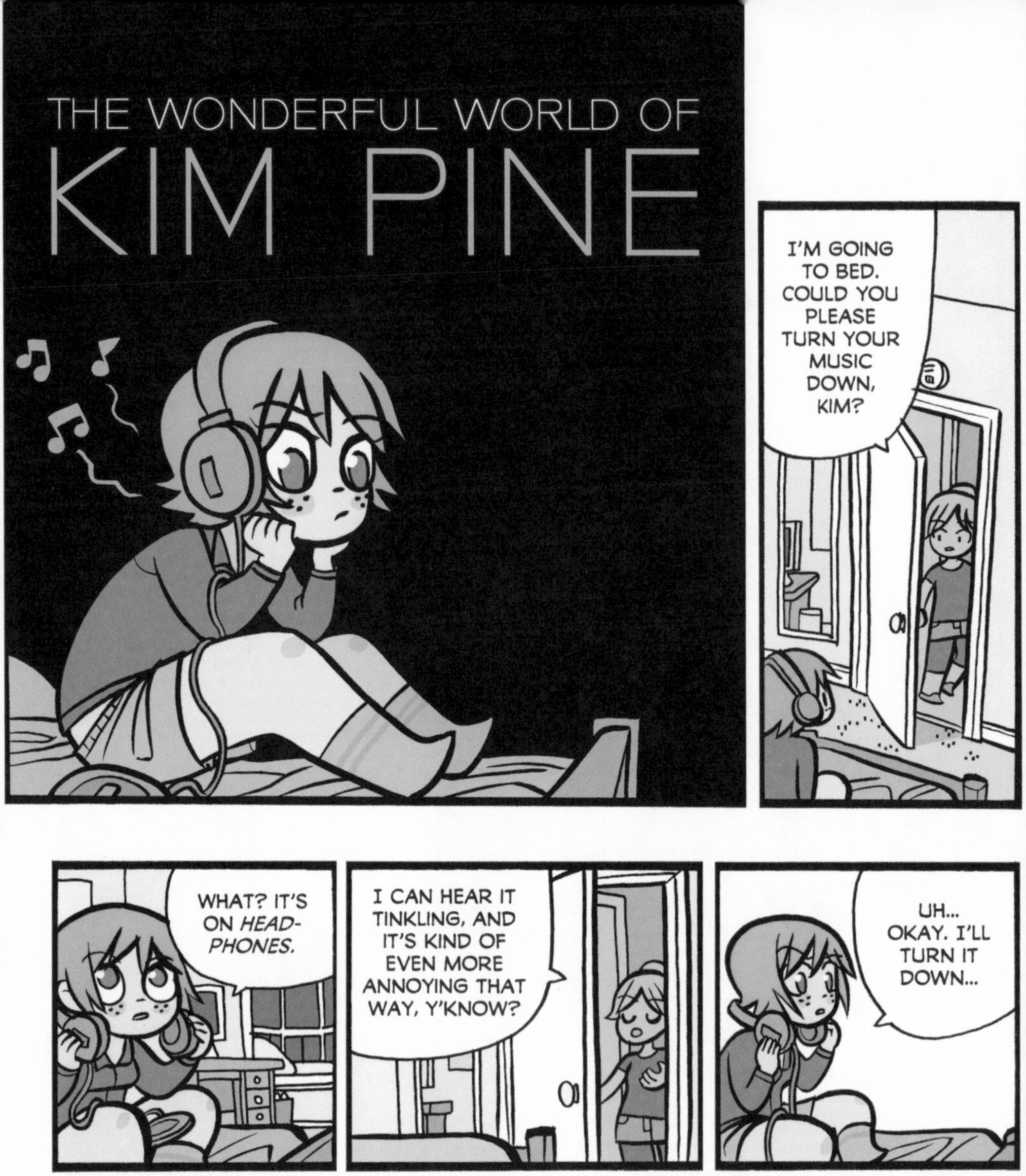
THE WONDERFUL WORLD OF
KIM PINE
I'M GOING TO BED. COULD YOU PLEASE TURN YOUR MUSIC DOWN, KIM?
WHAT? IT'S ON *HEAD-PHONES.*
I CAN HEAR IT TINKLING, AND IT'S KIND OF EVEN MORE ANNOYING THAT WAY, Y'KNOW?
UH... OKAY. I'LL TURN IT DOWN...

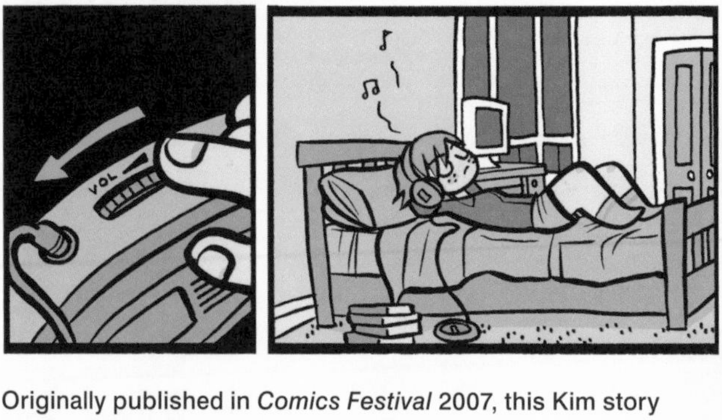
VOL

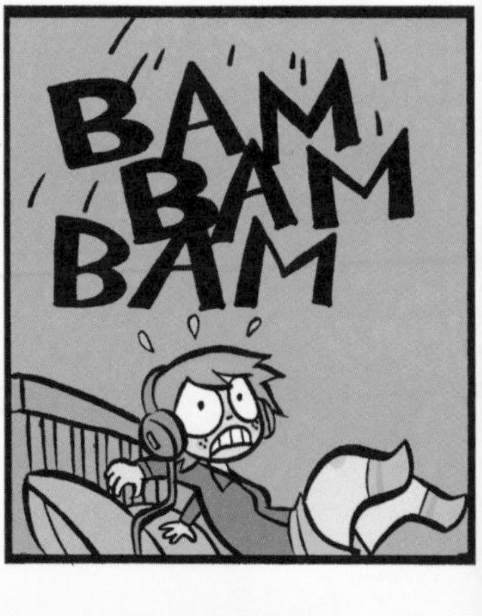
BAM BAM BAM

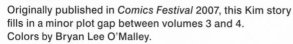

Originally published in *Comics Festival* 2007, this Kim story fills in a minor plot gap between volumes 3 and 4. Colors by Bryan Lee O'Malley.

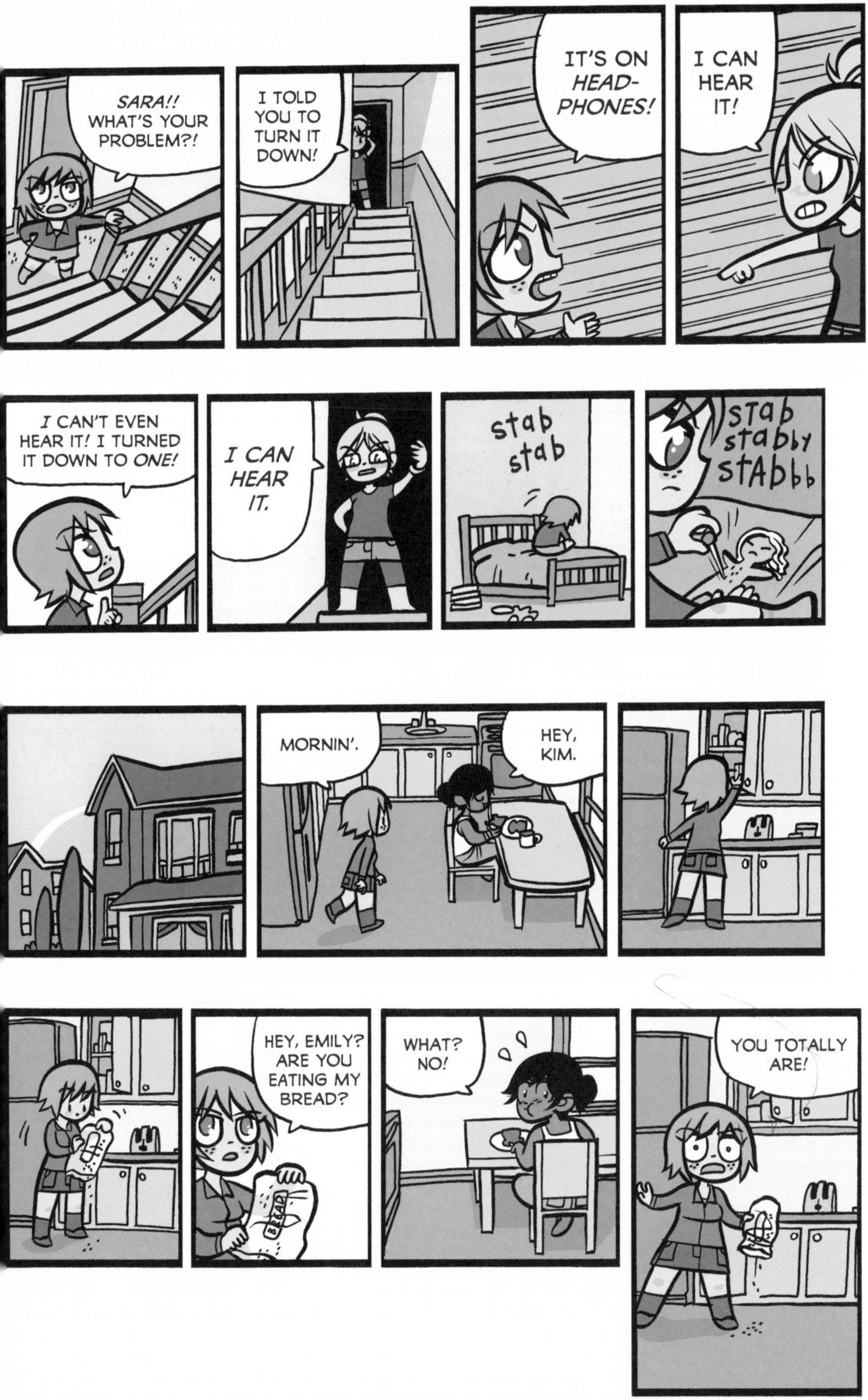
SARA!! WHAT'S YOUR PROBLEM?!
I TOLD YOU TO TURN IT DOWN!
IT'S ON HEAD-PHONES!
I CAN HEAR IT!
I CAN'T EVEN HEAR IT! I TURNED IT DOWN TO ONE!
I CAN HEAR IT.
stab stab
stab stabby stabbb
MORNIN'.
HEY, KIM.
HEY, EMILY? ARE YOU EATING MY BREAD?
BREAD
WHAT? NO!
YOU TOTALLY ARE!

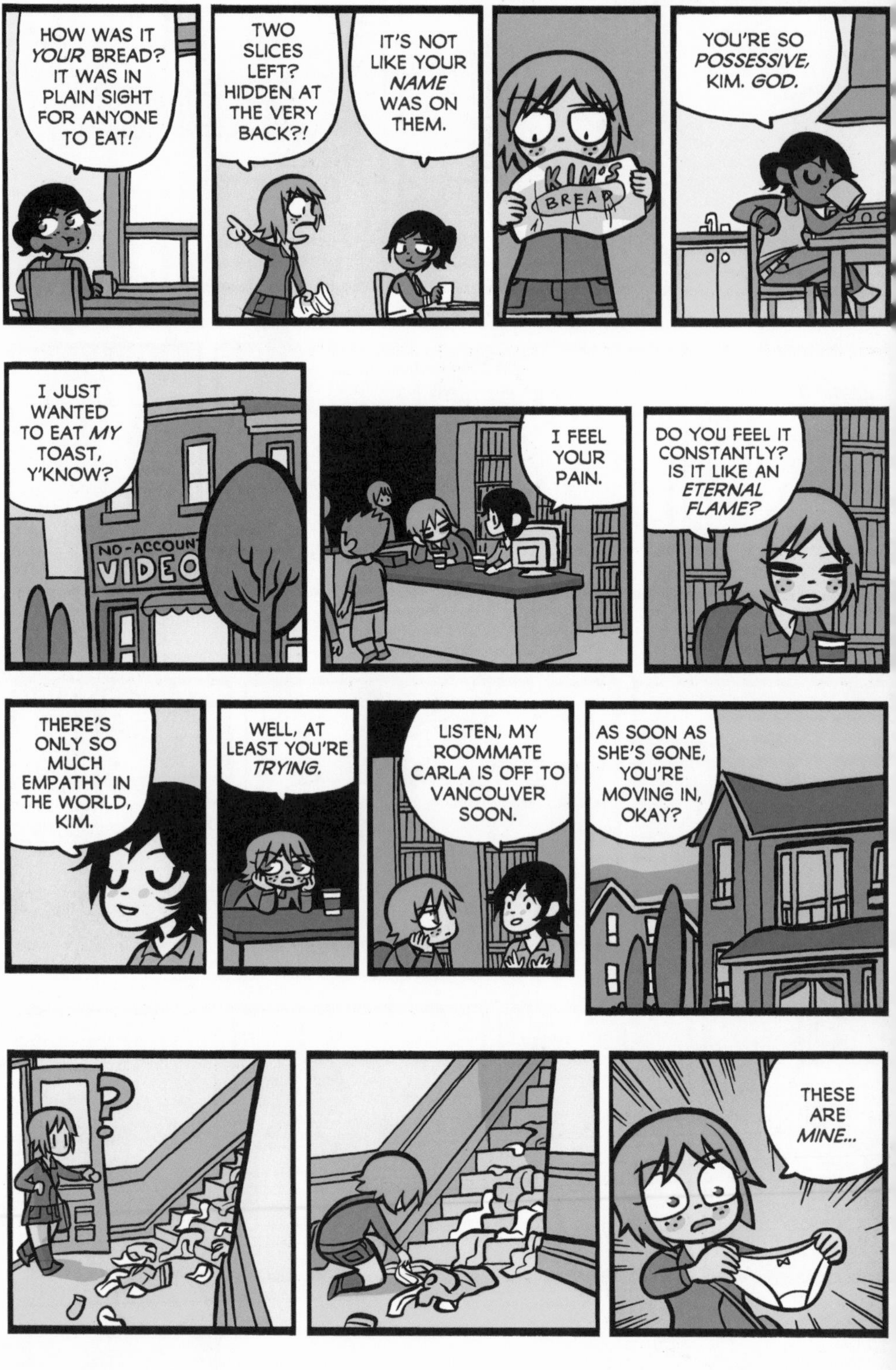

HOW WAS IT *YOUR* BREAD? IT WAS IN PLAIN SIGHT FOR ANYONE TO EAT!
TWO SLICES LEFT? HIDDEN AT THE VERY BACK?!
IT'S NOT LIKE YOUR *NAME* WAS ON THEM.
KIM'S BREAD
YOU'RE SO *POSSESSIVE,* KIM. *GOD.*
I JUST WANTED TO EAT *MY* TOAST, Y'KNOW?
NO-ACCOUNT VIDEO
I FEEL YOUR PAIN.
DO YOU FEEL IT CONSTANTLY? IS IT LIKE AN *ETERNAL FLAME?*
THERE'S ONLY SO MUCH EMPATHY IN THE WORLD, KIM.
WELL, AT LEAST YOU'RE *TRYING.*
LISTEN, MY ROOMMATE CARLA IS OFF TO VANCOUVER SOON.
AS SOON AS SHE'S GONE, YOU'RE MOVING IN, OKAY?
?
THESE ARE *MINE...*

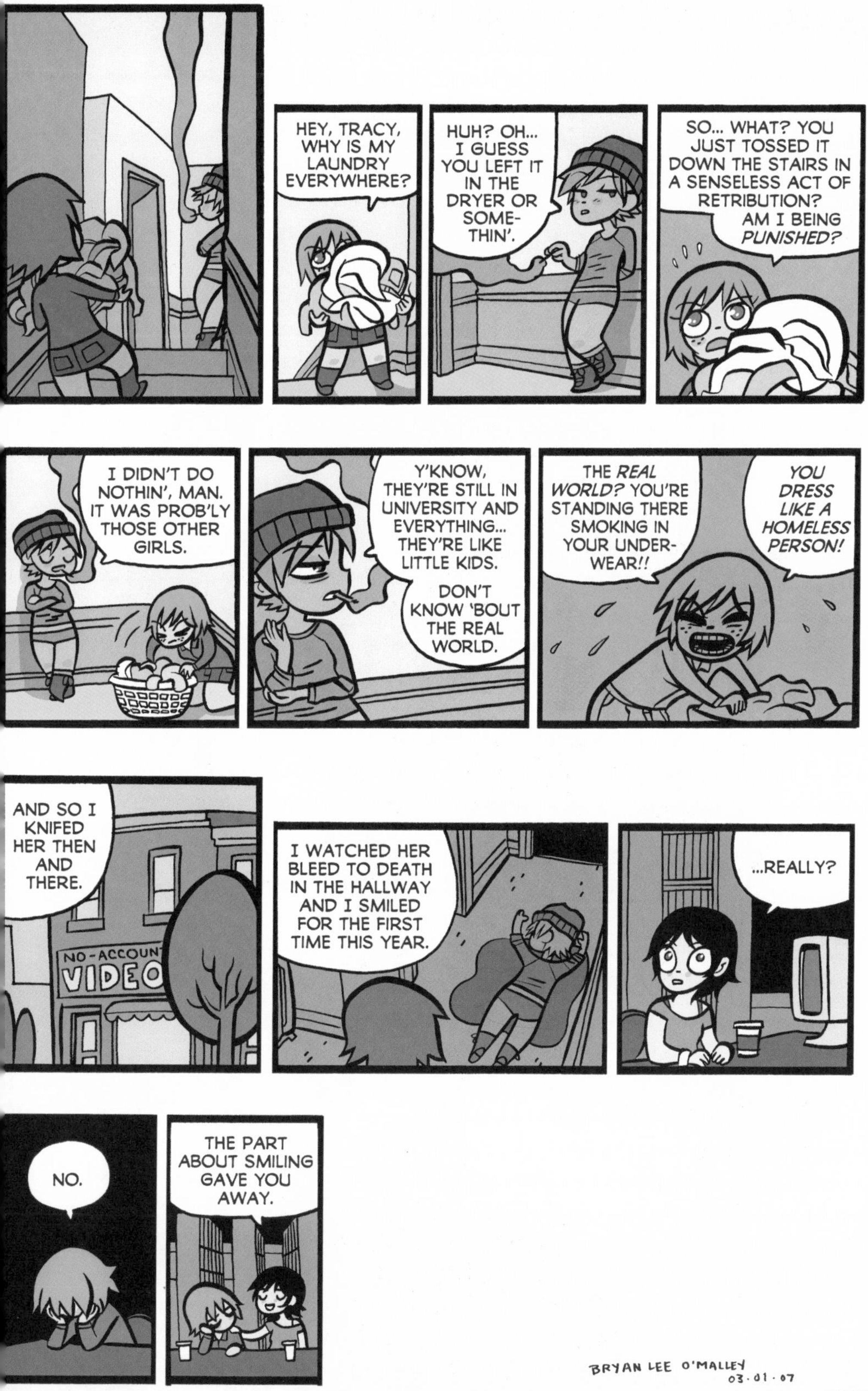
HEY, TRACY, WHY IS MY LAUNDRY EVERYWHERE?
HUH? OH... I GUESS YOU LEFT IT IN THE DRYER OR SOME-THIN'.
SO... WHAT? YOU JUST TOSSED IT DOWN THE STAIRS IN A SENSELESS ACT OF RETRIBUTION?
AM I BEING PUNISHED?
I DIDN'T DO NOTHIN', MAN. IT WAS PROB'LY THOSE OTHER GIRLS.
Y'KNOW, THEY'RE STILL IN UNIVERSITY AND EVERYTHING... THEY'RE LIKE LITTLE KIDS.
DON'T KNOW 'BOUT THE REAL WORLD.
THE REAL WORLD? YOU'RE STANDING THERE SMOKING IN YOUR UNDER-WEAR!!
YOU DRESS LIKE A HOMELESS PERSON!
AND SO I KNIFED HER THEN AND THERE.
NO-ACCOUNT VIDEO
I WATCHED HER BLEED TO DEATH IN THE HALLWAY AND I SMILED FOR THE FIRST TIME THIS YEAR.
...REALLY?
NO.
THE PART ABOUT SMILING GAVE YOU AWAY.

BRYAN LEE O'MALLEY
03·01·07

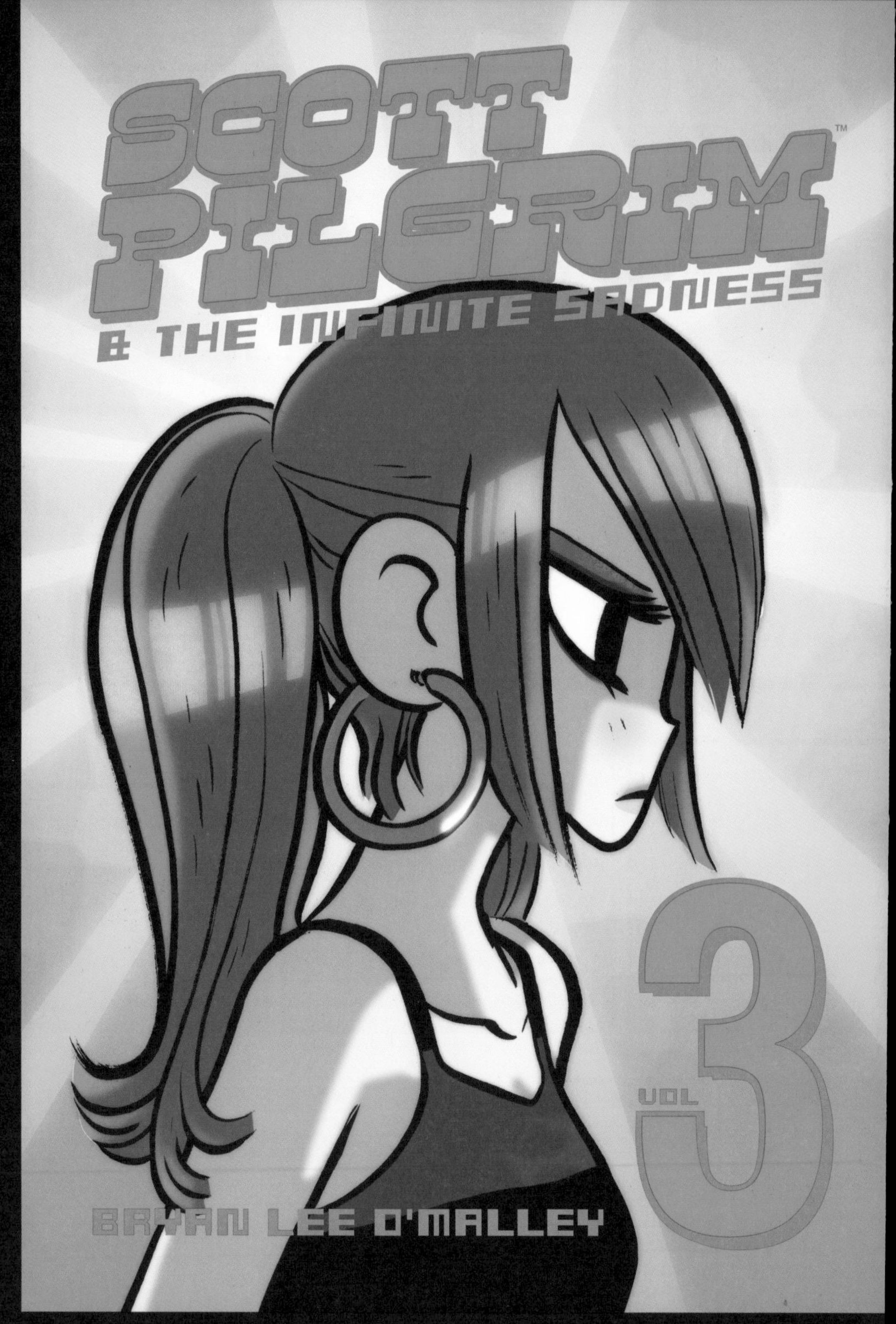
SCOTT PILGRIM™
& THE INFINITE SADNESS
VOL 3
BRYAN LEE O'MALLEY

 The cover for the original edition of *Scott Pilgrim* volume 3. Colors by Bryan Lee O'Malley.

The biggest,
most exciting
SCOTT PILGRIM™
adventure yet!

by **BRYAN LEE O'MALLEY**

Diamond code OCT05 3132 | *ISBN 1-932664-22-X*
www.scottpilgrim.com | *www.onipress.com*

OFFICIAL ONI PRESS
SEAL OF QUALITY

n Lee O'Malley.

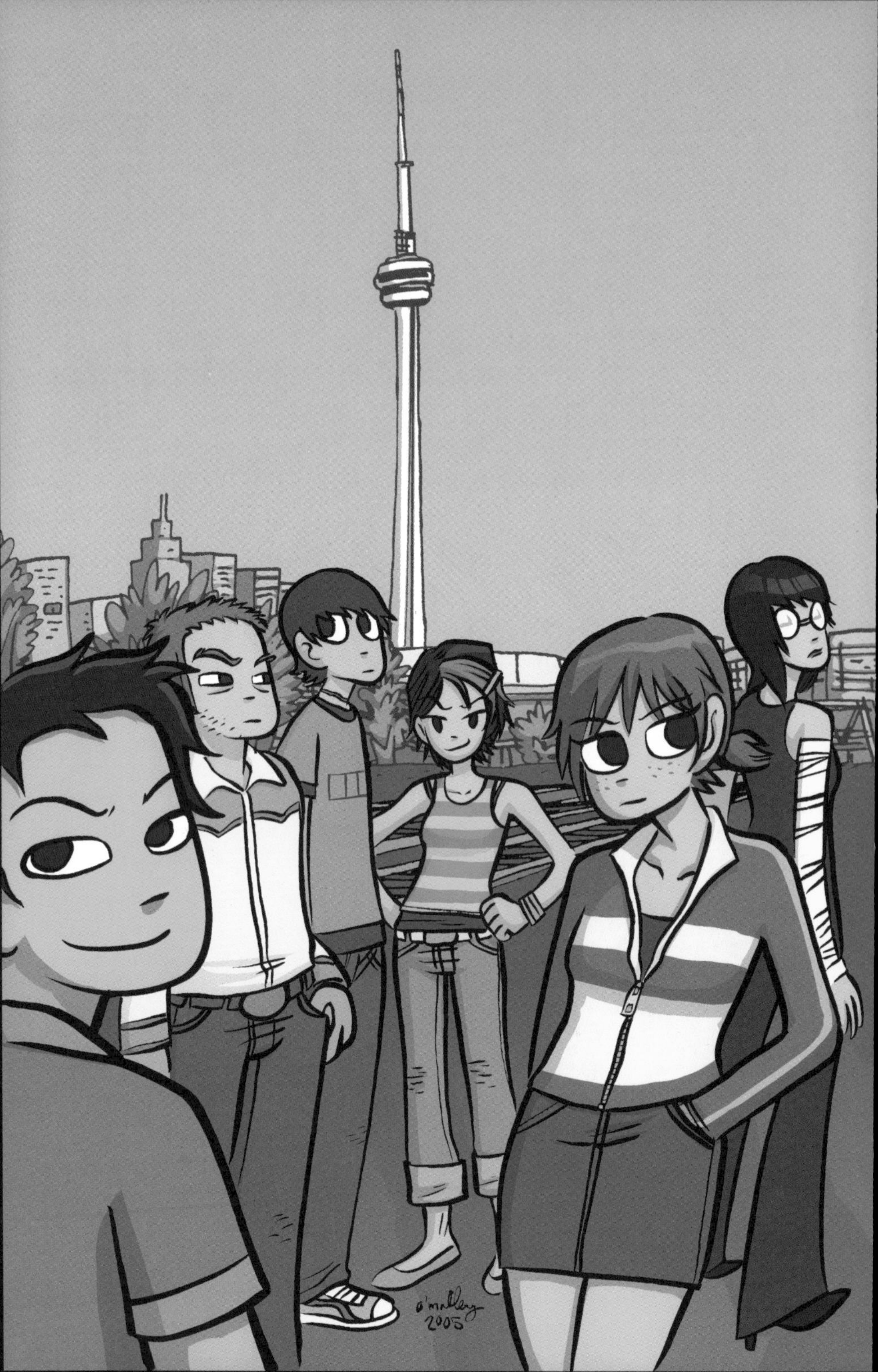
o'malley
2005

Unused cover concept for volume 3. New colors by Nathan Fairbairn.

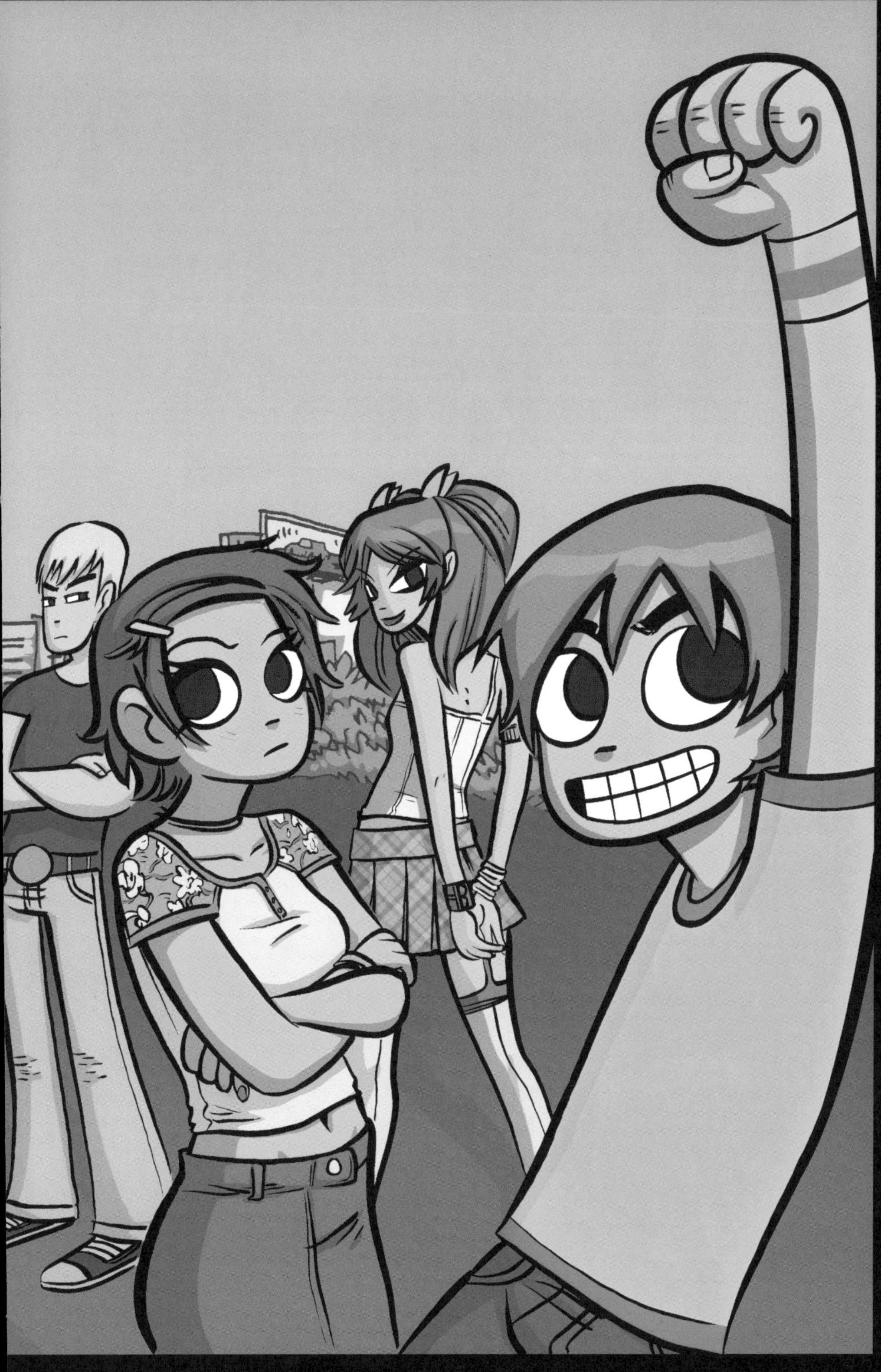

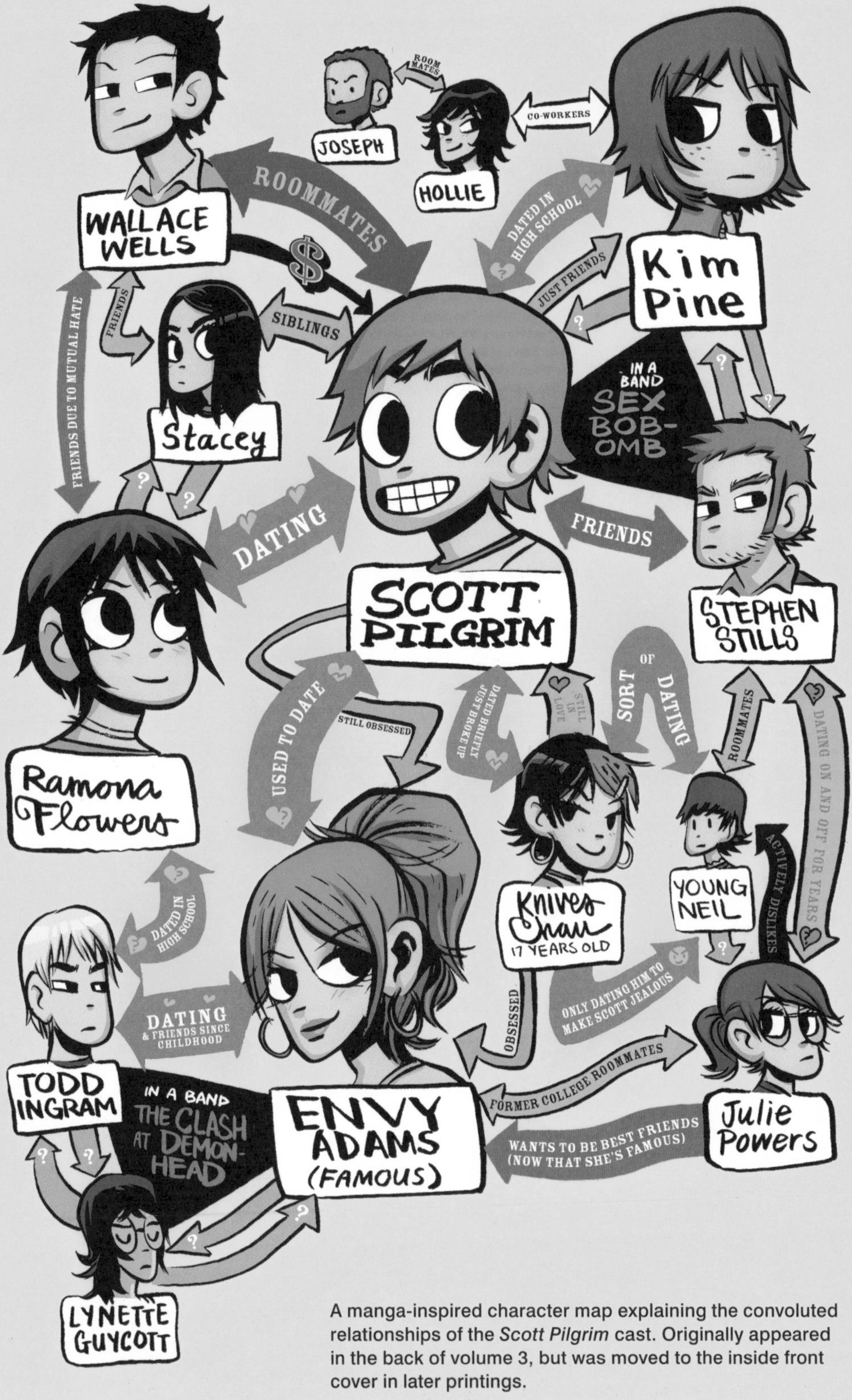
WALLACE WELLS
ROOMMATES
$
JOSEPH
ROOMMATES
HOLLIE
CO-WORKERS
Kim Pine
DATED IN HIGH SCHOOL
JUST FRIENDS
FRIENDS
SIBLINGS
Stacey
FRIENDS DUE TO MUTUAL HATE
IN A BAND
SEX BOB-OMB
DATING
FRIENDS
SCOTT PILGRIM
STEPHEN STILLS
Ramona Flowers
USED TO DATE
STILL OBSESSED
DATED BRIEFLY JUST BROKE UP
STILL IN LOVE
SORT OF DATING
ROOMMATES
DATING ON AND OFF FOR YEARS
ACTIVELY DISLIKES
Knives Chau
17 YEARS OLD
YOUNG NEIL
DATED IN HIGH SCHOOL
DATING & FRIENDS SINCE CHILDHOOD
OBSESSED
ONLY DATING HIM TO MAKE SCOTT JEALOUS
FORMER COLLEGE ROOMMATES
TODD INGRAM
IN A BAND
THE CLASH AT DEMONHEAD
ENVY ADAMS (FAMOUS)
WANTS TO BE BEST FRIENDS (NOW THAT SHE'S FAMOUS)
Julie Powers
LYNETTE GUYCOTT

A manga-inspired character map explaining the convoluted relationships of the *Scott Pilgrim* cast. Originally appeared in the back of volume 3, but was moved to the inside front cover in later printings.

PROCESS

The following pages present an unfiltered look at sketches and development material created during the production of *Scott Pilgrim* volume 3.

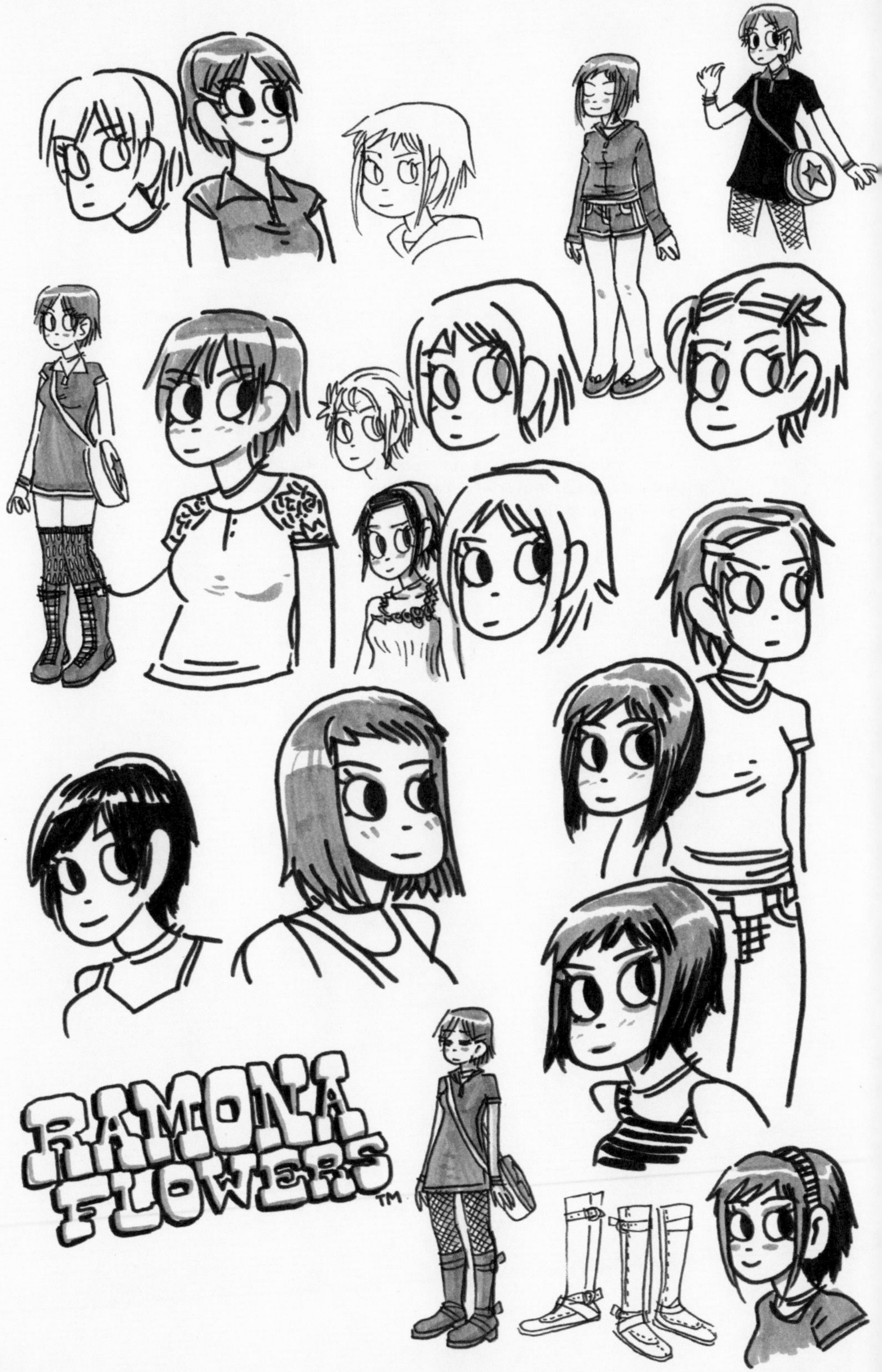
RAMONA FLOWERS™

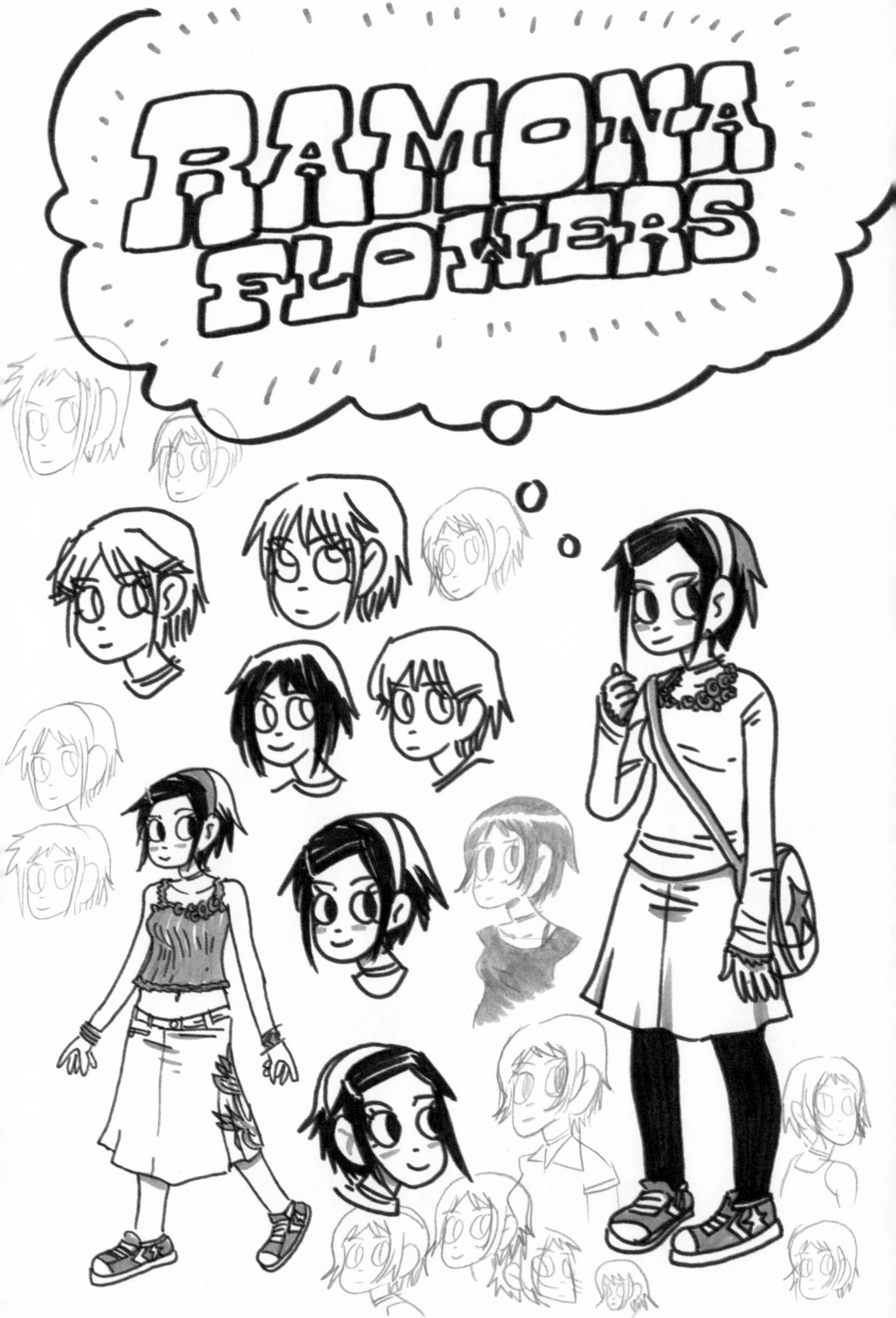
RAMONA FLOWERS

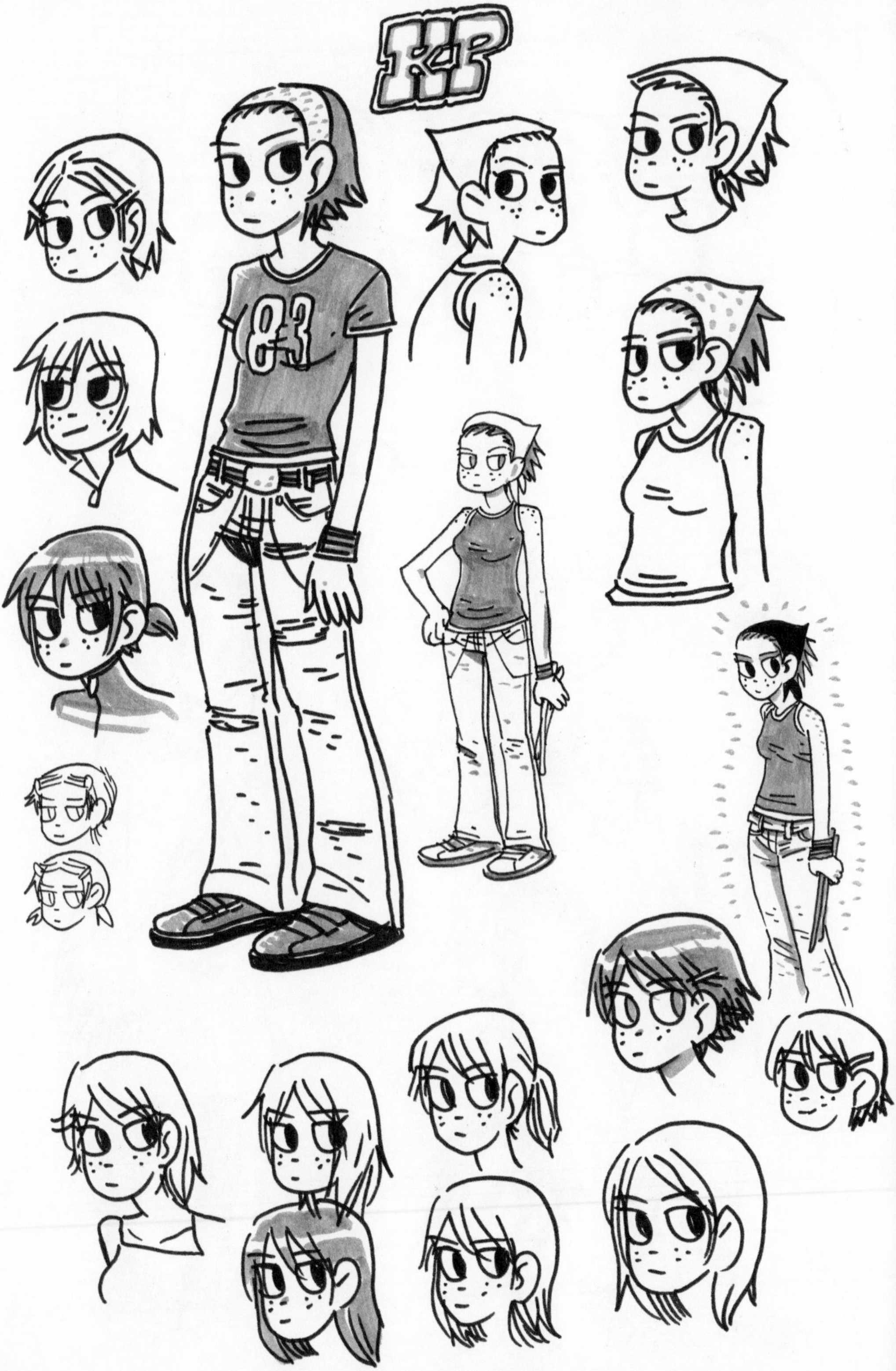
K-P
83

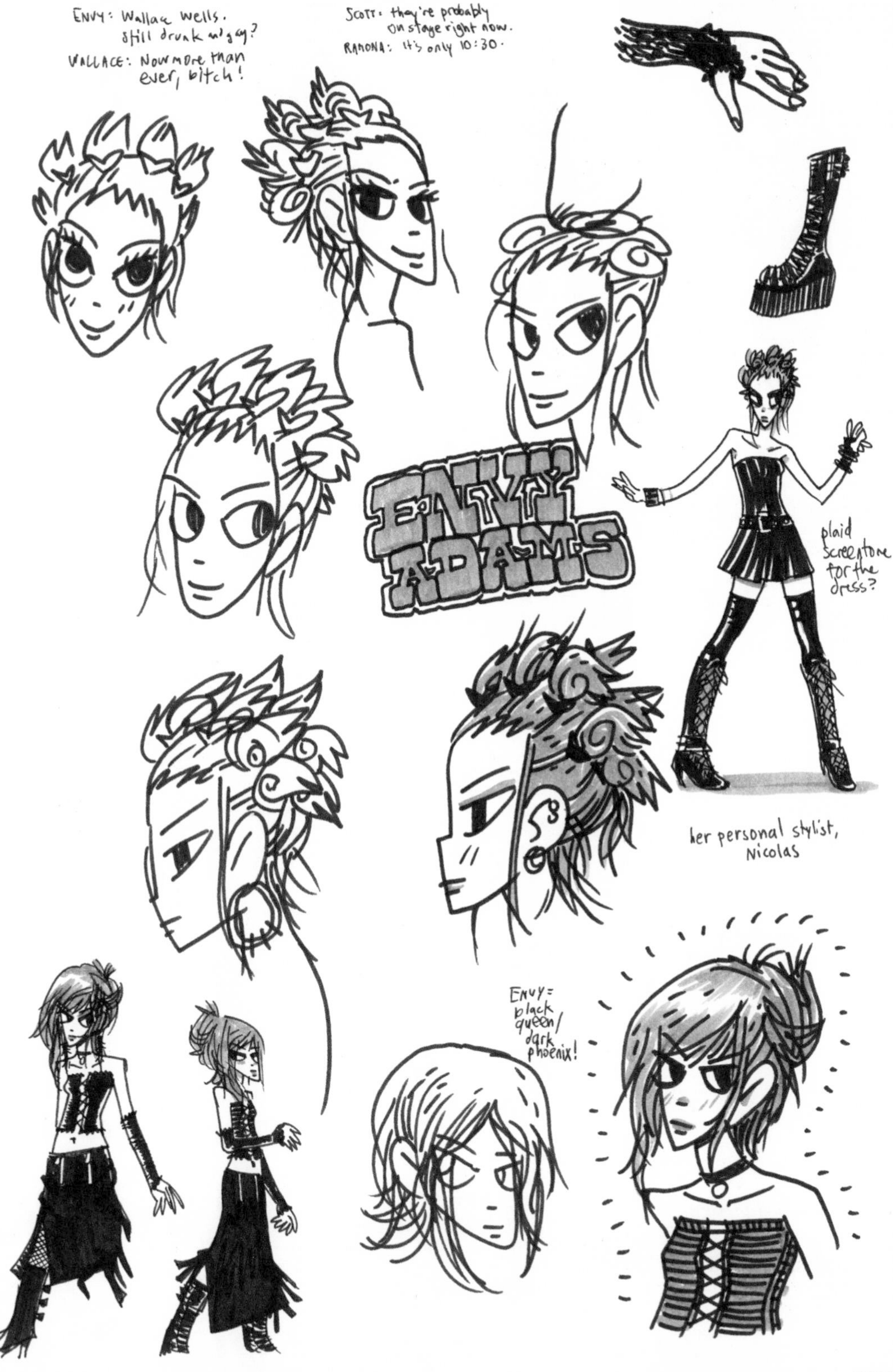
ENVY: Wallace Wells. still drunk and gay?
WALLACE: Now more than ever, bitch!
SCOTT: they're probably on stage right now.
RAMONA: It's only 10:30.
ENVY ADAMS
plaid screentone for the dress?
her personal stylist, Nicolas
ENVY = black queen/ dark phoenix!

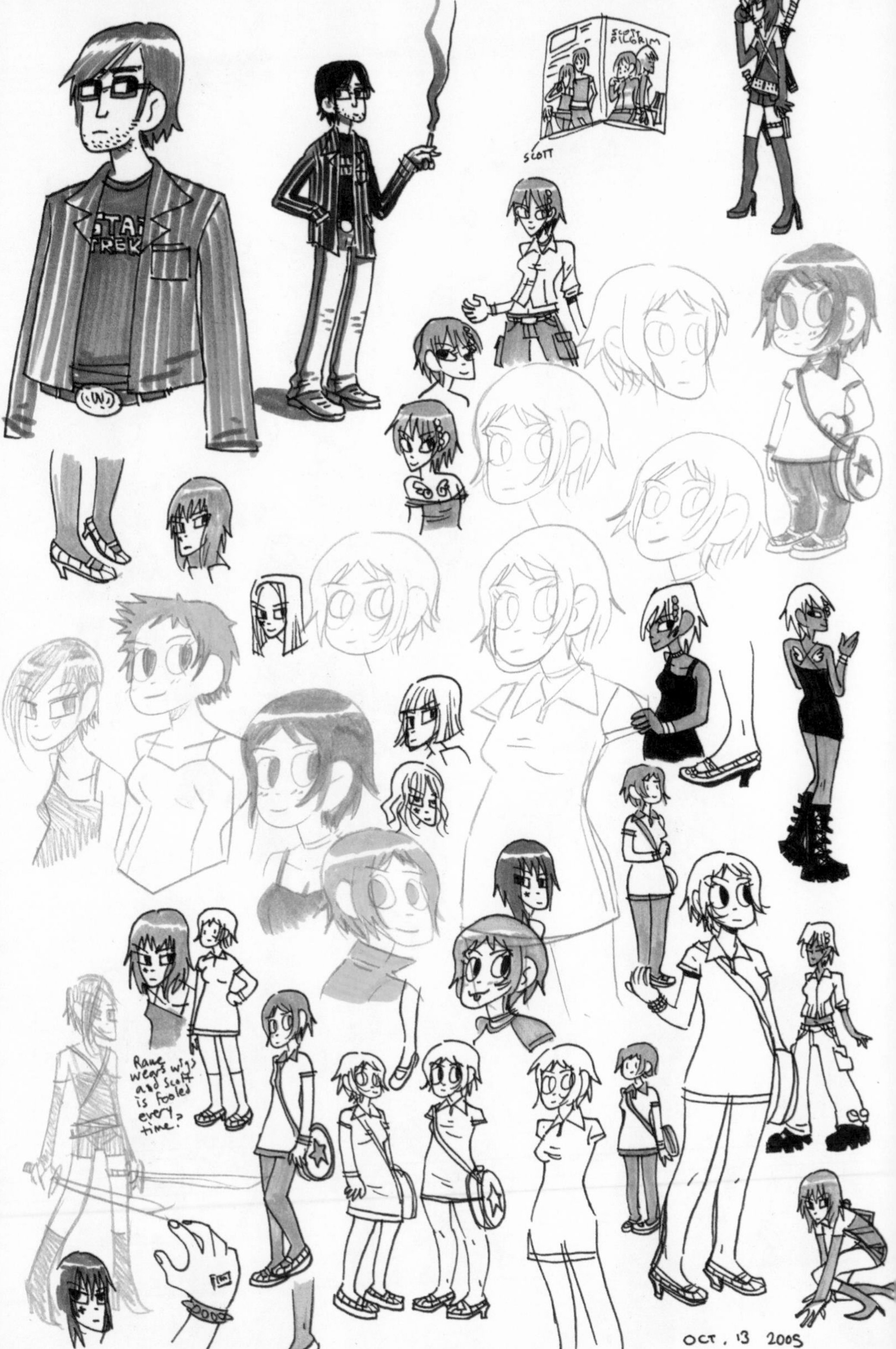
STAR TREK
SCOTT PILGRIM
SCOTT
Rame wears wigs and Scott is fooled every time?
OCT. 13 2005

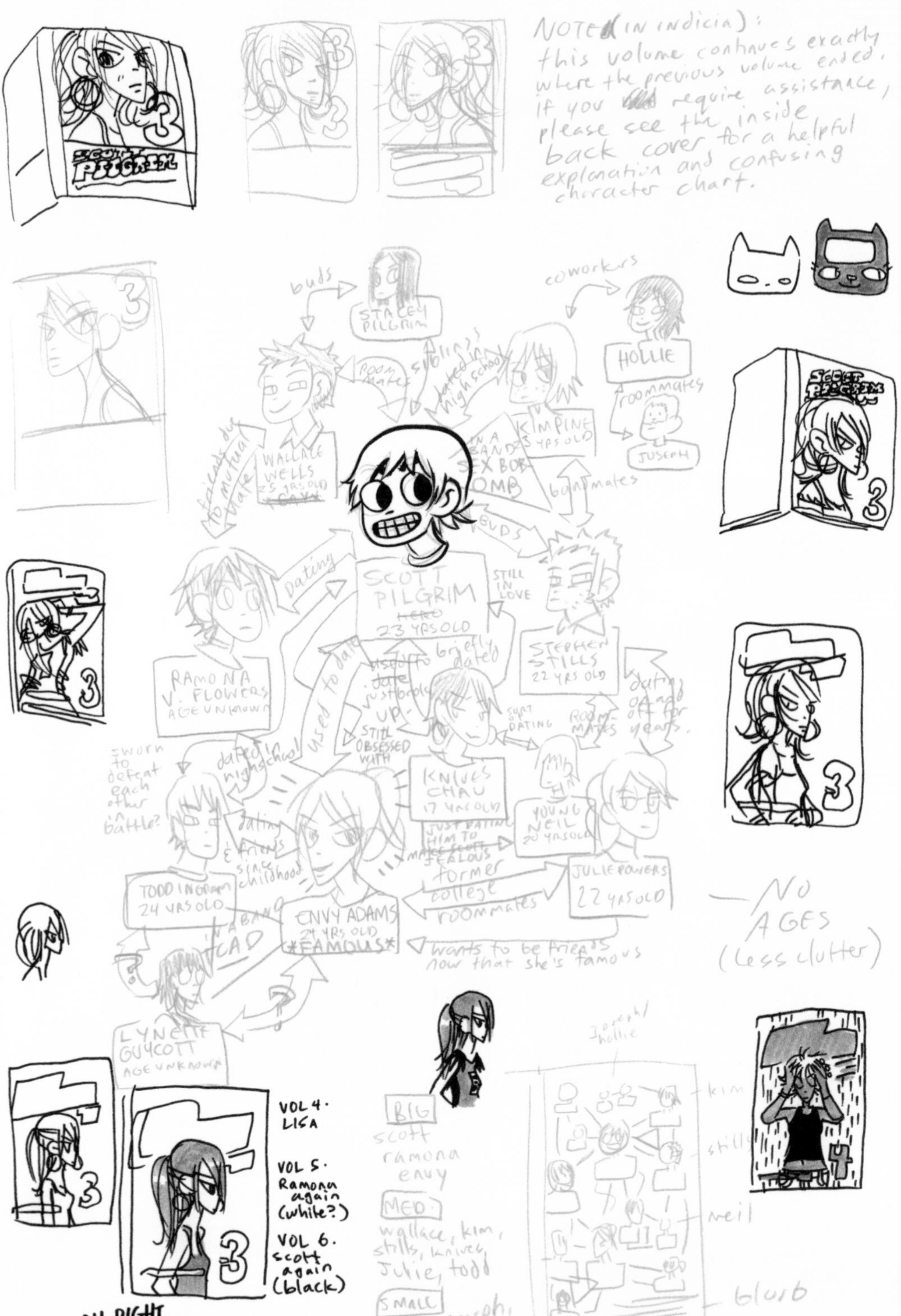
SCOTT PILGRIM
3
NOTE (in indicia): this volume continues exactly where the previous volume ended. If you require assistance, please see the inside back cover for a helpful explanation and confusing character chart.
buds
STACEY PILGRIM
coworkers
HOLLIE
roommates
JOSEPH
ROOMMATES
siblings
dated in highschool
KIM PINE 23 YRS OLD
IN A BAND SEX BOB-OMB
bandmates
WALLACE WELLS 23 YRS OLD GAY
friends due to mutual hate
BUDS
dating
SCOTT PILGRIM HERO 23 YRS OLD
STILL IN LOVE
STEPHEN STILLS 22 YRS OLD
RAMONA V. FLOWERS AGE UNKNOWN
used to date
briefly dated
used to date just broke up
STILL OBSESSED WITH
SORT OF DATING
ROOMMATES
dating on and off for years.
sworn to defeat each other in battle?
dated in highschool
KNIVES CHAU 17 YRS OLD
YOUNG NEIL 20 YRS OLD
JUST DATING HIM TO MAKE SCOTT JEALOUS
dating & friends since childhood
former college roommates
JULIE POWERS 22 YRS OLD
TODD INGRAM 24 YRS OLD
IN A BAND
CAD
ENVY ADAMS 24 YRS OLD *FAMOUS*
wants to be friends now that she's famous
LYNETTE GUYCOTT AGE UNKNOWN
—NO AGES (less clutter)
VOL 4. LISA
VOL 5. Ramona again (white?)
VOL 6. Scott again (black)
OH RIGHT
BIG scott ramona envy
MED. wallace, kim, stills, knives, julie, todd
SMALL stacey, joseph, hollie, neil, lynette
joseph/hollie
kim
stills
neil
blurb
4

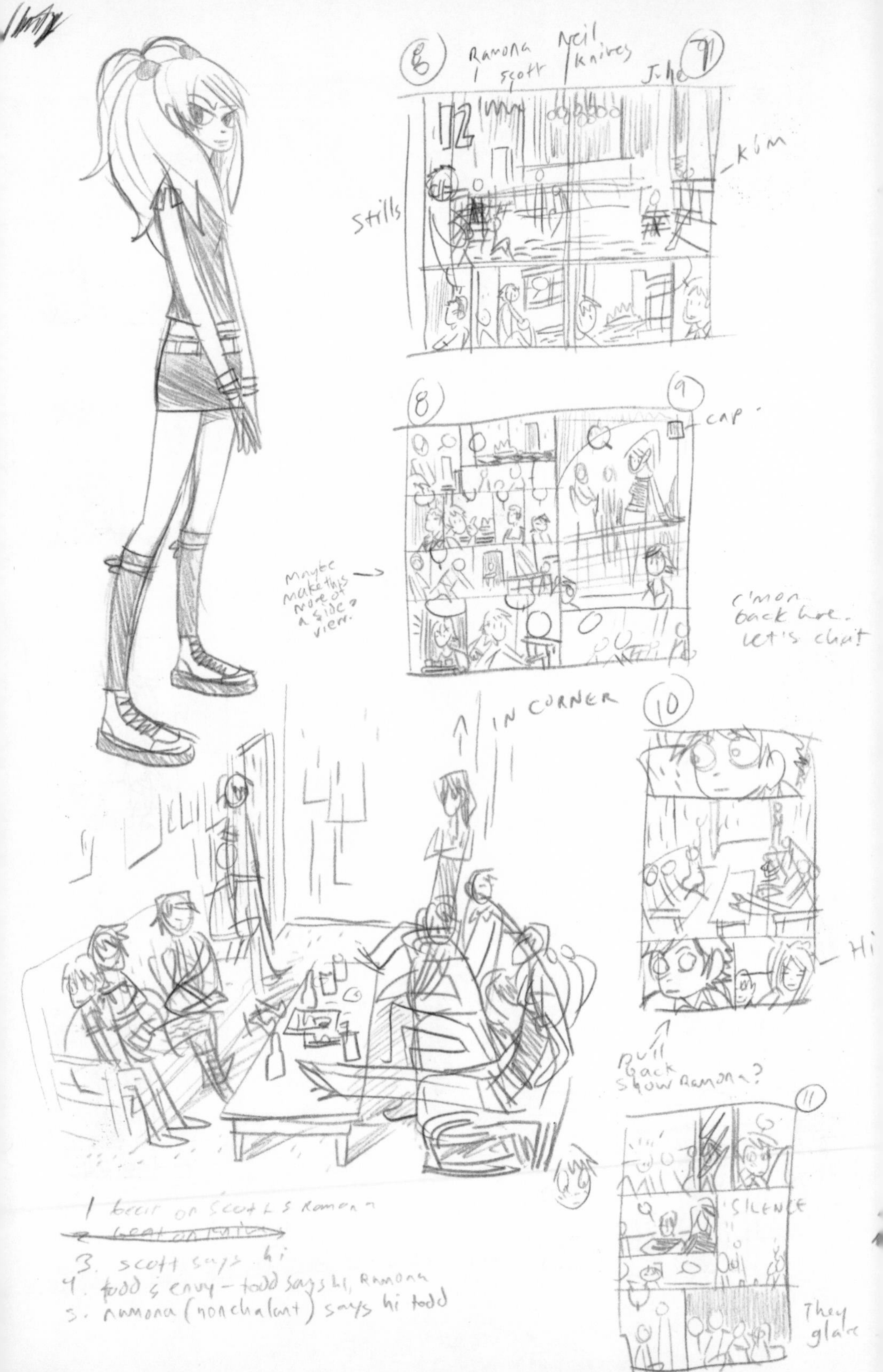

8
Ramona
scott
Neil
knives
9
Julie
Kim
Stills
8
9
cap
Maybe make this more of a side view.
c'mon back here. let's chat!
IN CORNER
10
Hi
pull back show Ramona?
11
SILENCE
They glare
1 beer on Scott & Ramona
3. scott says hi
4. todd & envy - todd says hi, Ramona
5. Ramona (nonchalant) says hi todd

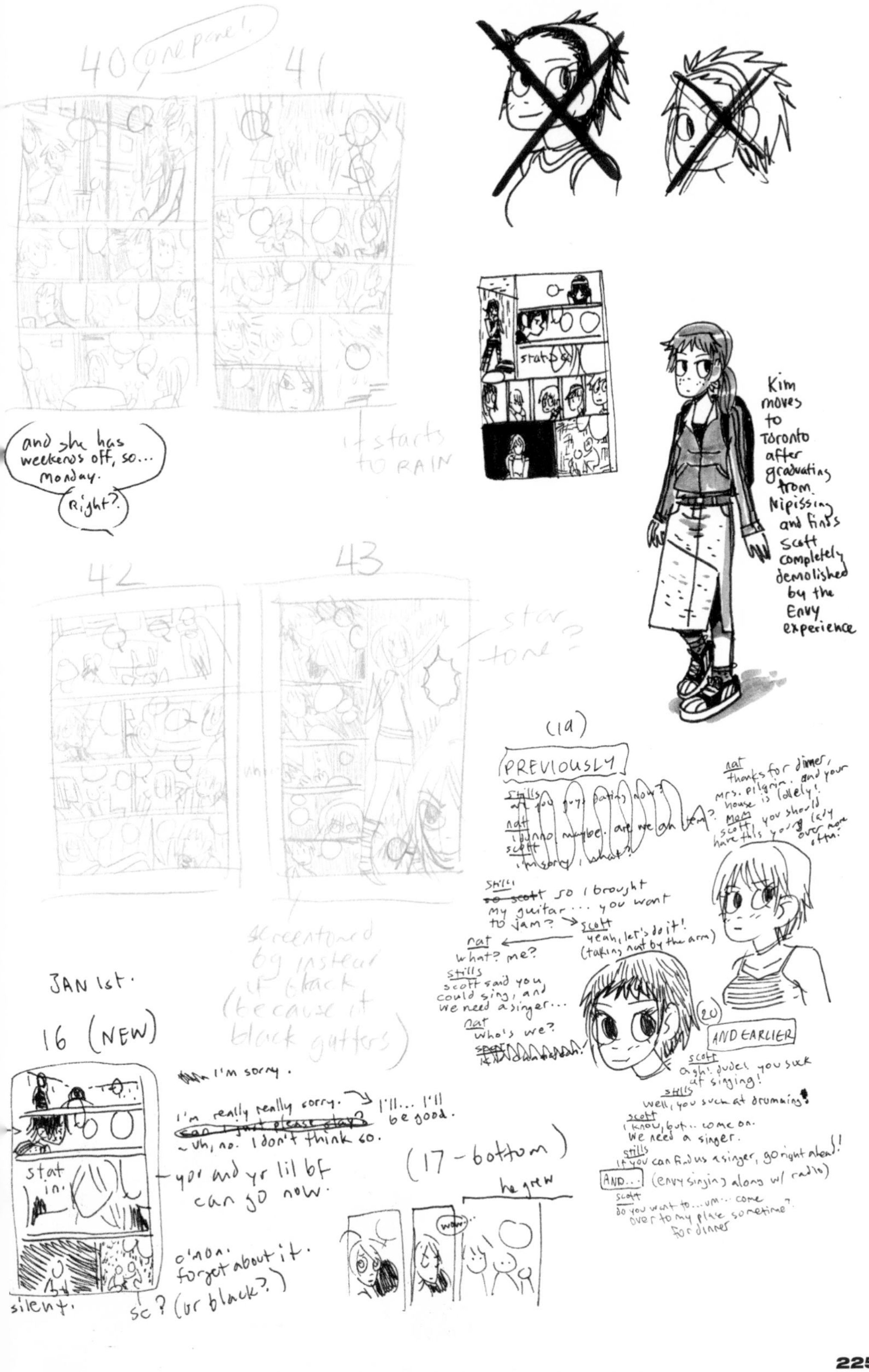
40 (one panel!) 41
and she has weekends off, so... monday.
Right?
it starts to RAIN
42 43
star tone?
screentoned bg instead of black (because of black gutters)
JAN 1st.
16 (NEW)
stat in.
silent.
I'm sorry.
I'm really really sorry.
I'll... I'll be good.
can I just please stay?
-uh, no. I don't think so.
you and yr lil bf can go now.
c'mon. forget about it.
sc? (or black?)
(17 - bottom)
he grew
wow...
Kim moves to Toronto after graduating from Nipissing and finds Scott completely demolished by the Envy experience
(19)
PREVIOUSLY
stills are you guys dating now?
nat I dunno maybe. are we an item?
scott I'm sorry, what?
nat thanks for dinner, Mrs. Pilgrim. and your house is lovely!
MOM scott, you should have this young lady over more often.
stills so I brought my guitar... you want to jam?
scott yeah, let's do it! (taking nat by the arm)
nat what? me?
stills scott said you could sing, and we need a singer...
nat who's we?
(20)
AND EARLIER
scott argh! dude! you suck at singing!
stills well, you suck at drumming!
scott I know, but... come on. We need a singer.
stills if you can find us a singer, go right ahead!
AND... (envy singing along w/ radio)
scott do you want to... um... come over to my place sometime? for dinner

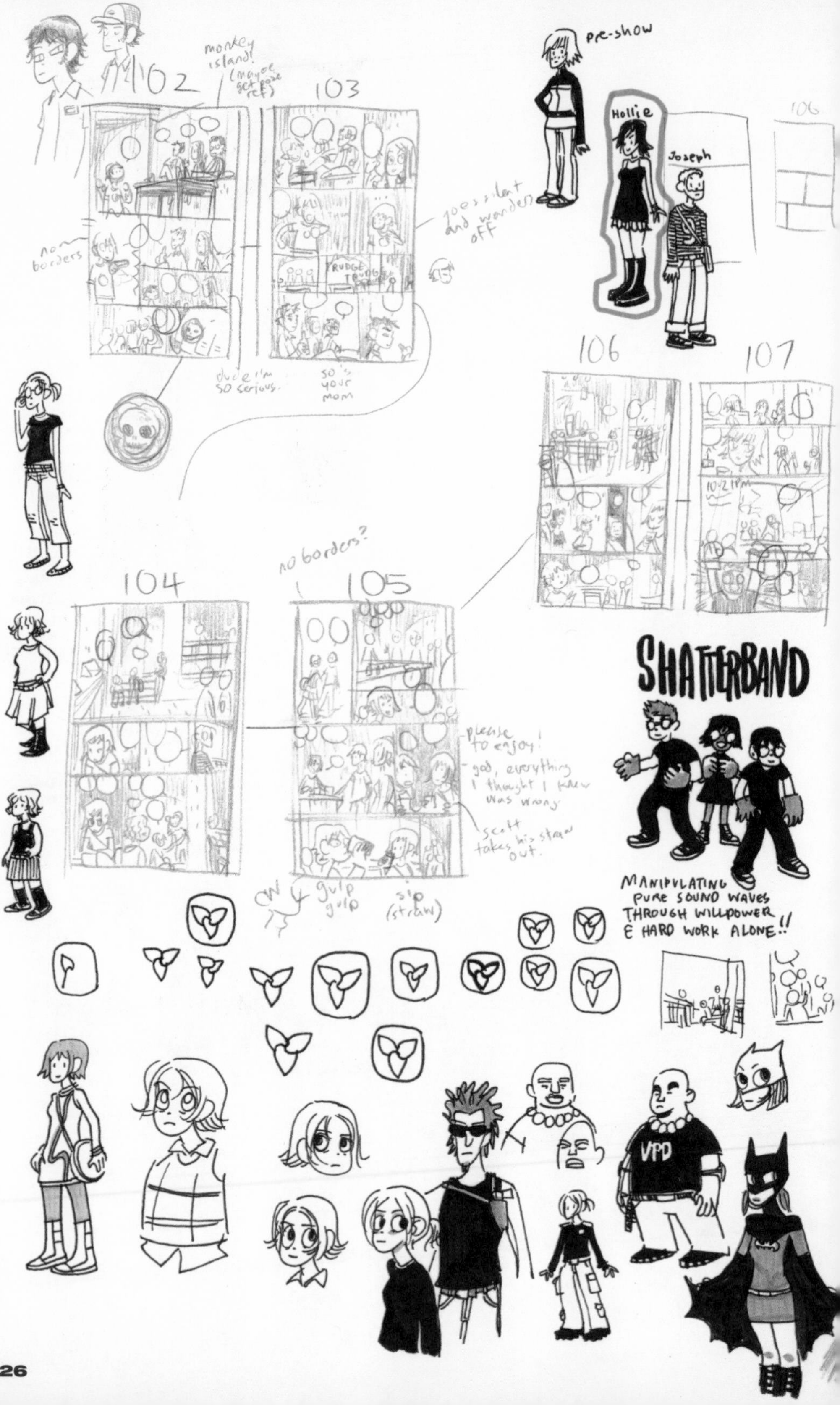
monkey island! (maybe get pose ref)
102
103
pre-show
Hollie
Joseph
106
no borders
goes silent and wanders off
TRUDGE TRUDGE
dude i'm so serious.
so's your mom
106
107
10:21PM
no borders?
104
105
please to enjoy!
god, everything I thought I knew was wrong
scott takes his straw out.
gulp gulp
sip (straw)
SHATTERBAND
MANIPULATING PURE SOUND WAVES THROUGH WILLPOWER & HARD WORK ALONE!!
VPD

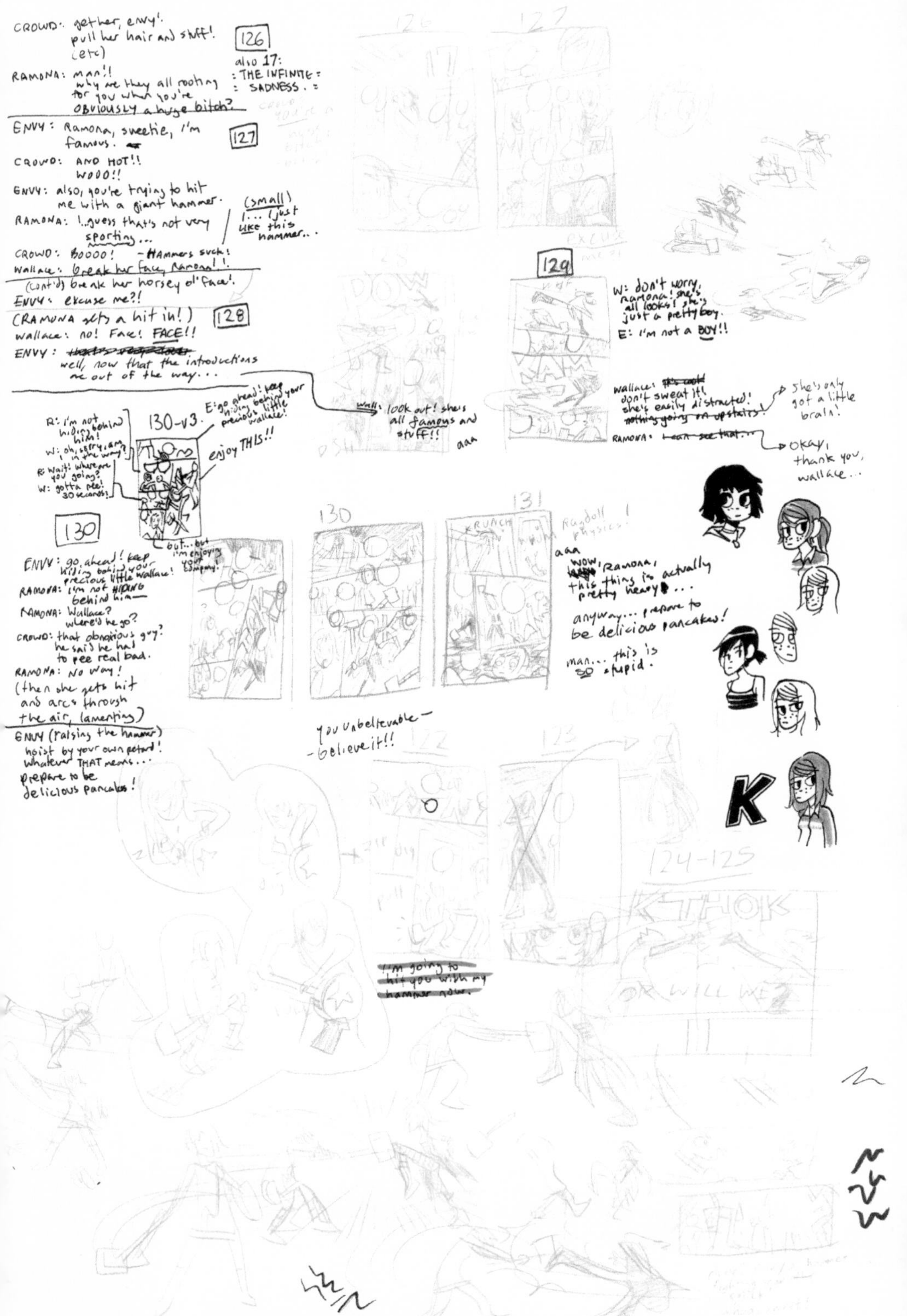
CROWD: get her, envy! pull her hair and stuff! (etc)
126
also 17: : THE INFINITE : : SADNESS. :
RAMONA: man!! why are they all rooting for you when you're OBVIOUSLY a huge bitch?
ENVY: Ramona, sweetie, I'm famous.
127
CROWD: AND HOT!! WOOO!!
ENVY: also, you're trying to hit me with a giant hammer.
RAMONA: I..guess that's not very sporting...
(small) I... I just LIKE this hammer...
CROWD: BOOOO! —Hammers suck!
Wallace: Break her face, Ramona!! (cont'd) break her horsey ol' face!
ENVY: excuse me?!
(RAMONA gets a hit in!)
128
Wallace: no! Face! FACE!!
ENVY: well, now that the introductions are out of the way...
Wall: look out! she's all famous and stuff!!
aaa
129
W: don't worry, Ramona! she's all looks! she's just a pretty boy.
E: I'm not a BOY!!
Wallace: don't sweat it! she's easily distracted! nothing going on upstairs!
She's only got a little brain!
RAMONA:
Okay, thank you, wallace...
R: I'm not hiding behind him!
W: oh, sorry, am I in the way?
R: Wait! where are you going?
W: gotta pee! 30 seconds!
130-v3.
E: go ahead! keep hiding behind your precious little wallace!
enjoy THIS!!
but... but I'm enjoying your company!
130
ENVY: go ahead! keep hiding behind your precious little Wallace!
RAMONA: I'm not HIDING behind him—
RAMONA: Wallace? where'd he go?
CROWD: that obnoxious guy? he said he had to pee real bad.
RAMONA: No Way!
(then she gets hit and arcs through the air, lamenting)
ENVY (raising the hammer) hoist by your own petard! Whatever THAT means... prepare to be delicious pancakes!
130
131
KRUNCH
Ragdoll physics!
aaa
WOW, Ramona, this thing is actually pretty heavy...
anyway... prepare to be delicious pancakes!
man... this is SO stupid.
you unbelievable— believe it!!
122
123
124-125
KTHOK
OR WILL WE?
I'm going to hit you with my hammer now.
K

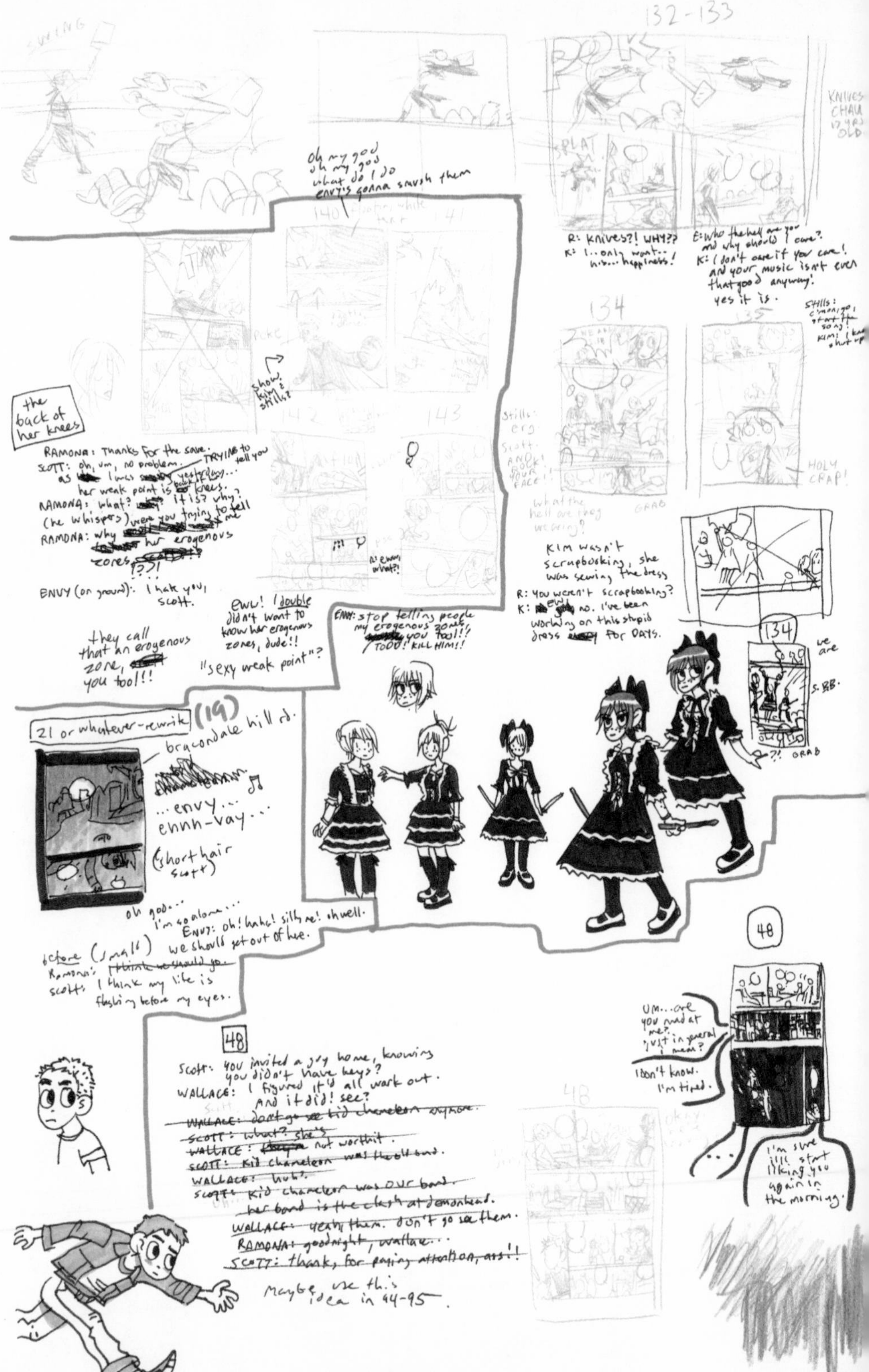
SWING
132-133
POOK
KNIVES CHAU 17 YRS OLD
SPLAT
oh my god
oh my god
what do I do
envy's gonna smush them
140
141
R: Knives?! WHY??
K: I... only want... his... happiness!
E: Who the hell are you and why should I care?
K: I don't care if you care! And your music isn't even that good anyway!
yes it is.
134
135
POKE
show Kim & Stills?
the back of her knees
142
143
Stills: erg
Scott: AND ROCK YOUR FACE!!
HOLY CRAP!
what the hell are they wearing?
GRAB
RAMONA: Thanks for the save.
SCOTT: oh, um, no problem. TRYING to tell you as I was saying yesterday... her weak point is her knees.
RAMONA: what? it is? why?
(he whispers) were you trying to tell me
RAMONA: why her erogenous zones?!?!
ENVY (on ground): I hate you, Scott.
Kim wasn't scrapbooking, she was sewing the dress
R: You weren't scrapbooking?
K: no. I've been working on this stupid dress for DAYS.
ew! I double didn't want to know her erogenous zones, dude!!
"sexy weak point"?
ENVY: stop telling people my erogenous zones, you tool!! TODD! KILL HIM!!
they call that an erogenous zone, you tool!!
134
we are S.BB.
GRAB
21 or whatever - rewrite
(19)
bracondale hill rd.
...envy...
ennh-vay...
(short hair Scott)
oh god...
I'm so alone...
ENVY: oh! haha! silly me! oh well.
before (small) we should get out of here.
Ramona: I think we should go.
Scott: I think my life is flashing before my eyes.
48
UM... are you mad at me? just in general I mean?
I don't know. I'm tired.
...
I'm sure I'll start liking you again in the morning.
48
Scott: You invited a guy home, knowing you didn't have keys?
WALLACE: I figured it'd all work out. And it did! see?
WALLACE: don't go see kid chameleon anymore.
SCOTT: what? she's
WALLACE: not worth it.
SCOTT: Kid chameleon was the old band.
WALLACE: huh?
SCOTT: Kid chameleon was our band. her band is the clash at demonhead.
WALLACE: yeah them. don't go see them.
RAMONA: goodnight, wallace...
SCOTT: thanks for paying attention, ass!!
Maybe use this idea in 94-95.
48

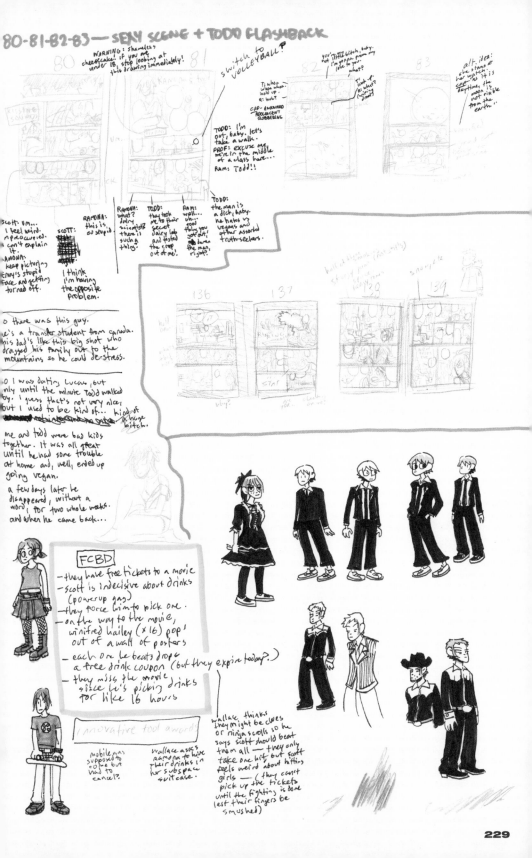

80-81-82-83 — SEXY SCENE + TODD FLASHBACK

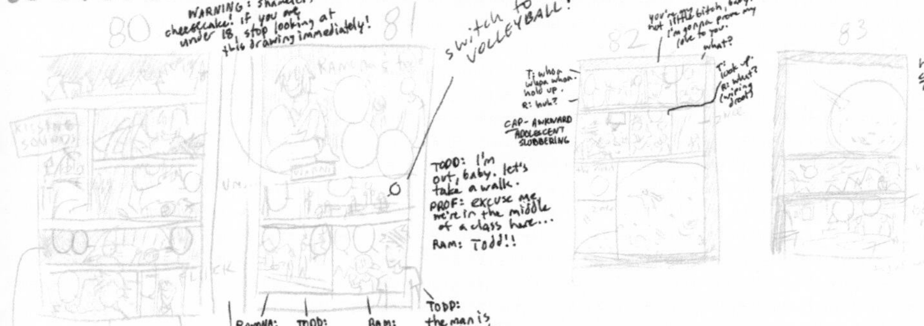
80
WARNING: shameless cheesecake! if you are under 18, stop looking at this drawing immediately!
81
switch to VOLLEYBALL?
TODD: I'm out, baby. let's take a walk.
PROF: excuse me, we're in the middle of a class here...
RAM: Todd!!
82
T: whoa whoa whoa. hold up.
R: huh?
CAP- AWKWARD ADOLESCENT SLOBBERING
you're not my little bitch, baby. I'm gonna prove my love to you.
what?
T: look up.
R: what? (wiping drool)
83
alt. idea: she stares at her watch. cap- as it is daytime, the moon is not visible from the earth...

RAMONA: this is so stupid.

RAMONA: what? dairy scientists? there is such a thing?

TODD: they took me to their secret dairy lab and tested the crap out of me!

RAM: well... uh... good thing you got out! damn the man, right?

TODD: the man is a dick, baby. he hates us vegans and other assorted truth-seekers.

SCOTT: UM... I feel weird. preoccupied. I can't explain it.
RAMONA: keep picturing Envy's stupid face and getting turned off.

SCOTT: [redacted] I think I'm having the opposite problem.

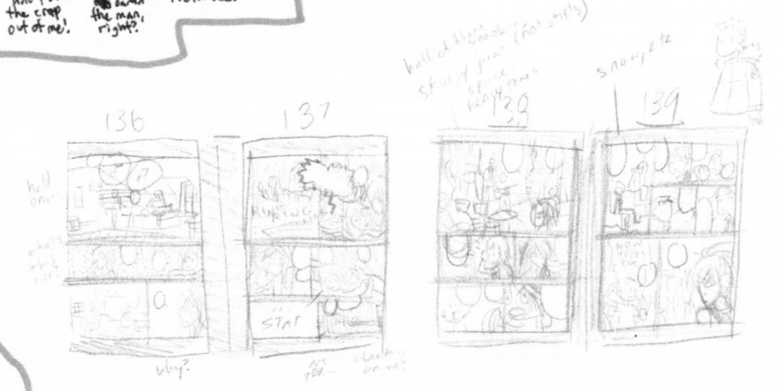
136
137
138
139

so there was this guy.
he's a transfer student from canada.
his dad's like this big shot who dragged his family out to the mountains so he could de-stress.

so I was dating Lucas, but only until the minute Todd walked by. I guess that's not very nice, but I used to be kind of... kind of ~~[illegible]~~ a huge bitch.

me and todd were bad kids together. It was all great until he had some trouble at home and, well, ended up going vegan.

a few days later he disappeared, without a word, for two whole weeks. and when he came back...

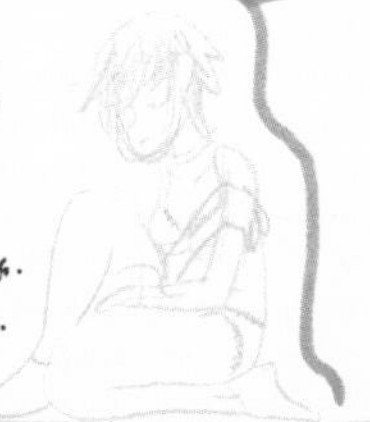

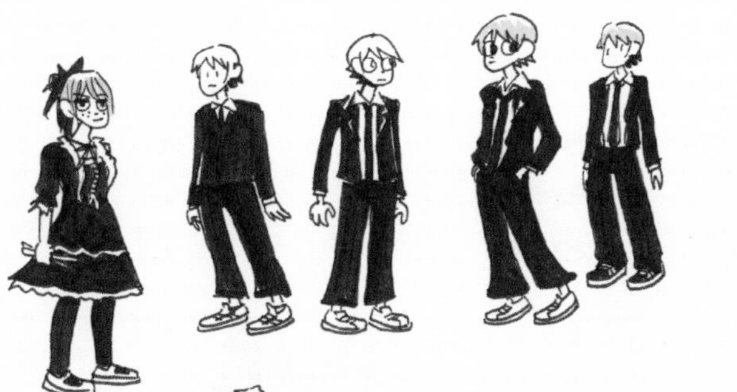

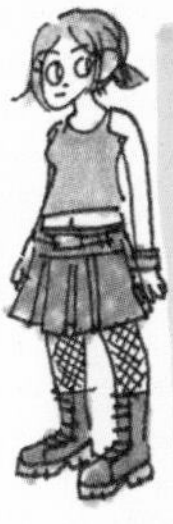

FCBD
- they have free tickets to a movie
- scott is indecisive about drinks (powerup gag)
- they force him to pick one.
- on the way to the movie, winifred hailey (x16) pop out of a wall of posters
- each one he beats drops a free drink coupon (but they expire today?)
- they miss the movie since he's picking drinks for like 16 hours

innovative tool awards

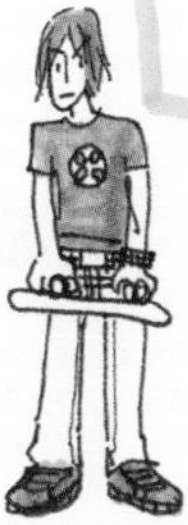

mobile was supposed to come but had to cancel?

wallace asks ramona to hide their drinks in her subspace suitcase.

wallace thinks they might be clones or ninja scrolls so he says scott should beat them all — they only take one hit but scott feels weird about hitting girls — (they can't pick up the tickets until the fighting is done lest their fingers be smushed)

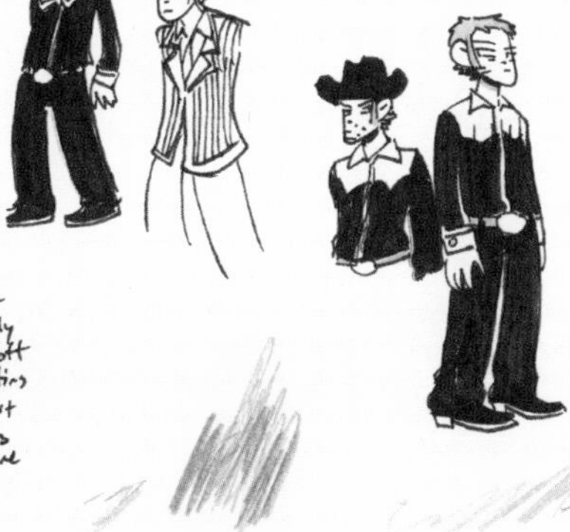

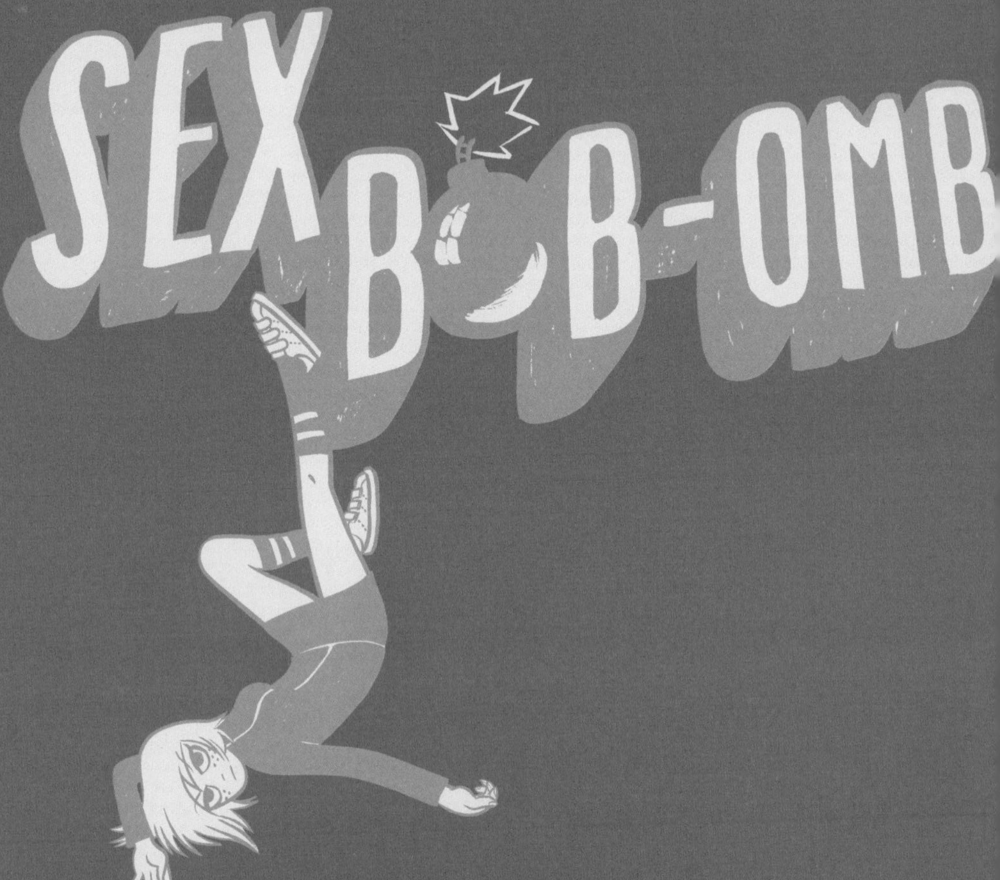
SEX BOB-OMB

This design was used for an official t-shirt in 2006.

DELETED
SCENES

The following pages were created during the making of this book but were ultimately not used in the original edition. They are presented here for the sake of completion.

Pages 232-233 feature a sequence originally intended to slot in after page 19 of this edition.

Page 234 would have continued from page 22.

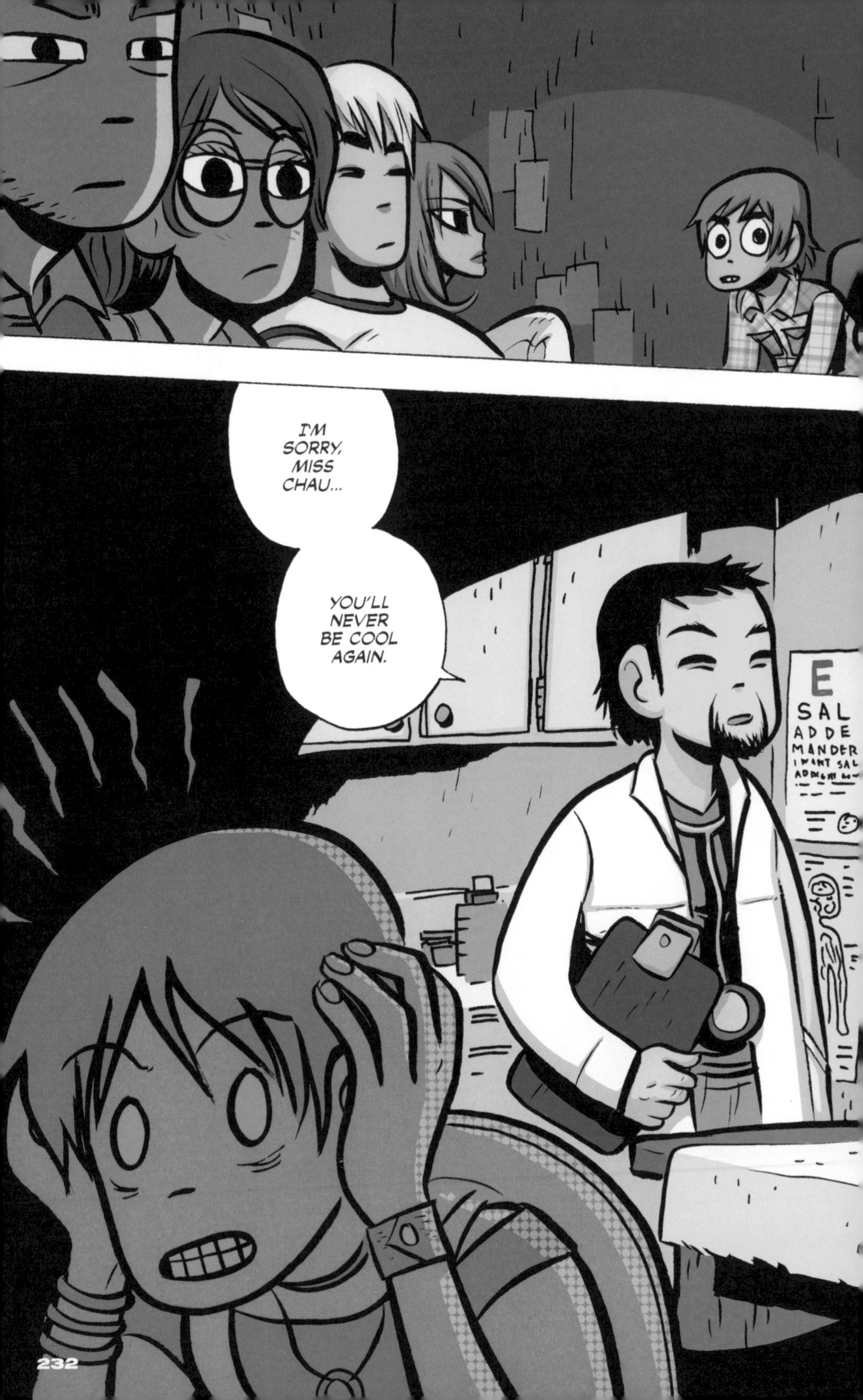
I'M SORRY, MISS CHAU...
YOU'LL NEVER BE COOL AGAIN.
E
SAL
ADDE
MANDER
I WANT SAL

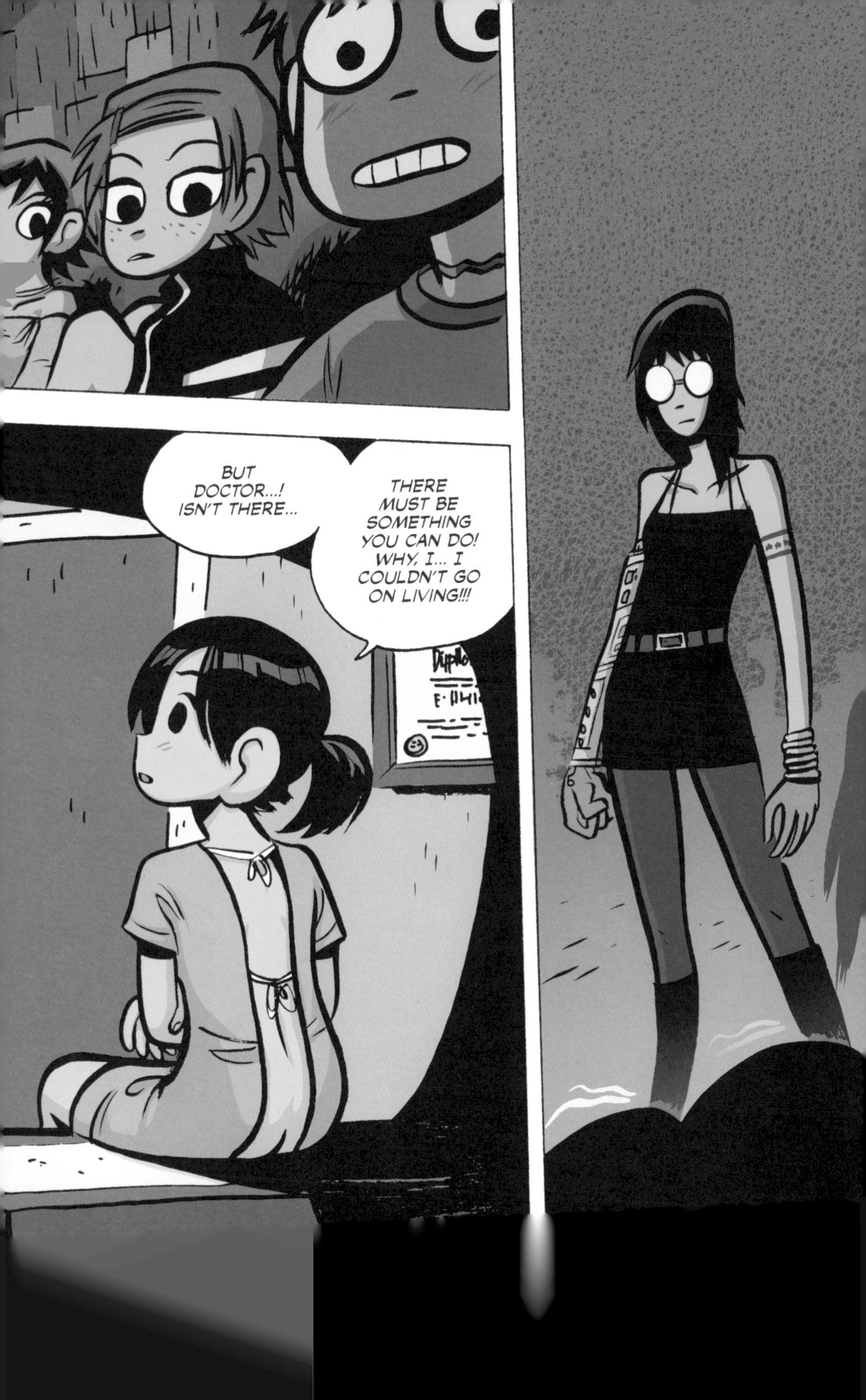
BUT DOCTOR...! ISN'T THERE...
THERE MUST BE SOMETHING YOU CAN DO! WHY, I... I COULDN'T GO ON LIVING!!!

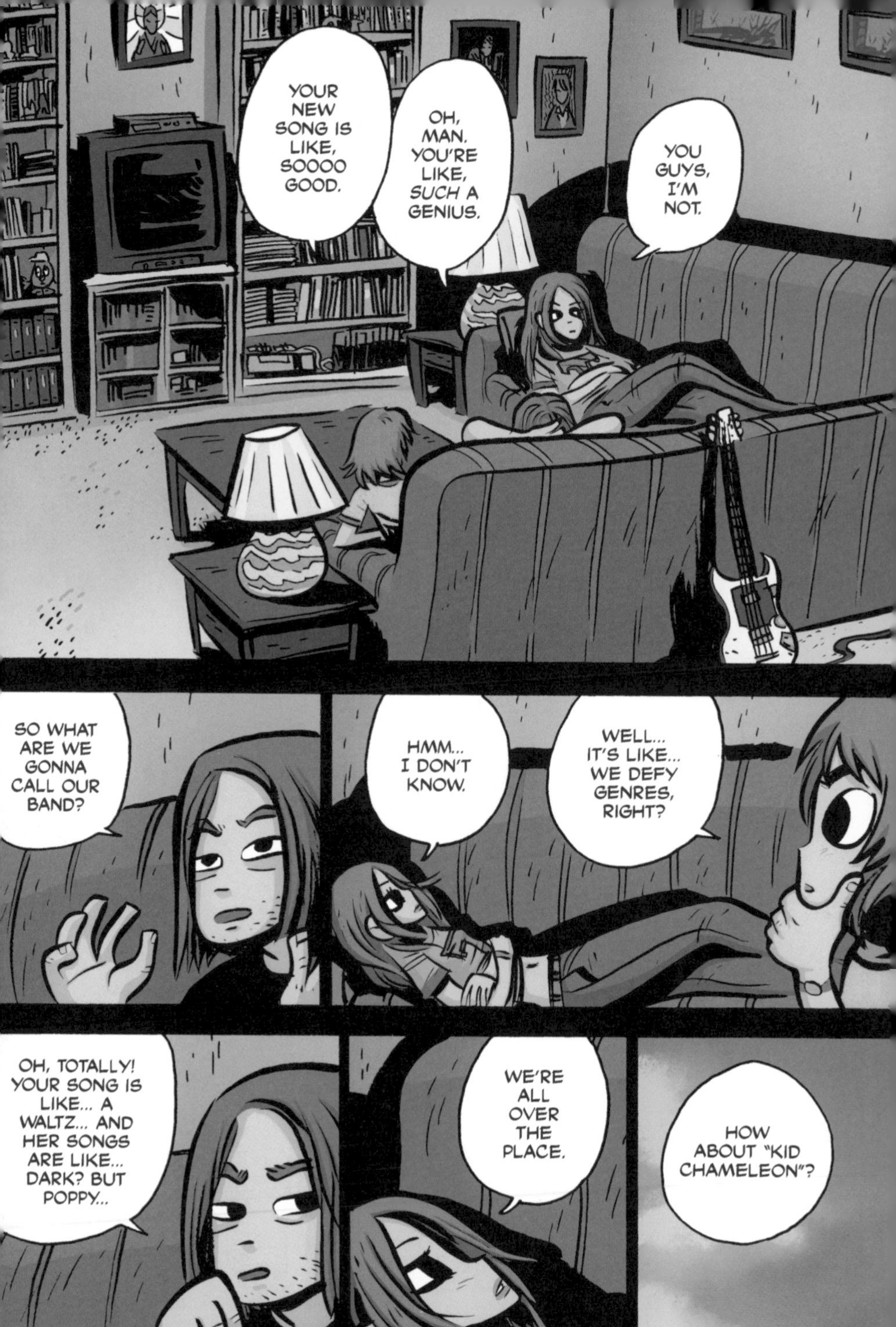
YOUR NEW SONG IS LIKE, SOOOO GOOD.
OH, MAN. YOU'RE LIKE, *SUCH* A GENIUS.
YOU GUYS, I'M NOT.
SO WHAT ARE WE GONNA CALL OUR BAND?
HMM... I DON'T KNOW.
WELL... IT'S LIKE... WE DEFY GENRES, RIGHT?
OH, TOTALLY! YOUR SONG IS LIKE... A WALTZ... AND HER SONGS ARE LIKE... DARK? BUT POPPY...
WE'RE ALL OVER THE PLACE.
HOW ABOUT "KID CHAMELEON"?

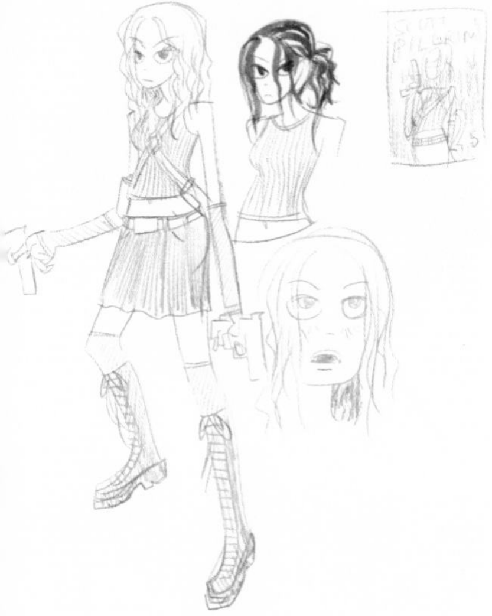

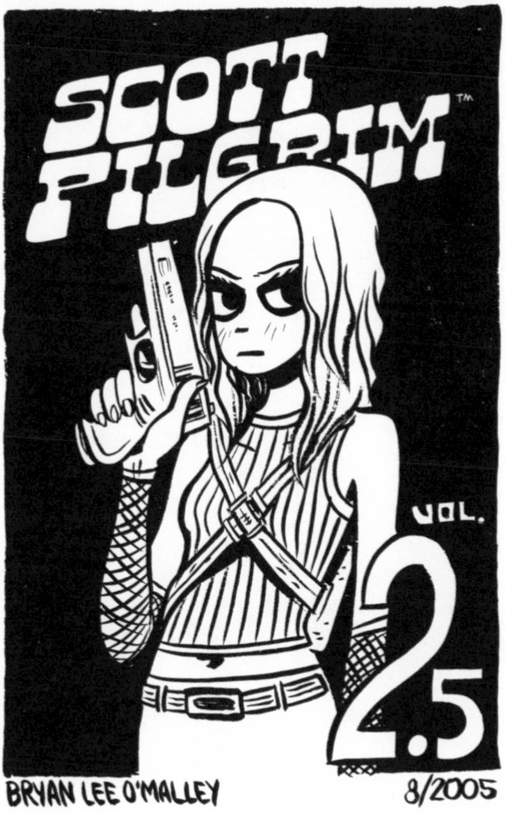
SCOTT PILGRIM™
VOL.
2.5
BRYAN LEE O'MALLEY
8/2005

Scott Pilgrim Volume 2.5 was planned as a minicomic featuring the character Winifred Hailey. It never made it past this cover sketch, but the idea was later used for *Free Scott Pilgrim*.

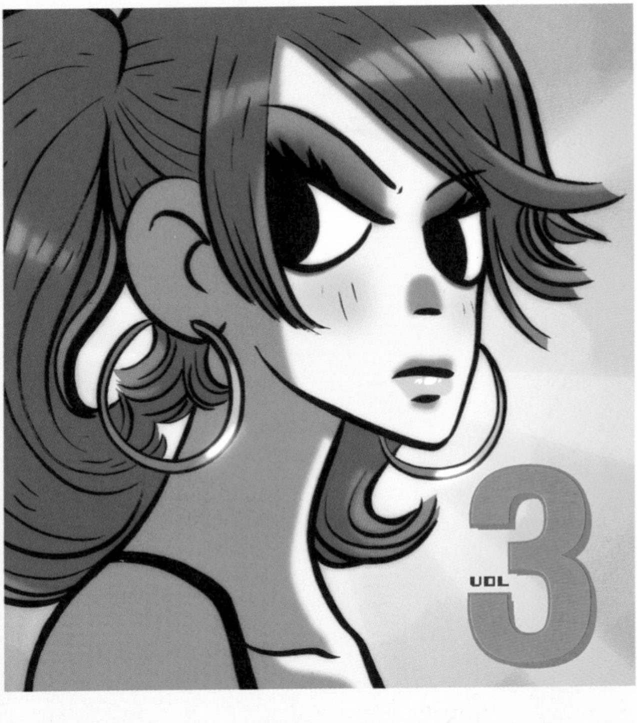
VOL
3

Unused cover concept for *Scott Pilgrim,* volume 3.

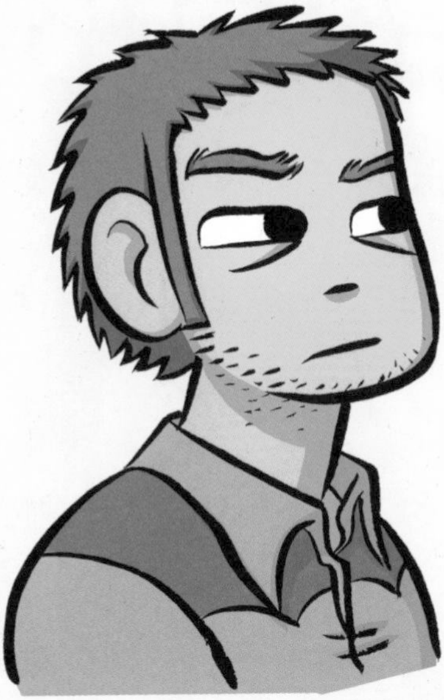

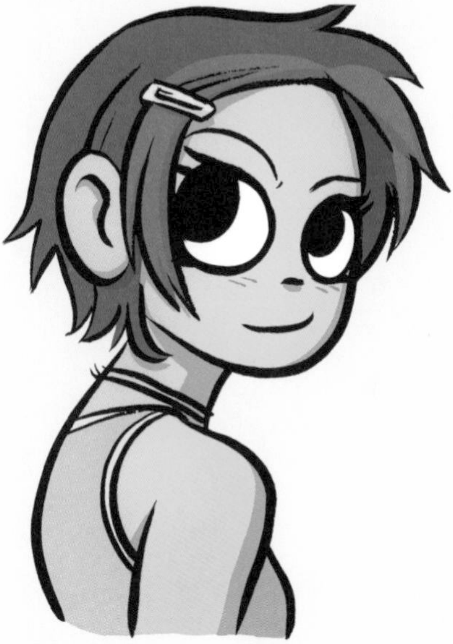

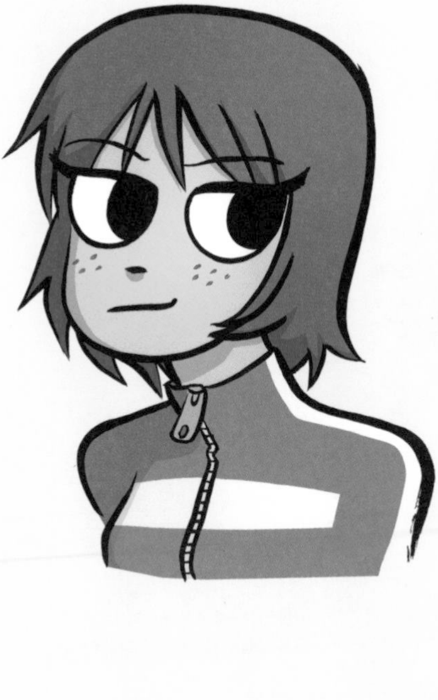

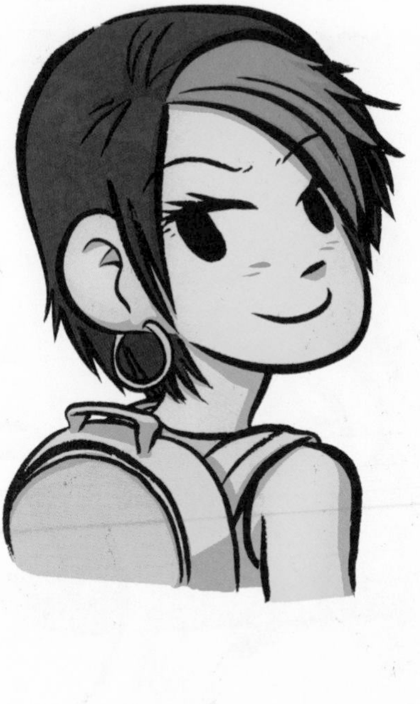

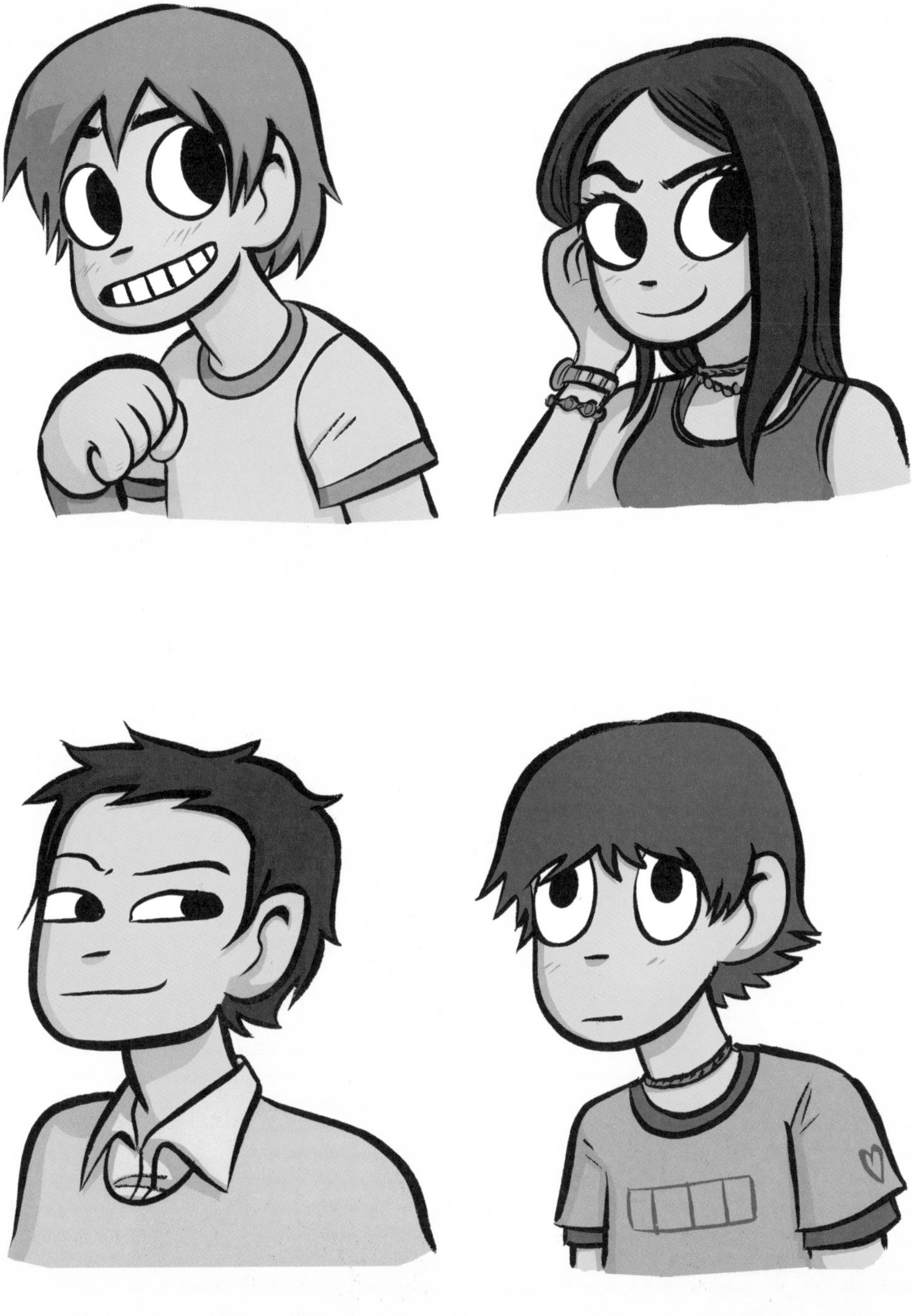

These character drawings were originally created for an early *Scott Pilgrim* website in 2005.
New colors by Nathan Fairbairn.

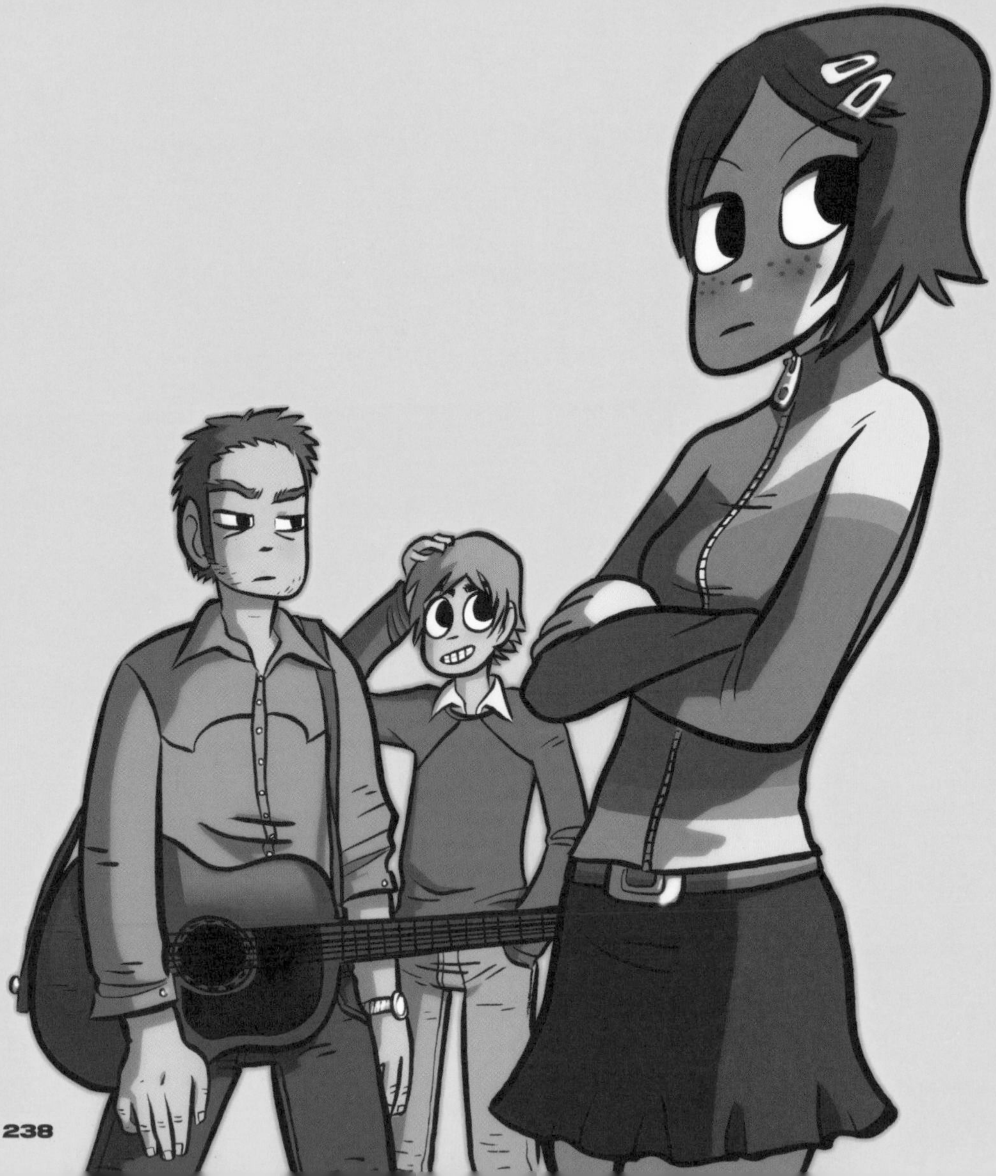

BRYAN LEE O'MALLEY

is a Canadian cartoonist. His six-volume *Scott Pilgrim* series was a New York Times bestseller, an LA Times Book Prize finalist, and won an Eisner Award, two Harvey Awards, a Doug Wright Award and a Joe Shuster Award. In 2010, *Scott Pilgrim* was adapted into a critically-acclaimed major motion picture (from Universal) and video game (from Ubisoft). O'Malley lives in Los Angeles.

NATHAN FAIRBAIRN

is a Canadian colorist who, since breaking into the industry in 2007, has worked extensively for DC, Marvel, Dark Horse, Top Cow, and Oni Press. He won the Shuster Award in 2010 for Outstanding Colourist. Titles he has worked on include *Batman Incorporated, Wolverine: Weapon X, Swamp Thing,* and the Eisner-nominated miniseries *Mystic.* Fairbairn lives in Vancouver, BC.

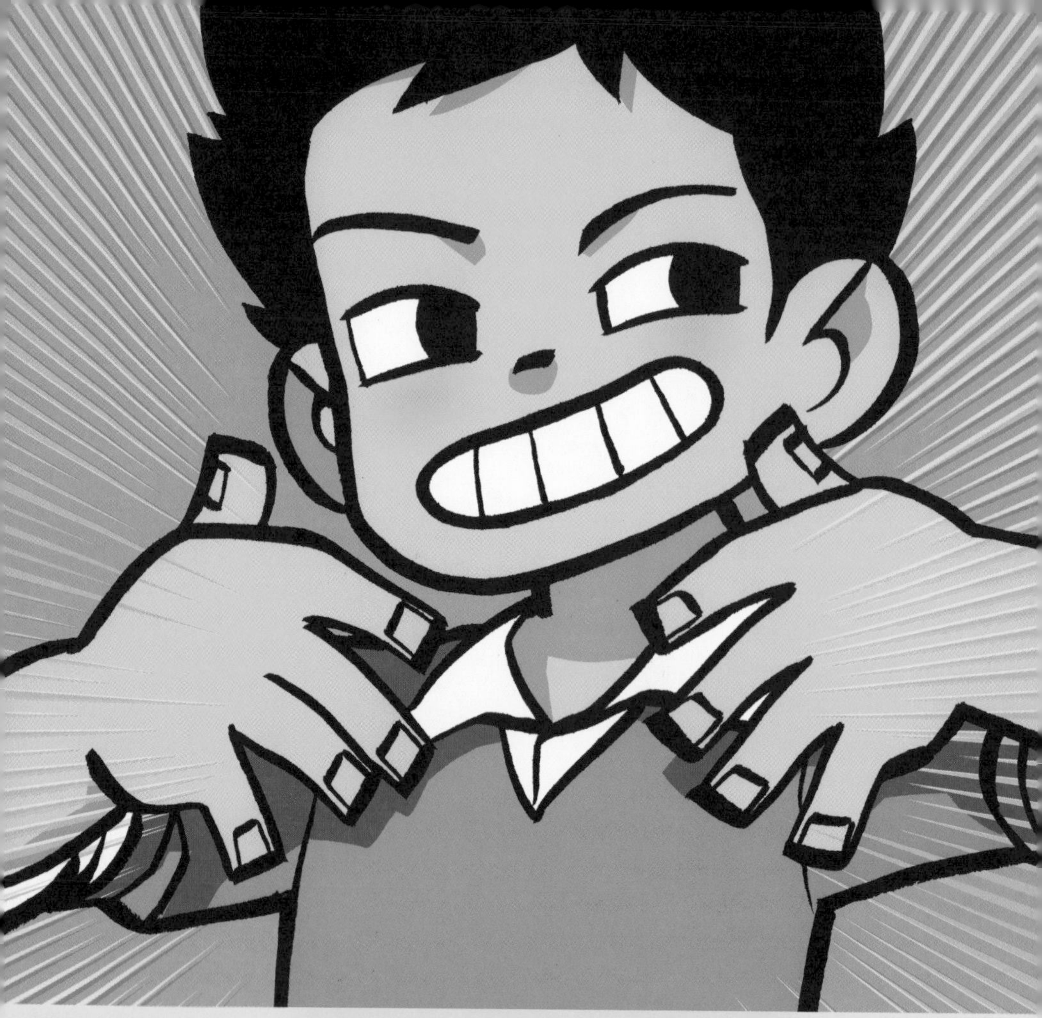

SCOTT PILGRIM'S STORY DOESN'T END HERE...

Scott Pilgrim Color Hardcover Volume 1
Scott Pilgrim's Precious Little Life
ISBN 978-1-62010-000-4
Available Now!

Scott Pilgrim Color Hardcover Volume 2
Scott Pilgrim Vs. The World
ISBN 978-1-62010-001-1
Available Now!

Scott Pilgrim Color Hardcover Volume 4
Scott Pilgrim Gets It Together
ISBN 978-1-62010-003-5
On Sale Fall 2013!

Scott Pilgrim Color Hardcover Volume 5
Scott Pilgrim vs. The Universe
ISBN 978-1-62010-004-2
On Sale Spring 2014!

Scott Pilgrim Color Hardcover Volume 6
Scott Pilgrim's Finest Hour
ISBN 978-1-62010-005-9
On Sale Summer 2014!

ALSO AVAILABLE NOW FROM BRYAN LEE O'MALLEY & ONI PRESS...
Lost at Sea
ISBN 978-1-932664-16-4

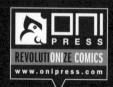

ONI PRESS
REVOLUTIONIZE COMICS
www.onipress.com

For more information on these and other fine Oni Press titles, visit our website at www.onipress.com